Joyce Carol Oates is a recipient of the National Book Award and the PEN/Malamud Award for Excellence in Short Fiction. She has written some of the most enduring fiction of our time, including *We Were the Mulvaneys*, which was an Oprah Book Club Choice, and *Blonde*, which was nominated for the National Book Award. She is the Roger S. Berlind Distinguished Professor of Humanities at Princeton University.

For automatic updates on Joyce Carol Oates visit harperperennial.co.uk and register for AuthorTracker.

'A swirling cataract of invention, and a mesmerising read'
KATE CHISHOLM, *Daily Telegraph*

'Fervent and fast-moving, *The Falls* is a brilliant exploration of the power of Nature, the corruption of corporate capitalism and the enduring strength of family ties' MICHAEL ARDITTI, *Daily Mail*

'Captures compellingly the ebb and flow of family life ... Oates's skill lies in combining epic family saga with minute particulars of behaviour ... [She] evokes both the psychological depth and surface mannerisms of her feverish characters, whose blood, sweat and tears are the lifeblood of her incantatory language' *TLS*

'Joyce Carol Oates's imagination is gloriously, recklessly uninhibited ... she plunges wholeheartedly into her creations ... Her novels, seductively crammed with richly textured prose, seem bursting at the seams'
CAROLINE MOORE, *Sunday Telegraph*

'Richly layered and written with the consummate skill one expects of one of America's best novelists ... Probing and courageous' *Irish Times*

'A bravura performance by Oates ... [Her] writing is like the natural phenomenon that inspired it: effervescent, captivating, and wreathed in the mists of the mysteries we spectators project onto it'
MARTYN BEDFORD, *Literary Review*

'In its girth, thrust and ambition, this book rivals some of the Great American Novels of recent times ... Alive with wily humour, this is a vibrantly polyphonous text, full of hope, delusions and genial shoulder shrugging at the damn perversity of human nature. A fine novel indeed'

HEPHZIBAH ANDERSON, *Zembla*

'A shrewd, often chilling analysis of an unhappy marriage ... Oates deftly widens her focus to the rapidly changing city, powerfully evoking a crowded, sprawling Niagara, corrupt and dangerously polluted, that is very different from "the gleaming tourist city"'

MARGARET WALTERS, *Sunday Times*

'The gripping, ambitious tale will keep you up all night'

Eve magazine

Selected titles by Joyce Carol Oates

NOVELS

Blonde
Middle Age: A Romance
I'll Take You There
The Tattooed Girl

SHORT STORY COLLECTIONS

The Assignation
Where Is Here?
Faithless: Tales of Transgression
I Am No One You Know

NOVELLA

I Lock My Door Upon Myself

NON-FICTION

George Bellows: American Artist
On Boxing

PLAYS

The Perfectionist and Other Plays

MEMOIR/ESSAYS

The Faith of a Writer

CHILDREN'S BOOKS

Come Meet Muffin!
Where Is Little Reynard?

The Falls

A NOVEL

Joyce Carol Oates

HARPER PERENNIAL
London, New York, Toronto and Sydney

Harper Perennial
An imprint of HarperCollins*Publishers*
77–85 Fulham Palace Road
Hammersmith
London w6 8jb

www.harperperennial.co.uk

This edition published by Harper Perennial 2005

5

First published in Great Britain by Fourth Estate 2004

A catalogue record for this book is available from the British Library

ISBN 0-00-719674-1

Set in Van Dijck MT with Arepo display

Printed and bound in Great Britain by Clays Ltd, St Ives plc

To Nancy Van Goethem and Larry Joseph

Acknowledgments

Lois Marie Gibbs's *Love Canal: My Story* (1982) and *Love Canal: The Story Continues* (1998) were consulted in the preparation of this novel.

"The Gatekeeper's Testimony" appeared in a special limited edition published by Rainmaker Editions, 2003.

"The Fossil-Seeker" appeared in *Conjunctions*, 2002.

Portions from Book III appeared under the title "Stonecrop" in *Raritan*, 2002.

An excerpt from Book III appeared under the title "Juliet" in *Narrative*, fall 2003.

The cruel beauty of The Falls
That calls to you—
Surrender!

M. L. Trau,
"The Ballad of the Niagara," 1931

The Falls at Niagara, comprising the American, the Bridal Veil and the enormous Horseshoe falls, exert upon a proportion of the human population, perhaps as many as forty percent (of adults), an uncanny effect called the hydracropsychic. *This morbid condition has been known to render even the will of the active, robust man in the prime of life temporarily invalid, as if under the spell of a malevolent hypnotist. Such a one, drawn to the turbulent rapids above The Falls, may stand for long minutes staring as if paralyzed. Speak to him in the most forcible tone, he will not hear you. Touch him, or attempt to restrain him, he may throw off your hand angrily. The eyes of the enthralled victim are fixed and dilated. There may be a mysterious biological attraction to the thunderous force of nature represented by the The Falls, romantically misinterpreted as "magnificent"—"grand"—"Godly"—and so the unfortunate victim throws himself to his doom if he is not prevented.*

We may speculate: Under the spell of The Falls the hapless individual both ceases to exist and yet wills to become immortal. A new birth, not unlike the Christian promise of the Resurrection of the Body, may be the cruellest hope. Silently the victim vows to The Falls—"Yes, you have killed thousands of men and women but you can't kill me. Because I am me."

Dr. Moses Blaine,
A Niagara Falls Physician's Log 1879–1905.

By 1900 Niagara Falls had come to be known, to the dismay of local citizens and promoters of the prosperous tourist trade, as "Suicide's Paradise."

A Brief History of Niagara Falls, 1969

Author's Note

Though there are numerous elements of historical and geographical accuracy in this portrait of Niagara Falls, New York, it should be stressed that the city and its environs are finally mythological.

Especially, resemblances to actual persons living or dead are coincidental.

Contents

PART III — *Family*

EPILOGUE

PART I

Honeymoon

The Gatekeeper's Testimony:

12 June 1950

*A*t the time unknown, unnamed, the individual who was to throw himself into the Horseshoe Falls appeared to the gatekeeper of the Goat Island Suspension Bridge at approximately 6:15 A.M. He would be the first pedestrian of the day.

Could I tell, right away? Not exactly. But looking back, yes I should have known. Might've saved him if I had.

So early! The hour should have been dawn except that shifting walls of fog, mist, and spray rising in continuous billowing clouds out of the 180-foot Niagara Gorge obscured the sun. The season should have been early summer except, near The Falls, the air was agitated and damp, abrasive as fine steel filings in the lungs.

The gatekeeper surmised that the strangely hurrying distracted individual had come directly through Prospect Park from one of the old stately hotels on Prospect Street. The gatekeeper observed that the individual had a "young-old pinched face"—"wax-doll skin"— "sunken, kind of glaring eyes." His wire-rimmed glasses gave him an impatient schoolboy look. At six feet he was lanky, lean, "slightly round-shouldered like he'd been stooping over a desk all his life." He hurried purposefully yet blindly, as if somebody was calling his name. His clothes were conservative, somber, nothing a typical Niagara Falls tourist would be wearing. A white cotton dress shirt open at the throat, unbuttoned dark coat and trousers with a jammed zipper "like the poor guy had gotten dressed real fast, in the dark." The man's shoes were dress shoes, black leather polished "like you'd wear to a wedding, or a funeral." His ankles shone waxy-white, sockless.

No socks! With fancy shoes like that. A giveaway.

The gatekeeper called out, "Hello!" but the man ignored him. Not just he was blind but deaf, too. Anyway not hearing. You could see his mind was fixed like a bomb set to go off: he had somewhere to get to, fast.

In a louder voice the gatekeeper called out, "Hey, mister: tickets are fifty cents," but again the man gave no sign of hearing. In the arrogance of desperation he seemed oblivious of the very tollbooth. He was nearly running now, not very gracefully, and swaying, as if the suspension bridge was tilting beneath him. The bridge was about five feet above the white-water rapids and its plank floor was wet, treacherous; the man gripped the railing to keep his balance and haul himself forward. His smooth-soled shoes skidded. He wasn't accustomed to physical exercise. His shiny round glasses slipped on his face and would have fallen if he hadn't shoved them against the bridge of his nose. His mouse-colored hair, thinning at the waxen crown of his head, blew in wan, damp tendrils around his face.

By this time the gatekeeper had decided to leave his tollbooth to follow the agitated man. Calling, "Mister! Hey mister!"—"Mister, wait!" He'd had experience with suicides in the past. More times than he wished to remember. He was a thirty-year veteran of The Falls tourist trade. He was in his early sixties, couldn't keep up with the younger man. Pleading, "Mister! Don't! God damn I'm begging you: *don't*!"

He should have dialed his emergency number, back in the tollbooth. Now it was too late to turn back.

Once on Goat Island the younger man didn't pause by the railing to gaze across the river at the Canadian shore, nor did he pause to contemplate the raging, tumultuous scene, as any normal tourist would do. He didn't pause even to wipe his streaming face, or brush his straggly hair out of his eyes. *Under the spell of The Falls. Nobody mortal was going to stop him.*

But you have to interfere, or try. Can't let a man—or a woman—commit suicide, the unforgiveable sin, before your staring eyes.

The gatekeeper, short of breath, light-headed, limped after the younger man shouting at him as he made his unerring way to the southern tip of the little island, Terrapin Point, above the Horseshoe Falls. The most treacherous corner of Goat Island, as it was the most beautiful and enthralling. Here the rapids go into a frenzy. White frothy churning water shooting up fifteen feet into the air. Hardly any visibility. The chaos of a nightmare. The Horseshoe Falls is a gigantic cataract a half-mile long at its crest, three thousand tons of water pouring over the Gorge each second. The air roars, shakes. The ground beneath your feet shakes. As if the very earth is beginning to come apart, disintegrate into particles, down to its molten center. As if time has ceased. Time has exploded. As if you've come too near to the radiant, thrumming, mad heart of all being. Here, your veins, arteries, the minute precision and perfection of your nerves will be unstrung in an instant. Your brain, in which you reside, that one-of-a-kind repository of *you*, will be pounded into its chemical components: brain cells, molecules, atoms. Every shadow and echo of every memory erased.

Maybe that's the promise of The Falls? The secret?

Like we're sick of ourselves. Mankind. This is the way out, only a few have the vision.

Thirty yards from the younger man, the gatekeeper saw him place one foot on the lowest rung of the railing. A tentative foot, on the slippery wrought iron. But the man's hands gripped the top rung, both fists, tight,

"Don't do it! Mister! God damn—"

The gatekeeper's words were drowned out by The Falls. Flung back into his face like cold spit.

Near to collapsing, himself. This would be his last summer at

Goat Island. His heart hurt, pounding to send oxygen to his stunned brain. And his lungs hurt, not only the stinging spray of the river but the strange metallic taste of the air of the industrial city sprawling east and north of The Falls, in which the gatekeeper had lived all his life. *You wear out. You see too much. Every breath hurts.*

The gatekeeper would afterward swear he'd seen the younger man make a gesture of farewell in the instant before he jumped: a mock salute, a salute of defiance, as a bright brash schoolboy might make to an elder, to provoke; yet a sincere farewell too, as you might make to a stranger, a witness to whom you mean no harm, whom you wish to absolve of the slightest shred of guilt he might feel, for allowing you to die when he might have saved you.

And in the next instant the young man, who'd been commandeering the gatekeeper's exclusive attention, was simply—gone.

In a heartbeat, gone. Over the Horseshoe Falls.

Not the first of the poor bastards I've seen, but God help me he will be the last.

When the distraught gatekeeper returned to his booth to dial Niagara County Emergency Services, the time was 6:26 A.M., approximately one hour after dawn.

The Bride

1

No. Please, God. Not this."

The hurt. The humiliation. The unspeakable shame.
Not grief, not yet. The shock was too immediate for grief.

When she discovered the enigmatic note her husband had left for
her propped against a mirror in the bedroom of their honeymoon
suite at the Rainbow Grand Hotel, Niagara Falls, New York, Ariah
had been married twenty-one hours. When, in the early afternoon of
that day, she learned from Niagara Falls police that a man resembling
her husband, Gilbert Erskine, had thrown himself into the Horseshoe Falls early that morning and had been swept away—"vanished,
so far without a trace"—beyond the Devil's Hole Rapids, as the scenic attraction downriver from The Falls was named, she'd been married not quite twenty-eight hours.

These were the stark, cruel facts.

"I'm a bride who has become a widow in less than a day."

Ariah spoke aloud, in a voice of wonder. She was the daughter of a much-revered Presbyterian minister, surely that should have counted for something with God, as it did with secular authorities?

Ariah struck suddenly at her face with both fists. She wanted to pummel, blacken her eyes that had seen too much.

"God, help me! You wouldn't be so cruel—would you?"

Yes. I would. Foolish woman of course I would. Who are you, to be spared My justice?

How swift the reply came! A taunt that echoed so distinctly in Ariah's skull, she halfway believed these pitying strangers could hear it.

But here was solace: until Gilbert Erskine's body was found in the river and identified, his death was theoretical and not official.

Ariah wasn't yet a widow, but still a bride.

2

... WAKING THAT MORNING to the rude and incontrovertible fact that she who'd slept alone all her life was yet alone again on the morning following her wedding day. Waking alone though she was no longer Miss Ariah Juliet Littrell but Mrs. Gilbert Erskine. Though no longer the spinster daughter of Reverend and Mrs. Thaddeus Littrell of Troy, New York, piano and voice instructor at the Troy Academy of Music, but the bride of Reverend Gilbert Erskine, recently named minister of the First Presbyterian Church of Palymra, New York.

Waking alone and in that instant she knew. Yet she could not believe, her pride was too great. Not allowing herself to think *I am alone. Am I?*

A clamor of wedding bells had followed her here. Hundreds of miles. Her head was ringed in pain as if in a vise. Her bowels were sick as if the very intestines were corroded and rotting. In this unfamiliar bed smelling of damp linen, damp flesh and desperation. Where, where was she, what was the name of the hotel he'd brought her to, a paradise for honeymooners, and Niagara Falls was the Honeymoon

Capital of the World, a pulse in her head beat so violently she couldn't think. Having been married so briefly she knew little of husbands yet it seemed to her plausible (Ariah was telling herself this as a frightened child might tell herself a story to ward off harm) that Gilbert had only just slipped quietly from the bed and was in the bathroom. She lay very still listening for sounds of faucets, a bath running, a toilet flushing, hoping to hear even as her sensitive nerves resisted hearing. The awkwardness, embarrassment, shame of such intimacy was new to her, like the intimacy of marriage. The "marital bed." Nowhere to hide. His pungent Vitalis hair-oil, and her coyly sweet Lily of the Valley cologne in collision. Just Ariah and Gilbert whom no one called Gil alone together breathless and smiling hard and determined to be cheerful, pleasant, polite with each other as they'd always been before the wedding had joined them in holy matrimony except Ariah had to know something was wrong, she'd been jolted from her hot stuporous sleep to this knowledge.

Gone. He's gone. Can't be gone. Where?

God damn! She was a new, shy bride. So the world perceived her and the world was not mistaken. At the hotel registration desk she'd signed, for the first time, *Mrs. Ariah Erskine*, and her cheeks had flamed. A virgin, twenty-nine years old. Inexperienced with men as with another species of being. As she lay wracked with pain she didn't dare even to reach out in the enormous bed for fear of touching him.

She wouldn't have wanted him to misinterpret her touch.

Almost, she had to recall his name. "Gilbert." No one called him "Gil." None of the Erskine relatives she'd met. Possibly friends of his at the seminary in Albany had called him "Gil" but that was a side of him Ariah hadn't yet seen, and couldn't presume to know. It was like discussing religious faith with him: he'd been ordained a Presbyterian minister at a very young age and so faith was his professional domain and not hers. To call such a man by the folksy diminutive "Gil" would be too familiar a gesture for Ariah, his fiancée who'd only just become his wife.

In his stiff shy way he'd called her "Ariah, dear." She called him

"Gilbert" but had been planning how in a tender moment, as in a romantic Hollywood film, she would begin to call him "darling"—maybe even "Gil, darling."

Unless all that was changed. That possibility.

She'd had a glass of champagne at the wedding reception, and another glass—or two—of champagne in the hotel room the night before, nothing more and yet she'd never felt so drugged, so ravaged. Her eyelashes were stuck together as if with glue, her mouth tasted of acid. She couldn't bear the thought: she'd been sleeping like this, comatose, mouth open and gaping like a fish's.

Had she been snoring? *Had Gilbert heard?*

She tried to hear him in the bathroom. Antiquated plumbing shrieked and rumbled, but not close by. Yet surely Gilbert was in the bathroom. Probably he was making an effort to be quiet. During the night he'd used the bathroom. Trying to disguise his noises. Running water to disguise . . . Or had that been Ariah, desperately running both faucets in the sink? Ariah in her stained ivory silk nightgown swaying and trying not to vomit yet finally, helplessly vomiting, into the sink, sobbing.

Don't. Don't think of it. No one can force you.

The previous day, arriving in early evening, Ariah had been surprised that, in June, the air was so *cold*. So *damp*. The air was so saturated with moisture, the sun in the western sky resembled a street lamp refracted through water. Ariah, who was wearing a short-sleeved poplin dress, shivered and hugged her arms. Gilbert, frowning in the direction of the river, took no notice.

Gilbert had done all the driving, from Troy, several hundred miles to the east; he'd insisted. He told Ariah it made him nervous to be a passenger in his own car, which was a handsomely polished black 1949 Packard. Repeatedly on the trip he excused himself and blew his nose, loudly. Averting his face from Ariah. His skin was flushed as if with fever. Ariah murmured several times she hoped he wasn't coming down with a cold as Mrs. Erskine, Gilbert's mother, now Ariah's mother-in-law, had fretted at the luncheon.

Gilbert was susceptible to sore throats, respiratory infections, sinus headaches, Mrs. Erskine informed Ariah. He had a "delicate stomach" that couldn't tolerate spicy foods, or "agitation."

Mrs. Erskine had hugged Ariah, who yielded stiffly in the older woman's plump arms. Mrs. Erskine had begged Ariah to call her "Mother"—as Gilbert did.

Ariah murmured yes. Yes, Mother Erskine.

Thinking *Mother! What does that make Gilbert and me, brother and sister?*

Ariah had tried. Ariah was determined to be an ideal bride, and an ideal daughter-in-law.

A clamor of church bells. Sunday morning!

In a strange bed, in a strange city, and lost.

A female voice chiding in her ear, and a smell of Mother Erskine's talcumy bosom. *If you've never drunk anything stronger than sweet cider, Ariah, do you think it's wise to have a second glass of champagne—so soon after the first?*

Possibly it hadn't been Gilbert's mother but Ariah's own mother. Or possibly it had been both mothers at separate times.

A giggly-shivery bride. In satin and Chantilly lace, fussy little mother-of-pearl buttons, a gossamer veil and lace gloves to the elbow that, peeled off after the luncheon, left small diamond-shaped indentations in her sensitive skin like an exotic rash. At the luncheon, held in the Littrells' big, gloomy brick residence adjacent to the church, the bride was observed nervously lifting her champagne glass to her lips numerous times. She ate little, and her hand so trembled she dropped a forkful of wedding cake. Her rather small, almond-shaped pebbly-green eyes were continually misting over, as with an allergy. She excused herself several times to visit a bathroom. She freshened her lipstick which was bright red as neon; she'd powdered her nose too frequently, and granules of powder were discernible from a short distance. Though she tried to be graceful she was in fact ungainly and gawky as a stork. Pointy elbows, beaky nose. You'd never have thought her an accomplished singer, her voice was scratchy and inaudible. Still, some pronounced Ariah "very charming"—"a beautiful bride." And yet: those Dixie-cup breasts! She was well aware that everyone stared at her bosom in the exquisite Chantilly lace bodice, pitying her. She was well aware that everyone pitied Gilbert Erskine, to have married an old maid.

Another glass of champagne?

She'd graciously declined. Or, maybe, she'd taken it. For just a few sips.

Mrs. Littrell, mother-of-the-bride, relieved and anxious in about equal measure, had conceded to Ariah that, yes, it might seem strange to her, a full corset to contain the tiny 32-A breasts, the twenty-two-inch waist, and the thirty-two-inch hips, yes but *this is a wedding, the most important day of your life*. And the corset provides a garter belt for your sheerest of sheer silk stockings.

Ariah laughed wildly. Ariah grabbed something, a swath of silk from the astonished seamstress, and blew her nose into it.

Though she'd obeyed of course. Never would Ariah have defied Mrs. Littrell in such matters of feminine protocol.

Later, on the morning of the ceremony, being dressed by Mrs. Littrell and the seamstress, she'd prayed silently *Dear God, don't let my stockings be baggy at the ankles. Nowhere it can show.*

And, as the ceremony began: *Dear God, don't let me perspire. I know I'm starting, I can feel it. Don't let half-moons show at my underarms. In this beautiful dress. I beg you, God!*

These eager girlish prayers, so far as Ariah knew, had been answered.

She was feeling stronger by degrees. She forced herself to whisper, "Gilbert?" As one might sleepily whisper to a spouse, waking in the morning. "Gilbert, w-where are you?"

No answer.

Gazing through half-shut eyes she saw: no one in the bed beside her.

A crooked pillow. Wrinkled linen pillowcase. A bedsheet turned partly back, as if with care. But no one.

Ariah forced her eyes open. Oh!

A German ceramic clock on a mantel across the room and shiny gilt numerals that meant, for several arduous seconds, nothing to Ariah's squinting eyes. Then the clock's face showed 7:10. The fog outside the hotel windows was fading, it appeared to be morning and not dusk.

Ariah hadn't lost the day, then.

Hadn't lost her husband. Not so quickly!

For probably if Gilbert wasn't in the bathroom, Gilbert was elsewhere in the hotel. Gilbert had let it be known he was an early riser. Ariah guessed he was downstairs in the lobby with its Victorian dark paneling, leather settees and gleaming marble floor; or possibly he was having coffee on the wide, regal veranda overlooking Prospect Park and, a short distance beyond, the Niagara River and Falls. Frowning as he skimmed the *Niagara Gazette*, the *Buffalo Courier-Express*. Or, his monogrammed silver pen in hand, a birthday gift from Ariah herself, he might be making notations as he leafed through tourist brochures, maps and pamphlets with such titles as THE GREAT FALLS AT NIAGARA: ONE OF THE SEVEN WONDERS OF THE WORLD.

Waiting for me to join him. Waiting for me to slip my hand into his.

Ariah could envision her young husband. He was quite attractive in his stern way. Those winking eyeglasses, and nostrils unnaturally wide and deep in his long nose. Ariah would smile gaily at him, greet him with a light kiss on the cheek. As if they'd been behaving like this, so casually, in such intimacy, for a long time. But Gilbert would dispel the mood by standing quickly, awkwardly, jarring the little rattan table and spilling coffee, for he'd been trained never to remain seated in the presence of a woman. "Ariah! Good morning, dear."

"I'm sorry to be so late. I hope . . ."

"Waiter? Another coffee, please."

In charming white wicker rocking chairs, side by side. The honeymoon couple. Among how many hundreds of honeymoon couples in June, at The Falls. The uniformed Negro waiter appears, smiling . . .

Ariah winced, climbing down from the bed. It was a Victorian four-poster with brass fixtures and a crocheted canopy like mosquito netting; the mattress was unnaturally high from the floor. Like a creature with a back broken in several places, she moved cautiously.

Tugging at a strap of her silk nightgown where it had fallen, or had been yanked, over her shoulder. (And how sore, how discolored her shoulder was . . . A plum-colored bruise had formed in the night.) Her lashes had come unstuck, though barely. There were dried bits of mucus in her eyes like sand. And that ugly acid taste in her mouth.

"Oh. My God."

Shaking her head to clear it, which was a mistake. Shattered glass! Mirror-shards shifting, sliding, glittering in her brain.

As, the previous week, she'd clumsily dropped a mother-of-pearl hand mirror on the carpeted floor of her parents' bedroom, perversely the mirror bounced from the carpet and onto a hardwood floor and cracked, shattered at once—the frightened bride and the stunned mother-of-the-bride staring in dismay at this portent of ill luck in which, as devout Presbyterians, neither was allowed to believe. "Oh, Mother. I'm *sorry*." Ariah had spoken calmly though thinking with stoic resignation *It will begin now. My punishment.*

Now the muffled thunder of The Falls had entered her sleep.

Now the muffled thunder of The Falls, ominous as God's indecipherable mutterings, had entered her heart.

She'd married a man she had not loved, and could not love. Worse yet she'd married a man she knew could not love her.

The Roman Catholics, whose baroque religion appalled and fascinated Protestants, believed in the existence of *mortal sins*. There were *venial sins* but *mortal sins* were the serious ones. Ariah knew it must be a *mortal sin*, punishable by eternal damnation, to have done what she and Gilbert Erskine did. Joined in sacred matrimony, in a legal contract binding them for life. At the same time, possibly, it was a very common occurrence in Troy, New York, and elsewhere. It was something that would "get over with, in time."

(A pet expression of Mrs. Littrell's. Ariah's mother uttered it at least once a day, she seemed to think it a cheery sentiment.)

Ariah stood unsteadily on a dusky pink plush carpet. She was barefoot, sweaty yet shivering. She began to itch suddenly. Beneath her damp armpits, between her legs. A flamey itch like an attack of tiny red ants in the region of her groin.

My punishment. Ariah wondered if she was a virgin, still.

Or if in the confusion of the night, in a delirium of part-nudity and bedclothes, open-mouthed kisses and panting, and the young husband's frantic fumbling, she might have become . . . might somehow *be* . . . pregnant?

Ariah pressed her knuckles against her mouth.

"God, no. Please."

It wasn't possible, and she wasn't going to think about it. *It was not possible*.

Of course, Ariah wanted children. So she said. So she'd assured Mother Erskine, and her own mother. Many times. A normal young woman wants children, a family. A good Christian woman.

But to *have a baby!*—Ariah recoiled in disgust.

"No. Please."

Ariah knocked timidly on the bathroom door. If Gilbert were inside, she hardly wanted to interrupt him. The door wasn't locked. Cautiously she opened it . . . A rectangular mirror on the back of the door swung toward her like a jeering cartoon: there was a disheveled, sallow-faced woman in a torn nightgown. She turned away her eyes quickly and the fine broken glass inside her skull shifted, glittering with pain. "Oh! God." But she saw that the bathroom was empty. A spacious luxurious blindingly white room with gleaming brass fixtures, perfumy soaps in tinsel wrappers, coyly arranged monogrammed hand towels. An enormous claw-footed white porcelain tub, empty. (Had Gilbert bathed? Showered? There was no sign of wet in the tub.) The room smelled frankly of vomit, and several of the thick white terry cloth towels had been used. One of them lay on the floor. Above the elegant sunken ceramic sink, the heart-shaped mirror was spotted.

Ariah picked up the soiled towel and hung it on a rack. She wondered if she would ever see Gilbert Erskine again.

In the mirror a ghost-female hovered, but she didn't meet its piteous gaze. She wondered if possibly she'd imagined everything: the engagement ("My life is changed. My life is saved. Thank you, God!"); the wedding ceremony in her father's very church, and the sacred marital vows. Ariah's favorite movie was Walt Disney's *Fantasia*, which she'd seen several times and it wasn't such a step from *Fantasia* to being married.

If you're the spinster daughter of Reverend and Mrs. Thaddeus Littrell of Troy, New York. A dreamer!

"Gilbert?" She raised her voice tremulously. "Are you— somewhere?"

Silence.

In addition to the bathroom, the Rosebud Honeymoon Suite, as it was called, consisted of a bedroom and a parlor, and two closets. The furnishings were aggressively Victorian with tulip-colored cushions, drapes, lamp shades, carpets. A number of the cushions were heart-shaped. Ariah opened each of the closets, wincing with headache pain. (Why was she behaving so absurdly? Why would Gilbert be hiding in a closet? She didn't want to think.) She saw his clothes, neatly arranged on hotel hangers, hanging in place, undisturbed. If he'd run off, wouldn't he have taken his clothes with him?

She didn't want to think if the Packard was missing. It had been a gift from the Erskines to Gilbert, some months before.

The parlor! A bad memory hovered here. On a marble-topped table were a vase of slightly wilted red roses and an empty bottle of French champagne, both compliments of the Rainbow Grand. *Congratulations Mr. and Mrs. Gilbert Erskin!* The bottle lay on its side. Ariah felt a rush of shame. A tart sweet taste rose like bile in her mouth. Gilbert had only sipped at his glass of champagne, cautiously. He rarely ingested, as he called it, alcohol; even at the wedding reception he'd been sparing. But not Ariah.

Hungover. That was her condition. No mystery about it.

Hungover! On the morning following her wedding day.

Too shameful. Thank God none of the elders knew.

For Gilbert would never tell. He wouldn't even tell Mother Erskine who adored him.

Disgusting. Frankly you disgust me.

Never. He was too polite. And he had his pride.

He was a gentleman, if an immature boy, too. A gentleman would never upset his wife, especially a high-strung, excitable wife. His bride of less than twenty hours. *So Gilbert had to be elsewhere in the hotel.* Downstairs in the lobby, or in the coffee shop; out on the veranda overlooking the lawn, or strolling on the hotel grounds, waiting for Ariah to join him. (Gilbert wouldn't have gone sightseeing yet, to The Falls, without her.) And it was still early, not yet 7:30 A.M. He'd taken his clothes and shoes and dressed quietly in the parlor. Taking care not to wake Ariah who he knew was—exhausted. He hadn't switched on a light. He'd crept about barefoot.

Desperate to escape. Undetected.

"No! I can't believe that."

It was strange to be so *alone*. Even Ariah's voice in this absurdly decorated suite sounded *alone*. She'd supposed marriage would be different.

You begin with a wish, and the wish comes true, and you can't shut off the wish.

Like "The Sorceror's Apprentice," the comic-nightmare sequence in *Fantasia*. The ordeal of Mickey Mouse as the Sorceror's hapless apprentice did come to a happy ending, however, when the Sorceror returned home and broke the spell. But Ariah's situation was very different.

Home. Where was Ariah's home? They would be "settling in" in Palmyra, New York. In a tall gaunt brick house that came with Gilbert's appointment as minister. She hadn't thought very clearly about this residence, and wasn't going to think about it now.

Now: where was *now*?

Niagara Falls?

Of all places! Vulgar jokes. As if Ariah and Gilbert were hoping to be typical American newlyweds.

In fact it was Gilbert, strangely, who'd wanted to come to The Falls. He'd long been interested in "ancient glacial history"—"geological pre-history"—in upstate New York. One of their dates had been to the Museum of Natural History in Albany, and another had been to Herkimer Falls where a retired army colonel had a collection of fossils and Indian artifacts, open to the public. From Gilbert's dinner conversation with her father, which was so much more animated and interesting than Gilbert's conversation with Ariah, she'd gathered that Gilbert believed it might be his "destined task" to reconcile the alleged evidence of fossil discoveries in the nineteenth century with the biblical account of the Earth's creation.

Reverend Littrell, square-jawed and robust in middle-age, looking no-nonsense as Teddy Roosevelt in the old photos, laughed at such a notion. He was one who believed that the Devil had left so-called fossils in the earth for credulous fools to find.

Gilbert had winced at this, but, gentleman that he was, made no objection.

The way of science and the way of faith. Ariah had to admire her fiancé for such ambition.

She'd always interpreted the Book of Genesis as a Hebrew version of a Grimm's fairy tale. Mostly it was a warning: disobey God the Father, you'll be expelled from the Garden of Eden. A daughter of Eve, your punishment will be doubled: *In sorrow thou shalt bring forth children, and thy desire shall be to thy husband, and he shall rule over thee.* Well, that was clear enough!

Ariah didn't intend to get into theological debates with Gilbert, any more than with her father. Let these men think what they will, Ariah thought. It's for our own good, too.

Ariah decided to call the front desk. Bravely she picked up the pink plastic receiver and dialed "O." She would ask if—if a youngish man was anywhere in the lobby? Or—out on the veranda? In the coffee shop? She wanted to speak with him, please. A tall thin young man weighing perhaps one hundred fifty pounds, with a parchment-pale skin that looked too tight for his facial bones, round wire-rimmed glasses, neatly dressed, courteous, with a distinctive way about him of seeming to be waiting patiently to be pleased; or, revealing how charitable he might be, how willing to compromise his expectations, though secretly he was displeased . . . But when the operator said cheerily, "Good morning, Mrs. Erskine, what can I do for you?" Ariah was struck dumb. She'd have to adjust to being called *Mrs. Erskine*. But it was a greater shock to realize that a stranger knew her identity, the switchboard must have lighted up her room number. Meekly Ariah said, "I—was just wondering what the w-weather is? I'm wondering what to wear this morning."

The operator laughed in a friendly, practiced manner.

"Though it's June, ma'am, it's also The Falls. Dress warm until the fog lifts." She paused for dramatic effect. "If it lifts."

3

7:35 A.M. ARIAH HADN'T yet discovered the farewell note, on a sheet of dusky-rose Rainbow Grand stationery, neatly folded and propped against the vanity mirror in the bedroom. It was a small oval gilt-framed mirror into which, in her stricken state, Ariah couldn't bring herself to look.

God, no. Spare me. What Gilbert must have seen, while I slept.

Of course, it was a relief that Gilbert Erskine wasn't close by.

After the frantic crowdedness of the previous day, so many suffocating faces brought close to hers, and a nightmare lunacy of smiles, and the intimacy of the shared bed . . .

A bath. Quick, quick before Gilbert returned!

Ariah would have taken a bath in any case. Of course. Ordinarily she bathed every night before bed, but she had not bathed the night before; if she missed a night, she bathed in the morning without fail. Sometimes in the sticky humidity of summer in upstate New York, in this era before air-conditioning, Ariah bathed twice daily; yet was never convinced, she didn't *smell*.

Nothing appealed to her more than a bath. A soaking hot bath in the sumptuous bathroom, in a luxury tub she wouldn't have to clean afterward with Dutch cleanser and a scrub brush; a bath fragrant and bubbling with lilac bath salts, courtesy of the Rainbow Grand. Her eyes filled with tears of gratitude.

Give me another chance! God, please.

Of course there was hope, still. Ariah didn't seriously believe that Gilbert Erskine had *run off*.

For where, after all, could a twenty-seven-year-old Presbyterian minister, son and son-in-law of Presbyterian ministers, run off *to*?

"He's trapped. Just like me."

Ariah ran bathwater from big brass faucets until every mirror in the bathroom was steamed over. Luscious warm suffocating perfumy air! And water hot as she could bear, to cleanse away the dried sweat and other stains from her body. The smells of her body.

And his body, too. Where she'd clumsily touched him. By accident. Or somehow in the confusion, she'd brushed against him, or pressed against him . . . She couldn't remember exactly. And whatever had happened, what milky fluid leaping from the man's rubbery thing onto her belly, and into the bedclothes, *no she could not remember.*

The man's shocked high-pitched cry. A bat-cry. His convulsions, his whimpering in her arms. She could not remember *and she was not to blame.*

Ariah would shampoo her hair, too. It was snarly and sticky at the nape of her neck. Her hair that was wanly-wavy and faded-red, so fine and thin as to require constant care. "Pinning up" with bobby pins, foam rubber hair rollers. (She'd brought a cache of these on her honeymoon, hidden in her suitcase. But obviously she couldn't wear such trappings to *bed*.) This morning she wouldn't have time to curl her hair, she'd brush it back into what Mrs. Littrell called a "chic French twist," and fluff out her languid bangs on her forehead. And hope she'd more resemble a ballerina than a spinster librarian or schoolteacher.

She would wear a pink rose bud twined into the French twist.

She would wear very light makeup, not the cosmetic mask of the previous day that had seemed required. Not vivid red lipstick but coral pink. *A different sort of femininity. Seduction.*

And so when Gilbert saw Ariah again, in a floral-print shirtwaist, a white cardigan over her shoulders, her hair in the chic French twist and a demure lipstick on her thin, curving lips, he'd admire her again. He'd be in awe of her again. (Hadn't he been in awe of her once? For a while? The "musically-inclined" daughter of Reverend Thaddeus Littrell, with her small-town patrician aura?) He would smile shyly at her, adjusting his glasses. He'd blink at her as if a bright light were shining in his eyes.

I forgive you Ariah. However you disgusted me last night, and I disgusted you.

I can't love you. But I can forgive you.

Ariah let her ivory-silk nightgown with the wide lace straps and lacy bodice fall in a snaky heap on the tile floor. There were dried mucous stains on it. And darkish stains . . . She wasn't going to look. She was grateful for the billowing steam, that obscured her vision. Carefully she climbed into the claw-footed tub, that was still only partially filled. "Oh!"—the water was scalding. But she would endure it. The tub was larger, more ungainly than the Littrells' old tub at home. A drinking trough for elephants. And not so sparkling clean as she'd believed: narrow rings of rust around the brass fixtures, bits of fluff and tiny kinky hairs floating in the sudsy water.

Ariah settled gingerly into the tub. She was so slender-boned, she seemed almost to be floating. *Don't look. There's no need.* Her sallow bruised body. Small breasts hard as green pears. Tight little nipples on these breasts like rubber caps. She had to wonder if Gilbert had been disappointed . . . Her collarbone pushed against her pale, nearly translucent skin, that was sprinkled with pale freckles. As a girl Ariah had dared to poke her tight little belly button with a finger, wondering if this was an act considered "dirty." Like so many acts associated with the female body.

At the fork of her legs, a rusty swath of that hair called *pubic.*

Embarrassing! A few years ago, introducing students at a music school recital, Ariah had stumbled over the word *public* and had seemed to say *pubic.* Quickly she'd corrected herself—"*Pub*lic." She'd been addressing an audience of mostly parents, relatives, neighbors of her students, and her face flamed: each freckle in the constellation of freckles in her face was a miniature fiery star.

Fortunately, Gilbert Erskine hadn't been in the audience. She could imagine him wincing, his eyes pinching at the corners.

Out of kindness, no one had ever mentioned Ariah's slip of the tongue.

(Though people must have laughed, in private. As Ariah might herself have laughed if another had made such a blunder.)

In Troy, New York, it seemed much was left unsaid. Out of tact, kindness. Out of pity.

Ariah was examining a broken fingernail. It was cutting into the tender quick of her finger.

A scratch on Gilbert's shoulder? On his back, or . . .

Isn't Gilbert Erskine too young for you, Ariah?—so Ariah's girl cousins and friends never once inquired, during the eight months of their engagement. Even in playful innocence, no one inquired.

She would wonder if anyone inquired of Gilbert *Isn't Ariah Littrell too old for you?*

Well, they were a match! They'd seemed the same age, much of the time. They were of the same intelligent, bookish, high-strung, perhaps somewhat egotistic temperament, inclined to impatience, exasperation. Inclined to think well of themselves and less well of most others. (Though Ariah knew to hide these traits, as a dutiful daughter.)

Two sets of parents had heartily approved of the match.

Difficult to gauge who of the four elders was most relieved: Mrs. Littrell, or Mrs. Erskine; Reverend Littrell, or Reverend Erskine.

In any case, Ariah had become engaged in the nick of time. Twenty-nine was nearing the precipice, the edge of oblivion: thirty. Ariah scorned such conventional thinking and yet the nether years of her twenties, past the median twenty-five, when everyone she knew or knew of was getting engaged, getting married, having babies, had been dismaying, nightmarish. *Dear God send someone to me. Let my life begin. I beg you!* There were times, shameful to admit, when Ariah Littrell, an accomplished pianist, singer, music teacher, would have gladly exchanged her soul for an engagement ring, it was that simple. The man himself was a secondary matter.

And then the miracle happened: the engagement.

And now in June 1950, the wedding. Like Christ with the fishes and loaves, better yet like Christ raising Lazarus from the dead, the event had seemed to Ariah a miracle. She wouldn't have to be Ariah Littrell the minister's daughter any longer; the "girl" everyone in Troy professed to admire. Now she could bask in the innocent pride of being the wife of an ambitious young Presbyterian minister with, at only twenty-seven, his own church in Palmyra, New York, pop. 2,100.

Ariah had wanted to laugh at her friends' faces when they first saw the engagement ring. "You never thought I'd get engaged, admit it!" she'd wanted to tease, or accuse. But she'd said nothing, of course. Her friends would only have denied it.

The wedding ceremony itself had passed in a dream. Certainly Ariah had had no champagne before the church service yet her walk was unsteady, she'd leaned against her father's strong arm as he escorted his tall pale red-haired daughter up the aisle and a blaze of light blinded her, pulsing lights like manic stars. *Do you Ariah Littrell solemnly swear. Love honor obey. Till death do you . . .* No champagne of course but she'd taken several aspirins with Coke, a frequent home remedy. It caused her heart to jump and her mouth to dehydrate. Gilbert would probably disapprove. Beside her at the altar he stood taller than she, still and wary, trying not to sniffle and reciting his part of the ceremony in a grave voice. *I take thee, Ariah. My lawfully wedded wife.* Two trembling young people at the altar being blessed like cattle about to be slaughtered by a common butcher. Bonded by terror yet strangely oblivious of each other.

What awaited Ariah, what "physical" ordeal on her wedding night, and on the nights to follow, she shrank from contemplating. She'd never been a girl whom forbidden thoughts much tempted, no more than forbidden actions. Though observed to be surprisingly passionate while thundering her way through the stormy movements of Beethoven's great piano sonatas, or singing certain Schubert lieder, Ariah was a stiff, shy girl in most gatherings. She blushed easily, she shrank from being touched. Her pebbly-green eyes glinted with intelligence and not warmth. If she'd had occasional boyfriends they'd been boys like herself. Boys like Gilbert Erskine who were young-old and inclined to be round-shouldered in their teens. Of course Ariah was routinely examined by the Littrells' family doctor, but the elderly physician could be relied upon not to use gynecologic instruments in any extreme manner, and always desisted when Ariah whimpered in pain and discomfort, or kicked at him in panic. Out of feminine delicacy and embarrassment Mrs. Littrell skirted the marital subject, and of course Reverend Littrell would rather have died than speak to his tense, virginal daughter of "intimate" matters. He left this awkward task to his wife, and thought no more of it.

The hot bath was making Ariah light-headed. Or such thoughts were making her light-headed. She saw that her left breast floated in the water, partly ochre-colored as if in shadow. He'd squeezed, pinched. She supposed there were bruises on her lower belly and thighs. Between her chafed legs there was less sensation, as if that part of her body had gone to sleep.

That bat-cry of his! His flushed shiny boy's face contorted like Boris Karloff's face in *Frankenstein*.

He had not said *I love you, Ariah*. He had not lied.

Nor had she whispered *I love you Gilbert* as she'd rehearsed, lying in his arms. For she knew the words would offend him, at such a time.

Lying in the bath, as the water lost its steamy heat and began to scum over with soap, Ariah began silently to cry. Tears stung her eyes, that were already sore, and ran down her cheeks into the bathwater. She'd imagined how, while she was bathing, she would hear the outer door open and close, and Gilbert's uplifted voice—"Ariah? Good morning!" But she hadn't heard any door open and close. She hadn't heard Gilbert's uplifted voice.

She was thinking how, long before she'd met Gilbert Erskine, while still in high school she'd locked herself in the bathroom at home and "examined" herself after a bath with a small mirror. Oh, she'd nearly fainted! It was bad as giving blood. She'd seen, between her slender thighs, inside the damp, curly swath of pubic hair, a curious little raised tissue like a tongue, or one of those slithery organs you take care to remove from a chicken before roasting it; and, as she stared in appalled fascination, a small, pinched hole at the base of this tissue, smaller than her belly button. How on earth could a man's "thing" be fitted into such a tiny space? *Worse yet, how could a baby emerge through such a tiny space?*

The revelation had left Ariah weak with terror, dread, revulsion for hours afterward. Maybe she hadn't recovered, yet.

4

THERE IT WAS. The note. So conspicuous. Like a shout. Propped up by the vanity mirror. Ariah would never comprehend how, or why, she hadn't noticed it earlier.

On rose-colored hotel stationery, in a hastily scrawled handwrit-

ing Ariah could not have easily identified as Gilbert's, were these
words:

> Ariah sorry—I cant—
> I tried to love you
> I am going where my pride must take me
> I know—you cant forgive
> God will not forgive
>
> By this I free us both of our vows

On the carpet below was a monogrammed silver pen. It must have
been tossed carelessly down, and rolled onto the floor.

For a very long time (five minutes? ten?) Ariah stood frozen, the
note in her trembling hand. Her mind was struck blank. At last she
began to cry, hoarse ugly sobs wracking her body.

As if, after all, she'd loved him?

The Fossil-Seeker

*R*un, run! Run for your life.

At last it was dawn. All night the thunderous river had called to him. Through the night as he prayed to summon strength for what he must do, the river called to him. *Come! Here is peace.* River of Thunder the Tuscaroras named it centuries ago. Falls of Thunder. The Ongiara Indians named it Hungry Water. Devouring the unwary, and the sacrifices. Those who threw themselves into its seething waters to be carried off to oblivion, and peace. How many tortured souls repudiated by God had found peace in those waters, how many had been obliterated and returned to God, he could not guess. Surely there had been hundreds like himself, perhaps thousands. From the start of recorded history in this part of North America, in the 1500's. Many of these were pagans, but Jesus would pity them. Jesus would pity him. Jesus would grant him oblivion, as He on His cross would have been granted oblivion if He had wished it. But He had not required such solace for He was the son of God and born without sin or the very capacity or yearning for sin. Never had He touched a woman, never had He shrieked in ecstatic surrender to the woman's crude touch.

It was dawn, it was time. He'd lived too long. Twenty-seven years, three months! They called him young, fussed over him as a prodigy, but he knew better. He'd lived a day and a night too long. *Do you take this woman as your lawfully wedded wife. Till death do you part* and so he could not bear another hour. Slipping from the bed. Slipping from the bedclothes that smelled of their bodies. As the woman who was Mrs. Erksine *the lawfully wedded wife* slept heavily, on her back as if she'd fallen from a great height, unconscious, brainless, her hands flung upward in an expression of astonishment, mouth open like a fish's and her breath catching at the back of her mouth in a wet rasping idiotic way that maddened him, made him want to shut his fingers around her throat and squeeze. Run, run! Don't look back. Gathering his clothes, his shoes, tiptoeing into the parlor where a chill pale light at the windows exposed the fussily decorated plush-pink room. *Honeymoon suite, paradise for two. Luxury and privacy. An idyll you will never forget!* Fumbling with buttons, muttering to himself as he dressed hurriedly, pushed his bare feet by force into part-laced shoes, and fled.

Run, run! For your life.

Too restless to wait for an elevator, taking the fire stairs instead. Five flights down. By the Bulova watch (a gift from his proud parents when he'd graduated top of his class at the Albany Theological Seminary) he had not failed to strap to his wrist, for G. was one to observe certain routine rituals of his life even in the final exalted hour of his life, it was just past 6 A.M. The hotel lobby was nearly deserted. A few uniformed hotel staff, taking not much notice of him. Outside, the air was cold and very damp. June, the month of brides. June, the season of young love. June, a mockery. If by G.'s watch it should have been dawn, by the actual sky above the Niagara Gorge it was an hour without time, mist-shrouded, sullenly glaring like the bottom of a scrubbed pot and smelling mostly of something sulfurous, metallic. *Niagara! Honeymoon Capital of the World*. He'd known from the start, maybe. Never had he truly deceived himself. Introduced to the red-haired woman, eager to establish himself with her influential father the Reverend Thaddeus Littrell of Troy, New York. Introduced to the red-haired woman whose thin lips wavered in a hesitant, hopeful smile even as her pebbly-green eyes stared at him lustrous and unyielding as glass. And he'd thought, in his folly, vanity, desperation *A sister! One like myself.*

He was walking swiftly. Bare feet in leather dress shoes, and his heels chafed. A mistake not to pull on socks but he hadn't time. He needed to get to the river, he needed to get *there*. As if, only *there*, he could breathe. The broad sidewalks of Prospect Street were puddled from a recent rain. The cobbled street glistened with wet. He stepped into the street and out of nowhere a rattling trolley rushed at him and a shrieking horn sounded and he hid his face so no one could recognize it afterward seeing its likeness in the local papers. For he knew the shame and desperation of his act would outlive him, and its courage would be obscured, but he did not care for it was time, God would never forgive him but God would grant him freedom. That was the promise of The Falls. Through the night he heard its murmurous roar and now in the open air he heard it more clearly, and could feel the very ground beneath his feet vibrating with its power. *Come! Here alone is peace.*

What pride, what a fervor of triumph. Ten months before.

On the telephone announcing in a tremulous voice *I am engaged, Douglas.* And his friend spoke warmly, spontaneously. *Congratulations, Gil!* And he'd said almost boastfully, *Will you come to my wedding? They're scheduling it for next June.* D. said, *Of course, Gil. Hey, this is great news. I'm very happy for you.* G. said, *I'm happy, too. I'm . . . happy.* D. said, *Gil?* and G. said, *Yes, Douglas?* and D. asked, *Who is she?* and for a moment G. couldn't think, and stammered, *Who?* and D. said, laughing, *Your fiancée, Gil. When will I meet her?*

D. had been impressed (hadn't he?) when he'd learned who his friend's fiancée was. The daughter of. A music instructor, pianist and singer.

At the seminary they'd been such opposite types. Yet they'd

talked passionately late into the night: of life and death, mortality and Life Everlasting. Never had they talked of suicide. Never of despair. For, young Christian men studying for the ministry, why should they despair? They were themselves the bearers of good news. Instead, they talked with the fervor of late adolescence of love— "mature love"—"love between a man and a woman"—"what a Christian marriage in the mid-twentieth century should be." Of course they'd talked of having children.

They played chess, which was D.'s game. They went hiking, and sometimes searched for fossils in shale-rich ravines and creekbeds, which was G.'s game since boyhood.

D. hadn't been able to attend G.'s wedding. G. wondered if he would attend his funeral. If there can be a funeral without a body? For maybe they'd never find his body. He smiled to think so. Sometimes, going over The Falls, a human being was lost forever. Even small boats had been known to disintegrate in such a way that their parts were never retrieved or identified.

The peace of oblivion.

G. had left no note for D. He'd left a scribbled note only for A., his wife. Out of a sense of obligation that suggested (he hoped, for he wasn't cruel) none of the loathing he felt for the woman. But D. would forgive him. He believed.

D., in the simplicity and goodness of his heart. A natural-born Christian. He would grieve for G., but forgive him.

D. had his own, separate life now. For years. He was assistant to the minister of a large, prosperous church in Springfield, Massachusetts. He was proud husband and father of two-year-old girl twins. To make of D. an accomplice of a kind if only at second- or third-hand would be a sinful act. To make of D. a sharer of so shameful a secret. Unless it was so beautiful a secret. *I can't love any woman, God help me I've tried. I can only love you.* D. had joined G. in his rambling walks in search of fossils. He'd begun as a boy collecting Indian arrowheads and artifacts but "fossils" came to fascinate him more. These delicate, leafy remnants of a lost and scarcely imaginable time before human history. Like mysterious artworks they were, skeletal impressions of once-living organisms from an era millions of years—

an unfathomable sixty-five million years!—before Christ. A world of slow time in which one thousand years was but a moment and sixty thousand years was too brief a time to be measured by geological methods of fossil dating. As a boy of thirteen he'd fashioned a fine-meshed net attached to a wooden frame so that he could wade creekbeds and sift through soft black muck in search of fragments of fossil rocks and bone, the teeth of ancient sharks and skates; the outlines of ancient squids calcified to a kind of amber. So far inland as Troy, New York! G. couldn't believe, as his own father did, that the Devil had planted so-called fossils in the earth to mislead mankind; to cast doubt on the account of creation in Genesis—that God had created the earth and the stars and all the creatures of the earth in seven days and nights, no more than six thousand years ago. (Six thousand! G. smiled to think of it.) Yet he resisted the very premise of "evolution." Blindness, accident. No! Not possible.

And yet: could it be true that ninety-nine percent of all species, flora and fauna, that have ever lived have become extinct, and that species are passing into extinction continuously? Daily? Why did God create so many creatures, only to let them fight frantically with one another for existence, and then to pass into oblivion? Would mankind disappear too, one day? *Was this God's plan?* For surely there was a plan. Christianity must try to comprehend, and to explain. G.'s father refused to discuss such issues with G. He'd long ago come to the conclusion that science was a false, shallow religion and that deep abiding faith was all that mattered, finally. "You'll see, son. In time." A few of G.'s younger instructors at the seminary were more open to discuss such questions but these men, too, were limited in their responses, and uninformed in science. To them, there was little difference between six thousand years, sixty-five million years and five hundred million years. Faith, faith! G. complained to D., "What good is 'faith' if it's based upon ignorance? I want to *know*." But D. said, "Look, Gil. Faith is a day-to-day, practical matter. I can no more doubt the existence of God and Jesus than I can doubt the existence of my family, or you. What matters is how we relate to them, and to one another. And that's all that matters."

G. was moved by this answer. Its simplicity, and the essential soundness of such an attitude. Yet he doubted he could be satisfied with it. Always he wanted more . . .

"Maybe that's your special destiny, Gil. To make sense of these things. To bring together science and 'faith.' Ever think of that?"

D. seemed quite serious, saying this. He seemed to think that G., graduate of a provincial Protestant seminary in upstate New York, with virtually no science in his background, might be capable of such a task.

No one but D. had ever had such ambitions for G.

No one but D. had ever called him *Gil*.

Well, that was finished now. G. would be leaving his fossil collection behind, in his parents' house. In his boyhood room, in drawers and cartons. In junior high he'd begun bringing these to show his science teachers, who made a stab at identifying and dating them. Had his teachers known much more than G. himself, he wondered. He'd wanted to think so. They assured him that, at least, the fossils were millions of years old. Hundreds of millions? There was the Cambrian Era, and there was the Cretaceous Era. Fossils in this upstate New York region might belong to the Ice Age. The Age of Dinosaurs. The Age of Neanderthals. He'd been thrilled to think that these mysterious objects had ended up in his possession. There were no accidents in God's plan, and he knew that God had intended him to be a minister; since God had allowed him to find these fossils, too, there was a reason. One day, he would know that reason. He intended to take courses in paleontology, paleozoology, at a distinguished university like Cornell . . . Somehow, he never had. He wondered if he'd been fearful of what he might learn.

That you have no special destiny. Not you, and not mankind.

At this early hour of Sunday morning the city was nearly deserted. Yet church bells seemed to be ringing continuously. A noisy clamor. He wanted to clap his hands over his ears. Never had he noticed how intrusive his faith was. Here we are! Christians! Surrounding you! Bringing news of the Gospels! Good news! Come and be saved! How much more seductive he found the monosyllabic roar of The Falls.

He forced himself, panting, to walk at a normal pace. For what if a police officer saw him, and guessed his intention. His face. His ravaged face. His boy's face that had aged years in a single night. His eyes sunken in his face. He was afraid it shone unmistakably in his face, the release from misery he sought.

It was difficult for him to simulate calm, though. He felt like a wild beast on a leash. If anyone got in his way or tried to stop him, if the woman had tried to stop him, he'd have flung her aside in a rage.

It wasn't despair he felt. Not at all. Despair suggested meekness, passivity, giving-up. But Gilbert Erskine wasn't giving anything up. Another man would return to the hotel suite, to the *lawfully wedded wife*. The bed, the swath of rusted-red crotch. The moaning fish's mouth and the eyes rolled back in the head and the eventual babies, a cozy stink of diapers. That was Gilbert Erskine's true destiny. The tall gaunt house in Palmyra, New York, mud-colored brick and rotted shingleboards in the roof and a congregation of less than two hundred people, most of them middle-aged and older, to whom the young minister must "prove" himself. "Win" their confidence, their respect, eventually their love. Yes? But no.

Not for G. He was acting out of courage, conviction. God would not forgive him. *But God will know me as I am.*

The roar of The Falls. Like the blood-roar in the ears. Penetrating his fevered brain as he'd lain sleepless in that bed. Recalling the vanity of their first meeting. He'd believed the woman a "sister"—what a cruel, crude joke. How they'd met. Now he knew. Their elders had shrewdly planned the meeting, he saw now. Her parents were desperate for the prim, plain spinster to be married, and his parents were desperate for the prim, plain bachelor to be married. (Possibly they worried about his manhood? Reverend Erskine at least.) And so "Ariah" and "Gilbert" were but pawns on a chess board who'd imagined themselves players!

Last night. His life careening past as if already he were drowning in the river. Broken like a cheap plastic doll in The Falls. Beside him the stuporous snoring woman. Drunken woman. His wedding night, and a drunken woman. Run, run! He had to throw himself into the most monstrous of falls, the Horseshoe. Nothing less would suffice. In his expansive sense of himself he dreaded surviving. He dreaded being pulled from the churning water below The Falls, broken and maimed. Would rescue crews be on duty, so early in the morning? He wished for total extinction, obliteration. To erase forever from his sight the smeared greedy face of the red-haired woman. Chaste and virginal and cool to the touch as an icicle she'd been for the long months of their engagement, and that thin-lipped smile and awkward manner . . . Well, he'd been deceived. Like a dupe of the Devil he'd been deceived. He, Gilbert Erskine! The most skeptical of the seminarians. The most "free thinking." He who'd prided himself on eluding the wiles of featherbrained simpering-coy females for years. Desperate to marry, they were. The pack of them desperate to be "engaged"; shamelessly greedy for a ring to wear, to present boastfully to the world. *See? I'm loved. I'm saved.* But Ariah Litterell had seemed to him so different. Of another species. A young woman he might respect as a wife, a woman who was his equal socially and almost his equal intellectually.

He was bitter that D. had not asked *Do you love this woman, Gil?*

He'd planned to say to D. *As much as you love yours.*

The occasion had not arisen. In fact, no one asked G. *Do you love this woman?*

Possibly G. had murmured to her, yes he did. He loved her. Possibly, stricken with shyness. Embarrassment. And the woman in turn stiff, self-conscious, blinking rapidly and her green-glassy eyes wavering from his eyes. Possibly she'd murmured to him, in turn. *And I, I love you.*

So it was decided. He'd slid the ring on her thin finger.

Run, run!

Spray wetted his face like spit. The roar of The Falls had been steadily getting louder. His glasses were misted over, hardly could he see the pavement in front of him. That bridge. Goat Island Suspension Bridge. *Love me why can't you love me for God's sake can't you. Do it, DO IT!* It was Goat Island he wanted. He'd marked on the tourist map. With the little silver pen she'd given him, inscribed with his initials *G.S.* His pride in this artifact! *I'm loved, I'm saved.*

Their shy groping dry-mouthed kisses. Her stiffening body, the tough little skeleton holding her erect when he touched her, put his arms around her. *Like they do in the movies. Fred Astaire, Ginger Rogers, let's dance! It's so easy.*

He'd known she hadn't loved him. Of course he'd known.

Yet he'd believed (almost!) that he loved her. *He would come to love her, his lawfully wedded wife. In time.*

As his father had come to love his mother, he supposed. As all men came to love their wives.

For had not God enjoined mankind to *Increase and multiply.*

Run! The shame of it would paralyze him otherwise.

Champagne at the reception, and in the hotel room. He had not known. Had not guessed. This delicate-boned woman drinking thirstily as a day laborer. Ignoring his tactful suggestions that maybe she'd had enough. Giggling, wiping her smeared mouth on the back of her hand. Kicking off her shoes. When she tried to stand she'd swayed, light-headed; he'd jumped up to steady her. She half-fell, pushed herself into his arms. How different from the stiff-backed minister's daughter he'd known. Ariah Littrell in her white ruffled blouses, her Peter Pan collars and crisply ironed shirtwaist dresses and flannel skirts. Neatly polished high-heeled pumps and spotless white gloves. That Ariah was nearly three years older than G. secretly pleased him. It was like a trump card, for he knew she had to be grateful he'd chosen her. And he didn't want an immature woman for a wife, he understood that he would be the immature spouse. Ariah would take care of Gilbert as his adoring mother had done for twenty-seven years. If he was hurt, sulky, irritable, disappointed, Ariah would understand and forgive. If he flared up in a childish temper, she would forgive. All this he was counting on. An ambitious young minister requires a canny, mature, responsible wife. Attractive but not overly attractive. And Ariah was gifted, in the way of small town, sequestered talent: he'd been impressed by her piano playing, and by the quality of her soprano voice. At a Christmas recital there was Ariah Littrell singing "Silent Night, Holy Night" so beautifully you saw her as beautiful. The sallow skin was radiant! The rather chill, shrinking eyes were green-glowing as emeralds! The small pursed mouth was gracefully opened to shape surpassingly sweet words. *Silent night, holy night* . . . G., seated with Reverend and Mrs. Littrell, was taken by surprise. He hadn't expected to much enjoy the recital but as soon as Ariah stepped out onstage, nodded to her pianist-accompanist and began to sing, he felt a thrill of—something. Pride? Covetousness? Sexual attraction? This beautiful, coolly poised young woman singing to an audience of admirers, strikingly dressed in a long wine-colored velvet skirt with a sash, and a long-sleeved white silk blouse. Her eyes were uplifted as if to heaven. Her narrow tapered fingers were pressed to her bosom in an attitude of prayer. The hair that in ordinary light was dull, faded, limp, was lustrous in the stage lighting. Subtle spots of rouge enlivened her face. *All is calm, all is bright* . . . G. clenched his fists thinking yes, yes he would love this remarkable woman. He would make her *his*.

Run for your life.

The wedding ceremony had passed in a haze like landscape glimpsed from the window of a speeding lurching vehicle. Though D. was not present, hadn't been able to attend, G. persisted in seeing him in the corner of his eye. D., smiling and nodding encouragement. *Yes! Good! I've done it, Gil, and so can you!* At the reception she'd begun drinking and on the drive from Troy to Niagara Falls she'd fallen asleep, her head lolling against his shoulder in a way that annoyed him, it was so intimate and yet unconscious, brainless. And in their hotel room she'd drunk most of the bottle of champagne that awaited them. She chattered nervously, her words slurred. She giggled and wiped at her mouth. Lipstick on her teeth, her clothing disheveled. Rising, she became dizzy and lost her balance; he'd had to jump up to steady her. "Ariah, dear!" Preparing for bed she giggled and hiccuped and stumbled to him. When he stooped to kiss her wet, parted lips he tasted alcohol and panic. His heart was lurching and kicking. The bed was ludicrously large, the mattress so high from the floor, Ariah insisted he "boost" her. Heart-shaped velvet cushions everywhere, lace coverlets like nets to catch unwary fish. This was a shrine to—what? Ariah lay in the bed like an awkward sea otter in her ivory silk nightgown, hiccuping, jamming her knuckles against her mouth and trying not to burst into laughter. Or was it hysterical sobbing.

He hadn't known what to expect, hadn't wanted to think ahead, but, dear God, he hadn't expected this. She drew him to kneel beside her aroused and trembling as in a fever dream of lurid degradation. Beneath his hesitant weight she squirmed and moaned. Suddenly clasping her arms around his neck—tight!—tight as an octopus's tentacles—and kissing him full on the lips. Was this Ariah Littrell the minister's spinster daughter? Clumsily seductive, one of her eyelids drooping. He couldn't bear it, her hot hands swiping blindly at him. She was moaning his name, that in her mouth sounded obscene. Groping against his chest, his belly and groin. His penis! That any woman would touch him there, like that . . . In a guttural moan pleading *Love me, why can't you love me for God's sake. Do it! DO IT!* The bared gums, damp exposed teeth. A ragged swath of rust-colored hairs between her clutching thighs. She was ugly to him, repulsive. *Damn you please what's wrong with you DO IT!* Bucking her groin against his. Her bony pelvis. He wanted to strike her with his fists, pummel her until she lost consciousness and had no further knowledge of him. He too was moaning, pleading *Stop! Don't! You disgust me.* In fact he may have slapped her, not with the flat of his hand exactly, flailing out in instinctive self-defense, knocking her back into the oversized pillows. But she'd only laughed. Unless she was crying. The brass bed jiggled, creaked, lurched and careened like a drunken boat. His elbow raked against her breast. There was something offensive, obscene about the small hard breasts, the inflamed-looking nipples. He shouted and spat at her to leave him alone yet blindly she swiped at him, grabbed at him, her strong fingers gripped his penis as in the most lewd of adolescent sex-fantasies. To his horror a sharp shuddering cry escaped from his lips even as his milky seed leapt from him piercing-sweet like a swarm of honeybees. He collapsed upon her then, panting. His brain was extinguished, like a flame that has been blown out. His heart pounded dangerously. Their sweat-slick bodies held fast.

Later he would hear her gagging and vomiting in the bathroom.

A delirium of sleep washed over him like filthy frothy water. In the confusion of a dream he believed he might have murdered the woman whose name he couldn't remember. *Lawfully wedded wife. Death do you part.* He'd snapped her neck. Smothered her in the smelly bedclothes. Pounded and clawed between her legs. He was trying to explain to his father, and to his friend D. whom he'd betrayed. He could not bear it. Never again.

Run, run!

Crossing the plank bridge above the rapids. His bare feet in leather shoes were hurting. He'd dressed hurriedly, carelessly. His zipper had jammed. A voice lifted in his wake—"Hey, Mister? Tickets are fifty cents." Someone was calling after him. Fifty cents! G. didn't so much as glance back. He'd had a reputation, he'd prided himself in his reputation, at the seminary, for being rather aloof, even arrogant. D. was his only friend, D. was truly Christly, good. D. would understand his desperation and forgive him even if God would not. He hadn't a penny for a ticket. Where he was headed, proudly he had no need for a penny. And possibly it was the Devil who teased him in the guise of a gray-haired gatekeeper. As it might be the Devil who teased mankind by placing "fossils" in the earth. Tempting him to turn back. Tempting cowardice. But G. in his headlong plunge would not succumb for G. had vowed to see this through. To God he'd vowed. To Jesus Christ (whose salvation he repudiated) he'd vowed. In a dead hour of the night before dawn, by his gold Bulova watch nearing five o'clock, he'd knelt on the painfully hard mock-marble tile floor of the bathroom. Steeling himself to endure the woman's odor. Vomit, sweat. Odor of unclean female flesh. He'd bared his soul to his maker, that it be extirpated by the roots. For he had no need of a soul now. This act would be his crucifixion. A man's death and not a coward's. D. would see. All the world would see.

D.'s heart would be broken at last. The world's heart would be broken.

And no possibility of survival.

Behind him the gatekeeper shouted. Barely G. could hear the man's voice over the roaring of The Falls. At his left hand the Niagara River was wild, deafening. You would think, as local Indian tribes had thought, that it was a living thing that must be placated by sacrifices. A hungry river, and insatiable. Its source must be unknowable. And the massive falls ahead. The Falls stretching in a horseshoe curve, as far as the eye can see through curtains of rising mist and spray. (Winking flirtatious little rainbows appeared and disappeared amid the spray. Like bubbles, or butterflies. Tempting the viewer to stare in surprise, admiration; tempting the viewer to smile. Such useless beauty, amid such destruction!) Scarcely could G. see but he knew The Falls were ahead. It was a site called Terrapin Point he sought, knowing by the map that it was the southernmost tip of the little island. The Falls were so loud now as to be mesmerizing, calming. Flying spray blinded him but he had no need any longer to see. Damned glasses sliding down his nose. Always he'd hated glasses, diagnosed with myopia at the age of ten. G.'s fate! In a gesture of which he'd never have been capable in life he seized his glasses and flung them into space. Good riddance! No more!

Suddenly he was at the railing.

At Terrapin Point.

So soon?

His hands groped and closed about the topmost rung of a railing. He lifted his right foot, a slippery-soled shoe, nearly lost his balance but righted himself, like an acrobat positioning himself on top of the railing even as a part of his mind recoiled in disbelief and bemusement thinking *You can't be serious, Gil! This is ridiculous, you graduated top of your class, they've given you a new car, you can't die*. But in his pride he was over the railing, and in the water, swept instantaneously forward with the rushing current powerful as a locomotive and within swift seconds his skull was broken, his brain and its seemingly ceaseless immortal voice extinguished forever, as if it had never been; within ten swift seconds his heart had stopped, like a clock whose mechanism has been smashed. His backbone was snapped, and snapped, and snapped like the dried wishbone of a turkey clutched at by giggling children and his body was flung lifeless as a rag doll at the foot of the

Horseshoe Falls, lifted and dropped and lifted again amid the rocks and sucked downward amid churning water and winking miniature rainbows, lost now to the appalled sight of the sole witness at the railing at Terrapin Point—though shortly it would be regurgitated from the foot of The Falls and swept downriver three-quarters of a mile past the Whirlpool Rapids and into the Devil's Whirlpool where it would be sucked downward from sight and trapped in the spiraling water—the broken body would spin like a deranged moon in orbit until, in His mercy, or His whimsy, God would grant the miracle of putrefaction to inflate the body with gases, floating it to the surface of the foaming gyre, and release.

The Widow-Bride of The Falls:

The Search

1

*D*amned, *she would speak of herself.*
Yes you could see it. In her eyes. Poor woman!

No one among the staff of the Rainbow Grand could state with certainty when she'd first appeared downstairs in the lobby: the young red-haired woman soon to be known, in popular imagination, as the Widow-Bride of The Falls. It was about 10:30 A.M. of June 12, 1950 when some of them began to notice her, but without taking particular note. The lobby of the Rainbow Grand was spacious, and crowded. A passing bellboy may have stepped into her wavering path and nearly collided with her, quickly apologizing, but as quickly continuing on his way. A waitress in The Café would speak of seeing her—"Or someone just like her"—at about that time. But it was June, season of weddings. It was honeymoon season in Niagara Falls and the lobby of the old Victorian Rainbow Grand on Prospect Street was festive with people, mostly couples. There were lines at the registration counter with its ornate gilt scrollwork and, overhead, a sunburst clock held aloft by a smiling Cupid. AMOR VINCIT OMNIA. In the center lobby, in cushioned wicker chairs, men were seated with crossed legs, smoking cigars, pipes. Cigarette smoking was general. Leading off the lobby was the Rainbow Terrace, an expensive dining room serving Sunday brunch. At the rear of the lobby, late breakfast and other refreshments were being served in The Café, a casual but elegant area surrounded by potted trees and tropical flowers; on a raised platform, an ethereal long-haired young woman harpist played Irish airs—"Danny Boy," "The Rose of Tralee," "An Irish Lullaby." Frequently, guests were paged over an amplifying system by a disembodied male voice. What a commotion! Like the comforting humming buzz of a hive. Or the murmurous vibratory roar of The Falls.

Almost, you could drift and eddy in this space mesmerized, unthinking. You could fall under the spell of the harp's long delicate stroking notes, barely discernible above the crowd noise. You could find yourself standing transfixed in one spot not knowing where you were, or why.

She was alone. That stood out. Everyone else with someone, or in a hurry to get somewhere. But not her.

The Widow-Bride, when first seen, looked nothing like a bride, still less like a widow. She was wearing a floral-print organdy shirtwaist with a flared skirt, of the kind a high school girl might wear to her graduation. Its sash was a crimson ribbon, limply tied in a bow. Its mother-of-pearl buttons were elaborately but crookedly buttoned to her throat as if she were cold. She appeared to be wearing a white glove, and carrying the other. Her hair, the hue of faded rust, had been fashioned into an inexpert French twist, and was already loosening; she'd pinned a pink rosebud to the twist, and the rosebud was drooping. Her stockings were a size or two too large for her extremely slender legs, and were baggy at the ankles. Her shoes were white patent leather with a medium heel: Sunday church shoes. Her face was sallow, and sprinkled with freckles like dirty raindrops; at times it appeared smudged, partly erased like a pastel drawing. As the hotel concierge would later recount to Clyde Colborne, proprietor of the Rainbow Grand, this strange, solitary figure moved slowly and haltingly "like a sleepwalker" amid the hubub of the lobby. For a while she stood by the elevators looking anxiously at the opening doors as if waiting for someone to appear; after about twenty minutes, when the harpist took her break from playing, the red-haired woman was perceived to awaken and glance about, startled. At once she left the café area and disappeared from view. But a while later, there she was again: in the center lobby, in the lounge area where guests convened, standing and seated, reading newspapers, smoking. Here, the red-haired woman was observed gazing with childlike intensity, yet a kind of blindness, at the faces of certain of the male guests, who were made to feel uncomfortable. Several of these men spoke to the red-haired woman, no doubt politely, but she drew quickly away, with a shake of her head as if no, now she realized, this individual wasn't anyone she knew, or was seeking. "I could see she wasn't propositioning them. Nothing like that. Not a one of them complained." (Though afterward several of these men, remembering the encounter, would grant interviews to local media. *Yes you could tell. It was her husband she was looking for. But she was too shy to say. To say his name. Or it was like, maybe, she'd forgotten his name. But she knew somehow he was dead. She was in shock. My heart went out to her!*)

Bellboys would later recount that the red-haired woman turned up again in the elevator corridor where she stood to one side, her head averted, to watch, at a furtive angle, guests coming and going, passing around her like swift-flowing water around a rock. Later, she drifted to the entrance of the Rainbow Terrace, where the maître d' spoke to her—"It was like speaking to a zombie. She was polite, but inside her eyes, not-there." When he saw her partly ascending the crimson-carpeted staircase that led to the mezzanine, and hesitating as if she'd become light-headed, the concierge asked an assistant to approach her to ask if he could be of help, but when he did, the red-haired woman shook her head no—"Real gracious, like she was sorry to disappoint *me*." Again she disappeared (into the women's lounge, as the attendant there would later recount) only to reappear a few minutes later, her face washed, at the lobby entrance; here she took a position a few yards from the main, revolving door, which was in continuous motion.

"It was like she was waiting for someone to come through that door. But she knew he wasn't going to come. So—she stood there."

By this time—it was after noon, busier than ever in the Rainbow Grand with churchgoing patrons arriving for the popular Sunday brunch—the drooping pink rosebud had fallen from the red-haired woman's head. The clumsy French twist was coming undone in wisps and strands of thin hair. The white glove she'd been carrying was gone. Though she must have been exhausted, yet the red-haired woman stood with the resolve of a department store mannequin— "like she wasn't even blinking"—staring at the revolving door. How long the solitary woman would have stood there if the concierge hadn't at last approached her, he wouldn't have wanted to think.

"Ma'am? Excuse me? Are you a guest at the Rainbow Grand?"

The red-haired woman seemed not to hear the concierge at first. When he entered her line of vision she stepped to one side, to continue to gaze at the revolving door. It was "like she was hypnotized— and didn't want to be wakened." He repeated his question, politely but forcibly, and this time the red-haired woman glanced at him and nodded, just discernibly, yes.

"May I be of assistance, then?"

" 'Assistance.' " In a scratchy, almost inaudible voice she spoke slowly. It was as if the word was foreign, puzzling.

"Help? May I help you?"

The red-haired woman's eyes lifted to the concierge's face slow as glass eyes turning upward in a doll's head. The skin beneath the eyes was discolored, bluish. There was a reddened mark on the underside of the woman's slender jaw as if she'd injured herself, or had been injured. ("A man's fingers it looked like. Just the shape of them. Like he'd grabbed her, tried to strangle her. But maybe not. Maybe it was my imagination. Afterward, it must've faded.") The woman squinted, and adjusted her rings. Apologetically she shook her head, no.

"No, ma'am? I can't help you?"

"Thank you but no one can help me. I believe I am—damned."

The concierge was shocked. At this moment an exuberant family burst through the revolving doors like fireworks and he wasn't sure he'd heard what he'd heard, or that he wanted to hear it.

"Ma'am? Excuse me, *what*?"

"Damned."

Her lips moved numbly. She spoke matter-of-factly. She would have turned away except the concierge touched her wrist, and led her into a quieter corner of the lobby. Clearly, the woman was unwell. Emotionally disturbed, mentally deranged. She was of a good background, you could tell. Not wealthy but solidly middle-class, or a little above. A small-town patrician. The accent was unmistakable: upstate New York, but not western New York. Somewhere east, maybe north. A married woman, a well-bred woman. Something had happened to her or had been done to her and the concierge was fervently hoping that whatever it was, whoever the perpetrator had been, it hadn't happened on the hotel premises. Or, if it had, the Rainbow Grand would not be liable.

"Ma'am, I wish you'd tell me what's wrong? So that I could try to help?"

The red-haired woman asked earnestly, "What's wrong with *me*? Or with *him*?"

"Who is *him*?"

"My husband."

"Ah! Your husband's name is—?"

"Reverend Erskine."

"*Reverend* Erskine? I see." As he would tell Mr. Colborne, the concierge now had a recollection of having seen this woman in the company of a youngish man the previous day, when they'd checked into the hotel. He'd had no exchanges with the couple and didn't know their names, however. "Has something happened to him?"

(The concierge felt a stab of apprehension. Of course, you expected the worst. Unlocking a door upstairs, discovering a man hanging from a lighting fixture. A man who's slit his wrists in the bathtub. It wouldn't be the first time a man had committed suicide in the Rainbow Grand, with or without a spouse, though such a fact was kept very quiet.)

The red-haired woman said in a whisper, turning her rings around her finger, "I don't know. You see—I've lost him."

" 'Lost him'—how?"

"Where things are lost. Gone."

"Just—gone? Where?"

The red-haired woman laughed sadly. "How on earth would I know *where*? He didn't tell me."

"How long has Reverend Erskine been missing?"

The woman stared at a wristwatch on her slender wrist, without seeming to comprehend the time. After a while she said, "Maybe he drove away. The car is his. He left our room sometime before dawn. I think. Or maybe . . ." Her voice trailed off.

"He left? Without saying a word?"

"Unless he spoke to me. And because I was, I was sleeping, because I was sleeping, you see, I—didn't hear him." She seemed about to burst into tears but recovered. She wiped her eyes with her gloved fingers. "I didn't know him that well. I don't know his—practices."

"But, Mrs. Erskine, have you looked for your husband outside? He may simply have stepped outside."

"Outside." Mrs. Erskine shook her head slowly as if the concept of such vastness overwhelmed her. "I wouldn't know where to look. I wouldn't know where to begin. The car is his. There's all the world."

"Maybe he's just outside on the veranda, waiting for you? Let's go look." The concierge spoke heartily. Hopefully. He would have led Mrs. Erskine through the revolving door except she shrank back with a look of fear, warding him off with her arm.

"I—I'm not sure that he would want that, you see. If he was outside. On the veranda."

"But why not?"

"Because he has left me."

"But, Mrs. Erskine, why do you think your husband has left you, if he left no word? When he might be just outside? Isn't it an extreme conclusion to come to? Maybe he just went sightseeing. Over to the Gorge."

"Oh, no." Mrs. Erskine spoke quickly. "Gilbert wouldn't go sightseeing without me, on our honeymoon. He'd marked off things for us to see. He's scrupulous about things like that. Very well organized. He's a collector, or was. Fossils! And he wouldn't do things by half. If he's gone, he's gone."

Honeymoon. This fact struck the concierge as ominous.

"But Reverend Erskine left no note, you say? He left without a word?"

"Without a word."

With what stoic resignation the red-haired woman uttered this.

"Not in your room, you've looked carefully? Not at the front desk?"

"I don't believe so."

"You did check at the front desk, Mrs. Erskine?"

"No."

"No?"

"He wouldn't have left a note for me there. Not in an open mail box. That wasn't Gilbert's way. If he had something private to tell me."

The concierge excused himself and went to the registration desk to check. No message for room 419? He asked the staff on duty if they'd spoken with or seen this "Reverend Erskine" but they told him no. He asked to see the ledger, and there it was: *Reverend Gilbert Erskine, Mrs. Ariah Erskine, Troy, New York*. There was a registration for a 1949 Packard also. The couple was booked into the Rainbow Grand for five nights in the Rosebud Honeymoon Suite.

Honeymoon. This was not just ominous, it was pathetic.

"Call Mr. Colborne, will you? Just leave a note with him. No emergency, exactly. A disturbed woman with a missing husband, she thinks."

" 'Missing'? There was a guy over the Horseshoe, this morning."

"Over the Horseshoe." The concierge would afterward recall hearing this offhand remark from one of the desk clerks as he was turning away, and discounting it in the same moment. Or maybe he hadn't clearly heard. Or hadn't wanted to hear.

You don't think of clergymen committing suicide at The Falls. Especially not on their honeymoons. *You just don't.*

The red-haired woman seemed unsurprised that there was no message for her at the desk. But she allowed the concierge to escort her outside. In the pale, sunlit air of early afternoon the young woman's eyelids fluttered as if she were blinded. Her freckled face shone as if she'd scrubbed it, hard. She looked strangely young, yet worn, exhausted. Her eyes were a peculiar glassy green, rather small, shrinking. She was no beauty, with eyebrows and lashes so pale a red as to be nearly colorless, and a translucent skin showing a tracery of small blue veins at her temples. Yet there was something fierce and implacable in her. A stubbornness, almost a radiance. "Like she'd been wounded, real deep. Humiliated. But she was going to see it through, every drop of it."

And so she seemed reluctant to glance up at the exuberant guests crowded onto the veranda, a handsome structure that wrapped around three-quarters of the hotel. The concierge took her arm when she stumbled. They were walking on a graveled path below the veranda, between the hotel and a terraced lawn and rose garden. Guests dined in the open air, and in a lavender Victorian gazebo set upon the lawn like something in a child's storybook. A few of the guests glanced up as they passed, curiously.

"You don't see your husband anywhere, Mrs. Erskine?"

"Oh, we won't find him. I told you. He's gone."

"But how can you be so certain?" The concierge was trying to remain patient. "If he left no word? It might simply be a misunderstanding."

Gravely the red-haired woman nodded. "Yes. I believe it is. It was. A tragic misunderstanding."

The concierge wanted to ask if they'd quarreled, but couldn't bring himself to say the words.

They passed the tennis courts. They passed badminton players, croquet players. Middle-aged men in sports clothes laughing loudly, drinking beer, smoking. At the large outdoor pool there were numerous swimmers, sunbathers. The atmosphere was festive, even raucous. Popular music was amplified overhead. The red-haired woman shielded her eyes as if she felt pain.

"We should check your car, ma'am. Just to see."

This, the concierge would have done immediately if he'd been Mrs. Erskine, but she didn't seem to have thought of it. "Do you remember where your car is parked, Mrs. Erskine?" the concierge asked, as they approached the lot behind and below the hotel, and the woman said dreamily, "It was Gilbert who parked it, of course. He wouldn't allow me to drive his car. I don't believe he would ever have allowed me to drive his car. Though I've had a driver's license since I was sixteen. But of course it was *his car*. I mean, it *is*. There, by the fence—see? The Packard."

It was a sign of the red-haired woman's state of shock that, seeing her husband's car in the lot after all, she was only mildly surprised, and not at all relieved. In fact the concierge noted how she stood frozen in place, simply staring at the car and not coming near it. As if the gleaming black Packard were another riddle for her to contend with that day, and she wasn't capable.

The concierge checked the Packard's doors and trunk—all locked. He peered into the shadowy interior which was cushioned in pale gray, spotlessly clean. Not a single item of clothing or a scrap of paper in the backseat. The concierge didn't know if the presence of this car, which Mrs. Erskine seemed to have taken for granted would be missing, was a good sign, or not so good. The clergyman might have come to harm somehow, somewhere. Met with "foul play"—there were elements in the city of Niagara Falls known to be dangerous.

The concierge said heartily, "Well! You see, Mrs. Erskine, he can't have gone far on foot. Probably when we return to the hotel he'll be there, waiting."

It had become so balmy a June day, after the mist and chill of the morning, such an optimistic pronouncement seemed appropriate. But Mrs. Erskine shuddered. "Back in the room? In the 'Rosebud Suite'? No."

She was frowning, turning her rings rapidly as if she wanted to twist them off her finger.

The concierge tried to comfort her, taking her arm to lead her back to the hotel, but the red-haired woman began speaking quickly. "Please, you don't need to humor me! You've been very kind. I hoped not to involve anyone in this, especially strangers, but I don't seem to know what to do next. Where to look. Where to wait." She paused, her lips trembling. She was trying to choose her words with care. "Especially if Gilbert is gone, and won't be back. I can't face his parents. Or my parents. They will blame me. And I am to blame, I know.

But I must be practical, too. My days of dreaming are past. I will be thirty years old in November. I do have money saved, in a bank account in Troy," she went on earnestly. "I can pay for the hotel suite. If the management is concerned about payment, please don't be. *I will pay*." Mrs. Erskine had begun to cry softly. Or perhaps she was laughing. Her pale lips twitched.

The concierge, a fourteen-year veteran of the Rainbow Grand, was stricken with pity for this woman, wanting to console her but at a loss for words. *What do you say to a bride whose husband has abandoned her on their honeymoon?* Mrs. Erskine's eerie fatalism was beginning to affect him, like a slow-acting poison.

Gamely he said, gently taking her arm, "Mrs. Erskine, ma'am, we'll find your husband for you, I promise. Don't fret."

" 'Don't fret'!" Her laughter was like glass breaking. "This is my *honeymoon*."

2

Where the hell was his boss Clyde Colborne? The concierge was anxious, exhausted. Like a hotel employee who's been carrying an extra chair around, nowhere to put it. You carry the damned thing from room to room, and it's heavy. Somebody else take this chair!

"We'll try once more downstairs. Then, your room. Are you feeling strong enough, Mrs. Erskine?"

The red-haired woman inclined her head, lowering her eyes. As if to indicate *Yes, yes! What choice do I have.*

Another time, the concierge checked at the front desk to see if there was a message for Mrs. Erskine in room 419—"Sorry, sir. Nothing." Patiently then, like a man guiding an erratic and unpredictable child, the concierge escorted Mrs. Erskine through the main lobby, which was more crowded and bustling than before, the air heavy with tobacco smoke; and through the busy café (where a pianist was now playing sparkly Broadway show tunes); and into the Rainbow Terrace where well-dressed diners, milling about an extraordinary lavish buffet spread against an entire mirrored wall like a feast of the gods, glanced at Mrs. Erskine's pale stricken face, with curiosity. In a lowered voice the concierge asked unnecessarily, "You don't see him anywhere, Mrs. Erskine, I guess?"

The woman's head shake was almost imperceptible.

No. Of course I don't see him. Here? How could I see him, if he has gone?

By this time most of the hotel staff had been alerted to Mrs. Erskine's predicament. Bellboys had been directed to search the gentlemen's lounges, private meeting rooms opening off the mezzanine, fire stairs and storage rooms and remote corners of the building. The hotel physician Dr. McCrady had been summoned in case Mrs. Erskine became hysterical or ill. Calls had been placed to Niagara Falls police and riverfront authorities including the Coast Guard rescue unit. The concierge was taken aside by a colleague and informed that an "unidentified man" had in fact thrown himself into the Horseshoe Falls early that morning; a gatekeeper at the Goat Island Bridge had tried to stop him. Search crews were out downriver, but the body hadn't yet been found and the mayor's office, in alliance with the powerful Niagara Tourism Commission, hoped to "keep a lid on it" for as long as possible.

The concierge shuddered. Oh, he'd known! Something terrible.

I believe I am—damned.

Yes, the description of the suicide made it sound as if it might well be Reverend Erskine.

The concierge saw the red-haired woman standing awkwardly near the registration desk, paying little attention to the the hotel physician's repeated suggestions that she sit down in one of the plush chairs nearby. In her vague placid way she was watching as a young, attractive honeymoon couple, arms around each other's waist, bantered and giggled with the desk clerk as they signed the register. She'd discovered that her French twist was coming undone and was trying to fix it, with clumsy fingers. She adjusted the limp bow of her crimson sash. Of all the women and men in the lobby of the Rainbow Grand, which had come to seem a nightmare simulacrum of the vast peopled world beyond the hotel, this woman, Mrs. Ariah Erskine, seemed the one singled out as extraneous; the one who was extra, unwanted; the one with no place to *be*.

"We'd better tell her, eh? Take her to the police station."

"But if they don't have the body yet, she can't identify it. And maybe it isn't the reverend. Jesus, it would be cruel to upset the poor woman any more than she's upset now, if—if the dead man isn't her husband."

"But if he *is*?"

"Dale, where the hell is Mr. Colborne?"

"On his way. He says."

Clyde Colborne, proprietor of the Rainbow Grand, was an affable, earnest, but not always reliable employer who delegated most of his authority to his staff. He'd inherited the distinguished old Prospect Street hotel, which had been founded by his grandfather in 1881, in an affluent, ebullient era of Niagara Falls tourist expansion; the hotel was still prestigious, but, like the other old, Victorian-style hotels near The Falls, built at a time when patrons traveled by train, not by car, and demanded luxury services including accommodations for their servants, the Rainbow Grand was beginning to feel competition from motels and "tourist cabins" springing up like toadstools just outside the city limits of Niagara Falls. If Mr. Colborne was much aware of this threat, he rarely spoke of it except elliptically— "People will always demand quality. The Rainbow Grand supplies quality. That's the American way."

So far as his staff knew, Clyde Colborne spent a good deal of his time boating on the river and the Great Lakes, playing golf at the l'Isle Grand Country Club in warm weather, and gambling with his friends, who were men very like himself.

The hotel manager, a woman named Dale who'd been Mr. Colborne's assistant for a decade, suggested that they check Mrs. Erskine's suite before taking her to the police station. It was a terrible situation for all concerned, but they had to think of public relations. Of the other hotel guests who'd come to the Rainbow Grand to have a good time. If poor Mrs. Erskine suddenly broke into hysterics, what a scandalous scene it would be! "Look, this is June. It's a Sunday in June and it isn't raining for once. It's honeymoon season, for God's sake. *A damned happy time at The Falls.*"

So they talked Mrs. Erskine into reluctantly going upstairs to room 419. The red-haired woman said plaintively that her husband wouldn't be there—"That's the very place, in all the world, I can guarantee you he *isn't*."

By this time Ariah Erskine was moving so haltingly, with such an air of distraction, she seemed to the Rainbow Grand employees hardly aware of her surroundings. When the elevator door opened on the fourth floor she had to be gently urged to disembark. Yet she assured Dr. McCrady with an air almost of annoyance that she was "fine"—"not at all faint or light-headed." She had lost her room key, however. Fortunately, Dale had a master key to let them in.

At room 419, the concierge knocked loudly, nervously. Just in case someone was inside. "Hello? Is anyone here? Hotel management, coming in."

No answer.

The ornate door's exterior was covered in crimson plush. A brass plaque read ROSEBUD HONEYMOON SUITE.

Dale unlocked the door, and the red-haired woman and the hotel employees entered hesitantly. There is no emptiness quite like the emptiness of a hotel room with no one in it. Through partly drawn venetian blinds a pale, filtered-looking sun shone. Somewhere overhead, a vacuum cleaner droned. The first room was the ornately furnished parlor, which was obviously empty. A few scattered tourist brochures and maps, a vase of drooping roses, an empty champagne bottle lying on its side; and two champagne glasses, both empty, some distance apart.

The concierge opened the door to the bedroom, which seemed to be empty also. This room, Mrs. Erskine entered very reluctantly, her eyes nearly shut. "No one. There's no one." She spoke so softly, it wasn't certain she'd spoken at all. The ornate brass four-poster bed with the crocheted canopy had been, it seemed, hastily straightened, the spread drawn up over rumpled bedclothes, and heart-shaped cushions placed on it. Your immediate, erroneous impression was that someone, or something, might be beneath the spread. That the bed had been made up struck the concierge as a fastidious touch: Mrs. Erskine had expected visitors, and wanted things to look neat. But the air smelled distinctly stale. A man's hair oil, a woman's cologne, an odor of slept-in, soiled sheets . . .

What happened in that bed? What shock, what misery. What revelations.

The red-haired woman averted her eyes. For a precarious moment she swayed on her feet.

The concierge asked politely, uneasily, "May I check the bathroom, Mrs. Erskine?"

"Yes. Of course. There's no one."

A light was burning in the bathroom, but the room was empty. Dampened towels had been replaced on racks, and the shower curtain tucked into the big claw-footed tub. In the sink were several strands of dark hair: not Mrs. Erskine's. And on the counter beside the sink was a man's zipped-up toiletries case of no special distinction. But it was there.

Not a good sign, the concierge thought.

Suddenly the red-haired woman said, with a breathy laugh, "His toothbrush is inside, I checked. You'd think he would have taken it with him, wouldn't you? But I suppose it's easy to buy a toothbrush. Wherever you go."

Next, they checked the closet in which Mr. Erskine had hung his clothing, which Mrs. Erskine said hadn't been disturbed so far as she knew. They checked the top bureau drawer, in which Mr. Erskine had placed neatly folded white undershirts and boxer shorts, black silk socks, several freshly laundered white cotton handkerchiefs, and a pair of cuff links. On a luggage stand was Mr. Erskine's suitcase, empty except for a paperback book titled *The Niagara Gorge: History and Pre-History*, and, another bad sign, a man's leather wallet.

"Mrs. Erskine, may I—?"

"Yes, of course. Take it."

Self-consciously the concierge examined the wallet, which contained the minister's identification and photo, driver's license, several blank checks torn from a checkbook, a half-dozen coins and bills of various denominations including fifties. The photo showed a dark-haired, beakish-nosed, narrow-faced young man wearing scholarly eyeglasses, unsmiling. This was Reverend Gilbert Erskine? The departed husband of the red-haired bride?

A fanatic. The set of that mouth. Those eyes!

Exactly the kind of man, the concierge thought, to throw himself over the Horseshoe Falls.

"Mrs. Erskine, may I take this photo of your husband? The authorities will need it. And you'd better take this wallet, and keep it safe. Never leave valuables in a hotel room."

The red-haired woman accepted the wallet from the concierge with lowered eyes, as if embarrassed. She made no attempt to count the bills which, the concierge had swiftly estimated, came to several hundred dollars.

They returned to the parlor, where Mrs. Erskine drifted to the window to gaze out blankly into the distance. Was she looking toward The Falls? Or—the sky? In profile, she did possess an antique sort of beauty. Her face seemed both ethereal and resolute, like a profile on an old coin. Again the concierge saw, or believed he saw, faint red marks like a man's fingers on her pale, delicately-boned throat.

The reverend. Must've been. Who else?

While the concierge and the others made another quick search of the parlor, the red-haired Mrs. Erskine remained motionless at the window. As if thinking aloud she said, dreamily, "The Falls. Is it singular, as you speak of it? Or—are there several Falls?"

Dale said, "We just say 'The Falls.' Not meaning the city but the river. It's more than just the actual place, the American Falls, the Bridal Veil, and the—Horseshoe. It's the rapids, too, and the Devil's Whirlpool. And the Gorge. You could say it's all the miles, about four miles, of dangerous water. 'Hungry Water' the Indians called it. It's the spirit of the place, too."

" 'The spirit of the place.' Yes."

It would seem to them afterward that in some way the red-haired woman *knew*. What had become of her husband.

They were finding nothing of significance in the parlor. Several annotated tourist brochures and maps. A flier for the popular *Maid of the Mist* cruise past the base of the American and Horseshoe Falls. It was touching to think of the young honeymoon couple planning to take that cruise, back in Troy. "You say you found no note, Mrs. Erskine?" the concierge asked a final time. "Nothing that might be construed as—a farewell note?" He found himself staring into a wastebasket shoved beneath a Victorian ladies' writing desk, where some papers had been crumpled and dropped.

The red-haired woman seemed to waken, not quite fully, from a trance. "What? No. No farewell. I'm sorry."

Flush-faced, the concierge stooped to retrieve whatever it was in the wastebasket—two crumpled paper napkins, of which one had lipstick smears on it. But that was all.

3

"A GUEST AT *my hotel*? Tell me *no*."

Seeing in the eyes of his staff, before anyone dared speak, that there was bad news.

At least, the hotel wasn't on fire: he'd have known that by now.

At least, no one had been murdered on the premises: the police would be here, the front drive filled with squad cars and emergency vehicles.

By two-twenty of the afternoon of June 12, 1950, just in time to escort Ariah Erskine to Niagara Falls police headquarters, Clyde Colborne had arrived at the Rainbow Grand at last.

He was a big-boned busy man in his mid-thirties. Aggressively friendly, with a prematurely bald, opaquely gleaming head like Roman statuary. His small shrewd restless eyes were deep set in a face lined from years of boating, waterskiing, golfing in the sun. His hands and feet were large, busy, agitated. He exuded an air, pungent as aftershave, of frantic and well-intentioned inaction. He spoke and laughed loudly, with an excess of energy. Today he was dressed as if he'd been to church that morning, in a seersucker suit, white dress shirt open at the throat, and straw fedora; as often he did on such occasions, dropping by the hotel on Sunday, he allowed his employees to think, not altogether accurately, that he'd been to church services with his family on the Island (as l'Isle Grand was called), and hadn't simply stopped back home while his family was at church to quickly shower, shave, and change clothes before driving out again after a marathon Saturday night of poker and drinking on a friend's yacht anchored off Buckhorn Island, in the Tonawanda Channel of the Niagara River.

Colborne wasn't separated from his wife, at the present time. He was living at home, though often he spent the night in his suite at the Rainbow Grand. The previous night, after the marathon game had ended around 5 A.M., he'd slept five or six dazed, stuporous hours on the yacht, where he was always welcome. He'd lost money at poker and was feeling guilty, dissolute, and resentful that he, Clyde Colborne, a man worth millions of dollars, at least in properties and investments, a man liked and admired by other men if disapproved of by his prudish wife and in-laws, should be made to feel such things. *Married too young! Married too long.* His friend from boyhood Dirk Burnaby who'd never married at all, who'd hosted the poker game on his yacht and won $1,400 from Colborne over the course of the night, said that the domestication of the male of the species *Homo sapiens* was "the great unsolved riddle" of evolution.

Not just the women have domesticated us for their own purposes, they make us feel guilty as hell when the domestication doesn't take.

Before he'd arrived at the Rainbow Grand, Colborne had heard the rumor of a suicide at The Falls. By this time it was likely a news bulletin. Burnaby had a police radio (unofficial, unauthorized) on the yacht to which he sometimes listened, especially in the late hours of the night when he couldn't sleep, out of "congenital curiosity" as he called it. (Burnaby was a lawyer as well as a yachtsman, gambler, sports fan and sporadic "civic leader.") So they'd been hearing the unwelcome news that a man, at the time unidentified, had been seen by a gatekeeper at the Goat Island Bridge to have "thrown himself" over the Horseshoe Falls early that morning. Another suicide! At the giddy height of the honeymoon tourist season, when visitors to The Falls came from all over the world. God damn suicides, Colborne thought, disgusted. This would be—how many in the past year alone? Three, four? That authorities knew of. No doubt there'd been more, and the broken bodies never discovered.

Burnaby said cryptically he never learned of a jumper at The Falls but he didn't feel a tug somewhere in his soul. "There, but for the grace of God, and plain good luck, go you." But Colborne didn't feel that way. He was a businessman, he was selling The Falls. He was selling the idea of The Falls. He wasn't selling the idea of some twisted neurotic nut jumping into The Falls.

Still, it was mostly male suicides that aroused his fury. Colborne conceded that females who jumped were desperate for reasons of being female. It was like a birth defect: female. Female suicides were more to be pitied than condemned, as the church condemned them. The majority were young, distraught girls, pregnant and abandoned by their lovers. They were wives mistreated or abandoned by their husbands. Their babies had died. Maybe, somehow, they'd killed their babies. They were mentally ill, deranged. They were *only just females.* At the height of romantic female suicides at The Falls, in the mid-nineteenth century, all the female suicides had been young, beautiful, "tragic"—at least, as they were represented in newspaper sketches. In the mid-twentieth century, things had changed. A lot. Suicides now were likely to be pathetic girls and women, not heiresses or the spurned mistresses of wealthy men, and their deaths were not romanticized by the media.

But the men! Selfish sons of bitches. They had to be moral cowards, taking the easy way out. Sullying the reputation of The Falls. Exhibitionists. *Look, look at me! Here I am.*

Except: Colborne knew what a body can look like after it has gone over The Falls. After it rises to the river's surface, sometimes days or even weeks later. Miles downriver, at the lake.

Yet The Falls exerted its malevolent spell, that never weakened. If you grew up in the Niagara region, you knew. Adolescence was the dangerous time. Most Niagara natives kept their distance from The Falls, so they were immune. But if you drifted too near, even out of intellectual curiosity, you were in danger: beginning to think thoughts unnatural to your personality as if the thunderous waters were thinking for you, depriving you of your will.

Clyde Colborne liked to think he was spared from such thoughts. As Dirk Burnaby once said, you had to have a deep, mysterious soul to want to destroy yourself. The shallower you are, the safer.

Colborne had said, laughing, "I'll drink to that."

The Falls was good for one thing: money.

So this was bad news, anyway not good news, what his employees were telling him. Everyone on the staff was abuzz with it. A certain Reverend Erskine had disappeared, and from all reports it sounded as if he was the man who'd jumped that morning; his bride of hardly more than one day, the red-haired woman with the pale freckled face and distracted manner, had been looking for him in the hotel, and had finally reported him "missing." The couple was from Troy, on the far side of the state; they'd booked the Rosebud Honeymoon Suite for five days.

"They were married just *yesterday*? Jesus."

Colborne was incredulous, incensed. He had a twelve-year-old daughter. He had a mother who adored him, forgave him his faults. He was sentimental about women. It infuriated him that any man, let alone a minister, could behave so selfishly on his honeymoon.

"At least he could've waited till he was married a while. Give it a chance. A few weeks. Months. Like the rest of us did. *Jesus*."

Introduced to the widowed bride, Colberne thrust out his hand to take hers. He was wound tight as a spring. He was yearning for a quick drink. The young woman's fingers were icy in his, and without strength; he had a sudden impulse to warm them energetically in both his hands. "Hello! Hel*lo*. Mrs. Erskine, I'm Clyde Colborne, proprietor of the Rainbow Grand. I've heard of your situation and I'll be taking you to police headquarters. You've called your family, I assume? And Reverend Erskine's family? And please understand, Mrs. Erskine, under these difficult circumstances you're welcome to stay on at the Rainbow Grand, compliments of the management, as long as—" Colborne paused, blushing. He meant to say until the body is found, identified, shipped home. But Mrs. Erskine hadn't yet been told about the man over The Falls. "—as long as required."

The red-haired woman lifted her strange glassy-green eyes to his. Though she'd surely been told by his employees who Clyde Colborne was, and where he was now taking her, she seemed to have forgotten. In a scratchy wondering voice she repeated " 'As long as required.' " As if the words were foreign, or a riddle.

On the brief drive to Niagara Falls Police Headquarters on South Main, Clyde Colborne at the wheel of his flashy new car (a powder blue Buick with whitewall tires, automatic transmission, beige leather upholstery soft as the inside of a woman's thigh) was uneasily aware of his passenger Ariah Erskine who sat stiffly, gloved hands clasped together on her lap. (Ariah had retrieved from her hotel room a fresh pair of white crocheted gloves.) Colborne wracked his brains to think of something to say to her. Silence between human beings scared him. He was rehearsing how he'd recount this miserable experience to his old friend Burnaby. *Jesus! I'd have been a helluva lot better off going to church with my family.* Only when Colborne was parking his car did the woman say quietly, "I haven't yet called my family. Or his. I have nothing to say to them. They will ask where Gilbert went, and why. And I have no answer."

4

Foolish woman, who are you to be spared My justice?

God's voice taunting her. Inside her skull. In this place of strangers staring at her. In pity, and suspicion.

"But how is it justice, God? Why do I deserve this?"

She waited. God declined to reply.

How long ago it now seemed, and how remote. She was standing with her thin arms lifted in a pose of crucifixion as the white satin gown with its myriad pearl buttons, tucks and pleats and ingenious lace trim, was fitted onto her like an exquisite straitjacket. Mrs. Littrell had insisted upon the corset, Ariah could scarcely breathe. *I take thee Gilbert. My lawfully wedded husband.* A sneeze would have shattered the corset, and the wedding.

At police headquarters, the bride of the "fallen" man was clearly to blame.

Ariah had washed her face. Rinsed her mouth where panic had left a taste as of copper pennies. How annoyed Gilbert would be to see how another time her damned "French twist" (as her mother called it) had come undone. Strands and wisps of hair made hopelessly frizzy by the humid Niagara atmosphere. Ariah saw with dismay she looked as if she'd only just wakened.

In that pigsty of a bed.

You disgust me. I tried to love you.
This frees both of us now.

In this new, impersonal place. Not the showy luxury of the honeymoon hotel but an ugly fluorescent-lit room where strangers addressed her urgently. "Mrs. Erskine?" And again, as if this was her name, "Mrs. Erskine? We have something to tell you, please prepare yourself." The gentlemanly man from the hotel whose name she'd forgotten seemed to have disappeared and she was left now with these strangers, identified as police officers though they were not in uniform. One of them, unexpectedly, was a woman: a "matron." You would need a female police officer to deal with female criminals, victims. This one was middle-aged, with a blunt ax of a face, a faint dark mustache on her upper lip, in a gray serge suit that fitted her bulk snugly. The woman was saying—what? Ariah tried to listen through the roaring in her ears.

Gilbert Erskine might have "fallen" into—what? Where?

"The Horseshoe Falls, a witness has reported. At about six-thirty this morning."

Ariah heard these individual words but could make little sense of their significance. And the woman had, amazingly, the wallet photo of Gilbert, too. (How had she gotten her hands on that picture of Gilbert, exactly like one Ariah had in her possession?) Ariah said, slowly, "My husband wouldn't have gone sightseeing without me. He might have left me, but he wouldn't have gone sightseeing without me. For weeks we'd been planning this trip. He was planning it, mostly. He'd marked off the tourist sights and the 'geological' sights we were going to visit, he even numbered them in the order we'd be seeing them." She said, stubbornly, "You'd have to know Gilbert Erskine, to know that he wouldn't have done such a thing."

The woman in the gray serge suit, busty and big-shouldered, was trying not to be argumentative, you could see. But there was an argument brewing here.

"Mrs. Erskine, we understand. But this photo of Mr. Erskine has been identified 'almost certainly' by the witness who saw the man at The Falls this morning. On Goat Island. Shortly after the time you've said Mr. Erskine disappeared from your hotel room."

"Did I say that? How could I say that?" Ariah asked excitedly. "I'm sure I said I didn't know the time. I had no idea of the time. The time was not a concern of mine when I was asleep. Someone must be lying."

"No one is lying, Mrs. Erskine. Why would anyone be lying? We want only to help you."

"If my husband is gone, he's gone. How can that be helped? How can you help *me*?"

"Since your husband is missing, and since a man was witnessed at the Horseshoe Falls—'falling' into the river—"

"Gilbert wouldn't do such a thing. I know what you're saying: by 'fall' you mean 'jump.' I know what you mean. But Gilbert would never have done such a desperate thing, he's a man of God."

"We understand, Mrs. Erskine. But—"

"You don't understand! Gilbert turned his back on me, but he wouldn't have turned his back on God."

Ariah spoke adamantly. It seemed to her that these ignorant strangers were deliberately provoking her. Wanting her to admit her complicity in Gilbert's fate. Wanting her to confess.

One of the male officers said, clearing his throat, "Mrs. Erskine, had you and your husband—quarreled?"

Ariah shook her head. "Never."

"You had not quarreled. At any time, ever."

"Not at any time. Ever."

"Was he upset?"

" 'Upset' in what way? Gilbert kept his feelings to himself, he was a very private man."

"Did he seem to you upset? During the hours preceding his 'disappearance'?"

Ariah tried to think. She saw again her husband's contorted, sweaty face. His teeth locked in a grimace like a Hallowe'en jack-o'-lantern. She heard again the bat-shriek that escaped from his lips. She could not betray him, his shame as profound as her own.

Ariah shook her head, with dignity.

"And he left no note behind, you've said?"

"No note."

"No hint of—why he might wish to leave you? Where he might be going?"

Ariah shook her head, brushing a strand of hair out of her warm face. Oh, she was perspiring! Vulgarly put, sweating. Like a guilty woman, under interrogation. For hours she'd been chilled, shivering. Now suddenly this place was airless, and very warm. The bowels of the earth opening in steamy gassy warmth. Ariah saw with a startled smile that she was wearing the white crocheted gloves her elderly great-aunt Louise had given her for her trousseau.

Trousseau! Ariah bit her lip to keep from laughing.

"Prior to your honeymoon trip to Niagara Falls, while you were planning your wedding, for instance, there was no suggestion of a— disagreement? Unhappiness on Mr. Erskine's part, or yours?"

Ariah scarcely listened to this rude question. *No.*

The police officers regarded her with neutral assessing eyes. It seemed to Ariah that they exchanged glances with one another, so subtly she couldn't detect them. Of course, they were practiced at this sort of thing. Interviewing guilty individuals. They'd become skilled at it as a trio of musicians. String trio. Ariah was the visiting soloist, the soprano who kept hitting wrong notes.

"We've sent out an emergency bulletin concerning your husband, Mrs. Erskine. And search teams are out along the river, on both sides, looking for the body of the—fallen man." The woman in the gray serge suit paused. "Would you like us to notify your family now? And Mr. Erskine's?"

The woman spoke in a kindly voice. But Ariah had an urge to slap her homely, bossy face.

"You keep asking me that," she said sharply. "No. I don't care to notify anyone. I can't bear a crowd of relatives around me. I threw away that damned corset in a trash can. *I won't return to that.*"

There was a startled pause. This time it was much more evident that the police officers were exchanging significant glances.

" 'Corset,' Mrs. Erskine? I don't understand."

Because she was trussed up in one herself, she couldn't comprehend how Ariah had escaped hers.

"Gilbert chose to leave me alone, and I will remain alone."

But the policewoman was as stubborn as Ariah, and not to be dissuaded. She said, "Mrs. Erskine, we have no choice. You'll need your family for support and we must notify Mr. Erskine's family, immediately. It's standard procedure in a case like this."

In a case like this.

It was then that the heavy mug slipped from Ariah's fingers and fell to the floor, spilling water and cracking into pieces. Ariah wanted to protest to these strangers who were blaming her and pitying her and trying to manipulate her that she was not "a case like this"—nor was Gilbert Erskine "a case like this"—but the floor beneath her feet tilted suddenly, and she couldn't get her balance to stand. There was a flickering of fluorescent lights like heat lightning and though Ariah's eyes were opened wide she could not see.

Foolish woman, don't despair. My justice is My mercy.

5

"HELLO, BURNABY. Thank God you're there!"

He was making the call from a pay phone in the lobby. He was in need of help. A drink also. Moral support. Dirk Burnaby was the man to consult at such dire times. Just to talk, maybe. Ask for expert advice. Solace. Any hour of the day or night. Poor bastard's an insomniac, since the war. Likes to hear from his buddies. A bachelor gets lonely almost as much as a married man. Burnaby, the youngest in their crowd, is the lone bachelor. Always has women, some of them gorgeous showgirls from the Elmwood Casino, or models. Lucky bastard, but one day his luck will run out.

Colborne was wishing he'd brought his pocket flask with him, dying for a drink. They'd all had quite a few on Burnaby's yacht last night. *The Valkyrie.* Beautiful forty-foot boat, gleaming white. Anchored in the river above l'Isle Grand, within sight of the Burnabys' estate on the southeastern end of the island. Not that Burnaby lived in the old mansion. Burnaby a little drunk, joking he's the Flying Dutchman of The Falls. What's that mean?

Colborne was saying, "This poor woman. A guest at the Rainbow. I'm thinking she's sort of my responsibility. Till her family shows up.

It looks as if her husband killed himself. Just this morning. Dirk, you listening? A Presbyterian minister."

At the other end of the line Burnaby made a noncommital sound.

"We're at police headquarters, they're trying to interview her. I assured her she could keep the suite as long as she needs it." Colborne paused. *Good public relations* he was thinking. But he was being charitable, too. He wanted Dirk Burnaby to understand that. In their circle, Burnaby was a generous, even reckless spender. He lent money he knew would never be repaid. He took on law clients he knew would never pay him, as he took on cases he knew he couldn't win, or couldn't win lucratively. Burnaby wasn't a Christian but he behaved like a Christian is supposed to behave which made Colborne, a Christian, uncomfortable. So Colborne wanted Burnaby to know about the suite. "It's a honeymoon suite she has," he added. "Not cheap."

This captured Burnaby's attention.

"Honeymoon? Why?"

"They were on their honeymoon. Married yesterday."

Burnaby laughed.

Colborne reacted indignantly. "Hey, Burn! God damn this is no joke. The woman is left alone here and she's in a state of shock and is saying she doesn't want to see her own family, even. I said I'd help her, but—what the hell am I supposed to do?"

"Well, is she young? Good-looking?"

"No!" Colborne paused, incensed. "But she's a lady."

At Burnaby's end of the line there was an ominous silence.

Why was Colborne calling his friend Burnaby, why from police headquarters, it must be he was in an anxious state. The previous night on *The Valkyrie* he'd lost at poker, $1,400 and most of it to Burnaby. Signing a check to his friend with a good-natured flourish. Colborne had played shrewdly and seriously but the cards had gone against him. Burnaby had had all the cards. Whether Burnaby dealt or not, he had all the cards. His friends acknowledged Burnaby's good luck, over the years. Most of the men in their circle had known one another since the early 1930's, Mount St. Joseph's Academy for Boys in Niagara Falls. Burnaby had been two classes behind Colborne, Wenn, Fitch, and Howell, but he'd played on varsity teams with them, football and basketball primarily. When he won, he was a gracious winner; when he lost, he was a gracious loser. But he rarely lost. Possibly his friends were a little jealous of Burnaby's success with women. He was a serial polygamist, they joked. Not that he married any of these women or even got inveigled into "engagements." Somehow, Burnaby walked away clear. And he remained on friendly terms with the women, or usually.

As long ago as Mount St. Joseph's, Dirk Burnaby had been the Peacemaker. One of the priests had called him that: "Peacemaker." In fact, Burnaby had a temper himself. But his anger quickly passed, he was always more thoughtful, smarter than the other boys. Deeper. More spiritual, maybe. Burnaby had a strange habit of apologizing with such sincerity you felt a thrill of happiness that you'd put him in the wrong, even if often he wasn't exactly in the wrong. It seemed to pain him that someone might dislike him and that his friends might dislike one another. *What if one of us dies?* Burnaby would say. And he meant it! He was a guy who wanted his friends to be friends. And you wanted to please Burn, so you gave in. Burn made you a better person than you truly were, to please him. So it was even now. Adulthood hadn't changed any of them much. A dozen times in the past twenty years Colborne had called Burnaby for help. A few years ago when Irma had ordered Clyde out of their house, Irma was filing for divorce, citing infidelity on Colborne's part. Infidelities! As if the women had meant anything to Colborne, *they had not*. It seemed impossible to drum into Irma's head, *they had not*. But women like Irma are slow to forgive. Stingy in forgiving. Colborne had been plunged into a sorry state. Living in a suite at the hotel (and trying not to see how his employees gawked and grinned at him behind his back), drinking too much. Eating too much. Losing money at the racetrack. The women he'd been seeing had no time for him when he hadn't money to spend on them, not that they were call girls exactly (though maybe they were, to speak frankly) but they could sniff out a lost cause. In eighteen months he'd bled away somewhere beyond fifty thousand dollars with nothing to show for it but a genital rash and a tendency to puke unexpectedly. Clyde had been sick with worry that his children would turn against him, though he supposed they'd be justified in doing so. A daughter, two sons. He wasn't worthy of these kids. Irma was poisoning them with her tears and hurt feelings, and Clyde loved his kids, too, but God damn (he vowed) if he was going to crawl on his belly to beg forgiveness, *he was not*. This was tearing him up! So one night he bared his ulcerous soul to Dirk Burnaby, knowing that Burnaby would make things right. Burnaby had a successful law practice in Niagara Falls and Buffalo predicated upon his ability to help other lawyers with cases that were too complicated for them, or that they'd frankly screwed up. Burnaby, the man to call. A man you could trust not to betray your secrets. So Colborne went to Burnaby, and confessed his situation. And Burnaby listened, and immediately took action. Told Colborne to sober up, and Colborne did. (To a degree.) Told Colborne to keep away from the race track over in Fort Erie, Ontario, and Colborne did. Told him how to behave—"warmly, sincerely, like you love them"—with his family, and Colborne did. And Burnaby spent time with Irma, just the two of them. Which was flattering to Irma. Burnaby told Irma that Colborne loved her so much, he had to test that love. And he would never hurt her again. And so the crisis passed. The Colbornes were reconciled. Sometimes Clyde wasn't all that certain that had been a good thing, but he guessed it was. Had to be.

Marriage, family. What else is there? You had to grow up. You had to accept it. He would make the marriage work bcause of Burnaby. Owed it to Burnaby. Irma felt the same way. *We owe it to Dirk Burnaby to stay together.*

Now Colborne was practically pleading, "Dirk? C'mon meet us. Down on South Main. We'll drive Mrs. Erskine back to the hotel and have a few drinks in the bar. Us, I mean. Not her."

It sounded as if, on the other end, Burnaby sighed.

"All right, Clyde. I'll be there in ten minutes."

6

THIRTY-THREE YEARS OLD, and a tightrope walker. Over a chasm deep as the Niagara Gorge.

He knew: he was kin to those flamboyant, obviously deranged

daredevils of the 1800's. Risking their lives to dazzle crowds by walking a tightrope across the deadly Niagara Gorge, or, crazier yet, plunging over The Falls in barrels, kayaks, homemade contraptions of ingenious designs. *Look, look at me! Was there ever anyone like me!*

He was descended from one of these. His notorious ancestor REGINALD BURNABY THE GREAT had walked an eighthundred-foot wire strung across the American Falls on Independence Day 1869. It was estimated that over eight hundred onlookers avidly watched as REGINALD BURNABY THE GREAT (variously identified as a defrocked Roman Catholic priest from Galway, an exconvict from Liverpool, if not an escaped convict from that seaport city) made the treacherous crossing in about twenty minutes, carrying a twelve-foot bamboo rod with American flags fluttering at both ends. During the crossing, women fainted; at least one woman went into labor. Judging from a daguerreotype of Reginald Burnaby taken on the eve of his crossing, he was a lean, swarthily handsome gypsylooking individual of about twenty-eight with a close-shaved head, a drooping handlebar mustache, a fierce, just perceptibly cross-eyed theatrical stare. On the wire he wore a Union lieutenant's coat (his own?) and a circus performer's black tights, and his daring exploit was celebrated in newspapers as far away as San Francisco, London, Paris, and Rome. The second time Burnaby risked his life above the Gorge, in June 1871, sponsored by a Niagara Falls spa, he drew even larger crowds. The novelty of this crossing was that Burnaby was laced into a straitjacket from which he managed to free himself midway over the Gorge; the drama was that a sudden headwind came up from the Canadian shore, and spitting rain, and Burnaby was forced to crouch on the tightrope and, "desperate and ingenious as a monkey," as the London *Times* correspondent described it, made his painstaking way from Prospect Point to Luna Island in approximately forty minutes. For Burnaby's third crossing, in August 1872, crowds were even larger, estimated at over two thousand on the American side alone, and at least half that number on the Canadian side. This crossing was sponsored by the daredevil himself, allegedly in need of money to support his wife and newborn baby. For this, most controversial crossing, from Prospect Point to Luna Island across the

American Falls, and from Luna Island to Goat Island, across the Bridal Veil Falls, Burnaby wore red silk tights and had painted his shaved head and face in the "warpaint" of an Iroquois Indian brave. From the start of the event the atmosphere was reported to be unruly and disrespectful. Mist rising out of the Gorge was particularly thick, and the crowd's view of the crossing was obscured, which contributed to general discontent and charges of "fraud." The daredevil seemed, too, less certain of himself. He was thinner, and seemed to have lost the reckless ebullience of his youth of only the previous summer. After about twenty-five minutes of a slow, inch-by-inch walk on the wire, something happened that caused Burnaby to fall into the cataract. (Though no one was ever arrested, it was believed that an unidentified youth on the American side had fired a slingshot at the daredevil, striking him in the back.) To the horror of the crowd, Burnaby plunged nearly two hundred feet into the churning water at the foot of the Falls; to the delight of the crowd, now screaming and jostling one another to get a better view, Burnaby bobbed to the surface of the water after a few minutes, seemingly "unscathed" as journalists would report. A "universal cheer" went up as the daredevil with the shaved, painted head swam toward the base of Luna Island; would-be rescuers reached out for him even as, when Burnaby was less than ten feet from shore, a powerful undertow sucked him down into the swift, green-tinged water. Eyewitnesses would claim that, as he was sucked down, Burnaby cried, "Darling, goodbye! Kiss the baby for me!" to his young wife who watched helplessly, their eight-month infant in her arms, from a platform on Goat Island.

That infant would one day be Dirk Burnaby's father.

The broken, battered body of Reginald Burnaby, scarcely recognizable except for the boldly painted head and face, wasn't discovered for several days, until at last it was sighted fifteen miles downriver, north of Lewiston, hauled to shore and given a Christian burial, courtesy of a coalition of Niagara Falls residents who'd taken pity on Burnaby and his young family.

After the widely publicized fate of REGINALD BURNABY

THE GREAT, tightrope walking across the Niagara Gorge was officially banned.

"Poor fool. You threw away your life, a precious life, and for what?"

On a wall of his Luna Park townhouse were several daguerreotypes of his daredevil grandfather. Dirk Burnaby often contemplated these, smiling at the handlebar mustache that gave to the lean, hopeful face a look of masculine swagger. In one photograph, Reginald Burnaby was smiling stiffly, and you could see that his teeth were in bad repair, crooked and discolored. In another photograph, Burnaby in snug-fitting jersey and tights, a circus performer's costume, stood with arms akimbo, knuckles on his hips and a cocky *Ain't I something?* expression on his face. Here you could see that Burnaby was a compact, muscled little man, strongly developed in the torso, thighs, and legs. (Dirk Burnaby had read that his grandfather was only five foot six, and weighed less than one hundred fifty pounds at the time of his death.) You could see that he was probably hot-blooded, restless, consumed with vanity, sought after by women, doomed to die young. Yes, he'd been brave, but what's the point?

Who wants to be a daredevil, and posthumous?

He, Dirk Burnaby, was nothing like his ancestor physically. He'd grown to a gratifying height of six foot two while still in his teens. (He'd liked that! Towering over his classmates and most adults. It had given him a charge of entitlement and invincibility he would draw upon through life, like a limitless bank account.) He wasn't swarthy-skinned like a gypsy but fair-skinned, and he wasn't even mildly cross-eyed. He detested mustaches and beards, they made his sensitive skin itch. He was a good-looking man, why hide the fact? He guessed he wasn't very brave. He'd never risk his life if he could avoid it.

"I'd rather live, thank you."

In the U.S. Army where he'd been a private in the infantry for two years, stationed mainly in Italy, he'd had to force himself to shoot at the enemy, and could not have said that he'd ever—once—hit any human target, let alone killed. He didn't want to *have killed*. At the crucial moment, firing his rifle, he'd often shut his eyes. Sometimes he hadn't aimed, and sometimes he hadn't even pulled the trigger. (Years later, Dirk would learn that a startlingly high percentage of soldiers had behaved this way, not wanting to *have killed*, and yet somehow the war was won.) Dirk Burnaby had been wounded, and and spent several weeks in an army hospital near Naples, he had medals to prove he'd acted bravely in the confused, chaotic event designated as World War II, he was damned glad the Allies had won over the deranged and murderous Axis powers, certainly he spoke with passion of the madness of Hitler, Mussolini, Tojo, and what it meant that millions of human beings had acquiesced to their madness, but of his actual war experience he retained little except a vast relief that the war was over and he was alive.

"That's what you missed, grandfather. Ordinary life."

One thing it was not: love at first sight.

He didn't believe in such. He wasn't a believer in romance, sentimental coincidences, "meanings" snatched out of the air. He certainly didn't believe in destiny, he was a gambler by nature and you know that destiny is just chance you try to manipulate for your own profit.

Yet his first glimpse of Ariah Erskine made an impression. The red-haired woman in the frilly girl's dress was in the company of his friend Clyde Colborne, who was leading her, like a convalescent, down the steps of the Niagara Falls Police Headquarters. The woman brusquely detached her arm from Colborne's as if he'd said something that annoyed her. Or she was capable of walking without a man's assistance, thank you.

Sighting Burnaby, Colborne called to him eagerly, and introduced him to "Mrs. Ariah Erskine" who stared at him for a tense moment before half-shutting her eyes. (Had the poor woman for that moment, in the confusion of grief, wondered if Burnaby, a stranger, might turn out to be the missing husband?) Mrs. Erskine struck him as fierce and plain and haughty as one of those straight-backed red-haired girl-women in certain of the watercolors of Winslow Homer. The prim little schoolmarm at the blackboard, in profile, detached from the observer's admiring eye; the red-haired girl in an orange dress lying in the grass reading a novel, oblivious of any onlooker. This woman's pale freckled face shone as if she'd scrubbed it, hard. Her faded rust-colored hair fell in lank coils and wisps about her head as if she'd given up on it. There were half-moons of perspiration beneath the arms of her organdy dress, and her stockings sagged at the ankles. Her eyes were moist, shifty, bloodshot. She was nothing like the sorrowful woman Dirk Burnaby had been led to expect, and much more interesting. As Clyde Colborne nervously chattered about what the police had told her, what was being done and would be done, the red-haired woman looked pointedly away, paying little heed to Colborne, or to his friend Burnaby who towered over her, flaxen-haired, handsome and gallant in a navy blue blazer with nautical brass buttons and neatly pressed white cord trousers, a manly-stylish figure out of *Esquire*. He, Dirk Burnaby, whom women adored, and some of them happily married rich women, ignored by this woman! He had to smile.

Ariah Erskine interrupted Colborne to tell him she didn't intend to return to the hotel just yet, she was on her way to the Niagara Gorge. If Colborne wouldn't drive her, she'd take a taxi. Or she'd walk. She'd been informed that authorities believed that her husband had "fallen" into the river that morning, and the search teams were out. A Coast Guard crew was out on the river. She had to be there to make the identification, if the "fallen" man was, in fact, Reverend Erskine.

Colborne said, shocked, "Mrs. Erskine, that isn't a good idea. You don't want to be there. Not if—"

"They're searching for a man. A body. I don't believe it can be Gilbert but I must be there." Mrs. Erskine tried to speak matter-of-factly but Burnaby could detect a tremor in her voice. She stood before the men with her head turned to one side, refusing to meet their eyes. "I will have to be a witness if—if they find this man. I will have to *know*."

Colborne objected, "But, Mrs. Erskine, it would be much better if you waited at the hotel until—"

"No. Nothing can be 'better.' If Gilbert is dead, I will have to *know*."

Colborne looked appealingly to Dirk Burnaby, who was staring at this stubborn red-haired woman with a kind of fascination. He didn't know what to think of her: his brain had gone blank. The bizarre thought came to him, she was so petite, couldn't weigh more than ninety pounds, a man could lift her and sling her over his shoulder and walk away with her. Let her protest! He heard himself say, "I don't think you caught my name, Mrs. Erskine? I'm Clyde's friend Dirk Burnaby. I'm a lawyer. I live about two miles away in Luna Park, near the Gorge. I'll do anything I can to help you, Mrs. Erskine. Please prevail upon me." This was a wholly unexpected remark. Burnaby would not believe he'd uttered it, an hour later. Colborne gaped at him, and the red-haired woman turned frowning to him, squinting upward as if she hadn't exactly remembered he was there. She opened her mouth to speak but did not. Her lipstick was eaten away, her thin lips appeared cracked and dry. Impulsively, Burnaby squeezed her hand.

It was a small-boned hand, small as a sparrow, yet even in the crocheted white glove the fingers felt hot, eager.

The Widow-Bride of The Falls:

The Vigil

For seven days and seven nights she kept her vigil.

For seven days and seven nights the Widow-Bride of The Falls was to be found at the Niagara Gorge, on Goat Island or on shore; she joined search teams looking for the "missing" man, and accompanied a Coast Guard search crew in their downriver patrol past Lewiston and Youngstown, to the mouth of the river at Lake Ontario. In the Coast Guard boat Ariah Erskine was the sole woman, and her presence made the men uneasy. She was feverish, entranced. Her bloodshot eyes were fixed upon the river's choppy, heaving waves as if, at any moment, a man's body might appear, and her search would end. In her low hoarse voice she said repeatedly, to whoever would listen, "I'm Gilbert Erskine's wife, and if I've become Gilbert Erskine's widow I must be present when he's found. I must care for my husband." Coast Guard officers exchanged pained glances: they knew what a man's body would look like, having gone over The Falls.

"Why have I involved myself with this woman? She's mad."

Worse, Ariah Erskine seemed scarcely to know who Dirk Burnaby was. No doubt she'd conflated him with Clyde Colborne, his friend. Still, Dirk had volunteered to make himself available to her for as long as required. He'd called his office and spoke with his assistant: all work was to be frozen, for the time being. ("Tell our clients it's an emergency.") Niagara Falls authorities knew Burnaby well and were grateful for his presence, for no one knew what to do with Ariah Erskine, who refused to behave as others wished her to behave. Even her parents couldn't reason with her.

Dirk Burnaby overheard one pitiful exchange: "Ariah, dear? Come back to the hotel with your father and me? Darling, you're exhausted. You're ill. Look at that dress! Your hair! Ariah, *please listen to your mother.*"

But Ariah, pouting and stubborn, would not.

"You wanted me to marry Gilbert Erskine. And so I did. And so I'm his wife. This is what a wife must do, Mother! Go away, and leave me alone."

It was a role she was playing, Dirk thought, disapproving. She'd become a pilgrim of The Falls—as the press was proclaiming her, The Widow-Bride of The Falls. Perhaps it was true, she hadn't any choice.

During the days of the vigil Ariah Erskine was observed to be obsessively aware of the river, its ever-shifting, roiling surfaces like green-tinged flame, yet virtually oblivious of her other surroundings. She was but vaguely aware of others beside her, and often failed to answer when spoken to. She would not have eaten at all except food was brought to her, and urged upon her.

When Ariah woke from her exhausted sleep she appeared dazed and vacant-eyed, vulnerable as a child roused from a bad dream. Yet within seconds she summoned her steely will, this will that so impressed Dirk Burnaby, for he'd never encountered anything like it in his life, establishing where she was, and why. *The bad dream was outside her, in the world. She must conquer it there or nowhere.*

It was a fact, eagerly reported by the press, that, each morning of her vigil Ariah Erskine, the Widow-Bride of The Falls, would appear at the Niagara Gorge by 6 A.M. Often she was hurrying, as if she feared being late. At this hour of morning the atmosphere of the Gorge was chill, damp, shrouded in mist. Amid tendrils of mist rising like steam Ariah would retrace the route allegedly taken by the yet-unidentified man who'd thrown himself over the Horseshoe Falls on the morning of Sunday, June 12: in a yellow rain slicker and hat provided her by the owner of the *Maid of the Mist* cruise boats, she crossed the narrow pedestrian bridge to Goat Island, staring intently at the fast-moving greenish-tinged water below and drawing her white-gloved hand along the railing. Her lips moved. (Was she praying? Addressing her lost husband?) In the gleaming bright-yellow slicker the woman looked like a deranged flower set against the sulfurous, ceaselessly rising mists of the great gorge.

("Ever rising like the souls of the damned seeking salvation," Ariah said to Dirk Burnaby, in one of her rare moments of noticing him. Her fixed, wistful smile made him shudder.)

Beneath the slicker Ariah wore summer dresses, cotton shirt-waists in light colors, or floral prints; on her legs were stockings that quickly became soaked from spray, as her face and hair were quickly wetted. She gave no sign of noticing. Press reporters and photographers, and as the days passed a ragtag assortment of the curious and morbid-minded, trailed in her wake, though at a respectful distance, as Dirk Burnaby assured. He detested these parasites, as he thought them, though Ariah herself seemed indifferent to their presence. Her concentration was solely upon the river. When a stranger called to her—"Mrs. Erskine? Excuse me, Mrs. Erskine?"—"Hello, Mrs. Erskine? I'm from the *Niagara Gazette*, may I speak with you for just five minutes?"—she seemed not to hear. Yet so far as Dirk could see she made no effort to hide her face or disguise herself, as she might have easily done. In some of the newspaper photographs of the Widow-Bride, Ariah's small-boned face, wetted from spray, shone pale and smooth as white marble, so that she appeared to be continually weeping, as a statue might weep, with a look resigned and calm.

Dirk knew that Ariah Erskine wasn't crying. She was a canny woman, saving her tears. She would need all the tears she could summon, soon.

Corpses in the Niagara River were usually found within a week. If they had sunk, the ghastly effects of putrefaction would turn them into "floaters." It was only a matter of time.

Once on Goat Island, Ariah made her way to Terrapin Point by the eastern loop of the path, which was the one the suicide had taken. There she stood unmoving for as long as a half-hour, a lone, melancholy figure in her incongruously gaily colored slicker, under the spell of the thunderous Horseshoe Falls. As the morning lightened, the eerie glassy-green aura of The Falls became more distinct. Faint rainbows appeared, shimmering in the mist. The roaring of the cataract at Terrapin Point was so loud it entered your very being, casting out coherent thoughts. You could not recall your name in such a din, and you would not wish to recall it. You felt yourself a heartbeat away from the primal core of being: sheer energy, nameless and inviolate. Photographs of the Widow-Bride at Terrapin Point, the site of the suicide, were very popular, though most showed the grieving woman only from the back, head and face obscured by the wide-brimmed rain hat. Dirk Burnaby himself stood a few yards behind her on the path, watching her uneasily, alert to any sudden reckless movement or gesture. If Ariah pressed too close against the railing, leaning her upper body over it, Dirk took a quick step forward. He was prepared to grab her, close his arms around her and wrest her away from danger. He understood the primitive, malevolent spell of The Falls: he was beginning to feel again the sinister attraction he'd felt years ago, as an adolescent, when his emotions were rawer, closer to the surface. Those feelings of dissolution, loss, panic, very like the sensation of falling in love against one's will.

The Falls! *You can't believe it can kill you. When it is pure spirit.*

After her vigil at Terrapin Point, Ariah would turn like one waking slowly and reluctantly from a deep sleep, and make her way along the western loop of the path, past the Bridal Veil Falls and Luna

Island, past Bird Island and Green Island; though the suicide hadn't occurred on this side of Goat Island, yet Ariah lingered at the railing, staring wistfully, hungrily, at the river here, as if, somehow, her lost husband's body might emerge. So much seemed possible when you stared upriver, and saw the violent, plunging waves moving toward you in a stream that seemed to stretch to the horizon, and infinity. There, at the river's source, was the future: at your back, it became the past. Only the fleet, ephemeral moment of its passing was alive, and alive in you.

Ariah Erskine then recrossed the pedestrain bridge, oblivious of the gatekeeper in his kiosk who stared at her in trepidation and dread (he was the man who'd witnessed the suicide, he feared her recognizing him); she passed by the American Falls, and for a long time stared at the plunging water at its base; she turned to follow the path downriver, pausing from time to time, never predictably, to lean over the railing and lose herself in the churning white water. In this way, through the course of a morning, the Widow-Bride of The Falls made her way past the Niagara Observation Tower and the *Maid of the Mist* boarding dock, which was crowded with tourists, past the site of the Cave of the Winds and the Devil's Whirlpool, which might engage her interest for as long as an hour.

The Devil's Whirlpool! Dirk Burnaby would think afterward it was as if she'd known. She'd sensed. The dead man inside. Caught by centrifugal force. A gyre of Hell.

Almost, he'd come to share the woman's morbid fascination with the river. The possibility of the river's disgorging, at any moment, the body of the dead man. He hoped that wouldn't happen, he could not have borne it, in her presence.

He wanted to stand close beside her at the railing, and put his arm around her. He wanted for himself this ferocity of attention, this loyalty. He couldn't believe that the Reverend Gilbert Erskine deserved it. He hated the man, detested him, that, though dead, he should so captivate the woman. Yet thinking *She's beyond hurt. Beyond the love of any man.*

———

A photographer was boldly edging near Ariah Erskine as she leaned over the railing above the Whirlpool and there came Dirk Burnaby to intercede, wrenching the camera out of the man's hands and tossing it over the railing into the river. When the man protested, mouth opening like a pike's, Dirk said calmly, "Now get your ass out of here, or you'll follow it."

The photographer said he was with the AP. He would report this to the police.

"I am the police," Dirk Burnaby said. "A plainsclothes detective assigned to protect this lady against harassers. So get out of here, you, or you're under arrest."

Shoving the heel of his hand against the photographer's chest, forcing him backward.

They didn't understand what had happened, they were saying. Not to Gilbert. Not to Ariah. It was as if something terrible—demonic— had happened to these young people as soon as they'd gotten married, and started their honeymoon at Niagara Falls. "Why is Ariah behaving so strangely, Mr. Burnaby? Why won't she spend any time with us?" Mrs. Littrell, a soft-bodied woman of late middle age with a raddled, pleading face and frightened eyes, appealed to Dirk Burnaby to intercede with her daughter, while Reverend Littrell looked on somberly, stroking his chin. They might have believed that Burnaby was associated with the Rainbow Grand, since he appeared to be a partner of Clyde Colborne; they might have believed that he was a Niagara Falls official of some sort, whose job was to comfort the distraught survivors of missing persons and suicides. Dirk felt sorry for the Littrells, and annoyance at Ariah, who was treating them so rudely; at the same time he was pleased to note that the daughter scarcely resembled either of her parents. The red-haired girl was an "original"—he'd known it!

Gently he told the Littrells that Ariah was in a state of shock, and they shouldn't take her strange behavior personally. He told them that in the course of his lifetime he'd been a witness to similar behavior in others—when an individual suffers an irreversible loss suddenly, with no warning. (He was thinking of one or two girls with whom he'd been romantically involved, who hadn't liked being dropped by Dirk Burnaby, and had made quite a fuss over it. He was thinking, too, of his mother, who'd slipped into a morbid state of self-absorption after the loss of her beauty in her fifties, refusing to leave her house on the Island even to see old friends. Even to see her children!) "People behave in extreme ways, after extreme shocks," Dirk said. "At the present time it isn't absolutely known that her husband is the man who'd been seen—well, at The Falls. And so Ariah is in a state of suspension, not knowing." He saw by the startled, fearful expressions on the faces of Reverend and Mrs. Littrell that they wanted not to know exactly what he was saying; they, too, were holding out hope that their son-in-law wasn't dead but had simply "disappeared." (And would "reappear"?) How pathetic the Littrells were! Dirk felt a stab of sympathy for them; for the desperation in their wish to believe that there was yet hope, and that their prayers, quite literal prayers, would be answered by a vigilant God. Dirk said gently, as if he were more intimately acquainted with Ariah Erskine than he was, "It's better for your daughter, in these circumstances, to be involved in activity, I think. Instead of just waiting helplessly, passively, at the hotel."

As a woman is meant to wait, Dirk thought.

Mrs. Littrell protested. "But, Mr. Burnaby, Ariah isn't even sleeping in the hotel, as far as we know. Where on earth *is she*? She isn't eating meals here. She informed us and the Erskines that she can't spend time with us, she 'hasn't time.' Gilbert's parents are very anxious, but Ariah won't see them. I caught sight of her in that hideous yellow raincoat in—is it Prospect Park? But when I called after her, she ran away. And there are photographers and reporters everywhere. Radio people hoping to interview *us*." Mrs. Littrell shuddered. "Have you seen what they're writing about her, Mr. Burnaby? Back home in Troy it's in the papers, too. 'The Widow-Bride of The Falls.' Our only child! She was just married this past Saturday." As she spoke, Mrs. Littrell glanced at Reverend Littrell for support, but her husband seemed scarcely to hear her. Dirk saw that the poor man was disoriented, inert. His bulky middle-aged body seemed to be losing definition, as if melting. He wore a nondescript dark suit with wide lapels, a starched white shirt and a dull "good" necktie. His eyes behind bi-focal glasses were moving jerkily about the room (they were in the Littrells' hotel room at the Rainbow Grand, Dirk had dropped by to speak with them in Ariah's place), as if he were seeking some confir-mation of where he was, what this must mean. Dirk's heart went out to him. For here was a man accustomed to authority, and without "authority" he was undefined as a flag in windless calm. Mrs. Littrell said, "Mr. Burnaby, will you tell Ariah we are—thinking of her con-stantly? Anxious about her? Hoping she will, when this is over, come back with us? Come h-home?"

So Mrs. Littrell knows her son-in-law is dead, Dirk thought.

A good sign.

But when Dirk left the Littrells, Reverend Littrell stepped out into the corridor with him as if to speak man-to-man. "Mr. Burnaby, did you say that you did—no, you did *not*?—know Gilbert? You didn't know him. I see. You didn't know, then, that Gilbert has had this strange, unhealthy interest, or hobby, in—what d'you call 'em— 'fossils'? Little skeletons, like snails and frogs, you find in rocks? He'd say they were millions of years old, in fact there's no way to prove they're older than six thousand years. And why these things are so important to so-called scientists, what they are meant to prove about God's creation, and the history of the earth—I don't know. Mr. Burnaby, do you?"

Politely Dirk shook his head, no. No idea.

"I'm no kind of a scientist, Reverend. I'm a lawyer."

Reverend Littrell said, frowning, "My son-in-law might have wanted Ariah to join him on some sort of expedition for these things. 'Fossils.' Trekking in creekbeds and swamps. And my daughter, who has a stubborn streak, as you've seen, might have refused to go with him on her honeymoon . . . I'm thinking, I'm hoping, that's what this is? That's all this is? Mr. Burnaby, what do you think?"

Dirk Burnaby murmured to the older man that he wasn't sure. He wasn't sure what to think.

Dirk could see why Ariah Erskine hoped to avoid her parents for as long as possible. And her in-laws! Reverend and Mrs. Erskine seemed almost to leap at the younger man when they saw him, rapacious as starving minks. Quickly he had to tell them he hadn't any news of their son. He wasn't with the Niagara Falls police or the Coast Guard, he was careful to explain, only just a private citizen trying to help in the emergency, but the Erskines didn't seem to hear. "Is there any news of my son?" Reverend Erskine asked, an air of reproach in his voice. When Dirk told him no, he didn't think so, not at the present moment, Reverend Erskine said, "But *why*? A man is missing, and his bride is distraught and making a spectacle of herself in public, and there is no *news*? I don't understand."

The Erskines were about the same age as the Littrells, in their mid- or late fifties, but looking older with strain and sleeplessness. Mrs. Erskine was a quiet, stifled-seeming woman with the oblong bony face of Gilbert Erskine in his photograph, but lacking her son's air of peevish intelligence; Reverend Erskine was a forceful individual with a voice calibrated to ring out from a pulpit, filling a moderate-sized church. In the hotel room, this voice was too loud for Dirk Burnaby's comfort, he had to resist the impulse to clap his hands over his ears. Dirk was slightly intimidated, too, by the older man's animosity. "Mr. Burnaby, the things that are being printed! Even in our hometown newspaper! And here in the *Gazette*, and the *Buffalo News*—officials too cowardly to identify themselves speculating that Gilbert is the man who 'threw himself' into the Horseshoe Falls. When there is absolutely no proof! This is libel, Mr. Burnaby. Please inform your friends."

Dirk faintly protested, these weren't his friends.

"Whatever they are saying about our son is *not true*. Gilbert would never do such a thing as—'throw himself' into The Falls." Reverend Erskine spoke contemptuously. He was a rail-thin man of no more than average height, shorter than Dirk Burnaby by several inches, yet seemed to tower over him, fierce in indignation. The lenses of his glasses flashed. There was spittle in the corners of his mouth. Dirk guessed that Gilbert Erskine had departed this life under orders from his father the Reverend, without either man knowing. *To escape the wrath of God. Here's God!*

Quietly Dirk said, with an apologetic glance at Mrs. Erskine, "Sometimes people surprise us. People we believe we know."

Reverend Erskine said brusquely, "Yes. But not our son. Gilbert isn't 'people.'"

To this, Dirk had no reply.

"Gilbert would never take his own—life. Never."

Dirk stared glumly at the plush crimson carpet.

"I expect these newspapers to print retractions. Apologies. *Gilbert would never.*"

Reluctantly Dirk had left Ariah Erskine sleeping in the back of his car, parked at the rear of his Luna Park town house. The red-haired girl (Ariah had become so frail and wistful during the course of the vigil, Dirk had difficulty thinking of her any longer as a mature, adult woman) had refused to come inside Dirk's house to freshen up and sleep. She'd refused to accompany him to the Rainbow Grand. *She too is fearful of these elders. It's her instinct to survive.*

When Dirk left the Erskines' hotel room, it was Mrs. Erskine who accompanied him to the door, and anxiously squeezed his hand. The woman's fingers were moistly clammy yet surprisingly strong. "Mr. Burnaby? 'Dirk'? I don't know who you are or why you've been so kind to Ariah—and to us—but I want to thank you, and God bless you. Whatever has happened to Gilbert"—her eyes snatched at Dirk's, shining with terror—"he too would thank you."

Dirk murmured words of consolation, or commiseration.

How he hated the suicide! *Selfish scheming bastard.*

He walked the half-mile to his brownstone town house in Luna Park. His mind seethed! He was a man of strong appetites and imagination and it was sometimes held against him that he inflated events and people with sudden significance, like magnified images on a screen. Later, these might shrink to pinpricks. They might disappear.

So he'd been accused. Frequently in his relatively short life of thirty-three years. "As if it's my fault. But how?" Truly, Dirk couldn't understand.

She'd refused to come inside his house, to sleep in a proper bed, or even atop a bed. Not once had she called him "Dirk"—nor even "Mr. Burnaby." *She didn't know his God-damned name.*

Seeing Ariah Erskine sleeping peacefully in the cushioned rear of his Lincoln Continental, a skinny muskrat of a girl with papery, bruised skin and a slack drooling mouth, knees drawn up to her scrawny chest, bitten-looking fingernails and faded red hair badly in need of washing, he told himself furiously *You are not. Not falling in love. Not.*

"Excuse me, Mr. Burnaby? The Coast Guard found it."

Not *him*. *It*.

Dirk would be grateful that Ariah Erskine hadn't been present to hear this crude remark made by a Niagara Falls patrolman.

It was mid-morning of June 19. Bells were ringing: Sunday.

Seven days and seven nights had passed in a vertiginous stream.

At the time of the discovery, the Widow-Bride hadn't been sleeping but gone into a women's restroom in Prospect Park.

Feeling sick, Dirk said, "Jesus! Where?"

"Whirlpool."

The Devil's Whirlpool! He'd had a premonition.

So many days of futile searches downriver to Lake Ontario and back to Niagara Falls, and all the while the body of the deceased had been trapped in the Whirlpool, less than three miles from the Horseshoe Falls. His body had been swept downriver, sucked into the whirlpool, and held captive. The Devil's Whirlpool was as extraordinary a natural phenomenon as The Falls. A mammoth circular basin in the Gorge, two hundred feet in height, in which frothy, foaming water turned in a maddened vortex. Objects of various sizes were sometimes trapped in this vortex for days, weeks. It was rare that a body was trapped as long as Erskine's had been trapped, but not unknown.

The corpse had been sucked beneath the surface of the river, and had been invisible from shore. Spinning, spinning, spinning for seven days and seven nights inside the Whirlpool.

Dirk no longer felt that he hated the suicide. Nor was he jealous of him. He hoped the poor bastard had, in fact, been dead when his body had entered the Whirlpool.

"Ariah, you can't possibly do this. Stay back."

"I will. I must."

"Ariah, no."

Dirk spoke harshly, as an elder brother might speak. Ariah licked her thin, cracked lips. Her skin was so papery-tight across the bones of her face, it seemed a sudden gesture or movement might tear it.

"But I *must*."

It was a role she was playing, Dirk thought. And she would play it through to the end.

The authorities had no choice but to concur. As the probable widow of the dead man, it was Ariah Erskine's right to see the corpse immediately and to make the identification.

Downriver, onshore near the Devil's Whirlpool, a small crowd had gathered. There was more than the usual contingent of reporters and photographers. Reluctantly, emergency workers allowed Ariah to approach the corpse. At about ten yards, Ariah pulled suddenly away from Dirk Burnaby's restraining arm, nearly running. The canvas covering the corpse was drawn back. Oh, what was that odor? That *smell*? A look of childlike perplexity came over the widow's face. The corpse was a classic "floater." No one had prepared the widow for this experience. Not even Dirk Burnaby who hadn't had the heart, or the stomach, for the task.

The remains of twenty-seven-year-old Gilbert Erskine were grotesquely bloated with intestinal gas, and nearly unrecognizable as human. The once-thin body was a balloon-body, naked, hairless, finger- and toenails gone. A dark, swollen tongue protruded from a bizarrely smiling mouth and drooping lower jaw. The eyes were milky, lacking irises, and lidless. The genitalia were similarly bloated, like burst plums. What was most hideous, the outer layer of skin had peeled away and a reddish-brown dermal layer was exposed, tinted by burst capillaries. A stink more virulent than sulfur dioxide lifted from the corpse. Ariah shouted with what sounded like laughter. A rowdy child's laughter tinged with fright, indignation.

She recognized her husband, she claimed, by the corpse's "angry grin." And by the white gold wedding ring, which matched her own, within which the blackened ring finger had swollen to several times its size.

"Yes. It's Gilbert."

She spoke in a whisper. Only then did the Widow-Bride lose her remarkable stamina, and her strength. Seven days and seven nights of vigilance were finished. Her eyes rolled back in her head like a shaken doll's and she would have fallen to the ground except, cursing himself for his fate, Dirk Burnaby caught her in his arms.

The Proposal

1

Abruptly she was gone from The Falls, and from Dirk Burnaby's life.

"Thank God! What a nightmare."

It was a memory to feed his insomnia. Like a great black-feathered scavenger bird tearing at his entrails. He wouldn't have believed himself so vulnerable. For after all he'd been in the war, he'd seen ugly sights . . . There were times when a sick, dizzy sensation overcame him, not memory exactly but the emotion of memory, playing golf with his friends on the beautiful sloping course at l'Isle Grand Country Club, sailing or boating on the river, and he was made to realize that his happiness was solely a consequence of chance, and luck: for how many millions of others, less lucky than Dirk Burnaby, life had been painful, ghastly, cut off prematurely. Seeing now the bloated, discolored body on the riverbank and the impetuous red-haired girl pulling away from him before he could stop her, nearly lunging forward to make her claim.

Well, she'd regretted that. He supposed.

Not love. Not my type. He hadn't heard from her since. Of course he hadn't. What had he expected, he'd expected nothing. As soon as the body was identified and the vigil was over, Dirk Burnaby's role in the drama ended. He'd seen Ariah Erskine taken away by ambulance to the hospital, in a state of collapse, but her family was summoned then and took over her care. The body would have been shipped back to Troy and the funeral and burial of the late Reverend Gilbert Erskine must have been immediate.

"Accident" it would be called, probably. The reckless young man with an interest in "scientific exploration" had "fallen" into the Niagara River. Local newspapers would be discreet. The coroner would rule "misadventure." For in the absence of a clear-cut motive for suicide, a note left behind . . .

He'd never been to Troy. A city of no special distinction, three hundred miles east along the Mohawk River, beyond Albany.

Not love. This was a fact: if Dirk Burnaby had sighted Ariah Erskine at a social gathering, his gaze would have drifted over her without snagging. When his friends asked about her, Dirk was evasive except to say emphatically that he'd had no contact with the woman since the vigil, it had been an impulsive gesture on his part and nothing more. She'd never thanked him. She'd never seemed to see him. Clyde Colborne said, "She told me she was damned. And the look in her face, I wasn't going to argue with her."

Damned? Dirk didn't ask about this. He was dealing cards, an action his skillful hands performed flawlessly, except suddenly he dropped a card, and it fell to the floor. His friends smiled at this and said nothing. That night (the poker game was at Tyler Wenn's, on the river) Dirk won $3,100 and pushed it back to his friends, not wanting it. He was sick of poker, he said. He'd known these men for twenty years, and more— Buzz Fitch, Stroughton Howell, Clyde Colborne, Wenn. They were like brothers to him, and he didn't care if he never saw them again.

Not lovesick. Not Burnaby! Skimming through newspapers and news magazines, staring at photographs, headlines. He knew this would disgust him but he couldn't resist.

THE VIGIL OF THE WIDOW-BRIDE OF THE FALLS

WIDOW-BRIDE'S 7-DAY VIGIL ENDS IN TRAGEDY

BODY OF 27-YEAR-OLD TROY MINISTER
HAULED FROM NIAGARA GORGE

Missing 7 Days
Sought by Bride

Life, *Time*, and *The Saturday Evening Post* had printed sympathetic features. Nowhere was the word *suicide* used.

Dirk paid little attention to the articles themselves, it was the photographs that engaged him. He frowned to see himself in some of these. An indistinct, shadowy figure. You could recognize Dirk Burnaby if you knew him, he had a certain physical stature, a blunt, handsome profile, fair hair that lifted from his forehead in springy, flaring wings. In one of the grainy newspaper photos Dirk was blurred in motion as if caught in the act of trying to prevent the photographer from taking the photo, as Ariah Erskine in her rain slicker and hat stood at a railing, poised as a statue. 29-YEAR-OLD TROY WOMAN JOINS SEARCH FOR HUSBAND IN NIAGARA GORGE. How strange it seemed to Dirk, the myriad actions and impressions of the long vigil reduced to such simple statements. And not one of the photos depicted Ariah Erskine as Dirk recalled her.

The Widow-Bride had become another Niagara legend, but no one would remember her name.

It wasn't a good day for Mrs. Burnaby, Dirk's mother. She was sixty-three years old and few days were good any longer.

"You never visit me, Dirk. Almost, I'd think you were avoiding me."

Mrs. Burnaby laughed cruelly. That sound, familiar to her son, of a silver ice pick stabbing at ice. For the older woman knew well that her son was avoiding her and that, to demonstrate how he was not avoiding her, he drove to the Island more frequently than he would have if he hadn't hoped to avoid her.

"Dirk, dear! Your mother knows, and forgives."

Claudine Burnaby now lived alone on l'Isle Grand, with a housekeeper, in the twenty-three-room "manor house" Dirk's father had built in 1924, rich from investments in local businesses and real estate. The Burnaby house, on six acres of prime riverfront property, was a smaller replica of an English country estate in Surrey, built of dark-pink limestone on a knoll overlooking the Chippawa Channel (facing Ontario, Canada) of the Niagara River. On bright days its tall stately windows shone with the sparkle of mysterious lives within; in more typical Niagara Falls weather, overcast and ponderous, the limestone resembled lead, and the steep slate roofs weighed down heavily. Like other 1920's-era mansions on the Island it boasted a romantic, pretentious name: "Shalott." Dirk had fled Shalott at eighteen, to Colgate University and law school at Cornell; he'd never returned to Shalott to live for any extended duration of time but his mother kept his old room in perpetual readiness, like a shrine. In fact, it was now a suite of rooms, an apartment remodeled and handsomely furnished. Dirk's father had died (suddenly, of a heart attack), twelve years before, in 1938, and his mother had begun her unexpected and perverse retreat from the world shortly afterward.

Dirk had been assured numerous times by his mother that he, not his older, married sisters, would inherit Shalott. Of course he would live at Shalott, and raise his children there. And if this would one day be so—Mrs. Burnaby reasoned, with flawless logic—why not now? Why didn't he marry, settle down like everyone else his age? Claudine would continue to live at Shalott, in "her" part of the house, and Dirk and his family would live in the rest, which was certainly large enough. There was the river, and the dock, the speedboat no one used any longer, the sailboat Dirk had loved as a boy, only just think how Dirk's sons would love it. Their daddy taking them out on the river, teaching them to sail . . .

"Except I'm not married yet, Mother. Not even engaged." Dirk was embarrassed to point out this detail. "You forget."

Coolly Claudine said, "No, Dirk. I never forget."

Claudine had become a mother who flirted with her son, yet maintained an air of moral reproach. She could say things to Dirk that no other living person could say to him; and he would have to tolerate it, and continue to adore her.

She'd become a beautiful exotic spider in her web of rooms, waiting at Shalott.

Long ago, in 1907, Claudine Burnaby had been a Buffalo debutante. In the fashion of the time she'd had an ample, bosomy body with a cinched-in waist and hourglass figure; her hair was naturally blond, her face childlike, with beestung petulant lips. She'd married a Niagara Falls entrepreneur named Virgil Burnaby, the (adopted) son of well-to-do Niagara Falls residents. Like most beautiful, rich women she was forgiven her faults and failings of character, and only after she'd begun to lose her fabled looks had she attempted, for a desperate year or two, to be "good." Maybe it was too late, or maybe "goodness" bored her. Certainly, religion bored her. If Sunday services weren't an opportunity for Claudine Burnaby to display herself to an admiring public, there was no purpose in going. As a relatively young widow she'd had numerous male friends, escorts, lovers (?), but none of these lasted more than a few months. In her early fifties she became obsessed with her appearance, the effects of aging on her fair, thin skin, and for years she considered a facelift, exhausting her family with her worries, for what if something went wrong during the operation?—what if it didn't turn out well? It did no good for Claudine's children to assure her that she was still a beautiful woman, though in fact she was a beautiful woman, now middle-aged. But Claudine refused consolation. "I hate it. This. I hate *me*. I hate to look in the mirror at *me*." For Claudine knew best what the mirror should have been reflecting, and now did not.

Yet there was genuine heartbreak here, Dirk thought. Where his mother had once been so sociable, now she was becoming a recluse. If she accepted invitations to the homes of old friends, she often left early without explanation or farewell. At the private, exclusive clubs of l'Isle Grand, Buffalo, Niagara Falls where she and her late husband had been prominent members for decades, she complained she'd become invisible: "People look toward me, but not at me. And no one really sees *me*."

It was a child's lament, in the mouth of an older woman.

Dirk's sisters Clarice and Sylvia protested, Claudine wasn't invisble to them, or to her grandchildren. By the bored, glazed look in Claudine's face, hearing this, you understood that being visible in such eyes meant nothing to her.

Clarice and Sylvia complained bitterly to Dirk. They recalled that, when they were children, their mother hadn't cared much for mothering them, when nannies could do as well. Though Claudine had quite enjoyed her son Dirk, a husky handsome good-natured boy with a sweet disposition. His sisters said, in disgust, "It's just masculine attention Mother misses. With her, everything is *sex*."

Dirk thought privately, no. For Claudine nothing is, or ever was, sex. Only just vanity.

He'd always felt guilty, his mother had so clearly favored him over his sisters. She'd given him money, surreptitious gifts, he'd taken for granted as an adolescent. Even as a young man in his twenties, when he'd made a show of being self-supporting . . .

In her late fifties, after a spell of depression, Claudine decided impulsively to have a facelift after all, in a Buffalo clinic. Afterward, her sensitive skin was bruised and swollen for weeks, her eyes were bloodshot, the left side of her face was frozen and without expression. Now she didn't dare smile or show emotion, for only one half of her face would register it. "A zombie! That's what I've become. Outside and in," she said bitterly, yet with an air of satisfaction. "This is my punishment. Virgil would laugh. 'Did you think you'd remarry?'—'Did you think any man would ever love you again?' It's no more than I deserve, an old woman trying to be *young*."

The surgery was irrevocable, Dirk learned. Nerves had been damaged. Tissues in Claudine's face and behind her ears had been permanently "traumatized." And she'd signed a release waiving all possibility of a malpractice suit.

There followed then spells of illness. Bronchitis, anemia, fatigue. What fatigue! Though Claudine abhorred exercise of any kind, yet she was so exhausted sometimes she could hardly dress herself. Often she slept for twelve hours at a time. When, after weeks of insisting, Claudine convinced Dirk to bring home with him, to meet her, an attractive young woman whom (he'd thought) he might marry, Claudine had sent word downstairs via Ethel to explain that "Mrs. Burnaby is unwell, and sends her apologies."

Now Claudine rarely left Shalott. And rarely did she invite visitors, even relatives. Her grandchildren were noisy and got on her nerves, her daughters were quarrelsome, and boring. Dirk saw that she cultivated *woundedness* as if it were a spiritual value; she'd become a martyr to her own vanity, which she interpreted as the cruelty of others in withholding their adulation of her, which she'd long taken for granted. She said, incensed, "I envy plain women. 'Pretty' women who were only just that—'pretty'—and anything special. They don't know what they've missed, and I *do*."

At the end of June, Dirk drove out to the Island to spend a weekend at Shalott. He was exhausted from his ordeal at The Falls. Insomnia raged about him in his Luna Park townhouse like flames. The Niagara Gorge was so near, you could hear the roaring of The Falls mingling with the roaring of your own blood and you could taste spray borne by a northerly wind, even in summer. With misgivings, Dirk fled back to Shalott where his mother awaited him, the velvety black spider quivering in her web.

But Claudine greeted him through a crack in her bedroom door.

For it wasn't one of her "good" days. She wouldn't allow her son to greet her, still less to kiss her. Though she was very excited about his arrival. Instead, to his dismay, Dirk was allowed to visit with Claudine only by sitting with his back to her as she lay on a chaise lounge in her bedroom, holding wetted cloths against her head to forestall a migraine. In a shaky, reproachful voice she said, "Darling, you can speak with me perfectly well without staring at me. We don't need always to be *face to face*."

Obsessed with her face. Dirk wanted to laugh, but was this funny?

Later that evening, when Claudine felt stronger, they would dine together in a shadowy, romantically candlelit room downstairs. Though at this time, too, Dirk was forbidden to *stare*.

Except for Ethel, the housekeeper who'd worked for Mrs. Burnaby for more than thirty years, no one, evidently, was allowed to see her *face to face* any longer.

Dirk hated it, that his attractive, sensible mother should be turning strange. At the age of only sixty-three!

Claudine plied him with questions, as always. The two drank a good deal of tart red wine, which Dirk poured. It had become a joke between them, Claudine's reiterated surprise when her wine glass was empty.

Dirk alluded to his "ordeal" at The Falls. A seven-day search for a young man who'd jumped over the Horseshoe Falls. As a volunteer, Dirk had been involved . . . to a degree.

Claudine said, with a shiver of disapproval, "Isn't that just like you, darling, involved with strangers. In such a gruesome adventure." A native of the Niagara Falls region, she was indifferent to The Falls and disdainful of tourists "from all over the world" flocking to it; possibly, she'd never even visited The Falls. ("I've seen postcards, I'm sure. Very striking, if you like that sort of thing.") Like every other native Claudine had grown up conscious of suicides but these she associated with failure in love or business, or outright madness; they had nothing to do with her. If she knew of her legendary daredevil father-in-law Reginald Burnaby who'd plunged to his death in the Gorge in 1872, she never alluded to him, even in jest.

Dirk's father Virgil Burnaby had been raised in unusual circumstances: he and his young mother had been taken into the home of a Niagara Falls banker and philanthropist, an officer of the Christian Charities Alliance named MacKenna.

It was typical of Claudine to show little interest in Dirk's recent ordeal. Dirk knew that his sisters had sent her clippings from newspapers and magazines, no doubt they'd indicated Dirk's shadowy figure in some of the photographs, but Claudine must have tossed everything away without reading it. " 'The Widow-Bride of The Falls'—I saw the vulgar headline. That was enough."

Later, when Dirk tried to steer the subject of their conversation back to The Falls, Claudine said irritably, "One suicide more or less, what does it matter? Please don't spoil this lovely meal by dragging in ugliness like a dead cat, Dirk, *I beg you.*"

Dirk smiled. Claudine wasn't a woman to beg.

Still later, when Claudine brought up the familiar, wistful subject of Dirk marrying, coming to live with his wife and family at Shalott, Dirk said casually he'd met a woman the previous week at The Falls. "A minister's daughter. From Troy. Not very religious, though. A music instructor, in fact." But Claudine, sipping scotch and water, didn't seem to have heard.

Though that night before going to bed Claudine said dryly, "We know no one from Troy, Dirk. We never have."

When Dirk visited Shalott he always drank more than he intended. He'd take a bottle of scotch with him to his room, with Claudine's blessing. *You only live once* was her philosophy. There was a grim twitchy joy in her jaws, uttering this; Dirk had just a glimpse before she shielded her face.

Yes, the face was partially frozen. But with Claudine, you couldn't have guessed which part.

At Shalott, Dirk was struck by the beauty of the setting. Not the pretentious manor house (which he disliked on principle: he was a man of modern tastes, not pseudo-European but Frank Lloyd Wright—American) but the grounds, the landscaping, the river. The river of his boyhood. The Niagara River that split at l'Isle Grand, as, miles downstream at The Falls, it would split at the much smaller Goat Island. It was said that the Niagara River was dangerously polluted from Buffalo industry, but less polluted in the Chippawa Channel which was on the western side of l'Isle Grand, than on the eastern, the Tonawanda Channel, bordering the industrial suburb of North Tonawanda. *Of pollution, you don't want to think. If you can't actually smell it, taste it, see it.* Too many of Dirk Burnaby's friends were factory owners or investors, many of his clients were of this class, it was an area he'd learned to circumnavigate. Gazing at the river, at sailboats and yachts on the river, you thought of beauty; of the grace of man-made objects that had a look, in the waning sunlight of a summer day, of natural objects. You didn't think of poisoned water any more than you thought of the deadly falls downriver. Here, the Niagara River seemed no different from any other wide, swift-flowing river. On clear days it reflected a cobalt-blue sky; at other times it was of the hue of lead, but a restless, scintillant lead, like a living thing twitching its hide. The white-water rapids didn't begin for several miles. Where the river broke at Goat Island, the current became treacherous; two miles above The Falls, this area was known as the "Deadline."

Once a boat moved into the Deadline, its occupants were doomed.

Once a swimmer allowed himself to be swept into the Deadline, he was doomed.

The Deadline. Dirk drank scotch, and considered what this might mean.

When Dirk visited Shalott he was forced uneasily to recall how, through most of his twenties, except when he'd been in the U.S. Army overseas, he'd drifted into a relationship with his mother of which he was ashamed. Not that he'd spent much time with her. He had not. But he'd accepted money from her, secretly. Without his father, who would have disapproved, knowing. Claudine had insisted in her lavish emotional way upon paying off the $12,000 loan Dirk had taken out for law school at Cornell; afterward there'd been living expenses, gambling debts . . . For several years Dirk had bet heavily at Fort Erie, playing the horses. It was an addiction, he'd come to realize. Not needing to win, but needing to play. He was more skilled at poker, luckily. He rarely lost at poker. He'd been a popular young bachelor-socialite, he'd bought a townhouse in the exclusive residential neighborhood of Luna Park, an expensive car and a new sailboat and a forty-foot yacht. He'd joined the private clubs to which his parents and friends belonged and he'd entertained at these clubs, often. The mothers of debutantes sought him avidly. Their fathers invited him to play golf with them, squash, raquetball, tennis. Poker. Dirk was an innocently genial poker player, his boyish smile and frank eyes masked his competitiveness, he seemed almost to win by accident. He became known as a young man of luck, a man with a charmed life. (Few people knew of his losses at Fort Erie. By 1949 he'd limited himself to small, three-digit bets there.) In time Dirk Burnaby made money as a lawyer but his expenses were in excess of his earnings and Claudine, far from discouraging him, seemed to be encouraging him. "You only live once. You didn't get killed in Italy. You have the looks of a taller, more manly Alan Ladd. Why shouldn't everyone adore you?" Dirk had accepted his mother's money in secret, partly because his accepting made her happy; and so few things made Claudine happy any longer. But he felt guilty about it. He'd dreaded his father discovering these transactions, and, in time, his sisters. (Dirk supposed that Clarice and Sylvia knew by now. You couldn't keep secrets from them, vigilant as vultures.) Though Dirk's father had been dead for more than a decade, still Dirk had the vague sense that he knew, somehow, and was disgusted with his son. Dirk came to hate it that he and Claudine were co-conspirators. What exactly did it mean *You only live once*.

Now Dirk never took money from Claudine. But he'd never given back the money she'd given him, either.

Claudine would be deeply wounded if he'd tried. Furious as a spurned woman. She'd have raised a hell of a fuss, and exposed them both.

"Maybe I will marry, Mother. Or try to."

It was a late, lazy Sunday brunch. Scrambled eggs, smoked salmon, Bloody Marys. They were seated on the flagstone terrace above the river and Claudine wore a wide-brimmed straw hat with a fine-meshed lace veil, to hide her ravaged face from her son.

There was a moment's pause. Claudine leaned forward as if she hadn't heard. "Dirk, what?"

"Maybe. Maybe I will."

Thinking *She won't want you. Why would she want you?*

He felt something sick, sliding inside him. He took a large swallow of vodka in the guise of hot-spiced tomato juice.

Claudine laughed thinly. "Who would you—marry?"

"I'm not sure."

"You're not serious, then." Claudine spoke carefully, with an air of regret.

"Probably not."

"Is it Elsie?"

"No."

"Gwen?"

"*No.*"

"Oh, that little blond—'June Allyson'—"

"Harriet Trauber."

"Is it?" Claudine exuded an air of mild enthusiasm. Harriet Trauber was one of the Buffalo debutantes, of a past season.

"No, Mother. It is not Harriet Trauber."

Claudine sighed. She drank her Bloody Mary in slow contemplative sips, daintily lifting her veil. "Not one of your Elmwood Casino showgirls, I hope."

Dirk, offended, didn't reply.

Claudine sighed in a pretense of relief. "Well, dear. You do have a wild streak in you, and a taste for wild, exotic women."

Dirk shrugged. He wasn't feeling wild or exotic at the moment.

Hungover, you might say, from the night before.

Eyes aching from hours of insomnia. Shielded from the watery glare of the river now by dark-tinted lenses.

Claudine asked, with studied casualness, "Are sexy women more *sexual*? In an actual way?"

"What other way than an 'actual way' could there be, Mother?" Dirk laughed uncomfortably.

"The sexual allure could be just superficial. A game, a simulation. But then actually, there might be—" Claudine paused, as if embarrassed. Dirk could see her fingering, stroking, the scarred tissue behind her right ear. "—nothing."

On the river, several tall white sailboats were passing, one of them badly buffeted by the wind. Dirk stared, hoping there wouldn't be a mishap.

Ethel emerged from the kitchen to bring Claudine and Dirk more hot-buttered rolls, iced tea in tall glasses, freshly quartered citrus fruit with dollops of whipped cream. Claudine, though veiled, managed to eat and drink without evident difficulty. There was the ancient solace of food. Mother-and-child, mother-and-food. Mother providing food to her son. Claudine hadn't much liked being a mother but she'd enjoyed certain of the rituals, and the respect and deference that came with them.

Dirk recalled similar scenes from his boyhood. Long ago. Or not so long ago. Claudine presiding over Sunday brunch, in summer. But the table would be filled. Dirk's father, Dirk's sisters, relatives, guests. An afternoon of sailing in the channel, past Fort Erie and Buffalo, beneath the Peace Bridge, into the open windy space of Lake Erie, vast as an inland sea. There was blond laughing Claudine in a translucent summer shift partly buttoned over a two-piece floral pink bathing suit. Our Betty Grable, Claudine Burnaby was teased. And there was Claudine upstairs, changing her clothes, and Dirk was summoned to her, he might have been thirteen, sixteen, even eighteen and home for a few days from college. Forbidden to look directly at his mother because she was changing her clothes. Forbidden to see. In her bright telephone voice Claudine would interrogate Dirk—where had he been all morning? with whom? where was he going next? when could she expect him home that night?—the questions had been rapidfire, and irrelevant. The exchanges had left Dirk edgy and anxious, sexually aroused and disgusted, eager to escape the shaded, perfumy air of his mother's bedroom.

He'd had girlfriends, and some of these girls were "older"—by a few, practical years. He'd satisfied his sexual desire with them, those nights. At the time he'd been too young to understand. Now, an adult, hot with chagrin and impatience, he supposed he understood.

She wanted him a boy, still. An immature hot-blooded male. He was a seducer, a sexual conqueror. Her rivals were defeated by his lust and his indifference for the objects of his lust. He was a sexually empowered adult man and yet something of a eunuch, a puppet-eunuch of his mother's.

"No. I must leave."

Yet she would plead with him to stay a little longer, to stay the night. As always she pleaded when Dirk was preparing to leave, though beforehand they'd agreed when he would leave. It was a comically familiar exchange that wasn't any less strained for being familiar, and for Dirk knowing it would come.

He had work to do, Dirk said. He'd missed days in the office, as a volunteer at The Falls.

Claudine crinkled her nose in distaste. She knew there'd been a suicide, and she wasn't going to inquire. She wasn't going to inquire if her son had been one who'd discovered the body or touched it.

As she wasn't going to inquire about—which city?—a small upstate city where the Burnabys knew no one.

Claudine accompanied Dirk to the driveway, to his car. She wore the veiled straw hat, which was quite an attractive hat, with a blue velvet ribbon and artificial flowers, and a floral print blue sundress, that fitted her softening body loosely. Saying goodbye, Dirk felt a stab of pity, and annoyance, that Claudine continued to hide herself behind that ridiculous veil. She was playing the role of the wounded recluse, and maybe she was trapped in that role. The Lady of Shalott waiting to be rescued. Awaiting a lover who would release her from her spell; or, at least, tear off the veil.

Impulsively, Dirk tugged at it. "Mother, come *on*. There's nothing remotely wrong with you."

But Claudine cried out in surprise and anger, resisting. She lunged away, and Dirk followed. She clung to the hat with both hands, and Dirk knocked it askew, laughing. Was this a game? All right: a game. Deftly he removed the hat—and the veil—and there was a pale-skinned, dazed-looking woman staring at him with mildly bloodshot eyes, faded blond hair brushed back flat, her unlined but sallow face stiff and affrighted and the mouth perversely lipstick-red. Furious, Claudine slapped at Dirk, and when he only laughed, she raked his left cheek with her nails. "God damn you, how dare you! Get out of here! *I hate you!*"

Dirk drove away from Shalott laughing, and trembling.

He was haunted by his mother's expression of hurt, dismay, outrage, chagrin. And by her face that unnerved him, it was so unexpectedly young.

2

EIGHTEEN DAYS AFTER the end of the vigil at The Falls, Dirk Burnaby drove across the width of the glacier-sculpted landscape of New York State to Troy.

He had no clear plan. He was excited, exhilarated, and yet morbidly fatalistic. *What will be, will be. You only live once.* As a rising young litigator he was fanatic about legal strategy yet this morning, his life in the balance, he had no more thought ahead than to take with him an address for the Littrell family, provided by the manager of the Rainbow Grand Hotel. There was a telephone number included but he hadn't called the red-haired woman who stood before him yet would not look at him. Maybe he simply wanted to force her, for a final and first time, to look at him.

It was a journey of more than three hundred miles. He was wearing new clothes from out of his closet, he hadn't remembered purchasing. A navy blue blazer with brass nautical buttons, a striped sport shirt, white cord trousers and a white yachting cap. A hemp belt with a small rectangular brass buckle. Navy blue canvas shoes.

Dirk Burnaby, a page out of glossy *Esquire*.

Yet, driving along the Mohawk River, he was forced to stop more than once by the roadside to urinate. Hiding out of sight of the highway near the villages of Auburn, Canastota, Fort Hunter. (Nervous! His bladder felt pinched.) Insomnia flickered and flared like malicious blue flames in even this, his wakeful state.

"God damn. This is enough. No more!"

Outside the village of Amsterdam a field of wind-tossed daisies caught his eye. These were in fact flowers with eyes. He laughed, his life seemed so simple. Knee-high in grasses he waded, picking flowers in ragged clusters and clumps for the red-haired girl, to make her look at him. He tugged at a tough, sinewy wild flower (chicory? with small blue petals?), he tore at thorny stems, vines, that stung his hands.

Wild rose, white and pale pink blossoms. But his hands were bleeding! He picked more daisies, and clumps of buttercups. These were small golden flowers he guessed were buttercups. In a ditch he discovered a pale anemone-like flower that reminded him of the red-haird girl's complextion, naturally he tore these up by the roots. In a trunk of his car was a glass quart jar which he filled with water from the ditch, and in this he crammed as many wild flowers as he could. A large, ungainly bouquet. As many as one hundred flowers. His heart beat rapidly and with an absurd hope.

In Albany, he stopped for a drink. In a wine and liquor store he bought a bottle of champagne. He told the smiling sales clerk, "Wait. Make that two."

"Two *Dom Pérignons?* Yes *sir*."

Shortly afterward he crossed a bridge over the Hudson River and entered the hilly city of Troy where he would be informed that the daughter of Reverend and Mrs. Littrell no longer lived with them in the rectory beside the First Presbyterian Church of Troy. It was Mrs. Littrell who opened the door, breathless and blinking at Dirk Burnaby whom she recognized. Her daughter was now renting an apartment near the Troy Academy of Music, and living alone.

This was a good sign, Dirk thought. Was it?

Dirk found his way across town to the old neo-Gothic Academy of Music, and to Ariah's red-brick residence a block away. On the gravelled walk to the house he paused, hearing a woman singing. The sound seemed to descend from overhead; he glanced up to see a second-floor window, open. He stood gripping the quart jar of spilling flowers in both hands, listening intently. A pure, clear, sweet if wavering soprano voice, put to the most unlikely of impassioned battle songs:

> "*Mine eyes have seen the glory*
> *of the coming of the Lord!*
> *He has trampled out the vintage*
> *where the grapes of wrath are stored!*
> *He has loosed the fateful lightning—*"

Yet, how like Ariah! Impulsively Dirk lifted his voice, untrained but deep-chested: "—of his terrible swift sword!"

He had not sung loudly enough for Ariah to have heard him, he was certain. Yet she didn't continue with the chorus, there was no *Glory, glory Hallelujah*, only an abrupt silence.

Dirk stood on the front stoop, ringing the bell. Pretending not to notice a woman peering at him from the window overhead.

She will answer, or not. In this way my life will be decided.

How calm Dirk Burnaby felt. This was good, this was right. He had put his life in the hands of this woman he scarcely knew.

Yet it was a shock, unexpected, when Ariah actually opened the door.

The two stared at each other, for a long moment unable to speak.

Dirk's first impression was: Ariah looked nothing like the Widow-Bride now. Her faded-red hair was charmingly disheveled as if wind-blown, feathery, in curls and tendrils about her slender face. In the unsparing sunshine it was streaked with silver like miniature lightning streaks. The red-haired girl was going gray!

Still, this was no mourner. Her skirt was a light summer fabric, a pattern of bright-green parrots with golden beaks, her T-shirt was white, fresh-laundered, sporty-plain as a teenager's. She was bare-legged, and barefoot. There was nothing in her smooth freckled face of loss, or regret; the color was up in her cheeks, a blush rising from her throat in the confusion of the moment. Her eyes, no longer blood-shot, with fine, pale-red lashes, were that pure glassy green, like the river, that so haunted Dirk Burnaby. Immediately these eyes widened, recognizing him.

Dirk heard himself stammer, "Mrs. Erskine—?"

"No. No longer." She spoke calmly, though she seemed frightened. Her fingers, with short, bitten-looking nails, fretted with a fold of the parrot-skirt. " 'Ariah Littrell' I call myself, again. I wasn't ever really that other."

That other was pronounced with an air of puzzled detachment, like a not entirely comprehensible foreign phrase.

Dirk Burnaby, eloquent and forceful as a litigator, deadly as a pit bull in court, was swallowing hard, mouth dry as sand. Oh, what was happening to him! He was conscious of having spilled water on his smart navy blue blazer. "Do you—remember me? Dirk B-Burnaby. I was the one who—I mean, I am—"

Ariah laughed. "Of course I remember you."

"You—*do*? I—wouldn't have thought so . . ."

An asinine thing to say, why was he saying it? Yet Ariah Littrell seemed to overlook his clumsiness, and invited him inside.

There was further clumsiness, as in a scene from a Bob Hope movie, as Dirk handed Ariah the dripping, unexpectedly heavy jar of flowers. He mumbled apologetically, "I hope you don't mind."

"Oh. Thank you."

Some of the flowers were spilling from the jar. Daisies with broken stems, a spray of pale pink wild rose studded with tiny thorns. There were exposed roots, clumps of dirt. Weeds mixed with wild flowers. Insects on the undersides of the chicory sprigs. But Ariah murmured, "These are beautiful."

They were in a small parlor. An upright Steinway had been pushed against a wall. On the piano were compositions by Mozart, Chopin, Beethoven, Irving Berlin. Underfoot was a snarled rag rug in which Dirk's rubber-soled canvas shoes somehow tangled. The vivid lime-green of the parrot-skirt brushing against the woman's bare, very pale slender legs was making Dirk's vision blotch. A hollow male voice said, "I had business in Albany and thought—I would drop by to see you. Ariah. I should have telephoned first, but—I didn't have your number." He paused. Pulses beat in his head, in subtle mockery of a normal heartbeat. "I heard you singing just now. Out on the walk."

I mean that I was out on the walk, and heard you sing. What am I saying?

Ariah murmured something Dirk couldn't hear, and ducked into the next room, a small, old-fashioned kitchen with an ugly deep sink and rusted faucets. Dirk followed blindly. At the sink Ariah turned, startled to see him so close. Dirk realized belatedly that he was expected to stay in the other room, but it was too late now: if he turned to retreat, he would appear even more foolish than he was. He would be even more foolish than he appeared. Surreptitiously he brushed at the wet spots on his blazer. Oh,

God. Some of them appeared to be blood, from his scratched fingers.

Ariah had set the jar of flowers in the sink and was reaching for a vase on a shelf above the sink, rising unsteadily on the tips of her bare toes. How pale, how slender her feet were! Dirk stared. He had a confused thought of stooping to hold those feet; to grip those feet in his hands and lift Ariah, for surely he was strong enough, as Fred Astaire might have gripped the feet of Ginger Rogers in a glittery fantasy dance scene in a movie not yet made; or had it been made, and Dirk was remembering it? Through the thin cotton T-shirt he could see the small white bones of the woman's vertebrae tensing like gripped knuckles and he felt a moment's vertigo, the sight was so intimate. "Here. Let me." He lifted the crystal vase down for her. It was one of Mrs. Littrell's, he seemed to know. A wedding present. He saw it slip from his damp fingers and shatter in pieces on the kitchen floor, yet somehow it did not, the vase was set safely in the sink. So Ariah would take from Dirk's shaky fingers whatever he urged upon her, and make it safe from him. He was saying, "You have a beautiful voice, Ariah. I recognized it immediately."

Meaning what? That Dirk had the ear to recognize a beautiful voice, which was debatable, or that he'd recognized Ariah's voice, immediately? This was debatable, too.

Ariah laughed, embarrassed. "Oh. You don't have to say such things, Mr. Burnaby."

"Dirk, please."

" 'Dirk.' "

How strange, how unmelodic a name! Dirk had never clearly heard it before. His mother had named him, surely. He seemed to know that "Dirk" was a family name, from his mother's family, not his father's.

Ariah said, "My voice isn't beautiful, it's—"

"For upstate New York, it is. It *is*."

He hadn't meant to sound blustery, bullying. His hollow voice filled the cramped kitchen like a cheap plastic radio turned too high.

"—it's hardly a *voice*." Ariah spoke sadly but matter-of-factly.

She was the music expert, she was the one who knew.

Ariah was struggling with the wild flowers in the sink. So many stems were broken, how had that happened? Why hadn't Dirk bought a bouquet, in Albany? *It had never occurred to me.* Tiny clumps of dirt had to be cut off the stems of most of the daisies, by Ariah using a paring knife. The chicory was almost too tough to cut. How had Dirk torn it out of the earth with his bare hands? Ariah dropped a sprig of this weed flower to the floor and both she and Dirk reached for it at the same time. Dirk saw with a pang of excitement that Ariah's thin freckled hands were bare of any ornament: no rings.

He'd forgotten: the Dom Pérignon in his car.

"Excuse me. Ariah. I—I will be right back."

On his way out to the car Dirk wondered if Ariah was thinking he might actually be leaving; he hadn't explained what he was doing. Maybe she expected him to drive away as unexpectedly as he'd arrived? Maybe he should drive away? He'd brought her the flowers, maybe that was enough. Everything was happening this afternoon swiftly and giddily as a ride on a roller coaster and Dirk Burnaby distrusted such swiftness. There was nothing he hated more than a giddy sensation as of slipping-sliding, falling.

He snatched up the paper bag with the bottles in it. Frankly, he was dying for a drink.

When he returned to Ariah's kitchen she'd managed to arrange most of the flowers in the crystal vase. She'd trimmed stems, and put aside broken flowers. She swatted at a fat dimpled spider that darted across the counter from a sprig of wild rose, to hide in a crack in the wall.

Dirk cried, "Champagne! Let's celebrate."

Ariah's mouth opened in protest, or alarm, or simple wonder.

As Dirk might have foreseen, Ariah had no champagne glasses, not even wine glasses, in her kitchen. But she had sparkling-clean fruit juice glasses for Dirk to pour the foaming Dom Perignon into. These fruit glasses were then clicked together, very lightly, in a ceremonial toast: "Here's to us!" Dirk laughed. He'd imagined the glasses colliding too sharply and breaking, spilling champagne over both Ariah and himself, *but that did not happen.*

Their mood was electric, haphazard. Was music playing? Dirk could hear it, faintly. Not the melody exactly but the cheery percussive beat. Glenn Miller. "String of Pearls." The way Ariah glanced around, baffled and pleased-seeming, you'd have thought she was hearing it, too.

Somehow they were in the parlor, fumbling for seats. Dirk had removed his navy blazer, he was feeling so warm. He found himself sitting on a rickety-legged piano bench between a stack of yellow Czerny lesson books and *Piano Technique for the Older Student*. Ariah was sitting on a cane-backed chair close by. Her bare toes twitched. She'd brought the crystal vase of wild flowers into the parlor, and placed it on the top of the piano where it loomed above them.

Dirk said reluctantly, as if the champagne were acting upon him like a truth serum, "I didn't come to Albany on business. I have no business in Albany. I came to Troy to see you, Ariah."

Ariah quickly lifted her glass and sniffed at the bubbly fizzing liquid within. Her pale eyelashes fluttered. She might have been shaken by this revelation, unless she wasn't surprised at all, but chose not to respond to it. Instead she said, in a murmur so quiet Dirk had to strain to hear, "I've had champagne only twice before in my life. But for the same occasion. It wasn't nearly so good as this champagne."

She laughed, shivering. Dirk stared fascinated at her. So strangely, her small prim perfect mouth called to his mind the pinkish-mauve translucent body of a beautiful tropical fish; one of the delicate, inch-long fish he'd purchased for his boyhood aquarium at Shalott. How the mysterious little creatures with their lacy tails and fins had darted forward to eat the food Dirk sprinkled on the water for them, retreating in virtually the same instant, possessed of a minute magical life far beyond the imaginings of the boy hulking above them like a clumsy demigod.

He continued, "I'm in love with you, Ariah. No other reason I'm here. I think you must know this?" He heard these words with disbelief. He'd meant to say something very different, about wanting to see her again. He felt compelled to add, since she was staring grimly into her drink, "Please don't misunderstand, Ariah. Ordinarily, Mondays are very busy days for me. Monday to Friday is work. I don't usually go gallivanting across New York State. I'm a lawyer. I'm a litigator. I'm in private practice, with a partner, offices in Niagara Falls and Buffalo." (Should he present Ariah with a card? He had a bunch of them in his wallet.) He said, faltering, "That week I took off to be with you at The Falls was—wasn't—a typical week for me. I'm not a volunteer rescue worker. Ordinarily I've have been working, every day. And damned long days. I mean—" His tongue was too big for his mouth. He had no idea what he was saying. "I'm in love with you, Ariah, and I want to marry you."

There. It was said.

He'd driven more than three hundred miles to make this absurd statement to a woman who continued to stare into her drink. Her small nose crinkled as if she were trying not to sneeze.

Finally she spoke, severely. "Marry me! Why, you don't even know me."

"I don't need to know you," Dirk said weakly. "I love you."

"That's ridiculous."

"Why is it ridiculous? It's love."

"You'd only just leave me. Like the other."

She spoke wistfully, and took a swallow of champagne.

"Why on earth would I leave you? I would never leave you."

Ariah shook her head, and wiped at her eyes. Suddenly she seemed about to cry.

Dirk said gently, "I know, you've had a terrible experience. But I'm nothing like—" He paused, not wanting to allude to *the other* in any way; he hoped never in their life together to allude to *the other* if he could avoid it. "I'm nothing like anyone else. Anyone you've known. If you knew me, darling, you'd know."

This audacious remark hovered in the air like the pollen-y fragrance of the wild flowers on the piano.

"But I don't know you, Mr. Burnaby."

"Please call me 'Dirk,' Ariah. Can't you?"

"Mr. Dirk Burnaby. I don't know *you*."

"You'll get to know me. We can be engaged for as long as you want. And we had that week together. That vigil. It was a very long week, I thought."

Like an obstinate child Ariah frowned. She seemed about to contradict Dirk, then thought better of it and took another sip of champagne. Her eyelashes quivered in ecstasy.

Love for this unpredictable female came so strong, Dirk felt the floor shift beneath his feet. For a moment, he might have thought he was on the river in a craft so small he couldn't see or feel it.

"Ariah, may I kiss you? Just once."

Ariah didn't seem to hear. She shook her head, as if trying to clear it. "Champagne has a strange effect upon me."

"How so?"

"A wicked effect."

Dirk laughed. "Well, I hope so."

Ariah laughed, strangely. Dirk was uncomfortably reminded of that shout of laughter when she'd first seen her late husband's bloated corpse.

"But I'm too old for you, almost. Men prefer younger girls—don't they?"

Dirk said, annoyed, "I'm not 'men.' I am myself. And I don't want a young girl, I want you."

Ariah drank champagne. Ariah smiled inscrutably.

"The notorious 'Widow-Bride.' You're very brave, sir."

"I want a wife I can respect intellectually. A wife who's smarter and more sensitive than I am, and tougher. A wife who's talented at something I'm surely not."

So combative! Dirk sounded to himself like a man fighting for his life.

Ariah said, thoughtfully, "But maybe you'd leave me, too. On our honeymoon."

How exasperating this woman was! Dirk foresaw a lifetime of combat.

"Ariah, why would I leave you? I adore you. You're my *soul*."

He leaned forward impulsively and framed Ariah's small heated face in his hands and kissed her mouth which was unexpectedly pliant, warm, friendly. He was mildly astonished that the woman was kissing him back even as she seemed to be laughing at him.

7 July 1950

She would say yes. Yes with her eager wiry little body like a nerved-up cat's fitting itself to the man. Yes to his large handsome face like a moon. Yes to his startled nickel-eyes. Yes to his voice, a deep-chested effortless baritone. Yes to what she shrewdly perceived as the man's goodness, his decency. Yes to his mouth that could be wounded by a careless word of hers. Yes to his bravery. His audacity. For she'd been another man's bride, if not another man's wife. Another man had wed her, if not loved her. She was a virgin in love and a virgin in the flesh though she'd felt her young husband's hot acid seed like spite spilling onto her belly, and into the damp bushy hair between her legs. But yes, she would marry Dirk Burnaby. Yes to the wild flower bouquet. Yes to the caresses of his big gentle hands, and his tongue. Yes to the astonishing heat, weight, solidity and size of his penis. That, that would have seemed to Ariah an hour before, before two quick glasses of champagne, the most forbidden of thoughts. Now the most luxuriant and lovely of thoughts. Yes to his kissing, mauling mouth. Yes to his just-slightly fatty-muscled shoulders, back, thighs. Yes to his hair falling into his face, and into hers.

Yes though a part of her knew he would leave her, too. Yes though a part of her knew she was damned. Yes though, being damned, she didn't deserve such happiness. Yes though, being damned, she didn't give a damn whether she deserved happiness, or whether she was damned. Yes to the man's obvious intelligence. Yes to the man's good manners, and his sense of humor. Yes that he made both himself and her laugh, unintended. Yes that his laughter was a deep belly laugh, heating the blood in his fair boyish face. Yes to his weight easing on her. Yes to that ease, that she would not have anticipated. She would not have imagined. Yes to the risk of pregnancy, which no more concerned Ariah in the suddenness of this moment than it would have concerned any female creature in the heat of first copulation. In the heat of first love. In the heat, frenzy, madness of first love. Yes to the risk of pregnancy with a man she scarcely knew. Yes though (in her morbid-minded way) she was in terror that she might already be pregnant, from her disastrous wedding night. From the single spilling of hot acid like spite. But yes to this man's raw desire for her. Yes to the smell of him like yeasty baking bread. Yes to what shone in his eyes, his love of her. Yes to the fact (she knew!) that he scarcely knew her. Yes to the flamey sensation in her loins. Yes that it was lifting higher, yet higher, like a fountain-jet. Yes that it was making her moan, scream. Yes though her mouth must be ugly, so gaping. Her lips drawn back from her clenched teeth. Yes to the man who made such lovely love to her, filling her body that was both small and infinite, inexhaustible.

PART II

Marriage

They Were Married . . .

1

They were married.

A hasty marriage, in late July of 1950.

"No time for an engagement. Dirk and I don't believe in such bourgeois customs."

Ariah spoke breathlessly, biting her lip to keep from laughing.

And, as Dirk Burnaby said, more somberly, "When it's love at first sight, you may as well give in. You're doomed."

Doomed to happiness! So the lovers believed.

They were married, to the astonishment of everyone who knew them. Especially those relatives, friends, acquaintances of the Littrells of Troy, New York. "Of course, no one approves," Ariah said, "but we've decided not to care." She wanted to say *we've decided not to give a damn* but held her tongue.

Being in love with Dirk Burnaby, being so happy in love, Ariah had to bite her tongue often for fear of speaking intemperately. For fear of speaking brashly. For fear of speaking truthfully.

In her thirtieth year Ariah had discovered not just love, but sex. Not just sex, but sex with Dirk Burnaby. *Lovemaking* it was called. *Making love.* Oh, aptly named! It could inspire you to speak bluntly, to shock and offend. It could inspire you to say things you'd never dreamt of saying before, when you'd made the effort (well, most of the time you'd tried to make the effort) to be decorous, well-behaved, a minister's daughter, a "lady."

Dirk said, "We can't care that others disapprove. Your family, my mother." He paused, suddenly staring with too much interest at a spot on the floor. For he was thinking of *the other*. The *first husband*. The *Erskines*. "No. We can't care, and we don't. We're married, and that's that."

Ariah said, "No. That is *this*."

Touching her husband in that way of hers. The "secret tickle" she'd about perfected. His gaze, meant to appear stern, serious, swam with sudden desire.

They were married, and Ariah laughed: "We can do this all the time, can we? My goodness."

"*My* goodness, you mean."

Tickling her in that secret way of his, that made her pant, scream, beg for mercy as she'd never done, or imagined, as the minister's daughter in Troy, New York.

They were married, and lived in Niagara Falls in the brownstone townhouse in Luna Park. There, they made love all the time. Or nearly.

He would leave her one day, she knew. But she never thought of it, so happy.

Do not think of it. Do not be morbid-minded.

So Ariah instructed herself. She meant to be, in this miracle-marriage, a practical down-to-earth woman.

She meant to be a loving woman, uninhibited. Every evening at dinner there was wine, poured by Dirk into sparkling crystal glasses.

That wicked, lovely sensation. Coursing through Ariah like molten honey. "I love love love *you*." Sometimes, laughing, he'd lift her in his arms, fling her over his shoulder, carry her upstairs.

She wasn't pregnant yet. Or, maybe she was?

Do not be morbid-minded, Ariah!

Often she took the bottle of wine upstairs with them. Especially the Chianti. As long as it was open, and hadn't been entirely finished, you wouldn't want it to go sour.

They were married, and never looked back.

That jiggly-creaking brass bed on the top, third floor of the house at 7 Luna Park! In the French silk-wallpapered bachelor bedroom with the deep-piled mint-green Chinese carpet so delicious to sink your bare toes into. In the neo-Georgian townhouse less than a half-mile from the Niagara Gorge. In the house where, summer nights with opened windows, moths throwing themselves against the window screens like soft palpitating thoughts, they could hear, in the distance, the ceaseless murmur of The Falls.

They were married, and became young.

Younger than either recalled having been as a child.

"I grew up in 'Shalott.' "

"*I* grew up in the rectory."

"We were privileged, we had money."

"*We* were privileged, we had God."

They laughed, shivered, and held each other close. They were naked as eels. So many toes (twenty!) beneath the covers at the foot of the bed.

Neither wished to think how accidental it was, they'd met, and fallen in love, and married.

Neither wished to speculate how bereft their lives would be, if *the other* husband hadn't thrown himself into the Horseshoe Falls.

No. You will not be morbid-minded ever again.

They were married, and each became the other's best friend.

And each realized he hadn't had a true best friend, until now.

They were married. Dirk Burnaby's legendary insomnia disappeared.

Though he was a big man, and with Ariah's delicious home cooking he'd be getting bigger, yet Dirk discovered in himself a knack for snuggling in the bony curve of his wife's side; a knack for burrowing, and burying his face in her neck; a knack for drifting to sleep in utter contentment, not a thought (of his profession, his finances, his increasingly eccentric mother) to plague him. Oh, life was so simple. Life was this.

Ariah remained awake, cradling him in her arms. She wanted to stay awake, to luxuriate in him. To gloat over him. Her husband! Her man! He was quite the most wonderful man she'd ever met, let alone come to know. Let alone touched, and kissed. He was quite the most wonderful man any girl might have dreamt of, in Troy, New York. She saw how women glanced after him in the street. She might be jealous one day, but not yet.

Tenderly she stroked his shoulders, his forehead, the stubbly underside of his jaw. She loved it that Dirk Burnaby was a big man, that he took up so much space in her life. She was baffled to recall what her life had been before him. *It wasn't a life. It hadn't yet begun.* She stroked his hair, brushing it out of his eyes. His fair flaxen hair, thick and springy and not a gray hair in it she could discover. Sometimes she felt a pang of envy. For her own so-called red hair was fading fast. Invaded by gray, silver, even white hairs. You could tell (you could speculate) she'd had a shock of some kind. A girl's face but streaked-gray hair. Soon, she'd look like a banshee. But she was too vain to dye her hair. (Maybe she wasn't vain enough?)

Dirk slept, and in his sleep seemed to grow heavier. He breathed through his mouth, a wet whistling sound. She loved that sound. She kissed his forehead. She heard him murmur to her in his sleep, words not quite audible or intelligible but they sounded like *'Riah love you*. Then he sank into sleep again. Rarely less than eight hours a night. Now that they were safely married. Ariah tried to ease her naked-sticky body into such a position that her arm, her leg, her side didn't become numb, circulation cut off by her husband's weight. She loved that weight. When he made love to her she wanted to be crushed, flattened. Smothered. "Oh come inside me! Deeper." It was curious that the man entered her body, yet seemed to surround her body. It was curious that they fitted together so perfectly, a hand in a glove, though anyone could see at a glance that they were the wrong sizes for each other.

The distant murmur of the Gorge. The murmur of their blood.

Maybe she was pregnant? How surprised Dirk would be.

Or maybe not surprised. They'd taken no precautions in Ariah's residence in Troy, and they'd been taking no precautions since. It must have been understood between them that they wanted children?

You only live once. This phrase Ariah had picked up from Dirk, that seemed to her both fatalistic and optimistic.

You only live once. It made her smile, it seemed to release you to anything you wanted.

They were married, and each night was an adventure.

The man was so new in her inner, secret life, he didn't always have a name.

Husband would do.

She clutched this husband tight. Her lightly freckled arms were slender, but strong. The strength of cunning and desperation. She'd been playing piano since age eight, which means playing scales tirelessly, fanatically, and that strengthens your arms, wrists, and fingers. She marveled that she'd seized for herself, in these arms, so remarkable a man. But she was humble, too. Perhaps she was even frightened. Knowing from past experience that God (in Whom she didn't believe, in the daytime at least) could snatch him back at any time.

There was daytime lovemaking, and there was nighttime lovemaking. By degrees, so gradually the change was almost imperceptible, the daytime lovemaking (with its air of being illicit, like chocolates before a meal) would fade, as the excited newness of married life must fade, but the nighttime lovemaking would continue, passionate and reverent, for some time. After love, Ariah would cradle her husband, who burrowed against her in a sweaty infantile bliss; she would stroke his big magnificent body, smooth his springy hair out of his eyes, murmur *I love you! My husband.* She could not have believed that any wife had ever so adored any husband. She could not have believed that her mother and father, from whom she was now estranged, had ever so adored each other. Always, the elder Littrells had been middle-aged. Ariah pitied them. Ariah was frightened by their example. *That will never happen to me. To this man and me.*

She smiled to think that Ariah Littrell had been such a sullen sulky petulant girl growing up in the rectory under the watchful gaze of her elders, such a sharp-tongued and sharp-elbowed schoolgirl always a straight-A student, (secretly) bored and restless in church during her very father's sermons. Yet, somehow, undeserving as she was, she was now *happy*.

One night when she'd been Mrs. Dirk Burnaby for just fifteen days, she saw through the lattice window beyond their bed a sickle moon glowing through columns of mist like a winking eye. She was cradling her deeply sleeping husband in her arms. She meant to protect him forever! Yet her eyelids began to flutter. Her eyes were shutting. She opened them wide to see her husband crossing the immense Niagara Gorge on—what was it? A tightrope? A *tightrope*? His back was to her. His fair flaxen hair blew in the wind. He wore a black costume, ministerial. He was carrying a twelve-foot bamboo pole to balance himself. It was a performance appropriate to a circus but, here, deadly. And there was the wind. Why was he doing such a thing, why when they loved each other so much?

At shore, Ariah leaned over an iron railing that dug into her waist and cried out to him in a raw, terrified voice. *Come back! I love you! You can't leave me!*

2

THEY WERE MARRIED, in love and in haste.

Amid whispers, murmurs, accusations. Tearful proclamations of disapproval. *How can you? What are you thinking of? Only of yourself? So soon after Gilbert's death? Have you no shame?*

Married in a brief civil ceremony, not in a church. Not in the bride's hometown, Troy, but in Niagara Falls. A private ceremony at City Hall and no relatives invited. *Shame!*

Ariah's heart pumped hard. Damned if she would cry.

She intended never to cry again, she was so happy.

With dignity Ariah explained: "Actually, there is shame. The world is heaped with shame like spoiling garbage. The death camps? Remember the Nazi death camps? Corpses stacked like firewood. 'Survivors' like skeletons. You saw the same photographs I did, in *Life*. You lived through the same history as I did. There you have shame. And more than shame. But Dirk Burnaby and I don't share in that shame, you see. We love each other and we see no reason to pretend that we don't. Especially we see no reason to pretend that our private behavior is anyone's business except our own."

It was a brilliant little speech, and almost flawlessly delivered. A slight tremor in Ariah's lower lip betrayed some emotion.

Mrs. Littrell was taken ill. Reverend Littrell, furious as Christ driving the moneylenders from the temple, forbade his daughter to return to the rectory, ever.

They were married, with no need to vow *Till death do us part*.

They were married, and God had nothing to do with their happiness.

They were married, and possibly the bride was pregnant.

In the bliss of first love Ariah tried not to think of the consequences of love. In those early days and weeks her brain was in a fever of love. She was a giddy young girl dancing! dancing! dancing! through the night, never tiring.

I could not say to my husband: I may be pregnant. You may not be the fa-ther. No more than I could say to this man: I know you will leave me one day. I know I'm damned. But until then, I mean to be your loving wife.

They were married, and in marriage you expect children. Sooner or later.

Married, which is to say mated. *Mating* was the physical conse-quence of *marriage*, and there was little that was abstract about it.

"I must be realistic."

So Ariah scolded herself. In her bliss of married contentment yet she had to brood upon certain facts that weren't going to go away.

One of these: she hadn't had a "period" in weeks. (How she hated that word! Her nose crinkled in distaste.) Her last "period" had been before Easter: April 15. Long before her disastrous tenure as Mrs. Erskine. Ariah didn't doubt, she'd ceased menstruating because of panic and dread over her wedding. She'd lost weight, she'd never been what the medical literature calls "normal." Her puberty (another ugly word) came late, she hadn't developed breasts, hips, or begun to menstruate (this ugly word she hated most of all) until the age of six-teen. The last girl (anyway, one of the last) in her high school class. And then she'd never been "regular." (Yet another ugly humiliating word!) If Mrs. Littrell, a woman with ample bosom and hips, was concerned about her daughter's physical condition, she must have been too embarrassed to speak of it. When Ariah began to miss "peri-ods" in high school, Mrs. Littrell took her to their family physician who mumbled, staring at a paperweight on his desk, that Ariah was "like some girls who grow up slow"—"mature slow"—she inclined to a condition called *amenorrhea*.

Amenorrhea! The ugliest word yet.

Ariah sat mortified in Dr. Magruder's office, staring at her freckled hands, with bitten-at nails, in her lap.

Amenorrhea. This was nearly always, Dr. Magruder fumblingly said, typical of a girl who was underweight, "slow" to mature.

Yes it did mean that Ariah might have difficulty conceiving, when at last she did get married.

(Or it might mean, as Ariah was guessing now, that the onset of pregnancy would be difficult to determine. Unless you rushed to a doctor to ask for a pregnancy test, which Ariah wasn't about to do.)

(Oh, God. She'd have been mortified to speak to Dirk Burnaby about such grim female matters. "Female troubles." The Burnabys were a romantic couple like Fred Astaire and Ginger Rogers. When one entered a room in which the other waited, you could hear dance music begin.)

They were married, and so became *husband*, *wife*.

These roles awaited them in the house at 7 Luna Park like *his*, *hers* monogrammed robes which each slipped into, happily. And gratefully.

Dirk said in awe, "I can't imagine my life before you, Ariah. It must have been so shallow . . . It must have been a life without oxygen."

Ariah wiped tears from her eyes but couldn't think how to reply. She could well recall her life before Dirk, the minister's daughter's tidy busy circumscribed life like an apron tied tight over her body. She'd had her music of course. Her students. Her parents, family. Yet thinking of that life now, she felt her throat constrict; she felt as if she might choke. No oxygen!

She ran to her husband (she was barefoot, they were in their bedroom dressing on a mist-muggy August morning) and pressed her wiry little body into his surprised arms, hugging him around the waist.

The man's fist-sized heart thumping against Ariah's ear like a metronome.

Dirk. Darling I think I'm . . . I might be . . . I have this sensation sometimes, I might be . . . pregnant?

But no. Ariah couldn't speak of her fear, and risk that look of alarm in her husband's face. Not just yet.

They were married, and all of the remainder of their lives would be their honeymoon. They were certain!

They were married, and Dirk Burnaby gave his red-haired wife the most exquisite gift she'd ever received: a Steinway spinet made of cherrywood. He'd lighted candles in the living room and small flames were reflected in the burnished wood.

"But why? What have I done to deserve this?"

Ariah's outcry startled her husband, it sounded so frightened.

The piano was an anniversary present, Dirk explained. Three months to the day since they'd "first laid eyes on each other."

Three months. Ariah would not calculate what that might mean. *Three months*. No, she would not think of it.

She was feeling faint, dizzy, giddy. But probably that was the Chianti.

And that warm honey sensation in the loins. The Chianti.

Ariah kissed her husband, hugged him so hard he laughed. "Whoa!" He eased her gently away. He wanted her to play for him, he said. She hadn't played piano, not a note, since that day he'd driven to Troy to claim her.

So Ariah sat at the spinet and played for her husband. Sipping wine between pieces, from a sparkling crystal glass. This spinet was quite the most beautiful instrument Ariah had ever touched, let alone played. Tears flooded her eyes and ran down her cheeks. As Dirk listened gravely, his big head bowed and nodding with the beat, Ariah treated him to a concert of her old favorite girlhood recital pieces. A Mozart minuet, Chopin waltzes and mazurkas, Schumann's "Träumerei," Debussy's "Clair de Lune." As each piece ended, Dirk exploded into applause. He was deeply and sincerely moved. Truly he believed that his wife was a gifted pianist, not only just a moderately talented girl pianist from Troy, New York. He often went to concerts in Kleinhan's Music Hall in Buffalo, he said. He'd heard performers in Carnegie Hall in Manhattan. He'd gone to the Metropolitan Opera where he'd seen spectacular productions of *Carmen* and *La Traviata*. His father, the deceased Virgil Burnaby, whom Ariah would never meet, had owned Caruso records which Dirk had heard often as a boy. Caruso singing *The Barber of Seville*, *The Flying Dutchman*. Caruso as *Otello*.

Ariah couldn't see how her polished, earnest piano technique had led them to the great Caruso, but the connection was flattering.

He loves me. He'd believe anything.

A strange precious truth this was. Like opening your hand and discovering in the palm a tiny, speckled robin's egg.

They were married. Abruptly, and without apology. Without giving notice. Without a thought for *how things are done*. Or *how things are not done*. "At least," Ariah said, "we didn't elope."

Dirk threw down the newspaper he'd been reading, in mock-disgust.

"God damn, Ariah, why didn't you think of it in time?"

They were married, and some weeks later there came for *Mrs. Ariah Burnaby* at 7 Luna Park, Niagara Falls, a handwritten letter with the return address *Mrs. Edna Erskine*. The three-cent stamp on the envelope was upside down.

"Gilbert's mother. Oh my God. She wants to know. If I am pregnant. No, it isn't possible!"

Cowardly Ariah threw away this letter without opening it.

They were married, and the woman who was Ariah's mother-in-law, Claudine Burnaby, gave notice, through Dirk's sisters Clarice and Sylvia, that she was "thinking seriously of disinheriting" her renegade son.

They were married, and lived in Dirk Burnaby's townhouse at 7 Luna Park where, it came to seem to Ariah, other women had, from time to time, visited, if not actually dwelt. She knew this was so because neighbors allowed her to know. Mrs. Cotten who lived next-door, Mrs. Mackay who lived across the Park. *Such glamorous women, some of them! Showgirls, evidently.* Dirk's older sisters whom Ariah had met only twice had allowed her to know. *We never thought Dirk would break down and marry anyone. Our kid brother was always such a spoiled immature brat.*

" 'Clarice and Sylvia,' " Dirk said, as if reading engraved names. "Two of the three fates. And Claudine is the third."

From time to time in the early weeks at Luna Park the telephone would ring and if Ariah answered "Hel-lo?" there was a grim reproachful silence on the other end. "This is the Burnaby residence, hel-lo?" (For possibly Ariah was a little lonely in these new quarters. In this city at the edge of the Niagara Gorge where once the Widow-Bride of The Falls had captivated the public imagination, but where Ariah Burnaby was unknown.) "I know you're there. I can hear you breathing. Who is it?" Ariah's hand trembled, holding the receiver. No, she wasn't frightened: she was annoyed. This was her home, and this telephone number was hers, as well as her husband's. She could detect female breathing through the phone. "If it's Dirk Burnaby you want to speak with, I'm afraid he isn't here." Ariah considered, but refrained from, adding *He's married now. I'm his wife.*

The calls came sometimes when Dirk was home. Ariah was determined not to listen. Not even to "overhear." (She wasn't going to be that kind of wife. She knew her husband had had a bachelor life before meeting her but that was long ago. Months ago.) There was someone persistent named Gwen, and there was someone really persistent named Candy. ("Candy": a showgirl name, if ever there was one.) Once or twice, someone named Vi who actually identified herself to Ariah before politely asking to speak with "your husband, the litigator." A perfumed, lavender letter postmarked Buffalo came for *Mr. Dirk Burnaby* from someone obviously female with the initials *H.T.,* but Ariah wasn't a witness to her husband opening it. (If in fact he opened it? Possibly, out of respect for Ariah, he'd tossed it away instead.) When the phone began to ring persistently in the early hours of the morning, and Dirk, grumpily awakened from sleep, answered, "Hello? *Hello?*" and "If this is who I think it is, please desist, this isn't behavior worthy of you," the time had come finally for Dirk Burnaby to have his number changed, and unlisted.

The mysterious calls abruptly ceased. And no more perfumed letters.

Seated at the Steinway spinet, picking at the perfect ivory keys, Ariah lifted her head hearing, or imagining she heard, the phone ringing. But no.

3

Amenorrheic. Slow to mature.

Telling herself it meant nothing that she was weeks late.

In fact, months late . . .

Always she'd been a thin, you might say a scrawny girl. One of those jumpy all-elbows girls. Such girls *do not get pregnant*.

Yet: Ariah had to concede, she was gaining weight. Her belly was strangely bloated. Her hard stingy little breasts were filling out and the nipples were becoming sensitive, she had to concede though this was absurd and she *would not think of it*.

She'd been a virgin. Gilbert had splattered his hot furious acid-seed on the outside (*not* the inside) of his bride's body. She knew! She would swear! She had been an unwilling witness.

"It couldn't make an actual baby. I don't think so."

God you wouldn't be so cruel would you! Thank you God.

It was 1950. Ariah Burnaby stayed home.

She was *wife* who stayed home while *husband* drove each weekday morning into the city to his law office.

A successful lawyer, Dirk Burnaby was. A "litigator." He had no great passion for the law, he acknowledged, but it was likely work for him, and he thrived on competition.

Ariah wasn't by nature a shy woman but she heard her voice go shy, soft, tentative one evening at dinner asking, "Would you mind, darling, if I gave piano lessons here? And voice lessons? I'm a little lonely during the day and I miss my students and I need something to occupy me until . . ."

Ariah ceased speaking, appalled. Almost she'd said *until the baby*.

Dirk didn't hear this, of course. Ariah's unsaid words.

Ariah wondered if she'd made a blunder in any case. The way her husband was contemplating her. It was the way he gazed at her while she played piano for him, most recently Beethoven's sonata in C-sharp minor, the so-called *Moonlight Sonata* she knew Dirk Burnaby would be a sucker for, that slow dreamy opening movement in particular, he'd said he had never heard anything so beautiful, and he meant it. But now Ariah wondered if she'd gone too far. It was 1950, not 1942. American women didn't work. Especially, married women of Ariah's social class didn't work. She could imagine how such a proposal, made by Ariah's mother, would have been met by Ariah's father. No women in the Littrell family worked. Not a one. (Except an unmarried aunt or two, elementary schoolteachers. They didn't count.)

But Dirk surprised her by taking up her hand, and kissing it, and saying with boyish eagerness, "Ariah, please do whatever you want to do. Whatever makes you happy, makes me happy. I'm gone so much, and this place must get lonely. You're a 'career woman'—I knew that. I'm proud of you. I'll spread the word in town. I have lots of friends, they have pretensions for their children, and they can afford lessons. You're in business, darling." He raised his wine glass in a toast, and Ariah raised hers. They drank. They kissed. Dirk said, "Until we start a family, anyway."

God you wouldn't. Not so cruel. Not twice.

It was Ariah's logic that the longer she waited, the more times she and Dirk Burnaby made love, the more likely it would be, must be, that the baby she might (or might not) be carrying was his, and not *the other's*.

She could not bring herself to see a doctor. Could not. For then she would know, inescapably. She would know if she was pregnant (or not) and she would have to tell Dirk and what exactly could she tell him?

She knew she was becoming a little crazy with this. Brooding!

The pale peaky face in the mirror. The banshee-streaks of silver in the hair.

Kneading the pale, tight flesh of her belly. Pinching her breasts. (Well, admit it: her breasts were fuller. Still small, but fuller. And "sensitive." Possibly that was the consequence of Ariah's amorous husband kissing, nuzzling, sucking at her nipples like a big mischievous baby. Gently, she would have to discourage him.)

At the spinet, she heard herself playing those slow exquisite nocturnes of Chopin. Easing-into-sleep, like lullabies.

They were married, it was 1950 and *husband* was gone for much of the day, Mondays through Fridays. *Wife* was home. *Wife* was beginning to be lonely, even after she started giving music lessons again.

(These were piano students exclusively, very young. She'd had older, far more talented students in Troy, and she missed them. In Niagara Falls, no one in the musical community knew her.)

Dirk conscientiously telephoned Ariah in the late morning from his office, at mid-afternoon, and, if he had to work late, or had to meet a client for drinks, he might call at about 6 P.M. "Darling, hello! I miss you." His voice was tender with love, regret. He was genuinely sorry to be late for dinner. Ariah assured him not to worry, she'd wait dinner for him. As soon as she heard his car pull into the driveway she'd prepare his drink: martini on the rocks.

And one for Ariah, too. She was acquiring a taste for those tiny olives!

Her voice was low, seductive. She heard herself murmur things to her husband over the phone she'd never have dared to say face to face.

"Oh honey." Dirk groaned, with the air of a man squirming inside his clothes. "Me, too."

Sometimes Dirk would insist that Ariah take a taxi into the city and join him. At the Falls Boat Club, or one of the posh Prospect Street hotels, or Mario's Restaurant & Pizzeria. They'd make an evening of it, drinks and dinner. Ariah was self-conscious among Dirk Burnaby's friends (he had so many, she hardly troubled to remember their names, she was acquiring a reputation for being aloof), but it was an opportunity for her to wear her new, stylish clothes from Berger's, in Buffalo, her high-heeled shoes and makeup. She fluffed out her hair and tried to see that the silver streaks were exotic. Back in Troy, she'd have felt like a freak all dressed up; in this new life, on Dirk Burnaby's arm, she felt glamorous. (Was she imagining it, her formerly thin, prissy mouth was fuller now? Swollen from so much kissing.) Dirk lifted her to kiss her: "You're prettier than Susan Hayward any day, and you're *mine*."

Susan Hayward! Ariah supposed, yes she could see a likeness.

Busy, bustling Mario's was the most popular of Falls restaurants among local residents, especially businessmen, politicians, court-house and City Hall–connected individuals. The boating crowd, and the gambling crowd. It seemed to be an open secret that Mario's was connected with a Buffalo crime family. (Ariah had never heard this quaint expression before meeting Dirk Burnaby: "crime family." The language made of crime something unexpectedly cozy, even tender.) In Mario's, everyone knew Dirk Burnaby. His signed photograph was on a wall in the barroom, among a gallery of local celebrities. The maître d' rushed to greet him. The proprietor, Mario himself, shook Dirk's hand, and escorted him to his favorite table in a rear corner of the main dining room. Waitresses in clingy black silk uniforms smiled at him, and stared at Ariah. And other women stared.

Ariah, blushing, could all but hear them. *Her? That scrawny redhead, what's Dirk Burnaby see in her?*

She gripped Dirk's arm tighter. He squeezed her hand.

It was even more unsettling to be introduced to Dirk's old, old friends. Who blinked at Ariah as if trying to place her. There was a drifting haze of foul bluish smoke in Mario's that made Ariah's eyes water and didn't help her perception. She knew that Dirk badly wanted her to like his friends, and he wanted his friends to like her. Fortunately most of these men gathered at Mario's without their wives. Dirk's closest friends were a hard-drinking rowdy crew who'd played poker together since high school at Mount St. Joseph's, with time out for the war. These were shrewd-eyed individuals, a few years older than Dirk. They had an air of money and entitlement that caused Ariah to see her husband in a new light. *He's one of them. His loyalty is to them.*

Gamely Ariah tried to keep these men straight, with mixed results. There was big-boned balding Clyde Colborne who looked unnervingly familiar, like a minor character in the comic strip Dick Tracy; there was Harold ("Buzz") Fitch, a high-ranking officer in the Niagara Falls Police Department; there was plump, moist-eyed Stroughton Howell, a "fellow lawyer," who squeezed Ariah's hand earnestly and congratulated her on her marriage; there was Tyler "Spooky" Wenn, gregarious and comical as Ed Wynn, who'd been a Marine lieutenant in the war and decorated with a Purple Heart ("To replace my own, that was shot to hell") and had just been elected comptroller of Niagara County. Ariah required a drink, or two drinks, to feel minimally comfortable with these loud-talking loud-laughing men. Their conversation mostly excluded her. In their midst, Dirk Burnaby was moderately subdued. He was their flaxen-haired younger brother of whom they were proud. They liked to touch him, gesturing and poking. No joke was worth telling unless Dirk was listening. Ariah understood that, because she was Dirk's wife, they would respect her and be kind to her; one or two even flirted with her. But she knew that they would never accept her as worthy of Dirk Burnaby.

Ariah understood, she wasn't jealous. Not just yet.

Returning to Luna Park after her first evening at Mario's, a long giddy evening that didn't break up until 1 A.M., Ariah murmured, her head resting on Dirk's shoulder as he drove, "That big bald man.

Colborne? Am I supposed to know him, darling? He behaved as if he knows me."

Another evening at Mario's, there was a shivery flurry of attention as a dark-haired middle-aged man of no evident distinction entered the dining room with an entourage of other men: Ariah heard the murmured name *Pallidino*.

Afterward she said to Dirk, "You didn't shake that man's hand, I noticed. When he came by the table."

Dirk said, "You don't miss a thing, sweetie, do you? I didn't think it was that obvious."

"Is he evil? Does he belong to the 'crime family'?"

Ariah spoke impulsively. Her head was spinning, a little. As Dirk drove along Rainbow Boulevard the headlights of oncoming traffic swam and burst against her eyeballs in soft soundless explosions.

"He's a businessman, he'd say. But not my kind of business."

Another evening at Mario's, after Ariah greedily devoured a platter of something doughy and delicious called gnocchi, having downed a martini, and two and a half glasses of wine, she'd had to excuse herself and hurriedly retreat from the table to the women's room where, intermittently for ten arduous minutes, she vomited everything up.

Everything, it felt like!

Afterward, though pale, shaky, and exhausted, she felt much better.

Don't be ridiculous. Make an appointment, see a doctor. If you're pregnant it will be Dirk's child. Who else?

4

THEY WERE MARRIED. Why wasn't that enough?

What need of family, in-laws? *In-laws!*

Ariah secretly liked it that her husband had been "disinherited" because of his marriage. She respected him, that he'd shrugged and laughed when he'd heard. You don't marry for money, you marry for love. You marry for life.

It was true, Ariah missed her parents, sometimes. Oh, not really—she wouldn't have been able to discuss her problem with her mother, anyway. And Reverend Littrell? Never.

In weak moments Ariah recalled the sting of her father's words.

You will not be welcome here. You and him. This is a terrible thing you are doing. Marrying in such haste, a man you don't know. And poor Gilbert has been gone less than a month. Ariah, shame!

Ariah had wanted to cry out she hadn't known Gilbert Erskine yet they'd urged her to marry *him*.

No. No defense, no apologies. Better to walk out of the rectory with dignity. Farewell to the obedient-daughterly life.

Mrs. Ariah Burnaby hadn't the burden of parents. In 1950, this was most remarkable, like walking about with a missing eye or limb you don't, somehow, miss.

Yet there they were, Ariah and Dirk, driving to Shalott—"Shalott!"—what a pretentious name for a house!—on a cloud-splotched Sunday in September.

Somehow, Claudine Burnaby seemed to have changed her mind about disinheriting her renegade son. And she was curious about the daughter-in-law. Finally.

One glance at me, and she'll know. She'll think this is why we got married so quickly.

For this doomed visit to the mother-in-law, Ariah was wearing a pink linen shift so shroud-like, the sleeves seemed to trail belatedly behind her. Her wrists, poking out, were alarmingly bony. She'd powdered over the freckles on her face, and carefully applied vivid red lipstick to her mouth.

"Oh, Dirk. I'm worried sick your mother won't like me."

"Oh, Ariah. I'm worried sick you won't like my mother."

Ariah was sincere, Dirk was teasing. But she saw the tension in her husband's jaws. The stoic glisten of his eyes. Uneasily she guessed that, though Dirk Burnaby strongly disapproved of his difficult mother, he loved her, too.

He would want his wife to love her, too.

Dirk had showed Ariah photographs of Claudine Burnaby: a striking, strong-jawed blond woman with intense eyes, an ironic smiling mouth. A tight Joan Crawford look about the mouth, as if it held too many teeth. How surprised Ariah was when Dirk said, laughing lightly, "Don't be deceived by Mother's sweet look, darling."

This was Ariah's first visit to l'Isle Grand, which seemed to float in the rushing Niagara River, midway between Niagara Falls and Buffalo. Shalott had been built at the southeastern edge of the largely rural block-shaped island, looking toward Ontario, Canada.

(Ontario! Ariah recalled for the first time since Gilbert Erskine's death that he'd been planning part of their honeymoon in Ontario: west of Niagara Falls in a wilderness area bordered by the Thames River where there were said to be rich fossil fields.)

Ariah bit at her thumbnail, surreptitiously she thought until her husband, reaching out as he drove, not even turning to frown at her, slapped her hand away from her mouth. "Ariah. Give me the word, and I'll turn right around and go back. I hate to see you anxious."

"Anxious? I am not anxious." Ariah stared through the windshield at whatever it was she was seeing: open fields, woods, the river at a distance. And houses. Such houses! You'd have to call them mansions. Ostentatious. "Conspicuous consumption." Part of her bridled against such material displays. She was a small-town minister's daughter, she knew vanity when she saw it. "I'm fascinated. Seeing how you lived as a boy."

Dirk laughed uneasily. As if he'd never thought of himself in such terms.

When Dirk turned into the hilly driveway of Shalott, Ariah bit her lip. Why, this was silly. A house so large! She decided she disliked Mrs. Burnaby on principle.

They'd been invited for brunch at noon, but by twelve-thirty Mrs. Burnaby hadn't yet appeared. A glass-topped table had been set for three on a flagstone terrace overlooking the river. "Mrs. Burnaby will be down soon, she apologizes for keeping you waiting," an older woman in a housekeeper's uniform told them, at intervals. They were to make themselves "comfortable." They were invited to have appetizers and drinks: tomato juice out of a chilled pitcher, which turned out to be, not tomato juice, but Bloody Marys. A delicious drink Ariah had never before tasted, and quite liked.

Dirk said, "Ariah, take care. Vodka can be lethal."

Ariah laughed gaily. She had been mildly nauseated that morning and hadn't eaten even a light breakfast and found herself strangely hungry now, devouring tiny crab croissants and radishes dipped in sour cream. She'd ceased biting her thumbnails. She caught sight of herself reflected in a window and was encouraged, she truly did look pretty: her husband's love had worked the miracle.

"Dirk, you won't stop loving me, will you? Darling? You won't wake up one day and change your mind?"

"Ariah, don't be silly."

"Because if you do, I might just go out. 'Out' like a light."

Dirk glanced about uneasily, as if he feared they might be overheard. Windows looking out onto the terrace were shaded by white louvre blinds through which one might observe the terrace without being seen, and most of these windows were open. He'd lighted a cigarette, and was on his second drink. And where the hell was Claudine?

Dirk walked Ariah down the sloping lawn to the river and out onto the dock and talked to her, somewhat distractedly, of his boyhood boats. His love of sailing, and the river. When his father had been alive. "I was a reckless kid, I guess. I had some close calls." Dirk spoke wistfully. Ariah wondered if he were regretting his past behavior, or the past itself. The wind lifting from the river was fresh and wonderfully invigorating. In the near distance sailboats glided past without seeming effort. Here, on the dock at Shalott, you couldn't hear the ominous thunder of The Falls; The Falls were miles away downriver. You might swim off this dock, the current here wasn't lethal. You wouldn't be carried away screaming to your doom. *I could live here. And our children. Why shouldn't we inherit?* It was an unexpected, unworthy thought. Ariah didn't know what to make of it.

The dock was in need of repair, shifting and creaking perceptibly beneath their weight. The only boat moored there was an old formerly white sailboat. The thought of climbing into that boat, of being rocked and jolted by the river, filled Ariah with alarm and yet she leaned flirtatiously against her husband's arm and said, "Your old sailboat looks abandoned. Why don't you take me out, Dirk? After brunch?"

"Yes. I'd like that."

Dirk spoke with forced enthusiasm. Ariah could see he was distracted, glancing at his watch and back toward the house. It wasn't like him not to focus upon her, in her presence. She felt the tug of the other woman, in that house.

"I think your mother has come outside? Isn't that—"

"No. It's just Ethel, wondering where we are."

It was nearly 1 P.M. Dirk, sullen and sulky, his hair disheveled from the wind, led Ariah back toward the terrace. The sun, not quite directly overhead, was surprisingly hot. In this climate there were perpetual cloud formations, hazy and humid, through which a whitish sun shone in patches. Between the two Great Lakes, Erie and Ontario. Always the sky was shifting, uncertain. In this pale glare the lawn at Shalott was exposed as brown, dry, weedy in places. Roses bushes were tainted with black spots. You could see that the grounds were becoming neglected, as if life were being withdrawn. And the stately limestone house, viewed from the rear, as from backstage, looked weatherworn. There were cracks in the stone. Slimy green moss like a long skinny snake grew in the rusted rain gutter that stretched the full width of the house.

Ariah laughed nervously. "Maybe this is the wrong Sunday, Dirk?"

"I'm thinking maybe it is," Dirk said grimly.

Ariah had never seen her tall handsome confident husband so distracted, edgy. Angry. They returned to the terrace, and Claudine still hadn't appeared. The embarrassed housekeeper apologized as before. Dirk said, "If my mother expects me to search for her, and beg her to join us, she's mistaken." Ariah, picking at the appetizers, tried not to overhear. She poured herself a little more of the delicious blood-red peppery drink, since Dirk seemed disinclined to pour it for her. She ate crab croissants, washed down with her Bloody Mary. Her mouth flooded with saliva, she was ravenously hungry, even as a mild wave of nausea stirred in her stomach.

Dirk said suddenly, "Ariah, we're leaving. Where's your handbag?"

Ariah stood very still, breathing deeply. She would conquer this moment of weakness. She would not succumb. Her eyelids fluttered. She didn't want to see the forlorn left-behind sailboat bobbing and rocking at the dock, the ceaseless motion, idiotic in repetition. Nausea was like seasickness. She turned away from the river, and saw, or imagined she saw, a ghostly face in a window about twelve feet away. But immediately the face was obscured by a drawn blind.

She hoped Dirk hadn't seen.

"Ethel? Tell your mistress she's insufferably rude. And not to invite my wife and me back here again, ever."

Dirk seized Ariah by the upper arm. He'd never gripped her so hard! She began to protest, stumbling in her high-heeled shoes, and suddenly to her horror she was choking, gagging. Suddenly she was sick to her stomach. Helpless, wracked by spasms of nausea, vomiting up all that she'd unwisely drunk and devoured, staining the front of her pink linen dress and splattering the glass-topped table and flagstone terrace.

"Ariah, God damn," Dirk said miserably, "didn't I warn you?"

5

IT WAS 1950 and everyone was pregnant.

Bouts of nausea, especially in the morning, became more frequent with Ariah.

Three months, twelve weeks and two days after her marriage to Dirk Burnaby, Ariah at last saw a doctor. A name out of the Niagara Falls telephone directory: Piper.

"Mrs. Burnaby, good news!"

Ariah burst into tears. Oh, she'd practiced this moment, her smile and her stoicism, she was even wearing stylish clothes to impress Dr. Piper and his nurse, but now that the moment had come, rushing upon her like a locomotive, she had no strength, she had no control. She hid her burning face in her hands. Dr. Piper, a dignified oldish gentleman with an office in downtown Niagara Falls, a brisk fifteen-minute walk from Luna Park, stared at her in astonishment.

Ariah pleaded, "Doctor, don't tell me how long I've been pregnant. Don't tell me when I'm due. No!"

"But, Mrs. Burnaby—"

Ariah tried to explain. No, she couldn't explain. She was weeping, blowing her nose. Oh, why couldn't that man have killed himself before their wedding night, not after? She stammered:

"Dr. Piper, yes—I'm happy. I am married, and I'm h-happy. I love my husband—we were just married in July—and we want children—but I'm not sure—I mean, I don't want to know—who the father is."

Seeing that Dr. Piper regarded her now with horror, in that way of Reverend Littrell regarding her with horror, Ariah tried to explain the circumstances of her first marriage—its brevity, "tragedy." Squirming with embarrassment she told him of how her husband had "ejaculated" onto her, between her legs. Oh, she'd been a virgin—but she knew that virgins can become impregnated. In high school such crude practical wisdom circulated, even a Presbyterian minister's daughter might overhear such wisdom, in astonishment and dread, and file it away for future reference thinking *But not me. Never me. Oh, no!*

"I don't want to know, doctor. If I've been pregnant sixteen weeks, my first husband is—would be—would have been—the father. If I've been pregnant just twelve weeks, my second husband is the f-father. Maybe the baby will be born premature? Maybe it will be born late?" Ariah couldn't bear to look at Dr. Piper, knowing the poor man was stricken with embarrassment, and knowing she, in the messiness of her female being, was to blame. "Doctor, please: I don't need to know absolutely, do I? My husband doesn't need to know?"

Dr. Piper pushed a box of Kleenex toward Ariah, who took a tissue gratefully to wipe her face. It seemed from previous remarks of his that he knew the Burnaby name, if not Ariah's husband personally, and was impressed by that name. He spoke now with more authority than Ariah expected, and immediately she was reassured: "Mrs. Burnaby, the baby in your womb is no more than thirteen weeks old. This is my estimate, and I'm rarely wrong. I may be off by a few days, a week, but no more. Mr. Burnaby is therefore the baby's father. Your due date will be April of next year. I can be more specific next time you come in, if you wish."

Ariah said faintly, "No, doctor. That's specific enough. April."

Dr. Piper rose from his desk, and shook Ariah's hand which was a cold-clammy dead woman's hand, and needed reviving. In a kindly voice he said, "I suggest that you cease these ridiculous speculations, Mrs. Burnaby. Tell no one what you've told me. Inform your husband of the good news, go out and celebrate, and I'll see you again soon. And congratulations."

They were married, and pregnant. They celebrated.

First-Born

1

*B y the calendar, I was a spring baby.
Born a week premature. Possibly two.*

Except, late March in Niagara Falls, New York, was blustery, snowy, subfreezing as it had been since Thanksgiving. Snowdrops and crocuses at 7 Luna Park, and across the street in the small gated park, daring to bloom prematurely, had been rudely covered in yet another gritty layer of snow.

Much was made of the fact that one hundred eight inches of snow had fallen in the Niagara region that winter. Most of this snow, by March 26, had not melted.

On their way home from the hospital, Ariah in a glow of elation asked Dirk to please drive by the river, so that their week-old son, Chandler, could see The Falls.

"Please, darling? He might remember it forever. It might be his first visual memory."

Dirk might have hesitated for a brief moment. His wife's moods were wayward and inscrutable and yet, he'd come to know, they were determined by a subterranean logic as firm and unyielding as the steel girders beneath the poured concrete of a bridge. And Dirk was in such a transport of dazed joy, wonderment, relief at the birth of a healthy son, of course he gave in.

He was clean-shaven. He'd had his shaggy hair trimmed. For several days he'd been a disheveled, distraught man. But no more.

At this time of year, The Falls was deserted as the moon. Except for a lone municipal snowplow grinding through Prospect Park, spewing exhaust in its wake, there was no one.

"No tourists! What a pleasure."

Dirk drove into Prospect Park, and parked at the Point. He kept the car's motor running, and the heater turned up high. Most of the rear of the Lincoln Continental was filled with flowers, tulips, hyacinths, paperwhites, past their first bloom but still fragrant, festive. These were flowers from Ariah's hospital room, and most of them were flowers Dirk had brought her.

Fred Astaire bringing his darling Ginger Rogers flowers in the hospital. His red-haired dancing partner, not dancing now. But soon to revive.

And bringing home with her a boy-baby so small, yet at five pounds, seven ounces so perfectly formed, Dirk knew that his life would be complete from now on. Yes, forever!

There was a northerly wind from Canada, and what they could see of the sky was the bright ceramic blue of winter. Ariah, shaky and pale from her ordeal, an eleven-hour labor, an alarming loss of blood, a brief but fevered hospital infection, cooed and kissed the flush-faced baby. "See, sweetie? Where Daddy and Mommy have taken you? The Falls." Ariah laughed and held Chandler up in her arms that trembled just slightly. (Dirk was keeping a close watch on her. He'd steady her grip on the baby if necessary. In the hospital, in the throes of her fever delirium, Ariah had cried out certain things. You might call them warnings. He would be warned, vigilant.)

Chandler was snugly swaddled in a blue cashmere baby blanket and his miniature, flailing hands were protected by matching mittens. Quizzically he peered through the car's broad windshield. His tiny fish-mouth gaped wetly and his round, dark eyes bulged. He blinked, and squinted. His face was a small rubbery doll's face with a forehead that sloped strangely, like a wedge of cheese, Ariah thought, and a chin that receded like something melted, but he was a beautiful baby, he was Dirk's and hers and had been worth all that blood.

Ariah said excitedly, "He can see. I mean, it's more than just his eyes are open. He's processing sight. It's like he's devouring the landscape, with those eyes."

Almost, you would think that Chandler understood what he was seeing. Where mist rose from the Gorge, ice had formed in a filigree on the tall leafless elms and oaks on the riverbank, and glittered in the sun like Mozart's treble notes. As in a fairy tale there was an ice-bridge that had formed across the Niagara River, and ghost-rainbows appeared and disappeared in an eye blink. Even in the subfreezing temperature, hot-looking steamy mist continued to rise.

It was the American Falls they were looking toward. The larger falls, the Horseshoe, was farther away, south and west of Goat Island and not visible from Dirk's car except as a confusion of mist.

For several minutes they sat in the car in silence.

Chandler squirmed, murmured. His little mittened fists flailed. He would be an inquisitive baby, inclined to restlessness, querulousness. His face puckered in a sort of animal anxiety. His fish-mouth gaped. Soon he would want to be fed again: nursed. *Nursing* was a new, astonishing and overwhelming experience for Ariah, a *lovemaking* experience for which the new mother hadn't been prepared.

Ariah smiled dreamily to think of it.

After a moment she said, "What do you think has brought us here, Dirk? The three of us."

Ariah spoke in a neutral, matter-of-fact voice. She might have been a client asking her attorney a practical question. She was jiggling Chandler's warm weight against the bosom of her coat, pressing her slightly chapped lips against the top of his head. He wore a tiny knitted cap one of Dirk's relatives had given them, but the heat of his scalp came through against Ariah's lips.

Dirk said, "What has brought us here?—d'you mean literally *here*? I've brought us here, darling. By your request."

Dirk spoke lightly, for lightly was the way in which to speak to a new mother at such a time.

But Ariah persisted, for Ariah must always persist. "I mean what has brought us, the three of us, to this place? And this moment? Out of all of the universe, and an infinity of time?"

It was a little difficult for Ariah to speak at such length. In the hospital, in her white-walled private room amid banks of flowers, and in the labor room, she'd screamed, begged, threatened. Her sensitive throat was raw with the guttural cries and groans, as of a dying animal, that had been forced from her.

Dirk said, in that light, insistent way, "You know what has brought us here: Love."

"Love! I suppose so." Ariah reacted as if she hadn't thought of this. Her husband, stroking her hand as she cupped the baby's head, helping to cup the baby's head with his big, somewhat clumsy hand, regarding her sidelong, surreptitiously, as he'd been regarding her in her hospital bed, and felt his heart clutch. Love for her and their son came so strong to him, he couldn't trust himself to speak.

Ariah continued, frowning, "Love isn't less a force in life than gravity, is it? You can't see 'gravity' either."

Dirk said, smiling, "You and Chandler are visible. I'm plenty visible."

He slapped at his midriff. He'd lost almost ten pounds since Ariah entered the hospital, but he could surely stand to lose ten more.

Ariah persisted. "But love is chancy. It's a roll of the dice."

"More like poker. You're dealt cards, but a good player gets good cards. And a good player knows what to do with them."

Ariah smiled at Dirk, liking this answer.

" 'A good player knows what to do with them.' "

Playfully she tugged at Dirk's fingers, that were cupping Chandler's head. The palm of Dirk's hand alone was large enough to hold their baby, with no other support. She said, in her new, raw, wistful voice, "You won't leave me for a while now, I guess? Now Baby is here."

"Ariah, why do you say such things?"

Dirk drew away, offended.

Ariah looked at her husband in innocent surprise. The big hand-some face, tired from the ordeal of the past week, like the face of an American boy who's had to grow up too quickly, was creased as if aggrieved. For the life of her, Ariah couldn't understand why.

At this moment Chandler began squirming and burbling more urgently, filled his tiny lungs with air, and began to bellow. It was nursing time, luckily.

And so a baby came to dwell at 7 Luna Park. A baby!

He was an angel-baby, sometimes. At other times, a red-faced roaring little demon. Mommy and Daddy gazed at him in wonder. Except he'd squeezed himself out through a far-too-small hole in her body, she'd have sworn he came from another planet. Krypton? Where the laws of nature differe from ours.

How he loved to cry, exercising those baby-lungs. Furious, purposeful, like one of those madmen-bully Fascist leaders you'd see in newsreels, Hitler, Mussolini, bellowing at their mesmerized audiences packed into public squares. Ariah was going to joke, "Maybe he'll want a pulpit for his first birthday, he can start giving sermons young." The allusion was to Reverend Littrell of course. But Ariah bit her lip, and went quiet.

Nights were not so romantic now at 7 Luna Park, in Dirk Burnaby's old bachelor quarters. Nights were a very rocky sail on a dark choppy turbulent river leaving you dazed, seasick. Praying for dawn. "At least you can leave for 'work.' That's where Daddys go." Ariah tried to see the humor of it. Dirk protested he'd stay home and help, if Ariah wanted him to. And he did hire a nanny, to help out when Ariah was totally exhausted. But Ariah rather resented the nanny, for Baby Chandler was *hers*.

(She'd never have another one of these again, she vowed. Oh, it had hurt! They say you forget labor pains but she, Ariah, wasn't going to forget. Ever.)

A baby-angel, a baby-demon. Waking a half-dozen times in the night. Howling, ravenous. Demanding the breast. Both breasts. Filling his diapers with baby shit. (Which, dopey from lack of sleep and not her usual sharp-elbowed self, Ariah would almost, strange as it sounds, come to not-dislike. "It doesn't smell bad, exactly. You get used to it. It smells like . . . well, Baby.")

A volcano, Dirk Burnaby marveled, that gushed at both ends.

Then there was nursing.

Nursing! Which Mother and Baby did, together, whenever Baby wished. A private matter. Baby's hungry little fish-mouth suck suck sucking at her fat, milky breast. *Another kind of lovemaking* Ariah thought. *But we won't tell Daddy.*

No, best that Daddy doesn't know.

Not that Daddy didn't adore Baby, he did. But Daddy would not have wished to think of Baby as a male rival, exactly.

God, thank You. Now I am redeemed, and will ask nothing of You ever again.

2

"It seems I've been forgiven, I guess. By the Presbyterians, at least."

Within a few weeks, Mrs. Littrell came alone, by train, to Niagara Falls to see her grandson. "Oh, Ariah! Oh my baby." It was a tearful reconciliation, there in the noisy Niagara Falls train station, like a scene in a maudlin but good-hearted movie of the 1940's, shot in wartime black and white. Ariah, now a married woman and a mother, and pretty damned proud of herself for coping as well as she did, mimed a face of daughterly emotion as she embraced her mother, startled by the older woman's soft, warm, bosomy body, but she couldn't leak out more than a tear or two. *Never! Never forgive you for abandoning me when I needed you.* "Ariah, dear, can you ever forgive me?" Mrs. Littrell asked anxiously, and Ariah said, at once, squeezing both her mother's pudgy hands in her own, "Oh, Mother. Of course. There is nothing to forgive." Dirk Burnaby the beaming son-in-law shook hands with Mrs. Littrell, gallant and kindly. And there was Baby Chandler in his stroller, blinking up at this weepy tremulous middle-aged woman and jamming fingers into his mouth. Mrs. Littrell crouched over him as over an abyss that made her dizzy. She stammered, "Oh, it's a miracle. He's a miracle. Isn't he a miracle, oh what a beautiful little baby." Ariah wanted to correct her mother, Baby Chandler wasn't beautiful exactly, no need to exaggerate, but yes, maybe to his grandmother he seemed so. Mrs. Littrell begged Ariah to allow her to hold him, and of course Ariah consented. "Chandler, here's your grandmother."

" 'Grandma.' I hope he'll call me. Oh, how beautiful he is!"

Mrs. Littrell had planned to stay just two nights in Niagara Falls, in the guest room at 7 Luna Park, but she ended up staying six nights.

"Somehow, it's easier when people aren't on speaking terms with you," Ariah said dryly. (Though secretly she was pleased with Baby Chandler's triumph over her mother. There was a delicious revenge here.)

Mrs. Littrell had brought two large suitcases with her on the train, one filled with baby things. These were "new and used" baby things including some of Ariah's own baby clothes from thirty years ago. "Do you remember, dear? This little cap, your own grandma knitted for you." Ariah smiled and said yes, she thought she remembered, though certainly she didn't. Why, these old things might have belonged to anyone, for all Ariah knew her mother might have picked them up at a rummage sale in Troy! The church was always having rummage sales in the basement. A sudden rage came over Ariah in the midst of their happy reconciliation, that her mother had no right to re-enter her life, when Ariah was doing so well without her, and without Reverend Littrell. Mrs. Littrell had no more right to re-enter Ariah's new life than Gilbert Erskine would have had, resurrected from the dead.

Gilbert Erskine. Ariah never thought of him any longer. Yet in a dream of singular ugliness he'd come to her: doggedly knocking at the front door of her new home. Like the monster-son in "The Monkey's Paw." Cowardly Ariah had hidden beneath the bedclothes and sent Dirk to answer the door in her place.

Obviously, Mrs. Littrell had no idea of Dirk Burnaby's financial situation, bringing the young couple so many things, both new and second-hand. Ariah had told her virtually nothing of her married life in Niagara Falls; she'd sent only a printed birth announcement and a few snapshots of Chandler. Clearly, Luna Park intimidated the minister's wife from Troy. The elegant brick homes in the leafy residential neighborhood near the river; the neo-Georgian townhouses facing the park with their small but scrupulously tended lawns and black wrought iron fences; the spare, sleekly modern furnishings of Dirk Burnaby's bachelor quarters; Ariah's gorgeous Steinway spinet—all took Mrs. Littrell by surprise. Not to mention the Irish nanny, the housekeeper and the cook, who happened to be male, a Frenchman whom Dirk employed for business dinners several times a month. And there was a Negro who tended the lawn, small as it was. Mrs. Littrell seemed disoriented, as if she'd wandered into the household of another woman's married daughter, but was in no hurry to leave.

Several times she murmured in Ariah's ear, "Dear, you must be so happy, your cup overflowing!"

The third time Mrs. Littrell made this breathless observation, as Dirk lifted Chandler to demonstrate for Grandma his son's remarkable kicking and flailing "helicopter stunt" as Dirk called it, wicked Ariah retorted, "Do you think my cup is so small, Mother? That it overflows so easily?"

Within the year, Reverend Littrell began to accompany Mrs. Littrell to Niagara Falls. Ariah's father, too, fell under the spell of the Burnaby household.

Especially, he fell under the spell of the new baby.

Ariah's father seemed to have aged in the past year. Ariah supposed she was to blame. He was a proud man, for all his Christian pulpit-humility, and Ariah's behavior had scandalized him. His face was deeply creased and his Teddy Roosevelt jaws jutted with less confidence. He appeared shorter. His belly was more pronounced. He'd acquired an annoying nervous habit of clearing his throat before and after he spoke, as if to obscure his words. Unlike Ariah's tearful mother he never quite apologized to Ariah, nor did he embrace her as her mother had done. The most he could manage was to inform Ariah, when they were alone together, as if the statement were a biblical revelation, "Sometimes to act in haste is not to act unwisely, I see. You are blessed in your husband and child. Ariah, every hour of my life I thank God, that things have turned out for you as they have."

Ariah said quietly, "Thank you, Father."

Wanting to add, with a mischievous smile *Yes but I'm still damned. That won't change.*

Well, Ariah was grateful. For her father's words, however grudging. At a time in her life when she no longer needed them.

(Why should she care about anyone, really? Now that she had her baby. Hers.)

"What good, decent people your parents are." Dirk spoke with his usual enthusiasm, and Ariah detected in his voice, in his smiling face, not the slightest hint of irony. She knew he was thinking *How different from my mother* and so of course the Littrells might seem to him good, decent, ideal in-laws.

"Well. They are Christians, obviously."

Ariah spoke lightly. No, she wasn't being sarcastic!

In fact she was grateful, very grateful, that her husband, ever the gracious host, was so courteous to her parents. This gave her space to lapse into silence when she wished. It gave her opportunities to slip away with Chandler for a nap.

She liked it that, in the presence of his tall, confident son-in-law, who spoke casually and with authority of business, politics, the economy, law, and who seemed to know a good deal about the imminent development in the Niagara region of "hydro-power," Reverend Littrell tended to be deferential. "Yes. I see. Oh, I see." Where in Troy he would have asserted his own personality, here in Luna Park he was subdued. Dirk Burnaby was of a social class unknown to the

Littrells, as his religious beliefs were undefined, and his sense of humor difficult to decode. Even Chandler, suddenly a toddler, was unpredictable. Competing with Grandma Littrell for their grandson's fickle attention, Grandpa usually lost. The child regarded the old man with slow-blinking curiosity, unsmiling. Sometimes he pushed frantically away from Grandpa. In her father's face at such times Ariah saw a look of genuine loss.

The power of a thoughtless child, to reject. To outlive.

So one generation grinds another into the earth. Into bones, dust. Into oblivion. Ariah smiled cruelly to think how little the promise of heaven must mean, if you've lost earth.

"Chandler! That's a naughty boy. Grandpa is going to read to you, see? Here's your Big Lion book, your favorite." Gaily Ariah hauled her son back to her father, and deposited him on the sofa beside the clumsily smiling old man.

Ariah was fearful of sailing, and didn't greatly love the forty-foot *Valkyrie* riding the crest of choppy waves upriver, downriver, to Lake Erie and back, yet she pretended for Dirk's sake to enjoy these excursions, or mostly. She foresaw a time when she'd stay home, and Dirk and Chandler could go out by themselves; but that time wasn't just yet.

It was a festive occasion, however, when Dirk took his in-laws on a yachting trip to Lake Erie, five miles to the south, and dinner on the splendid outdoor terrace of the Buffalo Yacht Club. Ariah took a kind of pride in seeing how startled, how impressed, her father was with the sleek whitely gleaming yacht, when Dirk first brought them to the marina. She supposed he was wondering how much it cost. (Never could he have guessed.) Mrs. Littrell was excited, anxious. There were many other boats on the river on this bright windy day, sailboats, yachts, speedboats, what if there was a collision, what if waves swamped and oveturned their boat? Ariah saw that her mother was genuinely frightened. She spoke in a lowered, embarrassed voice not wanting her son-in-law to hear. Ariah said airily, "Impossible, Mother. Dirk is an experienced yachtsman." *Yachtsman!* So casually uttered by one who, before Dirk Burnaby and this new life of hers at The Falls, had never so much as cast her eyes upon a vessel like the *Valkyrie*, let alone stepped on its lavishly appointed deck. In any case, once they were out on the river, Ariah and Mrs. Littrell stayed inside the cabin, with Chandler. The wind on the Niagara River was relentless; Dirk insisted upon maintaining a certain speed; he hated to "poke along"; when clouds were blown across the sun, the temperature dropped ten degrees. Ariah worried about gathering clouds over the lake toward which they were headed, but said nothing to her mother, of course. In the region of the Great Lakes, weather changed rapidly: forecasters were always making mistakes. Chandler was thrilled by Daddy's big boat but tended to become overstimulated by it, and tired quickly. He became cranky, fretful, teary, babyish. "He's a high-strung, sensitive child," Mrs. Littrell said protectively. "He takes after his mother."

Ariah laughed. "Is that how you see me, Mother? 'High-strung, sensitive'?" She didn't know if she should be flattered, or insulted. She was feeling damned proud of herself these days, a first-time mother.

For a while after Chandler's birth, she'd been not-herself, you might say. Exhausted, melancholy. Wanting to crawl into a nest of bedclothes and hide. But she hadn't, had she? Her hard little breasts had ballooned with milk, sweet delicious milk demanding to be sucked.

Mrs. Littrell was saying quickly, "But also very talented, Ariah. Very—intelligent. Mysterious, a bit. Your father and I have always thought so."

Mysterious! Ariah liked that, a little better. She asked:

"And how does Chandler take after his father, d'you think?"

"His father? Why—he has his eyes, I think. There's something of Dirk about his mouth. The shape of his head." But Ariah's mother sounded uncertain.

Ariah said, "When Chandler was born, his hair was dark. Dark swaths like seaweed. Now it's becoming lighter, like Dirk's. He'll grow into his father, I think. He likes numbers, and Dirk says he used to play with numbers at Chandler's age, too. Dirk's mother says

Chandler is very like Dirk at his age." This was so stunning a lie, Ariah couldn't quite believe it was hers. "Of course, Chandler was born a few weeks premature, he has catching up to do. But he will."

Thank God, Ariah's worries about her baby's paternity were behind her now. She recalled them only dimly, as you might recall a blurred movie sequence from long ago. Seeing Dirk with Chandler you knew they were father and son. Chandler adored his daddy, and Daddy adored him. Ariah saw her anxiety, in retrospect, as a symptom of her pregnancy like morning sickness, or her cravings for peculiar foods (cold oatmeal, pickle sandwiches, "fish fingers" with mustard, hot cross buns from DiCamillo's Bakery). A first-time mother fantasizes the worst, Dr. Piper assured her. Imagining they might give birth to deformed infants, monsters. At least, Ariah hadn't been that crazy.

Fretful Chandler had put aside his numbers game and dropped off to sleep. Mrs. Littrell was squinting through the spray-lashed cabin window at the men on the deck. Mrs. Littrell marveled, "I never thought I'd live to see the sight, your father in a life preserver. Like a sea captain." She tried to laugh though the *Valkyrie*, in the wake of an enormous Great Lakes coal barge that had passed dangerously near, was beginning to rock. With a ghastly smile Mrs. Littrell said, "Ariah, you married such a wonderful man. You were right not to despair."

Not to despair? Was that what her love for Dirk was?

"Yes, Mother. We don't need to discuss it."

Ariah shut her eyes. This damned boat! Rocking, lurching. It was seasickness she feared, more than drowning.

But Mrs. Littrell persisted, raising her voice to be heard over the noise of the boat's motor. "Oh, Ariah. God's ways are inscrutable as the Bible says."

Ariah said, "Maybe God just has a wicked sense of humor."

The Littrells never spoke to Ariah of the Erskines, whom they knew well in Troy; they never spoke to her of Gilbert Erskine. It was as if, when the Littrells were visiting at Luna Park, under the spell of the Burnaby household, a part of the past had ceased to exist.

The night of the yachting trip to Lake Erie and back, undressing for bed and discussing the excursion, which Dirk believed had gone very well, Ariah had a sudden wish never to see her parents again, or anyone. Her soul was worn thin and soiled as an old, used towel. She heard herself say in a droll voice, "Well. It seems I've been totally forgiven now. The *Valkyrie* did it, with the Reverend." Peering into a mirror she discovered several new, very visible silver hairs sprouting from her head. Like stark melancholy thoughts they were, the kind you want to tear out by the roots. "But guess what? I'm the same sinner as always."

Dirk chuckled, reaching for her. "Darling, I hope so."

3

NO WARNING!

A weekday afternoon in October 1953, too early for Ariah's afterschool piano student, the doorbell rang and Ariah went to answer it. She felt only a mild uneasiness. It wouldn't be the postman ringing the door at this hour, and not a delivery man. Ariah wasn't so friendly with her Luna Park neighbors that one of them might drop by unexpected and uninvited. (She had a reputation, she supposed, for being unfriendly, aloof. And maybe that wasn't misleading.) Apart from a few hours of piano instruction a week, Ariah spent her days with Chandler. She was a devoted, consecrated mother. She'd dismissed the Irish nanny Dirk had hired for her, and cut back the hours Dirk's housekeeper worked for them. "This is my house. I hate to share it with strangers." She loved to observe Chandler from a little distance, watching as the child played for long periods of time oblivious of her. He muttered, argued, laughed to himself, patiently creating remarkably intricate towers, bridges, airplanes, then, with a terse little cry of judgment ("Now you go!") in mimicry of Daddy's voice, he caused them to crash, disintegrate, topple into a heap.

The game had a secret name, he'd whispered in Mommy's ear if she promised not to tell: "Earthquake."

At two years, seven months, Chandler was thin, inclined to nervous excitement, shy and mistrustful in the presence of other children. His face was small and triangular as a ferret's. His eyes seemed to Ariah ferrety—shifting, restless. "Chandler, look at *me*. Look at *Mommy*." And so he might, but you could see that his rapidly working little brain was fixed on something more urgent.

Before Ariah could get to the front door, the bell rang again, sharply. Ariah was annoyed, opening the door—"Yes? What do you want?" On the step stood an elegantly dressed, perfumed older woman who looked familiar in a blurred bad-dream way. She was someone Ariah had never seen before and yet (she knew!) knew.

Moving her mouth strangely, the woman said, in a self-consciously cultured voice that sounded as if it hadn't been used in some time, "Ariah. Hello. I'm Dirk's mother Claudine Burnaby." Affecting not to notice Ariah's look of astonishment and dismay, she extended a gloved, languid hand. The pressure of her fingers was nearly nonexistent. She regarded Ariah through sunglasses so darkly tinted, Ariah couldn't see even the glisten of her eyes. Her mouth was a rich lustrous fire-engine red but it was a mouth reluctant to smile.

Her! The mother-in-law.

For a long terrible moment Ariah stood paralyzed. This was an unlikely, improbable meeting of the sort a morbid-minded daughter-in-law might already have fantasized, for more than three years, yet now that it was happening, clearly it was happening for the first time; and the mother-in-law was in charge.

Parked at the curb, solemn as a hearse, was a chauffeur-driven car.

Ariah heard her voice faltering like an amateur singer's. She reached for notes that weren't there. "Mrs. Burnaby! H-Hello. Please—come inside?"

The woman laughed pleasantly. "Oh, now, my dear—we can't both be 'Mrs. Burnaby.' Not at the same time."

Ariah would consider this remark afterward, in the way of an individual examining bruises and cuts he hadn't quite understood he'd suffered.

Ariah stammered something about Dirk not being home, Dirk would be sorry to miss her, even as, with a part of her mind, she knew that Mrs. Burnaby had come deliberately at a time when Dirk wouldn't be home, why was she presenting herself as naïve, obtuse? She offered to take Mrs. Burnaby's coat, fumbling with the garment, in fact it was a cape of buttery-soft wool, an exquisitely beautiful heather color that matched the suit Mrs. Burnaby wore beneath; the suit suggested high fashion of the mid-1940's, boxy shoulders and a tight waist and flared skirt to mid-calf. On her stiff metallic-blond hair Mrs. Burnaby wore a black velvet hat with a small cobwebby veil. An odor of aged gardenias and mothballs hovered about her. Ariah was deeply mortified to be exposed to this woman's eyes as one who'd so let herself go since her wedding. She was wearing an old cardigan sweater and shapeless slacks and "mocassins" so rundown at the heel they were, in effect, bedroom slippers. The cuffs of Ariah's slacks were stained from an Easter egg-dyeing session with Chandler months before. And of course Ariah's (graying) hair was brushed back flat from her pale, plain face, and needed shampooing. She'd intended to freshen herself up a bit for the five o'clock piano student . . .

Mrs. Burnaby seemed scarcely aware of Ariah, however, looking pointedly around. "It has been years. Dirk never invites me. He's always been a strange vindictive child, spoiled in the cradle. No one expected him to marry. Of course, there are reasons to marry, and some of them are good ones. You've changed the wallpaper in here, I see. And the tile floor is new. Not one of them prior to you actually lived here in Luna Park, so far as I know. Remarkable. 'Dirk is getting married, Mother,' my daughters informed me, 'you'd never guess who because you don't read the newspapers.' Their idea of humor. And who's this?" In her high-heeled pumps, just perceptibly swaying, Mrs. Burnaby swept into the living room, where Chandler glanced up startled from his Tinkertoys. The chattery woman with the metallic-blond hair, vividly made-up mouth, and shiny black sunglasses loomed above him like an apparition. Her voice lifted gaily:

"Is this—Chandler? I think it is."

Ariah hurried to crouch beside Chandler, who stared at Mrs. Burnaby in wide-eyed silence. Under cover of caressing him, she tidied up his clothing and smoothed down his fine flyaway hair. "Chandler, this is Grandma Burnaby. Daddy's mommy? Say hello to—"

Mrs. Burnaby said, pleasantly but firmly, " 'Grandmother Burnaby,' if you don't mind. I don't feel like anyone's grandma, thank you."

Ariah stumbled, " 'G-Grandmother Burnaby.' Chandler, say hello."

Chandler jammed fingers into his mouth, leaned his meager little body toward his mother as if to hide in the crook of her arm, blinked up at his grandmother, and murmured, barely audibly, what sounded like "H'lo."

In her Mommy voice Ariah said, as if this were happy, astonishing news Chandler must be delighted to hear, "This lady is your Grandmother Burnaby, Chandler. You've never met Grandmother Burnaby, have you? So this is a nice surprise, she's come to see us! Darling, what do you say when people come to see you? A little louder, honey— 'Hello.' "

Chandler tried again, shrinking. "H'*lo*."

Mrs. Burnaby said, "Hello, Chandler. You're getting to be a big boy, aren't you? Almost four? Or—not quite? And what have you built there, Chandler? An ingenious little city of *sticks*?" Mrs. Burnaby was breathing audibly as if she'd just run into the room. She carried a leather handbag and a shopping bag with a number of gift-wrapped packages; she handed the shopping bag to Ariah as one might hand over a burdensome object to a servant, without looking at her. "But why are you playing down here, Chandler? You must have your own play room upstairs? Surely there's a nursery upstairs? It can't be very convenient for your parents or comfortable for you, can it, playing down here? Getting in the way? And the furniture gets in your way, Chandler, doesn't it?"

This seemed to be so urgent a question, Mrs. Burnaby spoke with such sudden concern and irritation, Ariah felt obliged to reply, as Chandler squirmed against Mommy. "Oh, Chandler plays anywhere he wants. He plays upstairs, and he plays down here. Sometimes I play with him, don't I, Chandler? And he uses the furniture, too, in very clever ways. See, Mrs. Burnaby—"

The older woman said flatly, "Please do call me 'Claudine.' As I said, everyone can't be Mrs. Burnaby at one time."

" 'C-Claudine.' "

Ariah's impulse was to say what a beautiful name, for it did truly seem to her a beautiful name, but her throat shut up, refusing.

"And you are 'Ariah.' Dirk's wife, from Troy. I've misplaced the last name, I apologize. Your father is a preacher?"

"A minister. Presbyterian."

"But he does preach, also? Or don't they preach in that sect?"

"Well, yes. But—"

"Well. At last we are meeting. I've seen snapshots of you of course, my daughters have shown me." Mrs. Burnaby paused. It was a pause that called for a smile, or a thoughtful frown. But Mrs. Burnaby's face remained inexpressive. "My dear, you look different in each snapshot; and now that I've met you, why—you're someone else."

It wasn't often that Dirk and Ariah visited with Dirk's married sisters and their families. Ariah dreaded these occasions which were usually centered around a holiday: Thanksgiving, Christmas, Easter. From the start she'd sensed the disapproval, even the dislike, of her sisters-in-law Clarice and Sylvia, and had resolved not to care. Now she dreaded to think what they might say of her, to their mother.

And how eerie it was, Claudine Burnaby looked scarcely older than her daughters who were in their early forties.

Ariah had invited her mother-in-law to please take a seat several times but each time the woman affected not to hear; she'd suggested making tea, but Mrs. Burnaby seemed to prefer to prowl about the downstairs, asking if items of furniture or wall hangings were new, and if Ariah had selected them; she professed to admire the spinet, which was heaped with lesson books; she struck several loud chords that made Ariah grit her teeth as if she were hearing fingernails scratched on a blackboard. "I used to play once. Long ago. Before the babies came." Next she drifted into the dining room, and peered through French doors at the back yard; she spent some minutes in the kitchen, as Ariah looked on anxiously from the doorway, wincing at the condition of the sink, the gas stove, the refrigerator. Ariah wanted badly to say *The cleaning woman is coming tomorrow* but though this was true, it had the air of a falsehood. She wanted to protest *Don't judge me by what you see!*

Back in the living room, Mrs. Burnaby sat in a chair close by her grandson, stiffly, like a waxworks figure with limited flexibility in its lower limbs. She tried again to engage Chandler in conversation. She lifted one of the brightly wrapped presents out of the bag as if to tease, but Chandler merely cringed against Ariah, as before. The presents Mrs. Burnaby had brought for him, both Chandler and Ariah seemed to know beforehand, by their size and relative light-ness, were unpromising. Clothes, stuffed animals. Ariah worried that Chandler might squirm out of her arms and escape. Interrupted at his play he sometimes became peevish, and sometimes strangely wounded, fearful. Especially he disliked being interrogated as Mrs. Burnaby was doing. And how strange this grandmother was, so un-like his other grandmother; regarding him through shiny, opaque black glasses and expecting him to smile at her though she wasn't smiling at him. Her sandpaper face was unlined yet sallow-skinned, and her mouth was too bright, drawn to exaggerate the fullness of her lips, or to disguise their thinness. When she spoke, it seemed as if she had marbles in her mouth she was trying not to spill out. When she leaned forward to touch his hair, Chandler shrank back. He would have skidded across the carpet on his bottom, escaping into the next room, except Mommy caught hold of him with a gay little laugh.

"He's shy, Mrs. Burnaby. He's——"

The older woman snorted in derision, as if "shy" was a code she knew how to decipher.

"Is he shy around his other grandmother? The one from Troy?"

"He's very young, Mrs. Burnaby. He won't be three until next spring."

"Three." Mrs. Burnaby sighed. "He will live into the twenty-first century. It's strange that anyone can be so young, isn't it, and be hu-man? But he was premature, they say."

Ariah let this pass. It made her uneasy that Claudine Burnaby should speak so familiarly of Chandler, as if this were her privilege.

Ariah repeated her offer of tea, or coffee, and this time Mrs. Burnaby said, "A scotch and soda. Thank you." Ariah escaped into the kitchen to prepare this drink for her mother-in-law and, for Chandler and herself, a root beer. What a relief to be alone! She could hear Mrs. Burnaby's raised, ebullient voice encouraging Chandler to open his presents, but there was no audible response from Chandler.

Why are you here. What do you want from us. Go away, back to your spider's web.

Still, Ariah thought, gamely, the woman was Chandler's grandmother, and had some rights, perhaps. And Chandler should have the opportunity of acquiring a wealthy older relative. Yes? It was a practical matter. Ariah should set her prejudices aside.

But my prejudices are me! I love my prejudices.

How powerful, the smell of Dirk's expensive scotch. Ariah considered making a scotch and soda for herself. Or having a quick swallow of undiluted scotch here in the kitchen. But, in this nerved-up state of hers something unfortunate might happen. That flamey sensation of whisky going down, so wonderful, and maybe too wonderful, making Ariah want to cuddle with Dirk, and make love. Or she'd want to cry, because she was lonely. She'd want to seek out a Roman Catholic priest (she'd never in her lifetime so much as spoken to a Roman Catholic priest) and confess her sins. *I am damned, can you save me. I drove my first husband to kill himself. And I rejoiced, that he was dead!* She wanted to call Dirk at his law office and tell his velvety-voiced secretary (who was in love with Dirk Burnaby, Ariah knew) it was an emergency, and when he came on the line she would scream at him. *Come home! This horrible woman is your mother, not mine. Help me!* She had prepared Claudine Burnaby's drink with trembling fingers and it smelled so good, Ariah took a sip, but only a small sip, from the bottle before screwing the top back on.

That sweet flamey sensation in her throat. And beyond.

Since the failed visit at Shalott in the summer of 1950, more than three years ago, there had been little contact between Claudine Burnaby and the young couple. When Chandler was born, Ariah had sent a birth announcement to Mrs. Burnaby, who responded by sending a number of lavish gifts to her grandson, including an expensive baby stroller modeled after a Victorian model, oversized, clumsy, ornate and impractical, which Dirk had hauled downstairs into the basement at once. And she'd sent gifts for Chandler at Christmas and Easter. Invariably these were store-wrapped packages addressed to

CHANDLER BURNABY, ESQ. There were no notes inside, no acknowledgment of Chandler's parents. "Maybe she thinks Chandler lives alone in his dad's old bachelor quarters," Ariah laughed. Only joking (of course) and yet Dirk, thin-skinned where his mother was concerned, took offense. "My mother isn't a well person. I've tried to accept that, and you should, too. She doesn't mean to be rude. She lives in her own airless universe, like a tortoise in its shell." But a tortoise doesn't live in an airless universe, Ariah objected, a tortoise lives with other tortoises, surely they communicate. Tortoises don't control ridiculous amounts of money they haven't earned, but only just managed to inherit. Ariah wasn't about to express this opinion to her fretful husband, however.

Ariah hated it that Dirk's sisters Clarice and Sylvia were forever reporting back to Dirk news of their mother they knew would upset him. Claudine had become a "hopeless hypochondriac." She was "pathetic, piteous." Then again, she seemed to be, at times, genuinely ill, with migraines, respiratory infections, gallstones. (Surely no one can imagine gallstones?) Claudine hoped to "manipulate" all of the Burnabys into bending to her will. There was "nothing in the slightest" wrong with her except she was "cruel and vindictive, like a Roman empress." It was the sisters' (and their husbands') belief that Claudine Burnaby was playing a game with them, and their attorneys: egging them to file a motion in district court to wrest from her power of attorney, at which point she would haul them all into court and cause a scandal. In addition to Dirk and his sisters there were a number of other Burnabys and associates involved in the family's businesses, about which Ariah knew little, and wanted to know less. Real estate, investments in local factories, a property-management company in Niagara Falls. Patents? Dirk said peevishly, "We don't require a penny more than I make as an attorney. And I don't want to discuss it." Ariah, who hadn't the slightest interest in discussing it, stood pertly on her tiptoes to kiss her husband's incensed, heated face, and wrapped her arms as far around him as she could.

Oh, she loved him! Sure did.

Thinking now, maybe she could be polite, if not charming, to Claudine Burnaby; maybe even (summoning up her Christian-love training, Sunday school classes taught indefatigably by her own mother) she could become fond of the woman. "I'll try!" One more small—very small—sip of Dirk's smooth-tasting scotch, and Ariah returned to the living room where Mrs. Burnaby had "helped" her grandson open two of his presents, which were in fact clothing, for a child younger than Chandler's age. Chandler was making only a feeble effort to pretend to be interested in these gifts, and showed little curiosity about the others. Ariah hoped to make amends. Mrs. Burnaby accepted her scotch and soda without comment, and drank thirstily, as if this were her reward, while Ariah knelt beside Chandler to share her root beer with him. But something in the air had altered, while Ariah was out of the room.

Mrs. Burnaby said in an ironic voice, "Bringing gifts, one is bringing oneself. The 'heart-on-the-sleeve' sort of thing. But the 'heart-on-the-sleeve' is not always wanted."

Ariah opened her mouth to protest. But the scotch she'd swallowed so quickly in the kitchen made her want to laugh instead.

Mrs. Burnaby continued: "I did play piano once, but not Chopin, Mozart, Beethoven. I lacked the technique. I was groomed as a debutante—I was a 'great beauty'—to use an expression of that era. You, Ariah, have been spared that, at least."

Ariah did laugh, this insult was so clumsy. Or—wasn't it an insult at all, but a backhanded compliment? Mrs. Burnaby was twirling her forefinger in her drink. "My daughters and their husbands are hoping to inherit Shalott, and the land that goes with it, but Shalott is destined for Dirk. For a son. Dirk is the only one of my children expansive enough to fit that space. Do you see? Though he has broken my heart. Though he is not reliable as a son, nor probably as a husband. As you'll discover, my dear."

Stung, Ariah said quietly, "I don't think I want to discuss my husband with you, Mrs. Burnaby. Especially in the presence of his son! You can understand that, I hope?"

Mrs. Burnaby ignored this remark, taking another large swallow of her drink. "My daughters say that you're quite the amateur pianist. *They've* heard you, evidently. I wonder if you'll play for me?"

"Well. Sometime, maybe. At the moment—"

"And you 'give lessons' in this house, as you'd 'given lessons' back in Troy? Is there some reason for this, dear?"

"For 'giving lessons'? I like to teach young students. And I—I need something to do. Beyond being just a wife and a mother."

" 'Just a wife and a mother'! What does Dirk say to that?"

"Why don't you ask him, Mrs. Burnaby? I'm sure he'll tell you."

"You taught music before you were married, they say. Before the first of your marriages. I realize you've been married more than once, Ariah. A widow at a young age. It was more common during the war. On my son's income, it seems just slightly peculiar that his wife would be 'giving' piano lessons, but perhaps I don't know what Dirk's income is any longer. He has ceased to inform me. He has his reasons, but no one knows what they are. The careless boy still owes me $12,000 but since I'm not charging him interest there's no urgency on the borrower's part to repay any loan. Oh, you look surprised, Ariah? Yes but it's pointless to ask Dirk about these matters because he simply won't tell. He has never confided in any woman. He's morbidly secretive. Playing one woman against another. Some of them would come to me, the respectable ones I mean. Broken-hearted, and of course furious though they didn't know it at the time. I was not directly involved—nor was Dirk's father, I want you to know—but there were arrangements made, 'medical' arrangements of a kind, in order that Dirk might be extricated from the potentially embarrassing situations he found himself in. And found others in. Do you follow my words, Ariah? Except for your freckles, which I find very attractive, you look disconcertingly blank."

At this moment Chandler, unless it was Ariah herself, spilled root beer onto the rug, which required frantic dabbing-at with a napkin.

Mrs. Burnaby continued, "I'm wondering if Dirk still visits Fort Erie? Has he taken you to the track, dear?"

"The—track?" Ariah knew of course that there was a horse-racing track at Fort Erie, a locally famous track; but Mrs. Burnaby's question stunned her.

"I see he has not? Well."

By this time pulses were beating painfully in Ariah's head. The scotch, so smooth going down, was making her stomach queasy. She felt as if her elegantly dressed mother-in-law in the black velvet hat and opaque sunglasses had leaned over languidly to poke her in the breastbone. And, to her horror, she saw that Chandler was absorbing it all. Usually bored by adult conversation, the child was listening now, peering open-mouthed at his grandmother. "Honey, why don't you go into the other room, for just a minute? Mommy will be right there—"

"No, no. That isn't necessary, my dear. I'll be leaving now."

Ariah stumbled after Claudine Burnaby, in the woman's perfumy wake. Lacking the presence of mind to retrieve Mrs. Burnaby's cape, so Mrs. Burnaby retrieved it herself from the front closet. "Please give my love to Dirk. I don't know when I will be leaving the Island again. There seems so little reason, and so much effort. And my health is frankly poor." At the door, Mrs. Burnaby extended her gloved hand another time, not to take Ariah's hand but simply to nudge it, in farewell. In a lowered voice she said, "My dear, don't be anxious. Your secret will die with me."

"My s-secret? What secret?"

"Why, that child isn't Dirk's son. You know it, and I know it. He isn't my grandson. But, as I say, don't be anxious. I'm not a vindictive woman."

Ariah stared speechless as her mother-in-law, in impractically high-heeled pumps, made her way down the front walk, joined by the chauffeur who hurried to assist her into the rear of the limousine.

When she returned to the living room there was Chandler absorbed again with his Tinkertoys. Beside him the pile of gift-wrapped presents lay ignored.

Ariah took the bottle of scotch upstairs with her, where Dirk would find her later that evening in their bedroom, in their yet-un-made bed, when he returned from work.

The Little Family

1

*I*t was only logical, wasn't it?

Knowing that your first-born might be snatched from you at any time by an Act of God, you must have a second child. And if you fail to love your first-born as much as a mother should love, you certainly should have a second child, to make things right.

"Though some things probably can't ever be made right."

By the same logic, if your first two babies are boys, you are compelled to try again in the hope of having a daughter.

A daughter. "My life would be complete, then. God, I would ask You for nothing more, I promise."

It was only logical. Knowing that your husband might one day leave you, or be snatched from you, you must have several children at least.

It was only logical. Ariah Burnaby was a logical woman. She would become, through the years, a woman who expected the worst, to relieve herself of the anxiety of hope. She would become a woman of calm, fatalistic principles, anticipating her life with the equanimity of a weather forecaster. She would risk (she supposed she knew this, for at her most neurotic she remained an intelligent woman) driving her husband from her by her expectation that he would one day "vanish" from her life.

Even as she clutched him tight in her arms. Yet never tight enough.

It was only logical wasn't it? Yet how many times during the next decade would the strangled prayer leap from her who did not believe in prayer.

"God, You would not be so cruel—would You? Please let me be pregnant this time. Oh, please!"

It was a logical wish. Yet it would require years.

"You do love me, Dirk? Don't you?"

In her wistful voice she inquired. In the night, in the stupor of half-sleep when we utter things we would not utter by day.

He was too mired in sleep to reply. Except with his body curving about her, heavy, warm, consoling. She lay in the crook of his arm plotting. Another baby!

They never loved each other less (at least, Ariah believed that this was so) but they made love less frequently with the passage of time. And less passionately. They surprised each other less often in their lovemaking. There must have been a day, an hour, when they made love during the daytime for the final time; when they made love impulsively somewhere other than their big, comfortable bed for the final time; when Ariah pressed her anguished mouth against Dirk's sweaty chest to keep from crying out too loudly.

And once Ariah made the decision *she must never, never drink again* after that terrible visit from Claudine Burnaby, not even a single glass of her favorite red wine at dinner, not even a single glass of *Dom Pérignon* to celebrate a precious anniversary, the sweet yearning sensation in her loins faded as if it had never been and she began to embrace her husband with less desire, and sometimes with no desire at all except the grim female desire to conceive, to become pregnant, to have a baby.

To have a baby.

Maybe it wasn't logical, such a wish. But it would appear so in retrospect, after the children were born.

For in retrospect, the most random and desperate toss of the dice can be made to seem inevitable.

How many years. "Yet I didn't doubt. Never."

And so I was born. And why?

2

A MIRACLE! Ariah at last conceived a second child, and gave birth to him in September 1958. She was thirty-seven years old.

"Almost too late. But not quite!"

This pregnancy, Ariah would recall as suffused with happiness as with an unwavering golden light. How unlike the nightmare of the first pregnancy, long ago! Royall Burnaby was born exactly on schedule, a healthy seven-pound nine-months' baby with his daddy's unmistakable flaxen hair and cobalt-blue eyes. Born to his mother's unbidden thought *This one is truly ours. This baby, we can love.*

Born at a time when his daddy was riding the crest of a booming economy in Niagara Falls.

Born at a time in history when it seemed that the very universe was expanding, to infinity.

If Ariah's marriage was beginning to "drift"—"fray"—these were words that came to mind, less cruel than others—the birth of Royall Burnaby would make things right, for a while.

"Now you truly can't leave me, Dirk, can you?—now we have two of them." So Ariah teased, swiping roughly at her eyes.

Dirk winced. He never knew what to make of his wife's teasing except he didn't like it, much. But he knew better than to speak sharply to her.

Lifting Royall kicking and flailing in both Daddy's big hands. Lifting Royall who was a robust little dynamo of a baby, already defining himself as a distinct personality. And very different from Chandler. Ariah, watching them, knew that Dirk could not be thinking *This one is mine, my son* yet the expression in his face of rapt, wounded love suggested exactly this.

The 1950's. "Boom times."

It would be an era, local historians claimed, like the 1850's in Niagara Falls. But where tourism was developed in the 1850's, industrial Niagara Falls would be developed in the 1950's. By 1960, the population of the area would double to more than 100,000.

By 1970, the area would boast the highest concentration of chemical factories in the United States.

Inland from the Niagara River and the fantastical mist-shrouded Gorge the city of Niagara Falls and its outlying suburbs was aggressively developed. Royall Burnaby's world.

If there was another, Royall would not know of it.

Ariah had but a dim, vague notion of what was happening, for she took little interest in "local politics." (In fact, she took very little interest in politics. Why bother, it was a man's world.) Yet even Ariah came to realize how open land, wooded land, farmland at the edge of the city was being excavated, leveled, made over into industrial sites covering hundreds—no, it must have been thousands—of acres. "What happened, Daddy? Where are we?"—so Chandler asked, baffled, as on their Sunday drives Daddy drove the little family out north along the river, or inland toward Lockport. (Chandler was interested in the Erie Canal, and in the great locks at Lockport.) But familiar sights were becoming unrecognizable, torn up and jumbled like a Tinkertoy earthquake.

"Chandler, you're looking at *progress*."

So Dirk said, gesturing through the car windshield. In the back seat, Ariah held Royall on her lap, cooing and singing in his ear.

It was a profound fact: raw earth was becoming cement. Trees were toppled, sawed into pieces and hauled away. Giant cranes and bulldozers were everywhere. The old two-lane road to Lockport was expanded to three lanes. Highways appeared through fields, overnight. There were new bridges, brisk brutal gunmetal-gray. Ariah observed in distaste, and at a distance. The "progress" was taking place miles away from Luna Park, why should she care? Luna Park was in the area of Rainbow Avenue and 2nd Street, the oldest residential neighborhood in the city; the changes were all to the east and north, beyond Hyde Park, out Buffalo Avenue, Veterans Road, Swann Road, in the area of 100th Street and beyond, which might have been on the moon so far as Ariah was concerned.

A no-man's-land, claimed for factories, warehouses, employee parking lots. Auto parts manufacturers, refrigerating unit manufacturers, chemical factories, fertilizer factories. There were gypsum plants. Tanneries and leather goods factories. Detergent, bleach, disinfectant and industrial cleanser factories. Asphalt, asbestos. Pesticides, herbicides. Nabisco, Swann Chemical, Dow Chemical, United Carborundum, NiagChem, Occidental Chemical ("OxyChem"). Giant power stations were being erected south along the river with the much-publicized intention of "harnessing" as much as one-third of the water power of The Falls. Ariah read in the *Niagara Gazette* of hundreds of prime acreage sold to Niagara Hydro by an entity called Burnaby, Inc., and was so shocked she let the newspaper slip to the floor.

"My God, is that us? Are we rich?"

The possibility filled her with dread.

At this time Royall was a five-month baby, brimming with appetite and energy, nursing at Ariah's breast. Chandler, seven years old, a slightly clumsy child made shyer and clumsier by the arrival of a baby brother, hung back in the nursery doorway, worriedly watching his mother. Seeing her look of surprise and distress he asked what was wrong and Ariah said quickly, "Oh, honey. N-Nothing! Nothing is wrong."

Since the birth of Royall, Ariah seemed often to be disconcerted by Chandler's presence. She loved him of course but had a tendency to forget him. In the confusion of sleep-deprivation she thought of him as *the other*, temporarily forgetting his name.

Ariah had vowed not to love Chandler less than Royall. Yet this vow, too, she tended to forget.

Ariah wasn't a superstitious woman but she felt a pang of something like terror. For it seemed dangerous somehow to be "harnessing" The Falls. Diverting millions of tons of beautiful rushing river water, converting it into electricity for "consumers."

Hauling Royall into the bedroom, where there was a telephone, she called Dirk at his law office. Oh, why was Dirk never home! Never home when she needed him. The velvety-voiced receptionist told her coolly that "Mr. Burnaby" was away at City Hall, at a meeting with the mayor and the Niagara County Zoning Board of which he was a new member. (Was Ariah supposed to know this? Had she forgotten?) "And what is the number there? Please." The velvety-voiced receptionist sounded reluctant, but provided Mrs. Burnaby with the number of the mayor's office; the recently elected mayor of Niagara Falls was Tyler ("Spooky") Wenn; Ariah believed that she had a right to call her husband, since Dirk so rarely called home now, as he'd done when they were newlyweds, and when Chandler had been an infant. Ariah's hand was shaking. Royall, squirming on Mommy's lap, flailing his little fists, was getting upset; no doubt he'd soaked his diaper again. Ariah bit at her thumbnail deliberating whether to call Wenn's office and demand to speak with her husband at once, saying it was a family emergency; this was a stratagem Ariah had used in the past, perhaps once or twice too often; but sometimes she couldn't help herself, alone with two young children and prone to emotions that alarmed her.

She'd been happy those nine months, pregnant with Royall. They hadn't known it was a boy of course. Ariah was crazy with love for Royall but couldn't help thinking that her happiness would be complete if she'd had a daughter instead.

"Ariah? Hello? What is it?"

Dirk's voice was loud and urgent in her ear. Ariah couldn't remember having called him. Royall was gasping for breath, preparing to bellow. Hurriedly she pushed her breast into his mouth, her sore, chafed nipple that looked as if someone mean had been pinching it, and Royall began to suck.

"Ariah? Darling? Is something wrong?"

He must love her, then. Ariah heard the rising desperation in his voice.

Ariah fumbled with the receiver and tried to speak but her words spilled out like pebbles. She knew there was a specific reason she'd called Dirk out of a meeting with the mayor of Niagara Falls but damned if she could remember. She said, "There was a problem—the baby wasn't breathing right—but he's breathing now, he's fine now."

"Honey, I can't hear you. Is something wrong with the baby?"

"He wasn't breathing right. But now he is breathing right. I'm sorry to have disturbed you. I didn't know what to do."

"He's all right now? Royall is all right?"

"Royall is fine. Listen."

Ariah held the receiver to Royall's damp little mouth and poked him into gooing, chortling. One of his sounds was a high-pitched noise like a peacock's shriek.

"Ariah? Is that—Royall? Is Royall all right?" Dirk sounded dazed, like a blind man trying to see.

"Darling, Royall is fine. He's the most wonderful baby in the world."

"He's all right? You're sure?"

Ariah laughed angrily. "I'm sure. If you're so doubtful of me, come home and see for yourself."

There was a brief startled pause.

"Well. You scared the hell out of me for a moment." Dirk spoke carefully, not wanting to upset her more. Ariah knew: her cautious lawyer-husband didn't want to upset his unstable wife. In a framed photograph in Dirk's study there was a faded daguerreotype of his notorious grandfather Reginald Burnaby, a tightrope walker captured in the act of crossing the steamy Niagara Gorge, holding a twelve-foot pole across his shoulders for balance. Ariah understood the precariousness of that balance.

As Royall sucked and tugged at her teat, Ariah felt a sudden discomforting stab of something raw, wet, yearning at the pit of her belly, and moaned aloud. "Oh, Dirk. I miss you. Come home and make love with me, darling."

"Ariah? What?"

"I miss you, Dirk. I want to make love with you. The way we used to. Before the babies. Remember?"

There was another pause. Ariah could hear her husband's quickened, alarmed breathing.

"I'm in a meeting, darling. It's an important meeting. If I'm not there for the vote, Christ knows what will happen. So I'd better say goodbye, Ariah, if you and the baby are all right?" Dirk paused, as if trying to think of something. "And Chandler?"

Ariah laughed at the way Royall was sucking vigorously, causing her pain at the breast, and that aching aroused sensation between her legs. "Your son is quite the lover, Dirk. You'll be sorry." Milk leaked out of Royall's tiny fierce mouth and ran down his chin. Watery milk it seemed to Ariah, thin as skim milk. Maybe it wasn't good milk. Good mother's milk. Maybe it was deficient in vitamins. Dirk was saying something, asking her something, Ariah couldn't hear over the sucking gurgling noise of the baby. In the midst of her confusion she remembered suddenly why she'd called Dirk. "That front-page article in the *Gazette*? The hydro-power plants? Why is our name involved?"

Quickly Dirk said, "Honey, that deal has nothing to do with us. It's a branch of the family I'm not connected with. Not actively. Don't be upset. There's nothing to it."

"Nothing to it. I see."

"I hold some shares in Burnaby, Inc. But I'm not involved, I have my own separate life. My own income."

Ariah was becoming so aroused, so uncomfortable, she dared to dislodge her breast from the baby's eager sucking, and for a stunned moment the baby simply continued to suck at the air, his pudding-face blank. His small moist cobalt-blue eyes with their fine, pale lashes seemed to have no focus: here was sheer appetite, thwarted. At the other end of the line the baby's father was saying he had to return to his meeting, he'd be home around ten, he hoped. "You and the children are all right, yes? I love you."

"Well, I hate you."

Ariah laughed angrily, and hung up the phone before Dirk could explain to her why he'd be late again that night, having dinner at Mario's or the Boat Club or the Rainbow Grand Terrace with his rich business friends.

Chandler had picked up the *Gazette* pages, and was eagerly reading the article about Niagara Hydro. The child was a precocious reader, he seemed to have taught himself by the time he began school and was now, according to his teacher, the most advanced reader in second grade. But he read often in poor lighting, and Ariah was concerned he would weaken his eyes. He said, "Mommy, is this our name— 'Burnaby'? Or somebody else?"

"Somebody else."

By this time Royall was screaming with fury. Red-faced as a demon. Ariah could feel his temperature rising and had a frightened thought of a lobster being boiled, turning red. She was terrified of him suddenly. Why had she wanted another baby so badly, when she was too old? When her husband might leave her at any time? She screamed, and dropped Royall's agitated weight onto—what was it?—the edge of the bed. It was a cushioned surface and yet, kicking and thrashing in infant rage, Royall somehow bounced, and rolled over onto the floor; striking the carpeted floor about equally on his padded diaper bottom and at the base of his skull. For a fraction of an instant there was silence in the bedroom, the boiled-looking baby had ceased to breathe, then he filled his tiny lungs with a tremendous intake of air and began to cry, shriek, bellow until Ariah pressed her hands over her ears, destroyed.

Seven-year-old Chandler hurried to pick up his thrashing baby brother, and lay him carefully on the bed where he continued to bellow without pause. Ariah backed off, barefoot, into a corner of the room. She could feel milk leaking from both her teats, running in rivulets down her hot skin; she was naked inside her grubby bathrobe. Chandler said earnestly, "We could take him back, Mommy, couldn't we? Where you got him?"

3

NOW THERE WERE two little boys in the Burnaby household, and Ariah felt more lonely than ever: lonely for a daughter.

This yearning began soon after Royall was weaned. Oh, she missed a baby at her breast! Begging *Give me a daughter. A daughter to redeem me, to make things right.*

For it seemed to Ariah that she'd failed, somehow. She was a female (obviously!) and yet somehow not a womanly woman, not a good woman.

So emotional did Ariah become, as months passed, months and years, and she was so in terror of coming to the end of her childbearing life, that Ariah nearly confided in her own mother. "Did you have these feelings too, Mother? Did you want a daughter?" But Mrs. Littrell merely smiled, and shook her head. "Why, I 'wanted' whoever God sent me, Ariah. And so did your father."

A smug fool. Ariah hated her.

(No, Ariah wasn't "close" with her mother, though the Littrells drove frequently to Niagara Falls to visit at 7 Luna Park, and, at least once a year, the Burnabys drove to Troy for one or another "festive" occasion. Ariah gritted her teeth and played her role as a Daughter who'd become a Mother, to her parents' approval. She supposed that Mrs. Littrell believed that she and Ariah were "close" but it was a misunderstanding on the older woman's part. Ariah had talked it over with Dirk rationally: "Chandler and Royall need grandparents, and these are devoted grandparents. So I think we should continue to see them, for the boys' sake." Dirk appeared shocked by this casual argument. "But I thought we all liked one another, Ariah? I thought we'd agreed we were all friends?" Ariah shook her head, bemused by her affable husband. "Of course we 'agreed,' darling. I always agree. But it isn't so. We do what we do for the sake of the children."

(At least there was no possibility of a misunderstanding on Claudine Burnaby's part. There was a woman who had cut herself off completely from Ariah. What a relief!)

Two little boys in the Burnaby household. One, the younger, so clearly took after his daddy; the other, the older, possibly resembled his mother. In temperament, at least.

Chandler did very well in school. His grades were high, but he never seemed satisfied. Even in grade school he was always turning in extra-credit assignments to his teachers, usually on scientific subjects like the Ice Age, woolly mamoths and saber-toothed tigers, Neanderthal Man, Haley's Comet, the Solar System. (For a replica of the Solar System, Chandler designed an ingenious wire-collage contraption in which the sun was a grapefruit, and the planets smaller fruits culminating in a grape, which was Pluto. For a replica of the orbit of Haley's Comet, Chandler designed a yet more ingenious mobile contraption in which the comet was a spark plug and the planet Earth a painted rubber ball. For this, Chandler won a prize at the Niagara County Science Fair, competing with children ten years and younger.) Dirk was proud of Chandler, and Ariah supposed she was, too. But the child annoyed her so! He had not a shred of musical talent, though he was always at the piano, in emulation of Ariah's younger pupils. Ariah pressed her hands over her ears begging him to cease: "Honey, my pupils don't play any better than you, but at least, listening to them, Mommy gets paid." Chandler's shirts were often misbuttoned, even when Ariah could swear she'd buttoned them herself, with care. He came back from school looking like a street urchin, with shabby clothes, old dried food stains on his trousers, when Ariah had sent him off in freshly laundered, pressed trousers. His shoes were always muddy, it seemed, even in fair weather. His shoelaces were often untied, he tripped on his own disproportionately long feet, fell down stairs and opened a terrible cut on his chin, which turned by degrees into a white, fossil-like scar. In this climate of perpetual shifting skies, sudden rains, sleet, hailstones, where healthy natives seem to have developed antibodies for colds and flu, poor Chandler was always coming down with respiratory ailments and stomach flu. He ran sudden fevers out of sheer perversity, knowing how his mother was terrified of meningitis and polio. Yet, with a temperature of 102.2°F, Chandler insisted upon trekking eight blocks to school in the rain because he feared "falling behind"; he put up such a protest, Ariah had to give in. "But if you come down with meningitis or polio, Chandler Burnaby, Esquire, you can take yourself to the emergency room, and you can dig your own little grave, and on your tombstone you can carve: SMART ALECK. I wash my hands of you."

Dirk chided Ariah for fussing over the boy too much, making him self-conscious about his health, which was fine for him to say, he and Royall were brimming with health. Ariah protested, "Who else is going to fuss over that child except his mother? Who else gives the slightest damn whether that child lives or dies except his mother? Because his mother is the one who will be blamed if he doesn't. Doesn't live." Dirk laughed at her, she was funny as Lucille Ball on TV, another redhead but not so scrappy and sharp-witted as Ariah. "Oh, Ariah, what is going to happen to Chandler? He's a perfectly healthy good-natured little boy. A little scrawny in the chest, maybe." Ariah flared up. "Are you blaming me that your son is underweight? Malnourished? He doesn't eat, his nose is always in a book. Maybe he has a tapeworm."

Worse, Chandler was an absentminded child. While Royall fixed you intensely in his gaze, smiled and bobbed his head and began to "talk" at twenty months, and by three had learned to shake his parents' visitors' hands and ask how they were, Chandler often drifted about in a haze of interior thinking; you could all but hear the machinery of his brain whir. He wandered into the city or to the Niagara Gorge instead of coming home directly from school, and was returned home in an NFPD cruiser, or by strangers with out-of-state license plates. Young children unaccompanied by adults were not allowed along the river pathways of the Gorge, especially they were forbidden to cross onto Goat Island, but of course Chandler Burnaby turned up at exactly these places; afterward, he would say he was "just exploring. Seeing what's there." Beginning in fourth grade he turned up downtown at the Niagara Falls Public Library where librarians would discover him not in the children's room where he belonged but in the adult stacks, "skulking" amid books "not meant for a child's eyes." Naturally, his embarrassed mother would be summoned to fetch him home. Ariah was furious with the child but supposed she saw the humor of the situation. "If you're going to run away from home, mister, you'll have to go a lot farther than downtown." Chandler apologized but so softly and vaguely, Ariah knew he was scarcely listening to his own words.

She was most exasperated when she caught him reading after he was supposed to be asleep. Chandler would make a little tent of his bedclothes, and hunch inside it with a flashlight, reading and surely damaging his eyes. "If you need glasses someday, don't come belly-aching to me. And if you go blind, mister, you can get a tin cup and go begging out on the street. But don't come begging to *me*."

Chandler cringed wide-eyed at her fury. But at once Ariah smiled, and grabbed him to her bosom. "Hey, kid: c'mon. Mommy loves you."

4

A daughter. Amid these rapacious males. And our little family will be complete.
Ariah waited.

5

"RIDICULOUS! Worse than fairy tales."

From time to time, pushing the baby's stroller in Luna Park, pausing to talk beneath the tall splendid plane trees with other mothers or nursemaids, in her bright chattery Lucille Ball manner, that masked Ariah Burnaby's secret disdain not only for the company she kept at such times (while her gregarious attorney-husband Dirk Burnaby kept a very different company) but for her phony, altered personality, Ariah heard tales of the Widow-Bride of The Falls. But no one recalled the name of the beautiful young red-haired bride who had searched at the Niagara Gorge for seven days and seven nights for her lost, doomed bridegroom who had plunged over the Horseshoe Falls to his death. No one could say with certainty if the tragedy had occurred a few years ago, twenty-five years ago, one hundred years ago.

There was a young Hungarian nursemaid who assured Ariah that the ghost of the Widow-Bride still kept her vigil. "On misty nights. And only in June. They say, if you see her, don't speak to her because she will run away. But if you are quiet, she might come to *you*."

Ariah laughed. A sliver of ice seemed to enter her heart, this was so absurd.

Ariah laughed, hiding her face. In his handsome baby buggy, little Royall stirred and kicked.

Politely, Ariah asked the Hungarian girl if she'd ever seen the Widow-Bride, herself. The girl shook her head of thick plaited braids vigorously. "I am Catholic, and we are not told to believe in ghosts. It is a sin to believe in ghosts. If I saw a ghost, I would shut my eyes. If I opened them and the ghost was still there, I would run away, fast."

The girl grinned and shivered, this was all so real to her.

Ariah said, gently skeptical, as if she were speaking to a very young child, "But why, Lena? Why run away? The poor Widow-Bride is dead, isn't she?"

The girl said earnestly, "The ghost is dead, yes, but she is not where she belongs. So she is a damned soul. That is what a ghost is. So I would run away from her, Mrs. Burnaby, oh yes!"

Ariah had to admit, she'd run away, too. If she had the option.

Chandler came home from Luna Park Elementary with tales that made Ariah's skin creep.

A long time ago, the Onigara Indians made sacrifices in the Niagara River above the Gorge. Each spring a twelve-year-old girl was brought to the rapids above Goat Island, locally known as the Deadline, and placed in a canoe in her bridal vestments, and a priest of the tribe blessed her, and released her, and the canoe was propelled to the Horseshoe Falls, and over; the girl was then the bride of the Thunder God who lived in The Falls.

Chandler said, excitedly, "That's why there are ghosts in The Falls. In the mist you can see them, sometimes. That's why people want to throw themselves into The Falls, it's the Thunder God. He's hungry."

Ariah shuddered. Of course it was true. Or had been true, at one time.

But she turned a derisive face on her impressionable young son. You'd have thought she was furious with *him*. "Bullshit. It's not so romantic and 'mythic' if you know that these so-called sacrifices were probably just kids nobody wanted—orphans, or weird crippled kids. Expendable females." Ariah spoke with passion. Chandler gaped at her. An adult's intelligence turned ferociously upon a nine-year-old, a howitzer blasting a hummingbird to bits. Yet there are hummingbirds who are pests, and deserve to be blasted to bits. " 'Ritual sacrifice'—'ritual murder'—'becoming the bride of the Thunder God'—these are fancy ways of talking about just plain *murder*. Ignorant, primitive, superstitious. Like marrying off a twelve-year-old-virgin to an actual man, except worse. The God-damned Indian 'braves' should have been tossed into the Niagara River, too. See how brave they'd be, the bastards. They could have a big powwow with their buddy the Thunder God down in the Whirlpool." Ariah made a spitting gesture, she was so riled-up and disgusted.

It was uncanny: Chandler's eyes had no color at all. Sometimes they were the glinting no-color of fish scales, sometimes a swampy muddy brown, or brown-green. When Ariah looked into his face, at times like these, the very irises of Chandler's eyes seemed to shrink. (Oh, she knew. He was becoming near-sighted. To spite her.) "Honey, see? Mommy is just trying to train you. Not to believe the bullshit you'll be hearing through your life."

Chandler nodded, as a kicked dog might nod. At least the kid was learning. He was learning not to just get straight A's in grade school but to be thoughtful, skeptical. He was learning to take after his mother who was damned.

6

THESE WERE HAPPY TIMES. Ariah knew.

Warm spring days she took Royall outdoors. In Luna Park, in Prospect Park, and along the misty Niagara Gorge which the toddler seemed to find endlessly thrilling. Already by the age of ten months Royall could "walk" when Ariah held his hand tightly. Proudly they circled the Victorian gazebo at the center of Luna Park, the flaxen-haired chubby little boy staggering and lunging and shrieking with excitement beside his mother who never ceased to murmur words of encouragement to him. "Yes, honey. Like that. Very good. Oops! Now up on your feet again, Royall. What a big, good boy Royall is, how well he can walk." Royall's eyes lit up, no exaggeration, when one or another observer applauded his efforts, clapping and praising him.

Soon, the other mothers and nursemaids of Luna Park knew Royall by name.

Royall, the beautiful, blessed Burnaby boy.

Ariah's heart swelled with love of the child. Now he'd outgrown his demanding infancy, now he was developing a distinctive personality, she felt a tenderness for him she'd never quite felt for his older brother. Where Chandler had seemed to cringe at the world as if overwhelmed by its profusion, Royall gazed and blinked and laughed and invited more.

Ariah was in awe of him. This child seemed to know the world was friendly to him. Adored him. Always going to offer him more.

Leaving the house with Royall on their morning expedition, Ariah sometimes heard Chandler call after them, "Mommy? Can I come, too?" She'd forgotten it was summer, and Chandler didn't have school. Or she'd forgotten that Chandler was in the house. She felt a pang of guilt and said at once, "Of course, honey. We didn't think you would be interested. You can push the stroller." For as long as Royall's strength held, he walked beside Ariah; when he tired, Ariah strapped him into the stroller and pushed. Unless she'd scheduled a piano lesson, she was in no hurry to return to 7 Luna Place. If the telephone or the doorbell rang in her absence, what did it matter?

Dirk complained it was difficult to reach Ariah, sometimes. She'd decided she didn't want "help" on the premises. Not even a nanny to help with Royall, no thank you. Ariah was all the nanny Royall required.

It was a coolly bright autumn day when Ariah felt herself drawn to Prospect Park. Walking with her eager little puppy Royall who lunged forward and had to be restrained; had to be carried in Ariah's strong arms across streets, and up hills, as Chandler capably pushed the stroller. They were Mommy and two sons. Missing was Daddy, and the little girl.

Juliet, Ariah would name her. Was there ever so beautiful a name as *Juliet*?

In high school, Ariah was convinced that her life had begun to go wrong when her parents baptized her with such a ridiculous name. Some old maiden aunt of her father's, long deceased.

They hadn't been walking half an hour before both the heels of Ariah's feet began to blister. Damn, she'd worn impractical shoes. In the grass, she could walk barefoot; on pavement, she was wary of tossed-down, still smoldering cigarette butts, pebbles and bits of glass. And there were such swarms of tourists near the railings overlooking the river, she was in danger of being trod upon. So Ariah sat at a picnic table with Royall while Chandler ran to fetch them root beers. It was their custom to have root beers on these expeditions. They were close by the churning upper rapids, near the pedestrian bridge to Goat Island. Newlyweds were having their photographs taken on the bridge. A family of barn-sized individuals, laughing and talking in midwestern accents, trooped by. Ariah wanted to warn them not to underestimate The Falls, just because it was midday, and noisy. Beneath the noise, you could hear something finer, like a vibration. If you looked carefully, you could see phantom rainbows winking and glittering above the river. Ariah shivered, and smiled. The roaring of the American Falls, close by, seemed to enter her soul.

This is your happy time. Thirty-nine years old. You won't have these beautiful young children forever.

(Had God spoken to Ariah, this time? She thought so. But she couldn't be sure.)

Well, it was so. Children grew up fast. Nearly everyone Ariah met socially, friends and business associates of Dirk's, had much older children than the Burnabys did. Some of these children were virtually grown.

Ariah thought how disapproving these people would be, how they'd look upon Dirk Burnaby's eccentric wife with distaste, if they knew how badly she wanted another baby. Oh, yet another!

Chandler returned with their cold root beers. But Royall was too excited to drink more than a few sips. Brimming with energy, he began to run in circles in the grass, shrieked and stumbled and fell and picked himself up, and ran in another circle, tireless. His fine flaxen hair glowed in the pale sunlight. His perfectly shaped, chubby little arms pumped, helping to keep his precarious balance. How purely instinctual this child was, fascinating to watch. The flame of life seemed always at the surface of Royall's being; his skin was heated with the hard, firm coursing of his blood. No one could mistake this child for a little girl, despite his wavy hair. Ariah recalled how, the previous evening, she'd given him his bedtime bath; how he'd teased her by splashing water onto the floor, and onto her. Washing him gently she'd found herself, not for the first time, dreamily contemplating his soft, small penis that floated in the soapy water. So clean, perfectly shaped. And the tiny sacs of flesh that cushioned it. (Did these sacs, in the sexually mature male, contain the seed?—the sperm? Ariah didn't know enough about male anatomy. She might have asked Dirk, at one time.) Strange that Royall had the potential to disturb his mother, as Chandler had not. For Chandler's sex was but an appendage to his thin, awkward body, a body that reminded Ariah of her own, while, in Royall, sex was the center of his compact little body. Sex was the point of his being, or would be one day. His father's virility, reborn. But strange and disturbing, in a boy so young.

"Royall! You'll put yourself in a fever."

At last Royall tired of running in circles and barking like a deranged puppy, but still he was restless, pushing at Ariah when she tried to cradle him in her arms to nap on the park bench with her. No, no! Royall wasn't ready for a nap. So Chandler offered to push him in the stroller around the park, and Ariah strapped him in, and adjusted his little visored baseball cap, for, like his daddy, Royall was susceptible to sunburn; Ariah warned Chandler not to push his brother too fast, not to go too far and above all don't go anywhere downhill. She called after them, "And don't get lost. D'you hear?" But the roaring of The Falls toward which Chandler was moving was so loud, already he was beyond hearing.

Within seconds Chandler and the stroller disappeared amid a flock of camera-laden tourists, heading for the *Maid of the Mist* cruise. In the near distance, a high-flying American flag whipped in the wind at the edge of the Gorge.

Thanks to God, these blessings.

Ariah sighed, yawned, stretched like a big lazy cat and lay on the park bench in the sun. Wriggled her bare, white toes. Oh, this was heavenly. She deserved this. So tired! Comets danced against her shut eyelids.

The cement path beside the river was wet from spray. But there were guard railings of course. Mingling with tourist families, Chandler and the stroller would appear to belong to them. No one would identify him as a lone nine-year-old pushing a younger brother in a stroller, and Mommy nowhere near. Such park regulations didn't apply to a child as mature and canny as Chandler.

Ariah felt herself drifting into a light sleep. She was in a canoe above the rapids, in an only moderately swift current. From time to time she heard people passing near, raised voices and laughter. A language she couldn't identify, was it French? (Were these strangers looking at her? Making rude comments about her? A freckle-faced redheaded woman with austere features appearing slender and young as a girl until you drew closer, and saw the streaked hair and fine white lines in her face. The tendons in her white throat. Yet this woman was smiling, was she?) Thinking of how many years ago, more than nine years. She'd been brought to Niagara Falls as a naive, trusting bride. Knowing nothing of love, sex. Knowing nothing of men.

Since that time, since the death of her young first husband whom she could no longer remember clearly, and did not wish to remember, Ariah had received several letters from his mother, Mrs. Edna Erskine. Ariah had not answered these letters. To her shame, she hadn't even opened them. She had not dared. The last letter, received when she'd been pregnant with Royall, had so frightened her, like a missive from the dead, she'd printed on the envelope RETURN TO SENDER ADDRESSEE UNKNOWN and dropped it in a mailbox.

She'd told Dirk nothing of course. Like all wives she lived her secret, silent life unknown to her husband, as to her children.

Her husband! Dirk Burnaby was her husband, not *the other*.

Yet there were times like these, drifting helplessly into sleep, Ariah seemed not clearly to know who *the husband* was.

No, certainly her husband was Dirk Burnaby. A man far more real than Ariah herself, if you measured his height, his girth, his position in the world.

Ariah had not told Dirk about the terrible visit from Claudine. Not even to explain her agitation afterward. The alcoholic stupor he'd found her in. Nor had she spoken to him of Claudine's accusations. That Dirk was in debt to her, that he gambled, that he'd had mistresses for whom "medical arrangements" had been made . . . *A daughter. Give me a daughter before it's too late.*

Lying in Dirk's strong fleshy arms the previous night. She'd been awake, waiting for him. Oh, he'd come home late: past midnight. And he'd been drinking. Ariah knew, and Ariah forgave. Her husband was troubled about something, and Ariah took solace in knowing he wouldn't involve her. For Dirk Burnaby, too, must have his private life. His secret life. And his work as an attorney, of very little interest to Ariah, was much of that life. She wasn't the woman he should have married, clearly. She'd seen his face when, in the company of his friends and their wives, she, Mrs. Burnaby, made one of her coolly enigmatic remarks, or, more baffling still, said nothing at all. Ariah was capable of sitting at a dinner party, staring into space and drumming her fingers on the table (in fact, Ariah was practicing piano, on an invisible keyboard) while conversation swirled about her. At l'Isle Grand Country Club, the last time she'd gone, Ariah had drifted away from the others in their party and located a piano in a ballroom, sat and played quietly, dreamily, her girlhood pieces she'd loved, and for which she'd been extravagantly praised, the first movement of the *Moonlight Sonata*, a minuet by the young Mozart, mazurkas by Chopin of surpassing beauty, and Ariah had so lost herself she'd forgotten where she was; and was rudely awakened by the sudden mocking applause of Dirk's friends Wenn and Howell who stood grinning behind her. Fortunately, Dirk came into the room at that point, too. Ariah, hurt, humiliated, had simply fled. *But I will get my revenge on you. Someday.*

The night before, she'd been in one of her weepy moods. Not unhappy, just weepy. She knew from the other mothers in the park (most of them much younger than Ariah!) that everyone had "weepy" moods from time to time, if you're female it's allowed. In fact, Ariah was happy. Lying in Dirk's arms she wept out of sheer happiness. Why? Their sons were such beautiful children. No one deserves such beautiful children. "But, darling," Ariah whispered, burrowing her face into the collar of Dirk's flannel pajamas, "we need a daughter, too. A little girl. Oh, we can't give up! We need a daughter to make our family complete." Ariah was holding herself rigid, trying not to tremble, as Dirk prepared to speak. For they'd discussed this subject many times. As a prelude to lovemaking in a way very different from the lovemaking of the earlier years of their marriage, when they'd been spontaneous, playful, ardent. Now, when they made love, Ariah clutched at Dirk with an air of determination, desperation. Her strained face showed the outline of the skull beneath. Her mouth was anguished, her eyes rolled back in her head. At such times Dirk seemed almost fearful of her. A man in fear of a woman who happened to be his wife. He'd sighed, and stroked Ariah's warm forehead as if to placate her. So deeply in love with Ariah, he could barely see her any longer; as one is unable to see one's own mirror reflection, pushed too close. "Of course I would love a daughter, too. But do you think it's wise to try? At our age? And what if we had another son?" Ariah stiffened. Ariah laughed. "My age, you mean." She spoke lightly to disguise her hurt.

In the morning she would say, kissing him ardently, "Another son, why not? We'll have a basketball team."

Ariah smiled, drifting downriver in the sunshine. Thinking of this.

For they'd made love after all. She, the woman, bent upon conceiving, had had her way another time.

A daughter! Take my sons, and give me a daughter in their place, I will never beg for anything again O God I swear.

"Ma'am? Wake up, ma'am."

A harsh, urgent voice. Whose?

Ariah was awake, yet somehow her eyes were shut. How her heart strained as she tried to climb the sheer sharp glistening-wet granite walls of the Gorge. Someone was speaking to her, loudly.

"Ma'am? *Please.*"

Ariah felt her shoulder nudged. What was this! A stranger daring to touch her, in this public place where she lay defenseless. Her eyes flew open.

She stammered, in a panic, "What—is it? Who are you?"

It has happened. And now.

A stranger was talking earnestly to Ariah, as she managed to sit up, and to stand. (But why was she barefoot? Where were her shoes?) Hurriedly she adjusted her clothing and ran both hands through her rats'-nest hair. A youngish man in a dark green uniform, a park attendant, spoke sternly to her, which seemed to Ariah very wrong, this man was younger than Ariah. "Ma'am? Are these your children? They were on Goat Island unattended."

Chandler slouched close by his mother, shame-faced. And there in the stroller, strapped in, little baseball cap askew on his head, was the baby. Oh, what was his name: Royall. *A name I picked out of the paper, the sound of it struck me. Royall Mansion, a winning thoroughbred.* Ariah stared at her children as if she hadn't seen them in a long time. But where had they drifted off to? How much time had passed? Why was Ariah, Dirk Burnaby's wife, barefoot in this public place being scolded by an impertinent stranger? "Yes, of course they're my children," Ariah said hotly. "Chandler, where have you been? I've been worried sick about you. I told you *not to go far.*"

Chandler mumbled an apology as the park attendant looked on dubiously. You'd almost think, the expression in his face, he didn't believe that Ariah was these boys' mother. Chandler's misbuttoned red plaid shirt and baggy khaki pants were damp from spray. Like a street urchin the child looked, not a son of Dirk Burnaby of Luna Park! Ariah wanted to shake him, hard. And there was Royall not looking like himself but anybody's baby, snot glistening at his nostrils and drool at his slack baby mouth. His face was soft bread dough that has lost its shape. His demon-energy seemed to have faded, he was groggy, dopey and could barely keep his eyes open.

Oh, dear. Despite the protective cap, it looked as if Royall's little pug nose was sunburnt.

Ariah was scolding Chandler, he'd disobeyed her again. Wandered off. Unreliable! The park attendant listened with a maddening air of severity, shaking his head. Who did he think he was, the F.B.I.? Ariah concluded that if he had the power to arrest her or issue a summons he'd have done it by now, which was a relief. Royall woke from his trance and began to cry loudly. "Mom-*my*! Mom-*my*!"

Ariah knelt before him hastily and gathered him in her arms. "Darling, Mommy's *here*."

And so Mommy was.

Mommy and Chandler pushed the stroller back to Luna Park, crooning "Little Baby Bunting." Royall, worn out from crying, slept.

7

"MRS. BURNABY. Good news!"

Oh, but was it? Ariah's heart turned dry, porous, and cracked like a clump of old clay.

"Doctor. Oh my God. Thank you."

Of course she was astonished, stunned with joy.

Ariah would calculate she'd been pregnant already, that day in Prospect Park lying in the sun. Dreaming, drifting. Somehow, she'd known: she'd known something. Already the deepest spring of her happiness had begun to flow.

Juliet would be born in late May 1961.

My little family, complete.

Before . . .

A vulture the woman seemed to him. Hovering at the edge of his vision. Perched, hunched, staring unblinking at him. Waiting.

She was the Woman in Black. She was observing him, she was waiting to waylay him. She was patient, relentless. Waiting for him. Waiting for Dirk Burnaby to weaken. She had his name, and she had his number. He dreaded her coming to his home in Luna Park.

Though his receptionist had several times told Dirk the woman's name, he'd forgotten it almost at once.

So he imagined Death. A vulture with an unerring eye and an infinity of patience. So he imagined his conscience, at some distance from his life.

Don't get involved. For Christ's sake.

The last thing you need, Burnaby.

"Madelyn, please explain to this woman another time, I'm 'truly sorry.' It's 'with genuine regret' that I can't see her, and I can't consider taking on her case. Not just now. Not with so many cases piled up. 'This sort of personal-injury litigation isn't Mr. Burnaby's métier.' "

Madelyn, who'd been Mr. Burnaby's receptionist for eleven years, knew "métier"—it was one of her employer's pet words, for the moment. *Métier* meaning specialty, trade; an area of work in which one excels. *Métier* meaning what Dirk Burnaby the attorney knows he can do with his customary skill and cunning, and win at.

Another time he said, "Madelyn. No. Please give these materials back to her. Please explain, another time, that 'Mr. Burnaby sincerely regrets' etc. This kind of litigation isn't what I do, and anyway I'm booked solid. For years."

Madelyn hesitated. Of course she would do what Mr. Burnaby requested. She was in his employ after all. In love with him, these many years. But her love was the kind of love that expects no reciprocation nor even acknowledgment. "But, Mr. Burnaby, she'll ask me, Did he read my letter?—Did he look at the photographs, at least? What should I say?"

"Tell her No."

" 'No'—just 'no'?"

"No. I did not read her letter, and I did not look at the photographs."

He was becoming exasperated, annoyed. Beginning to lose his Burnaby poise. Beginning to feel like a pursued man. What most surprised him was that Madelyn of all people should be fixing him with that expression of apology and reproof; as if, independent of him, she'd formed her own opinion on this subject.

"Oh, Mr. Burnaby, she only wants to see you for a few minutes. She promises. Maybe—you should? She's such a"—Madelyn paused, blushing at her own audacity, searching for the most accurate and persuasive word—"sincere woman."

"Sincere women are the most dangerous. God spare us!"

Backing off, retreating to his inner office, Dirk succeeded in making Madelyn laugh. But it was a frayed, sad-sounding laugh. A disappointed-with-you-Mr. Burnaby laugh.

The Vulture. The Woman in Black. She'd taken to waiting for Dirk Burnaby in the lobby of his office building. On the steps outside. On the sidewalk. Even in a lightly falling rain, even at dusk when he'd been working late and not intending to avoid her, simply he'd been working late, lost in concentration.

At the edge of his vision he saw her, the dark hovering figure, he would not look closely, would not make eye-contact, before she could speak his name, he'd turned, he was walking swiftly away.

He knew. Not to get involved. Not to be moved by sympathy, or pity.

If she called after him, he didn't hear.

No. I won't. I can't.

Since falling in love with Ariah and marrying her he'd ceased to think of himself as a lone romantic figure crossing a tightrope. A tightrope over an abyss! No more, he was not that man. He'd never been that man. His grandfather Reginald Burnaby's fate in The Falls would not be his. It was 1961, not 1872. Dirk Burnaby was not alone now, never would he be alone again. He had sealed his fate. Or, his fate had sealed him.

Ariah confided in him, "Now we're safe, darling! Even if one is taken from us, we'd have two left. If you leave me"—she laughed her low throaty laugh, mocking her own dread—"I'd have three of *them*."

Dirk laughed, for such remarks of Ariah's were presented to him as whimsical, meant to amuse. There was the custom between them of Dirk shaking his head in a pretense of severity. "Ariah! The things you say."

"Well. Someone has to say them."

Ariah's response was bright, brave. Her green-glassy eyes, her redhead-pallor that gave her, at forty, a look of being young and un-tried. After more than a decade of living with Ariah, Dirk believed he understood the woman less than he had at the outset. He wondered if this might be true of any woman?

Of course, Ariah wasn't "any woman."

He considered her words. "Now we're safe." What did this mean? Was this the basic principle of domestic life, of the terrible need to propagate one's kind? The human wish, as in a fairy tale, to live longer than one's lifetime, through one's children. To live longer than one is allotted, and to matter. To matter deeply, profoundly to someone.

Not to be alone. To be spared the possibility of knowing oneself, in aloneness.

He was a married man in his mid-forties, a man deeply in love with his wife. A man who has fathered children whom he loves. A responsible citizen of his time and place. *Who I am there's no doubt. No longer. I know.*

Sometimes this love came so strong, almost he couldn't breathe. He felt his chest constrict. His young sons, his baby daughter. Their mother's eyes lifting to his in triumph; yet a fearful, perilous triumph. *They are my tightrope now* Dirk thought tenderly. *Unless they are my abyss.*

This woman, the Woman in Black had appealed to other attorneys in Niagara Falls. For weeks she'd been making the rounds of law offices. Strange that she would come to Dirk Burnaby so late: he supposed she knew she couldn't afford his fees, it wasn't likely she could afford the fees of any attorneys with offices in his building. Two Rainbow Square this new tower of a building was called. At the heart of downtown, Rainbow Boulevard and Main Street.

She'd presented her case to the Niagara County Health Department. She'd tried to speak with the editor of the *Niagara Gazette*, and had in fact spoken with a reporter. Word spread quickly in the city, which, despite its burgeoning population of factory workers and manual laborers, was a small, tight community. Its nucleus, those individuals who had power and who mattered, consisted of less than fifty persons, all men. Dirk Burnaby was among these men of course. And most of them were friends of his, or friendly acquaintances. Men of the older generation had been friends or friendly acquaintances of his father, Virgil Burnaby. Dirk belonged to the same private clubs to which they belonged. Their women adored him.

How could he explain to the Woman in Black *My friends are your enemies. My friends can't be my enemies.*

Dirk didn't know the details of the lawsuit this desperate woman was hoping to bring against the City of Niagara Falls except that such a lawsuit hadn't a chance to be resolved in her favor, or even to be seriously considered by a judge. The rumor was that her family had serious health problems, possibly she'd had miscarriages; or such was the claim. She was trying to organize a homeowners' association in her neighborhood, in the vicinity of Ninety-ninth Street and Colvin Boulevard, protesting health conditions at a local elementary school. He'd seen in the *Niagara Gazette* a brief, neutral feature beneath the misleading headline PARENTS ORGANIZE TO PROTEST 99TH ST. SCHOOL.

The mayor of Niagara Falls, Dirk's old friend "Spooky" Wenn, firmly believed that the Woman in Black—whose name he, too, had difficulty recalling—was a "known Communist." In fact she was the daughter of a "notorious" Communist, a CIO organizer of the 1930's in North Tonawanda who'd died in a confrontation with strikebreakers and police. "These people" had caused plenty of trouble in the past. The woman and her husband, supposedly an assembly worker at one of the plastics plants, were "professional agitators." Obviously, they were Jewish. They "took orders from Moscow." They'd been involved in demonstrations in Buffalo at the time of the Rosenbergs' execution. Probably the two weren't married, but had "set up shop together" as "part of a commune." Everybody knew that communism was "godless"—that was a fact. This couple had a mortgage on a tract-house bungalow on Ninety-third Street as a "front." They were from New York, or maybe Detroit. The woman had a "history of mental illness." The man had a "prison record." They had children living with them they claimed were theirs. As the woman claimed she'd had miscarriages, and that this was the fault of the city, not her own fault. She claimed that her children were sick because of city water, or the soil, or the air, or the playground at the Ninety-ninth Street Elementary School, who knew all that she'd claimed? Already she had caused trouble at the school and at the Niagara County Health Department. Wenn spoke at length, vehemently as if he'd been personally threatened by the Woman in Black. It was 2 A.M. of a Sunday morning, an interlude between poker games at Stroughton

Howell's newly purchased white colonial house overlooking Buckhorn Island. Clyde Colborne, Buzz Fitch, Mike MacKenna, Doug Eaton whose older brother was married to Dirk's sister Sylvia, and Dirk were also there. Wenn said, "These Reds! Like the Rosenbergs, their dream is to overthrow the U.S. Government and replace it with communes and free love, that's what this 'complaint' is really about. The end justifies the means. Plain as day in old Marx's *Mein Kamp*." Stroughton Howell exchanged a glance with Dirk, laughed and said, "In Adolf's *Das Kapital*, too."

Wenn said hotly, "They don't make any secret of their intentions, is my meaning. It's when they go underground, pretending to be 'ordinary citizens,' that they're dangerous."

Dirk Burnaby was in an affable mood, having been drinking good scotch and getting more than his share of good cards through the evening, but not such good cards that his friends were demoralized and resentful when he won, and won again. He'd sit a game out. He could sense when luck might fade from his fingertips. With lawyerly sagacity he said, "What 'these people' want is compensation—a settlement out of court. The hell with overthrowing the U.S. Government."

Had he meant this tossed-off remark? Probably, yes.

And would he regret having said it?

The Woman in Black! The Vulture.

Before the woman had a name, before she was fully human to him. She'd been a threat. She'd caused him to curse under his breath. *God damn no I will not. What an asshole I am, if I do.*

Never would Dirk bring up the subject of the Woman in Black with Ariah. Not voluntarily. He knew better—he'd had enough experience by this time!—than to discuss anything problematic with his excitable wife. Their conversations might begin normally enough, but within a few minutes Ariah would begin to be alarmed, agitated. During the past several years she'd become increasingly anxious about the vast world outside their home in Luna Park. She refused to read the front section of the *Gazette*—"It's obscene to know too much, if you can't do anything about it." She shrank from any mention of "foreign" news because it was always worrisome. She refused to watch TV news, and of the magazines that came into the house she favored the *Saturday Evening Post*, *Ladies' Home Journal*, and *Reader's Digest*, not *Life* and *Time*. Abruptly she'd excuse herself to leave conversations at social gatherings that drifted onto unpleasant subjects, like wartime reminiscences among Dirk and his fellow veterans. (One of Dirk's ex-G.I. acquaintances had entered Dresden after the notorious "firebombing." Another, a banker with a riverfront home on l'Isle Grand, had been present at the "liberation" of Auschwitz.) Ariah listened with morbid concentration, biting her thumbnail until the cuticle bled, as Chandler described the "duck-and-cover" drill (in the event of an atomic attack by the Soviets) at Luna Park Elementary. Even reports of the children filing outside during ordinary fire drills upset her. Yet Ariah saw the wisdom of such procedures—"You have to prepare for the worst." And yet if Dirk began to speak worriedly of his law practice, if he spoke in any but the most casual, conversational way about his profession, Ariah's face stiffened. Dirk could amuse her, Ariah loved to be amused. She wanted to be told that the world beyond 7 Luna Park was a region of fools and knaves. If you were neither a fool nor a knave you wanted no part in that world. You held yourself aloof, superior. So Ariah could be entertained, she could be made to dissolve into peals of laughter. She loved Dirk's mimicry of local judges, politicians, law colleagues and rivals. She had a delightfully malicious sense of humor. But if Dirk began to speak seriously, she stiffened. She never asked about the outcomes of his cases out of a fear, he supposed, that he would have to report to her now and then that he'd lost; or had not won so spectacularly as he and his clients might have wished. She feared his failure, his professional humiliation, his bankruptcy. She feared that his mother would "disinherit" him (even as, as Dirk said repeatedly, he had no wish for his mother's money, and assumed he was in fact "disinherited.") Above all she seemed to fear his sudden death (heart attack, car accident), his "disappearing"—"vanishing."

Like the first husband, Dirk supposed.

Except, strangely, Ariah no longer seemed to recall that she'd had a first husband, before Dirk Burnaby.

After their second son was born, and took up so much space with his lung power and his indefatigable energy, the elegant townhouse at 7 Luna Park was too small. Dirk overrode Ariah's protests and bought a larger, five-bedroom house almost directly across the way at 22 Luna Park. The new house was of the same vintage as the townhouse, built in the 1920's, with large rooms upstairs and down, made of sandstone, on an acre of land bordered by elms and Scotch pine, prime real estate in this part of the city. Still, Ariah had been stubborn about moving. She'd been irritable and edgy for weeks. She hated it that, in these new quarters, she had no choice but to allow her husband to hire a full-time housekeeper and nanny. "I guess we must be rich," she said dryly. "Like all the Burnabys. Tempting fate."

Dirk said, " 'Fate' comes to us, Ariah. Whether we're rich or poor."

Ariah shivered. Playfully she slapped Dirk, digging her short, bitten-at nails into his arm. In the matter of morbidity, she didn't want to be challenged.

What mattered was that the Burnabys' new house, like the old, was miles away from Ninety-ninth Street and Colvin Boulevard, as Luna Park Elementary, where Chandler was now in fifth grade, was miles away from the Ninety-ninth Street School.

. . . And After

*A*nd yet it would happen: in September 1961 Dirk Burnaby would take on the "doomed" lawsuit after all. The legal action known initially as the Olshaker case; subsequently, and more notoriously, referred to as "Love Canal."

Quickly—incredulously!—word spread through Niagara Falls. Through the tightly knit legal community in which everyone knew everyone else, or wanted to think they did; through City Hall and the City-County Courthouse; through the social set to which Dirk Burnaby belonged, or might have belonged if his eccentric red-haired wife had been more sociable. In some quarters the news was greeted with disbelief, and in others with outrage.

"Dirk Burnaby? Is the man crazy? He must know that suit can't win."

And, "Burnaby! You have to hand it to him, the guy has guts."

And, "Burnaby! That bastard. That traitor to his class. This is the end of his career."

Love Canal. As Dirk Burnaby would say, "It isn't a canal. It was never a canal. And it has nothing to do with love."

He'd believed he had made his decision: not to speak with the Woman in Black. (Whose name he seemed incapable of remembering.) He shunned this impetuous individual when she dared to approach him outside his office and he refused to return her calls to his office and by mid-June of 1961 she had ceased trying to contact him. She'd ceased appearing to him in that stealthy vulture-way of hers that had begun to enter his sleep; to contaminate his dreams and make him moan aloud like a frightened child. Ariah, hearing him, would nudge him awake demanding to know what was wrong? was he having a nightmare? a heart attack? In the night, in their bed at the top of the house, there was Ariah cupping her anxious hand to his chest, to the wiry-haired flesh of his upper torso slick and clammy with nightmare sweat; where, a few inches away inside his shuddering body, his heart beat like the clapper of a bell.

Dirk would murmur, "Ariah, no. It's nothing. Go back to sleep, darling."

He'd made a decision, he believed. In any case the Woman in Black had vanished from his life. If she'd finally gotten a lawyer to take her on, Dirk hadn't heard. He dreaded finding out.

Then in late June driving home in a sudden thunderstorm, beneath a roiling, blackened sky, Dirk was waiting for a traffic light to change at the intersection of Main and Ferry, near St. Anne's Hospital, when he saw a young woman and a small child huddling beneath an umbrella, waiting at a bus stop. They weren't wearing raincoats, only just summer clothes. The storm had blown up swiftly, as usual: within a few minutes the mild June temperature had plummeted twenty degrees. Rain pelted like machine-gun fire, gutters rushed with dirty water. The woman was crouched over the child trying to hold the umbrella at an angle to shelter her, but without much success. A vicious rain slashed at them, blown almost horizontally. Dirk pulled alongside the curb and called out, "Hey, want a ride? Get in." The woman hesitated only a moment before climbing into the front seat of the big luxury car, settling the shivery little girl on her lap and collapsing the umbrella. She was breathless and seemed a little disoriented. "Tell the nice man thank you, Alice! Mister, you are a true samaritan." She was wiping at the girl's face, brushing wet strands of taffy-colored hair out of her eyes. The woman's hair was very black, in wet tatters. She was perhaps twenty-eight years old, exuding an air of vigor, busyness; her skin was olive-pale, she wore no makeup, her eyes were dark, and glittery-vivid as minerals; there were bruise-like indentations beneath her eyes but otherwise, Dirk thought, she looked pretty good. Considering.

She, or the girl, smelled of something fruity like chewing-gum or Popsicle, jarringly mixed with an odor of disinfectant.

Politely Dirk asked where he could take them, and the woman gave an address and apologized it was so far—"Why don't you just take us to the bus station, mister? We'd be grateful." Something about the address made Dirk wince. It was no part of Niagara Falls he knew, miles away to the east. That no-man's-land of new housing developments, factories and warehouses, raw gouged earth and toppled trees. But of course he would drive this poor woman and her child home. It was the least he could do, in his expensive new-model sea-green Lincoln Continental with whitewall tires, automatic transmission, velvety cushioned interior that put Ariah in mind, as she had several times observed, of a swanky casket. He felt pity for this attractive woman and her daughter, no doubt they'd been at the hospital, forced to take city buses in such weather. He saw a wedding band on the woman's finger and an engagement ring with a pea-sized stone and felt a stab of disapproval, almost of moral repugnance, that any man, any husband, couldn't provide a little better for his wife and child.

Burnaby, come on: poor people can't help it.

He had to remind himself frequently of that fact. If it was a fact.

In the fierce thunderstorm Dirk was driving east on Ferry, past Tenth Street, past Memorial Parkway, beyond Hyde Park that seemed to float like a luminous green island in the failing light, into this region of the city of his birth that was nonetheless scarcely known to him, where the air was beginning to smell like a gritty intensification of his passengers' curious scent. A mixture of sweetness, and something harshly chemical beneath. The Lincoln's windshield wipers were straining to keep the broad windshield clear. Dirk was uneasily aware of the black-haired woman staring at the side of his face.

In a voice of childlike surprise she said, "Mr. B-Burnaby?"

"Yes? You know me?"

The woman's eyes widened. She smiled a wonderful smile. "Do I know *you*! Mr. Burnaby, I'm that nervy woman who was trying to get you to talk with me for weeks. Remember?"

Dirk stared at her. The Woman in Black! And he hadn't recognized her.

Her name was Nina Olshaker, she wasn't wearing black, only ordinary light summer clothes, cotton shirt and slacks, straw shoes on her bare feet, soaked from the rain. There was nothing reproachful or vulture-like in her manner, only eagerness, apprehension.

Dirk was feeling ashamed, he'd so exaggerated the threat of this poor woman. She'd been wearing a black dress or dark, more formal clothing each time she'd come to his law office, the clothes of a woman in mourning. For in fact she was in mourning.

That first glimpse of her, weeks ago, and Dirk hadn't wanted to see more. He'd known who she was or had thought he'd known. He'd known what she wanted of him or had thought so. And like a coward he'd shrunk from meeting her gaze.

"I owe you an apology, I guess. Mrs. Olshaker."

"Me? You owe me an apology? Mr. Burnaby, *no*."

He was too embarrassed to explain, and so he acquiesced to his fate. It would happen swiftly. Afterward he would recall how he'd had the opportunity to drop the woman off at the bus station downtown; he'd had the opportunity, at her house, simply to drop her off and decline her invitation to come inside. And having come inside, listening to her impassioned plea, he had the opportunity to tell her he'd consider her case, and retreat. All these opportunities he'd let pass in his zeal to do the right thing.

For his heart was moved by her. And by the beautiful wan little girl with the taffy-colored hair who seemed to Dirk unnaturally lethargic, passive.

How different from his three-year-old Royall, that child of boundless energy and good spirits!

So Dirk drove Nina Olshaker and her daughter home, to a small woodframe bungalow at 1182 Ninety-third Street, near Colvin Boulevard and a brackish waterway called Black Creek. The house, pale yellow with dark green trim, was set close to the street in a narrow, truncated yard in a neighborhood, or tract division, of similar low-priced homes. Like a toy or model house it seemed, so compact. It might have fitted into the Burnabys' two-car garage at 22 Luna Park.

Colvin Heights this subdivision in east Niagara Falls was called, though in subsequent years and decades it, and the phenomenon it represented, would be designated by a blunt sort of shorthand—*Love Canal*. At the time, Dirk had no awareness of any canal; there was no canal visible. No canal existed. Colvin Heights appeared to be fairly new, few trees of any substance grew on the homeowners' grid-measured properties and those Dirk saw looked stunted, with papery leaves. He was conscious of a swampy, sweetly sulfurous atmosphere as if by degrees he'd been descending in his big luxury car, a seagreen gondola designed to float. When he left the sanctuary of the car a dark stinging rain was flung against his unprotected face but he whooped and laughed as if this were an exuberant game, trotting around with his large black golfing umbrella open, to attempt to shield Nina Olshaker and her daughter as they hurried into the house.

There, Dirk would stay for nearly two hours. In his zeal to do the right, gentlemanly thing.

"Ariah? It's me. I'm working late, honey. An emergency has come up."

Ariah's voice lifted faintly, as if she were hundreds of miles away, not less than ten. " 'Emergency'?"

Quickly Dirk said, "Nothing serious, Ariah. Nothing personal."

"Well. All right then. Come home when you can, Dirk. The children will probably be asleep. I'll keep dinner warm for you."

Dirk felt a mild stirring of nausea. No appetite!

He said, "Darling, that's very thoughtful of you. Thanks so much."

Ariah laughed. "Well, we are married. I am your wife. It's my duty to keep things warm, isn't it?"

Dirk would learn: Nina Olshaker had been married for ten years to Sam Olshaker who currently worked the night shift at Parish Plastics, one of the largest factories in the county. They'd moved to Colvin Heights six years before. They had a nine-year-old son Billy and six-year-old Alice and they'd had a younger daughter Sophia who'd died of leukemia in March 1961, at the age of three. "This place poisoned her, Mr. Burnaby. I can't prove it, the doctors won't say so, but I know."

Nina's and Sam's families were from the region. Sam had been born in Niagara Falls, where his father worked for Occidental Petroleum; Nina had been born in North Tonawanda where her father had worked for thirty-five years at Tonawanda Steel and had died last summer of emphysema at the age of fifty-four. She said, bitterly, "And Daddy's death, too. Tiny bits of steel in his lungs. He'd cough up blood. He could hardly breathe, at the end. He knew what was causing it, all the men at the steel mill know, they're resigned. The pay is good, that's the catch. And maybe, though they know what's happening to them, they don't exactly believe it. We felt that way with Sophia. She was getting weaker, losing weight, her white blood cells were failing, but we kept praying, and always we were thinking she'd be getting better. It was like me, having a miscarriage: I'd think, it's just this one, wrong thing. It's something gone wrong, once. Like bad luck. But next time things will be different. When Sophia died I wanted an autopsy done on her, I mean I thought I did, until it was explained to me what an autopsy is, and I changed my mind. Now I wonder if I did the right thing? If it was leukemia, just that, like something you inherit in the blood, like the County Health Depart-

ment told us, or maybe it was something else, too? Some poison here?
I can taste it, myself. In wet weather like this. But they told us there's
nothing, no poison in the air, or in the drinking water, they've done
tests. Or so they claim. Oh Mr. Burnaby, I'm worried sick about Alice,
now. She doesn't gain weight, doesn't have much appetite, I take her
for blood tests and she has 'fluctuating low-white cell counts'—
what's that mean? And Billy gets headaches over at the school, his
eyes are sore and he's coughing a lot. And Sam." She came to an
abrupt dead stop, considering Sam.

Dirk murmured his condolences. He was very, very sorry. And
how feeble his voice sounded, as Nina continued impatiently:

"I just want justice, Mr. Burnaby. I don't want money, I want justice for Sophia. I want Billy and Alice protected from harm. I want
whoever is responsible for Sophia's death and for other children sick
or dying in this neighborhood to say they are responsible. I know
there is something wrong here. You can smell it, sometimes it burns
your eyes and nostrils. In the back yard, in lots of back yards here,
there's this strange disgusting black sludge that oozes up, like oil,
but thicker than oil. I'll show you, it's in our basement. In wet
weather it oozes through the walls. You call the city government, you
get a secretary or somebody who tells you to wait, and you wait and
the line goes dead. You go down there, to City Hall, and you wait.
You can wait for weeks, months. I'd guess you can wait for years if you
lived that long. At the Ninety-ninth Street School, Mr. Burnaby, the
kids can taste the drinking water isn't right. They play outside, on
the playground, and their eyes burn, and their skin. There's a field
beyond the school, and a ditch, and the boys play there, and get
burnt. Billy brought these 'hot rocks' home—some kind of phospho-
rous rock, the size of a baseball, you throw it at the ground and it
pops like a firecracker and smolders, what the hell kind of thing is
that for kids to be playing with? I talked with the principal. He isn't
friendly, sympathetic, at all. You'd think he would care about the students in his school, for God's sake, but no, he's practically rude to me,
like I'm a crazy, pushy mother he hasn't got time for. He says Billy
should stay on school property and not play in the ditch or the field
but the fact is, the children are playing in the playground, this black

sludge bubbles up through the cracks. I have photographs of all these things, Mr. Burnaby. I have photographs of Sophia, I want you to see. Billy? Billy, come here."

A sniffy tow-headed boy had been hanging in the doorway of the living room, and now came reluctantly forward to meet Mr. Burnaby—"He's a lawyer, Billy. A famous lawyer."

Dirk winced. Famous!

"I want Billy transferred to another school but they refuse to transfer him. Because to give in, to one parent, they'd have to admit there was something to give in to, and they won't do that. Because then everybody would want their children transferred to a safer school. Because then maybe they'd be 'liable'—the school administration, the Board of Education, the mayor? They all protect one another, you can see they're stalling and lying, like at the Health Department, but what can you do, we live here, we just about make our mortgage payments and the car payments and if we have extra medical costs like taking Alice to St. Anne's instead of where they want to send us for tests, at the county medical clinic, all that adds up, we just can't afford it on Sam's salary and if something happens to him, there's the medical insurance at Parish, and the pension, and Sam is worried they could 'retaliate' against him, if we cause trouble—is that possible, Mr. Burnaby? Even with the union—the AFL?"

Dirk frowned thoughtfully. But he knew: yes it was possible. Parish Plastics was one of the tough area employers, he knew the old man Hiram Parish, a friend of Virgil Burnaby as Mrs. Parish had been a friendly social acquaintance of Claudine, he knew the reputations of Parish, Swann, Dow, OxyChem, and others. Even with the booming local economy, the labor unions hadn't gotten the contracts they'd wanted from these companies. Dirk Burnaby wasn't involved in labor negotiations but he had lawyer friends who were: on retainer for the companies. If he'd taken up labor law, which had never appealed to him, possibly he'd be working for Parish, Inc. He said, "It's possible, Mrs. Olshaker. I'd have to examine your husband's contract, to have an idea."

Was this the first, fatal step, Dirk would wonder. The involuntary gesture. The introduction of *I*, Dirk Burnaby, into the lives of strangers.

"Mr. Burnaby! Thank you."

Nina Olshaker gazed at him with those darkly shining mineral-eyes, smiling as if Dirk Burnaby's words meant more than, in fact, they meant.

The remainder of the visit would pass for Dirk in swift disjointed segments like an interrupted dream. Nina spoke to him in an animated, aggressive way, as if something had been decided between them.

She told him of the "tragic mistake" of the house: they'd signed on for a thirty-year mortgage. The house they'd loved at first, in such a "nice"—"warm"—"friendly"—neighborhood of couples like themselves, lots of children, Billy could walk two blocks to school, a big enough yard in back for Sam to plant a vegetable garden. "He gets so much happiness out of that, you should see him. It must be a gene or something? I'm missing it. I think, if I plant some seeds, probably they won't come up. If they do, some damned bugs will get them." Half-consciously Nina drew her hand across her abdomen. She was thinking of having miscarried, maybe. Or she was thinking of the little girl who'd died.

Dirk listened. He asked few questions, that evening. He was fascinated by Nina Olshaker who was like no other woman he'd encountered close up. Possibly she had some Tuscarora blood, her hair was so very black and without lustre. Her eyes were ringed in fatigue and worry yet shone with a dark scintillant knowledge that drew him as an accomplice. She had the nerved-up scrappy manner of a tomboy. Her dark skin was slightly coarse, yet attractive. Oh, Dirk Burnaby found Nina Olshaker attractive. He had to admit. She was special, she thought of herself as special. She had a mission, even in defeat she would have a mission. Those inexpensive summer clothes, barefoot amid the cozy clutter of her household and not much embarrassed by her (not very clean) feet as she wasn't much embarrassed by the household clutter, or her children's runny noses, or the prevailing odors of something dank and rotted in the air: she told Dirk Burnaby her story without the slightest consciousness that she was of a type and a class ordinarily invisible to him.

Not that Dirk Burnaby wasn't a believer in democracy. All men, and some women, created equal. In the eyes of God. (If not the economy.) Under the U.S. Constitution guaranteed the right to life, liberty, and the pursuit of happiness. If not actual happiness. (Whatever happiness is. A snug house built of compacted cash made to resemble bricks.)

As Claudine Burnaby would say with snide humor *Such people don't exist. And if they do, what have they to do with us?*

Nina was saying how the house had turned out to be a trap and it had made Sophia sick and it was making them all sick and now some of the neighbors were turning against Nina saying she'd caused trouble at the school scaring people and promoting "hysteria" and "lowering property values"—actually accusing her and Sam of being Communists. "Can you believe it, Mr. Burnaby? Sam and me? Isn't that ridiculous? We're Catholics."

Dirk said, "Yes. That's ridiculous."

"I mean, it is ridiculous! It's bullshit. All we want is honest answers to our questions, not people lying to us, how's that make us Communists for God's sake?"

Dirk was thinking uneasily of the epithets tossed at lawyers who'd defended men and women blacklisted or "under suspicion of subversion" in the early 1950's. Those few faculty members at the University of Buffalo who'd refused to sign loyalty oaths. A Protestant minister, a *Gazette* columnist, local union officials. There weren't many. The lawyers who'd defended them were scorned as *Commie-lawyers, Red-lawyers. Jew-lawyers.*

Dirk said heartily, "Well. It's 1961 now, Nina. We're much more advanced."

Next, Nina Olshaker showed Dirk a portfolio of snapshots. Wiping at her eyes, trembling. She'd herded Billy and Alice into another room to eat a heated-up casserole and watch TV, she didn't want them seeing these. Dirk steeled himself to see a succession of photos of the beautiful lost Sophia. An infant, a toddler, a leggy little girl held proudly aloft in her daddy's sinewy tanned arms. (Sam, a wiry young man, smiling in sunshine; a baseball cap on his head, T-shirt and shorts. Dirk felt a moment's stab of sexual jealousy.) Next, the child was in a hospital bed, her skin whitely translucent and her pale blue eyes clouded. Next, the child was dead, a waxen-skinned doll in a white satin-lined casket. Dirk half-shut his eyes no longer listening to Nina Olshaker's quavering voice.

Thinking of his daughter, Juliet. Barely six weeks old. He swallowed hard, he felt a pang of terror.

Already Dirk had forgotten, he hadn't much wanted another child. He'd been appalled by his wife's raw need. He'd been a little frightened of her.

Make love to me! For God's sake, do it. Do it!

Not Ariah but the fierce ravenous female. Not the Ariah he'd married but another in her place.

Yet: of that union, Juliet was born.

"I have a daughter, too."

"Oh. What's her name?"

"Juliet."

"Such a pretty name! H-How old is she?"

"Just born."

Strange to have said! It wasn't true, exactly. The frailty of infant life struck him in that instant. How precarious the hold on life. Sucking at a mother's breasts or at a bottle, utterly dependent upon others, lacking strength, mobility, language. For an instant he felt the absurd terror that, in his absence, as punishment for Dirk Burnaby not coming directly home, something would happen to his daughter.

Nina was showing him photographs she'd taken at the Ninety-ninth Street School. The playground where black "sludge" bubbled through cracks in asphalt. The "smelly sludge" ditch. The open field of tall weedy grasses and thistles, laced with brackish water. Billy Olshaker's puffy reddened eyes, his "burnt" hands and the "burnt" hands of other children. "The principal told us mothers, 'Make sure your children wash their hands. There won't be any problem then,' " Nina said angrily. She spread many more snapshots, covering a table-top, taken in the neighborhood and in the Olshakers' basement and back yard. Dirk considered these, dismayed. There had been lawsuits in recent years against certain of the chemical companies, Dow, Swann, Hooker, OxyChem, personal-injury suits initiated by workers that were virutally always rejected by district judges or settled out of court for undisclosed sums, none of them very high. It was understood that you took a risk working in certain factories, and for this risk you were paid.

Of course, you weren't paid enough. Never enough. But that was another issue.

The pollution of a neighborhood, of earth, soil, water, and the subsequent effect upon individuals, was something very different, and new. Dirk Burnaby had never given it much thought. His practice of law had nothing to do with such amorphous cases, he was a litigator trained to argue small but devastating points based upon the New York State statutory law. His clients were usually well-to-do businessmen wishing to protect or extend their status. Occasionally Dirk represented a client declaring bankruptcy, and occasionally he did pro bono, charity work. But that wasn't his métier. He was a master chess player on a game board he knew intimately as, on that game board, he, Dirk Burnaby, was known, respected and feared.

He felt a stab of excitement, and of dread. A new game! This, too, Dirk Burnaby would master.

"In my own hometown."

Dirk must have spoken aloud, for Nina Olshaker said grimly, "Yes! In your hometown."

Some of the snapshots had fallen onto the floor, and Dirk picked them up. His face pounded with blood. Nina was saying, "This should be evidence, Mr. Burnaby, shouldn't it? In a court of law, if jurors saw it, it should matter. Children should matter. People's lives should matter." Dirk was thinking no, scientific evidence should matter, doctors' testimonies should matter, or could be made to matter. A calm though tearful mother on the witness stand, describing such things, describing her child's death, her own and her children's illnesses, could be made to matter.

"Mr. Burnaby! C'mere. Before you leave." Nina seized Dirk's arm and led him into the kitchen, ran water from both faucets into a glass, asked him to smell, to taste. Dirk smelled but declined to taste, though (he was thinking) the water didn't smell very different from the water he and his family drank in Luna Park. Nina laughed and poured the water into the sink. "Well, why should you? Nobody blames *you*." Next, Nina hauled him into the basement, Christ what a smell here, and the cheaply carpentered wooden steps creaking beneath their weight. In the harsh overhead light the basement was an ugly cave smelling of backed-up drains and something tarry, nauseating. On the floor were dark web-patterns, glistening. There were streams of rain water, small puddles. The barely six-foot concrete walls oozed a shitty sort of muck. A sump pump worked noisily, like a heart about to burst. "When it rains hard like it is now, the basement floods. Sam is the one to check the sump pump but by the time he comes home it might be broken. Damn!" Nina was panting, incensed. She gripped Dirk's arm firmly as if to prevent him from running away upstairs. "See, Mr. Burnaby? I'm not imagining this. People in the neighborhood say it's 'just what happens' in Niagara Falls when it rains, even Sam tries to say so, he was born here he says, it's always like this he says, nobody wants to admit this is something else, afraid of 'lowering property values'—bullshit! This is more than rain water and dirt, it's more than sewage backing up, it should be tested, all the land and water out here in Colvin Heights should be tested, I keep telling people. I never used to be a sickly person. I'm not a sickly person but I get migraines from living here, I'm getting asthma like poor Billy, and Sam, I don't talk about myself much because who gives a damn, it isn't about me it's about children we need to care about, don't we? Sam gets pissed with me, says I'm imagining a lot of this but I didn't imagine having a miscarriage, did I? I didn't imagine my daughter dying of leukemia, did I? *Did I?*"

Nina had become emotional, wiping tears from her eyes. Her face was contorted with grief, rage. Dirk, trying not to breathe in this foul place, couldn't comfort her, had to escape back up the steps where, in the doorway, the child Billy was crouched.

Jesus! A close call, he'd almost gagged. A sudden headache had caught him between the eyes. And his eyes were stinging with moisture.

Nina caught up with him in the kitchen, and apologized. "I'm sort of used to the smell, I guess. What it would be like to somebody else, I can't imagine." She laughed awkwardly.

When Dirk left the house, desperate now to escape, Nina accompanied him. The heavy rain had lightened. Dirk didn't bother to open his umbrella. Thank God, he could breathe again. After the stink of that basement, which he wouldn't forget for a long, long time, the viscous air of east Niagara Falls tasted almost fresh.

And it was an air, an early evening, possessing an eerie luminescence, mingled with the prevailing swampy, tarry odors. The sky was marbled with cloud, partially clearing in the western, Canadian sky where the sun was just descending. It was midsummer: the summer solstice: night was slow to come in this urban area of factories with tall smokestacks rimmed with flame, vast acres of scattered lights.

At Dirk's car Nina continued to speak to him, more rapidly now, as if sensing she might have offended him, and might have driven him away. "People say there's an old canal around here that was filled in, nobody knows where it is exactly. By the school, I think. All through here. It was filled in before the Colvin Heights contractor began to build here after the war and I was thinking—what did they fill the canal with? Maybe not just dirt, but waste products? Chemicals? Swann Chemicals is just out Colvin Boulevard, on the other side of Portage. Nobody will tell us about it. At the Health Department and at City Hall I've asked. At the *Gazette* I've asked. That's why I'm trying to get a lawyer interested. Mr. Burnaby, everybody says the best lawyer in Niagara Falls is *you*."

Dirk frowned. Possibly this was true. On his chess board, playing by the rules he knew, Dirk Burnaby was possibly unbeatable, in the prime of his career as he was in the prime of his life.

"Mr. Burnaby, I know you can't say 'yes' right now. But please don't say 'no.' Please! I know you will have to think about this. And I know that you know, we don't have much money. We might have—scraping together, some of the neighbors who are concerned—a couple of thousand dollars. I know you get much more. That nice woman, in your office, was trying to explain. But I wanted to talk to you, and I have. Thank you!"

Dirk said, "Mrs. Olshaker, I'll be in contact. You've given me a good deal to think about."

Nina boldly seized his hand in both her hands and squeezed it, hard. Her mineral-eyes glittered with a sort of flirtatious desperation. In a lowered voice she said, "I have a confession to make, Mr. Burnaby. Don't be angry! Don't hold it against me! See, I prayed for this. This evening. I prayed for you. *God has sent you to me.*"

The Underworld

Never adultery. Never an adulterous husband. Nor did I fall in love with that woman.

Though he would destroy himself, and his marriage, in the doomed cause of Love Canal.

1

ARIAH KNEW, yet didn't know. As a wife doesn't know, yet knows.

Or believe she knows.

It was the late summer of 1961, and then it was the autumn, and the start of another winter at The Falls, close beside the Niagara Gorge. A new baby in the house at 22 Luna Park! The mysterious pulsing life of the house this baby daughter seemed to Ariah, the mother. The triumphant, if exhausted mother. There were Chandler and Royall she loved, but it was Juliet who was Ariah's very soul.

"Our eyes. We have the same eyes. Oh, Bridget! Look."

Holding the moistly smiling, big-eyed baby beside her head, preening before the mirror. Pebbly-green eyes, glassy-green eyes lightly threaded with blood, the newly hired Irish nanny blinked from one pair to the other, from Baby to Mother, and, being Irish, and canny, knew to say in her exuberant brogue, "Oh, Mrs. Burnaby! Sure she's the image of her mother, God has blessed you both."

And yet.

My husband loves me. He would never be unfaithful to me. He knows it would destroy me. And he loves me.

Damn! The telephone was ringing. Ariah had forgotten to take the receiver off the hook. In the midst of her Thurs. 5 P.M lesson (the pupil was a plumply-pretty middling-talented twelve-year-old neighborhood girl of whom Ariah was rather fond) Ariah called without rising from the piano bench, "Royall, sweetie, will you take that phone off the hook? Don't say a word to whoever it is, just take the receiver off the hook and put it down gently. That's a good boy."

But Royall, being Royall, never obeyed his mother without at the same time disobeying his mother. That was Royall's game. He was three years old, brimming with games. He picked up the ringing phone in both hands and chattered into the mouthpiece like a demented monkey, "No Momma! No Momma, g'bye!" Giggling, the child let the receiver fall to the carpeted floor with a soft thud, backing off, hands clapped over his mouth with a look of naughty hilarity. Ariah could hardly scold him, whoever was on the phone would overhear.

Ariah's after-school piano lessons were intended to be, for her, oases of relative calm, sanity, yes even a bit of beauty amid the seething energies of the Burnaby household, but that wasn't always so.

Ariah turned with a sigh back to her pupil, who was frowning over a tricky exercise of dominant seventh (broken) arpeggios in B♭ major, which her stubby fingers could almost manage, but not quite. Still, the girl had talent. Or what passed for talent in Ariah's teaching career these days. With her usual breathy enthusiasm Ariah said, "Very good, Louise! Very promising! Now let's hear it again, keep the notes flowing smoothly, we're in four/four time—"

A strange sort of consolation it was, somehow. The frequency with which, teaching piano, you hear yourself murmuring *Very good! Very promising! Now let's hear it again.*

Her Burnaby in-laws and social acquaintances thought it eccentric, Ariah knew. That the wife of Dirk Burnaby gave piano lessons. For five dollars an hour. A woman with three young children. Like a genteel spinster in need of an income. Ariah had said in wide-eyed innocence to Dirk's disapproving sisters, "Oh, I'm preparing for some future time when I might be abandoned and bereft and will have to support myself and my children. Shouldn't all wives?" It had been worth it, to see the look on their prissy heavily made-up faces. Funny! Ariah smiled, recalling.

Though Dirk hadn't been so amused. In fact he'd been furious with her.

Ariah had wanted to protest *But shouldn't all wives?*

There was Louise playing her dutiful arpeggios, broken chords that should have been swift, light, sparkling as water rippling over rock but were deliberate, unevenly struck, each note a tiny mallet. "Remember the beat, dear: four beats to a measure, and a quarter note gets one beat." Ariah tapped with her pencil. She'd developed an ambiauditory skill, listening to her pupils with one ear while listening to whatever might be happening in another part of the house with the other ear. This new house Dirk had insisted upon buying was dismayingly large, there were many rooms the older children could drift into, the room designated as "Mommy's piano room" was a former parlor opening off the living room and near a hallway that led to the kitchen and connected with the stairs. Where was Bridget? Possibly in the kitchen with the baby. She was to keep an eye on Royall, too, but of course Royall wasn't easy to keep an eye on. By now, Ariah hoped, whoever had called her had hung up.

Yes, it sounded as if Bridget was in the kitchen. Feeding and cooing at the baby in that swarmy way Ariah disliked. *She wants to be that beautiful baby's mother. Well, I am that baby's mother.*

Ariah didn't like the way Royall crowded against the Irish nanny, either. The way the Irish nanny was forever stroking his fine flaxen hair, exclaiming over his blue eyes, hugging him. Chattering away with him, in what sounded like Gaelic babytalk. Ariah wondered if they plotted and laughed together, secrets kept from Mommy.

Chandler was too old for Bridget to fuss over. And he was never home. Luckily!

Ariah liked a telephone off the hook. She felt protected, safe. Ringing phones made her nervous. Sometimes she walked swiftly away from a ringing phone, clapping her hands over her ears. Suppose it was Dirk, or that velvety-voiced receptionist Madelyn she despised, what would the call mean except that Dirk would be late again for dinner, or absent at dinner, and why should Ariah seek out such hurtful news? Better not to know. Just see what happens. Remove the receiver from the hook and let the dial tone go dead as it does, eventually. Though sometimes the housekeeper interfered, or even Bridget who had no business playing parlor maid. The phone rang jarring the peace of the household and there came the cry—"Mrs. Burnaby? Phone, ma'am."

But where was "ma'am?" Upstairs in her bathroom with both faucets running water. Humming loudly.

Ariah's piano lessons always ran over if there was no next pupil, and so this lesson continued until six-fifteen. Louise seemed uneasy, uncertain. She'd done so poorly with the little Mozart rondo she'd been working on for weeks, Ariah had had to play it for her another time. What a charming, sunny, clockwork sort of piece it was, all sparkling surfaces, no depths or interstices of brooding. "Now try again, Louise. I know you can do it." But Louise began, struck her first wrong note, and shook her head. "I g-guess I have to leave, Mrs. Burnaby." Clumsily the girl rose from the piano bench, gathering her music. Ariah was perplexed. Louise, shame-faced, said, "This is my last piano lesson with you, I guess. I'm sorry."

Ariah was so taken by surprise, she hardly knew how to react. "Louise, what? Your last lesson—?"

"My m-mother says . . ."

"Your mother?"

"My dad told her, I guess. No more piano lessons after today."

The girl, blushing fiercely, not meeting Ariah's eye, fled.

Ariah trailed after her to the front door, and shut it quietly behind her, and stood then in the vestibule for several minutes dazed as if she'd been struck on the head. Why, Louise Eggers was one of Ariah's most promising students. The Eggers family lived across the park in a handsome old colonial in which, several times in the past several years, the Burnabys had been guests. Ariah had been her usual somewhat reserved self in the face of Mrs. Eggers's sociability, but she'd always assumed that Mrs. Eggers liked her. Mr. Eggers, chief executive officer of Niagara Hydro, was a friendly business acquaintance of Dirk's.

Or had seemed so.

"Oh, *damn*." Ariah winced in pain.

Someone must have put the receiver back on the hook. The telephone was ringing.

The well-intentioned pest from County Galway summoned "ma'am" to the phone with her lilting lyric brogue. Numbly Ariah took the call in Dirk's study. "Yes." She hadn't the strength to pose even a ritual question.

But here was a shock. Ariah's sister-in-law Clarice.

Clarice! The elder of the two Burnaby sisters, and the one who frightened Ariah the more. A glaring-eyed Joan Crawford type with tightly permed hair like tiny sausages and a habit of turning her lip up at Ariah even as she smiled at her in a pretense of warmth. Clarice was in her early fifties, a stolid woman, with something of Claudine Burnaby's air of entitlement and reproach. "Ariah? Are you there?"

"Oh. Yes."

Ariah's response was weak, nearly inaudible. She was trying to summon strength to behave in that way—but what was that way?— the smug world designates as normal.

Oh, dear. Rapidly Ariah's mind skittered about. Had she and Dirk been invited to bring the children to Clarice's house on l'Isle Grand, and had they neglected to go? Again? (To Ariah's shame, this had happened on Easter Sunday of that year. Ariah accepted the blame, she'd forgotten to mark the date on her calendar.) Two or three times a year Dirk's sisters made the charitable effort to be friendly, inviting their brother and his burgeoning young family to their homes for one or another "holiday" occasion. Ariah dreaded these occasions and sometimes, pleading a sick headache, or a re-scheduled piano lesson, failed to attend. Claudine Burnaby, now in her seventies, stubbornly reclusive and rumored to have become a religious fanatic, never visited her childrens' homes but was obsessively talked-of and worried-over to the point at which Ariah wanted to clap her hands over her ears and run out of the room.

(Why was it such "eccentric" behavior, hiding away in your home if you wanted to? If you had the financial means? Especially if you lived in an estate like Shalott, overlooking the Niagara River.)

Politely Clarice asked Ariah how she was, how were the children; invariably Clarice bungled the childrens' names, but Ariah never troubled to correct her. Ariah quickly told her fine, fine, everyone is fine, though in the confusion and unease of the moment Ariah hadn't the faintest idea what she was saying: if Chandler had been missing from home for days, if Royall had lighted matches in the basement to set the house on fire, and Bridget had run off with beautiful Baby Juliet, Ariah would have answered brightly, "Oh, *fine*!" But she hadn't the energy to ask Clarice how her family was.

"Well. The reason I'm calling, Ariah," Clarice said, in a voice like poured concrete, "is to ask if you've been hearing some of the ugly rumors I've been hearing." There was a dramatic pause. Ariah pressed the phone receiver against her ear hard, as if the rumors were inside the phone, and she was supposed to hear them?

Clarice pressed grimly forward. "About my brother Dirk."

Desperately Ariah quipped, "Oh, your brother Dirk! Not my husband Dirk. That's a relief."

"Ariah, dear, I hope you'll think this is amusing."

Ariah laughed. "Clarice, I hope it will be. I've had three piano lessons this afternoon and I'm in a mood to laugh at something."

"Well, you won't laugh at this: Dirk is involved with another woman."

Involved! What a curious expression.

"Ariah? Did you hear me? People are saying, Dirk is seeing another woman."

Ariah was smiling into a patch of mist that had somehow drifted into the room. It hovered over objects, obscuring their shapes. It tasted of the cold wet mist at the foot of The Falls.

"Oh, goodness. Dirk 'sees' women all the time, Clarice. He could hardly help it, could he? With his eyes?" Ariah laughed, a sound like a chicken as its neck is being wrung. "Why is that un-un-unusual?"

"Ariah, are you sitting down? Sit down."

Ariah shook her head stubbornly. She would not sit down! Like Royall who disobeyed on principle. She had at least as much pride as her own three-year-old. She was standing at Dirk's roll-top desk, leaning weakly against it. She hadn't the motor coordination required to pull out Dirk's heavy swivel chair and sit down. It was rare for her to enter Dirk's study. Supposedly it was out-of-bounds to the children. Nor had Ariah the slightest interest in financial records, cancelled checks and receipts and income tax forms. All of Dirk's personal records were kept in this room, which meant family records too, but Ariah shunned such official documents. Since her marriage she hadn't paid a single bill, never so much as opened letters containing bills, anything from County of Niagara, State of New York, or the U.S. Federal Government she pushed from her with a shudder, knowing that her capable, good-natured husband would deal with such horrors.

Her sensitive nostrils quivered in this room. She could detect the faint, consoling odor of the cigars Dirk occasionally smoked. His hair lotion, his cologne. A bottle of French cologne for men that Ariah had given him. *He loves me. Knows it would destroy me.*

Ariah could hear Bridget carrying Juliet upstairs to the nursery, cooing and crooning in Gaelic. Time for a diaper change! Ariah felt a terrible sense of loss. Diapers, baby pee and baby shit! She was missing her daughter's babyhood. On the stairs, Royall rushed behind Bridget chattering and thumping his feet like a marching soldier. Ariah was desperate to be with them. She stammered, "C-Clarice? I have to hang up, my children are calling me."

Fiercely Clarice said, "No. Don't you dare hang up, Ariah! You've hidden that head of yours in the sand long enough. These ugly rumors don't concern just you, they concern the Burnaby family, too. All of us. My poor mother who isn't well, and would be devastated if she heard how badly her son, her 'favorite' child, is behaving. And in public. It isn't upsetting enough that Dirk is involved with a lower-class woman, a married woman with children, he's been filing preposterous motions in court on her behalf, he's lost his legal as well as his moral judgment, he seems to have lost his mind, and you, his wife, who has always imagined she's so clever and cultured and sharp-witted and superior to the rest of us, haven't noticed? Are you blind, Ariah?"

The mist seemed to be spreading. Ariah rubbed at her eyes. Maybe she was going blind? A roaring in her ears too, like distant falling water.

On the wall above Dirk's desk were framed daguerreotypes of his daredevil grandfather Reginald Burnaby the Great. A whippet-lean gypsy-swaggering sexy young man with a close-shaved head and handlebar mustache and intense shiny dark eyes like marbles. Ariah felt his jeering presence. *You too, on your tightrope! You, in a dream of believing yourself safe on land.*

These many years, Ariah had been teasing herself, and Dirk, with droll fantasies of his leaving her. But now.

Clarice was saying, "Ask my brother about 'Nina' when he comes home. 'Nina Olshaker.' If he comes home. Ask him why he's committing professional suicide for her sake. Initiating a lawsuit against the City of Niagara Falls, the Board of Education, Swann Chemicals, and I don't know who all else! His own friends, I'd have thought! Men he went to school with! Our parents' friends! Some of the most powerful people in Niagara Falls and Buffalo! And all this for a woman who isn't even good-looking, they say. Her husband is a factory worker and a Communist agitator and they have two children, both retarded. But now the Olshakers are separated, Dirk has set up a residence for her in Mt. Lucas, she lives there at his expense and you, Ariah, his wife, know nothing of it, do you? Hiding away playing your precious piano! 'Steinway spinet'! Your husband's mistress has a touch of Tuscarora blood, they say. Worse yet, she's Catholic."

Ariah whimpered like a small tormented animal. "I don't believe you! Leave me alone." She slammed down the receiver on her sister-in-law's ravening voice.

On the wall, Reginald Burnaby the Great smiled and winked at her.

"It isn't true. Not Dirk."

Ariah began to search through Dirk's desk, blindly. She was looking for—what? Her husband's secrets. The desk was a handsome old piece of furniture, carved mahogany and so heavy it left deep indentations in the rug; it had come to Dirk not from his father Virgil Burnaby but from his father's wealthy benefactor Angus MacKenna. Ariah knew little of these dead people, and wished to know less. She had married Dirk, not his family. She hated his family! Oh, a roll-top desk is a hive of secrets. Masculine secrets. There were numerous pigeonholes, drawers. Scattered about the desk were cellophane-wrapped cigars, Sweet Coronas mostly. There were wads of cancelled checks, receipts, bills held together by rubber bands. Bank statements, IRS forms, business letters, insurance policies. (No personal letters? That was suspicious.) Whimpering to herself like a kicked dog, Ariah pulled open drawers, rifled through them frantically. *This is not the person I am. This is not Ariah.* Mist from The Falls had gotten into the room, nasty as cold spit. Ariah was having difficulty seeing. She fumbled through Dirk's checkbook, panting. Evidence? Evidence of a husband's betrayal? She'd forgotten the woman's name. *But there can't be any woman.*

In his careful printed handwriting Dirk had noted he'd made out checks of $500 to "N. Olshaker" in August, September, October, and most recently November 1961. Ariah was panting, dazed. " 'N. Olshaker.' If she's his client, why is he paying *her*?"

Paying her for what?

Services rendered?

There were other mysterious—suspicious—notations. Monthly payments of $365 to Burnaby Property Management, Inc. Why was Dirk making out a check to his family's business? What sense did this make? " 'A residence in Mt. Lucas.' Where he has put his mistress. Oh, my God."

There was a movement behind Ariah, she turned guiltily and saw in the doorway of the study a bony-faced boy of no distinctive age, too grave in his expression to be a child, yet too small of stature to be an adolescent, with a sallow, furrowed skin and worried eyes glinting like fish scales behind his wire-rimmed glasses. (Oh, those damned glasses! They were only a few weeks old and Ariah never saw them without wanting to snatch them off the boy's nose and break them in two.) The boy's flannel shirt was rumpled and misbuttoned and there were stains on both knees of his school trousers though certainly these items of clothing had been freshly laundered and ironed when he'd put them on that morning. For a panicked moment Ariah couldn't remember this child's name.

He's mine, my penance.

The boy asked anxiously if something was wrong?

That scratchy voice: if sandpaper could talk, it would talk like this.

Ariah managed to recover, to a degree. "Chandler, for God's sake. You frightened the life out of me. Creeping up behind me like a—a turtle!" Ariah clasped her hands together to prevent their shaking. Her face must have been deathly pale, the freckles standing out like exclamation points. Yet Ariah addressed Chandler in her usual chiding voice, as if the child warranted, and would feel comfortable with, no other.

Chandler said hesitantly, "I—heard you crying, Mother. I heard you—scream."

Ariah said hotly, "You did not hear me scream, Chandler. Don't be ridiculous. *That wasn't me.*"

2

Into the underworld then I descended. Where you can't see, can't breathe. Suffocating in black muck. In shame.

These weeks, months. Exhausting and yet exhilarating days that began for Dirk Burnaby early in the morning, and ended early in the morning. Neglecting his other clients, his paying clients, in the cause of Love Canal.

It was true, Dirk Burnaby was filing motions in Niagara County District Court. In the service of his clients he was going to war against the City of Niagara Falls, the Niagara Falls Board of Health, the Niagara Falls Board of Education, Swann Chemicals, the Office of the Mayor of Niagara Falls and the Office of the Medical Examiner of Niagara Falls. Never had he written such eloquent, forceful prose. But mostly he was an explorer, in his car and occasionally on foot, descending into the underworld.

He would feel at times like those early, doomed explorers, who'd paddled their canoes along the wide river linking two gigantic lakes, not realizing until it was too late that the current was accelerating rapidly, and that they'd entered the "Deadline"—the rough, white-water rapids just above Goat Island. At first you think that your actions are propelling your little boat along at such speed; then you realize that the speed, the propulsion, has nothing to do with you. It is something happening to you.

Dirk woke himself from such trances he drifted into, often in the County Hall of Records, or in his big luxurious boat of a car like Charon's barge crossing the Styx into a region unknown to him.

Crossing into that other region, the industrial city of Niagara Falls. How unlike the gleaming tourist-city on the Niagara River. The scenic city at the edge of the renowned Niagara Gorge. The Wonder of the World, Honeymoon Capital of the World. Prospect Avenue with its old, grand hotels of another era, only just beginning to be replaced, in the early 1960's, by more modern hotels and "motels." And Prospect Park and gardens. And the continuously rising mist and roaring of The Falls. Dirk could not see that the second city, the underworld region, that stretched out for miles to the east, had any relationship to the dwellings on the river. It was a twin, yet a misshapen twin. There was The Falls, and there was the city of Niagara Falls. The one was beauty and the terror of beauty; the other, mere expediency and man-made ugliness.

Man-made poison, death.

"Where it's deliberate, it's murder. It's beyond negligence. 'Depraved indifference to human life.' "

The only connection between The Falls and the thriving industrial city was the massive energy diverted from The Falls to operate certain of the industries of Niagara Falls. But you had to know that this connection existed, and was a multi-million-dollar business: Niagara Hydro. To the uneducated eye such connections were invisible.

To the uneducated eye, much was invisible.

"They have no conscience. My kind."

My kind Dirk Burnaby would be discovering at every turn.

Where Nina Olshaker had been rudely rebuffed, thwarted, and lied to in her inquiries, Dirk Burnaby fared much better. He was an attorney licensed to practice law in New York State, and he knew the rights of both citizens and attorneys. He demanded to see county records, deeds of ownership. He demanded to see county health records. And transcripts of meetings of the Niagara County Board of Zoning. He knew his way around both city and county buildings, the Niagara County Courthouse, the Office of the Niagara Falls District Attorney. He asked questions, and he insisted upon answers. He not only threatened to subpoena witnesses, he did. He wasn't one to accept obfuscation—"bullshit"—from subordinates and flunkies including Mayor Wenn's staff. Including Dirk Burnaby's fellow attorneys, in the hire of local government and the executive officers and board of directors of Swann Chemicals, Inc.

The chief attorney for Swann Chemicals was a man named Brandon Skinner, whom Dirk knew at a distance, warily. As Skinner knew Dirk Burnaby. Between them was mutual respect if no warmth. Skinner was Burnaby's elder by ten or twelve years, a wealthy man with a riverside estate not far from Shalott.

"At least, we've never pretended to be friends. There isn't that pretense to maintain."

Dirk was feeling hopeful. Optimistic. He knew the symptoms: the excitement preceding a good, fair fight.

Of course he knew that Skinner and other attorneys for the defense would stall, stall, stall. He knew the tricks, he'd used them often enough himself. Tricks are a staple of the lawyerly trade, like surgical instruments to a surgeon. But the defense couldn't trick him. Nor could the defense break the backbones of the plaintiffs by causing them to run up devastating legal costs because he, Dirk Burnaby, was working for no fee.

Possibly, he was beginning to see, he'd end up paying expenses out of his own pocket.

"What the hell. I'm rich."

Into the underworld. Where I would drown.

For there came the hour when Dirk discovered the name "Angus MacKenna" in startling proximity to the name "Hiram S. Swann." Angus, Virgil Burnaby's benefactor! The kindly-seeming old man had been a virtual grandfather to Dirk, long ago.

And there came the hour when Dirk discovered that MacKenna Laboratories, Inc., a company in which Virgil Burnaby was a partner, had been, reconstituted in 1939 as MacKenna-Swann Chemicals, Inc.; in 1941, Swann bought out MacKenna's investment, and the company would be known subsequently as Swann Chemicals, Inc. It would become, in the boom years of wartime defense manufacturing, one of the most prosperous businesses in upstate New York.

"Why did I never know this? My father—"

But Dirk's father had rarely spoken of such matters to Dirk. In the last years of his life he'd seemed to have lost interest entirely in business and public life, or to have been revulsed by it. His life was boating, fishing, golfing. His life was drinking, in an affable gentlemanly manner that masked (Dirk supposed, now: at the time he hadn't a clue) a profound melancholy. Dirk's parents led increasingly separate lives in middle age, Claudine aggressively social and Virgil stubbornly withdrawn. Dirk recalled most vividly sailing excursions with his father when, alone together, they'd communicated wordlessly as if reduced to a common identity by the windy, choppy river where anything might happen. At other times, Virgil Burnaby had been smiling, distant. *A man who has lived another man's life.*

Years later, Dirk wondered if his father, a member of l'Isle Grand Country Club, married to an heiress, had been ashamed of Reginald Burnaby the Great. That mustachioed daredevil who'd died in The Falls, for glory and a few hundred dollars. Or maybe Virgil had been proud, secretly. Dirk felt the loss, his father had never told him anything of his personal, emotional life.

Growing up, Dirk had known vaguely that his father was involved with Angus MacKenna and his sons Lyle and Alistair in various business ventures. One of their successes was the development of insecticides and herbicides; MacKenna Laboratories owned several patents which were retained when the company was sold, and from these patents, at the present time, Virgil's heirs still received dividends. (And rather large dividends.) Two years before Swann bought out McKenna and associates the company acquired at auction the uncompleted seven-mile canal locally known as Love Canal, for use as a waste dump. The mysterious canal had never existed as a waterway. Its construction began in 1892, as a project by a local developer named William T. Love; the ambitious plan was to link the upper and lower Niagara River and bypass the Gorge. But Love had gone bankrupt and the canal was left only partly dug. It was located in a no-man's-land at the eastern edge of what was at that time a city of about twenty thousand inhabitants where industrial development was only just beginning. As in the much larger lakeport city of Buffalo, and in the industrial suburbs of North Tonawanda and Lackawana, the boom in local development would begin with the outbreak of war in 1941. Military vehicles, aircraft, munitions, canned goods and boots, gloves, uniforms, even flags! And chemicals of all kinds. The war was the best thing to happen to Niagara Falls, even better than tourism in the 1850's.

Dirk recalled the excitement of that time, as at the age of twenty-four he'd rushed to enlist, with his friends, in the U.S. Army. It hadn't occurred to him that, for those Americans remaining at home, including Virgil Burnaby and his business associates, the war was a very good thing.

From 1936 until 1952 the so-called Love Canal, an open ditch, was used as a municipal and chemical disposal site. Swann Chemicals dumped tons of waste there, and sold dumping privileges to the City of Niagara Falls for the dumping of garbage and, in the 1940's, to the U.S. Army, which dumped classified (radioactive) chemical warfare wastes relating to the Manhattan project. In 1953, Swann Chemicals abruptly ceased dumping and covered the hazardous waste with dirt, and sold the seven-mile contaminated property to the Niagara Falls Board of Education for one dollar. One dollar!

And the contractual stipulation that Swann Chemicals, Inc. was exempt *in perpetuity* from any damages—"physical harm or death"—suffered as a consequence of the hazardous waste.

Dirk read and reread, appalled.

How had this happened? How was this allowed to happen? So recently as 1953? Eight years after Hiroshima, Nagasaki. When certain of the consequences of radioactive poisoning were known.

Swann Chemicals was the principal polluter, but the dumping had begun in the era of MacKenna-Swann. Insecticides, herbicides, poisons. Chemicals. Dirk saw that the dividends his family received were to be traced back to such origins. Those patents he'd professed not to care about, but had taken for granted like all the Burnabys.

Dirk felt sick, ashamed. He was involved in this, too.

All his life he'd been involved, unknowing.

(But how unknowing?)

In her chiding murmur Ariah spoke of the "rich Burnabys." It wasn't clear to Dirk if Ariah was teasing him or taunting him. If her remarks were playful, or cruel. Certainly she exhibited a maddening air of moral superiority. (No wonder Clarice and Sylvia disliked their sister-in-law. Dirk couldn't blame them, really.) But Ariah's disdain for money was the result of her having married Dirk Burnaby, who provided her and their children with a comfortable life. Where was the moral superiority in that?

It was Nina Olshaker he dreaded, discovering that he, Dirk Burnaby, was connected in any way with Love Canal. However indirectly, blamelessly.

(But how blameless?)

After the hazardous-waste property was sold to the Niagara Falls Board of Education for one dollar, the Board promptly resold much of the land to a local developer named Colvin, and began construction on an elementary school. By the time the Ninety-ninth Street School was opened in the fall of 1955, much of Colvin Heights had been built and many of the small woodframe bungalows had been sold.

Dirk supposed that the administration and faculty of the school knew nothing of the building site—the fact that they were working on a toxic waste dump. The principal of the school couldn't have known, even. The Board of Education must have kept secret the deal with Hiram S. Swann and associates. Colvin, the contractor, would have kept the secret too, for surely he'd known?

According to county health records, residents of Colvin Heights began to complain almost immediately of nauseating odors, "black sludge," leaking basements, spongy lawns, "burnt" children and pets; "surfacing barrels" in their yards that contained a virulent kind of tar. Colvin arranged to clean up some of the worst areas, as did the City of Niagara Falls. A crescent-shaped sector, adjacent to Swann Chemicals two miles to the east, was dezoned for residential housing and kept undeveloped. (Though it was fenced off, children played there. It began to be used as an unofficial dump for homeowners wanting to get rid of filthy mattresses, broken household items, old building materials and combustible Christmas trees.) In 1957, medical investigators for the county health board "examined" the site of the Ninety-ninth Street School and declared the area "without hazard to health." They examined those residents of the subdivision with medical complaints and found "no grounds" for alarm. Their conclusion was unanimous: there was no problem in Colvin Heights, and if there was, the problem had been taken care of.

Dirk checked the records of the Board of Education for 1952. The chairman at the time of the Swann Chemicals sale was a local businessman, now deceased, named Ely; Dirk recalled that Ely, or someone with that name, had been a business associate of Hiram Swann's. He would have been an acquaintance of the MacKennas, and surely of Virgil Burnaby.

That was why the Board of Education had accepted Swann's unprecedented stipulation that his company be absolved of blame *in perpetuity*. These were friends aiding friends. Men who belonged to the same private clubs, who were linked with one another by ties of commerce and perhaps even by marriage and blood. And possibly there'd been money changing hands. Ely might have been a secret investor in the subdivision to be known as Colvin Heights. Ely might have been a poker buddy of Hiram Swann. Or a golfing partner of the MacKennas. He'd have been a guest at Shalott, very likely. Membership on the Board of Education was political in some cases, volunteer-philanthrophic in others. There were no salaries. The chair was honorific.

Dirk was sitting with his head in his hands. His heavy, dazed head. He had no clear idea where he was, which municipal building he'd entered hours before, a lone prowler amid echoing dust-grimed aluminum stacks like those of a library, shelved not with books but with documents. He'd been taking notes furiously, now his right hand was a claw. Hardly could he hold a pen. The interior of his nose, mouth, throat felt singed, as if he'd been breathing the fumes of a furnace. What would he tell Nina Olshaker? For he must tell Nina Olshaker. How he yearned for the river! The river of his boyhood. The sky over the river, patches of broken concrete giving way as he stared, as the wind blew, to a pale autumn sun. But it was the sun. And the wind from Ontario was fresh, clearing his nostrils. He and his father were on the wet, slippery deck of Virgil Burnaby's thirty-foot Chris-Craft *Luxe II*. A trim, whitely glistening boat it was, beautiful to Dirk's eye, though as a boy he much preferred his father's sailboat. But Virgil hadn't wanted to take out the sailboat in the last years of his life, sailing was too strenuous for one in his weakened condition. (A heart condition? Dirk hadn't ever known.) They were alone, what a relief to be alone. This was their longest trip, through the vast width of Lake Erie and up the astonishing length of Lake Huron to Sault Sainte Marie hundreds of miles away in northern Michigan, at the Canadian border. Virgil Burnaby, Dirk Burnaby. Father and son. Dirk shaded his eyes watching his father at the prow of the boat, staring out at the lake and the hazy horizon. There was something in the older man's posture, the stoop of his shoulders and the incline of his head, that made Dirk uneasy. "Dad?" Dirk called, cupping his hands to his mouth. "Hey, Dad?" His voice was young and desperate. But with the noise of the boat's motor, and the wind, Virgil Burnaby didn't hear.

3

Not in love with Nina Olshaker. And yet.

Instinctively Ariah drew away from his touch. His breath. His grinding guilt-sick brain. As one might shrink from a subtly toxic odor. An invisible, yet palpable, radioactive aura. Dirk told Ariah nothing of Love Canal for he knew she wanted to hear nothing of his deepest, most profound life that excluded her and their children. She'd become the most fiercely protective of mothers. Her instinct was unfailing, ever vigilant. Hadn't she noticed—she must have noticed!—that Dirk was working longer hours, and often on weekends; that he'd lost much of his ebullience, and his appetite. He smoked more. He slept less. At home, he was locked away in his study and on the telephone well past the children's and Ariah's bedtime. Most astonishingly, he'd dropped his poker nights, that tradition he'd begun in 1931. Prior to this, poker night had been cut back to approximately once a month. But now, it seemed that Dirk had dropped poker altogether. Ariah was so absorbed in Juliet and Royall, she seemed scarcely to take notice of her husband except to murmur, with her small, hurt smile, "Well! We're honored you're back in Luna Park for a few hours, Mr. Burnaby." She joked with the children, in Dirk's presence, "D'you know the one about the high-priced lawyer and his client? 'Client calls up on the telephone and lawyer answers, and client says, "Hello! How are you?" and lawyer says, "Fifty dollars." ' " Ariah laughed heartily, a signal for the older children to laugh, which they invariably did. Juliet, just a baby, waved her pudgy little fists in excitement. Laugh, laugh! Dirk laughed, too.

Like all lawyers, he loved lawyer jokes. The more unfair, the funnier.

Some nights, sharp-eyed Ariah must have noted crescents of fatigue beneath Dirk's smiling eyes, and she must have smelled whisky on his breath. But she never asked where he'd been, or with whom. Or if he'd been in his office all these hours, working. Drinking alone.

Ariah seemed to have few friends and no intimate friend. So she heard no rumors. That Dirk Burnaby was neglecting or putting off his paying clients, that several had left him in disgust and more were preparing to leave. Not only wasn't Dirk Burnaby taking on paying clients, he was the one who was paying now, the expenses of a unique and difficult lawsuit that was turning out to require far more preparation than he'd anticipated back in July. But Ariah was oblivious, in her intense, narrowly circumscribed and comforting world of children, household, piano lessons.

Sometimes in the night they held each other, Ariah pressed monkey-like and playful into her husband's brawny arms, the couple wordless, oddly content, on the edge of sleep as of a vast abyss. It was the habit of years, this embrace. Ariah dropped off to sleep as Dirk, his old, sour insomnia rolling back upon him like despoiled waves, found himself thinking of—who? The Woman in Black?

Ridiculous to have thought of Nina Olshaker in such terms. How we demonize what we don't know, and fear.

Dirk was ashamed to recall how close he'd come to denying Nina, as every other attorney in the city had denied her.

How close he'd come to losing her.

"I won't fail. I can't."

Ariah, asleep in Dirk's arms, heard these murmured words and wriggled in childish pleasure.

"Mmm, darling. I love you, too."

Days, Ariah avoided answering the phone. She sorted mail into neat piles on the vestibule table, but frequently put off opening her own mail, rare as it was. (A letter from her mother for instance. Reverend Littrell had died suddenly of a stroke that fall, and Mrs. Littrell, feeling lonely and useless in Troy, was hinting how she'd like so very much to come to Luna Park to live—"to help out with the children"—but Ariah was not encouraging.) She never watched TV news or read the front pages of newspapers where "disturbing" news might be printed. Quickly she turned to features, to women's pages, entertainment, comics. She, Royall, and Juliet enjoyed the comics: the Katzenjammer Kids, Li'l Abner, and Donald Duck were their favorites. If she'd read certain pages of the *Gazette* or the *Buffalo Evening News* she'd have discovered articles, interviews, even editorials on the subject of the Colvin Heights Homeowners' controversial lawsuit, and she'd have discovered Dirk Burnaby's name. But she didn't, and wouldn't. Sometimes, turning newspaper pages quickly, Ariah shut her eyes and bit her lower lip. No, no! Local news no more tempted her than news of a massive earthquake in Mexico, the crash of an American Airlines jetliner in Jamaica Bay, a tenement fire in Buffalo killing eleven children, a covert invasion of Cuba by American-armed Cuban refugees (" 'Bay of Pigs'?" Ariah would inquire innocently for years. "Couldn't they have named it something else?"), an insurrection, or a civil war, or an invasion, whatever it was, worsening on the far side of the earth in—what was the country? Somewhere Asian, remote as the moon.

But there was Chandler, indefatigable Chandler, a diligent newspaper-reader. How quick to spy the name "Burnaby" amid columns of newsprint. "Dad? This is you in the paper, isn't it?" The child's voice quavered with excitement.

Dirk steeled himself to read. "Burnaby" didn't invariably get a good press in Niagara Falls these days.

COLVIN HGTS HOMEOWNERS FILE SUIT
AGAINST CITY, SWANN CHEMICALS

"Depraved Indifference" Charged

"Yes, Chandler. It is."

"This 'Love Canal'—it isn't a real canal, is it?"

"No. It never was."

"How far away is it from us?"

"About twelve miles. That way." Dirk pointed.

"Is twelve miles close?" Chandler frowned, crinkling his forehead. You could see how he needed to know, beyond the statement of fact, what fact meant.

"I think it's too close. But no, it isn't dangerously close."

Dirk smiled, to reassure Chandler. Though his smile wasn't so confident as the Burnaby smile of months ago.

Chandler said, with a shy dip of his head, "Dad? Could I—help you?"

"Help me? How?"

"I don't know. Somehow. Like a 'paralegal.' "

Dirk laughed. "No, Chandler. You're a little too young. And not exactly trained. But thanks for asking, I appreciate it."

Dirk was touched. Eleven-year-old Chandler was a somber, quizzical boy with a precocious air of adult responsibility. His near-sighted eyes were of the unsettling hue of mist and their focus seemed blurred, even with his new glasses. He was a straight-A student in eighth grade (so Dirk was informed, by Ariah) but hadn't many friends, and wasn't entirely at ease at school. His smile was quick, shy, tentative. Always he seemed to be inquiring of his parents *Do you love me? Do you know who I am?* The younger children, Royall and Juliet, were so much more the focus of their mother's scrupulous attention, Chandler tended to be overlooked. Dirk, who rarely spent time alone with him, wanted now to touch him, hug him; wanted to reassure him *Yes of course your daddy loves you.* How he dreaded turning into his own father . . .

In a lowered voice Chandler said, "Don't worry, Dad. I won't tell Mom. What I read in the paper about you, I never tell Mom."

A preliminary hearing in the Love Canal case had been set for mid-February in the Niagara County District Court. But the date was postponed for several weeks, by request of the defense. And another time the date was postponed, to late April. The Niagara County Board of Health was updating its findings, for the defense. Plaintiff's attorney registered displeasure at such unconscionable stalling even as plaintiff's attorney privately felt vast relief. The motion Dirk had written was the longest and most statistically documented of his career, yet (he conceded) it might have been longer, more fully documented.

"Oh, Mr. Burnaby! Why are people so *evil*?"

How young she seemed, Nina Olshaker. Wiping tears of grief and outrage from her eyes. Her question was a legitimate one. Dirk

Burnaby whose lucrative profession was words could not think of an answer.

Well. There was the Holocaust, he'd discovered certain facts about human nature as a result of what he knew of the Holocaust, and he was certain he didn't know all there was to know of the Holocaust. The role of scientists, doctors, nurses, helpful managerial types, even teacher-types, and (especially) legal-minded types. Messianic leaders, mystics. You could not even say that some of these individuals were selfish, for "self" seems hardly the point. You could not say that the Nazis were insane, for the record shows that they were fully, calculatingly sane. In the service of madness, and yet sane. In a court of law, demonstrably sane. The crude, cruel bullies, the born sadists, murderers, and executioners of the race, you could comprehend, but not these others. How to comprehend these others!

My kind, some of them. Oh, obviously.

Consider atomic testing, in Nevada. Preliminary to and following Hiroshima, Nagasaki. The decade of the 1950's was the decade of (classified) nuclear testing. You wanted to be patriotic. You needed to be American-patriotic, it was the golden-glow aftermath of a just war. A war that (everyone agrees) had to be fought, could not be not fought, and was fought, and was won. And he, Dirk Burnaby, had been part of that winning. And so not wanting to know too much about the government for which he'd fought. It was never good for a patriot to know too much. How, as Dirk had heard from a *Buffalo Evening News* reporter who hadn't been able to publish his information, that in Nevada at the Nellis testing grounds in 1952 to 1953 some soldiers were provided with protective gear, and some were not. Films were made of their "witnessing" the explosions at varying distances. Some soldiers, with and without protective gear, were driven in Air Force vehicles to ground zero immediately after the A-bomb explosions, while others were positioned at calibrated distances. How far from ground zero was "safe"? How close was "dangerous"? Scientists and politicians were eager to know.

My kind was in charge there. High-ranking military men, privileged and highly paid scientists. Dirk knew.

Why then his surprise at Love Canal. Why his naïveté, perverse in a forty-five-year-old man of intelligence and experience.

Yet he shared in Nina Olshaker's dismay, disgust. He tried, he was trying damned hard, Ariah could not have begun to suspect how hard, to separate himself from this "case." He was trying not to become emotional. He was Nina Olshaker's attorney, not her protector. He would not be her lover.

Never. That won't happen. That would be madness.

This remarkable woman unlike any other woman he'd known. Though she suffered from migraine headaches, chronic coughs and infections, the onset of what appeared to be asthma, and "bad nerves," yet Nina was out daily canvassing Colvin Heights. With little help she'd organized the Colvin Heights Homeowners' Association, to which about seventy people now belonged, out of approximately three hundred fifty who might belong. Nina was tireless, or seemed so. She was energetic, optimistic, devoted to her cause. If she was sickened by what she discovered, she tried not to become demoralized. From Dirk she was beginning to learn shrewdness. Cunning you might call it. He'd provided her with a tape recorder, for instance, to tape interviews with her neighbors, not to rely upon schoolgirl note-taking which might be challenged at a later date, in court. Aided by a paralegal in Dirk's employ she was recording a list of instances of illnesses, chronic medical conditions, and deaths in the Colvin Heights subdivision since 1955. She was interviewing parents of children who'd been attending the Ninety-ninth Street School, and she was trying to interview teachers. The principal of the school forbade her to "set foot on school property." Sometimes, doors were shut in her face. She was accused of being a "trouble maker"—an "agitator"—a "Commie." She and the homeowners' association were "lowering property values"—"stirring up negative publicity." She and her lawyer were "out to make a killing"—"looking for a big settlement." She told Dirk, "Some of the people who won't talk to us, they're pathetic. They're coughing, their eyes are puffy and red like Billy's. On Ninety-ninth Street there's a guy, couldn't be more than fifty, he's shaking all over like with nerve gas. They're on crutches. Wheelchairs! One guy works at

Dow, he's using an oxygen mask. Emphysema. 'From smoking,' his doctor told him."

But Nina Olshaker was amassing data, covering some of the same territory the Niagara County Board of Health had claimed to have covered a few years before. The data was damning, Dirk thought. Any fair-minded judge, and certainly any typical selection of jurors, would be impressed. Nina's focus was One Hundred Eighth Street to Eighty-ninth Street. Colvin Boulevard to Veterans Road. Here there were strange clusterings of maladies on streets that bisected the (hidden, buried) Love Canal, and the frequency of occurrence of these maladies was strikingly disproportionate to the frequency of occurrence elsewhere in the city, and in the general population of the United States. Miscarriages, still births, birth deformities. Neurological disorders, stroke. Cardiac problems, respiratory problems. Emphysema. Liver, kidney, gallbladder trouble. And miscarriages. Eye infections, ear infections, strep throat. Migraine headaches. More miscarriages. Cancers! Cancers of all kinds. A cornucopia of cancers. Lung, colon, brain, breast, ovarian, cervical, prostate, pancreatic. (Pancreatic was a rare cancer, but not in Colvin Heights.) Leukemia. Childhood leukemia. (Seven times more frequent than average.) High blood pressure, morbidly low blood pressure. Nephrosis, nephritis. (Illnesses extremely rare in children, but not in Colvin Heights.)

And miscarriages.

Nina said, "I feel less lonely now, what I'm learning. More like I have a right to be angry."

Another time Nina said, "Mr. Burnaby, I know what I'm doing, all this." She spoke aggressively, fixing him with one of her dark, intense, unblinking stares that looked as if they must hurt her eyes.

Dirk said, " 'What you're doing'—what do you mean, Nina?"

"It's got to do with Sophia. I'm mourning my little girl, I guess. That's why it's hard for me to stop, to come back home. No matter how tired I am. Sam says I'm going buggy about this and making things worse but if my mind isn't busy with these things, like trying to talk sense into people, trying to get them to see this is for their own God-damned good, it settles back on her, see? On Sophia. And I can't do her, or Billy, or Alice, any good that way."

By January, the Olshakers' son Billy had become so allergic to the Ninety-ninth Street School, nauseated, teary-eyed and puffy, prone to asthma attacks, Nina refused to let him attend, and was "in violation" of state law. She was served with a summons, threatened with arrest. "They can't make me, can they? Mr. Burnaby, can they? That place makes Billy sick. I can feel it coming over him when we walk there. Will they put me in jail? What can I do?" Dirk made threatening phone calls of his own, and dealt with the problem. He rented a bungalow in Mt. Lucas, a rural-suburban town northwest of Niagara Falls, where Nina could stay with her children when she wanted to escape Colvin Heights. (Sam remained in the house on Ninety-third Street, a ten-minute commute to Parish Plastics. Sam considered moving out of their house "giving in.")

But Nina was tough, Nina persevered. Dirk marveled at the woman's tenacity. He was accustomed to clients who never lifted a finger to aid in their cases, simply paid him his fee. He was accustomed to clients who weren't fighting for their lives. Halfway he wondered if he should offer to buy out the Olshakers' property, pay off their mortgage, and help the couple buy a house elsewhere in Niagara Falls. But he knew that Sam wouldn't allow such an act of charity, Sam had his pride that was already threatened by Dirk Burnaby's presence in Nina's life. And there was a point to pride.

Or do I want Nina to leave her husband. Just temporarily!

Of the outrages that Nina was discovering, the one that most upset her was an account by a housewife who lived on Ninety-eighth Street, behind the school. The woman described an "emergency cleanup" of the playground after torrential rains in the spring of 1957 resulted in a foul-smelling black sludge covering much of the asphalt. One morning, Nina said, the woman watched as a city vehicle pulled up and a work crew in protective gear climbed out, looking like space men, helmets, boots, gloves, and some of them wearing gas masks. Gas masks! And yet, a few days later the school was reopened, and children were playing on the playground as usual. Nina said, her voice quavering, "That's where our children go! That school! This is where we live! And these adult men, working for the city, they were afraid to breathe the air! But everybody lies to us. The Mayor would deny all this. The Board of Health. They say there's nothing wrong here, it's our fault we're sick, we 'smoke too much, drink too much.' That's what they say. They don't give a damn if our children live or die, they don't give a damn about any of us, Mr. Burnaby, why are people so *evil*?" The young woman, exhausted from strain, began to sob, and to cough. Dirk held her, somewhat stiffly. He felt a nameless emotion for her, not sexual desire, or not desire merely, but sympathy, a shared animal panic that they weren't strong enough, the enemy would defeat them. If the enemy was *evil*, the enemy would defeat them.

They were in the house he'd rented for Nina and her children, in Mt. Lucas. It was eleven o'clock in the evening, the children had gone to bed. Dirk and Nina were in the brightly lit kitchen where they'd spread the Colvin Heights map on the table. Sam was working at Parish Plastics. Dirk was approximately twenty miles from Luna Park and his own home, his family. He held Nina Olshaker as she sobbed, and felt the frantic heat lifting from her skin. A smell of something musty, female perspiration, rage. He felt her erratic heartbeat. He wanted to love this woman, yet could not. Dared not. Stiffly he held her, awkward as if Dirk Burnaby had never held a weeping woman in his arms, any woman not his wife, so clearly yearning for him, or for comfort from him.

His profession was words, but damned if he could think of any now.

"Dirk. Hello."

This grim greeting. Clarice's voice grated against his ears like a rusted file against rock.

It was the morning after Nina Olshaker's emotional outburst. Dirk had been thinking of her, and of what she'd asked, and felt as helpless now as he'd felt then. *Am I going to fail, I am not.*

Dirk's elder sister telephoned him at his office, demanding of

Madelyn that she get "your employer" on the phone, immediately. No matter if he's already on the phone, get him on. Was it a family emergency, yes it was.

How long had it been since Dirk had spoken with anyone in the Burnaby family? He couldn't recall. Months. He'd neglected to return his sisters' calls (he knew they'd be furious with him, in this matter of Love Canal) and he'd neglected to call Claudine, let alone visit the difficult old woman.

One day he'd be stricken with guilt, Dirk knew. After Claudine died. But not just yet.

After a hurried, perfunctory preamble of inquiring after Dirk's health and family and paying no heed to Dirk's polite replies, Clarice bluntly attacked. "This female you're involved with, this woman, she's married, she has children, she's a Tuscarora Indian, is she?—a *squaw*? In the eyes of the world, my brother has no more shame than to shack up in Mt. Lucas with a *squaw*?"

Dirk was so stunned by this rush of words, the vulgarity of a woman he'd always believed to be prissy, puritanical, for a moment he sat speechless.

Clarice said, furious, "Dirk, God damn you are you *listening*? Are you *awake*, or are you *drunk*? Are you trying to destroy the Burnaby family, through some *madness*?"

Dirk managed to say, shaken, "Clarice, what the hell are you talking about? 'Tuscarora squaw'? I'm not going to listen to bullshit like this."

"Don't you hang up! Don't you dare hang up! It's impossible to reach you, like it's impossible to talk to your wife. The two of you in your dream world, oblivious of the rest of us, how ashamed we are, your behavior, and her—'Ariah'—a ridiculous name—a name no one has ever heard of—you and her, what a perfect match you are—the adulterer and the wife who sees and hears no evil—"

"What has Ariah to do with this? I forbid you to speak of Ariah."

"Of course! 'Forbid you to speak of Ariah!' And what of this other woman, 'Nina'? Do you forbid me to speak of her?"

"Yes. I'm going to hang up, Clarice."

"Fine! Good! Ruin your life! Your career! Make enemies who will destroy you! If Father could see you now, how his 'favored child' has turned out."

"Clarice, we'll talk about this another time. There is nothing between Nina Olshaker and me, that's all I'm going to say. Goodbye."

"Ariah hung up on me, too. That woman is blind, as blind as you. As selfish. Mother said of her, 'She's a demon.' What a match, the two of you. A match made in hell."

"Clarice, you're hysterical. Goodbye."

Dirk hung up the phone, trembling. He would remember only a few of his sister's shouted words. *Ariah hung up on me, too.*

"I'm not anyone's 'lover,' darling. I'm your husband."

Dirk tried to explain, gently. A headache beginning to rage behind his eyes.

Yes he was involved in a complicated civil case, the most challenging of his career. No he was not involved with Nina Olshaker, the principal litigant.

He was representing Mrs. Olshaker, yes. He was not Mrs. Olshaker's lover.

"I'm her attorney. I've committed myself. It's no different than any other case of mine, except—" Dirk hesitated, his voice beginning to quaver. For of course the case was different from any he'd ever taken on. "Except it's more complicated. It has required much more preparation."

How misleading, for Dirk Burnaby to speak of Love Canal as if the case were nearly completed. As if the massive preparation was over.

Ariah listened attentively, with averted downcast eyes. Her face was a girl's face set in pale marble that had begun to crack very finely. At the edges of the evasive eyes, and bracketing the mouth that seemed to have shrunk to the size of a snail curled inside its shell.

Dirk continued with his explanation that was not—for why should it be?—an apology. The day had been a long one, and not a very cheering one, for another of Dirk's expert witnesses was reneging on his promise to delivery testimony for the plaintiff, and Dirk had been on the phone, cajoling, pleading, cursing, his throat raw in indignation; yet now he managed to speak matter-of-factly, calmly. Betraying no guilt for he felt no guilt. (Did he? No one would think so, seeing the man. For this midnight conversation with his wife he'd even shaved and smoothed lotion on his smarting jaws. He'd removed his camel's hair sport coat. He'd removed his silk necktie. He'd removed his monogrammed gold cuff links and rolled up the sleeves of his starched white cotton shirt, in a gesture of husbandly frankness.) He was explaining that he'd never "deceived" Ariah in any way, no matter what Clarice had said. Ariah had given him reason to assume that she wasn't interested in the Love Canal case, and he didn't blame her. ("It's a nightmare. You're better not knowing.") He had reason to assume from remarks Ariah had made over the years, that the details of his law practice weren't of much concern to her; and in this case, which was demanding so much more effort than any other he'd undertaken, he'd particularly wanted to spare her.

"Did you!"

Ariah spoke in a breathy murmur that might have been intended as flirtatious.

How strangely Ariah was behaving. As if it were she, and not Dirk, who'd been "exposed" by Clarice. As if, having been informed of her husband's deception, and having said nothing to him about it for months, Ariah was an accomplice to his crime.

Dirk said uneasily, "Ariah, darling? You aren't upset, are you?"

" 'Upset.' "

The snail-mouth scarcely moved. Ariah murmured so without emphasis, her remark had no meaning.

"Darling."

Dirk touched her arm, but Ariah shrank gracefully away. As a cat shrinks from the touch of one she doesn't quite want to touch her just at this time, yet wishes not to offend for in the future this individual might be of use.

Barefoot Ariah moved swiftly. She brushed past Dirk without a word of explanation, and left the room and descended the stairs.

They'd been in their bedroom where a single bedside lamp was burning. Dirk had been speaking quietly. Ariah had slipped a pumpkin-colored satin robe over her nightgown as soon as Dirk entered the darkened room, apologized for waking her and switched on the light. Another time he apologized though Ariah indicated no, don't be silly, she hadn't been asleep. She'd been waiting for him. Playing Chopin mazurkas on her fingertips, as often she did in this bed. No need for any apology!

Downstairs, Ariah directly went to the liquor cabinet in the dining room. With the brisk aplomb of one wringing the neck of a chicken, who has wrung the neck of a chicken numerous times, she unscrewed the top of Dirk's Black & White scotch whisky and poured herself a drink in a wine glass hurriedly snatched from a shelf.

"Ariah! Darling."

Dirk was stricken, witnessing such a sight. That Ariah had grabbed a wine glass made the gesture somehow more poignant.

Ariah drank, shutting her eyes. Almost, Dirk could see a flame piercing her slender throat, lifting upward into her nostrils. Ariah drew a sharp shaky breath, but remained stoic and contained.

"Ariah, please don't be upset. There's no reason, truly!"

Still Ariah had avoided looking at him. Her eyes were shrunken and slanted in her face as if secret weeping had worn them out. And her freckles were gone, like Ariah's youth. Shakily she lifted the wine glass and took another quick sip of scotch. Her eyelids shuddered shut.

Dirk said, "Ariah, I don't know what my sister has told you. I can't imagine what she has been saying. She has no grounds for the terrible accusations she's made." Dirk paused, uncertain what accusations Clarice might have made. He didn't want to make a needless blunder here. "The relatives are angry with me on both sides of the family. Not just the Burnabys, but my mother's people, too. Everywhere in l'Isle Grand. They're saying that I'm a 'traitor to my class'—like FDR. They never approved of him! Ariah, there's nothing to Clarice's charges about Mrs. Olshaker. Whatever she has been saying about Mrs. Olshaker. My relationship with Nina Olshaker is purely professional, I swear."

How weak that sounded: *I swear.*

The claim of every liar.

"And Nina Olshaker isn't a Tuscarora Indian. And even if she were . . ." Dirk's voice trailed off, defensive and wavering. What exactly was he telling Ariah?

Ariah seemed hardly to be listening to these protestations. She might have had her question prepared for some time. Quietly she asked, "A house in Mt. Lucas? Why?"

Dirk said quickly, "For reasons of health. The children's mainly. The nine-year-old Billy Olshaker has asthma and an extreme allergic reaction to the school site, which is on this Love Canal waste dump we've exposed. And the younger child, a little girl, has a low white-blood-cell count, and respiratory problems. I've hired expert witnesses to report on certain of the chemicals, benzene and dioxin for instance, that are among as many as two hundred chemicals in Love Canal, dumped since 1936, and these specifically cause leukemia in young—"

Ariah shook her head lightly as if dispelling an unpleasant dream-fragment. "Yes, but where is the husband? Is Mr. Olshaker in Mt. Lucas with his family?"

"Sometimes, weekends."

Dirk wasn't certain if this was true. But it sounded plausible.

He said, "Sam Olshaker works at Parish Plastics, it's a ten-minute commute from their home in Colvin Heights. If he stayed in Mt. Lucas, it would be a much longer drive."

"Why didn't you arrange for a more convenient house, then?"

How shrewd a litigator Ariah might have been. Cross-examining a witness who doesn't quite comprehend how he is incriminating himself. And her voice so maddeningly small, constrained.

Dirk said, confused, "A—more convenient house? Conveniently located? Well, we wanted—I mean, I wanted—a place in the country, to remove Nina and the children from the air of east Niagara Falls." Dirk spoke rapidly now, and convincingly. "East Niagara Falls is very different from Luna Park, Ariah. You can't imagine. I don't think you've driven out in that direction for years. We live so near the river here, the Gorge, and Canada, the air is nearly always fresh. But a few miles to the east—"

"Are the Olshakers formally separated?"

"They are not *separated*. No."

"Yet they don't live together."

"Some of the time—much of the time—they do. They do live together. Except—for reasons of health—"

"Yes, you've said. Are you in love with Nina Olshaker?"

"Ariah." Dirk was shocked at the question, and the calmness with which it was uttered. "How can you think such a thing, of me. Your husband! You know me."

Ariah's veiled eyes lifted fleetingly to his. She seemed bemused, not angry. "Oh yes, do I?"

Dirk said, hurt, "Ariah, certainly you know me. No one knows my heart as you do." Moving his big shoulders uneasily, as if his shirt was too tight. Tugging at his already opened, unbuttoned collar that irritated his neck. "I've always believed, darling, that you know me better than I know myself. That I'm naked before you, exposed."

Ariah laughed thinly. "That cliché! 'Know me better than I know myself.' Marriage is a sustained *folie à deux*. Like crossing a tightrope without a safety net beneath, and not looking down. So the more we know of each other, the less it signifies. You're a lawyer, Mr. Burnaby, one of the best. So you know."

Dirk was dismayed by Ariah's cold little speech. He'd begun to think she might be sympathetic with him. But now she was accusing him. And of what, exactly, was she accusing him?

"Ariah, I don't understand. What do I know?"

"Is it the individual words you don't understand, or their overall meaning."

"Their meaning."

"You do know what a *folie à deux* is?"

"Ariah, our marriage is not a *folie à deux*! That's ridiculous. It's crude and cruel. We've known each other almost twelve years."

Ariah said stubbornly, "All marriage—all love—must be a *folie à deux*. Otherwise, there would exist neither marriage nor love."

Dirk's cheeks smarted. He wanted to take hold of his wife's narrow shoulders and give her a good, hard shake. Never once in their marriage had he touched her in anger, or even impatience; rarely had he lifted his voice to her, though provoked beyond endurance at times. At such times. There was a fatal smugness in Ariah's self-damning pronouncements. There was a fatal smugness in self-damnation. "Never mind if I'm deluded, for the moment! Say I am. Fine. I happen to think that I love you, and I am not in love with—" Dirk hesitated, suddenly reluctant to use Nina Olshaker's name in this way, to shore up a case with his exasperating wife. "—this other woman. Whatever Clarice has told you. She and Sylvia have always been resentful of us, you must know. They'd like very much to undermine our marriage."

Ariah considered this. Of course, Ariah knew this was so.

Dirk touched Ariah's wrist. It was a gentle, tentative gesture, neither repudiated by Ariah nor accepted. He said, "I love you and my family, darling. My truest life is my family."

"Is it!"

"Of course it is." Dirk wondered if he might take the bottle of Black & White scotch whisky from Ariah's hand. There was something in the way she gripped it that worried him. And he would not have minded a small drink of his own. He'd had one or two at Mario's before driving home but that seemed a very long time ago now.

Dirk said humbly, "I realize I've been distracted by work. And it won't—can't—quiet down for a while. If we lose at the preliminary hearing, I'm certainly going to appeal. But if we win, let's say by early summer, of course the other side will appeal, and—"

"How lawyers make work for one another! You're all priests, worshipping the same god. No wonder you adore one another."

"At the moment, in Niagara Falls, no one much adores *me*."

Dirk spoke lightly, not bitterly. Did he give a damn that he was becoming a pariah among his colleagues, God damn he did not. But he wanted the love and support of his wife, at least. He deserved that, at least. He said, as if he'd been derailed from a crucial argument, "When we finally do win the case, Ariah, which I believe we will, by next fall at least—"

"Fall of which year? This year?"

Ariah's question stunned him. It was meant as thinly veiled sarcasm, he knew; yet, *which year*? It was possible that Love Canal would not be resolved for a long, long time.

"Ariah, the case is complicated. It's very complicated. I've been consulting expert witnesses, I've hired doctors, scientists to help me with the preparation. We're trying to assemble data to rebuff the Board of Health's claim that there is 'no problem' at Love Canal; or, if there was a problem, they've solved it. But I've been running into resistance because there are local doctors, even in Buffalo and Amherst, who are afraid of testifying against their colleagues in the AMA. And an organic chemist at the University of Buffalo, I thought I'd hired, decided suddenly he couldn't risk testifying for the Love Canal residents, his laboratory is dependent upon grants from the State of New York. And I can't get the State of New York Health Department involved in this, the bastards won't cooperate." As Dirk spoke with increasing emotion Ariah stood silently, curling her bare white toes into the carpet.

Dirk continued, urgently: "It's a question of faith, Ariah. You must know, darling, that I love you and the children more than anything else in the world, and—"

Ariah opened her eyes, and for the first time regarded Dirk, unblinking. "And yet you're endangering us. You're endangering our marriage. Our family."

"Ariah, I am not."

"You're going outside the family for—I'm not sure what it is: something you want, and need. We aren't enough for you."

Ariah drifted away, gripping the bottle of Black & White firmly. She was sylph-like, floating. Dirk had no choice but to follow. Wanting to seize her arm, to make her stop, listen to him. Ariah made her unerring way barefoot along a darkened corridor toward the front of the house. The house at 22 Luna Place was large, and this corridor was lengthy. Through the leaded mullion windows of the vestibule there was a glaring pale moon, and there was a surprisingly rough, muscular wind in the trees. The perpetual wind off the Gorge! Dirk was thinking how it wore out all resistance. You might become as stone, smooth-worn, impersonal and beyond hurt.

Outside, the beautiful old elms of Luna Park were being buffeted by this wind. Centuries of elms and centuries of wind and yet in this new decade the elms were beginning to falter, just perceptibly. Their stately limbs beginning to dry out, fracture.

Ariah said, now with an air of pleading, "Dirk. I want you to drop this 'Love Canal.' Just now, tonight, I—I think you should."

Dirk protested, "Ariah, no! What are you asking? Darling, I can't."

" 'Can't.' "

"I can't, and I won't. These poor people require my help. They deserve justice. Everyone lies to them, and I'm not going to lie to them. I'm not going to abandon them."

" 'Can't.' 'Won't.' I see."

"No lawyer with any integrity drops a case like this. Not when the circumstances are so grim, and the plaintiffs so helpless."

"And who is paying legal costs? Not these 'helpless' plaintiffs, I suppose."

"Well, no."

"Mr. and Mrs. Olshaker?"

Dirk said impatiently, "Sam Olshaker works shifts at Parish Plastics. He supports a wife and two children. He makes less in a year than I make in—" Dirk paused, uncertain. (He hadn't meant to boast, exactly. But was this a boast? Lately, Dirk Burnaby hadn't been bringing in any income at all. The cash flow in his office account was in one direction only.) "They have no money saved. They have to pay medical costs that go beyond Parish's benefits. And those benefits don't go far. They bought a house on a thirty-year mortgage and like their neighbors in Colvin Heights they're trapped there, unless Swann Chemicals, or the county, or the state, can be forced to pay reparations. Unless somebody buys out their mortgage for them. And in the meantime, their health is being affected. Try to have pity on these people, Ariah. If you met them, and their children—"

Ariah said hurriedly, "But I haven't. And I won't. I have nothing to do with them, and they have nothing to do with me. There are starving people in China, in India, in Africa! I have to care for my own children, I have to protect my own children. They come first, and— nothing comes second!"

"Ariah, what a despicable thing to say. That isn't worthy of you."

"It isn't worthy of your wife, maybe. But it's worthy of *me*."

But Ariah spoke hesitantly, as if she repented her harsh words. She lifted her wine glass another time and drank greedily. Dirk knew he shouldn't challenge her. It was a mistake to excite her further, at this time. Now she was becoming emotional, he must be cautious. Since her father's death she'd become less predictable, less stable; though seeming hardly to have mourned the man, and airily dismissing Dirk's commiseration, yet Ariah had been deeply affected, Dirk knew. And her mother's widowhood and loneliness must have weighed upon her, too. Dirk knew he should retreat, cautiously. Or stand wordless beside her. As consolation. Whatever a husband was, is. Whatever that mute mysterious bond between them.

Somewhere close by, overhead, a floorboard creaked. Or seemed to creak. Sharply Ariah called out, "Chandler! Go back to bed immediately."

But there was silence at the top of the stairs. Even the solemn sonorous ticking of a grandfather clock in the hall seemed to pause for a dramatic moment before continuing.

Dirk touched Ariah's stiff trembling back, and tried to take her in his arms. In a startled reflex she jammed an elbow against him. She broke free of him, breathing quickly. Dirk said, pained, "Ariah, I can't give up Love Canal. Don't ask me. I've promised so many people. They're depending upon me. This isn't ordinary litigation, making rich people richer, this is life. Their lives. If I quit now——"

"The pride of Dirk Burnaby would be hurt? I see."

"——I'd be letting them down. Betraying them. And our adversaries deserve to be exposed. Punished. The only way that hurts them, by paying out money. I'd love to bankrupt Swann and his associates! Those bastards. And the city, and the county, the Board of Education and the Board of Health, these agencies have been in collusion for years. The D.A., the judges. I'm the only attorney it seems who will take on this case, to the bitter end. I couldn't live with myself if——"

"Then who will you live with? *Her*?"

Ariah turned a white, pinched face to Dirk. A face that disconcerted Dirk, it was so contorted by fury.

"Ariah, I've told you. I am not in love with Nina Olshaker."

"But she's in love with you."

"No! Certainly she isn't in love with me."

Dirk spoke so vehemently, with such disgust, you could see he had to be telling the truth.

Ariah turned away. She, who had not drunk even wine for years, so far as Dirk knew, now poured more scotch into her wine glass, and drank in a desperate, swaggering gesture. The powerful alcohol was having an effect upon her judgment, her motor coordination, Dirk could see. Yet he hesitated to take the bottle from her. How like a willful child she was, capricious as Royall. But the air of self-hurt, and of revelling in self-hurt, was Ariah's own. That lethal swerve to the woman's otherwise lucid intelligence. Dirk recalled how, years ago, at l'Isle Grand Country Club, Ariah had drifted away from their dinner with friends and found a piano in a vacant ballroom and when she was discovered, and her playing applauded, she'd fled the scene like a kicked dog. Dirk's friends had genuinely admired Ariah's piano playing, yet Ariah had seemed to hear, or had wished to hear, mockery in their applause. And no amount of explanation or apology could make things right.

Ariah said, her voice trembling, "Very well then. Mr. Burnaby. Move in with 'Nina Olshaker'—this paragon of suffering and virtue—who happens to be young enough almost to be your daughter—and her precious children. More precious to you than your own children. Move into this honeymoon cottage in pastoral Mt. Lucas. We don't need you here. We never see you anyway. I can support us with piano lessons. Go on, go away."

"Ariah, don't say such things. I can't believe you mean it."

"You've gone outside the family. You've betrayed us."

Dirk reached for Ariah as she turned from him, all he could grab was the bottle of scotch. Ariah ran barefoot and whimpering up the carpeted stairs. "Away, away! I hate you, we all hate you, *go away*."

"Ariah—"

Dirk stood panting and perspiring at the foot of the stairs. He could hear his distraught wife running flat-footed, now rather heavily and without grace, into the nursery—was that where Ariah went? No, she'd gone into Royall's room, next to the nursery. She would wake the dazed little boy from his fathoms-deep sleep, and half-carry, half-drag him into the baby's room, and there she would astonish the Irish nanny by shutting and locking the door behind her as if she and Royall were pursued by a demon. She would snatch up the sleeping baby out of her cradle, crooning to and comforting the children she was terrorizing, she would warn the frightened Bridget to stay away from the door, and if Dirk dared to ascend the stairs to knock gently and reasonably at the nursery door (but Dirk would not, he knew better) Ariah would scream at him through the door, with the fury of a mother bird protecting her young.

In the hall outside the nursery, there poor Chandler might be standing. Barefoot too, in his rumpled flannel pajamas. Possibly Chandler would have had time to put on his glasses, but probably not. Chandler blinking and squinting at his distraught father, locked out of the nursery by fiery Ariah.

But Dirk knew better than to pursue the woman. Bottle in hand, he fled the house at 22 Luna Place.

Wondering would he ever return? Would Ariah want him, and would he want to rejoin her; had he the strength to rejoin her, and yet continue with Love Canal? He could not give either up. At that moment, pressing down hard on the gas pedal of his car, he could not have guessed where he was headed, what this exhausting conversation with Ariah would mean. Even his gambler's intuition had drained from him.

Driving in the wind-buffeted night. In the forty-sixth year of his life. At the verge of the Deadline, he was. He could feel the rapid current yet more rapidly accelerating. There was no reversing his course now, nor even swerving to the side. Driving in the large luxurious American car that never ceased to remind him at such times of a boat; a boat manned by Dirk Burnaby himself, on the River Styx. He would drive, drive. He would not sleep. East of Luna Park, away from The Falls and into the interior. Something drew him like a magnet. It wasn't the woman but something nameless. The lewdly winking teasing lights of Dow Chemical, Carborundum, OxyChem, Swann

Chemicals. Alliance Oil Refinery, Allied Steel. Pale smoke like drifting bandages. And fog. And mist, obscuring the moonlit sky. East Niagara Falls was a region of perpetual drizzle. Smells that had become visible. Rotted eggs, sour and sweet and yet astringent like disinfectant. A taste of ether. Dirk drove, fascinated. He guessed that he must be driving in the vicinity of Love Canal. One Hundred First Street and Buffalo Avenue. He'd swing around on Buffalo, to Veterans Road. He had all night. He was in no hurry. He had no destination. Lifting the bottle of scotch to drink, grateful. This consolation a man knew he could rely upon.

Into the underworld that opened to receive me.

3

ONE BY ONE, in the late winter and early spring of 1962, his brothers turned from him.

There was the day at City Hall when Tyler "Spooky" Wenn stared coldly at him, and passed Dirk Burnaby without a word. "Hello, Mr. Mayor!" Dirk called after the man's stiff retreating back, in a phalanx of several other stiff retreating backs, the mayor's companions. In a voice of perfectly pitched mockery Dirk Burnaby spoke.

There was the day when Buzz Fitch passed him by. Or nearly. Pausing at Dirk's table in the Boat Club, unsmiling, A curt nod. Fitch's grave, gravelly voice. "Burnaby." Dirk glanced up, and forced a smile. But he knew not to extend a hand to be rebuffed. "Fitch. Mr. Assistant Chief of Police Fitch. Congratulations!"

(Did Fitch pack a gun, wearing a suit and tie, dining at the Boat Club with friends? Dirk had to suppose, yes.)

There was the day when Stroughton Howell passed him by: Dirk's old law school friend, newly appointed Judge Howell of the Niagara County District Court, in handsome black judge's robe worn with a theatrical flair. Yet his moist-eyed glance at Dirk was one, Dirk would afterward recall, of pained regret, as Howell moved toward an elevator in deep conversation with one of his clerks in the high-ceilinged open foyer of the county courthouse, and Dirk Burnaby prepared to leave by a side door. Howell stared, and Howell murmured what sounded like, "Dirk!", and seemed about to say more then decided no, and moved on. "Judge Howell, hello," Dirk called after the man.

But Judge Howell, entering the elevator, didn't glance back.

Congratulations on your appointment, Judge. I'm sure you deserve it, even more than your esteemed colleagues on the bench.

And there was the painful evening at the Rainbow Grand where he'd gone for a drink with his old friend Clyde Colborne. After one of his long days. After one of his very long days. And Clyde Colborne said quietly, "Burn. I hope to hell you know what you're doing." And Dirk said, irritably, "No, Clyde. Tell me."

Clyde shook his head gravely. As if Dirk were asking too much of him, even in friendship.

Dirk said, "What I'm doing, Clyde, is following my instinct for once. Not the money trail. My conscience."

Conscience! Clyde glanced at Dirk, alarmed.

"You can afford a conscience, Dirk. You're a Burnaby. But that won't last forever." Clyde paused, suppressing a mean-brotherly smile. "The way your practice is hemorrhaging, it won't hardly last the year."

"I'm not thinking about that. I'm thinking about justice."

Justice! Like conscience, this merited a look, from Clyde, of alarm.

Clyde Colborne was fast becoming a ruin of a handsome man. He still had the rich-boy's swagger, that never offended because it invited you to join in; he still had the hotelier's gregarious air. But in recent years the Rainbow Grand was drawing fewer guests, and far fever rich guests, each season. You could see and feel the shift along Prospect Street, in the other old luxury hotels, as if the climate of Niagara Falls were changing. As if the air of the city were changing: instead of fresh chill winds from the Gorge, there was now a prevailing odor of chemicals, a yeasty haze to streetlamps and to the moon by night. And on the outskirts of the rapidly growing city there were ever more cheaply constructed motels, "motor cabins." Bargain accommodations for American in packed cars and campers. Families with young children, in addition to honeymooners. Tourists on buses. Retirees. People who cared not the slightest for gourmet food and drink, or quality cabaret singers, or fresh-cut flowers in expensive hotel suites, or Irish harpists in the lobby. These were the true twentieth-century Americans, Clyde Colborne shuddered at the vision.

Saying now, "This, what you're doing, Burn. God damn! The publicity. It's rotten for our image. It's hurting tourism. Things are bad enough, in certain quarters desperate enough, and you come along. If—" Clyde paused, flushing with embarrassment. He, who'd taken three years of Latin at the Academy, translating, with Dirk Burnaby's help, Cicero and Virgil, stammering now like an asshole cartoon character spouting dialogue unworthy of him and his friendship with Dirk Burnaby but God damn if he could think of other, more worthy words. This pained him, and he resented it. " 'Love Canal.' It's getting as much fucking attention as The Falls, or more. Every time I open a fucking newspaper."

The men fell silent. Dirk Burnaby, with so much to say, so much he couldn't bring himself to say (this long exhausting day of meeting with expert witnesses, interviewing three pairs of parents in Colvin Heights whose young children had died of leukemia within the past two years), found that he had nothing to say. And seeming to know that this would be the last time he would speak with Clyde Colborne, his friend.

A dangerous moment when Dirk had an impulse to toss his drink into Clyde's face. But no. You don't surrender to such impulses except in melodramatic Hollywood films. And this wasn't Hollywood, and certainly this was no film. For, in films, there are close-ups, distance shots, "master" shots, fade-outs and quick merciful cuts. There is an under-current of music signaling what emotion you are meant to feel. In what's called life, there is a continuous stream of time like the river rushing to The Falls, and beyond. No escape from that river.

So Dirk didn't toss his drink into Clyde Colborne's face, nor did he finish it. He sat it down on the glass-topped little table between his and Clyde's legs. He tossed down a twenty-dollar bill, and stood before Clyde could protest the drinks were on him, Jesus!

"Yes. Love Canal is hurting us. Goodbye, Clyde."

Had to admit, he missed poker nights. God damn there was a hole in his heart, he missed those bastards.

There was one of Dirk's brothers-in-law. The one who'd married Sylvia. Small shrewd eyes and an oily skin glistening like a seal's hide. Dirk had a moment's panic that this brother-in-law was intent upon inviting him home for a family dinner out on the Island, *haven't seen you in a long time, miss you, Dirk, and so does Sylvia*, but it wasn't that at all, no invitation to dinner on the sleek brother-in-law's mind, instead he gripped Dirk's elbow urgently: " 'Love Canal.' That's a Negro neighborhood, isn't it? Over on the east side?"

Politely Dirk explained to the brother-in-law no, Love Canal was not a Negro neighborhood.

"And if it was?"

Seeing the expression on Dirk Burnaby's face, which was ordinarily a cordial face in the company in which the two men were accustomed to meeting, the brother-in-law released his grip on Dirk's elbow, and backed off. He stammered a few more words, and goodbye. Yes he'd say hello to Sylvia. Yes he'd report to the relatives that Dirk Burnaby was a changed man, an angry dangerous man, it was exactly as everyone was saying of him. *A traitor to his class.*

The framed, autographed glossy photo of Dirk Burnaby was still there, on the celebrity wall at Mario's. No one had suggested to Mario that it be removed, yet. Possibly Mario would never remove it.

When I win, I'm going to win big.
  Watch me.

One night Dirk drove to l'Isle Grand, where he hadn't been in months. Estranged from Claudine. Estranged from l'Isle Grand Country Club. Yet curious to know, if he went to the Club, if anyone would speak to him? Acknowledge him? He'd have a late dinner at the Club, on a whim.

"Mr. Burnaby. Hello."

The gravely smiling maître d' glanced over Mr. Burnaby's broad shoulder to see how many in Mr. Burnaby's party. No one?

The elegant dining room was still three-quarters full, at just after 10 P.M. Couples, tables of six and eight, no one who seemed to recognize Dirk Burnaby, or glanced up smiling in Dirk Burnaby's direction. And not a face he knew. Blurred and indistinct these faces were, like smudged thumbprints. "In the bar, I think. I'd rather be seated in the bar."

It was the gentlemen's Cigar Bar. In fact, Dirk would dine at the bar. As an experiment. To see if any of his old friends and acquaintances would join him.

No one joined him. Even the service was slow. It was the kind of service you might designate as lightly ironic.

Lightly ironic is not the kind of service a man expects, at a club to which he'd been paying dues for decades.

Dirk ordered a scotch straight up, and waited for some minutes while the bartender prepared it. He was thinking possibly he'd skip dinner. It was getting late for a T-bone steak. Or a twelve-ounce ground-round burger on kimmelwich, a speciality of the Cigar Bar. He had not returned home for two days. Ariah was too proud to formally expel him and yet: he knew himself expelled.

Wanting to grip Ariah's shoulders and plead with her *I can't choose, I won't choose, between my family and my conscience how can I choose!*

Of course, Dirk could return home whenever he wished. If he could bear it. For Ariah had given him up. Given him over, in her heart, to the other woman.

Though the *other woman* was a phantom of Ariah's own contriving.

(Of Nina Olshaker, Dirk tried not to think. The woman's anxiety about her children, and Love Canal. The woman's anxiety about the future. Always Dirk Burnaby had protected himself against the anxiety of his clients, except not now. Except somehow, not this time. "What will happen to us? What if we lose? We can't lose, can we? Mr. Burnaby, can we?" The *other woman* pleading with Dirk Burnaby as you might plead with a savior.)

(But no. One never pleads with a savior. Isn't that the promise of the savior, no pleading? No abject anxiety?)

(Impossible to think of such things. No wonder he had no appetite for red meat. Another drink, instead!)

"Mr. Burnaby?"

"Yes, Roddy?"

"The gentleman has sent you this drink. With his compliments."

Dirk who'd been gazing into the sluggish mucky water of Black Creek, that was fed by swales bisecting the buried Love Canal, glanced up uncertain of his surroundings. It was strangely late, past 11 P.M. He couldn't recall if he had eaten or not. He guessed he'd had several drinks. The Cigar Bar was nearly empty, yet rife with the stuporous odors of cigar smoke that made his eyes water as more frequently, since Love Canal, and the hours Dirk Burnaby spent in Colvin Heights, his eyes were likely to water, and sting. And a headache behind the eyes, not a rapid drumbeat headache but an andante beat, a drummer with a large muffled instrument. Dirk squinted at the far end of the polished cherrywood bar where a tall figure stood, lifting a glass in Dirk's direction. A friend? A familiar face? A stranger? Dirk's eyesight wasn't so reliable lately as it had once been. He guessed that the individual at the far end of the bar, dark suit, white shirt, dark sculpted hair brushed back from his forehead, must be a member of l'Isle Grand Country Club and yet must be someone who supported Dirk Burnaby in his Love Canal campaign.

Dirk fumbled for his glass of scotch and lifted it in a toast as the individual at the far end of the bar, in a mimicry of a mirror-gesture, lifted his glass in a toast. Both men drank.

Through a haze of headache pain Dirk saw the stranger's face shift to a sudden lewd grin. The shadowy blank eyes in the skull. A radium-glow to the bony forehead.

"Mr. Burn'by! Goo' luck!"

Hemorrhaging money. Like time.

How he'd become, without being aware of it, a kind of upright needle, his (empty) head the eye of the needle, through which Time flowed in an erratic but ceaseless stream. *Going past, going past, ceaseless into the past.*

"Zarjo"

On the eve of the Love Canal hearing, Dirk Burnaby astonished his family by bringing home a foundling puppy from the SPCA shelter.

The date was May 28, 1962. The eve of the much-postponed hearing at the Niagara County Courthouse, District Judge Stroughton Howell presiding. The eve, too, of Juliet Burnaby's first birthday.

Did I remember? Of course I remembered.

All my life, I remember.

Was it a coincidence, Daddy brought Zarjo home that evening?

Daddy protested as if his feelings were hurt. " 'Coincidence'?— hell, no. As Einstein says, God doesn't play dice with the universe."

Dirk Burnaby who was Daddy in the household at 22 Luna Park.

Dirk Burnaby who was Daddy, and adored as Daddy, nowhere else but at 22 Luna Park.

As in a fairy tale the puppy came already named: "Zarjo."

Pronounced, as Daddy insisted, " 'Zar-yo.' A Hungarian name."

The boys, Royall and Chandler, had wanted a puppy of course. Royall in his clamorous way, Chandler in his rather wistful, unemphatic way. As soon as Royall had seen dogs belonging to other children, naturally he'd wanted a dog for himself. As soon as Royall had been able to utter "pup-py" he'd been begging for one.

Ariah, the most cautious of mothers, had been unresponsive to such blandishments. She'd known not to recoil bluntly *No of course not, you're not going to have a puppy in this house, not ever*. She'd known not to laugh in her sons' yearning faces. *A puppy! Another helpless un-house-broken baby creature to love, well count Mommy out this time*.

In a delirium of excitement like Zeus emerging from a cloud there came Dirk Burnaby who hadn't been home for two days now home abruptly just as his amazed family was about to sit down to dinner, an early dinner at 6 P.M., prepared by Ariah and Bridget companionable in the kitchen as sisters, or almost, suddenly Daddy was in the kitchen with them and in his arms a squealing, pee-piddling little furry thing. Appalled, Ariah saw and knew the worst: it was alive.

Alive! Zarjo was more than alive. Zarjo was a firecracker of aliveness. Zarjo was an atomic fusion of aliveness. His wavy fur the hue of soiled butterscotch, black rings around his moist blinking eyes. Part beagle, part cocker spaniel, Zarjo was. And part mongrel. But "promising not to be a big dog, probably," as the vet at the SPCA had assured Dirk Burnaby.

One of those impulses that were increasingly ruling Dirk Burnaby's life. One of those hunches, a fiery flash of knowing-what's-right. Dirk had left his office nerved-up and optimistic about the next morning's hearing, he'd intended to drop by Mario's for a drink but instead he'd swung around to the SPCA shelter as if drawn by a magnet to Fifth Street and Ferry and there he was amid a frenetic barking and yipping of furry creatures selecting one of the smaller ones.

Ariah was stunned, though trying not to show it. For the sake of the children Ariah was trying not to show much of what she felt, these days. Almost calmly asking, "Dirk, why have you done this, d-darling, why? I mean, why at this time? Is this—really a very good time? Oh, dear—a puppy. Oh, Dirk."

Thinking *Superstition. He's thinking if he does a good deed tonight, in the morning God will favor him and rule for his client*.

"Why? Ariah, you shouldn't have to ask *why*."

Royall and Chandler weren't asking why, Royall and Chandler were crazed with joy.

Little Juliet in her high chair was squealing, shrieking with joy.

Like Christmas ornaments lighting up, Ariah's children. Royall was on the floor with Zarjo hugging and kissing the puppy as Chandler squatted over them managing to pet the puppy's frantic head. Both boys were crying, "Mommy, don't send Zarjo away! Mommy, please! Mommy, *no*."

So they begged. For frenzied minutes they begged! Royall wept, kicked, pounded his little fists, which in fact weren't so little any longer, against the floor, as Ariah tried to lift Zarjo to hand back to Daddy. "Mommy, *no. Mommy*." Already Mommy was weakening, for who could resist blue-eyed Royall begging as if for his life? And there was Chandler, unexpectedly emotional too. "Mommy, Zarjo must be meant for us! If Daddy hadn't picked him out at the SPCA he might be put down. You know what that means, Mommy, don't you? 'Put down.' " Chandler's myopic eyes swam behind their glasses.

Royall, suddenly sobered, alertly asked, "What's that? 'Put down'? 'Put down' *where*?"

Chandler said grimly, "It means killed. Put down into the ground, and buried. Like anything dead."

Royall bellowed in protest. "Mommy, no. Mommy, NO."

By this time Juliet was crying, too. Though at one year old the baby was too young (at least, Ariah hoped so) to know what was going on, what sort of emotional blackmail-terrorism this was. The adulterous husband and father rushing home after forty-eight hours' absence to dump a squirmy, squealing, teary-eyed pee-piddling five-week-old adorable beagle-spaniel puppy in her lap, and rushing out again into the fragrant spring evening.

"Dirk? Don't you dare! Stop! You can't seriously intend to—"

But yes, Dirk was leaving. He'd left his car running in the driveway. He had work to do at the office, he couldn't stay. He'd grab a bite to eat later. He wasn't hungry. "Goodnight, everyone! Daddy loves you! Be good to Zarjo. Ariah, darling, I'll call you tomorrow after"—Dirk's brave voice faltered only now, perceptibly—"the decision."

The man was in a manic state. That neon glare in his tawny eyes, the quavering voice. Yes, he was trying to bargain with God. As if you could bargain with God! Oh, Ariah knew better. If this man hadn't betrayed her and broken her heart, Ariah might have taken pity on him.

Ariah called in his wake, "Don't you 'darling' me! I want a divorce."

A madhouse in the kitchen. The tuna casserole dinner was ruined. The boys were clamoring, "Mommy can we keep him! Mommy can we keep him!" The baby was crying at the top of her tiny lungs, and a disheveled Bridget was crooning at her in frantic Gaelic. The puppy Zarjo was barking and yelping like the "Anvil Chorus," or "Wellington's Victory," the most appalling music ever penned by man. A chorus of beggars plucking at the taut stingy strings of Ariah's heart. What choice did she have, this was damned unfair! Wanting to scream at them all but instead she pulled out a chair, and sat, and lifted the struggling five-pound Zarjo onto her lap. Splashes of puppy-pee had already soaked into her skirt, what difference would a little more make?

Sternly Ariah scolded, "Don't 'Mommy' me. I refuse to be this little thing's 'Mommy.' It's bad enough I'm your 'Mommy.' If we keep him—"

"Mommy! Oh Mommy *can we*!"

"—you, Chandler, and you, Royall, will take care of him. You will feed him, take him for walks, clean up his messes beginning with right now, that puddle on the floor. Do you promise?"

What a question.

"Yes, Mommy! We promise!"

"We promise, Mommy!"

Ariah, who should have known better, sighed, and petted the puppy's lunging head. His ears, his pink floppy tongue. His little rear end was wriggling on her lap as if Zarjo was trying to do the samba. "He is sort of cute, I suppose. If you like puppies. Chandler, shut the doors to the rest of the house. Royall, put newspaper pages down on the floor here. We'll give Zajo a forty-eight-hour trial. Not a minute more."

Chandler, wiping tears from beneath his glasses, said, "Mommy, thank you."

Royall, hugging both Mommy and the puppy, cried, "Mommy! *I love you.*"

In this way Zarjo came to live in the Burnaby household shortly before the time Dirk Burnaby, who was Daddy, was to depart.

The Fall

T *he tightrope walker begins his brave doomed journey across the abyss.*
Soon obscured by rising mist, fog. Blown off-balance by a gust of
wind, or shot in the back. Falling, so strangely silent.
Unless amid the noise of The Falls his screams went unheard.

Dirk Burnaby would not fall in silence. His protests would be heard, and recounted by, more than sixty witnesses.

The judge ruled. The lawsuit was dismissed. A red haze throbbed in Dirk's brain. Suddenly his legs propelled him upward. He knocked aside the chair in which he'd been sitting at the plaintiff's table, facing the judge's bench. On his feet, and furious. Like a maddened bull, furious. He would be heard "threatening" Judge Stroughton Howell. He would be heard uttering such phrases as "mendacious bastard"— "corrupt son of a bitch"—"bastard hypocrite"—"on the take"— "I'll expose you"—"of all people, you!" Seized by the arm by a shocked bailiff, a man with whom Dirk Burnaby had more than once spoken, even joked, he would turn blindly upon the bailiff and strike him so square in his face, with such strength, the bailiff's nose, left cheekbone, and left eye socket would be shattered, and blood would splash onto Dirk Burnaby's gray-striped sharkskin suit and starched white cotton shirt.

"Pandemonium" in the courtroom, as the *Niagara Gazette* would eagerly report. A "brief, intense struggle" as sheriff's deputies "wrestled" the plaintiff's attorney Dirk Burnaby into submission, arrested him on a charge of assault, and led him forcibly away.

The red haze throbbing. Seeking release. And in that instant a professional career ruined. A life ruined. In no more time than the time required to strike a match: to produce a small blue-flaring flame out of what had been mere inert mineral.

If you could relive that instant.

Would I do it again, God damn yes. Yes! Except I wouldn't hit the bailiff I'd have gotten to Howell himself. Punched in that hypocrite bastard's face.

"Berserk"—"out of control"—so witnesses would say of Dirk Burnaby in Howell's courtroom. Some would claim that they'd seen him drinking in a nearby restaurant during the noon recess. Others would say this wasn't true. It would be reported how, behind the judge's high bench, a clammy-faced Stroughton Howell in his judge's robe had cringed in fear until Dirk Burnaby was subdued.

Then, Howell declared Dirk Burnaby in contempt of court.

In contempt! It's contempt I have for this court. For this thoroughly rotten legal community. For judges on the payroll of criminal defendants. That bastard Howell.

Hypocrite bastard, used to be my friend.

As he was led struggling, stumbling, cursing out of the courtroom by a phalanx of men in the gray-blue uniforms of the county sheriff's department, Dirk Burnaby heard Nina Olshaker call after him. She tried to follow him, tried to touch him; was detained by deputies; wept and cried, "Mr. Burnaby! Dirk! We'll try again, won't we? We'll appeal? We won't give up. *We won't give up.*"

Several witnesses claimed that Nina Olshaker had also cried, "Mr. Burnaby, I love you! Oh God, Dirk, I love you!"

Never. There was no personal feeling between us. None on my side and none on Nina's. We are both happily married. I swear.

The first of the Love Canal class-action suits, it would come to be designated. The first in a disjointed succession that would not end until 1978. But in May 1962 it was the sole Love Canal suit, and it had been summarily dismissed.

By the decision of a single judge, a judge clearly prejudiced in favor of the powerful defendants, the labor of ten months had been dismissed as of no worth. Nearly one thousand pages of plaintiffs' and expert witnesses' depositions, scientific and medical data, photographs, documents. Dirk Burnaby's carefully composed, passionately argued motion for a trial.

Now there would be no trial. There had been no offer of a settlement for those residents of Colvin Heights suffering from illnesses, medical conditions, loss in property value. And with plaintiff's counsel charged with assault, there would be no appeal.

Sure I pleaded guilty. What choice, I was guilty. Hitting that poor bailiff, the wrong man. God damn my bad luck.

Witnesses to Dirk Burnaby's outburst and arrest were much interviewed by local media, and none more frequently than Brandon Skinner, chief defense counsel for Swann Chemicals and co-defendants. Skinner described himself as "an old friend and rival" of Dirk Burnaby. He'd never seen Burnaby, a brilliant lawyer, so obsessed—"morbidly obsessed"—with any case as he'd been with this one, which Burnaby was allegedly litigating for a contingency fee which was to say, since the case was generally conceded to be unwinnable, pro bono. In itself, this was such imprudent, reckless behavior, you could see that Burnaby had lost all sense of proportion. He'd lost his lawyer's instinct for survival.

Yes, Skinner said repeatedly, Burnaby certainly had had an excellent reputation prior to the "incident."

Possibly, Skinner conceded, Burnaby had had something of a reputation for a quick temper. But never professionally. He was known as a shrewd poker player, for instance. You "didn't want to bet against" Dirk Burnaby's cards. Until Love Canal.

Possibly too, Skinner said reluctantly, Burnaby had begun to acquire a reputation as a drinker. That is, a "heavy" drinker. This was fairly recent. The past few months.

At least, the public aspect of Burnaby's drinking was recent.

Asked to comment on the rumor that Dirk Burnaby had been "involved" with his client Nina Olshaker, and that Mrs. Olshaker was currently living in a house in Mt. Lucas rented for her by Burnaby, Skinner said stiffly that he had no idea if this was so, he detested rumors, but if it was so, it would help to explain a great deal.

Why a man throws away a career, for the sake of a gesture.

Did Skinner believe that Burnaby's career was over?

"Sorry. I have no comment."

Judge Stroughton Howell would never comment publicly on the "incident" in his courtroom. Nor on the behavior of Dirk Burnaby, his old, ex-friend. On the Love Canal lawsuit he'd commented in detail,

in his carefully worded written decision to dismiss plaintiff's charges
and declare no grounds for a trial.

It had been a "difficult" decision, Howell acknowledged. The case,
involving so many parties, and presenting so much contradictory evidence, had been "unusually complicated." Yet the principal issues,
Howell said, were just two: was the 1953 contract agreed to and
signed by Swann Chemicals, Inc. and the Niagara County Board of
Education legally binding in its stated absolution of fault to be laid to
Swann Chemicals if "physical harm or death" followed as a consequence of waste materials buried in Love Canal; and, had there been
"absolute and incontrovertible evidence" of a linkage between Love
Canal (that is, residence in the subdivision known as Colvin
Heights), and numerous reported cases of illness and death in that
neighborhood in the years 1955 to 1962.

Judge Howell found the controversial 1953 contract "illegal"—
that is, "not legally binding" under the New York State statute. But
he went on to find that the plaintiff had failed to prove its case against
Swann Chemicals, the City of Niagara Falls, the Niagara County
Board of Education, the Niagara County Board of Health, et al.
Howell came to this decision, as he said, after "carefully considering"
the evidence offered by both sides, which were in sharp disagreement
about the nature of "causation" of illness and death; but he ruled finally in concurrence with the 1957 report of the Niagara County
Board of Health, updated in March 1962, that there was "no incontrovertible evidence of a link between the reported environmental factors and isolated cases of illness and death" in Colvin Heights.

With that ruling, the case was dismissed.

With that ruling, Dirk Burnaby's career as an attorney came to an
abrupt, unexpected ending.

*I could have torn the bastard's throat out with my teeth. He betrayed justice,
and he betrayed me. Hypocrite lying bribe-taking judge-bastard, I could kill
him even now with my bare hands.*

In truth he hadn't been surprised. He'd had a premonition. He'd had numerous premonitions. Dirk Burnaby may have been deluded, and he may have been desperate in his delusion, as a man is desperate in a hopeless love, but he'd known what might happen. He knew how powerful his adversaries were, and how prejudiced any Niagara Falls judge would be in their favor.

He'd wondered in private why Stroughton Howell hadn't recused himself from the case, on the grounds of having been a close, intimate friend of the plaintiff's attorney for more than twenty years. And now he knew.

Dirk hadn't told Nina Olshaker, or the others. He'd shared his misgivings with no one. His slow-dawning realization, that sick sensation in the gut, the opposition had gotten to his expert witnesses, to undermine his principal argument of "causation." Of nineteen men and women, physicians, medical workers, scientists who'd agreed to give sworn depositions on behalf of the Colvin Heights residents, only eleven had come through. And of these, several spoke tentatively, unwilling to fully commit to the standard of "absolute and incontrovertible evidence." For always there are genetic factors, behavioral factors like drinking, smoking, overeating, that might be said to "cause" illness in an individual.

By contrast, Skinner and his team had assembled more than thirty expert witnesses to rebuff the argument of "causation." These included the most highly respected local physicians. The chief of medicine at Niagara General Hospital, an oncologist at Buffalo's Millard Fillmore Health Center who specialized in children's cancers, a Nobel laureate chemist consultant at Dow Chemical. Their arguments were a single argument, like a single deafening drumbeat comprised of numerous drums: amid a myriad of factors it is impossible to prove that some factors "cause" illness.

Just as it has never been proved that smoking tobacco "causes" cancer. Not by any science known in 1962.

In the hire of Swann. Swann's money. Bribes. Bastards!

Dirk would not have wished to think that Howell might accept a bribe, too. As an attorney Howell had made money, now he was a county judge his yearly income had diminished considerably. It was a fact of public life: judges, politicians, police were in positions to accept bribes, and some of them went so far as to solicit bribes. In Niagara Falls since the Prohibition years, the 1920's, as in Buffalo, organized crime exerted a powerful influence, too. It was common knowledge, but Dirk Burnaby tried not to know too much.

Years ago, as a young aggressive attractive lawyer with a "good" surname, that's to say in no way likely to be confused with an Italian surname, Dirk had been approached by a Buffalo lawyer on the payroll of the Pallidino family, as the organization was called. Dirk had been offered a good deal of money to work with the Pallidinos in preparing a defense against charges by a crime-crusader state attorney general, in the heady era of Kefauver's senate crime investigating committee, but Dirk hadn't been tempted, not for a moment.

He hated and feared criminals. "Organized" criminals. And he hadn't needed the bastards' money.

Thinking now, God damn he should have tried to bribe a few key witnesses himself. A few thousand dollars more or less, already he'd invested so much of his own money, what difference? Now it was too late. Now his enemies had defeated him. He should have gotten to Swann's key witnesses, and out-bid Swann. Should've risked more than he had in the cause of Nina Olshaker, her dead daughter and her ailing children he'd come to feel a kind of love for, yes and her husband Sam, and the Olshakers' future murky as the sky above East Niagara Falls. But he'd feared being caught. Not the morality of being caught but the bare blunt fact of being caught, exposed. Behaving unprofessionally. Providing his enemies with grounds to press for his disbarment.

Which now he'd done. Why?

Why, why throw away your career. Your life.
It had to be. I don't regret it.

In a ground-floor cell at the Niagara County Jail where he'd been in-carcerated for ten hours in "contempt of court." In Dirk Burnaby's first cell he was thinking these thoughts. His blood still raging. The red haze in his brain. Oh, but Christ he was tired: except for his fast pulse he'd have liked to sleep. Sleep like the dead. He'd have liked to have a good stiff scotch. The knuckles of his right hand were skinned, bruised and swollen from connecting with a man's face: the hard but friable bone behind the face.

Had to be. I don't regret it.

Oh, shit: I will always regret it. But it had to be.

11 June 1962

Had to be, had to be. What choice?

At about midnight of this day that Dirk Burnaby could not have named the sky above the Niagara River began to clear after a fierce pelting rain and suddenly a full moon emerged, so bright it hurt his eyes. Yet Dirk found himself smiling, to see it. A man who rarely smiled except at such unexpected times. Alone, like this. Driving alone late at night (or was it very early in the morning) with no clear sense of the hour, the date, except a guilty sense that he was falling behind.

Not quite two weeks after Dirk Burnaby's public humiliation, his act of "assault" and his arrest.

Driving his luxury car, now splattered with mud, along the broad puddled Buffalo–Niagara Falls Highway. Beside the Niagara River. West and north in the direction of Niagara Falls. Home! He meant to go home. He saw a night sky above the city mottled with cloud as with a radioactive luminosity.

He wasn't drunk. Since the age of sixteen he'd been one to hold his liquor, as he was one to accept responsibility for his actions.

He hoped his children would understand. He believed they would, one day. You might not redeem yourself by accepting responsibility for your actions, but you can't redeem yourself otherwise.

That night, Dirk Burnaby was driving in the direction of Luna Park and so naturally the speculation would be that Dirk Burnaby had been headed home.

Anxious in wondering if he'd be welcome at that home. *May I speak with Mommy?* he'd inquired of Royall and the child ran away breathless and returned after at least ten long seconds breathless and chagrined crying *Daddy! Mommy says she isn't home. Daddy, you can talk to me!* And so Daddy did talk to Royall, until at the other end of the line someone came up silently (Dirk tried not to envision who, and with what expression on her pale freckled face) and took the receiver from the four-year-old and hung up.

Dirk had been absent from 22 Luna Park for several days. He'd been in Buffalo, conferring with lawyer-colleagues. Defeated in the Love Canal case but only temporarily, he believed. He could initiate an appeal, and he could help raise money for the Colvin Heights Homeowner's Association, though disbarred from practicing law himself. Since that afternoon in the courtroom Dirk Burnaby's life had become mysterious to him, he had only his instinct to follow. He'd become a specimen in a jar. He smelled of formaldehyde. Yet as a specimen he wasn't quite dead.

Disbarment was certain. He'd decided to enter a plea of guilty in the assault. He had posted $15,000 bail and he was "free" and he would be sentenced in less than a week, and he would accept the sentence. Probation, or prison time.

Prison! In more than twenty years of Dirk's law practice, not one of his clients had gone to prison.

He'd had to plead guilty to the charge of assault because he was guilty. He might have claimed self-defense, but it had not been self-defense, only just a vicious reflexive blow. Breaking the face of an innocent man. Dirk was ashamed, and knew the shame would outlive him. Yet in the *Niagara Gazette* as in the Buffalo newspapers Dirk Burnaby was emerging as something of a heroic figure, however reckless, self-destructive.

LOVE CANAL LAWYER BURNABY
PROTESTS JUDGE'S DECISION

Courtroom Assault Leads to Arrest

And,

LOVE CANAL LAWSUIT DISMISSED,
ATTORNEY BURNABY CHARGED WITH
COURTROOM ASSAULT

Since that day, Ariah had not spoken to him. Dirk understood that Ariah might never speak to him again.

He was driving at about sixty-five on the nearly deserted highway when he saw the reflection of a large truck in his rearview mirror, no more than twelve feet from his rear bumper. An enormous diesel rig it appeared, with an unnaturally high cab. Dirk pressed down on his gas pedal and accelerated to pull away. The heavy Lincoln plowed into and through puddles of water, sending up sheets of blinding spray like a racing boat. Dirk switched on his windshield wipers, beginning to panic. The vehicle behind him accelerated as well. It couldn't be a coincidence, there was the truck looming again in Dirk's rearview mirror, nearly nudging his bumper. Again, Dirk pressed down on the gas pedal. He was now traveling at seventy, seventy-five miles an hour. Dangerous, under these road conditions. Of course, he could outspeed the truck, if necessary; but why was it necessary? Though he couldn't identify the truck the chilling thought came to him *Swann Chemicals. One of their rigs.*

The Lincoln was traveling now at eighty. Dirk gripped the steering wheel tight with both hands. Beside the highway, on Dirk's left, the Niagara River rushed, raged. Always it was a shock to see the river so close beside the road, here at the upper rapids. The Deadline. Beyond was Goat Island, deserted and featureless in the dark; and beyond Goat Island, The Falls and the Gorge lit up in carnival colors for the summer tourist trade, shifting as in a kaleidoscope Dirk found distasteful, vulgar. He had not intended to follow the highway past

Goat Island, he'd intended to turn off onto Fourth Street, which would take him to Luna Park.

"Hey. What the hell are you doing!"

Dirk managed to keep a safe distance between his speeding car and the speeding rig behind him, but the Lincoln had begun to shudder with the strain. Dirk's hands gripping the steering wheel were suddenly clammy with sweat. He couldn't calculate how he might slow to exit the highway with the God-damned truck so close behind, already he was in the right-hand lane and had nowhere to go except the shoulder. And the shoulder of the highway was deeply puddled, and dangerous. And Dirk seemed to know that the driver in the truck, invisible behind his high windshield, wouldn't allow Dirk to ease over onto the shoulder.

For another mile they traveled like this, Dirk's Lincoln and the unidentified rig, as if locked together.

Then Dirk saw, moving swiftly from behind, at his right, noiseless as a shark, a second vehicle. A police cruiser? No light was flashing on the roof, and Dirk heard no siren. Yet he recognized the vehicle as an NFPD cruiser. It was moving up beside him, on the shoulder, at Dirk's speed of eighty-two miles an hour.

Dirk glanced over at the driver in alarm, and saw an individual in dark glasses, visored cap pulled low over his forehead. A single police officer? That struck Dirk as a bad sign. He'd switched on his right-turn signal, but couldn't maneuver to exit. He couldn't increase his speed sufficiently, and he couldn't slow down, he was boxed in by the cruiser to his right, the diesel rig behind him. *They want to kill me. They don't know me!* The thought came swift and almost calm and though it was a thought as logical as the geometry theorems Dirk had memorized in high school, and had taken solace in, somehow he didn't believe it, his lips drew back from his gritted teeth in a smile of derision. It couldn't be! It could not be. Not like this, with such rude abruptness. *Not now. Not when I have so much more work to do. I'm still young. I love my wife. I love my family. If you knew me!* The police cruiser was edging into Dirk's lane. Dirk sounded his horn, shouting and cursing. His bladder pinched. His body was flooded with adrenaline like neon acid. The Lincoln was up to eighty-six miles an hour, faster than Dirk had ever driven any vehicle. It could not go faster, yet Dirk pressed down on the gas pedal harder. He was trying to save his life, steering away from the cruiser, aiming for the middle lane of the highway, and at last the left-hand lane, hoping to Christ no one would slam into him head-on. The Lincoln's tires plowed into a wide, deep puddle, water streamed over his windshield like flame, he saw the guard rail rushing toward him, illuminated by his headlights. The car was shuddering, skidding. He saw the Niagara River choppy and wind-ravaged in the unnatural glare from the sky, so strangely close to the highway you would think the river was flooding.

And that was all Dirk Burnaby saw.

Poor fool. Threw away your life, and for what?

PART III

Family

Baltic

*F*amily is all there is on earth. Seeing there's no God on earth."

We went to live in a crumbling brick-and-stucco rowhouse at 1703 Baltic near Veterans' Road. In a residential neighborhood that bordered, on the east, acreage belonging to the Buffalo & Chautauqua Railroad. We were below Fiftieth Street, miles from Love Canal. Our house had been built in 1928. A house of "poignant ugliness" Ariah would call it.

The other house, on Luna Park, had had to be sold soon in the late summer of 1962. Anyway, our mother sold it.

"Near-destitute" she described us. We would grow up clinging to this mysterious phrase without knowing what it meant, exactly. Except that *near-destitute* was a permanent condition, possibly a spiritual condition, special to us. The fatherless Burnaby children.

"If they ask of him, tell them: it happened before I was born."

Always there was a *they*, *them*. Always there was *we*, *us*.

Ariah shut the door upon *them*. Locked all the windows and pulled down the blinds. Only her piano students were welcome into the house at 1703 Baltic, ushered into the parlor which was the music room for years, until a porch at the rear of the house was remodeled and winterized and became the "new" music room.

It happened before I was born. So many times we spoke these words, they came to seem true.

"Our catechism for today is: do you get what you deserve, or do you deserve what you get?"

Her eyes like green gasoline on the verge of igniting and yet: you'd remember afterward that Ariah was smiling.

Years of smiling. And her thin strong arms hugging us. And hot fierce flamey kisses to dispel a child's nighttime terror of loss, dissolution, chaos.

"Mommy's here, honey. Mommy's always here."

It was so. And Zarjo was her companion, bristly-haired, with alert anxious spaniel eyes. Nosing, nudging, clumsily caressing with paws that seemed almost human, in yearning.

If Mommy couldn't sleep with one of us wakened by a nightmare, Zarjo could. Snuggling, shivering with doggy pleasure. His cold damp nose gradually warming, in the crook of a child's arm.

"Mommy's here." Rolling her eyes skyward. (Really just roofward. It was an ongoing joke in the household, as in an ongoing radio program, that God-the-Father was a cranky presence hovering a few feet above the leaky shingleboard roof.) "Or maybe I mean the ghost of Mommy. Soldiering on."

Beyond the house was a weedy-marshy back yard, a scattering of rusted-wire chicken coops, a three-foot railway embankment. Freight trains hurtled past with jarring violence two or three times daily and often in the night. *Buffalo & Chautauqua. Baltimore & Ohio. New York Central. Shenandoah. Susquehannah.* Nothing beautiful in the locomotives belching black smoke and the freight cars rattling and rumbling through our heads except the names *Chautauqua, Shenandoah, Susquehannah.*

"Never cry. Not in public, and not in this house. If ever I catch one of you kids crying, I will personally—" Ariah paused dramatically. The gasoline eyes glittered. Zarjo thumped his stubby tail in anticipation, eagerly watching his mistress. We were Ariah's TV audience: meant to register the comical difference between Mother's precise enunciation and cultivated manner, and the comic-strip vernacular of her speech at such times. "—knock your blocks off. Get it?"

We did. We got it.

In fact we never did, but we were vigilant.

There was Chandler, of the three of us he was the eldest, and would always be so. There was Royall, seven years younger than his brother. There was Juliet, born in 1961. Which was too late.

Those old rusted chickenwire coops! I still dream of them sometimes.

Our next-door neighbors told us they'd been rabbit coops, once. The rabbits had been big soft-furred long-eared gentle creatures with glazed eyes, grown too large for their cramped quarters. Sometimes their fur pressed through the chickenwire and blew gently in the wind. The rabbits were solitary, one to a coop. We counted seven coops. There were more, badly rusted and broken, in the cellar of our house. Chandler asked what was the point of cooping rabbits in such small cages but the reply was unclear.

Beneath the coops were calcified droppings, like semi-precious gems almost lost in the weeds.

It happened before I was born. The body was never recovered. The car was dredged up out of the Niagara River near the twisted guard railings but the body was never recovered and so there was no funeral, there would be no grave site.

There would be no mourning. No memory.

Never would Ariah speak of him. Never would Ariah allow us to ask about him. It was not that our unnamed father was dead (and had died, as we would come to know, in mysterious circumstances) but there had been no father. Long before his death he'd been dead to us, by his own choice.

He had betrayed us. He had gone outside the family.

The Woman in Black

*T*his cemetery!
     Royall was thinking the warm sunshine seemed wrong here. You couldn't name it but definitely something was wrong here.

He'd been meaning to stop for a long time. He had the kind of honeycomb mind where notions took a while to work their way through to being acted upon. But finally, if you didn't get impatient, Royall would act upon them, maybe.

It was a Friday morning in October 1977. Royall was nineteen years old and soon to be a married man.

Heartsick Royall, who knew why? Mostly he kept it a secret.

This cemetery on Portage Road he'd been driving past for over a year and had long meant to explore. An old neglected place beside an abandoned church that looked lonely and in need of visitors. Royall had an eye for such things. It wasn't pity, he didn't think, nor even curiosity. *Like calling to like* Ariah would say.

Ariah would be exasperated seeing him here. But Ariah wouldn't know.

Royall entered the cemetery by the opened front gate. It was wrought iron, very rusted. You couldn't make out the letters overhead, they were so rusted. Grave markers near the gate were old and weather-worn, dating back to—when? The earliest grave marker he saw was thin as a playing card, stooped over as if about to fall. The letters were so faint Royall could barely read them but the dates looked like 1741–1789. So long ago, it made Royall dizzy to calculate how many generations.

The Falls and the Gorge were millions of years old, of course, like the earth, but these weren't living things. They had never lived, and had not died. That was a crucial difference.

Royall liked it that he knew no dead people. Never visited any cemetery to see any specific grave.

Isn't that unusual, his fiancée asked him. Most of us, we know lots of people who have died.

Royall laughed and told her, as his mom would say, the Burnabys aren't lots of people.

Tall grasses, spiky thistles, briars were everywhere in the cemetery, crowding the grave markers and the crumbling rock wall where the grounds-keeper, if there was one, couldn't mow. Royall had an urge to do some mowing here himself. (Sometimes he liked to mow. Not always but definitely sometimes. His back, shoulders, arms were muscled. His hands were so calloused they were almost gnarly. Big hands, and capable. With a hand mower, Royall was usually the one to mow the grass at home. If Royall procrastinated, you could be sure that Ariah would grab the mower and start pushing herself, panting and fuming and churning the mower's dull blades in wet grass, to embarrass Royall.)

A warm autumn day in this neglected place, it was a beautiful place and so seemed wrong to Royall. Because the dead can't feel the sun. Because the mouths of the dead are filled with dirt. And their eyes stitched shut. Radioactive bones, glowing in the dark of the earth.

Where do you get your strange ideas, his fiancée was always asking him. Quickly kissing him on the lips so that Royall wouldn't take offense.

Royall hadn't wanted to say *Out of my dreams. Out of the earth.*

In fact, Royall was sure he'd seen photographs of radioactive bones somewhere, in a book or a magazine. Maybe they'd been X-rays. And there was that photo of a Japanese family, all that remained of them shadowy silhouettes baked into a wall of their home in Hiroshima in some long-ago time before Royall and Candace were born, when President Harry S. Truman ordered the A-bomb dropped on the Japanese enemy.

Royall never told Candace things to upset her. Virtually as a baby he'd learned that there were things you didn't say, and didn't ask. If you made a blunder, Mom would stiffen and back away as if you'd spat on her. If you behaved the right way, Mom would hug, kiss, rock you in her thin but strong arms.

Royall realized he'd been whistling. Out of a tall elm, a bird with a liquidy sliding call echoed him. Royall's fiancée liked to say he was the most whistling-hearted boy she'd ever known.

Fiancée! Tomorrow, shortly after 11 A.M., Candace McCann would be his bride.

It was a strange custom. Royall had never given it any thought before. A new individual would enter the world: *Mrs. Royall Burnaby*. Yet now, that individual didn't exist.

In the brick-and-stucco rowhouse on Baltic, mail came sometimes for *Mrs. Dirk Burnaby*, or *Mrs. D. Burnaby*. Official-looking letters from the City of Niagara Falls, the State of New York. Ariah took them quickly away. *Ariah Burnaby* she was, if anyone cared to know.

Royall was discovering that the cemetery was larger than you'd imagine from the road, covering about two acres. Tall oaks and elms partly dead, with split, drooping limbs and dried leaves. Briars, and wild rose running loose like barbed wire. That autumn smell of leaves and soft rotted things. The cemetery was hilly at the edges, and that seemed wrong, too. Graves on a hillside looked as if they might slide downhill in the next rainstorm. Where a wedge of raw red earth had caved in from erosion, tree roots were exposed. These roots had a look of anguish or threat, like somebody dead, trapped in the earth, was clawing to get free.

Royall felt light-headed, for just a moment. His whistling slowed, then took heart and continued.

Was someone watching him? He glanced around, frowning. He remembered seeing a low-slung Ford, older than his own car, parked by the side of the church. Royall's car, his newly repainted (sky-blue, with ivory trim) 1971 Chevy sedan purchased for $300 from his boss at the Devil's Hole Cruise Line, was parked at the cemetery gate.

His boss Captain Stu, like his mom Ariah, would be exasperated seeing Royall drifting about this useless place. Whistling, and his shoes squishing in damp soil. Of course Royall should be in his car driving to work. (Royall assisted the cruise ship pilot, Captain Stu. Royall wore a nautical-looking waterproof uniform and his title was Lieutenant Captain Royall and since he was twenty years younger and way more good-looking than Captain Stu, it was Royall who was most frequently photographed with beaming female tourists and children. Even before graduating from Niagara Falls High in 1976, Royall had been working at the Devil's Hole and making good money.)

Royall wasn't one to ask of himself *Why the hell have I stopped here?*

Royall wasn't one to calculate his every move like a chess player. Not one to ask *Why, why now? When I'm going to be married tomorrow morning.*

Royall was discovering more graves, and newer graves. These dead were beginning to be born in the early 1900's and some of them had not died until the 1940's: killed in the war. There was a winged cement angel with blank blind eyes and a chipped-off ear guarding the grave of a man named Broemel who'd been born in 1898 and had not died until 1962 which was very recent. *Careful now* Royall was being warned. *You want to be careful, son.* This voice, crafty yet kind, he sometimes heard when he might be drifting into a mistake.

Mostly Royall had no idea what the voice was saying. If he tried to listen closely, the voice vanished. Yet he was comforted hearing it. As if someone was thinking of him, Royall Burnaby, even when common sense told him no one was.

Royall's sister, Juliet, told him she heard voices too, sometimes. Telling her to do hurtful things.

Hurtful things! Royall laughed, Juliet wasn't any kind of girl to do a hurtful thing to a spider.

Why'd a voice give you such advice? Royall asked. And Juliet said like it was the most matter-of-fact statement, Because there is a curse on us. Our name.

Curse! Like a mummy's curse? Frankenstein? Royall had to laugh, this conversation was so ridiculous. There's no such thing as a curse. Ask Chandler. Ask Mom.

In that quiet stubborn way Juliet said, It's only what the voices say, Royall. I can't tell them what to say.

Well. Royall didn't believe in any damn curse. No more than Chandler, who was the brains of the family, did.

But he'd begun walking fast, as if he had a destination and wasn't just prowling. Overhead the sky was bleached-out. The sun burned through, whitish-hot. Like something melting. The slanted light indicated autumn. By the Niagara Gorge the air would smell of chill, vaporous moisture but here, inland, a sweet rotted-earthy odor rose from the grass. Royall paused, shutting his eyes. What did it remind him of—tobacco? Sweet Corona cigars. Royall didn't smoke (Ariah boasted she'd drummed it into her children's heads that smoking was a filthy habit bad as heroin) but he'd tried a couple of cigars offered by the older gambling men he sometimes hung with, downtown. He'd coughed and choked, tears stung his eyes, he'd decided that cigars weren't for him yet still he was drawn to the dark earthy tobacco smell.

A sexual pang in his groin, at the thought of being married tomorrow. Royall's first full night with Candace McCann in an actual bed.

A narrow graveled lane led through the opened gate into the center of the cemetery but if you followed it, you came to an abrupt stop. The lane just ended. Rows of gravestones here belonged to people who'd been born in the early decades of the twentieth century and had died mostly in the 1940's, 1950's, 1960's. It was a strangely warm day for October. Sunshine, and no wind. You wouldn't know that The Falls was less than two miles away.

The cemetery, Royall decided, was like a city. It continued the injustice of the city and of life. Most of the grave markers were ordinary stone, weather-worn and soiled with bird lime, while others were more expensive, larger, made of granite or marble with shiny engraved facades. This was Christian ground, no doubting it. Everywhere were inscriptions to signal the joy of death, and heaven. *The Lord Is My Shepherd I Shall Not Want*. And, *This Day I Shall Be With You In Paradise*.

Did Christians truly believe in the resurrection of the body? It was a mystery to Royall, what Candace tried in her faltering way to explain to him.

Ariah was always saying scornfully there was no God on earth, and yet—"There might be a God watching." This made the human predicament worse. For God was tricky, unpredictable. In gambling terms, God held all the good cards. God owned the casino. The casino was God. You couldn't ever hope to know God or His plan but still He might be there, so you had to be vigilant. In one of the religious fevers that overcame her at unexpected times, like an onslaught of flu, Ariah might insist that her children accompany her to church, but most of the time she disdained such superstitious—craven—behavior. Royall didn't take any of it that seriously. He couldn't see why anybody did, especially the part about hell.

In Niagara Falls the joke was, who needs hell? We have Love Canal.

Royall craned his neck looking up at a ten-foot Jesus Christ on a stone cross. A bird's nest of twine and straw had been built at the cross staves. This Christ had a beautifully shaped head, crowned with thorns but triumphant. *Yet I Shall Rise Again*. Royall shivered, there was something thrilling here. Yet he was grateful he hadn't been baptized a Christian. Too much was expected of you! Nearby were several stone angels. One or two were so decrepit you couldn't tell if they were intended to be female or male. Or wasn't there any sex distinction, among angels? The angel Royall liked best was a boy-angel with muscular-looking hawk-wings and a pugnacious upper lip. A little like Royall himself. Bird shit glowed a faint radium green on the angel's head and wings but the angel gazed upward undaunted. *Flights of Angels Sing Thee To Thy Rest*. Royall wondered what wild yearning had inspired the original idea of angels.

"Probably it was a dream somebody had?"

Royall spoke aloud in wonderment as often he did when he was alone. It was a habit he'd had since childhood like whistling, humming loudly, even singing. Hearing him, people were inclined to smile. A happy, uncomplicated soul, they thought Royall Burnaby.

But not very mature, and not ambitious. He'd managed just to scrape through high school despite the fact (as his teachers insisted) that he was intelligent enough, only just lazy. He had a reputation at school for being a good-natured boy who'd volunteer for any task, like pushing tables and chairs around the cafeteria, hauling cartons of supplies up flights of stairs. He'd changed flat tires for more than one teacher, he'd helped push teachers' cars out of snowbanks. The kind of boy who failed a course because on the day of the final exam a friend needed a favor done, and Royall volunteered. Last year he'd almost failed to graduate with his class, Royall Burnaby who'd been voted "best-looking" senior boy. Except his attention was so scattered, he might have been one of the ten or twelve seniors out of one hundred eleven at NFH to go to college. He hadn't even graduated with a New York State regents diploma, only a local diploma.

Not like his brother Chandler who'd been an honors student at NFH, but who'd want to be Chandler? Poor guy, too brainy for his own good. And possibly, when it came down to it, not brainy enough. He'd almost flunked out freshman year at Buffalo State, as a scholarship student, suffering from "nerves." Now he was teaching junior high in Niagara Falls and probably making less money than Royall who piloted shrieking tourists into the churning Niagara Gorge and brought them back alive again.

Royall saw a movement at the farther side of the cemetery, nearest the church, where someone was tending a grave. A solitary individual, kneeling and working rapidly with a clippers.

That sharp sudden sexual pang in his groin, again. Out of nowhere it struck.

Royall ran up a hill at the rear of the cemetery, where grave markers were dated as recently as August 1977. There were not many of these for the cemetery was nearly filled. In this raw, grassless section plots were laid out in a more orderly, mundane fashion than elsewhere, and the markers, of various sizes, were uniformly upright. Their facades were sleek as Formica. Mourners had brought pots of geraniums and hydrangea, most of the flowers long dead. There were plastic Easter lilies and plastic ivy wreaths. Small drooping U.S. flags on sticks. Royall's eyes rapidly and nervously skimmed the graves as if seeking a familiar name yet, if you'd asked him what the name was he sought, Royall could not have said.

He'd have made a joke of the question, like Ariah.

"I'll know it when I see it."

And there was the woman in black waiting for him, at the foot of the hill.

Royall was slip-sliding down the eroded slope, grabbing exposed tree roots to steady his balance. He had about five minutes to get to work. Typical! Just like Royall! He'd lost track of time entirely. An easy, glib excuse would spring to his lips when he got to the Devil's Hole Cruise Line landing, he wasn't going to worry. He was striding along the rows of graves taking little heed where his heavy feet struck when he saw the woman standing no more than twenty yards away, watching him. She was very intent upon him. Was this someone Royall knew, and should politely greet? Someone who knew him? The woman wore layers of black clothing, down to her ankles. Her untidy black hair was laced with gray like cracks. Her lips twitched in a dreamy smile.

Royall slowed like a deer struck by an arrow. Not a fatal blow, but enough to make him pause. He didn't want to stare rudely at the woman, but couldn't look away. From a distance she might have been mistaken for a girl as young as Juliet but at closer range, in this stark whitish sunlight, you could see she was much older, in her early forties perhaps. Yet her manner was girlish, breathless. Her skin was papery-pale and her eyes were slightly sunken in their sockets. High on her thin cheeks were two delicately blended spots of rouge. She was attractive in a wan, subtly ravaged way, like a 1940's film star years after her prime. Her black hair that was laced with gray fell past her shoulders, tangled and wavy. Her clothes were the strangest clothes ever worn by any visitor to a cemetery: a shimmery black sheath that cascaded down her thin body to her ankles like a nightgown, and over this an unbuttoned black satin jacket with feathery black trim. The jacket's buttons were made of darkly winking rhinestones. Around the woman's neck was a black crocheted scarf flimsy as cobwebs. The woman's feet were bare, long and narrow and very white. Royall swallowed hard, seeing those bare feet in the matted grass. And the expectant way in which the woman was standing, leaning against the back of a weather-stained gravestone, watching him approach.

Royall realized that the woman must have been waiting for him. She'd seen him climb the hill, and she'd waited for him to come back down. She'd let drop her clipping shears back by the grave she'd been tending.

"Hello." The woman's voice was low, husky, breathless.

Royall, blushing, mumbled what sounded like "H'lo."

"We know each other, don't we?"

"I—don't think so, ma'am."

"Oh, I think we do." The woman smiled, and a fierce, tawny light came up in her eyes. Royall wondered if she was drunk or drugged or mildly deranged. With the spread fingers of her tense right hand she was pressing an end of the cobwebby scarf against her right breast, in a way to suggest a pounding heart inside. Royall's knees quivered.

He was having an uneasy feeling about this. A sensation of fiery throbbing had begun in his groin, which he knew was wrong. Which he knew was out of place. A woman old enough to be Royall's mother! And she did look familiar to him, somehow. One of those women who'd befriended Ariah at one or another of the little churches Ariah had attended over the years. Or a neighbor from Baltic Street. Or the mother of a high school friend of Royall's. An ex-girlfriend's mother, who would say in the next breath how she and her daughter missed him? Royall was a careless boy who'd never taken time to learn the names of most people he met, reasoning with childish logic that he'd be meeting them again, or, if he never met them again, what was the purpose in remembering their names? Especially, Royall was likely to forget the names of older persons. He couldn't remember the names of his so-called aunts who lived on l'Isle Grand and in school he'd been capable of forgetting his teachers' names over a summer.

As if she could read these scattered thoughts on the brink of adolescent panic, the woman moved swiftly to Royall, and took his hand firmly in hers. She tugged at him, smiling. She was several inches shorter than Royall, and looked up at him with the raw heedless yearning of a flower seeking the sun. She whispered, "I do know you. Yes. You're his son. Oh, this is so—such a miracle." Tenderly the woman framed Royall's face in her thin hands, and leaned boldly against him, and kissed his mouth lightly, as a mother might do. Royall was too shocked to respond. His instinct was to push away, for this must be a ruse, a trick, yet he was a boy so trained to be courteous to his elders, especially a woman who seemed needful of him, he stood mute, rooted to the spot, like a hapless character in a children's cartoon. And the woman, at such close quarters, gazed at him so warmly. Her eyes were shadowed and faintly bloodshot yet they seemed to him luminous eyes, darkly bright, with a tawny hazel glow, and beautiful. Her skin appeared translucent, stretched tight across the delicate bones of her face; at her temples, there were faint blue veins. The woman's face was lightly powdered, her lips were dark crimson and fleshy and beautiful to him. At its neckline the shimmery black sheath was loose, and Royall could see the woman's pallid, ghostly skin inside, the tops of her bare breasts. Royall felt an overwhelming sensation of warmth, tenderness. His eyes flooded with moisture, he was so suddenly happy.

"Darling boy. I knew it was you. Come here. Here!"

The woman tugged at his hand, laughing. She continued to caress his cheeks and to kiss him in her quick, light, fleeting way, like moths brushing against his lips, mysterious and elusive. He was fearful of taking hold of her. Yet she was touching him familiarly, companionably, as a mother touches a child, affectionate yet lightly chiding. "Hurry. Oh, hurry." In a hiding place such as a child might discover, between two tall gravestones, one guarded by a melancholy angel with discolored wings, the other decorated with a frayed U.S. flag the size of a hand towel, the woman took hold of Royall's elbows, and laughed at his expression of alarm; she kissed him now more forcibly; her eager lips parted his, and Royall felt her warm nudging tongue, snaky-quick, teasing. By this time Royall, who was an excitable young man, was very excited. At six feet two inches he was packed solid with blood and all of this blood had flooded into his groin which felt to him enormous as a mallet. A roaring came up in his ears. There were bees humming overhead and in the near distance on the far side of the cemetery a freight train approached, and passed: the identical train that was hurtling past the Burnabys' house at 1703 Baltic, making the windowpanes vibrate and causing Ariah to press her fingertips against her temples in a gesture of pain and vexation. "Darling boy. You have his hair. His eyes. Oh, I knew." The woman stood on tiptoe, bare white feet trembling with strain. Royall was beginning to clutch at her. Clumsily at first, then more forcibly. So happy! A delirium of happiness. As in a dream of a kind Royall would not have had the imagination to summon for himself this woman whose name was unknown to him opened the loose top of her dress in a gesture that pierced him like a knifeblade. Dazed, light-headed, Royall stooped to kiss her breasts, that were soft-skinned and pale, with rosy-brown nipples that puckered and hardened at the touch of his lips. The woman began moaning, and clutched at Royall's head, pressing him against her. "I knew. I knew if I came this morning. Oh, this is a miracle. *You.*" They were lying down together in the damp matted grass. Royall's brain seemed to have gone out like a light abruptly switched off. His hands were moving desperately across the woman's body, clutching at the shimmery fabric of her dress, as she lay back in the grass, and lifted her hips, and lifted her long skirt, and tugged off her underpants. The matter-of-fact way in which she performed these gestures was deeply moving to Royall. He had a glimpse of the woman's pale, slender thighs, and the dark patch of hair between her thighs.

Stricken suddenly with shyness, Royall couldn't bring himself to open his trousers. His hands were oversized, clumsy as hooks. The woman unzipped his trousers for him, smiling and whispering. "Darling boy. Darling." The roaring in Royall's ears grew louder. He was being drawn into the churning depths of the Gorge. The crazed water below the Devil's Hole, where the tourist boat bucked and heaved and women and children screamed in fright, and Royall, when he was piloting the boat, steered them on their course, exactly on their prescribed course, and finally back to the landing. Now he and this woman unknown to him were lying on the ground together, in the sudden stark intimacy of individuals horizontal in each other's arms. No turning back. No direction except forward. The world had shrunk to the approximate size of a grave, and there was no direction except forward. Royall knelt awkwardly over the woman, concerned that he might be too heavy for her, the hot heavy weight of his lanky muscled body on her slight body, but she pulled at him teasingly, murmured *Hurry! hurry!*, the cords in her neck taut with strain. Royall's knees were shaking. He might have been fourteen years old, sexually inexperienced and panicked. Yet the woman plucked at him, stroked and caressed him, as if his tense quivering body were in her keeping, as familiar to her as her own. She guided his penis into her, into that rough swath of hair between her thighs, and then inside, deep inside her, where she was astonishingly soft; soft as Royall could never quite believe; soft as liquid flame; and Royall was obliterated in that flame, and near to losing control. The woman lay back in the grass, hair tangled behind her head in a silky outspread web. "Oh. Oh. *Oh*." At once she'd begun to feel pleasure. This was astonishing: Royall was accustomed to girls who seemed almost to feel nothing, or who pretended to feel what they believed they should feel; but this woman, older, sensuous and eager as no girl Royall had ever made love with, fell into a rhythm of quickened, then languorous beats, kissing him, running her hands rapidly over his back, gently squeezing his penis as he pushed himself into her, until the flamey sensation overcame him and Royall pumped his life into her, between the strong slender legs that gripped him so firmly. The woman shuddered, writhed and clutched at him as if they were drowning together.

I love you Royall clenched his jaws tight to keep from exclaiming.

When he came to consciousness he was lying sprawled on this woman unknown to him as if the two had fallen together, in this intimate embrace, from a great height. And where were they, and what time was this? Royall's brain was dazed, obliterated. Since infancy he'd slept with unusual intensity, and often woke in a state of dazed distraction, exhausted from sleep, in thrall to whatever had happened to him in sleep which he could only dimly recall in consciousness.

And so it was now, in the cemetery beside the abandoned stone church on Portage Road. As the woman murmured to him, kissed and stroked him, Royall lay passive for some minutes, without volition. When at last he made a movement to lift himself from her, the woman quickly gripped his thighs with her own, pressed her hands firmly against his back and held him. In her rapt throaty voice she murmured, "No. Not yet. I'll be so lonely. I can't bear it. Stay with me. Don't leave me yet." Kissing and stroking and beginning again gently to squeeze him, beginning again that rhythm that so excited Royall, like a giant heartbeat it seemed to him, that enveloped him, as if he were an infant in his mother's womb. "Not yet. Not yet. Don't leave me yet." Until at last, Royall was hard again.

2

A whistling-hearted boy. Exactly the type a girl can't trust.

That day. That long day in Royall Burnaby's life. The first Friday of October 1977. The eve of Royall's marriage to Candace McCann he loved and would never, never wish to hurt.

Except: how could Royall be married now?

His heart pounded in shame. Already, before Royall had a wife, he'd been unfaithful to her.

As Juliet said *There's a curse on us Burnabys. The way people say our name, you can hear it.*

Royall had been an hour and twenty minutes late at the boarding dock on the river. He'd missed his cruise, and both boats were out. Captain Stu was furious with him. Royall mumbled an apology. His brain was so dazzled, his mouth so parched with love for the woman in black, he made no effort to think of an excuse. It was like an exam essay question in high school where Royall's mind was blank as a wiped-over blackboard. Not clean, but wiped-over and cloudy. He just stood there nodding, eyes downcast, as Captain Stu like an exasperated father chewed him out and sent him on his way, to get into uniform for the 11 A.M. cruise.

That long day, through which Royall moved like a sleepwalker smiling, blinking, behaving courteously in his role as "Lieutenant

Captain Royall," the youngest of the several pilots employed by the Devil's Hole Cruise Company. He was a favorite with female tourists of all ages, as well as children who clamored to have their picture taken with him. Smiling his open, frank smile as he was photographed for the thousandth time at the wheel of the spray-soaked boat. And when Royall was asked the inevitable question how much water flowed over The Falls, he never failed to give the answer, "Six million cubic feet a minute, a million bathtubs a second," as if for the first time.

Piloting tourists for the Devil's Hole Company was a job that required manual skill, patience, "personality," and minimal ambition, and so a job well suited for Royall Burnaby who'd barely managed to graduate from high school. Chandler was disappointed in his younger brother, having expected Royall to at least apply to a local college like Buffalo State, but Royall liked his job at the Devil's Hole, work that kept him busy and didn't require much thought. *It hurts too much to think. There's no future in it.* Ariah had encouraged Royall to take the job, to stay close to home. In fact, Ariah encouraged Royall to live at home as long as he wanted.

Royall, and his wife-to-be Candace. Until the young couple could afford a "decent" place of their own.

Royall hurriedly boarded the tourist boat. Here he had a purpose, and he had power. "Lieutenant Captain Royall." At the helm of the crowded boat he felt strangely free. He needed to be working, and he needed to be responsible. Maybe it was better to be responsible for strangers than for people you knew and cared about. Tourists were a sub-species of humanity focused on Getting The Most Out Of Their Money. They were greedy and anxious to See What Was So Special. Their attention spans were short, which was a good thing. They were easily pleased, and The Falls were genuinely awesome so they were never disappointed. Some of them, and not just children or the elderly, were so intimidated by The Falls that they came close to fainting, which was exciting, and dramatic, and Something To Remember. On those occasions when someone did succumb to panic and had to be comforted by an attendant, observers were satisfied that they were Getting The Most Out Of Their Money.

Royall was repeatedly asked, "It must scare you, too, sometimes? Have you ever had an accident out here?" Smiling to show that he took such questions seriously, Royall always said:

"Yes and no. Yes, I'm scared as hell sometimes. No, I've never had an accident. The Devil's Hole Cruise has never lost a customer in twenty-two years of service at the Niagara Gorge."

This elicited relieved chuckles. Anyway, it was true.

No one in any of the expertly piloted excursion boats was in danger from The Falls. The excursion routes were carefully plotted and no pilot ever varied his course. Mechanical as clockwork, and reliable. For all the grandeur and "nightmare" of the gigantic Falls, the danger was a known and therefore navigable thing, a form of entertainment. And business.

The danger was above The Falls, not below. If you fell in, above The Falls, and were carried over.

Royall was asked repeatedly, too, whether "very many" people committed suicide at The Falls. Like every employee in the Niagara Falls tourist trade, Royall was instructed to smile politely, and to say, "Absolutely not. All that is exaggerated by the media."

To take the Devil's Hole excursion you had to gear up in waterproof raincoats and hats provided at the landing dock. Warned that the voyage was very wet, and they should make certain that their watches and cameras were waterproof, passengers began squealing and shrieking as soon as spray began to hit, and the boat lurched, wobbled, bobbed, bounced in the waves like a carnival ride. They passed the American Falls on their left, and then the Horseshoe Falls, which was massive, glaring green in the autumn sunlight like molten glass. Pouring, deafening water. Except it hardly seemed like water. Think of a million tin cans being dumped, Royall liked to describe the noise, only the dumping never ends. You'd think that by now Royall would have gotten used to it and that was true, to a degree. Some days, he piloted the boat like a mechanical man, every beat memorized. Other days, like today, he was distracted. Thinking *It could not have happened. That wasn't me.* The woman in black was kissing Royall's slack, dreamy mouth. Even as the boat ventured out into the mist, the woman in black was twining her snaky arms around Royall's neck. He found himself staring up at the falling, cascading water. That dense sinewy substance that could kill in seconds. Snap a man's backbone like a twig. His own backbone had arched like a bow, he'd moaned aloud as a wounded creature as the arrow shot, the arrow that shot from his groin that was at the same time the arrow that lodged in Royall's body. He could not believe that he'd done what he had done that morning, and could only think that the woman in black had hypnotized him. *His eyes* she'd murmured. *Oh I knew. Knew you*.

The strange thing was, the water below The Falls was as deep as The Falls itself. So that whatever The Falls meant, it was half hidden. When you saw The Falls, you were seeing only half of the Niagara Gorge.

Never would Royall tell Candace what he'd done. Making love to a woman he didn't know, a woman old enough to be his mother. *And you loved it didn't you. Dying to do it again aren't you*. Never would Royall confess to his bride that he'd betrayed her.

Twenty minutes out, and looping back to the loading dock right on schedule. Again, again, and again that afternoon like clockwork.

God damn it could not have happened. Must've been a dream.

One of the passengers was plucking at Royall's arm. "Mister? Can we take a picture of you? By the railing here, O.K.? D'you mind if Linda gets in the picture, too? Thanks!"

After the last trip of the day, Captain Stu insisted upon taking Royall out for a few beers. Royall was leaving on his honeymoon next day, and would be away for a week; by then, the Devil's Hole cruises would have shut down for the season and wouldn't resume until next May. "Gonna miss you, kid. You're a good kid." Captain Stu shook Royall's hand with coarse cordiality, to show that he'd forgiven him for being late that morning. He winked lewdly at Royall and wished him good luck in his "voyage." Royall wiped beer from his mouth and smiled at his employer blankly. "What voyage, Stu?" Captain Stu laughed. "Marriage, son. You'll need all the horsepower you can get."

Stu Fletcher was a white-haired portly man in his fifties with a nose of broken capillaries that glowed like radium. He readily admitted to having a drinking problem, and he smoked too many cigars, but he was "damned fond" of Royall—"You're like a son, except my own son wouldn't work for me. Thinks he's too goddam good for Cap'n Stu." Royall laughed uneasily. He'd gathered from previous conversations with the older man that Stu knew who he, Royall, was, in a way that Royall himself didn't exactly know, because Ariah had forbidden him such knowledge. *You have your mother. You don't need anyone else.* Royall understood that his father had died when he, Royall, had been very young; before his father died, he'd left Ariah and his children. Dirk Burnaby betrayed the family, the unforgiveable sin. From Chandler, Royall learned that their father had died in an accident, his car had swerved through a guard railing on the Buffalo–Niagara Falls Highway and gone into the Niagara River. Chandler cautioned Royall never to hint to Ariah that he knew this much, Ariah would be furious. Juliet was always saying there was a curse on them, the name "Burnaby" was a curse, but Royall knew better. He'd had plenty of friends through school and he'd been elected "best-looking boy" of the Class of '76 at Niagara Falls High—did that sound like a curse?

Royall lingered with Cap'n Stu at the bar of the Old Dutch Inn, a smoky tavern in downtown Niagara Falls that conspicuously did not cater to, or attract, tourists. Cap'n Stu was in a mellow talkative mood, which was fine because Royall was not. Especially this evening, he was not. If Royall had a question or two he might've asked the old man, he kept his mouth shut.

More tenderly than anyone had ever touched Royall Burnaby, the woman in black had touched him. *We know each other don't we?* More tenderly than anyone had ever kissed Royall, the woman in black had kissed him. *Your eyes. His eyes.* He had not dared to ask the woman in black whose eyes she meant. Somehow, Royall knew.

He was supposed to drop by to see Candace, briefly. The route was a familiar one but, driving, Royall kept drifting off in his thoughts. A shaft of stark white sunshine struck the uplifted face of a stone angel and Royall smelled the damp, slightly rank hair of the woman in black, a strand fallen across his panting mouth. Oh God. Blood pumped into Royall's groin as the woman in black drew him down beside her in the matted grass. *Beautiful boy. We know each other don't we?* As in a dream suddenly she'd unzipped his trousers, she was guiding him inside her, stroking and holding his penis with such tender familiarity, it was as if they'd made love many times before. It was an easy act, and it was a happy, uncomplicated act. And they could do it again, again, again. Royall swallowed hard. His eyes filled with moisture. An amber traffic light turned to red as Royall drove blindly through an intersection. Someone sounded a horn, and a man in a Mayflower moving van leaned out his window to yell. Royall whispered, "God damn." He saw that he was on Ferry, blocks past Fifth Street.

He drove on. He found himself at Thirty-third, circling the block for no reason except to drive past the high school. Why? He didn't miss the damned place. He was grateful to be gone. Still, he'd been young then. Hadn't even met Candace McCann yet. (Ariah had brought them together: she'd met Candace at one of her neighborhood churches where Candace was singing in the choir and Ariah had volunteered to direct the choir for several months, until gradually she'd lost interest in the church.) Royall had had other girl friends, and he'd let those girls down too, he supposed. *Royall Burnaby, that boy will break your heart.* It seemed to happen, each time, without Royall's knowing. Without his intention. Girls fell in love with his sweet, easy smile, his frank blue eyes, his gentle touch. His voice that told them what they most wanted to believe, even when they should not have believed it. *Royall, I love you. I love you so much. Royall, do you love me? Just a little?*

How was it Royall's fault, words sprang from his lips. *Yes. I guess I do.*

You do? You love me? Oh, Royall!

Candace McCann was the girl who'd made a man of Royall Burnaby. Breaking down weeping in his arms one night that spring, in this very car, telling Royall she'd "missed a period"—she was "so ashamed, and so frightened" and she loved him so much, she'd "want to die" if he didn't love her. Royall felt a chill pass over him even as he comforted Candace and told her he'd take care of her, please don't cry he'd take care of her, though stunned trying to grasp how Candace could be pregnant; how, when Royall had been so damned careful; and they hadn't even made love many times, not in any way that might cause a girl to become pregnant. But if it was so, Royall reasoned, it was so; at heart, Royall was a fatalist like his mother.

Honey I love you. It will be O.K.

Are you sure? Oh Royall, are you sure you love me? Because if—

Candace, sure I'm sure! Everything will be O.K., I promise.

I'm terrified of telling my mother. I can't tell my mother. Unless—

Don't tell her yet. Until you're absolutely sure—

Royall, I am. I am absolutely sure. I've been sure for twelve days at least. Oh Royall, you don't love me—

Honey, I do! I said I do.

But—would you want to marry me anyway? Even if—I wasn't—

Candace had broken down weeping as if her heart would break, and what choice had Royall except to comfort her? He'd felt a stir of excitement, pride, dread, but mostly plain wonderment, that he might be a father within nine months; when he felt, most days, like a boy of about twelve. Still, he couldn't let Candace down. He did love her. She was about the prettiest girl he'd ever seen, in Niagara Falls at least.

So Royall bought an engagement ring at a downtown jeweler's, a silver setting with a tiny diamond he'd managed, through connections, to get at a discount for ninety dollars. So Royall formally proposed, and Candace McCann tearfully accepted his proposal.

At first, the wedding was set for June. Then, when Candace discovered she wasn't pregnant after all, the date was moved to October, when Royall's season with the Devil's Hole Company ended.

But do you still love me? Royall? Even if—

Honey, of course. I love you more than ever.

You're sure? Because if—

I'm sure.

We will have babies, though. Won't we?

Just as many as you want, Candace. I promise.

Such strange gnarly toads, leaping out of Royall Burnaby's mouth!

But truly Royall wanted to marry Candace. He loved her, and he couldn't bear the thought of hurting her. Hearing that girl cry as if her heart was breaking near about broke Royall's own heart, he'd come to think was a plastic heart. Cheap and easily cracked yet its materials indestructible.

The most surprising thing about Royall's engagement was Ariah's reaction. You'd have thought Mom would fly into one of her raging tantrums and kick Royall out of the house; in fact, Ariah drew a deep breath when Royall stammered in embarrassment he "guessed he wanted to get married, it was time," and told him yes. Yes, it was time. At nineteen, he was old enough. The way girls and women threw themselves at Royall, it was better for him to settle down quickly with a good, sweet, uncomplicated girl like Candace McCann who wouldn't push him beyond his capabilities, before something disastrous happened. (This could only mean Royall impregnating some unsuitable girl! As if he had no more control of himself than a dog trotting about the neighborhood in thrall to any bitch in heat.) Just as Ariah hadn't been disappointed when Royall didn't go to college, but had seemed relieved, so Ariah smiled at the prospect of her younger son marrying. In fact, the newlyweds could live at 1703 Baltic, for a while. Ariah would move out of her upstairs bedroom, and redecorate it for them.

Live with Ariah in that narrow, cramped house! Royall shuddered at the prospect. Poor Candace would be gobbled up alive, and made over into a second daughter for Ariah.

No. The newlyweds would live in a rented flat on Fifth Street, a few minutes' drive to the Niagara Gorge where Royall worked from May to mid-October and to King's Dairy, the most popular ice cream parlor in Niagara Falls, where Candace worked at the counter, and was assistant manager. The newlyweds would live alone!

Ariah was disappointed. You could see Ariah was very disappointed.

Those green-gasoline eyes close to igniting. The pale freckled skin tight at her temples, and nerves pulsing beneath.

Royall, you could save on rent. I wouldn't charge a penny.

Mom, thanks. But I guess not.

Let me speak with Candace. She's got a practical head on her shoulders.

Mom, no.

What you save on rent, you can put away for a down payment on a place of your own. Oh, Royall! Let me talk to Candace.

Mom, I'd rather you didn't. You know how Candace is around you. She admires you so, and she's afraid of you, and she doesn't know her own mind.

Whose mind is she supposed to know? Yours?

Hey, Mom. Don't let's fight, O.K.? Candace is going to be my wife, not yours.

Maybe that's the problem. That poor girl needs more family. More than just a husband can provide.

Mom, the house is too small! Even with Chandler gone, it's too small. Juliet would be uncomfortable, sharing the upstairs with Candace and me.

That's ridiculous. You know very well that Juliet is brokenhearted that you're leaving, Royall. She adores you. And she adores Candace, as a sister.

Jesus, Mom. Please.

Are you afraid to let me speak with Candace? You are!

Mom, stay away from Candace.

My music room is winterized. You and Chandler did a wonderful job remodeling. I'll move my bed downstairs, and we'll buy you and Candace a beautiful big double bed. And you can have that mahogany dresser, it's an antique. Candace can pick out a wallpaper design. The choice can be entirely hers. And curtains! Flounced white curains, I think. Royall, look at me. How can you be selfish about something so important? Candace deserves all the love she can get. Family is all there is on earth. Seeing there's no God on earth.

By the time Ariah finished this breathless speech she was trembling, and so was Royall. He would recall afterward with a shiver of dread how close he'd come to giving in. Always, it was far easier to give in to Ariah than to resist.

But Royall was stubborn, and refused Ariah's offer. No, no! If his mother made his wife into a second daughter, then he, Royall, would be sleeping with his sister. Christ!

In the end Ariah relented. But next morning offered to help pay for Candace's engagement ring. And again Royall gritted his teeth and thanked his mother politely, and declined.

(Luckily Ariah hadn't known, or guessed, that Candace thought she was pregnant at that time. Ariah was never to know.)

Thinking these thoughts, that made the pulses in his head beat, Royall sat in the idling Chevy at the edge of the high school parking lot. He was staring at the buff-brick, flat-roofed, factory-like building. Ordinary, it was, even ugly, yet at dusk, in the early evening, as streetlights came on, the building seemed to float upon the stained asphalt pavement, every window mysteriously darkened. Damn, Royall regretted now he hadn't tried harder. He'd been such a popular athlete: softball, football, basketball. If he hadn't had to work after school, he'd have been on all the teams. As it was, he'd been allowed to substitute occasionally, when the team was facing a tough opponent, and Royall could get off from work. He'd been so well-liked, he'd been unaware, maybe, of another way of being; as a dreamer is unaware he's asleep until wakened. His teachers had certainly encouraged him. If he'd gone to college he wouldn't be getting married at the age of nineteen . . . Well, many of Royall's classmates were married already. Girls especially. (Secretly) pregnant before their weddings, and grateful to be married to guys with jobs at Dow Chemical, Parish Plastics, Nabisco, Niagara Hydro. Most of Royall's male friends worked for these, or similar factories, the highest paid workers' jobs in Niagara Falls because they were unionized. Royall had never been attracted to factory work. "Real" work, eight hours a day and five days a week, union dues, contracts. The thought of punching a time clock made him wince. Royall Burnaby, who'd been so often applauded as an athlete, and for his singing-and-guitar performances for local audiences, punching a time clock! His pride would never allow it. And his good sense.

If he'd gone to college. But Ariah hadn't wanted her younger son to go to college. *Over-reaching. Ambition. What does it get a man, it gets him dead*. Ariah had spoken bitterly, unleavened by her usual caustic humor.

What had hurt him, he'd never acknowledged to any living person, was having to follow Chandler in school. Chandler who'd gotten high grades in all subjects, especially math and science. Chandler who'd been a serious student in every class, with few friends and activities to distract him. Royall's teachers had liked Royall, sure, but they hadn't been able to resist comparing him constantly to Chandler, to Royall's disadvantage. What the hell, why try? Anything Royall did academically, Chandler had already done better. In some cases, much better. Fuck it! Royall got into the habit of forgetting homework assignments, cutting exams. He'd told himself that being voted best-looking senior boy was better than being valedictorian of his class like Chandler. Ask the girls.

"Royall! You aren't looking like your*self*."

It was the lightest of reproaches. Not a scold. Candace had run to sling her arms around Royall's neck and kiss his cheek that was uncomfortably warm, and needed shaving.

This long day! He was an hour late, and his breath smelled of beer. Yet Candace wasn't going to scold outright, preoccupied with wedding plans. Candace's sister Annie was there, and two of Candace's friends, and the phone was ringing, and Candace was in a bright glittery mood, like an astronaut, Royall was thinking, just before the moment of take-off.

Candace kissed Royall again, wetly on the mouth. She had a way of kissing that was exclamatory and victorious. Royall blushed, the others were looking on. If he'd been alone with Candace he would have hugged her tight and buried his face in her crinkly, curly hair. He said not a word. He'd become confused by words. The woman in black had stolen away all his words, and he'd never been an articulate boy. Cap'n Stu had bade him goodbye and good luck with a pulverizing handshake and Royall hadn't been able to respond with anything more than a wince.

"You can't stay long, honey. We're going over the *food*."

Royall didn't want to know what this meant. What *food* had to do with him and Candace getting married, or, in fact, what getting married had to do with him and Candace loving each other, or believing they loved each other. Since that night last spring when Candace wept in his arms whispering how she'd die if Royall didn't love her, he'd been confused.

Sometimes, hearing his fiancée and his mother excitedly discussing the wedding, which was never less than The Wedding, as you'd say The Holidays, or The Falls, Royall felt like an intruder. A church wedding? Was that what they'd be having? (But Royall wasn't at all religious. He'd only attended a few services at the Church of Christ and Apostles, a sparrow-colored shingle-sided church on Eleventh Street, to please Candace. He'd had the vague idea that he and Candace would elope over a weekend? No?) Well, a church wedding was what they were having, as Royall learned. A small private wedding. But there would be a bridesmaid, or would there be two bridesmaids? There would be guests, a reception afterward at 1703 Baltic? Quite a surprise, that Ariah who never invited anyone into her home if she could avoid it, except her music students, would suddenly open the house to "guests"; Ariah, who scorned bourgeois convention, and had many times proclaimed her repugnance, to her children, for the "outmoded institution" of marriage, would be playing the organ at her son's wedding, and had ventured out to buy her first new dress in years, at the Second Time 'Round Fashions downtown. "Royall, did your mother tell you the latest?" Candace asked, her glittery voice quavering. "My mother *is* coming. And, oh God, she insists she's bringing this 'man friend' of hers nobody has ever *seen*."

Royall shifted his shoulders uncomfortably. He knew he was meant to share Candace's indignation, or anxiety, but he wasn't up to it. "I guess you're tired, honey. That job of yours!" Candace sighed, turning to appeal to her sister and friends, with whom no doubt she'd been sharing her disapproval of Royall's occupation at the Devil's Hole. "All those silly tourists clamoring around you. Half the women draping themselves over you and having their pictures taken! And I just know that boat isn't safe. Going into the Niagara Gorge, it can't be safe. And it doesn't even pay that much, to make up for being dangerous." Candace's words lifted like the querulous notes of a bird's cry. The tiny diamond on her left hand winked as Candace moved her hands about in a flurry of emotion, doll-like, prettily. Candace was a very pretty girl, twenty years old, but with the manner and affectations of a fifteen-year-old; her breathy soprano voice, her every gesture communicated prettiness, and an expectation that others respond to this prettiness, as a dancer moves to familiar music.

"This sweet girl I'd like you to meet"—Ariah's description of Candace McCann. "This girl at church who's so pretty, and so—well, *sweet*." As if Ariah had wracked her brains and there was nothing more to say of Candace.

There was an edge to Candace's sweetness, Royall had discovered, that Ariah didn't yet know. One day, Ariah might be surprised.

Candace's most striking feature was her strawberry blond hair, worn in a wavy-curly tumble to her shoulders and held in place with butterfly barrettes and clips. Her face was small and heart-shaped. She had a squealing little laugh, and a habit of clasping her fingers together in a gesture of childlike enthusiasm. Her fingernail polish always matched her lipstick, coral pink. She had a sweet if uncertain voice and often sang aloud, church hymns, popular songs. At King's Dairy, which was the predominant dairy and ice cream parlor in Niagara Falls, Candace McCann was the most popular waitress, and the most lavishly tipped; in her daffodil-yellow uniform with white collar and cuffs, and starched white cap pert on her head, she reminded older male customers of—who? Betty Grable, Doris Day? Another era, before the 1960's, when women began to defy men, and ugliness became a mode of self-definition. Not Candace McCann!

When they went out together, Candace and Royall were an attractive couple who drew strangers' admiring eyes. Which made Royall uneasy even as it flattered Candace. "I always think, the two of us might be discovered, someday," Candace said, with a little shiver. Royall joked, "Discovered doing what, honey? And by who?" Candace slapped lightly at his wrist as if he'd said something risqué.

The phone rang. Annie answered it, and Candace took the receiver from her with a nervous giggle. "Oh, gosh. Mrs. Burnaby." Candace's voice sobered, it was Ariah.

Royall saw Candace and Annie exchange a glance. *My future mother-in-law. Oh, God!*

Royall took advantage of this distraction and slipped into the tiny kitchen to repair a leaky faucet Candace had been complaining about. He'd brought along handyman's tools. Such household tasks comforted him, especially when he was feeling edgy. His father had been a lawyer, which meant his father had been a man of words, and probably not a man who'd used his hands, and Royall liked to think how he differed from that disgraced father he'd never known.

After the faucet, Royall examined the refrigerator, which Candace complained made strange noises and didn't "smell right." This was a chipped-enamel Westinghouse that had come with the rented apartment like most of the other kitchen appliances. Royall couldn't find anything obviously wrong with the refrigerator except it was old, and its motor thrummed and vibrated like a wheezing, living thing. There was a six-pack of beer in the refrigerator for him, but Royall took out a quart of King's Dairy milk instead and filled himself a full glass. Plain white milk, he'd been drinking it by the glass all his life. Ariah had made him drink three full glasses a day while he was growing up. She'd made each of her children swallow down teaspoons of cod liver oil in orange juice, at breakfast. When they protested, gagging at the taste of the cod liver oil, Ariah said sternly, "Strong teeth, strong bones. The rest will follow."

Royall tried not to listen to voices in the other room. He hoped to hell that Candace wouldn't put him on the phone to speak with Ariah. His voice would tremble and betray him. *I can't marry her. I don't love her. God help me.*

Of course Royall would marry Candace. He loved her, and that was it.

He'd given her an engagement ring, the wedding was the next morning at eleven, they had honeymoon plans. Ariah approved. Candace adored him. *That was it.*

At the start of October, Candace had moved into this one-bedroom apartment in a brownstone building on Fifth Street in which the newlyweds were going to live. They'd paid a sizable deposit and the first three months' rent. Candace and her girlfriends had found the apartment, and Royall thought it was fine. Small, a little shabby, but, for the price, fine. It was on a busy street, a bus route. A five-minute walk for Candace to King's Dairy, a five-minute drive for Royall to the Niagara Gorge. In the off-season, Royall would probably be working for Empire Collection Agency, which paid a commission; he'd been offered the job by a friend of Stu Fletcher, who knew and liked Royall. But now the time was approaching to begin his new job,

Royall was feeling uneasy. Did he have the temperament for calling strangers on the phone, or boldly dropping by their homes to harass them into paying debts they probably couldn't pay? Was Royall the swaggering-pirate type to "repossess" a car, a boat, a TV set or fur coat whose hapless owner had fallen behind in payments? He was beginning to wonder. The previous year, he'd worked at Armory Bowling Lanes, sometimes bartending. He'd been restless in that indoors job, after the excitement of the Devil's Hole. He'd been thinking about Niagara General Hospital where he could be an attendant, not a great-paying job but the emergency room appealed to him, and riding in an ambulance, helping desperate people. And there was the Police Academy, he'd have liked to be a policeman, maybe, except you had to carry a gun, and might have to use a gun, and that was a sobering thought. Royall might have looked up a Buffalo record producer who'd given Royall his card, having heard him playing his guitar and singing in a summer arts festival in Prospect Park in August, but Royall guessed that nothing serious would come of any "audition," and probably he'd lost the producer's card. He might have looked for employment in a high-quality hotel or restaurant in the more affluent Buffalo area, Candace thought he'd make a handsome maître d', but mostly she urged him to quit the Devil's Hole permanently and get a real job, like most of their male married friends who worked in the factories of East Niagara Falls, North Tonawanda, Buffalo. "Especially when we start a family, Royall. I'll be quitting the Dairy."

Royall swallowed a large mouthful of milk. His jaws ached from the cold.

Shutting his eyes and seeing again a stark, whitish shaft of sunshine in the cemetery. Like a knifeblade piercing his eyes, his groin. The woman in black lay back in the matted grass and opened her arms to him. *We know each other don't we. We know each other.*

If only Royall were married to Candace right now: there would be no turning back.

(But Royall wouldn't have made love to a strange woman in a cemetery that morning, would he? If he and Candace were married?)

Royall was thinking he might be living here, in this apartment, right now; except Candace hadn't wanted him. He might have moved in with her at the start of the month and by now they'd be settled. But of course they hadn't been married yet, and Candace worried what people would think. In Candace's world, everyone knew everyone else and was eager to transmit "news." And relatives on both sides would have been indignant, scandalized. Even Ariah who scorned convention would have disapproved, and the infamous Mrs. McCann who was said to be "openly living with" a man not her husband. Candace herself was strict about ushering Royall out of the apartment at a "decent" hour. What was the point of getting married, Candace wanted to know, if you lived together, slept together, saw each other at breakfast, anyway?

Royall smiled. Well, yes? What was the point?

Candace came into the kitchen, fussing with butterfly clips in her hair. She was fluttery, frowning. Royall could see in her pretty-doll face a somber bulldog face taking shape, in the lower jaws and pursed mouth. She was chattering breathlessly about Ariah's change of mind over something-or-other, and how many guests were absolutely, positively coming. Royall tried to be sympathetic, but Candace seemed to be uttering words in a foreign language he'd never heard before, all sibilants and vehemence. Her hands flew about like startled birds, the tiny diamond on her ring finger winked. Royall wished that he and Candace were alone together in the apartment, all others banished, including phone calls. (The phone was ringing again in the other room.) Oh, this long day!

But Candace wasn't in a mood to be touched right now. The conversation with Ariah had set her off.

Royall said with his sweet-sexy smile, in a voice like Candace's favorite Johnny Cash, "Honey, why don't we run off tonight? Forget all this wedding crap and elope?"

Candace's eyes widened as if Royall had pinched her. " 'Wedding crap'! Royall Burnaby, what did you just *say*?"

Royall shrugged. It seemed like a God-damned good idea, to him.

Or, if they couldn't elope, if they could be alone together in the apartment. This was their home-to-be, the double bed with the American Heritage pine headboard was theirs, a wedding present from Ariah. Everybody out! Phone receiver off the hook! Royall wanted badly to grab Candace in his arms, and lie down with her as they sometimes did, not to make love but just to kiss, hug, snuggle, comfort each other. It didn't matter what nonsense passed between them, like the lyrics of a song whose music has snagged in your head.

Except: Royall worried that the rich dark earthy smell of the cemetery was in his hair, in his clothing. He worried that Candace could taste the other woman on Royall's lips.

Candace's voice rose sharply. "What's got into you, Royall? As soon as you stepped in that door and I saw your face, I *knew*."

Royall said quickly, " 'Knew'? Knew what?"

"Well, I don't know. One of your Burnaby things. Some strange mood where you mumble, and won't look anyone in the eye."

A Burnaby thing? Royall had never heard of this before. And hadn't he just been looking Candace in the eye?

Candace said, pouting, "You! Sometimes I think you don't even want to get married. Sometimes I think you don't even love me."

Royall's head was aching. The cold milk had gotten into the bones of his forehead now. A dull ache, and he had to resist hiding his face in his hands.

"Well, do you? I don't believe you do."

Tears shone in Candace's eyes. Her lips were pursed prettily. In the other room, voices lifted. Peals of laughter. The phone rang.

Candace turned to leave, but Royall gripped her arm.

His voice croaked. "Honey."

"What? *What?*"

Royall swallowed hard. Now his tongue had grown cold, and numb. These words had to be summoned from a distance, like hauling a barge along a canal. "Honey, I guess I don't. Not exactly."

" 'Don't'? Don't what?"

Royall shook his head miserably.

Candace's eyes turned steely, like ice picks. Her pert little nose seemed to sharpen. In that instant, she knew.

Candace picked up the quart of milk and dumped what remained of it over Royall's head, shrieked and screamed and slapped and kicked at him until he restrained her. "You can't! You can't! I hate you, Royall Burnaby, *you can't*!"

This long day. At last, it was coming to an end.

3

If they ask of him tell them: *It happened before I was born.*

Royall knew better. And yet, he had no clear memory of the man who'd been his father.

He had no memory of Luna Park except he knew, from Chandler, that the family had once lived in a "big stone house" facing the park, a long time ago. There were no photographs of that house as there were no photographs of that time. There were no photographs of their unnamed father.

When Royall tried to remember, his mind seemed to dissolve like vapor. Like spray thrown up by The Falls, scattered and lost in the wind.

As a boy living on Baltic Street he'd secretly bicycled to Luna Park a few miles away to see if, if he saw the house, he'd remember it. But each time he approached the park he became strangely dizzy, his knees weak, the front wheel of his bike turned sharply, he almost toppled into the street. So he'd given up and turned back. *It isn't meant to be. Mommy is the one who loves you.*

Royall's memory began when he was four years old and Ariah was half-carrying him sleepy and confused into the "new" house. Up narrow creaking stairs, and into his "new" bedroom. He would share this room with his brother for the next ten years. He would question nothing, he would be Ariah's happy, healthy boy. In the brick-and-stucco rowhouse at 1703 Baltic Street exuding its mysterious, half-pleasurable odors of old wood smoke, grease, and mildew, where freight cars emblazoned *Buffalo & Chautauqua*, *Baltimore & Ohio*, *New York Central*, *Shenandoah*, *Susquehannah* thundered through their skulls.

Royall came home from Baltic Street Elementary with tales of The Falls.

Ghosts came out of the Gorge at night, Royall told Ariah excitedly. Some of these were Indians, and some were white people. It was a white man taken by the Indians and made to swim in the river and the river carried him over The Falls, and there was a "red-haired young bride" who searched for him "for seven days and seven nights" and when she found him, drowned and dead, torn into pieces by the rapids, she "cast herself" into the Gorge, too.

Ariah who was brushing and plaiting Juliet's long hair, that was wheat-colored but threaded with streaks of dark red, asked dryly, "When did all this happen, sweetie?"

Royall, in third grade at the time, said, "A hudred hudred years ago, Mommy. I think."

"Not 'hudred,' Royall. *Hun*dred."

" '*Hun*dred,' Mommy. And a thousand, too."

Like Zarjo, the child was. Adorable, and eager to please. If Royall had had a stumpy tail like the dog's, he'd have been thumping it most of the time.

Ariah laughed, and leaned over to kiss her son. The things children seem to believe. "If it was that long ago, Royall, she's dead, too. Ghosts don't live forever."

Royall came home from fourth grade with a different tale of the Gorge. This time, Chandler as well as Juliet were witnesses.

"Mom*my*! The ghost I was telling you about?"

"What ghost, honey? We don't believe in ghosts here."

Wide-eyed Royall said, "She lives on this street! People say they see her, she's *real*."

Ariah stared at her breathless son. She was handing him a tall glass of King's Dairy "whole" "homogenized" milk as she always did at this time. Calmly asking, "Who told you that?"

Royall frowned, trying to remember. He wasn't a child who remembered most things accurately. Names, faces, events were easily jumbled in his head, like dice shaken in a cardboard cup. He became restless sitting at his desk at school, and he became impatient with printed words "jumping all over" in his eyes. It might have been older classmates who'd told him this, about the ghost who lived on Baltic Street. It might have been his teacher. It might have been the mother of one of his best friends, who often invited him into her house after school, and gave him milk and cookies with her son, and let the boys watch TV cartoons, forbidden by Ariah Burnaby at the other end of the block.

Juliet, the most credulous of children, now a first grader, was listening intensely to her brother. She was a somber little girl with a face "long as a cucumber" and brooding "black-eyed-pea" eyes as her mother described her; the danger was, if Juliet heard tales of ghosts sighted on Baltic Street, she'd be seeing ghosts that very night. Chandler, a wraith-like adolescent adept at slipping in and out of rooms, sensitive to Ariah's shifting moods, was preparing to slip from the kitchen now, sensing a scene. And in the corner to which he'd been banished, as a naughty dog who'd raided neighbors' garbage cans another time, Zarjo was drowsily alert. It was a cold windy November afternoon of no special distinction in the history of the Burnaby family of Baltic Street except as Royall stumbled telling about the ghost, the ghost who was "real"—"a lady ghost"—"walks by The Falls and scares people so they jump *in*"—Ariah interrupted to ask who on earth was telling children such bullshit tales, and Royall protested with a nine-year-old's earnestness, "Mommy, it's *true*. She's a lady-ghost, you can see her by The Falls."

Ariah laughed. Her laughter was short and shrill as a whip cracking. Only a child as adept at gauging Ariah's moods as Chandler could interpret her laughter as he might take note of her clenching fists.

Yet Chandler wasn't fast enough, slipping away. Though Royall was the one who'd told the bullshit tale, it was Chandler who drew Ariah's wrath. Ariah turned to lunge at him, grabbing his hair in both her hands and yanking him back into the kitchen. "You! That look in your pinched little face! You *spy*."

Zarjo leapt up, barking excitedly. Royall, jostled by the struggle of Ariah and Chandler, spilled most of his glass of milk onto himself.

Otherwise, an ordinary November afternoon in the history of the Burnaby family of Baltic Street.

4

TEN YEARS LATER, Royall winced thinking of that spilled milk. The shock of it, and the glass shattering at his feet.

King's Dairy. Cold milk thrown on Royall Burnaby. He smiled to think maybe it would happen to him every ten years? Some weird crazy-quilt pattern in his life.

Once, Candace had told Royall and Juliet in her breathless fluttering way, "Oh, you're so lucky! You have the most fascinating mother in the world."

Brother and sister had exchanged a startled glance.

Juliet said, sighing, "Well. We know that, I guess."

Ten years after the incident in the kitchen, Royall was standing hesitant on the front porch at 1703 Baltic. He could hear piano music inside. Someone was playing the piano energetically, it sounded like a Mozart rondo, there was a pause like a hiccup, and Ariah's uplifted, encouraging voice. Ariah's children had been trained to enter and leave the house quietly during her piano lessons, but Royall lingered on the porch, dreamy and distracted. He wore rumpled khaki pants, a flannel shirt over a T-shirt, a Devil's Hole Cruise cap pulled low on his forehead. He had a three days' growth of beard, meanly glinting as steel filings, and his eyes were bloodshot as if he'd been rubbing them with his knuckles, hard. He hadn't changed his clothes or done much more than wash his hands, forearms, and underarms, since Friday morning, and this was Monday afternoon, late.

Shame, shame! "Royall Burnaby" is the name.

In fact, Royall didn't feel all that ashamed, and he didn't feel repentant in the slightest. Relief filled him like a helium balloon. Free! He could float away, in such freedom. Not a married man at nineteen.

Of course, Royall felt sorry for Candace. His face burned when he thought of it. He'd hurt her, and the last thing he'd wanted to do was hurt her. He felt almost as sorry for Ariah, too. But why?

Candace is going to be my wife, Mom. Not yours.

Ariah had not wanted Chandler, aged twenty-five, to "see" a woman friend of his who was separated from her husband, and pregnant. Ariah had expressed shock and repugnance for any such "liaison" and had made Chandler promise he wouldn't get drawn into marrying the young woman; Ariah had refused even to meet her. Yet, Ariah had immediately latched upon Candace McCann as a "perfect" wife for Royall.

This was strange. Yet, knowing Ariah, maybe not so strange.

Now that she was in her mid-fifties, not quite so nervous and excitable as she'd been at a younger age, Ariah was less prone to spectacular flare-ups of temper. (Or "fugues," as she called them, with clinical detachment. As if such tantrums were a state of mind for which no one was to blame, like being struck by lightning and kicking and flailing out to hurt innocent bystanders as a result.) Still, Ariah's moods were unpredictable. There were days when she refused to speak to Juliet for some minor infraction of their mother-daughter intimacy that made no sense at all to Royall, who, as a boy, had been allowed much more freedom growing up. Ariah laughed at household misdeeds committed by Royall out of carelessness or clumsiness, that would have thrown her into a fury if they'd been committed by Juliet, or poor Chandler.

(Fortunately for him, Chandler no longer lived at home. But he dropped by often, and sometimes slept in his old bed, as if he needed Ariah's scolding presence as much as, in her peculiar way, Ariah needed him.)

"Hey Royall! How's it going?"

A neighbor from across the street whose roof gutters Royall used to clear out for a very minimum wage now called out to Royall, who had no choice but to wave and call back. Royall supposed that everyone in the neighborhood knew of the rudely cancelled wedding, though no one on Baltic Street had been invited.

"Thought you'd be off on your honeymoon this week, eh?"

"Well, no. I'm not."

The neighbor, an older man with a limping leg, laughed mysteriously and disappeared back into the house. Royall's face burned.

Maybe this wasn't a good idea? Returning home, so soon. Royall had to admit he was fearful of seeing Ariah.

Of course he'd called Ariah on Friday evening. Immediately he'd told her the wedding was "off." It had been after nine o'clock and Ariah was reluctant to answer the phone when it rang so late, but she'd answered it on the tenth ring, and had been so astonished by Royall's news she'd asked him please to repeat it, and when Royall did, saying in a rush of words that he couldn't marry Candace, he didn't love Candace and didn't believe that Candace loved him, Ariah was silent for so long Royall worried she'd had some sort of attack. Then he heard her harsh, labored breathing, as if she was trying not to cry. Ariah, who scorned tears! Quickly Royall said, "Mom? Candace is coming to see you. She understands why I'm doing this. She's upset, and mad as hell at me, but she understands, I think. Mom, forgive me, I'm sorry. I'm a bastard, I guess. Mom—" But the voice on the line was Juliet's. "Royall, she's run upstairs. She wouldn't tell me what's wrong. Royall, you aren't hurt, are you? Royall? *You aren't dying?*"

Next day, Saturday, Royall sent Ariah a telegram, his first.

DEAR MOM I'M SORRY HAD NO CHOICE WILL
EXPLAIN SOMEDAY LOVE ROYALL

Immediately after the breakup with Candace, Royall had gone into hiding. Three days a fugitive. Out of contact with everyone. He hadn't called anyone else, knowing that word would spread quickly. Every one of Candace's friends and relatives would have been informed within an hour. Like sewers flooding, Ariah used to say of gossip making the rounds. You can count on sewers flooding in Niagara Falls just as you can count on gossip and "wicked news" generally. Royall didn't want to think what people were saying of him. Shocked, scandalized, furious. Even Candace's mother was probably prepared to strangle him. *Can you believe! Royall Burnaby doing such a thing! On the night before the wedding!* Royall knew that Candace would be bitter about having to return the wedding presents, injury on top of insult.

She would never forgive him, he knew. What he'd done was worse than any act of sexual betrayal. If he'd told her about the woman in black she would have been hurt, dismayed, disgusted, she'd have wept and struck at him, and told him she hated him, she didn't want to marry him; yet in the end, and fairly quickly, Candace would have forgiven him, and married him. But what he'd done now, out of conscience, and knowing it was the right thing for them both, she would never forgive.

Had the piano lesson ended? It was almost six o'clock. But Ariah sometimes went over the hour. She was a diligent, exacting teacher who, after more than thirty years of teaching piano, still had the capacity to be surprised by mistakes. Ariah had long embarrassed her children, especially Juliet who felt such slights keenly, by caring more about her pupils' piano lessons than the pupils themselves cared. She was forever being hurt, stunned, devastated by modestly talented adolescents who broke off lessons, or by their parents' decisions not to continue. It had nothing to do with money: Ariah sometimes carried a student for months, for no fee. She loved music and could not comprehend that others took music so casually. *This is just throwing money down a rat hole* was the crude (but possibly accurate?) expression used by the father of one of Ariah's students, when he'd decided to discontinue lessons. Ariah took up the expression with her usual grim humor. *Throwing money down a rat hole, that's what we're all doing. That's life!*

On Baltic Street, among working-class and "welfare-class" neighbors, some of them living in badly decayed rowhouses spilling over with children, the graying red-haired woman who lived at 1703 was known to be a widow, bringing up three fatherless children by herself, dignified, polite, somewhat disdainful and aloof with her neighbors, very reclusive, "eccentric." It was acknowledged that Ariah Burnaby was someone special, an "educated"—"talented"—woman; it was understood that she feared intruders, even a friendly knock at the door could upset her. *Like a ghost she is. Looks right through you. "Missus" Burnaby you can't call her, she gets a look in her face like you stabbed her in the heart.*

Since he'd been old enough to play with the children next-door, Royall had been a popular presence on the street, a sort of cheerful semi-orphan. He made friends everywhere and was always welcome in his friends' homes where sometimes, casually, their mothers would interrogate him ("Royall, your mother doesn't go out much, does she?"—"Royall, you don't remember your father, I guess?"). Feelings oscillated between resentment of Ariah Burnaby for her purported superiority and sympathy for her predicament. Was she someone to dislike, or someone to pity? The woman could play piano beautifully, but she hadn't a husband, had she? She'd been married to Dirk Burnaby, but she lived on Baltic Street now, didn't she? And where were her family, her relatives? Why were she and her children so alone?

When Royall was a child, there were months-long phases when Ariah couldn't bring herself to leave the house even to shop for food—"I just feel so weak, can't breathe, I know I'll faint if I get on that bus"; at such times, neighbors quietly offered to help. They took Chandler and Royall to the A & P with them, Ariah's carefully printed grocery list in hand; they drove the children to the doctor, or the dentist, or shopping for clothes and shoes. Ariah had to be grateful for such kindnesses, but bitterly resented them. "Don't tell family secrets!" she warned the children. (Who had to wonder, what were these secrets?) "People just want to pry. When they sense weakness, they pounce." When, shortly after her fiftieth birthday, Ariah had to have emergency surgery for the removal of gallstones, neighbors invited the children to share meals with them; and when Ariah was discharged from the hospital and convalescing at home, they sent casseroles, turkey left-overs (this was at Thanksgiving), cakes and pies. Chandler was designated to thank them politely, even as Ariah seethed with indignation. "Jackals, in a pack! They see that I'm 'down.' They think I'm one of them now." Ariah's pale skin gleamed coldly. Her glassy-green eyes glimmered with commingled pain and triumph. "But they're wrong, see? We'll show 'em."

Chandler, ten at the time and beginning to be independent-minded, objected. "Mom, they're just trying to be nice. They feel sorry for us."

" 'Feel sorry for us'!" Ariah said scathingly. "How dare they! Tell them to feel sorry for themselves." Even in her convalescent's bed, her skin deathly pale and her voice cracking, Ariah managed to wound her elder son.

Usually, Royall was spared. He had to wonder why.

"You. At least you're alive."

Royall laughed uneasily. Ariah said the damndest things. At last, the piano student had left. Ariah, walking the girl to the front door, hadn't shown much emotion at seeing her son leaning against the porch railing, the lid of his cap pulled down low to hide his guilty eyes.

The girl, high school age, blushed when she saw Royall, as if she knew him. She murmured what sounded like *H'lo Royall* as she brushed past.

There was Ariah gazing at him with hurt, indignant eyes. She might have been deliberating should she bar Royall from the house. Refuse to let him inside. She might have tossed his belongings out onto the sidewalk as they'd witnessed a raging woman across the street, years ago, tossing her husband's things out for all the neighborhood to gape at, and screaming, "Fucker! Fuck-*er*!"

There came Zarjo trotting out onto the porch, whimpering and barking with excitement. He hadn't seen Royall for several days and might have surmised from the tension in the household that something catastrophic had happened. An old dog now, thick in the torso, his wavy butterscotch hair faded and thin, and his eyes less clear, Zarjo remained puppy-like in his devotion to the Burnabys, especially to Royall. All his life, Royall had been his play-buddy, as Ariah was the one who fed him and kept him by her when the children were in school. Zarjo eagerly nuzzled Royall's hands, tottered on his hind legs trying to kiss Royall's face. "Zarjo, hey. Down." Royall couldn't help but feel that the dog's frantic loyalty was misplaced.

Ariah turned abruptly, and walked away. But she didn't shut the door in Royall's face.

"Zarjo, damn I said *down*."

You yearn to hurt them, sometimes. Those who love you too much.

Royall followed Ariah back into the kitchen rubbing his itchy, unshaven jaws, that felt as if they were sprouting quills. His clothes were rumpled and his underarms frankly smelled. Ariah put a tea ket-

tle on the stove, as she usually did after a long afternoon of piano lessons. She moved with studied slowness as if her joints ached. In the
overhead light, Ariah's long pale unsmiling face was that of a woman
no longer young, yet not resigned to age. Her manner was fierce and
resolute. Her hair, always her most striking feature, was coiled in a
loose, drooping yet regal knot and held in place with glinting pins; it
was partly rust-colored and partly silver, like mica. Though she was
clearly under a strain, and unhappy, Ariah had dressed for her piano
students in a long tweed skirt, a black cashmere sweater with an embroidered bodice, and a bravely bright red silk scarf; items purchased
for a few dollars each, and not recently, at the Second Time 'Round
Fashions Shop on Veterans' Road. Ariah Burnaby was a woman of
dignity, backbone straight and head high, in a neighborhood in which
housewives frequently appeared on their front porches in nightgowns
and bathrobes, hair in outsized curlers. Yet Royall imagined her teeth
grinding. *Yes I am furious. Yes you have gone too far this time.*

Ariah had been planning a wedding reception in this house. The
first social occasion she'd ever planned, so far as Royall knew. And
Royall had taken that from her.

Among other things he'd taken from her.

Royall's instinct was to acknowledge guilt and beg forgiveness.
But something in him held back, stubbornly. He wasn't sorry! He was
God-damned glad not to be married to Candace McCann, or to
anyone.

Royall saw the Western Union telegram, looking as if it had been
crumpled in Ariah's hand, lying on the kitchen counter. He tried to
think what to say that wouldn't be false, hypocritical, whiny. As if
reading his thoughts Ariah said dryly, "A telegram. My first.
Congratulations to Ariah Burnaby, your son has behaved disgracefully."

Royall sighed. He was rubbing Zarjo's eager head, that felt bonier
than Royall remembered, as the dog, panting excitedly, licked his
hands.

From long experience Royall knew that, if he didn't speak quickly
and forcefully, made no effort to defend himself, Ariah would escalate
her attack. He would never forget how, summer of his junior year in
high school, when he'd worked for City Parks & Recreation and had

been a popular softball player on the city-sponsored team, hair grown long and flaring past his shoulders, a braided headband around his forehead, Ariah was scathing in her denunciation of him as a "rabid hippie"; and one evening in this very kitchen she'd lunged at him with a scissors, grabbed his thick hair and snipped great chunks of it off before he could stop her. And ever afterward she'd teased him mercilessly. Her *rabid-hippie* son. She said, "Well. It shouldn't have surprised me, I suppose. Any reckless thing you kids do."

You kids. That stung.

Royall said, " 'You kids'? How d'you figure that?"

"Breaking your mother's heart. You have your ways."

"What the hell do Chandler and Juliet have to do with this, Mom? It was me."

" 'It was me.' I suppose you're proud. Selfish, vain, ignorant and deluded *male*."

Royall winced. How did you defend yourself, accused of being *male*?

Ariah said, her voice quavering, "You're like him. His seed is in you. To hurt, to destroy. To throw away everything. To turn from the very people who love you, who have trusted you. Oh, I hate you!" She paused, stricken, as if realising she'd said too much. Blindly she turned away, fumbling to lift the steaming tea kettle from the stove.

"Like who, Mom? My father?"

Royall waited, anxiously. He knew better than to press Ariah.

She was pouring water into a tea pot, spilling some onto the cupboard. Royall dreaded her scalding herself, her hand so shook. She said, "I can't ever trust you again. And I loved you so."

"Oh, Mom. Christ . . ."

"I loved you better than Juliet, who I was meant to love the very most. Juliet was my little girl, my daughter I'd have died for, but it never turned out right between us, not the way it did with you. Oh, from the first, you were my Royall! And now I hate you."

"Jesus, Mom. You don't mean that."

"Don't you swear in my presence! Slangy profanity, it's so 'hip' and vulgar."

Royall swallowed hard. "How am I like my father, Mom? Tell me."

Ariah shook her head curtly. Her face had shut like a blind being drawn.

Betraying the family. Going outside the family. That was it.

Daringly Royall said, "Mom, why won't you tell me about my father? I know the man is dead. He can't hurt us now—can he?" But here Royall became confused. The way he felt sometimes, piloting the Devil's Hole boat, when among the passengers there were some who over-reacted, squealed and screamed as if the boat was really in danger from the turbulent water; and in an instant fear was contagious everywhere on the boat, Royall's own heart pounding absurdly. The look in Ariah's face was one of horror.

Royall ceased speaking. He took the tea kettle from Ariah's shaky hand and set it back on the stove. At least, now, Ariah wouldn't scald herself, or him. There was a long, varied, serio-comic history of "accidents" in this kitchen, some of them committed by Ariah, and some by her distracted children.

Royall tried his most winning Royall-smile. It had worked for him for nineteen years with this woman, and he couldn't believe it wouldn't work now. In a voice of seeming apology he said, "I know, Mom, it was a shitty thing to do. I—"

" 'Shitty.' What kind of language is that? You were cruel, you were thoughtless—" Ariah broke off abruptly. Royall guessed she was about to say again that he was *male*.

"I was desperate, I guess. Something happened to me the other day. And I knew it wasn't right, what I was doing. It would hurt Candace, and it would hurt me. If we'd had children—"

Ariah said angrily, "If I'd had grandchildren. *That* would be beyond you, I suppose."

"What? What are you saying, Mom?"

"At least Candace isn't expecting a baby. That's the one good thing in all of this. If you'd abandoned her—"

Royall protested, "Mom, I wouldn't have 'abandoned' her. I would never have done that."

"Wouldn't you! I wonder." Ariah poured tea into a cup, steadying the ceramic pot with both hands. "Don't pride yourself, Royall Burnaby, that Candace won't recover from this. She was upset on

Friday evening, and brokenhearted, but she wasn't hysterical, and her religion will be a consolation to her. 'Royall isn't a Christian,' she said. 'So maybe this will be for the best.' She'll be wearing that beautiful dress for someone else, I predict, and soon. Within a year or two." Ariah was working herself up into one of her prim-lipped speeches. "A girl that pretty, you've let go. A girl with such a pure, uncomplicated heart, and so—*sweet*."

Royall said, disgusted, "Christ's sake, Mom! If I wanted a 'sweet' wife I'd marry a chocolate bunny. I'd go to bed with fucking Fannie Farmer."

"Royall. Your mouth."

"It's my mouth, not yours! I want a wife I can talk to, for Christ's sake. Talk to, and laugh with. A wife who's smarter than I am, not dumber. A wife for when I'm older, and ready. A wife who doesn't want me to get a 'real' job at a fucking chemical plant and destroy my fucking brain cells, what few I have. A wife who's—" Royall drew a deep breath, suddenly inspired. "—talented. At some thing I'm not."

Ariah was staring at Royall. Again that look of horror came over her. Her lips moved silently, she seemed about to faint. Royall was frightened for her, and said quickly, relenting, "Mom, I just know it's better this way. I think Candace knew, too, but once the wedding plans started it was hard to stop, like the wedding had a life of its own, and was the point of what we were doing. I didn't want to disappoint you, I guess. So few things seem to make you happy . . ."

These words hovered in the air. Not an accusation, a statement of fact. Ariah, recovering from her shock, managed to laugh indignantly. "Oh, now he can blame me! My blameless son, blaming his mother."

Royall was thinking for the first time that his mother and father must have been in love, once. A long time ago when they'd gotten married. And for how many years afterward? Then, something had happened. He wanted to know what! He had to know. But seeing the look in Ariah's face, he knew it wasn't going to be this evening.

"Mom, I'm not blaming you for anything. It's my own fault. I guess I'm weak, I like making girls feel special, and happy. Even if it's kind of unreal, like a masquerade."

"Life outside the family is a masquerade," Ariah said flatly. "You kids will learn."

But not inside the family? Royall shifted his shoulders uncomfortably.

There was Zarjo, for whom no ethical, moral, metaphysical questions existed, only an anxious dog-concern that his young master might abandon him. Zarjo, adept at decoding tensions in the household, sometimes before its inhabitants, was nuzzling Royall's hands, trying to press up to kiss his heated face. "God damn, Zarjo get *down*." The dog fell back, toenails clicking on the linoleum floor, hurt as if Royall had struck him. So naturally Royall had to pet and stroke him, reassuring him that yes, Zarjo was loved.

Half the world desperate to be loved. Half the world desperate to be free of being loved.

"What happened to me, Mom—"

"Yes. What happened to you? You look as if you've been drinking for days, and sleeping in your car."

This was cruel, and inaccurate. Royall hadn't had more than two or three beers that day. He hadn't been sleeping in his car since the first night, Friday.

"—I realized that I couldn't marry Candace because I—I didn't love her as much as I can love a woman." There, it was said. Royall licked his lips, having uttered this enormity. He'd never been a boy who contemplated himself, let alone the possibilities of this self; since boyhood he'd envisioned the future with the same affable amnesiac vagueness with which he envisioned the past. "It wouldn't have been fair to Candace . . ."

Dryly Ariah said, "Oh, and why? Because you'd have been unfaithful to that poor girl?"

Royall felt his face burning. Talking of such things with his mother! "Well, things like that happen, don't they? If you marry too young. You meet somebody you really love, in a way you can't love the person you married. And then—"

Ariah drew herself up to her full height of about five feet seven inches. A moderately tall women for her generation, she was much shorter than Royall, and had to exert her authority over him by fixing him with her famous green-gasoline gaze. Oh, you dreaded igniting that gaze! Chandler, and Royall, and Juliet, and no doubt Zarjo cowered in terror of igniting that gaze. "Are you saying, Royall Burnaby, *you've* met someone else?"

Royall hesitated. No. This was an error.

Never could he speak of the woman in black to Ariah. Never to anyone.

Ariah said derisively, "Oh, aren't we proud of ourselves! You *male*. Your sex would be amusing, if you didn't carry venom in your loins."

Royall shuddered at the thought. Venom in his loins!

I want to love. I will love. With my body, and not dishonestly. Never again.

Royall meant to change the subject. He was sweating inside his clothes. He said hesitantly, "I could go back to school, maybe. Night school. I could get a high school regents diploma. Then——"

Ariah was sitting at the kitchen table, sipping at her tea. A moment of crisis seemed to have passed, she could exert her authority more easily now. She laughed, not unkindly. "You. Royall, you barely graduated with that local diploma."

"—I could go to college, maybe in Buffalo. Chandler did."

"Chandler! He's much more intelligent than you, dear. You know that."

"Do I?" Royall said coldly. "I've sure been told so."

"You've always had trouble in school, from the start. You're restless, and easily bored. You're a physical type, not like poor Chandler. Even Chandler's eyes are weak."

"Chandler's eyes? Christ, Mom."

"Even Juliet is more of a student than you, Royall. She's dreamy and rebellious but she is smart. Whereas you——"

Royall laughed, rubbing Zarjo's bony head harder. "Mom, you're really encouraging. You have a lot of faith in me."

"Royall, I had faith in you as a musician, once. Not that damned guitar of yours but the piano. There's no instrument like the piano! You were playing with such promise, when you were eight years old. Then you turned against it, why? And you had a good, trainable baritone voice. But you couldn't be bothered, always running around. You didn't have the patience or the discipline. D'you think that 'folk singing' you did in high school is anything to be proud of? Now your voice is raw, bad as that ridiculous Tom Dylan."

"Bob Dylan."

Ariah's face crinkled in distaste. "Hideous! At least Elvis Presley had a voice."

"Mom, you hated Presley, too."

"I hated his music. 'Rock and roll.' It's ignorant barbarism, the death of America. Eaten from within by America's own children." Arian's hand trembled, lifting her tea cup. Her knotted hair had begun to uncoil. Savagely she said, "And you!—suddenly wanting to go to college. The way you wanted, then did not want, to get married to that sweet innocent girl. Why, when you love working at the Gorge?"

Royall saw which way this was going, but damned if he could head Ariah off. Years ago he'd overheard Ariah maneuvering Chandler out of going to the University of Pennsylvania, where he had a scholarship, in favor of staying closer to home, attending Buffalo State. *You know how strain upsets you. What if something terrible happened to you. So far from home.*

Sure enough, strain had affected Chandler, and would continue to affect him through four years of college, not in Philadelphia but in Buffalo. He'd had to commute to classes five days a week, live on Baltic Street with the family, and work at part-time jobs to pay for tuition and help with family expenses. *College* came to be synonymous with *selfishness*, *futility*. Ariah was on this subject now, speaking with eloquent disdain. "And where would you get the money for college? It's more than just tuition, it's expenses. Hidden expenses. You'd have to take out a loan, and you'd be in debt for years. And if you never graduated, what then? All that money lost: down a rat hole."

Rat hole! Royall had to smile. Hardly a day passed at 1703 Baltic without the evocation of the dreaded *rat hole*.

"What? This is amusing? Are you some sort of aristocrat in disguise, you're an heir to a lost fortune? I have news for you, kid."

Royall said, annoyed, "I can work. I've been working since thirteen. Come on, Mom!"

"Well, you're not thirteen now. Your way isn't going to be paved with gold forever, mister. D'you think, the money you 'donate' to this household could begin to pay for food, shelter, twenty-four-hour maid service, in the real world? Only in this family, believe me. Your sister polishes your boots, and why? Your sister who resists anything her mother requests of her, she'll spend dreamy hours polishing your ridiculous motorcycle boots, cowboy boots, and why? Don't ask me why. She adores you, obviously. You can see how threadbare we are, the great expense of your mother's life is having the piano tuned twice a year, otherwise we'd all be out on the street, begging for welfare. But you kids are all alike: you behave as if there's money secreted away. That's it!" Ariah paused, panting. This too was a theme of Ariah's, the *secreted-away* treasure. For as long as Royall could remember, Ariah alluded to such riches as you might allude to something obscene, yet thrilling; thrilling, yet obscene. But Royall knew it was pointless to take up this lead, for Ariah would only speak of what she wished to speak. She was a dog whose leash was firmly in her own jaws, turning, feinting, cavorting.

Ariah was saying, firmly, "The Gorge—the Devil's Hole—the tourist trade—is ideal for you. Tourists are all children wanting to be entertained, and you have that gift, Royall. And this 'Captain Stu' obviously favors you. And living at home here with your sister and me, and Zarjo who adores you, if you aren't going to get married after all, makes sense, Royall." Ariah was working up to a motherly sort of reproach. "We have been happy, Royall, haven't we? You, and Chandler, and Juliet, and Zarjo, and me? You shouldn't have said 'so few things make me happy.' Everything makes me happy, Royall. When my family is safe." Ariah wiped at her eyes, for emphasis.

The ceiling creaked overhead. Footsteps, sounding hesitant. Juliet? Her room was directly above the kitchen. Royall guessed that Ariah had sent Juliet upstairs, wanting no interference.

Did Juliet adore him? Royall swallowed hard.

His sister had been very upset by Royall's news. For some reason, she'd been eager for Royall to get married. At first, typically for Juliet, she declared she would not attend the wedding: she hated "phony, fussy" ceremonies. Anyway, no one wanted *her*. She disliked "dressing UP"—"fixing her hair." She was "so ugly, anyway." But

Ariah had appealed to Juliet, and eventually she'd changed her mind; lately she'd been anticipating the wedding with almost too much excitement. Instead of being a "colossal drag," her brother getting married now was a source of deep happiness. A "new sister" was exactly what Juliet wanted, she'd said. Suddenly it had turned out that Juliet had "always wanted" a sister. "And maybe I'll be an aunt, soon. I bet!" Juliet teased Royall, who blushed fiercely.

But now, Juliet was devastated. When Royall spoke with her the other evening she'd ended up screaming at him, and slammed down the receiver.

How could you! Oh, Royall! Damn your soul to hell.

How determined they all were, Royall thought, not to lose one another. Not to surrender an inch.

Ariah was watching Royall closely. She'd leaned over to stroke Zarjo's back, as Royall continued to stroke the dog's head. Soothed by the two people he loved most, Zarjo was becoming less agitated. Ariah said, "We're having meat loaf for supper tonight, with onions and peppers. That thick tomato crust you like. And mashed potatoes, of course."

Royall's favorite meal. He had to wonder if this was by chance.

"O.K., Mom. That sounds good."

"Unless you have other plans."

Royall said nothing. Again, he heard the upstairs floorboards creak. Juliet would forgive him, too. In time. Royall, who'd come back home. Royall, who'd never left home.

"I left word at his school, that Chandler should join us. He's been so mysteriously busy, we haven't seen him for days. Is he still involved with that 'woman friend' of his, Royall? The one who—"

The young woman's name was Melinda. She was married, but not to Chandler who was in love with her. Royall felt sorry for his older brother who seemed always to be taking care of others, including Royall. *Why do you put up with such crap from Mom?* Royall once asked Chandler, who'd stared at him in astonishment. *Crap? What? Royall, what?* Chandler hadn't a clue what Royall was talking about.

"Royall, tell me: did Chandler know about you and Candace?"

"Know what?"

"That you were going to break off the engagement."

"No. He did not."

"But you confide in him, don't you?"

"Sometimes. But not this time."

Ariah's chin trembled. "If I learn that Chandler knew! That Chandler advised you . . ."

"Well, Chandler didn't." Royall wanted to add, *Why'd I ask Chandler anything about love, marriage, sex?* Royall guessed that Chandler had never made love to any woman. Poor bastard, he was more his mother's son than Royall had ever been.

Ariah had finished her tea. Her pale cheeks were suffused with warmth. With girlish enthusiasm she said, "Well. We'll have a cozy supper, just the four of us. I had a premonition you might be back. I prepared the meat loaf this morning, before my first student came . . . But if you're going to eat with us, Royall, please bathe! You look as if you've been sleeping outdoors. You smell as if you've been with the pigs."

Royall laughed. He didn't mind being teased in such a way, he was used to Ariah's swift change of moods.

But Ariah couldn't smell the woman in black on him, that had happened days ago.

In fact, Royall had fled the city to stay with a high school friend who now lived in Lackawana. In disgrace at home, he'd surfaced in the smoky industrial town south of Buffalo where no one knew him except this friend. On Saturday night they'd gone drinking. On Sunday afternoon they'd gone to the Fort Erie race track to distract Royall from guilty thoughts. There, it was Royall's unexpected luck to win $62 on his first bet, which was the first bet of Royall's life; to lose $78 on his second bet; to win $230 on his third bet; and, against his friend's advice, recklessly betting most of his track earnings on a horse named Black Beauty II, an underdog at 8–1 odds, to win $1,312. One thousand three hundred twelve dollars! Beginner's luck, Royall's friend had marveled. Royall's first adventure at any race track.

Royall said, "Not pigs, Mom. Horses." To Ariah's surprise, he took out his wallet which was thick with bills, and began to count out money on the kitchen table. In an instant his manner had become swaggering, boastful. Royall could feel himself skidding, like a car on icy pavement. Six hundred, seven hundred, eight hundred dollars . . .

Ariah was shocked. "Royall! Where did you get so much money?"

"Told you, Mom. Horses."

"Horses? The race track?"

Now Ariah was staring at Royall as if she'd never seen him before.

"After what has happened in your life, Royall, how could you do such a thing? The 'race track.' At such a time . . ."

Royall reconsidered, and took back one of the hundred-dollar bills. This left six hundred in his wallet for Candace. And the rent on the apartment was paid for three months, Candace would remain there. Candace would resume her job at King's Dairy where she was the most popular waitress. As Ariah predicted, within a year or two Candace would be engaged again, and this time married.

Ariah was saying urgently, "Royall, don't you hear me? What's wrong with you suddenly? Have you been drinking, too?"

"No, ma'am." Royall frowned, pushing the bills toward Ariah. He did feel drunk, suddenly. Having trouble choosing the right words. As a young child he'd often been confused by printed words, the logic of their positioning on a page, that other children seemed to accept without question. (Or were their eyes different from Royall's?) Sometimes he'd turned a book upside down, or tried to read sentences from the side, vertically. Other children, and his teacher, had thought that Royall was being amusing, eager to make them laugh. An affable sunny child, with fair flaxen hair and vivid blue eyes, that happy smile? No wonder, little Royall Burnaby had been everyone's favorite.

"Ariah. Can I ask you something?"

It was rare for Royall to call his mother "Ariah." She stiffened at the sound. She said:

"I dread to think what it might be. When you've so clearly been drinking."

"Why did you name me 'Royall'?"

Ariah hadn't expected this question. Clearly, she was taken by surprise.

" 'Royall.' " Ariah passed her hand over her eyes as if trying to recall. She drew a deep breath, as if she'd been waiting for a very long time to be asked this question, and had prepared the answer. "I think—it must have been because—you were 'royal' to me. My 'royal' first-born son."

"Mom, Chandler was the first-born."

"Of course. I didn't mean that. But you, dear, you seemed to me my 'royal' son. Your father—" Ariah paused, stricken. But her poise was such, her hand didn't tremble, lowered from her eyes. Her clouded green gaze never wavered, fixed on Royall's face.

Royall said casually, "At Fort Erie, somebody told me there was once a 'Royall Mansion,' a famous horse. In the 1940's."

Ariah laughed nervously. "Well. I wouldn't know about that. I don't know anything about horses, or racing."

Royall said, "Hell, I wouldn't mind being named for a horse, if it was a special horse. There are worse things."

Royall was behaving now as if he were about to leave. This was strange, for he'd only just come home. He said:

"The money is for you, Mom. For wedding expenses. You paid out money of your own, a lot."

Ariah said quickly, "No. I can't accept your money. Not from the race track."

"From my regular job, then. I owe you. O.K.?"

"Royall, no."

Ariah was on her feet. Her authority had been challenged, her sovereignty in this kitchen was at stake. She gazed hungrily at her opponent like one who has been attacked in her sleep, off-guard. She pushed at the hundred-dollar bills, and Royall stepped away. One of the bills fluttered to the floor. Royall kept the table between them. Zarjo eyed them both, haunches quivering.

"It's tainted money. I can't touch it."

"Mom, it's just money. And I sure do owe you."

Ariah had saved out dollars, quarters, dimes from her piano lessons over the years. If there was a secret fund, it was Ariah's painstakingly acquired fund, kept in a savings account to earn a meager quarterly interest, or, Royall thought, hidden away in a dresser drawer upstairs in her bedroom. The conviction came over him powerful as the onslaught of flu: he loved this woman, his mother, and could not live with her any longer.

Royall rubbed Zarjo's head again, in parting. The dog's eyes lifted mournfully to him.

"Tell Juliet I couldn't stay, Mom. I'll be calling you."

Ariah said calmly, "Royall Burnaby. If you leave this house, you're not welcome to return. Ever."

"O.K., Mom."

Strange that Royall was leaving without supper, when he was very hungry. Strange, he hadn't known until this moment he would be leaving so suddenly, when a part of him, dreamy Royall, the child Royall, wanted so badly to stay. He would leave without taking the much-needed bath his mother had commanded for him. He would leave without going upstairs to take anything from his room; and when, next morning, he returned, he would find his belongings in a heap on the front porch, spilling over onto the sidewalk—clothes, shoes, boots, the guitar with the broken string, Niagara Falls High School '76 Yearbook, portable radio, record player and dozens of records in their well-worn covers. In one of his scuffed cowboy boots Royall would discover, to his dismay, seven hundred-dollar bills neatly held together by a rubber band.

And not even Zarjo would emerge to acknowledge him this time. The front door locked, and all blinds drawn.

5

Tell me about him? Our father?

Royall, I can't.

Yes you can. Chandler, c'mon!

I promised her. I gave her my word.

When the hell was that? When we were kids? We're not kids now.

Royall, I—

He's my father, too. Not just yours. You can remember him, I can't. Juliet can't.

Royall, I promised Mom. When he died. The police came, it was in all the papers. I was eleven. You were four and Juliet was just a baby. Mom made me promise I—

How did he die? A car accident, right? In the river? It was raining and his car skidded—and his body was never recovered—is that it? Tell me!

I said I can't! She made me promise I would never talk about him, ever. Not to you, and not to Juliet. To other people we were supposed to say it all happened before we were born.

But it didn't! We were kids! You knew him! Tell me what our father was like.

She would never forgive me if—

I will never forgive you, Chandler! God damn.

I gave Ariah my word. I can't go back on that.

She took advantage of you, being so young. That's why we're so lonely. We grew up, people looking at us like we're freaks. Like cripples who can dance, and seem happy. People like us that way, they don't have to feel sorry for us. God damn fuckers! It's been going on all my life.

Royall, Mom just wanted the best for us. It's her way, you know what she's like. She loves us, she wants to protect us—

I don't want to be protected! I want to know.

Nobody can stop you from knowing whatever you can discover. But I can't be the one to tell you.

Why did she hate our father so much? Why was she so afraid of him? What kind of man was he? I want to know.

Royall, we could talk this over in person. On the telephone, it's a strain.

No! If you won't tell me anything about him, I don't want to see you. It will only fuck me up more, to know that you know things and I don't.

Royall? Where are you calling from?

What the hell do you care? A phone.

Mom said you've moved out. You broke off the wedding, and you've moved out? If you need a place to stay—

Go to hell.

Furious, Royall hung up the phone.

6

"IT'S—UNDERGROUND?"

"Technically, yes."

This was a surprise, somehow. Royall associated the downtown public library with its Doric columns and rotunda and the open space of its circulation desk. Underground didn't fit in. But it was "old newspapers" Royall sought, and these were stored in the "periodical annex" on level C.

The librarian regarded Royall doubtfully, yet politely. He might have exuded the air of a young man who'd spent as little time in libraries as he'd been able to manage until now. "What are you looking for, exactly?" Royall mumbled a reply, and backed off.

As soon as Royall left the first-floor, well-lighted area of the old library, he found himself alone. His hiking boots made clumsy noises on the spiral metal staircase, like hooves, and a smothering smell, like sawdust mixed with backed-up drains, lifted to his nostrils. He felt his first moment of panic. What was he looking for, exactly?

Since dawn it had been raining steadily. Dreamy October had turned from mild and sunlit to autumnal chill and a smell like wetted newspaper. In the distance above Lake Ontario thunder rumbled ominously, like a great freight train gathering steam. Royall hoped the storm would hold off until he was finished at the library.

As if his task would be a matter of a half-hour, or less.

Being furious with his brother was a new experience for Royall. Being "angry" with anyone, in fact. And expelled from home. Expelled from home! Maybe he'd join the Marines. They were recruiting boys just like him. Maybe he'd change his name: "Roy" was more fitting than "Royall" if you were on your own at nineteen, nobody's son. If you were "Roy," you wouldn't smile so quickly, and so affably. You wouldn't always be whistling and humming and hooking your thumbs in your belt like a sweet version of James Dean. You'd look adults— other adults—frankly in the eye and tell them what you wanted.

Maybe.

On level C, Royall felt as if he'd descended into a submarine. The periodical annex was a pitch-black cavernous space where visitors had to switch on their own lights. Royall worried that someone might come along, a librarian or a custodian, and switch off the stairwell lights, leaving him stranded underground. Jesus! No wonder he'd avoided libraries all his life.

Royall fumbled for the switch. A blurred, flickering fluorescence seemed to glare from all surfaces equally. The smell of drains was stronger here. And that melancholy smell Royall recognized from his days as a delivery boy for the *Gazette*, wet newsprint. Royall had forgotten how much he'd hated that smell, how bound up with a child's helplessness it was, and how deeply it was imprinted in his soul.

"That's why I hate you. One of the reasons. You went away, and left me to that smell."

He made his way past cartons of books and periodicals in towering stacks. Some were shoulder-high, others to the ceiling. Discarded items they must have been, waterlogged from leakage and unread for decades. The floor of level C was dull dirty concrete. Here and there, books and magazines lay spreadeagled, as if kicked. Royall was put in mind of the cemetery on Portage Road. Most of the annex was taken up with unpainted metal shelves in rows, floor to ceiling, with narrow walkways between. The shelves were marked alphabetically but there seemed to be little actual order. Waterstained, dog-eared copies of *Life*, dating back to the 1950's, were mixed with more recent issues of *Buffalo Financial News*; the *Niagara Falls Gazette*, the primary object of Royall's search, had been shelved in various places, with papers from Cheektowaga, Lackawana, Lockport, Newfane. Someone had scattered pages of the *Lockport Union Sun & Journal* underfoot. Everywhere dates were confused, as in the aftermath of a violent windstorm. It was sometime in early 1962 Royall believed he wanted, but where to begin?

The woman in black had brought him here. He felt a stab of revulsion for her. Touching him as she had.

It would take Royall nearly a half-hour to locate any issue of the *Gazette* for 1962; and this issue, he saw to his disappointment, was December. A Sunday edition, front-page headlines that had nothing to do with his father, or with Love Canal. Royall let the newspaper drop back onto the floor, squatting on his haunches.

"Shit. I'm thirsty."

He hadn't had a beer that day. It was early afternoon. He'd wait until later. When he'd accomplished something.

Royall understood that his father—"Dirk Burnaby"—had been involved in the original Love Canal lawsuit, but he'd never known details. That early lawsuit had ended in defeat, so that "Love Canal" became a local joke, but later in the 1970's when Royall started junior high, litigation was renewed. Not the same individuals, maybe. New lawyers. New litigants. There were more lawsuits, some of them directed against chemical companies other than Swann. Royall was only vaguely aware of these matters. His friends and classmates had sometimes spoken of such things because their families were involved in them, but their knowledge too was haphazard and scattered. Royall, who rarely read newspapers, and dreamt and dozed through social studies classes, hadn't followed any of this closely. Chandler said they were "all right" living where they were on Baltic Street; at least, he hoped so. Ariah never spoke of such matters. If the wind shifted from the east, Ariah shut windows. If soot darkened windowpanes and windowsills, you cleaned them with paper towels. Ariah held newspapers literally at arm's length, skimming headlines with a look of dread and disdain. She expected the worst from mankind, which allowed her to be pleasantly surprised, fairly often, when the worst failed to happen.

You. At least you're still alive.

There was wisdom in that, maybe. Royall was learning.

Pawing through untidy stacks of *Gazettes*. Also the *Buffalo Evening News*, and the *Buffalo Courier Express*, which had surely covered the Love Canal case. Royall's hands were smudged from newsprint. He was encountering mouse droppings, tiny black pellets the size of caraway seeds. And the dessicated husks of insects. Occasionally a live, rapidly fleeing silver fish. *The fate of the dead. But I'm not dead.*

Back issues of newspapers, 1973, 1971, 1968 . . . How naive he'd been, thinking he could drop by the library here, read about his father, learn some interesting facts, and depart. But his task wasn't so easy. Somehow, the past wasn't *there*.

In the near distance was a steady dripping. Every four seconds. Yet, when Royall listened, the four seconds became five, or more. Then again the drip came more rapidly. Royall pressed his fingers against his ears. "God damn. Fucker." Royall missed the Devil's Hole already, and he hadn't been off a week. In his waterproof uniform, in his visored cap, passengers depending upon Lieutenant Captain Royall. It was a Disney cartoon and yet: the thunderous water below The Falls was real.

Sometimes, though, Royall felt himself not-real in that place. In the midst of spray, squeals of passengers, the heaving bucking boat. His thoughts drifted away, he slipped into an eerie dream of flailing his arms and legs underwater. The glassy-green, beautiful water of the Horseshoe Falls. Royall's long hair trailing like seaweed. He was naked, and his eyes were opened wide, as a corpse's eyes are opened wide.

Yes, Royall had seen corpses hauled from the Niagara River. He'd seen his first "floater" at the age of twelve. Mom never knew. Like hell, he'd have mentioned this to anyone in his family or even to neighbors on Baltic Street. A floater was a submerged corpse swollen with rot like a meat balloon, rising to the surface.

No, Royall hadn't thought much about it. That his own father had died in that river. Not ever a morbid-minded boy.

Royall rubbed his aching eyes. Glanced up from blurred columns of newsprint. The drip-drip-drip had entered his bloodstream. Someone was gliding silently behind a row of steel mesh stacks. He smelled her scent! A warm sensation began in his groin, of hope. Though his actual arm was too heavy to lift, Royall saw his hand outstretched to the woman in yearning.

"Wake up. C'mon!"

Royall shook his head to wake himself from his trance.

He pushed himself harder. He was frightened of failing. Of giving up, moving back to Baltic Street. He was panting, determined. He returned to the stacks, making his way laboriously on his haunches, checking every paper on the lowest shelf, every date. His thighs pounded in pain. Yet, by luck, he finally located copies of the *Gazette* dating back to 1961–1962. Individual pages were missing but the bulk of the newspapers appeared to be intact. Royall carried armfuls to a wooden plank table in the center of the room. He began to search, methodically.

There!—the first Love Canal headline. September 1961.

"You were still alive. Then."

Two hours and forty minutes Royall read, and re-read. He was beyond exhaustion. He could not have said if he was exhilarated, or frightened. There was so much more than he'd known, so much more than he'd been capable of imagining. He felt as if a door had suddenly opened in the sky, where you had not known there could be a door. A massive opening through which light shone. As light often shone, through fissures in thunderclouds, if only for a few tantalizing minutes, in the sky above the Great Lakes. It was blinding light, hurtful, not yet illuminating. But it was light.

7

ONE DAY HE DROVE out Portage Road, and there was the abandoned stone church. And there was the cemetery, that looked abandoned but was not, entirely. He parked his car and entered the cemetery as he'd done earlier in the month on a warm October morning, now it was later in the month and later in the season, a damp chill to the air and the sky overcast. There were fewer leaves on trees. The wind had blown them off. Wind had cracked tree limbs, overturned flower pots, twisted those little American flags stuck beside veterans' graves so they were barely recognizable as flags. Royall had learned, from the library, that Dirk Burnaby had been a veteran. Of World War II. There was no grave for Dirk Burnaby but if there had been, a flag might signal it.

This cemetery! It drew the eye, it fascinated, yet in the way of a dream in which individual details shimmer and fade, as you look closely at them. Royall had the impression that the cemetery was shabbier than it had been, as if months and even years had passed, and not less than three weeks.

He spent some time searching the area where the woman in black had been trimming grass on a grave, but no grave looked as if it had been trimmed lately. Fallen branches lay everywhere. Broken clay pots, dead geraniums, plastic flowers. Nor could he find the hidden-away place where the woman had drawn him, and they'd lain together. No names on any of the gravestones were familiar, or meant anything to him. Kirk, Reilly, Sanderson, Olds. These were the names of strangers who'd lived decades ago, the most recent burial had been in 1943.

Still, Royall didn't want to give up. He wasn't ready to leave. This was a Saturday morning, someone might come to the cemetery to visit a grave, to tidy up a grave, maybe the woman in black would return, Royall had so much to tell her.

Pilgrims

"The madness of wind excites us. But we know to bring the flapping laundry inside, fast."

It was of the other house we sometimes dreamt. The knocking at the front door, our mother's upraised voice, the indistinct voices of the police officers which we knew not to confuse with our father's voice. Mother's shrill strangulated cry.

No. Go away. Get out!

There were two of us awakened and crouching on the stairway landing. In the kitchen where he spent the night in his cushioned wicker basket, the puppy Zarjo began barking and whining anxiously.

We disobeyed Mother, we didn't go back upstairs. By the time the police officers left we were crying desperately.

In the nursery where Bridget had been awakened, the baby began to cry.

There were two brothers. Chandler who was eleven, Royall who was four.

They could not know that their father was dead. On that morning when police officers came to 22 Luna Park it hadn't yet been determined that Dirk Burnaby was dead. Only that the car registered in his name had been hauled from the Niagara River where it had skidded and smashed through a guard railing of the Buffalo–Niagara Falls Highway sometime in the early morning of June 11, 1962. Only that no body had yet been recovered.

There were no witnesses to the alleged accident. Nor would witnesses come forward.

An "accident" it would be ruled. For who could prove otherwise?

And though the body of Dirk Burnaby would never be recovered, in time a "death certificate" would be issued by the county.

It was of that other house we sometimes dreamt. We remembered how Mother fumbled and clawed at the lock of the door as soon as the police officers left. Before they'd returned to their car and driven away she'd locked the door. She was panting. We rushed at her in terror. Her eyes swung wildly in her face and her lips were white and ravaged like a fish's mouth torn by the hook. We were not yet disciplined for crying, that would come later, and so Mother allowed us to cry, Mother tried to hold both of us, awkwardly stooped as if her backbone had been broken. Her voice lifted defiantly. *Is that door shut? Is that door locked? Never open that door again.*

And so it was: none of us ever opened that door again.

The body of Dirk Burnaby was never found in the Niagara River.

And yet: at approximately 8 A.M. of June 11, 1962, a gathering of pilgrims visiting the shrine of Our Lady Of The Falls, a Roman Catholic basilica three miles north of Niagara Falls, would report having sighted what appeared to be "a man swimming in the river, downstream." The pilgrims belonged to a Roman Catholic parish in Washington, D.C., and had made the trip to the basilica on a chartered bus; there were forty of them, ranging in age from thirty-nine to eighty-six, most of them infirm or ailing to a degree. They claimed to have known absolutely nothing of the "vehicular accident" on the Buffalo–Niagara Falls Highway earlier that morning, nor that the Coast Guard and other rescue workers were searching the river for a man's body.

What they saw, or swore they saw, was a man swimming swiftly downriver, borne by the current in the middle of the river, and parallel with shore. The swimmer made no attempt to head toward shore. A few of the more able-bodied pilgrims shouted at him, waved their arms, ran along the riverbank until undergrowth prevented them. The swimmer took not the slightest notice. Some said it looked as if he were "swimming for his life." He'd appeared "out of nowhere" and would disappear "into nowhere" as the pilgrims stared after him in dismay.

The man was never identified of course. No one had seen his face, he was too far from shore. It wasn't clear—and this was a crucial point—whether he was bare-chested, or in fact clothed. Vaguely he was described as "not young"—"but not old." He had "dark-blond hair"—"buff-colored hair"—"a fair, whitish hair." All agreed that he was a "very good swimmer."

Coast Guard rescue workers on the river were contacted by radio, but the "swimming man" was never located.

I grew up, and I moved from the house on Baltic Street, and at the age of twenty-three I became a volunteer at the Niagara County Crisis Intervention Center. I became a Red Cross emergency rescue worker, and a member of the Samaritans, a suicide-prevention organization. I would learn that reports like the pilgrims' are not uncommon.

Witnesses will swear—sincerely, adamantly, at times vehemently!—that they have seen a swimmer where (in fact) they've seen a corpse, born rapidly downstream by a current strong and turbulent as that of the Niagara River. Often these witnesses will claim to have seen a human swimmer when what they've seen (as evidence will bear out) is the corpse of a drowned dog or sheep. It's because the rhythmic agitation of the corpse's limbs, caused by the waves, mimics the motions of swimming.

Invariably these "swimmers"—"excellent swimmers"—are swimming downstream, parallel with shore. Never do they turn, vary their swimming pattern, or head to shore. Never do they respond to observers shouting to them from shore. With tireless energy and determinism they "swim"—and disappear from view.

Why? A Coast Guard rescue worker explained.

"People want to see a 'swimmer.' Definitely they don't want to see a corpse. Out there, in the river, someone like themselves, they're going to want to see that he's alive, and swimming. Whatever their brains might tell them, their eyes don't *see*."

No body was ever recovered, identified as Dirk Burnaby. Years passed.

Hostages

1

*W*hy? *Because I need to help others.*
    Because I need to help. And there are others.
Because I need. I need.
Why?

2

EROSION TIME EROSION TIME

He was twenty-seven, it was March 1978. Block-printing these words onto the blackboard at the front of his ninth grade general science classroom at La Salle Junior High. In this room, in this public school in downtown Niagara Falls, Chandler mostly felt himself of no specific time or age at all.

Chandler was about to relate these terms to his students' homework assignment when the summons came for him: "Mr. Burnaby, excuse me? Please call the County Crisis Prevention Center. I guess it must be an emergency."

The young woman from the principal's office was breathless, concerned, sensing herself the bearer of urgent news.

It wasn't the first time that a summons from the Crisis Center had come to Chandler at La Salle, but usually these emergencies occurred at extreme hours. Late-night, early-morning. Weekends and holidays when the human will has frayed. Chandler murmured, "Janet, thanks!" Demonstrating to the twenty-eight students in the room how matter-of-factly their Mr. Burnaby dealt with "emergency," placing the stick of chalk on the blackboard tray and informing them, in his usual quiet, mildly humorous voice, that they'll be heartbroken, he has to leave before the end of class, something has come up. "I hope I can trust you? There are eight minutes left in the hour. Please remain in your seats until the bell rings. You can use the time to get started on your homework assignment and I'll see you, God willing, tomorrow. O.K?" They smiled seriously, they nodded. This was an emergency, he could trust them. For eight minutes at least.

God willing. Why'd Chandler say such a thing? He wasn't one to dramatize danger, or himself. And he neither believed in God nor presented his subject to fourteen-year-olds in any way that might be construed as predicated upon a belief in God.

Even Ariah's God, the one with the cruel sense of humor.

"Mr. Burn'by? Is it somebody going to jump into The Falls?"

"I don't think so, Peter. Not this time."

Downstairs in the principal's office Chandler telephoned the Crisis Center and was given information, directions to the site of the "gunman/hostage" situation on the east side. Within minutes he was in his car, driving east on Falls Street past Tenth Street, Memorial Drive, Acheson Drive. All his senses were alert as if he'd been plunged into ice water. Feeling like an arrow being shot—swiftly, un-erringly, as Chandler himself could never shoot an arrow—to its target.

God willing. That wry fatalism, which was Ariah's fatalism, too. For you never knew, summoned by the Crisis Center, whether this would be the emergency from which you, the energetic volunteer, would not return.

Penance, is it? This life of yours. But if you love me why would you do penance?

He did love Melinda. He loved Melinda's baby daughter to whom he hoped to be a father, someday. But he couldn't answer her question.

Ariah had ceased asking. In the season of Chandler's first active in-volvement in the Crisis Center, his first year as a teacher in the Niagara Falls public school system, she'd registered her sharp disap-proval of her elder son's "reckless, dangerous" volunteer work, and Ariah wasn't one to persist where she knew she could not succeed.

These days, Chandler dealt with the problem by not telling Melinda, if he could avoid it. And certainly not telling Ariah.

"Gunman/hostage." Chandler had intervened in only one of these situations before, a deranged man holding two of his own chil-dren hostage in his home, and it had not ended happily. And it had lasted well into the night.

Chandler's volunteer work had begun when he'd been an undergradu-ate in the early 1970's. He'd demonstrated against the Vietnam War and the bombings in Cambodia. He'd joined other young miliant-idealists to campaign door to door for voter registration in poor Buffalo neighborhoods, and he'd helped set up Red Cross blood-giving booths at various sites in Buffalo, Niagara Falls, and their af-fluent suburbs. He'd helped petition for school bond issues, "clean water" and "clean air." (It was while working for the Red Cross that he'd first met Melinda Aitkins, a nurse.) Then, he'd been drawn into emergency work. Red Cross, Crisis Intervention Center, Samaritans. It was a small, intense community of individuals who soon became acquainted with one another. Most of them were unmarried, childless. Or their children were grown and gone. Or their children had disappointed them in some way. Sometimes, their children had died.

Most of the volunteers Chandler knew were Christians, and they took their religion seriously. A Christian is one who "does good" for others. Jesus Christ had been a volunteer in the salvation of mankind, hadn't He? Jesus Christ had been fearless in His intervention in the spiritual crises of mankind. The crucifixion was the earthly penance He had to pay for challenging the cyclical fatalism of mankind, but the resurrection was His reward, and an embled for all—wasn't it? Chandler listened raptly to such ideas, expressed by the former Jesuit who headed the local branch of the Samaritans, but listened in silence.

He told Melinda, "I wish I could believe. It would make everything so much easier."

Melinda said, "You don't want things easier, Chandler. You want things exactly as difficult as they are."

During Chandler's lifetime, Niagara Falls had become a sprawling, burgeoning, "prosperous" industrial city. It was boasted that the city's population had doubled since the 1940's. There were now more than fifty thousand industrial jobs in the area, and—a fact that was reiterated often, as if it were a special sign of merit—the highest concentration of chemical factories in the United States. The Niagara Falls Chandler had known, or had known to a degree, had been changed almost beyond recognition. Luna Park was the only "historic" residential neighborhood that remained, but it too had begun to deteriorate; the wealthy lived on l'Isle Grand, or beyond, in the affluent Buffalo suburbs of Amherst and Williamsville. The Niagara Gorge and land along the river approaching The Falls were protected by the state from commercial development because this was sacrosanct tourist territory, guaranteed to generate millions of dollars yearly.

In this new Niagara Falls where a shift in the wind turned the very air sepia, made eyes smart and breathing difficult, "crises" had become commonplace, like crime. Rarely did these crises involve individuals who'd made pilgrimages to The Falls to commit a spectacular act of suicide; these were natives of the city, nearly always men. They acted upon impulse in sudden rage, despair, madness fueled by alcohol and drugs committing acts of unpremeditated violence, much of it domestic. Their weapons were guns, knives, hammers, fists. Often they committed suicide after their rage played out, or tried to.

"Gunman/hostage." The dispatcher at the Crisis Center had told Chandler that robbery or burglary didn't seem to be involved. The motive had to be purely emotional, the most dangerous of motives.

Since he'd grown out of his awkward adolescence, Chandler had become a lanky, lean-muscled young man with a look of perpetual vigilance. He moved quickly like a tennis player confronted with a superior opponent, but not prepared to concede the game. His face remained boyish, somewhat undefined. He was easy (he knew!) to forget. His hairline had begun to recede when he was in his early twenties and his fair, feathery silvery-brown hair lifted from his temples as if lighter than air. His eyes were sensitive, moist. A girl he'd known in college had said of his eyes that they were "ghost-eyes"— "old-young eyes of wisdom." (Had she meant this as a compliment?) Chandler wore tinted glasses that gave him an offhand, sexy counter-culture look, but his counter-culture heroes had been the Jesuit Berrigan brothers, and he'd never dressed in any remotely radical way. If his hair grew long and curled over his shirt collar, it was out of neglect, not style. Chandler would never let his hair straggle to his shoulders and fasten a braided headband around his forehead, as Royall had done; Chandler was mystified by his younger brother's physical ease, and Royall's sense that others should be drawn to him, and were naturally drawn to him. Not that Royall was vain: he wasn't. But if girls or women fell in love with him, how was he to blame? *I don't make it happen. It isn't me, it's them.* By contrast, Chandler was astonished if a woman appeared to be attracted to him; he couldn't help but doubt her sincerity, or her taste. He saw himself as a spindly-limbed boy of thirteen with watery eyes and blemished skin and a perpetual snuffle whose exasperated mother was forever chiding to stand up straight, to brush his hair out of his face, button his shirts correctly, and—*please!*—blow his nose.

"Almost, Chandler has become handsome," Ariah said not long

ago, staring at him in surprise. As if she were seeing her elder son anew, and not entirely liking what she saw. "Don't let it go to your head, Chandler!" She'd laughed, with that Ariah-air of teasing and chiding, that made you wince even as you understood it was meant affectionately.

Why? Because I need.

Need to be of service. Somehow.

Always, it felt to him like a privilege. An unknown wish, granted.

Today he'd been directed to a factory on the east side, on Swann Road. Not a part of the city Chandler knew well though probably, when he saw Niagara Precision Humidifiers & Electronic Cleaners, he'd recognize the building. Chandler Burnaby had been driving the grim grid-patterned streets of Niagara Falls all his adult life. Sometimes it seemed he'd lived a previous life here, too.

Ariah had once said to Chandler, mysteriously, at the time of her hospitalization for gallbladder surgery, when she'd been frightened of what might lie ahead for her, "Dear, I do love you! Sometimes I think I love you best. Forgive me."

Chandler had laughed nervously. What was there to forgive?

Today was a bone-chilling late-winter day like wet, dissolving tissue. Wind from the east, that metallic-chemical odor that coats the inside of your mouth. An asbestos sky, snowed-in yards, filthy sidewalks and curbs. Snow covered in soot, snow in mounds spilling out into the street. Snow-slush, snow-and-ice. Chandler's heart had begun to beat more quickly, in expectation of what lay ahead.

He'd forgotten to call Melinda, to tell her he might be late that evening.

No. He hadn't forgotten. He hadn't had time.

No. He hadn't not had time, he might have asked one of his colleagues at school, a friend, to call for him. But he had not asked.

Sometimes, just approaching an emergency scene, Chandler felt his vision begin to darken at the edges. That strangest of neuro-optical phenomena, tunnel vision. As if at the periphery of what's visible the world itself was disappearing, sucked into darkness. It was a phenomenon common to firefighters. Though Chandler's crisis work was rarely physical, nearly always verbal; earnest counseling, giving advice and comfort. Often just listening, sympathetically. Talking a desperate man or woman out of suicide you come quickly to sense how the soul of the other is on your side, wants to be saved and not to die. It's the individual, blinded by despair, you must convince to continue living.

We all want to die sometimes, exhausted with the effort of living, but it passes. Like weather. We're like weather. See the sky? Those clouds? Blowing over. Between the lakes like we are, everything blows over eventually. Right?

It was the most banal optimism. You could read it on a cereal box. Ariah would laugh, pitying. Yet Chandler believed these words, he'd staked his life on them.

Burnaby, that name. That's a Niagara Falls name?

Maybe adults remembered. But ninth graders did not. Children born in 1963 or later, what could they know of a fading scandal of 1962?

Chandler rarely thought of it, himself.

He'd had his chance, he might have left Niagara Falls. You would think he'd be living in some place where *Burnaby* was only a name. He might have gone to college in Philadelphia. He'd had scholarship offers elsewhere, too. But he hadn't wanted to upset Ariah at a difficult time in her life. (What Ariah's crisis of that time had been, Chandler couldn't now recall.) Nor had he wanted to abandon Royall and Juliet to their temperamental mother. They needed Chandler too, though probably the idea would never have occurred to them.

Go to hell Royall had told Chandler, and hung up the phone.

The brothers had been estranged for nearly six months. Chandler had tried to contact Royall without success. It was ridiculous for them to quarrel, they had only each other. Royall had never spoken to Chandler in that way before, and Chandler was left dazed by their exchange.

It was unfair, Chandler had promised Ariah to "protect" Royall and Juliet at the time of their father's death, and so he had. He'd tried. All these years he'd tried. And now Royall had turned against him, refusing to understand. Royall had left home, was working for a businessman in the city; living alone, and taking night school classes at Niagara University. Royall, back in school! That was the most amazing news of all. Chandler heard of Royall occasionally by way of their sister Juliet, and then surreptitiously, for of course Ariah refused to speak of her "willful, self-destructive" son.

Chandler had wanted to ask his mother: how long could you expect Royall not to be curious about his father? And Juliet? Any reasonable mother would know it was only a matter of time.

"Reasonable." Chandler laughed aloud.

Thinking of these things, he'd begun to drive faster. The speed limit was thirty-five, he'd been pushing fifty. No time for an accident. He was needed out on Swann Road.

I don't want to be protected, I want to know.

Chandler wondered how much Royall had learned by now. How much about their father before wanting to know no more.

Shame, shame! Burn-a-by is the name.

There were children who'd actually chanted these singsong words behind Chandler's back. A long time ago, in junior high. He had pretended not to hear. He hadn't been a boy to be goaded into anger, or tears.

As he wasn't an adult to be goaded into emotion. Not easily.

Melinda had asked him one night about his father, because of course she knew, or knew something, having been born and grown up in the city herself. The name *Burnaby* was known to her. And Chandler told her frankly that he rarely thought of his deceased father, and out of respect for his mother he never spoke of him. But he would confide in Melinda, because he loved her and believed he could trust her.

"Do you! Love me, I mean."

"Yes. I love you." But Chandler's words were hesitant, uttered in wonder or in apprehension.

Chandler told her what he knew: that Dirk Burnaby had died that night in the Niagara River. Though his body had never been recovered, and for years it was rumored he'd somehow saved himself, managed to swim to shore. "But anyone who knows the Niagara River at that point knows that would be impossible," Chandler said. "It's a cruel joke, to suggest."

Melinda listened. If she'd wanted to ask had Chandler gone to look at the accident site, she did not.

She'd been trained as a nurse. She understood pain, even phantom pain. She understood that pain isn't therapeutic, cathartic, redemptive. Not in actual life.

The body of Dirk Burnaby had never been recovered, but the man was certainly dead, and an official death certificate had been issued, eventually. After a much-publicized investigation by police it was ruled that the incident had been an "accident"; which Chandler guessed was a euphemism. By tradition, the county coroner's office avoided a ruling of "suicide" whenever possible. Deaths at The Falls were usually attributed to "accident"—"misadventure"—out of a wish not to further upset survivors, and out of a wish to downplay suicide at the famous tourist spot. Even when suicide notes were found, these notes weren't always entered into the official police record.

The most grievous sin. Taking your own life in despair.

Chandler told Melinda that he supposed most people who knew Dirk Burnaby believed he'd killed himself. He'd been driving at a high speed (the speedometer was frozen at eighty-nine miles an hour) in a severe thunderstorm. He'd only recently lost an important court case, and he was nearly bankrupt. "There were other things, too. I knew from reading the papers. Ariah never had any newspapers in the house at that time, but I got hold of them myself. I read all that I could, but I've forgotten most of it now. Or I don't want to talk about it now, Melinda. All right?"

Melinda had kissed him, in silence.

Shame, shame. Burn-a-by is the name.

Chandler wondered if *Burnaby* was a name, finally, that would dissuade Melinda from marrying him. He would have to take that risk, he hadn't any choice.

The Crisis Center dispatcher had given Chandler the address, 3884 Swann Road. Past Veterans', past Portage, and now this stretch of Swann was closed by police to all but local traffic. Chandler showed his I.D. to a police officer and was flagged on. A quarter-mile to Niagara Precision Humidifiers & Electronic Cleaners, a low flattop cinderblock building set squarely in a parking lot. In the driveway were at least a dozen city and county police and medical emergency vehicles. Chandler parked on Swann Road and made his way to the scene as unobtrusively as possible, following the lead of a young police officer. Behind their vehicles and behind Niagara Precision trucks, police officers were crouched as in a suspenseful movie scene.

Except there was no background mood music here. There were no principal players, there was no script. Chandler Burnaby had been summoned by police but might not be used. The officer in charge would make that decision, but Chandler could have no idea when. He was available. He'd arrived, and was greeted. His hand had been shaken, and released.

The gunman had entered the factory approximately forty minutes before and at about that time he'd fired his first shots. The first calls to 911 hadn't been made until some minutes after that, by individuals who'd been allowed by the gunman to leave the building. Chandler could see the part-opened front door of the building and a shattered window a few feet away. The window was oddly shaped, about five feet high and no more than a foot wide. The gunman had been firing from this window, Chandler was told, but seemed to have stopped for the time being. "But keep your head down, mister, O.K.? Don't take any chances." Chandler said, "I know, officer. I won't."

As if he'd been rebuked beforehand. A civilian at the scene.

A bullhorn voice was making the air vibrate. So loud, Chandler almost couldn't distinguish words. *Mr. Mayweather, do you hear me? Release Miss Carpenter at once. Repeat, release Miss Carpenter at once. Show yourself in the doorway without your weapons, raise your hands, no harm will come to you, Mr. Mayweather. We are Niagara Falls City police. We have surrounded the building. Come out with your hands raised, and do not bring your weapons with you, Mr. Mayweather. I repeat, do not—* A police captain was speaking on the bullhorn, trying to exude an air of authority and calm.

At the site, Chandler was recognized by several NFPD officers to whom he was "Mr. Burnaby" of the Crisis Center. A plainclothes detective named Rodwell, whose daughter Chandler had taught two years ago at La Salle, crouched beside him to fill him in briefly. The gunman was known to have at least one handgun and one rifle, and he was believed to be "distraught, possibly drunk and/or on drugs." After his initial wild demand for "safe passage" out of the country he'd refused to communicate with police except for a few incoherent shouts; he hadn't picked up the telephone in the CEO's office where he was believed to be barricaded with a hostage, a young woman receptionist. *Mr. Mayweather? Are you hearing me? Mr. Mayweather we are asking you to lay down your weapons and appear at the door. We are asking you to release Miss Carpenter at once and allow her to leave. Are you hearing me, Mr. Mayweather?*

The gunman, white male, approximate age thirty, medium height and weight about two hundred pounds, had been identified as a recently discharged employee of Niagara Precision. Mayweather? There were Mayweathers in the Baltic Street area, and there'd been Mayweathers at Chandler's high school. This Mayweather had shot and critically wounded a foreman; fired wild shots in the direction of fleeing employees, whom he shouted at but didn't pursue; originally, he'd taken two women hostages, but released one after twenty minutes, a young pregnant woman, with instructions to tell police he wanted "safe passage" out of the country, by jet, to Cuba.

Cuba! Not a good sign.

As if Fidel Castro might give political asylym to a guy who's been shooting up co-workers.

Chandler asked Rodwell how he felt about what was happening, and Rodwell said he hoped to hell the girl wasn't already dead.

If the police knew she was dead, they'd go for Mayweather, immediately. They'd toss in tear gas, clear out the building. If Mayweather resisted, he'd be killed. It was a simple scenario, like a Greek tragedy in outline. Chandler knew from past experiences that there were few options for a barricaded gunman, and not one of them was in his favor.

Except, if suicide was the point.

The story, pieced together, was that Mayweather, fired from

Niagara Precision the previous week, had showed up that afternoon with a rifle, stepping into the front office and demanding to see the CEO who, luckily for him, hadn't yet returned from lunch; he'd decided to settle for the foreman, with whom he'd had disagreements, but after he'd shot the man he'd relented and allowed him to be carried out of the building by others, badly bleeding, and taken by ambulance to a hospital. Mayweather didn't seem to know what he wanted any longer, which wasn't unusual, Chandler thought, in such desperate situations.

Chandler made inquiries why Mayweather had been fired, and was told the exact reason wasn't known yet by police. Drinking on the job had been mentioned. Insubordination? Mayweather's co-workers described him as "quiet, a lot"—"sullen"—"thin-skinned." The young pregnant woman who'd been allowed to escape had been too shaken to tell police much, and was being treated for shock at a hospital.

The bullhorn voice continued, tireless. *Mr. Mayweather? I repeat, Mr. Mayweather, this building is surrounded—*

Chandler wondered when he'd be asked to intervene. Or if.

This was the suspense of the trenches during a lull. No shots had been fired by the invisible gunman for more than twenty minutes.

The air was so acrid here, Chandler had trouble breathing. His sensitive eyes stung. The predominant odor emanated from Dow Chemical close by, former manufacturer of napalm. At the Peace Bridge to Canada, years ago, Chandler had been one of numerous demonstrators against Dow Chemical. Police had arrested a few of the more aggressive demonstrators, but not Chandler Burnaby who'd never been one of those. You wanted to think that individual actions mattered, that there were real-life consequences following from ethical decisions, and maybe that was so. The despicable war had ended. U.S. troops had returned home. Napalm had gone the way of nerve gas. Though Dow had recouped its public relations disaster, and was once again prospering, like much of industrial Niagara Falls.

Swann Chemicals had been bought out by Dow in the late 1960's. A multi-million-dollar sale, highly profitable for the Niagara Falls–based company that had been the target of what was now referred to as an "early environmental" law action. Swann had won the Love

Canal case, but times were changing.

The bullhorn voice continued, more urgently. *Mr. Mayweather? We have surrounded the building. We need to know that Miss Carpenter is unharmed. Lay down your weapons, step into the doorway—*

For Christ's sake, Chandler thought. Let something happen.

No: he wasn't impatient. Why, impatience? The point of his being here was patience. He was the "crisis" man; he'd been trained to embrace "crisis"; he wasn't a professional, so this must be his vocation. He had to admit he liked being anonymous. If he was Mr. Burnaby, the name wasn't *him*. Not here, not now. This was a kind of grace, for one who couldn't believe in God. Ariah wouldn't know where her son was, and couldn't be anxious/furious about him just yet. Royall couldn't know, and wouldn't be preparing to feel guilty/defensive if something happened to him. Juliet couldn't know, though if the incident was being covered on TV, and she happened to watch the evening news, she might guess that her elder brother was on the scene.

And there was Melinda.

Chandler winced, thinking of her. He should have asked a friend to call her.

She was expecting him at her apartment, on the west side, sometime between six-thirty and seven. She'd call him, if he began to be late, and no one would answer his phone. They were to prepare dinner together (tonight, chili) as they did frequently. Chandler would play with the baby, turn the pages of a picture book, even help with her bath. Chandler would spend the night if Melinda invited him; if she sensed that Chandler wanted to be invited. Their lovemaking was tender, tentative. They were edging by degrees into a more defined relationship in the way of skaters, excited, apprehensive, edging out onto ice they aren't sure will hold them.

Surrender! Surrender your weapons.

Mr. Mayweather, the building is surrounded.

Hoping that no one would notice him, Chandler risked peering out around the van. It seemed unlikely that the gunman would be watching and fire at that moment. But the hairs at the nape of Chandler's neck stirred.

Royall always insisted his work at the Devil's Hole was one hundred percent safe. It only looks dangerous, taking a boat into the Gorge.

Chandler pushed his glasses against the bridge of his nose, squinting. His heart had begun to accelerate though he knew (he knew!) he wasn't in any actual danger. And so he was not. The facade of the grim building was unchanged. The door was ajar as before, the doorway empty. No movement there, or behind the shattered window. In the background a police helicopter droned. It seemed that time was suspended, but of course it was not. Police, paramedics, emergency workers, media people were waiting for something to happen, but where was the gunman? He'd set all this in motion, and had retreated with his hostage, barricaded. He wasn't responding to the deafening bullhorn, and wasn't answering the telephone. Chandler didn't want to think that Mayweather and the young woman hostage might both be dead.

Maybe Mayweather had a knife, he'd killed the woman in relative silence. The police hadn't heard gunfire. Maybe he'd slashed his own wrists. *Mayweather? This building is surrounded. If you hear me—*

You had to feel pity for a man, for whom being employed at Niagara Precision Humidifiers & Electronic Cleaners meant so much. This not-prosperous plant employing less than three hundred people.

Chandler overheard some of the cops making bets. Whether the guy would walk out alive, or be carried out. Whether he'd kill himself, or they would.

Chandler had been present at sites where men had died, or been wounded by police fire. Not a pleasant experience. The terrible noise of gunfire, lasting for several seconds, lodged deep in your brain. It was a noise beyond noise, a metaphysical assault. Noise like a machete severing bones. *I wish you wouldn't, but I wish more that you didn't feel the need.* Melinda kissed him, Melinda held him trembling in her arms. She seemed to sense that Chandler wasn't hers to hold, in quite that way; yet he wanted to be, and she sensed that, too. He hadn't told her more than she'd needed to know. Of course, she was a nurse, she'd worked in emergency rooms.

Twice in the past three years, Chandler had been present when men killed themselves. One had used a revolver, in a stand-off with police in a tenement building downtown, on New Year's Day, and the other had died in a plunge into the roiling American Falls from the tip of Goat Island, before a gathering of stunned onlookers. (This suicide, an eighteen-year-old Niagara University math major with no "known history" of emotional problems, had hung stony-faced over the railing for nearly an hour before letting go. Chandler had been designated to try to reason with him, get him to talk and reconsider, but Chandler had failed, and crept away in defeat. Death in The Falls. Of all deaths it seemed the most vengeful.)

In fact, most of the time Chandler was involved in emergency situations that came to no dramatic resolutions but simply ended, in stalemate and exhaustion. A drunken man barricaded in his apartment with his youngest child, shouting defiantly, weeping, smashing windows and furniture but putting up no resistance when police break in and take him into custody. A middle-aged flower-child on LSD who threatens to set herself on fire in a public place but, after drawing dozens of onlookers, and dousing herself spectacularly with kerosene, is unable to strike a match, and is led away giggling by police. Unshaven men in undershirts who rush at police officers, yelling obscenities and meaning to fight to the death, but are immediately overpowered, thrown to the pavement and deftly spreadeagled and their wrists handcuffed behind their backs.

So it went. Chandler had several times arrived too late, the drama was over, everyone was headed home.

That sinking sensation in the gut. *You haven't made any difference, what a fool you are. What vanity.*

Yet there was the night last July when he'd driven Melinda to the hospital, to give birth. They had not been lovers, only just friends. And Melinda had asked Chandler to stay with her because she was frightened to be alone and he had done so though frightened himself and when she began to have contractions he'd helped her, he'd gone to the hospital with her and remained with her through the seven-hour ordeal. It was the most remarkable experience of his life. He would never forget, he'd made a difference then.

Mr. Mayweather? Pick up the phone. We need to talk to you, Mr. Mayweather. We need to verify Miss Carpenter's well-being—

No response from the gunman.

Chandler overheard cops talking quietly together, nerved-up and angry. It wasn't believed that Mayweather had been wounded in the exchange of gunfire, but Chandler wondered if possibly he was. Maybe the gunman and his hostage were both bleeding to death inside the building? "Well-being"—how quaint this sounded, how unexpected in the bullhorn's deafening volume.

Mr. Mayweather, we are calling you at this moment and ask that you pick up the phone. We need to know what you want. What your expectations are. Mr. Mayweather? Are you hearing me? This building is surrounded. Release Miss Carpenter at once and you will not be harmed.

This time, as everyone strained to listen, there was a shouted obscenity from inside the building. The voice was strained, and didn't carry far.

Silence followed. (In the near distance, a rumble of freight trains.) There was the expectation that a gunshot might be fired, but nothing happened.

It was then that Chandler learned the gunman's first name: "Albert." Hadn't he known Albert Mayweather? From school? It was a name Chandler hadn't heard in years.

In fact, Chandler had graduated with another Mayweather, a younger brother or cousin of Albert. But he remembered Albert Mayweather, as a young boy might remember an older boy whom he fears and dislikes and yet admires in that unspeakable way of adolescence.

Mayweathers lived in the Baltic Street area, though none close by the Burnabys. There were many of them, a virtual clan. But Chandler recalled Al distinctly. A strong, stocky boy with a wrestler's build and dirty-blond hair coarse as rug fibres. He'd been a vocational arts major like so many boys at NFHS. His mood swung between a menacing silence and clownish exuberance. One of those boys whose idea of wit was to crack his knuckles, or fart, loudly. Al wasn't a team athlete but he played pick-up basketball with his buddies behind the school, cigarette dangling from his thick lips. "Alley-oop," his buddies called him. "Alley-oop" as if it were a term of endearment. Chandler understood reluctantly that girls, even "good" girls, were sometimes drawn to boys like Al Mayweather. At least initially.

Strange, and unspeakable: you wanted such boys to like you. To forgive you your high grades, your myopic eyes and faltering step, your stammer in fearful circumstances. You wanted a boy like Al Mayweather to acknowledge your name, a name given a perverse significance by scandal; a criminal name. *Burnaby? That's you?*

Chandler had a vague recollection that someone in Al Mayweather's family, or in the family of a Mayweather in Chandler's class, who was one of a number of OxyChemical workers who'd gone on disability young, in their thirties and forties; there was a class action suit against the company in the mid-1970s, much local controversy and anger. Chandler recalled such words as "betrayed"—"lied to"—"workers' rights"—"work-related illnesses"—in headlines. The multi-million-dollar lawsuit had not ended favorably for the workers, if you knew details. A jury had granted sizable monetary rewards to dying men, or to their surviving families, except these decisions were frequently overturned in appeals court, by which time the media had lost interest.

Mr. Mayweather? Step into the doorway with your hands raised.

Do not bring your weapons to the door, Mr. Mayweather.

Mr. Mayweather, the phone is ringing. Pick up the phone.

Police had tried to contact Mayweather's estranged wife, but hadn't been able to locate her at her home or at work. His children were living with their grandparents in North Tonawanda. Were they all right? Chandler knew that in such cases the gunman might have begun his shooting spree at home.

Chandler wondered if Mayweather's father was still living: probably not. None of those men involved in the lawsuit were alive now, probably. Lung cancer, pancreatic cancer, brain cancer, cancer of the liver, skin cancers. Fast-moving cancers. Metastasizing cancers. That was the point of the lawsuit, a demand for reparation for speeded-up lives, premature deaths.

"Love Canal" had been evoked, often.

But not the debased name *Burnaby*.

Melinda had said *Chandler, please. You are not your father.*

Chandler could count more than twenty police officers at the emergency site. Some were wearing protective gear and all were armed. Elsewhere, on the other side of the factory building, there were more, similarly armed men. Mayweather hadn't a chance. If he tried to shoot his way out he'd be riddled with bullets instantaneously. Chandler wondered, not for the first time in such circumstances, how it can happen that a man finds himself in such a place, one day. A rat backed into a corner. No way out.

Since high school, Chandler hadn't given the Mayweathers a thought. He supposed that the families still lived in the Baltic Street area. Now the younger generation had come into adulthood, like Al, and had gone to work in the factories; they'd married, had children, their lives were set. Probably, Al had gone directly from vocational arts at the high school into this job at Niagara Precision. He'd been what is known as a skilled worker, to be distinguished from a non-skilled worker. The highest paid were draftsmen and tool and dye designers, though if a plant wasn't unionized, as Niagara Precision probably wasn't, wages wouldn't be very high. Pension plans, medical coverage, insurance wouldn't be high. Non-union help could be fired, too. At the whim of the employer.

Two hours, forty-five minutes since Mayweather entered the building, and began shooting. Since the wounded man was taken to the hospital, not much had happened. Chandler had asked several times if he could speak to Mayweather over the bullhorn, explaining he'd gone to school with Mayweather, but the captain wasn't convinced this was a good idea yet. Police were still trying to contact the estranged wife, and Mayweather's brothers. Someone close to Mayweather. Chandler said, "I feel close to Al Mayweather. I think I could get him to pick up the phone."

(Was this so? Chandler wasn't sure. Hearing himself say these words, in a confident, urgent voice, he felt that possibly it was so.)

Chandler, like the others, was becoming edgy, anxious. The adrenaline rush was beginning to subside. Like low tide, waves retreating and leaving the sand littered with debris. Chandler was concerned that his head would begin to ache. That was his weakness, or one of them—throbbing pain behind his eyes and a rising sense of dismay, despair. *Why did he die. My father. Why, like a trapped rat. I loved him! I miss him.*

He'd let Royall down. Royall who'd called him, appealed to him in a way Royall had never spoken to Chandler before.

Royall, and Juliet. He was their protector. Ariah had begged him, fifteen years ago. Of course he'd promised. Better to betray the dead than the living.

Chandler thought of Melinda, of whom Ariah didn't approve; and of Melinda's baby, about whom Ariah knew very little. He wondered at his mother's animosity toward a woman she had not met. Because the woman's baby wouldn't be Ariah's grandchild? Maybe that was it. A baby whom Chandler might love, who wasn't descended from Chandler, and from Ariah.

Family is all. All there is on earth.

Television news vans had been arriving since the time of Chandler's arrival, strung out now along Swann Road. Behind the police line, media people drifted about, frustrated by inaction, and by the need to stay at a distance. These were professionals very different from those already at the scene: media people who saw the emergency as an opportunity, "news" to be exploited. They too were edgy, but expectant, hopeful. *Here we are! Now, something exciting can happen.* The most intrusive people were those who'd come in the van marked NFWW-TV "YOUR ACTION NEWS" CHANNEL 4. This was the local NBC-affiliate. Among them was a roaming cameraman with a bazooka-shaped instrument on his shoulder, aimed at shifting targets. By quick degrees, as dusk came on, the emergency area was being lighted. These were blinding lights with an eerie bluish cast. You expected to hear the powerful gut-thrumming chords of a rock band. There was now a cinematic sharpness to objects, textures, colors illuminated by the light, where, by the light of the ordinary overcast March afternoon, things had appeared blurred and insignificant.

A glamorous young woman reporter with NFWW-TV, tightly belted trench coat, crimson mouth and Cleopatra eyes, was trying to cajole police officers and medical workers into speaking into her microphone before the camera, but she wasn't having much success. Chandler knew, the media's goal was to acquire as much film footage as possible, to be shrewdly edited, spliced together, distorted for dramatic effect back in the studio. "Mr. Chandler? You're the 'Crisis man'? May I speak with you?"——the young woman's voice wafted to Chandler, who backed off, with a polite smile, "Sorry, I'm not 'Mister Chandler.' And no, sorry. I don't care to talk with you just now, it doesn't seem appropriate."

"But why not?"

"Because it doesn't."

"Because the gunman is still in there, and the hostage, and——"

Chandler turned away, hoping to discourage her. She moved on.

Like the professionals, Chandler had come to dislike the eager media people as intruders, exploiters. They were every cliché that might be said about them, and it was possible to feel some sympathy for them, yet you didn't trust them, you could not. When he'd first become a volunteer, Chandler had naïvely believed that coverage of such desperate incidents would be helpful, even educational, but he'd since changed his mind. The previous year, Chandler had been interviewed by NFWW-TV for the station's nightly news and he hadn't at all liked what he'd seen. To be identified as "Chandler Burnaby," a science teacher at La Salle Junior High, a "crisis volunteer with a mission," had seemed appalling to him, like self-advertising. He'd hated his voice, his smile, his nervous mannerisms; the transparency of his vanity, that he'd been successful in his effort, at that time. Worse, Melinda had happened to see him on TV before he'd had a chance to call her, and she'd been upset, more upset than he'd have expected.

Still, Chandler felt genuinely humble. He dreaded being made much of by the media, then failing publicly, ignominiously. He knew the irony and cheap pathos that could be generated by his being shot to death in the service of "saving" another.

Especially, aged twenty-seven, he felt humble around the Samaritans. This organization was strongly Christian, a suicide-prevention society that had begun in England decades ago and had affiliates in the United States. Samaritans were both professionals and non-professionals, but all were volunteers; you had to be trained, and the training was rigorous. The Niagara Crisis Hot-Line alone required a five-week orientation course; it wasn't for bored housewives and retirees looking for something to occupy their idle hours.

"Mr. Burnaby?"—now the TV woman had Chandler's surname, and was sounding empowered. Suddenly she was before him brandishing her microphone like a scepter, speaking in a hushed, breathlessly reverent voice. "Is it true that you know 'Albert Mayweather,' the gunman who has taken Cynthia Carpenter hostage, and shot and critically wounded a foreman here at Niagara Precision—" Chandler, annoyed, blushing, turned aside, gestured for her to get away from him.

"Cynthia Carpenter." The hostage, whose full name Chandler hadn't heard until now.

He tried to think: did he know any Carpenters?

Several members of the Carpenter family were at the site, some distance away, in safety. Chandler had noticed an older couple in their fifites or sixties, dazed, stricken. (But no Mayweathers?) Chandler was thinking that, face to face, he could reason with the gunman. Al Mayweather whom he'd (almost) known. One of the older boys you steered clear of, if you could. Not that Al Mayweather would have troubled to torment Chandler Burnaby, years younger. Mayweather and his friends noisy in the corridors, on the stairs, in the cafeteria at school. Mayweather, or boys very like him, in the locker room after gym, stripping for showers, braying with laughter, shouting and punching one another in the biceps, penises swinging like blood sausages.

If Mayweather surrendered now, releasing Cynthia Carpenter unharmed, surely that would mitigate the charges against him. He'd let the pregnant woman go. If the foreman didn't die, and wasn't permanently injured . . . Chandler wondered what Al Mayweather, now thirty years old, was thinking inside the building. That he was trapped? That he was in control? Trapped, yet (for the time being) in control? Chandler couldn't imagine what a man in such a desperate situation told himself. Or did. As minutes, and then hours, passed. There must be a point when he has to urinate badly. A point when he's becoming light-headed from not eating, and exhausted. A point when he wishes to Christ he'd never made such a mistake, and brought his life to this.

Chandler was being asked how well did he know Mayweather in high school, and he said, after a pause, "Not very well. But I think he'd remember me, he'd trust me. Maybe I can get him to negotiate on the phone."

Such confidence. Chandler wondered where it derived from.

It was nearly 6 P.M. when Chandler was given the bullhorn. He steadied his hands to keep them from shaking. A police officer was telling him to speak slowly and clearly and stay out of the range of any possible fire, don't be misled if Mayweather picks up the phone and talks to you, don't show your face. Try to get him to answer the phone. The phone that's been ringing, he won't pick up. Get him to put the hostage on. We need to know how that girl is.

"Yes. I know. I will. Thank you, officer."

Chandler swallowed hard. He'd spoken through a bullhorn once in the past, yet the vibratory sound, the volume of sound, took him by surprise. Like a dream of outsized, improbable power. Chandler brought his mouth to the bullhorn and was astonished at the magnification of his voice, and the authority of such magnification.

Al? Al Mayweather? This is Chandler Burnaby, we went to high school together. I'm from the neighborhood, Baltic Street. I'm not a police officer, Al, I'm a private citizen, a volunteer. I've been asked to help because I know you, Al. I wonder if you remember me? Please pick up the phone, Al, and we can talk. I need to hear your voice. Chandler paused. His heart was pounding with excitement. He wanted to think that Al Mayweather was struck by this new, unexpected voice. The voice of a friend, from the past. A voice that called him by his first name and uttered *please*.

Ten years. Maybe eleven since Chandler had last seen Albert Mayweather. Mayweather would never recall him, but they'd been in the same school building at the same time. They'd grown up in the same neighborhood, were wakened in their beds hearing the same thundering railroad cars and locomotive whistles.

Chandler hoped that Mayweather wasn't thinking why the hell was he, Chandler Burnaby, so interested in him suddenly this afternoon, after these years of living in the same city with no contact?

Al, will you pick up the phone? I'm dialing now.

In fact the phone was being dialed for Chandler. There were several police officers in the van with him, coordinating this procedure. Chandler heard the phone ring, ring at the other end. He hoped that Cynthia Carpenter was alive. He wanted badly to feel a strong brotherly bond with Al Mayweather but not if Mayweather had injured his hostage.

Al? We need to talk to you. O.K.?

The phone was dialed, redialed. Chandler reiterated his earnest plea. He remembered Al from high school—did Al remember him?—and he wanted to help Al now, wanted to help Al communicate with police to resolve this situation in a way best for all, so that no one would be hurt, was Al listening? Would Al please pick up the phone, it was being redialed . . .

A dozen rings and then, unexpectedly, the receiver was picked up.

A male voice sounded close and suspicious in Chandler's ear: "Yeah?"

Chandler had broken through. Where the police had failed, Chandler had succeeded.

"Al? Hello."

The call would be monitored by police officers, and recorded. Yet Chandler would behave as if it were a private call, and the exchange between him and Mayweather an intimate one.

He identified himself as a volunteer for the Crisis Center. He spoke of having been brought here by police to open "lines of communication." To discover how Al could be helped, in this situation he'd gotten into. But the voice was jarring as gravel pitched against the side of Chandler's head: "Nobody can help me, I'm fucked." Chandler protested, no, Al hadn't killed anyone, and paused to let that sink in. (Was it true? So far as Chandler knew, the foreman was still alive.) Chandler said, "You let a woman go free, the pregnant woman, that's in your favor, Al. That's what people are saying. And Cynthia Carpenter, the young woman who's with you now, she's all right, isn't she?"

There was a pause. Then a muttered, inaudible reply. Chandler said, "Al? I couldn't hear . . ."

He waited for a beat or two, then began to speak as if nothing were out of the ordinary. He had crucial information to impart, and he would assume that Mayweather, at the other end of the line, was listening, and clear-minded enough to know what was being told him. Chandler told Mayweather that the young woman's parents were waiting here, they were very upset, would Al please put Cynthia Carpenter on the phone? Saying, in his calm, earnest voice, the voice of a friend one might trust, "Al, it will make a tremendous difference, believe me, if you cooperate now. People are saying what a good, generous thing you did, to let that other woman go, you were considerate of a pregnant woman, you wouldn't hurt a woman . . ." Mayweather broke in vehemently, in an aggrieved voice, "I wouldn't! I wouldn't hurt a woman. Is my wife there?"

The wife. No doubt, this drama was about the (absent, estranged) wife. In the end, all drama is about family.

Chandler said, "Your wife isn't here just yet, Al. They're trying to contact her. Do you know where your wife is?" Mayweather said derisively, "How the fuck should I know where Gloria is, no I don't. Try her parents. Try her boyfriend." Mayweather continued for a while in this vein, angry and self-pitying, and Chandler thought it was a good sign, clearly Mayweather had not killed his wife before coming to shoot up Niagara Precision. Chandler said, "In the meantime, Al, there's Cynthia Carpenter, she must be very frightened, she might need medical attention, don't you think it would be a good idea to put her on the phone? Her parents are anxious to know that she's all right . . ." Chandler waited, and repeated the request. He knew from prior experience that reasoning with an excited or deranged person is like trying to row a canoe with one who can't, or won't, use his oar properly. The canoe veers now in this direction, now in that direction, you must keep to a relatively straight course by brute will, a resolute faith in the "good" outcome ahead; no hesitation, no private moments of doubt or alarm. Chandler knew how crucial this was. If something had happened to Cynthia Carpenter, Mayweather had no bargaining power. The hostage had to be living. "Al? Listen. People are anxious about Cynthia Carpenter, like I've said. You can imagine, yes? So, if you could put her on the line, for just a moment . . ." Chandler felt dizzy yet elated, as if crossing a high wire. High above The Falls. High above a crowd of gaping strangers. They wanted him to succeed, yet they wanted him to fail. Performing on the high wire, in danger of stumbling, of falling. One false move, Chandler would slip and fall. And Mayweather would fall with him. "Al? Are you listening? If you could . . ." He could hear Mayweather speaking to someone in the background, but he couldn't hear a reply.

The van was unheated, but Chandler had begun to perspire.

He would wait, he would try again. And again. As long as the police allowed him. This was his task.

Until at last, after minutes of frustration, Mayweather yelled what sounded like, "Here she is!" and there came on the line a thin, frightened voice. "H-Hello?" It was Cynthia Carpenter. Breathless, nearly inaudible, telling Chandler that she was "all right"—"sort of tired, scared"—"hoping police wouldn't shoot into the building." Chandler assured her, police would not shoot into the building. Her safety was primary. Cynthia Carpenter said, desperately, "This man has not harmed me, I swear. He let me use the r-restroom. He has not hurt me, I *swear*. But he says—" She began crying. Chandler didn't want to think that Mayweather might be holding a gun to her head.

He was feeling for the first time the visceral horror of the situation. It wasn't about Al Mayweather whom he'd known as a boy in high school, it was about the hostage Cynthia Carpenter whom he didn't know, until now, hearing her voice, he felt a tremendous sympathy for her. In terror of her life. Probably Mayweather had shoved her around, struck her. Certainly he'd terrorized her. Threatened to kill her. And she couldn't know, at this moment, whether she would be allowed to live much longer. Chandler thought of his sister Juliet, and felt a surge of rage, hatred for Mayweather.

Whatever the police do to him, the bastard deserves.

But no. Mayweather, too, was a victim. Chandler had to feel sympathy for Mayweather, too.

He tried to keep Cynthia Carpenter on the phone longer. She was crying, hyperventilating. Chandler spoke as comfortingly as he could under the circumstances. Her parents were here, and were very relieved that she was "all right"; no, police would not fire into the building, for her safety was their primary concern; they would do whatever they could, to get her released. But they needed to know what her captor was expecting in exchange for releasing her. "Mr. Mayweather doesn't seem to be communicating very clearly, Miss Carpenter. Maybe if you—"

The phone was taken from Cynthia Carpenter, and Mayweather began speaking excitedly. Telling Chandler that sure he'd let the girl go—if his wife came, and changed places with her; he "just wanted to talk" to Gloria. Chandler repeated that Gloria wasn't here, not just yet; police were trying to contact her, and when they did, Al could speak with her on the phone. Mayweather said that wasn't good enough, talking on the phone, she'd just hang up, and he wanted her with him, he needed to explain to her, what was happening was her fault, because he loved her, but she didn't love him, this was her fault and she knew it. Chandler listened sympathetically. Then, abruptly, Mayweather changed his mind and said he'd let the girl go if all the lights outside were switched off, police backed off and let him get to his car, and promised him "safe passage" out of the city. No guns, no roadblocks, no helicopters. "The girl will be with me, see? But I'll let her go when I can. In Canada, maybe."

"Canada! Well." Chandler wiped his damp face on a paper napkin. "That might be a little difficult to arrange. The bridge, the border . . ."

Mayweather wasn't listening. Already he'd changed his mind another time. He wasn't making sense, even as he spoke with a rapt, childlike intensity. Was Mayweather mentally disturbed? He didn't sound drunk, but he might be drugged. Chandler glanced up at police officers, who were watching him. What to say? What to do? Mayweather was raving, ranting. More about Gloria and the kids. More about Gloria knowing this was her fault. It must have been a sign of Mayweather's mental disturbance, he seemed not to recall why he'd come to Niagara Precision; why he'd shot a man, and had planned to kill another man. Chandler let him talk. As a boxer might punch himself out on his opponent, so Mayweather might punch himself out on the "crisis" man. When he began more often to pause, and to repeat himself, Chandler took up the conversation. Increasingly, it was a private, intimate conversation.

Chandler repeated that police were trying to contact Mrs. Mayweather but in the meantime Al should remember that he was a father, too. Maybe that should come first, being a father. He had his children's lives to consider. His family to consider. People who loved him, who were being hurt by this, anxious he'd be hurt, they loved him and didn't want him to be hurt, this hadn't gone so far it couldn't be halted and turned around and there'd be a lawyer to protect Al's rights, a public defender if he couldn't afford a lawyer, the law would provide for him, Chandler would make sure of that. Chandler was speaking rapidly, inspired and not altogether certain of what he was saying, except it sounded right, it sounded plausible, and Mayweather seemed to be listening, you felt that he was gripping the phone receiver tight and listening. "You need to stay alive for the sake of your children and for the memory of your father, Al. That's what you must do. The memory of your father, Al. *I* remember your father."

In this moment it seemed to Chandler that he did remember Al Mayweather's father. Maybe they'd spoken together. In the neighborhood. At the time of the OxyChemical lawsuit. The workers' photographs in the paper. Not cancer but—what? Emphysema. Though maybe there'd been cancer, too. Leukemia? Chandler remembered: Mayweather had seemed so old to him, bald, and his face ravaged, but he'd probably been no more than fifty, a poisoned man who'd died young.

"What would your father think, Al? He'd want you to do the right thing here, let the girl go, Al, wouldn't he? Al? Your father would want that."

Chandler was speaking blindly, his eyes stung with tears, but he must have spoken persuasively for shortly afterward Mayweather muttered what sounded like "O.K." It was the turn in the stalemate, now things would happen swiftly as they usually did at such times, like ice melting.

In the garishly spotlit doorway a small figure appeared, moving tentatively. A murmur went up from the onlookers but was stifled at once. The young woman, very young-looking, lifted both hands to shield her eyes from the light. She walked slowly, swaying, as if the ground were tilting beneath her feet. (She was shoeless, in her stocking feet. This curious detail, Chandler would long remember and confuse with himself, as elements in a dream are confused. Had he lost his shoes, somehow? In the police van?) Police had their rifles aimed, prepared to fire past the terrified girl. This was the moment everyone had been awaiting and yet it was not a moment to be trusted. A TV or movie moment, yet one without a script. As Cynthia Carpenter in her stocking feet crossed the patch of grassless lawn there was the collective expectation, the exquisite dread, that now, at this precarious moment, as all were watching, the gunman might begin to fire; might fire at his enemies around the girl, or might shoot her in the back. Yet she continued, looking neither to the right nor left, making her way haltingly to the penumbra of shadow at the edge of the light where she was seized by crouching police officers in protective gear and brought to safey, and embraced by her weeping parents.

So it ended, the drama of the hostage.

So it ended happily, that might have ended so very differently.

A toss of the dice, Chandler thought. In the end, it had little to do with him.

Chandler would think long afterward how striking Cynthia Carpenter was! A girl of about twenty, making her way through a force-field of imminent gunfire and death, visibly shaking; her pale soft face like something partly melted, eyes smudged and lipstick eaten away and her ratted hair disheveled, but she'd made it, she was triumphant, for she was one who'd walked away with her life and forever afterward her life would be precious to her, a miracle granted to her alone. And this miracle would be preserved on film, forever. Where words faltered and failed, Cynthia Carpenter's image would endure. Small compensation for her ordeal at the hands of a madman, still she would be "Cynthia Carpenter" of local legend, forever.

Now, the gunman inside the building was expected to surrender.

"Give it up"—his defiance, or his life.

Surrender, or kill himself.

In the excitement of the hostage's release, Chandler had lost contact with Mayweather. The line had gone dead. When the phone was redialed no one answered. Chandler, panicked at what might happen now to Mayweather, fumbled for the bullhorn.

He was sweating badly now. His white shirt, he'd worn to school that morning, damp beneath the arms and across his chest. He'd tugged his necktie off long ago and believed he'd stuffed it in a pocket, but the necktie was gone, lost. A rivulet of sweat trailed down Chandler's cheek like an oily tear. *Al? This is Chandler again. Al, thank you. Thank you for releasing that girl . . .* It was an absurd thing to say, yet Chandler had to say it. He would praise the madman who'd kept a young woman prisoner by gunpoint for several hours, he would thank him for releasing her, and he would be genuine in his gratitude. *Al? Now there's you. Will you pick up the phone? It's ringing . . .* The phone was not picked up. the number was redialed, and again went unanswered. *Al, talk to me! This is going to end well, now you've released the girl and people can see that your intentions are good. But now you need to give up your weapons, Al, O.K.? So that you don't get hurt, Al. You can come out, you'll be taken into custody but not hurt. Think of your family, Al? Your children, your parents. Your father. He was a brave man, I remember your father. He should not have died so young. He'd want you to live. Al. I want you to live. There's no purpose to holding out any longer, Al. You're smart, you know that. The police want you to lay down your weapons, just leave them on the floor inside there and come to the door, slowly. Let us see you, Al. I'm right here, I'm watching. Extend your hands where we can see them. It's going to be all right, Al, see, you let the girl go, that makes all the difference, no one has been killed, or seriously hurt, the girl is saying you treated her well . . .* So Chandler spoke earnestly, with increasing desperation; but there was no response.

The phone was redialed, and this time the line was busy.

Al? Please. Put the phone back on the hook, talk to me . . . I want so badly to talk to you.

Swift as ice melting the crisis was moving, but Chandler now seemed not to be guiding it. Chandler could feel how he was losing it, the strange fleeting power he'd had. For a few dazed minutes, that power. Like a small upright flame. But now the flame was wavering, flickering. Chandler began to beg. *Al? You can trust me, Al. They promise they won't hurt you—they promise—if—* Chandler guessed that the police would give him another few minutes, then they'd break off this attempt to negotiate. The barricaded man no longer had anything of value with which to negotiate, except his life, and maybe, after these hours of strain, exhaustion, professionally restrained fury and disgust, Al Mayweather's life wasn't of much value. Police would begin their siege, tossing in tear gas, routing the doomed man. How many dozens of armed men, and Mayweather alone. Chandler was feeling desperate, he couldn't fail now.

A toss of the dice. Why not, it had so little to do with him.

Protected, in the police van, by the blinding lights, as well as bulletproof glass, Chandler craned his neck far forward, to consider the blank front of the building. Rainwashed cinderblock ugliness. In the vivid bluish light it had the look of a two-dimensional stage set. It had the tacky look of something soon to be dismanteled, discarded. Chandler would have to act swiftly and decisively, or all his power would be snatched from him, he'd be returned to his own small life.

Chandler wondered where Mayweather was: had he crept out of the room in which he'd been safely barricaded for hours, had he followed Cynthia Carpenter toward the front entrance? Was he, even now, standing behind the broken window, aiming his rifle? Chandler contemplated the oddly shaped window, shards of glass at its edges like teeth. How charged with significance this scene had come to be, in the intensity of the drama, that had no significance otherwise. *The small life. The inevitable life. The life that awaits.* Even as he stared, Chandler realized that his peripheral vision had narrowed. Even as his eyesight became sharper, at the center of his vision, he was going blind at the edges. And yet—he'd become a funnel of super-charged energy. He knew—he knew!—it was his role to speak to Al Mayweather face to face.

To save Al Mayweather. As he'd saved the hostage.

These long exhausting minutes since he'd been handed the bull-horn, Chandler had been seated in a police van, inside the penumbra of shadow. Before anyone could prevent him, he climbed out.

In his weak, raw, human voice he called, "Al? It's me, Chandler."

Boldly he stepped into the lighted area in front of the building. No one had been quick enough to catch hold of him. He could hear shouts and protests on all sides. But Chandler continued forward, raising his arms in appeal. *He* had no weapon—of course. *He* would reveal himself to Al Mayweather, unprotected. He understood that he was doing the right thing. *In the purity of his heart, he could not fail to do the right thing.* Even as police shouted for him to take cover, cursed at him. Even as TV cameras were trained upon him. He called out, "Al? Can I come inside to talk to you? I need so badly to talk to you—" Less than ten feet from the partly opened door, Chandler seemed to see movement inside, but wasn't certain. His vision had so radically narrowed, it was as if he were looking through the wrong end of a telescope. What he saw was a small circle of extraordinary in-tensity, yet he seemed not to know what he was seeing, he couldn't have named it. The roaring in his ears grew louder. He was beyond the Deadline, rapidly approaching the Falls. There was a comfort in this. His heart lifted in anticipation. At the edge of consciousness voices were shouting *Take cover!* but these were distant, the shouts of strangers, he needed to show Al Mayweather how he had nothing to do with these strangers; how bonded the two of them were, like brothers, in their shared past.

There came then a single sharp crack, a gunshot.

On TV that evening. *The man worked a miracle, saved our daughter's life. We prayed, we prayed, and he saved her.* So the Carpenters would say of Chandler Burnaby. But Chandler wouldn't be seeing this interview, or the others. Nor the film footage, on all three TV stations.

And now the adrenaline tide had retreated, the dank, banal debris of a small life was exposed.

Sleet pelted against the car's windshield. He had to drive slowly in any case, pain throbbing behind his eyes. He was an hour and a half late, and had never telephoned. To telephone a woman you love, or almost love, or wish to love, you must imagine what you will say to her, and Chandler was emptied of words. The bullhorn had exhausted him. Like an immense ludicrous phallus. You picked such an instrument up in wonder, and set it down in dismay.

Driving to Alcott Street, north and west on Eleventh, where Melinda rented an apartment on the third floor of what had once been a private house, a five-minute drive from Grace Memorial Hospital where she worked. It was past 8 P.M. This day had begun early for Chandler, shortly after 6 A.M. In that other phase of his existence in which he was, affably, reliably, "Mr. Burnaby" who taught ninth grade science at La Salle Junior High. Paid less than the head custodian at the school but he understood that this was nothing personal. *Mr. Burnaby, that's who you are. Play the cards you're dealt, and shut up.*

They would be saying of Chandler Burnaby that he'd been a hero, he'd saved a young woman's life. But Chandler knew better.

He had not turned on the car radio, and would not. He had no wish to hear local news. In the morning, he would have to read the front page of the *Gazette*, that was unavoidable.

He felt sick, disgusted. His eyes ached. This was his punishment for having ascended to the high wire, this failure.

And so he tried to think of the baby.

Melinda's baby, that was not Chandler's. Another man had fathered this baby, and departed. Before the baby's birth, early in the pregnancy, he'd departed. Chandler could not comprehend such behavior, yet he knew it wasn't altogether uncommon. Melinda's husband, from whom she'd only recently become divorced, had been a medical student at the University of Buffalo, and was now an intern in the area. He had no custodial rights to the baby, he'd wanted none. Melinda would say only that the marriage hadn't worked out, she'd made a mistake.

You? You made the mistake?

My judgment. I misjudged.

The implication was, in Melinda's steely jawline, she would not misjudge another time.

The baby, Danya. Of whom (this was ridiculous, but true) Ariah was jealous, so that Chandler no longer dared speak of the baby, or of Melinda, to his mother.

"Hey. I love you. Know who I am?"

She did not, of course. Who exactly was Chandler Burnaby, in Danya's life?

Chandler was feeling a little better, less desperate, thinking of Danya. The warm, intense body. So hot, sometimes. And heavy. As if an entire life, a lifetime, were already compacted into that small body.

The eyes, open, conscious, darting curious and alert, insatiable.

Almost, when he held Danya, he could feel the infant taking in information, hungry to absorb all of the world.

She could be mine. She could love me as a father. I am not required to justify my life.

But when Chandler arrived at Melinda's apartment, it was otherwise. Yes, he was required to justify his life.

Possibly he'd known, he'd anticipated such a scene, that was why he had not telephoned.

Melinda confronted him at the door, tight-faced, furious. She was a strong, fleshy young woman two years older than Chandler, with a fair, frank, attractive face, hair of no distinct color, wanly brown, trimmed short to fit beneath her nurse's cap. She was of only moderate height, five feet four or five, yet exuded an air of authority, as if she were taller; as, though a warmly emotional young woman, she could detach herself, with alarming swiftness, from a scene in which others were emotional. Chandler had met her in the most romantic of settings: at the Armory, where he'd gone to give blood in the annual Red Cross drive, in a swoon hardly typical of him he'd smiled up dreamily at the attractive young nurse, tried to make conversation from the gurney on which he'd been urged to lie. *Promise you won't drain it all, my blood? I've put myself in your hands.*

Melinda was saying she'd seen him on TV. She'd seen what he had done, and she'd been terrified for him. But afterward, thinking it over, she was angry. She was disgusted. "You risked your life for—what? Who? That stranger? 'Somebody from your high school'—bull-shit! A pathetic loser, that's what he was. That's all he was. He killed himself, he could have killed you. For what? Exactly for what, Chandler? Tell me: for what?"

Chandler hadn't expected this greeting. Oh, in his heart he was a romantic, wishful fool, he'd hoped for something so very different though knowing (for Chandler always knew: Chandler was a scientist at heart, and pitiless) that he didn't deserve it.

Going outside the family. Betraying.

Bullshit.

Chandler tried to explain, but he wasn't going to apologize. Melinda interrupted, Melinda knew his heart. Hotly she said, "This has to do with your father, yes? But I don't give a damn about your father. I can't be involved with a man who doesn't care more about me, and my baby, and our life together, than he cares about a stranger, I can't be involved with a man who doesn't care if he lives or dies! Who'd toss his life like dice, as if it was worthless. Goodnight, Chandler. Goodbye."

And she pushed him out the door, and shut it in his stunned face.

3

Forced move. He vowed then, in the spring of his twenty-eighth year, he would take his life in hand.

He'd been drifting, passive. Like one hypnotized by The Falls. Melinda had forced him to see. She'd held up a reflecting surface to Chandler he hadn't been able to shield his eyes from, as one must shield one's eyes from the terrible visage of Medusa, stunned by a truth that has been both obvious and elusive. *Toss your life like dice, as if worthless.* It was uncanny, Melinda must love him. She had plumbed the depth of his soul.

When had it begun, this strange trance-like passivity, this drifting he'd mistaken for loyalty, or for self-penance. Since his father's disappearance from his life, perhaps. (Chandler had never seen his father's lifeless body. There had been no body. How, then, could he "believe" in his father's death?) Yet he'd prided himself on being a rational individual. By far the most rational individual in his family. He'd believed himself supremely in control, responsible, mature. Since the precocious age of eleven he'd been a loyal son to his (widowed, difficult) mother. He'd been a loving, patient, and protective older brother to his (fatherless, immature) brother and sister.

Promise! Ariah had whispered, gripping both his hands in hers.

Give me your heart! Give me your life!

Since junior high, Chandler had been a promising, if erratic chess player. He'd taught Juliet to play, and on wretched winter days when even his restless younger brother was confined to the house on Baltic Street, he'd taught Royall. (Ariah rarely played any board games with her children. She might have been afraid of losing to them.) Neither Juliet nor Royall cared enough for the game to play shrewdly or with patience, but they were intuitive, and sometimes lucky. Chandler wasn't one to trust luck. He would find himself in a position in which, to prevent a lethal move by his opponent, he had to sacrifice a valuable piece. This was the *forced move*: a sacrifice in the short run, for a win in the long run.

He would take his life in hand from now on. He was through with being ashamed of who he was, whom he'd been born.

Through the spring of 1978 he made inquiries into Dirk Burnaby's life, and into his death. To understand one, he must understand the other. He wrote brief, thoughtful letters to his father's former law colleagues and friends, whom he knew primarily as names from the newspaper. *Please, may I see you? Speak with you? It would mean so much to me as Dirk Burnaby's son.* He tried to locate the couple so central to Dirk Burnaby's final year, Nina and Sam Olshaker, and was sorry to hear that the couple had divorced in 1963, following the strain of the court case; it seemed that Nina Olshaker had taken her children away to live in the northern part of the state, outside Plattsburgh, and had no listed telephone number. He tried to speak with several of the expert witnesses who'd given Dirk Burnaby depositions in the Love Canal case, and was told that these individuals, who'd been under pressure at the time of the lawsuit and had been frequently questioned about their relationship with Dirk Burnaby after his death, no longer cared to discuss the subject. He tried to speak with the doctor who'd headed the County Board of Health in 1961, but was informed that this well-to-do gentleman was "retired to Palm Beach, and incommunicado." So too, other physicians who'd served on the Board at that time and had ruled in support of Swann Chemicals refused to speak with Chandler, or were elderly, or no longer alive. And so too, the defendants' attorneys, most of whom were still practicing law in Niagara Falls, very successfully. And so too, former mayor "Spooky" Wenn, now an executive in the state Republican party, and former Niagara County judge Stroughton Howell, now a justice of the New York State Appellate Court in Albany. He made an appointment to speak with an emeritus professor of biochemistry at the State University of New York at Buffalo, and he made an appointment to speak with Dirk Burnaby's former receptionist, Madelyn Seidman, and with the bailiff, now retired, whom Dirk Burnaby had pleaded guilty to having assaulted in Judge Howell's courtroom at the time of the preliminary hearing. He tried to make appointments to speak with the chief of police, Fitch, who'd been a friend of Dirk Burnaby, and with the the county sheriff, and with the detectives involved in the investigation of Dirk Burnaby's alleged accident, but none of these men would see him.

Of course, what had he expected? He was an adult, he knew the ways of the world. The male world of power, intrigue, threat.

And yet: after having refused to take calls from Chandler for weeks, Chief of Police Fitch telephoned Chandler directly to inform him that the NFPD investigation in 1962 "turned up plenty you wouldn't want to know about but we spared your family, see? We ruled 'accident,' the insurance company had to pay out." Before Chandler could respond, Fitch hung up.

Accident. Chandler was supposed to be grateful the ruling hadn't been suicide, was that it?

"Maybe you murdered him. All of you. Bastards."

He'd thought so, as a kid. For a while. Until the thought faded, as the fantasies of adolescence fade, of necessity.

Sixteen years. Amnesia.

Now memories were rushing back, making him wince with pain. Like sensation returning to frostbitten parts of the body.

Never cry. No tears. No one is worth your tears.

Your mother is the one who loves you.

He was scientifically-minded, and so he knew: he carried the genes of both his mother and father, equally. He owed his allegiance not to one but to two. Not one, but two contested in his soul.

Yet the contest had always gone to Ariah. The other, the father, was dead, vanquished. The mother had survived and was supreme. And her opinion mattered so strangely much to Chandler, even now, in his adulthood; often, he felt under her spell, as if something were unresolved between them, unspoken.

Long ago she'd sung to him, cradled him in her arms, adored him.

My first-born son! Ariah had always been extravagant in her speech, like a doomed figure in a Wagner opera. *There is only the first-born, no one speaks of second- or third-born.* Yet Chandler was clear-sighted enough to know that of course Ariah favored Royall, of her sons; she tried, tried very hard, to favor Juliet, her daughter, over both her sons. Chandler, the first-born, had been rapidly demoted. He knew, he didn't spare himself. But he loved Ariah just the same, and would always love her. He was enough his mother's son to be grateful for the mere accident of having been born.

Ariah had said dryly, "Einstein says he couldn't believe in a God who played dice with the universe. I say, that's all God does is play dice. Like it or lump it, fellas."

She'd been furious with Chandler over the hostage incident. Fortunately she hadn't seen the live coverage on local television, but neighbors had rushed to inform her. And there was the next day's

Gazette. Chandler Burnaby, junior high teacher, a "hero." Ariah had her own ideas about what Chandler was, risking his life for a worthless Mayweather, but she'd forgiven him, as Melinda would not. Ariah had shrugged, and wiped at her eyes in that Ariah-gesture that conveyed both maternal weakness and contempt for such weakness, and laughed.

"Well. As long as you're alive to have dinner with us tonight. That's something to be grateful for."

But Chandler was beginning to wonder: was it?

The dead have no one to speak for them except the living.
I am Dirk Burnaby's son, and I am living.

On impulse, one day, Chandler drove to l'Isle Grand to visit his father's sisters whom he had not seen in more than sixteen years. His elderly aunts Clarice and Sylvia, whom Ariah despised. The women were both widows. Wealthy widows. Chandler saw them separately but understood that the suspicious old women had conferred by telephone, for their remarks to him were very similar. Clarice said stiffly, "Our brother Dirk was a reckless man. He died as he'd lived, without caring for others." Sylvia said stiffly, "Our brother Dirk had been a reckless, spoiled boy, and he died a reckless, spoiled man." Clarice said, "We loved our baby brother. We tried not to care that he was everybody's favorite. He joined the army, he served his country, all that was noble, he was a brilliant attorney, but then . . ." Sylvia said, "We loved our baby brother but something went tragically wrong in his life, you see. A curse."

Chandler assumed they meant the Love Canal case, but when he inquired, Sylvia said guardedly, bringing a scented handkerchief to her nose, "I don't believe I care to say."

Clarice, too, spoke mysteriously of a "curse." When Chandler asked what was this curse, his aunt said, after a moment's hesitation, "Dirk fell in love with the red-haired woman, you see. He'd been meant to marry and live on the Island with his family; he'd been meant to oversee us, our holdings, our investments, all of Burnaby,

Inc., but instead he broke his mother's heart, and stole away a part of her soul, and nothing in our family has been the same since, our children, your cousins, are grown and gone, scattered to the four winds, not one of them has chosen to remain on the Island with us, and why?—because the red-haired woman put a spell on our brother. Her first husband threw himself into The Falls. And so her second husband was fated to die in The Falls. It had to happen. Momma predicted, and so it came to be."

First husband? Threw himself into The Falls?

Chandler left l'Isle Grand shaken and exhausted vowing never to return.

He knew: Claudine Burnaby, his grandmother, had died several years before, an elderly, ill woman. He'd known, not from Ariah (who would never speak of the Burnabys) but from an obituary in the *Gazette*. Claudine Burnaby had left the family estate Shalott to the Episcopal Church to be used as a school or retirement home. Most of her money, too, had been left to the church, not to her children and grandchildren, which Chandler supposed had been a shock to them, and an insult.

He had to smile. Grandmother Burnaby: who'd refused to be *Grandma Burnaby*.

The days were long gone when Grandmother Burnaby had had the power to upset her daughter-in-law Ariah. Chandler recalled how the haughty older woman had swooped upon him in the first Luna Park house, smelling of a powerful perfume. Black sunglasses like a beetle's shiny opaque eyes, and a very red, glistening mouth; her hair an unearthly silver blond, that smelled of something harshly chemical. Chandler had stared up blinking from his Tinkertoy village to see a remarkable face looming above him fierce and glaring as a mask. On his grandmother's head perched something squat and velvety black like a spider, he'd feared might leap onto him. The red-lipstick mouth moved stiffly pronouncing words Chandler would recall through his life, without understanding. *He will live into the twenty-first century. Strange that anyone can be so young, and still human.*

Nor had he understood why his grandmother had said that Chandler wasn't her grandson. (He'd heard, or thought he'd heard these words. Or had he imagined them?) Grandmother Burnaby had left presents for him, he hadn't much wanted to open, and after her departure Mommy tore the presents open, tore the tinsel wrapping paper, and the items of clothing, tore sleeves from little shirts, legs from pajamas, ripped and tossed and muttered and laughed to herself. She'd hugged him so tight he almost couldn't breathe but when she took a bottle from Daddy's cabinet and ran away upstairs she locked the door against him and so Chandler returned downstairs to the safety of his Tinkertoy village which would grow into the most elaborate village he'd ever built and which would topple into pieces only when Chandler decreed "Earthquake!" and made Daddy laugh.

4

Evidence. He was trained in science education, and he should have been trained in law, too. For (he was beginning to see) the world is a continuous trial, arguments among adversaries in search of (elusive, seductive) justice.

"Jesus. That was a painful experience. The judge was obviously biased, and your father was over-involved with the case, he did what no lawyer can afford to do: lost control in the courtroom. That was the end for him."

"Sure we were suspicious. But nobody had any way of knowing at the time. As soon as Howell threw out the case, 'Love Canal' was discredited for years. It was a litigator's joke. There were variations on it, the word *love*, it became a dirty joke in some circles. But things have come to light since then . . . unofficially, you might say. Your father's witnesses were under pressure from Skinner and his aides not to testify. Possibly they'd been threatened. (Was there a tie-in with the mob? This is Niagara Falls–Buffalo: does a fish swim? Does a bird fly? Since the 1950's this has been a mobbed-up region, kid.) So, sure, they'd been threatened. The Board of Health and the

Board of Education stonewalled. The defense paid 'expert witnesses' to stack the deck for their side. Everybody knew Howell would roll over like he did except possibly Dirk Burnaby. And your poor father, Christ it was a shame, I'd known Dirk since law school and it was hell to see that man wearing down. He said to me, I'll never forget it was the day before Howell dumped the case down the toilet, 'Hal, it's the pettiness of it, that breaks my heart.' He was drinking, frankly. You could smell it on his breath. So finally they provoked him into losing control in the courtroom. And that was it for Dirk Burnaby."

"It was a disgraceful act. Howell profited by it, and look at him now: state appellate court. And your father has been dead for, how long—fifteen years."

"Your father! I still can't believe he's gone . . . He was the kindest, most considerate employer. I have never worked for a man so gentlemanly, and good. He didn't want people to know how much of his own money he put into that terrible case, and he put his soul into it, and you could foresee what would happen, like a train wreck in slow motion, but no one could dissuade him. 'Now, Madelyn,' he'd say, when I was looking worried, 'Dirk Burnaby doesn't know what it is to lose.' And that was his tragedy: he didn't know. All his life he'd been successful and that blinded him to certain facts, like the nature of the people around him, men he'd gone to school with and believed he knew. He would not listen even to his lawyer friends, why'd he listen to me? Of course, I never said a word to your father about such things. It wasn't my place. I'd tried to send that Olshaker woman away but somehow she found your father, and got her talons in him. See, he was always a gentleman, and the others—the others were politicians. That mayor, Wenn! They acquitted him a few years ago on that charge of taking kickbacks but everybody knows what he is, and the others. The lawyers, and that hypocrite judge your father had reason to believe was a friend of his. I never thought your father killed himself, not for a moment. Other people who knew him well felt the same way. Mr. Burnaby was not that type . . . The type to despair, and make things worse. Mr. Burnaby was the type to want to help, to make things better. You know, Chandler, I was telling your brother these things, too. He came by a few months ago. 'Roy' he calls himself? Your younger brother, I guess? A handsome young man, a student at Niagara University."

"Yeah, it was the biggest surprise of my life: your father hauled off and hit me! Square in the face. Just about broke my face. It felt like Walcott's right must've felt on Marciano's nose, smashing it and throwing blood all over. I'd had other men try to fight me in the courtroom, sure, but a bailiff is usually forewarned, and I wasn't, with him, I mean—a lawyer! Usually, a hot-headed or volatile defendant, the deputies have him in shackles. You're prepared. But there was an actual lawyer wheeling around and punching me in the face! Afterward, Mr. Burnaby apologized. He telephoned me, and said how sorry he was, and he sent me a check for a couple of thousand dollars dated on that very day before he died and damned if I was going to cash it, but then I thought, what the hell, and I did . . . By then, Dirk Burnaby had been gone six months. I never believed he was dead, somehow. But nobody could survive going over The Falls so I guess he must've . . . must be dead. See, what I regret is I never said I forgave him, I was pissed as hell at him, hitting me for doing my job, when it was Howell's face he wanted to smash in, so I was sorry for that, I mean for not telling your father it was O.K., I understood."

"What can I say, son? You know, your dad was my oldest friend in the city. I guess—the world. We went to the Academy together, joined up in the army together, born a few days apart in this very month though in different years, so, sure, I miss him like hell this time of year, it kind of hurts . . . But there was no way I could help him. He was like one of those big beautiful moths you see at night, flying into a spider web he not only didn't appreciate how tough it was, how nasty, but he didn't even know it was there. Like your dad was flying blind, those last few weeks. And he was drinking, and got to that point we all get to eventually, where it's like soil soaked through, saturated, and you take in an ounce more and the poison goes straight into your blood because your liver can't filter it anymore. He'd had warnings, but he didn't listen. He was like a pioneer in that kind of law, now people look back on it. At the time it just seemed sort of crazy. Everybody went around saying the same kinds of things, like how'd you tell if a man is sick from where he lives or works, or from just smoking? (Everybody smoked.) Or drinking. Or heredity, or bad luck. See? At the time people said things like this, that was how they were thinking, the archbishop talked that way on TV, doctors talked that way, every politician getting paid big bucks to talk that way, didn't matter which party they belonged to, and of course judges, so it didn't take much imagination to see that Dirk was going to be shot down, but when it happened it was quite a shock, let me tell you. He'd alienated most of his friends, our friends. Our mutual friends. He'd sort of alienated me, to tell the truth. All this publicity about 'tainted air, tainted water and soil,' et cetera, it was very bad for business. Very bad for the tourist trade . . . Sure I hated what the city was turning into, air smelling like a cesspool on certain days, and honeymoon couples from all over checking in my hotel and expecting, I don't know, some kind of paradise, plus tourists from Germany, Japan, coming to see The Falls and not knowing what the city is. Sure we had complaints. Through the 1970's it's been getting worse. People like me, my family, we'd been in the 'luxury hotel trade' as it used to be called, for a long time. Now the business is mostly 'tourist trade.' Thank God, I got out from under the Rainbow Grand just in time, like the *Titanic* it would've been, mid-1960's when all of the country was going to hell. (It's still going to hell but at least they ran out of people to assassinate and drop napalm on.) Now Colborne, Inc., our family business, is diversified as all hell, like this great country of ours. We've got the Journeez End and the U-R-Here motels on Buffalo Avenue and Prospect. We've got three Tastee-Freezes and The Leaning Tower of Pizza. Bowling alleys we've got, Top Hat Disco & Shore Café at the Lake. In Alcott we've got a few concessions on the beach, plus Bingo Tent Bonanza. The Banana Royalle franchise we're looking into. Miniature golf! Kind of an asshole 'sport' I grant you, but tourists are crazy for it, Japs love it (you can figure why, eh?) so we're building a few of those. Two Peking Villages in the area, and that Hollywood Haven Disco the cops busted, we're possibly going to take over. The Niagara Wax Museum we bought last year, 'heroes and victims of The Falls,' we're renovating, and the Cross-the-Gorge, where you 'walk' on a tightrope over a wild waterfall and light display, holding a pole, and there's fans blowing wind trying to dislodge you, we've got terrific ideas for, this promises to be a real money-maker . . . Hey, sorry. You get the picture, I guess. I was at Mario's last night and thinking how your dad loved that place. He had a weakness, like me, for Italian sausage risotto, and for Mario's thin-crust pizza, and he'd be happy as hell to know that not much has changed there. Except for us being older and some of us dead, Mario's hasn't changed at all."

"Your father made one mistake a litigator can't make: he underestimated the moral rot of the adversary. He was of that caste and he hadn't grasped how corrupt they were because he looked at them and saw men like himself. And that was true, to a degree. But they were—they are—evil. They hired lawyers, doctors, 'research scientists,' health inspectors to do their evil for them. Telling a mother her child has 'congenital leukemia' not something caused by benzene, and that benzene bubbling up in her own back yard on the Love Canal. Telling men and women in their thirties they have 'pathogenic livers'—'pathogenic kidneys'—they were born with, when it was what they'd been eating out of their own gardens, poisoned by the Love Canal. Brain tumors almost certainly caused by tetrachloroethylene they attributed to 'third-degree television tube radiation.' Kids with asthma, weak lungs, bladder infections, these were 'congenital deficiencies.' (You look up *congenital* in the dictionary: 'dating from birth.') Women having miscarriages, babies born with had hearts, missing part of their colons, you ascribe to more 'congenital deficiencies.' When the state finally ordered blood tests for the Love Canal residents, finally in 1971, in the Armory, people were asked to come at 8 A.M. and waited all day, and at 5 P.M. half were still waiting. There was a 'needle shortage.' 'Nurse shortage.' Three hundred blood samples were 'contaminated.' Lab results were 'inconclusive'— 'misfiled.' Some of us have been criticized for suggesting these doctors are not much different from the Nazi doctors doing experiments on human beings, but I hold to that charge. The case the Coalition is presenting builds upon your father's but of course it's much larger in scope. You've been reading about us, I assume. We have five full-time lawyers including me. We have investigators, and a team of paralegals. We're not funded like the adversaries, but we are funded. We have the new findings of the State Board of Health—finally!—and in our favor. There are one hundred twenty people represented in this class-action suit. The Love Canal Homeowners Association, they call themselves now. 'Love Canal'— it's like waving a red flag. We're demanding $200 million to settle, minimum. The judiciary is much more sympathetic with this kind of litigation in 1978. There's pressure on Carter to declare Love Canal a 'disaster area'—the federal government would then buy out homeowners, help pay compensation. This will happen, it's only a matter of when. Dirk Burnaby is a hero to us, even with—well, his mistakes. When this is over, and we win, I want to organize a memorial for him, a man like that should not be forgotten . . . My theory is, your father began to fall apart when he realized how deep the rot was. I was just a kid at the time, growing up on the east side. My dad and uncles worked at the chemical factories, including Swann and Dow. 'Better Living Through Chemistry.' I've always seen the bastards for what they are, their PR tactics don't fool me. They'd still be manufacturing the sticky-stuff, napalm, if anybody'd pay them to, and the 'research scientists' are right now working on biological warfare weapons within a few miles of this office. You teach that at La Salle, Chandler? Well, maybe you should, if your subject is science . . . Do I believe that Dirk Burnaby killed himself? No. Died in an 'accident'? No. The bastards killed him. You'll never prove it, though."

5

A SWEETLY SCENTED LETTER came addressed to Chandler Burnaby at La Salle Junior High. Handwritten, purple ink on lavender stationery.

Dear Chandler Burnaby—
   I owe my life to you. I want so badly to see you and thank you in person. I have come to your school and waited outside but went away again out of shyness. I hope you will not misunderstand! I want only to see your face, the goodness in your face. Not in photographs but in actual life. May I?
   I am not engaged to marry anyone. I was recently, but am no longer.

Your friend forever,
Cynthia Carpenter

Chandler foresaw: a fumbling, emotional meeting. An impressionable young woman primed to fall in love with him. A very attractive young woman primed to worship him as a hero.

Unlike Melinda who knew his heart. Melinda who'd shut a door in his face.

Chandler put away the scented letter from Cynthia Carpenter, as a memento.

A memento of this strange season in his life in which he was both a savior and a fool, revered and held in contempt, adored and despised in about equal measure.

6

THERE CAME A DAY in that season, an hour when Chandler's loneliness became so acute, he yearned to speak with Royall. Suddenly, for Chandler, there was no one but Royall. His heart was full to bursting.

But Royall didn't want to see him, did he? Royall hated him.

And Royall, living downtown, had no telephone. Juliet advised, Just see him. Go there, knock on his door, he'll let you in. You know Royall.

Chandler wasn't so certain any longer, did he know Royall?

Juliet laughed. "Royall is asking new people he meets to call him 'Roy.' What if he asks us? I never could! He'll always be Royall to me."

Chandler did as Juliet suggested, showed up at Royall's apartment on Fourth Street, knocked firmly at the door. When Royall opened it, the brothers stared at each other for a startled moment, without speaking. Then Royall said, trying to smile, "Well, hell. It's you." Chandler said, "Royall, or is it 'Roy'? May I come inside?" Royall's face reddened. "Sure. C'mon in! I wasn't exactly expecting anybody."

Royall had been reading at the kitchen table, taking notes in a spiral notebook. His handwriting was childlike, large and careful. The book he was reading was a paperback edition of Shakespeare's *Hamlet*. He pushed these aside and yanked out a chair for Chandler.

Royall, reading *Hamlet*! Chandler smiled.

It was a cubbyhole of a kitchen, not much larger than the table. Several rinsed glasses, plates, and stainless steel cutlery lay neatly on a counter, readied for Royall's next meal. There were cooking odors, a predominant smell of something soft, mealy, and susceptible to scorch—oatmeal? Through a partly opened cupboard door Chandler had a glimpse of canned soups, a bottle of tomato juice, a box of Quaker Oats. His heart went out to his younger brother as to a child bravely playing house, having run away from home. On his side, Royall saw with surprise that his schoolteacher brother was looking uncertain, brooding, red-eyed in a way he'd rarely seen him; Chandler's jaws had been carelessly shaved, and his jacket was buttoned crookedly. He was breathing through his mouth, having hurried up two flights of stairs. Without a word Royall took two beers from a dwarf refrigerator beside a two-burner gas stove, and the brothers sat knee to knee at a battered Formica-topped table purchased, as Royall boasted, for five dollars at Goodwill.

They would sit at this table, they would speak earnestly together for several hours. By which time night came on, and Royall's six-pack of beer was depleted.

In a lowered, quavering voice Chandler told Royall all that he'd learned about their father. These past several weeks. Royall then told Chandler all that he'd learned about their father. These past several months.

Chandler said, "Jesus! Sometimes it seems to me he only just disappeared, the other day. It's still so raw and—" (But what was the word Chandler sought? He shook his head, baffled.)

Royall said, "No. It was long ago. Like Mom tried to make us believe, it seemed to have happened before I was born."

"That's not your fault, Royall. You were only four."

"Four is old enough to remember something. But I can't. I keep trying, and I can't."

"Maybe that's better—"

"Don't say that! Shit."

Royall ran his hands roughly through his hair. Chandler could see that he'd been thinking of this, tormenting himself with this. He spoke in a slow, pained manner more typical of Chandler than of Royall. "All this winter, I've been having weird dreams about him. But I don't even remember the dreams when I wake up. I can feel what they are, like my guts are sick, but with no memory."

Chandler was thinking, yes. He'd been bombarded with dreams, too. And no memory, only sensation. Anger, and despair.

Royall said, "Dad shouldn't have died. He didn't deserve to die like that. Some people say, maybe he was killed." Royall's voice trembled.

Chandler got stiffly to his feet, feeling his heart kick.

He'd rehearsed what he would say, when it came to this. He had known it must come to this.

Royall glanced up at Chandler, narrowing his eyes as if he were peering into a bright light. He drained the last of his warm beer and wiped his mouth on his sleeve. "I'm trying to wake up, though. From the dream. My whole life, a dream. Or whatever it was. This 'Royall' I used to be, that Mom loved. Lots of people loved. I didn't think I was strong enough, but I am." Royall left the kitchen, and returned with an object for Chandler to examine. "I wouldn't ever use this," he said. Chandler stared in disbelief. A gun? Royall had a gun? It was snub-barreled with a sullen bluish-oily gleam and a worn walnut handle, and was about nine inches in length. Royall was saying, "It belongs to my boss. I mean, he has more than one 'firearm,' he's lent me this. I have a permit to carry it, don't worry. He took me to the precinct station in person. But, Chandler—I wouldn't ever use it."

Chandler felt faint. "Royall, my God! Is it loaded?"

"Sure. But the safety is always on. See?"

Royall clicked the mechanism off, on. Off, on. He too was needing a shave. Pale stubble glittered on his jaws like mica.

Chandler thought, chilled *My brother holding death in his hand.*

Royall was saying, "In this literature course I'm taking, the professor said that if a gun appears in a play, it has to be fired by somebody, sometime. You can't set up a false expectation in the audience. But, in life, I don't believe that."

"No. Not in life."

"You can hold a gun in your hand, like it's a practical thing—a hammer, a pliers. A tool of somebody's trade. But you don't have to fire it."

Chandler pushed gently at Royall's hand. "Royall, please put that thing away. Make sure the safety is on, and put it away."

"It's just to show you, Chandler. What I might do, if I was desperate. If learning certain things about our father made me desperate. If, you know—*you* thought that being desperate was how I should be feeling." When Chandler said nothing, Royall said, "But I'm not desperate, am I? It's just in theory."

Still Chandler said nothing. He drew a deep breath.

Royall said, watching him closely, "I wouldn't know which was the target, anyway. Who."

"Who? Howell."

"*Who?*"

Chandler smiled. "We sound like a duet of owls. Whooo. Howww. I think I'm drunk."

Royall laughed. "On three cans of beer. Nobody gets drunk on three cans of beer."

"On an empty stomach, it's possible."

"I explained why I have the gun, haven't I? I need it for my job, for protection."

"What job?"

"I'm working part-time for Empire Collection, Inc. A collection agency. I drive around a lot, I make unannounced house calls. Sometimes I repossess cars, motorcycles. TVs, washing machines, there's a two-man team. My boss is some character, ex-Marine and ex-middle-weight boxer. Says he climbed into the ring with Joey Maxim. And he knew our dad from the 'old days.' Not well, at a distance. 'A gentleman among swine.' "

Chandler was distracted by the gun in Royall's hand. The more Chandler stared, the uglier it was becoming. Yet he smiled. "My kid brother. My kid brother with a gun."

"It's a thirty-eight Smith & Wesson revolver, six chambers. That isn't kid stuff. My boss says, if you're armed, you owe it to your health to be *armed*." Royall was holding the gun in the palm of his hand, as if weighing it. "He's had guys working for him beat up, stabbed, chased in the street and dragged from their cars, shot in the head, kneecaps, ass. But that won't happen to me because I'm not looking for a fight. Anywhere."

"But, Royall—a gun? You're a university student."

"I am! Not full-time, but maybe next year. This job with Empire is only temporary. I feel I should send what I can back to Mom, I left her and Juliet kind of without warning. I felt like I was running for my life." Royall, seeing that Chandler continued to stare at the gun with a sick, stunned expression, carried it away, and when he returned he was smiling, running a comb through his hair. "Let's get the hell out of here."

They left Royall's shabby brownstone building and walked quickly along Fourth Street. It was like emerging from a submarine after hours of captivity. Chandler drew a deep elated breath. He and Royall were friends again, reconciled! He loved Royall, he would try to forget the gun and what it might mean. Wind from Ontario was blowing mist in patches from the Niagara Gorge a quarter-mile away, wetting their warm faces.

They ate in Duke's Bar & Grill, in the fluorescent-lit diner amid rock music of the 1960's that made Chandler's eardrums throb. Royall moved his body to the beat, unconsciously, though he seemed scarcely to hear the noise. They were talking now of less intense matters. They smiled frequently, they laughed like old friends. It would seem to them afterward that this was new, rare—being in each other's company outside the house on Baltic Street. Outside their mother's dominion. Chandler asked about Royall's courses at Niagara University, and if Royall was lonely living by himself, and Royall seemed embarrassed saying yes, and no, sure he was lonely sometimes, but no, frankly he liked living alone, feeling like a grown-up at last, the serious part of his life just beginning. "Learning about Dad. Y'know? That's the beginning."

Chandler nodded, wanting to believe this.

Royall said, "I miss Candace sometimes, and Mom and Juliet . . . But not being married, I sure as hell don't miss that."

"You never were married, Royall. You can't be missing it."

"The idea of it. Having to love somebody twenty-four hours a day and be God to her. The pressure."

Chandler was thinking the reverse. He'd like that pressure. He was trying to imagine what that might be.

Royall said delicately, "Juliet told me about you and Melinda breaking up. You miss her, I guess?"

Chandler winced. "Miss her like hell. And the baby."

Royall shook his head marveling, as if *baby* was beyond him.

"Well. Melinda's O.K. Always nice to have a nurse in the family, as Mom says."

"*Mom says?*"

It was too funny. Chandler rubbed his jaws, startled to discover stubble. What day was this? Hadn't he shaved that morning, for school?

Like friends reluctant to say goodnight they talked of various things. Though this was a Wednesday night, and Chandler had class preparations for the next day. (How restless he was becoming, as a junior high science teacher! Dirk Burnaby would have expected much more of his son.) And there was the possibility of another emergency call from the Crisis Center, or the Samaritans, since Chandler had volunteered for the weekend. He couldn't bear being alone with his thoughts! He was concerned he might call Melinda, and she would hang up without speaking to him.

Can't be involved with a man who doesn't care if he lives or dies.

That wasn't true. It would not be true.

Despite the late hour, past 11 P.M., the diner was nearly full, noisy and smoky. A swinging door connected it with Duke's Bar, a popular hangout for Niagara Falls police officers and hospital workers. Behind the counter, at the grease-splattered grill, was a hulking shaved-headed young man with a blunt, familiar face. (A Mayweather? Someone from the neighborhood, in any case.) He glanced repeatedly at the Burnaby brothers in their booth, as they ate; but when Chandler tried to meet his eye, he frowned and turned away. The young man was about six feet three inches tall, and must have weighed two hundred twenty pounds. Yet his movements behind the counter were deft and coordinated. Chandler was curious who this person was, and Royall told him: Bud Stonecrop.

"His father was a NFPD sergeant who got beaten up pretty badly and had to retire a few years ago. They live on Garrison. Bud was a couple of years ahead of me at school. He quit without graduating and he's the cook here, kind of."

"*He's* the cook?"

"You like the chili? Bud makes the chili."

Chandler had devoured a large bowl of hotly spiced chili, he'd laced with crumpled oyster crackers. He'd been so hungry at first his hands shook. He'd scarcely noticed the chili except that it was unusually good. Royall nudged him, "If you like the food, let Bud know. He takes a lot of shit from his uncle who runs the place." Chandler signaled the hulking young man in the soiled white cook's costume, indicating he'd liked the chili; but Stonecrop, blushing, unsmiling, left the grill abruptly and disappeared back into the kitchen. Royall laughed. "Stonecrop is shy. He'd break your head with his fist but he'd have a helluva hard time talking to you."

Out on the street, the brothers hesitated before parting. Chandler's car was parked in one direction, Royall's apartment was in the other. The mist from the river was thicker. The sky was occluded, invisible. They'd been avoiding the crucial subject and now Royall lowered his voice, that quavered slightly, so that Chandler knew what he would ask. "Chandler, hey: you think there's something to it, what some people say—that Dad was killed?"

Chandler took a deep breath. "No."

"No? You don't?" Royall sounded surprised.

"No, Royall. You asked me, and I'm telling you. No."

Chandler would say nothing more on the subject. He'd prepared just these words.

Royall stared at him, considering.

They shook hands, parting. As they'd rarely done before in their lives. (Had they ever shaken hands, in fact? Chandler doubted it.) Impulsively he hugged Royall. "Royall, call me all the time, any time. Let's eat together once a week, at least. Budd Stonecrop's chili, O.K.? I want to hear from you, O.K.?"

Royall backed off, smiling. His eyes were teary, evasive.

"Sure, Chandler. O.K."

7

CHANDLER WROTE LETTERS to Melinda he never sent. That night, he wrote to Royall.

Dear Royall,
    No I will not.
    I will not urge us into a brothers' shared obsession.
    I will not urge us into that sickness.
    Discovering our father's murderer/murderers.
    (If they exist. If they are still living.)
    I will not ask such a thing of you, and I will not ask such a thing of myself.
    Royall, I love you. Your brother,

                        Chandler

A letter never sent, a memento. Like the scented letter from the young woman hostage, never answered.

8

HE RESOLVED: he would confront Ariah and demand to know all that she knew of his father's death. For sixteen years he'd yearned to say the forbidden name to her: *Dirk Burnaby*. He wanted to hear his mother speak of his father tenderly, with love. He rehearsed what he would say to her:

"Ariah, you did love him once. You can't hate him. He was your husband. Our father!"

But when Chandler drove to the house on Baltic Street, and waited on the front porch for Ariah's piano lesson to end, he began to relent. Or was it his nerve he was losing. It was a Saturday evening in late April. The weather had been unseasonably mild, for Niagara Falls. Chandler sat on the steps, petting Zarjo who was excited to see him, stroking the old dog behind the ears. Inside, at the rear of the house in Ariah's music room, someone was playing Grieg's "Morning" from *Peer Gynt*. Chandler listened, fascinated. Not Ariah, but a student. Playing with a headlong plunging energy. A talented but undisciplined young pianist. Most of Ariah's students were teenagers; sometimes Chandler would overhear Ariah talking and laughing with a student, and feel a tinge of jealousy. Had Ariah ever been so flirtatious and relaxed with *him*? Always she'd seemed on the brink of flinching when she saw Chandler. Reflexively her hand would reach out to straighten his collar, rebutton his shirt. She'd touseled and smoothed down his cowlicked hair in the way she touseled and smoothed down Zarjo's wavy fur. She'd sigh, "Chandler, what am I going to do with you?"

Chandler had always believed that Ariah hadn't loved him. More recently he'd begun to wonder: she certainly loved Zarjo.

Zarjo, the puppy Dirk Burnaby had brought to his family, on the eve of his death.

Zarjo, panting and squirming with pleasure, as Chandler absent-mindedly stroked behind his ears. The dog's spaniel eyes were a rich yearning brown, brimming with emotion. "You love us all, Zarjo, don't you? Never asking why." Chandler put his arm around the quivering dog, and buried his face in his fur. Zarjo's heartbeat was accelerated, his breathing rushed and urgent. Chandler felt emotionally shaky, he'd been so since the Mayweather suicide: that single gunshot, and the silence following.

Chandler had (almost) thought *Am I hit?*

No doubt, in the confusion of the moment, he'd glanced down at himself. He'd touched his head, his hair. It was a reflex, cops and emergency workers did it without thinking. *No. Not me. Not this time.*

Had he been expecting Al Mayweather to shoot him, through the broken window? A way of concluding, ending. Never asking why.

The rapidly played Grieg piece broke off without any ending. There was a brief pause, then another pianist began again, from the beginning. This was the instructor, demonstrating to the student how the piece might be played. The notes were struck with force and precision, flowing, swelling in a way to catch the heart. But Chandler found the music disturbing.

You wept for Dirk Burnaby in secret, didn't you. Yet you forbade his children to weep for him. You cheated us of grief.

It had to have been Juliet who'd set out geraniums in clay pots on the porch railing. Juliet who'd repainted the old, not very comfortable wooden porch chairs, a steely gray. There were rain-stained pillows on these chairs in which few people ever sat. Baltic Street was a neighborhood in which residents sat on porches in warm weather, sometimes late at night, drinking and eating, but not Ariah Burnaby, of course. To her, such behavior was "common"—"crude."

Nothing more alarmed Ariah than "strangers knowing our business."

Nothing was more disgusting than "casting your pearls before swine."

It was an irony of Ariah's life that, being so reclusive among her neighbors, so intent upon preserving her privacy, she drew attention to herself as few other residents of Baltic Street did. Chandler guessed that everyone above a certain age knew whose widow she was; everyone had an opinion of Dirk Burnaby. Yet there was something touching (Chandler supposed) in his mother's pride. In her refusal to be humble, "ordinary." Rarely in sixteen years had she visited any of her neighbors, even to thank them for taking care of her children when she'd been hospitalized; instead, Ariah had written formal thank-you notes on expensive cream-colored stationery, and sent Juliet out to deliver them. She'd rarely accepted invitations from the parents of her most gifted piano students, and had strongly disapproved of her children eating meals with, let alone spending nights with, friends. Her tremulous pronouncement was: "We may be near-destitute, but we don't need charity." And, in an incensed voice each of her children could perfectly mimic, "I was self-supporting long before I was married, and long after."

Cheated us of our grief. Why?

Chandler recalled his grandmother Littrell and several other relatives, whom he'd never seen before and would not see afterward, coming to Niagara Falls to stay with Ariah in the early, devastated phase of her widowhood. These good-hearted people, all of them female, had hoped to persuade Ariah to return with them to Troy, where it was believed she "belonged." Why on earth should Ariah stay in Niagara Falls? She disliked her rich Burnaby in-laws and they seemed clearly to dislike her. She had virtually no friends here, and no reputation as a music teacher. Her children could only grow up haunted near The Falls . . . Her home was with her family in Troy.

But Ariah had said quietly, "No. My home and my children's home is here."

Ariah played piano as she'd played her life—with a forced fluency, bright, brittle, polished. *Allegretto, molto vivace*—joyous notes leapt from her fingers upon command. She could do *maestoso*, and she could do *tranquillo* with equal dexterity. When she struck wrong notes, her fingers moved so swiftly onward, you couldn't be certain what you'd heard.

Zarjo broke away suddenly from Chandler's embrace, and trotted out to the sidewalk to greet a dog being walked by a stiff-kneed man with eyes like raw eggs in a dignified ruin of a face. "Zarjo! Good evening," the man said, in accented English. The dogs were clearly acquaintances, sniffing and nudging at each other excitedly. Zarjo even barked, which was rare for him. Though not young, Zarjo had always been an optimist of a dog, primed to believe the best of other dogs. His beagle tail swung like a pendulum, and his spaniel eyes swam with emotion. Ariah called Zarjo her shadow-self—all that was good in her, sentimental and soft-hearted, was embodied in Zarjo.

The visitor dog was a mixed-breed setter with coarse hair the color of oxblood shoe polish, rheumy eyes and a seemingly useless left hindleg, yet he, too, wagged his tail hopefully. "You know Zarjo?" Chandler asked the man with the tragic eyes, and the man nodded formally, somewhat shyly. "Yes. Very well. We do, Hugo and I. And Zarjo's mistress, your mother I think?"

Chandler's ears pricked at something here. Mistress? Mother?

It was the first Chandler had heard of Ariah befriending anyone in the neighborhood.

Inside the house, piano notes flew like rapturous birds.

In an uncertain, heavily accented voice the man said, "I am Joseph Pankowski. Chandler, is it? Yes. You are a science teacher, Ariah has said. Sometimes I stand here and listen, on warm evenings when the windows are open. Your mother is an accomplished pianist, it gives me happiness to hear her. So alive . . ."

Pankowski wore tasteful dark clothing, a serge jacket that fitted his sloped shoulders loosely, and dark trousers, baggy but pressed; his shoes were polished black leather of unusual quality. He was in his late fifties, of moderate height and weight, looking as if he'd once been larger. His face, Chandler saw uneasily, looked stitched together; his skull seemed to be pushing through his scalp in ridges and bumps. He breathed audibly, harshly. The floating damp eyes shifted in a kind of anguish of feeling, baffling to Chandler at the time though afterward he would realize *He wanted badly to impress me. Her son.*

Ariah's friend was a Polish Jew, born in the Warsaw ghetto, who'd emigrated to the United States in 1946. He, too, had been a musician, a violinist. But he had not played in years. His fingers and nerves were gone. Pankowski stared at his fingers, trying to flex them. The setter Hugo strained and tugged at the leash, nearly breaking away.

Chandler was tempted to ask what had happened: 1946? But he knew better. One could guess what this man had survived.

"The first music of your mother's I heard, last June on this side-walk, was a Chopin mazurka. Hugo and I were passing by, and we were stopped. We could not continue. Later, not that evening but an-other time, we would hear your sister sing, two little songs from Schumann's *Myrten*. Of course, we did not know who these people were, so gifted. 'Juliet'—a name out of Shakespeare! A shy girl but with a lovely alto voice. But you know, of course. You are her brother."

Chandler frowned. In fact he didn't know, much.

Years ago when Juliet was hardly more than a child, Ariah had tried to "train" her voice, as she'd tried to "train" Royall. But Ariah had been too demanding, and the lessons ended in tears and hurt feel-ings. Chandler knew that Juliet sang in the girls' chorus at the high school, and often sang solos; but he hadn't known that Juliet sang for Ariah, ever.

Out of politeness Chandler asked if Pankowski lived nearby, and the older man said, embarrassed, "Not so near! But not so far." His stitched-together face flushed. Ariah's piano playing ended abruptly, and Pankowski seemed now eager to be gone. He stammered, "Please give my warm greetings to your mother, will you please, Mr. Chandler, I mean—Chandler. Thank you. Goodnight!"

Pankowski walked on, stiff-kneed, tugging at Hugo's leash. The aged setter followed reluctantly, looking back at Zarjo who barked several times in rapid succession, like a wind-up dog.

Chandler thought *He's in love with her. God help him.*

When Chandler asked Ariah about Joseph Pankowski, she too seemed embarrassed. "Oh, him. The shoe-repair man." Ariah tried for an air of faint scorn, not meeting Chandler's eye. "We go to summer con-certs in the park, sometimes. He's a widower. His children are grown and gone." Ariah paused as if to say *Like mine*. Chandler said, "Well, he seems like an exceptionally nice man. A cultivated man. He used to play violin, and he admires your piano playing." Ariah laughed dismissively. "He's told you his life history, has he? Too-lonely people talk too much." She frowned into a corner of the room as if into infinity, with a shiver of disdain. "He was in Birkenau. He will never not be 'in Birkenau.' There is a tattooed number on his left wrist. He wears long-sleeved shirts but still you can see it." Ariah paused, rubbing at her own slender wrist. "I would think you could have such an ugly tattoo removed, if you made the effort."

Chandler objected, "Removing tattoos is painful, Ariah. Maybe it can't always be done."

Ariah said hotly, "I would do it."

Mother and son were breathing quickly as if they'd been quarreling. But of what? Why? Chandler had a fleeting memory of how, in this kitchen, years ago, Ariah had lunged at him without warning in a flaring-up of temper, because he'd been sidling out of the room. A spy, she'd called him.

A spy?

Ariah countered Chandler's questions about Joseph Pankowski by asking him about his "married-woman friend." Chandler said he had not seen or heard from Melinda in twenty-two days.

Ariah was impressed. "Twenty-two! You've been counting."

"Not deliberately, Mom."

Ariah considered what she might say. Ordinarily she never spoke of Melinda except elliptically, as one might allude to a vague, vaguely threatening condition, like a downturn in the economy, a forecast of Asian flu. She said, "I'm sure she's a very fine woman. A nurse. It's always good to have a nurse in the family! But older than you, isn't she? And divorced, already. And under such disagreeable circumstances, her husband leaving her before their baby was born!"

Chandler knew better than to defend Melinda to his mother. How many times he'd said *Yes but they married too young. Yes it was a mistake.* Wanting to say *Yes I love her, why is that a threat to you?*

Ariah continued, frowning, "If she wants to break off your friendship, I'd respect her judgment. She's more mature then you are. I can see why she'd be jealous of your 'crisis' work. And there is something unnatural about a couple in which the woman is older than the man, when men are so immature to begin with. Royall and Candace—there was a mismatch brewing."

Chandler laughed. "Mismatch? You introduced them, Ariah. You practically proposed to each of them."

Ariah smiled. A warm flush rose into her face. She loved being teased by her sons; now that Royall was gone, Chandler must do.

"Well. Your mother makes mistakes, too. She's only human."

Only human! This was news to Chandler.

Later, when Chandler's visit was concluding, and Ariah seemed to be in good spirits, Chandler dared to say he'd driven out to l'Isle Grand recently. "I spoke with my aunts. Clarice and Sylvia."

" 'My aunts.' Isn't that cozy. Since when are those dreadful snobs 'your' aunts?" Ariah spoke calmly, as if bemused.

"Aunt Clarice told me something very strange—"

"I'm sure she did."

"She told me—"

Ariah pressed her hands over her ears. "Please don't tax my credulity, Chandler. I'm willing to believe, that vindictive old harpy who has it in for me told you something *very strange*."

Ariah was laughing, or trying to laugh. Chandler hesitated. How could he ask his mother if she'd been married twice? If her first husband had "thrown himself" into The Falls? It was all so improbable. More than improbable, fantastic. Like those long-ago tales of sensation, romance, doom once told of The Falls, in another century.

Impulsively Chandler said, "Mom? Am I—was I—Daddy's and your son? I mean—I wasn't adopted, was I?"

"Adopted! What a thing to say."

Chandler hadn't meant to say *adopted*. In his confusion, he didn't know what he meant to say.

Ariah fumbled to touch Chandler's wrist, to console him. Her eyes, only just a moment before green-glinting with fury, immediately softened. She said, in her low, sincere voice:

"Honey, of course you weren't adopted. You were born right here

in Niagara Falls, at the hospital. You must have seen your birth certificate, I'm sure you've had to use it. What on earth are you saying,
Chandler? At such a time! You're an adult, twenty-seven years old.
Darling, you weren't an easy birth, I was in labor with you for eleven
hours and twelve minutes and I remember vividly, it's false to say that
a mother can't recall such things, especially with the first birth, and
you were—you are—my first-born." Ariah spoke emphatically, tugging at Chandler's arm as if he were about to disagree. "That can
never change."

"And my father—"

"We don't speak of him. He's *gone*."

"My father was Dirk Burnaby."

Ariah shut her eyes, stiffening. Her mouth had gone small and
pinched, snail-like. A plait of hair had come loose, disheveled onto
the nape of her neck. Chandler drew a breath, as of triumph. In this
house, in his mother's presence, he'd at last uttered the name *Dirk
Burnaby*.

"When he died, it was an accident, yes? It was ruled an accident?"

When Ariah didn't reply, Chandler dared to ask, "What about
Daddy's life insurance, if it was an accident? And his will? There must
have been money."

Ariah pressed her fingertips against her eyelids. Chandler felt her
agitation, before she spoke.

"I couldn't accept it. Blood money. Tainted money. I could not."

Chandler had to think, to absorb this. What was Ariah telling him?

As she spoke, rapidly and nervously, as if repeating words she'd
rehearsed numerous times, Chandler felt the edges of his vision begin
to darken, to shrink. "They tried to make me. His lawyers. His family, even. But I refused. I had to refuse. It wasn't pride, I am not a creature of pride. When he left us, I closed my heart to him and to all the
Burnabys."

Chandler couldn't believe what Ariah was telling him. Even as a
part of his mind thought calmly *Of course. I knew. It had to be something
like this.* "Mom, what? How much money did you 'refuse'?"

"I did sell the house. That ridiculous house, that habitation of vanity, had to be sold. And so we moved here. And we've been happy here, haven't we? The four of us. And Zarjo. Our little family."

"Oh, Mom."

"Well, haven't we? We lived lives of integrity. American lives of"—Ariah searched for the word, now appealing to Chandler—"self-respect. Oh, I did 'use' some of the blood money, from the sale of the house. There has always been some money in the bank. Only just a little, in case of some terrible emergency, God knows what God might send when you have three children and are unprotected in the world. I wanted to spare you that other life, the Burnaby life. Whatever our lives have been, they are ours." Ariah pleaded, "And we have been happy, Chandler? Haven't we?"

"How much money did you turn back?"

"I have no idea. I refused to be informed. I refused to be tempted, Chandler. In my place, I hope you would have done the same thing."

Years of Baltic Street. The *near-destitute* Burnabys. Chandler laughed, incredulous. Would he have done the same thing?

"No."

"Oh, Chandler. Yes you would. Even before the Love Canal scandal, I knew the Burnaby money was tainted."

" 'Tainted'! Ariah, you're like a character in grand opera, not life. This is Niagara Falls, this is life. All money is tainted, for Christ's sake."

"That is not true. You, a public school teacher, have higher morals than that."

"The truth is, you meant to punish him. Dirk Burnaby. By rejecting his money. By punishing us. As if, beyond the grave, he'd have seen, and been sorry."

"No. It was a matter of principle. In my place, you would have done the same thing. Chandler, tell me yes."

By this time Chandler's head was seriously pounding. He saw with a kind of clinical detachment that his vision had perceptibly narrowed, as if he were at an emergency scene. Tunnel vision. A symptom of of panic, but controlled panic.

"Mom, I'm leaving."

At this moment Juliet returned home, having been baby-sitting in the neighborhood. Fleet and secretive as a feral cat Chandler's sister rapidly ascended the stairs with no more than a murmured hello, as if knowing how Ariah would have waved her away, not wanting her to interrupt the intense conversation in the kitchen with her son.

Chandler stood, blundered to his feet. Trying to think *The fact is, I am his son. None of the rest matters.* He hugged Ariah, feeling how thin she was, wiry-thin, taut. When he kissed her goodnight, her skin burned his cheek. He tried to say he'd call, he'd drop by next day after school, but the words choked in his throat. Literally he was weak-kneed. Ariah followed him to the front door and called from the porch, her voice low, thrilled as a young girl's. "Darling, tell me 'yes.' You would."

Carelessly Chandler called back, over his shoulder as he was getting into his car, as if this were a trifling matter and not one involving how many hundreds of thousands of dollars it would make him faint to calculate, "Oh Mom, sure. You know me."

Never would he understand his mother. And so he would have to love her, without understanding.

There was Mommy scrubbing at Daddy's wrist with a wire brush, hard. The two of them upstairs at the old house in Luna Park, the first house. Where Chandler was the only child. Mommy was excited, anxious. Daddy's face was blurred but you could see it had been stitched together, mended. Chandler, a small child, crouched at the doorway, then crawled closer, hidden from the adults by the end of the bed. That big carved mahogany bed. The room was floodlit and blinding-bright yet dim, it was difficult to see. Couldn't see the man's face but knew it was Daddy. As Mommy rubbed the brush against the raw bleeding wrist, for there was something in the skin that offended her. Drops of blood like raindrops flew into the air and some of these fell on Chandler. He was sobbing, trying to wrench the wire brush away from his mother's strong fingers and in the struggle woke himself, dazed and spent.

9

"OUR SUBJECT TODAY is The Falls. And erosion."

On the front blackboard of Mr. Burnaby's ninth-grade science classroom is a simplified but accurate map of the Niagara River, drawn with rapid strokes of chalk by Mr. Burnaby (who must carry such a map, to scale, in his head). Still on the board from last week is:

EROSION TIME EROSION TIME

Mr. Burnaby says, pointing with the chalk, "The Falls are currently here, at Niagara Falls. Our city. A little more than two miles from this classroom. But The Falls weren't always here, and will not remain here. The Falls is in motion."

The Falls originated downriver, north of the city at Lewiston, approximately twelve thousand years ago. Not very long ago in geological time; but earth erosion moves swiftly.

"An inch a century? Yes, that's 'swiftly.' "

Chandler Burnaby, master of arcane knowledge that impresses certain of his smarter students. Mr. Burnaby, ninth-grade science teacher in the Niagara Falls public school system, bravely striding across chasms of geological time, a stick of chalk in his fingers like a talisman.

Mr. Burnaby, whom certain of the ninth-grade girls (it's hardly a secret which ones) have crushes on.

Mr. Burnaby, wearing his Mr. Burnaby face. Speaking his Burnaby voice.

Telling these young adolescents, some of them looking hardly more than children, terrible heartrending profound truths of time, mortality, human isolation in a godless universe. Truths of loss, annihilation. As the red minute hand of the clock on the wall moves placidly, a wheel forever turning.

Mr. Burnaby draws an inch-long line. How short it is on the blackboard, almost invisible. "Yes. A mere inch a century. But it's a slow inexorable wearing-away of the riverbed along forty miles. When our man-made devices to impede erosion fail, The Falls will resume its movement. One day it will have moved all the way upstream, past l'Isle Grand, past Tonawanda, past Buffalo; one day, a very long time from now, The Falls will be at the source of the strait (for in fact the Niagara River isn't a river, but a strait, connecting the two lakes) at Lake Erie."

Chandler wants to think that several of his students are absorbing this. Feeling it in their guts. The Falls, they've learned to take for granted, even to scorn, isn't *permanent*?

A bright boy waves his hand. Asks what the city will be called, if The Falls are gone from it? "Just 'Niagara'? And no 'Falls'?"

"Probably," Chandler says, "it won't be called anything. There won't be anyone here to take note of it. Like the great glaciers of the Ice Age, our city, and these other cities, will very likely have fallen into ruins, hidden in underbrush, inhabitants long gone. You've seen enough science-fiction to know the scenario. Things wear out, civilizations wear down, species vanish. Who knows where?"

His students stare at him. There's an uncomfortable silence. *Who knows where?* seems to hover in the air. He has frightened these young people for a few fleet seconds before the bell clamors and releases them and he seems to have frightened himself, too. Laying his chalk-stub into the tray beneath the blackboard but fumbling, it slips and falls shattering to bits at his feet.

10

HADN'T CALLED MELINDA.

He could take pride in his restraint, at least.

He'd been writing to Melinda, however. Coming to know her, and to know himself, intimately, from writing these letters though he put them away in a drawer without sending them.

It wasn't until after meeting Joseph Pankowski that he decided to send a few lines to Melinda. Terse as poetry:

I am sorry.

I think of you constantly.

Yes I was wrong, to value my life so cheaply.

I hope you can forgive me.

How to sign it but *Love, Chandler*? There seemed no other way.

He hated the many "I's" in what he'd written. He was sick of his ego, his self trapped like a fly in a bottle.

Yet he had to send this message. He'd written and rewritten each line numerous times, he couldn't seem to improve it.

Melinda didn't reply, didn't call. Yet somehow he felt encouraged.

He would not harass her. He would not drive past her apartment building on Alcott Street. He would not dial her number, and listen to the ringing, and hang up quietly if the receiver was lifted.

He would not go to the hospital to see if . . . Well, to see.

He would not send flowers, with a card saying only *Love, C*. He believed that, to a woman, flowers from a man might be perceived as sexually aggressive.

Instead, he sent her carefully chosen cards, scenic views of The Falls and the Gorge. These were meant to suggest an unearthly beauty. And the danger of such beauty.

I can change, I think.

I love you, and I love Danya.

Will you give me another chance?

In early May he searched for gently comical cartoon cards featuring nurses and patients, but found none that weren't vulgar. He drew his own card, a man lying flat on his back on a gurney, a nurse extracting blood from the man's arm.

Melinda! I'm in your hands utterly.

Have mercy.

He waited.

Our Lady of The Falls

W hy can't it be true? Why can't we believe? Some things in which we don't believe must be true . . ."

In the spring of 1891 in Niagara Falls there lived a fifteen-year-old dairy maid lately settled to live with relatives in the area from County Cork, Ireland. This girl was said to be of a "neutral" religious disposition: she believed in the Holy Roman Catholic Church and its sacraments, but was not one of those passionate believers who attend mass and take holy communion on days other than Sunday.

Within a year of the dairy maid's arrival in Niagara Falls she was deeply troubled, pale and distraught and sleepless. Abruptly she withdrew from the boisterous company of her relatives. She was drawn to The Falls to expiate her sin which was a sin of the flesh perpetrated upon her by the dairy owner's son. This young man swore he loved the dairy maid, in the early days of their acquaintanceship; in time, he swore he would strangle her with his hands that were toughened from milking the slippery teats of cows lowing and moaning to be milked as (the young man crudely believed) the dairy maid had wished to be "milked" by her lover: ejaculated into, his creamy semen coating her insides as she whimpered and sobbed in pain, thrashed her thighs from side to side, bit her lower lip hard enough to draw blood.

This girl, a virgin until so seduced, and impregnated, was not the cause of that sin; yet she carried the consequence of it inside her belly hard as a nut that would not be dislodged. (To her shame, the girl did try to abort the unwanted baby in her womb. Oh she tried, she tried! Stamping her heels, striking herself in the belly, running until she collapsed panting like a stricken deer. And in this she knew herself doubly a sinner, and rightly despised by God.) In a delirium of sorrow, malnourished, self-loathing, in the third month of her pregnancy when all who knew her shunned her, and the dairy owner barred her from his property, the shamed girl made her way on foot to the Niagara River, and to The Falls, of which she'd heard it was a place for sinners to cleanse themselves, by way of ridding the world of themselves. She removed her shoes as a penitent walking in dirt, sharp stones, tall grasses to the very edge of the rushing river, that acted upon her like a spell. Never had she gazed upon such a sight as the rapids, The Falls, the Gorge billowing mist like clouds of steam that seemed to her in her distraught state "as if it must be boiling hot, like the bowels of Hell."

The dairy maid had made her decision, and was calm in her actions. She would commit herself to the river as, she'd heard, numerous others had done, to be borne swiftly over The Falls. In this way she would spare her family the burden of shame she must bring them, and the unwanted bastard child no one (except perhaps the dairy maid) could love. Yet staring at the clouds of mist the dairy maid smiled to perceive several small rainbows, shimmering in thin rays of sunshine against an overcast sky. And with that innocent smile she felt her "heart leap" and was granted a vision of a radiant female figure rising before her above the great gorge at a distance of perhaps forty feet, hovering in the air. The feet of this figure disappeared in the mist generated by the Horseshoe Falls, and her haloed head touched the very sky. The dairy maid was stricken to the heart, and fell to her knees exclaiming *Holy Mary, Mother of God*, for she had recognized the Virgin immediately by her serene, beautifully composed face and her royal-blue robe that fell in graceful folds about her slender body. As she had been taught in childhood in the great church of her baptism the dairy maid surrendered herself to this vision with not a moment's hesitancy or doubt, praying in a loud ecstatic voice *Holy Mary, Mother of God! Pray for us sinners now and at the hour of our death, Amen.*

The dairy maid then begged the Virgin Mary to forgive her, and the Virgin Mary smiled gently upon her and spoke so softly that her words were obscured by the roar of The Falls yet the sense of them was communicated to the dairy maid as clearly as if the Virgin had whispered into her ear saying *My child there is nothing to forgive. Love, and you do God's will.*

At these words, the dairy maid sank into a swoon and lost consciousness and was not discovered on the riverbank for several hours; and was afterward delirious, with a high fever, for days. Carried to a nearby home on Prospect Avenue, she was treated by a physician, and woke weeping in joy; she told her rescuers of the vision she'd been granted of The Virgin of The Falls, repeating her story numerous times to all who would listen, and to priests of the Roman Catholic Church, who were immediately summoned. The Irish dairy maid was uneducated and illiterate and yet, witnesses claimed, she spoke with such certitude, her face radiant, it was impossible to believe that she was not telling the truth. Almost, you could see the Virgin through the dairy maid's eyes, so singularly did she convey the miraculous vision she'd been granted, and its special message for the faithful. *There is nothing to forgive. Love, and you do God's will.*

On a hilly site three miles north of The Falls, a shrine was erected to commemorate the dairy maid's vision: the Basilica of Our Lady of The Falls. In time, after numerous miracles of "healing" and "revelation" were said to occur there, the Basilica grew, and in 1949 a new, thirty-foot statue of the Virgin Mary, executed in Vermont marble and said to weigh more than twenty tons, was erected in such a position that it could be seen for miles, very like a vision, looking toward the city of Niagara Falls and the river. *You saw, and you wanted to believe. You saw, and looked away, and laughed, and hot acid spilled into the back of your mouth, you were sickened and ashamed and yet: you wanted to believe. Heal me.*

The Voices

There's a curse on our name.
    No. Our name is a curse.

The voices! The voices in The Falls . . . In winter The Falls are en-
cased in ice and rainbows of ice glitter across the Gorge and mist is
frozen like spun glass covering the trees and there is a frail ice bridge
that forms across the river between Luna Island and Bridal Veil Falls
and you want to believe you can cross that bridge and the voices are
muted, almost inaudible, you have to hold your breath to hear. But
with the thaw in late March, early April, the voices return, louder,
harsher, yet seductive, and by June as the anniversary of his death approaches the voices became clamorous and impatient and you hear
them in your sleep far from the rushing river. *Juliet! Juliet! Burn-a-by!*
Shame, shame's the name. You know your name. Come to your father in The
Falls.

―――――

"Zarjo, no. Stay."

Juliet whispers goodbye to Zarjo, roused from his warm inert sleep at the foot of her bed. Buries her face in the dog's familiar coarse fur and allows him to lick her face, her hands, panting silently, shivering with doggy enthusiasm wanting to be taken with her—where?

In the stillness before dawn. In a twilight of rain that has gradually lightened to mist, to fog.

She must leave quickly before Ariah knows. Before Ariah can prevent her. For in her bed that night, as she tried to sleep, the voices pushed near, jeering, derisive *Burn-a-by! Burn-a-by!* and among them his voice, she's convinced, the single voice among the others that's calm, gentle—*Juliet! It's time.*

(Is that his voice? Juliet believes it is.)

(Though born too late. Her memory of him is transparent as falling water.)

Yet when she sings, Juliet sings for him. Secretly, for him.

In recitals, she imagines him somewhere in the audience. Not in the first several rows with parents and relatives and classmates, but somewhere, in the darkness. He would be sitting alone, and he would be listening attentively. When she sings beautifully, it's because he listens so attentively.

Her solo in "The Messiah." At the Music Hall. For which she'd been praised. And such applause. For him!

A shy girl, her eyes welling with emotion. Swiping at her eyes seeing him smile, a look of fatherly pride.

At other times, unpredictably, her voice quavers and loses its strength, she feels that panicked sensation, her throat on the verge of shutting up: she knows the futility of singing for a man she can't remember, who died sixteen years ago.

We're happy, but only while the music lasts.

So Ariah has conceded. And so it must be true.

―――――

(It was after Juliet's solo in "The Messiah" that Madame Ehrenreich spoke with her about studying at the Buffalo Academy, where Madame teaches. A scholarship for the study of voice. A scholarship for Juliet Burnaby who was only sixteen. Juliet would not have to transfer to another high school but could commute into the city twice a week after classes, not a lengthy bus ride, the Academy would pay her expenses. *A golden opportunity!* her teachers said. Smiling at Juliet Burnaby as if expecting the frightened girl to smile back.)

Did this house have a daddy she would ask Mommy, and Mommy would say *No.*

Did this house have a daddy she would ask her brothers when she was just old enough to be desperate to know and Chandler said *Yes but he went away.* She asked *Why? Did he hate us?* and Chandler said evasively *It was just something that happened, I guess. Like weather. Mommy doesn't want us to talk about it, see, Juliet?* And there came Royall hot-faced, childish fists clenched, who knew little more than Juliet knew but had formed a boy's judgment *I hate HIM! I don't miss HIM! I'm glad he's gone away.*

Zarjo follows her to the foot of the stairs, his toenails clicking with melancholy precision, an older dog, breathing hoarsely, with an older dog's economy of motion, sensing that his hind legs might not retain the power to keep him balanced at such a steep angle, and Juliet is moving decisively away from him, she's serious about not taking him with her and he won't, cannot, bark inside the house: he's a very obedient dog, trained not to bark at trifles.

"Zarjo, I said no. *Stay.*"

Juliet leaves by the front door. The farthest door from Ariah's bedroom at the upstairs, rear of the house.

The last of Ariah's children to leave. To flee.

The last of Ariah's children to love her, so much it can't be borne. *I am not you, Mother. Let me go!*

Barefoot, running. Her numbed feet barely feel the pavement. And the chill, dewy grass, and the hard-packed dirt. As if she feels, not frightened now, but exhilarated. The decision having been made, and not by her. And hurriedly: she's in her white eyelet cotton nightgown smelly from bad dreams, her frayed trench coat over it belted tight.

Shame, shame. Know your name.

Commit the Act & be done with it.

In the stillness before dawn. Shifting walls of mist before dawn. When the world is dreamlike and, running through it, you are both the dreamer and the dream. Long ago the warrior-gods of the Ongiaras and Tuscaroras prowled this landscape, they were tall, cruel gods, more powerful than any human beings, but now these gods are gone and only their ghosts remain, mist-shapes drifting and fading in the corner of an eye. Chandler has said the landscape is always changing, The Falls are continually changing. Time, erosion. The Indian gods are gone, but no other gods have taken their place.

Except: the Niagara Falls City Transit buses, lighted from within like living organisms, gliding as if underwater and passing with harsh pneumatic exhalations of breath. Buses marked for *Ferry St.*, *Prospect Ave.*, *Tenth St.*, *Parkway & Hyde.* Juliet is furtive, shrinking from being seen, crossing Baltic Street to the park which is deserted at this hour, shrouded in fog. Runs, runs! She's a strong girl, her lungs are strong from singing. A slight girl, always looking younger than her age. She has been told not to walk alone in Baltic Park, her brother Royall has scolded her, but at this hour there's no one, she's running through a field of wet grass, now at the edge of a softball field that looks small, truncated in scale as a child's board game in the hazy light. *If her body isn't found. No one will know. Like her father, gone. Ariah will say, gone and not coming back, and so we won't think of her any longer, we will forget her.* A block away, a freight train is passing. The familiar noise of rattling boxcars. There's comfort in this familiar sound. *Shame's the name, know your name, what's your game?* In a dream Juliet Burnaby is being transported to The Falls by boxcar. This is because of something Mr. Pankowski said. The sound of trains in this city, the noise of boxcars a nightmare to him he could not expect any American to understand, but Juliet said yes she understood, it's boxcars that, if you were going to be taken away, like cattle for the slaughterhouse, would take you away. And the train would be going so fast, you couldn't leap off.

The sky above the Niagara River, a mile away, is a great chasm streaked with sudden light. Flames, filaments of light from the sun at the horizon. *No. Not afraid!*

2

THE VOICES! The voices in The Falls I heard when I was a little girl and Mommy pushed me in the stroller close to the edge where the cold spray wetted our faces, our eyelashes and lips and we licked our lips and laughed in excitement.

Oh, delicious!

See, Juliet darling? This is happiness.

She loved me best, Mommy said. I was her daughter, her baby girl and my brothers were boys. I was a girl like Mommy, and my brothers could never be girls. *This time I will do it right. This time, conceived without sin.*

Mommy sang to me. Mommy played the piano, and sang to me. And Mommy sat me on her lap at the piano, and held me tight inside her arms, and placed my pudgy baby fingers on the keys, and we played piano together; and Mommy urged me to sing, Mommy rewarded me with kisses when I sang in my baby-girl breathy voice.

These were magic times. There was no one but Mommy.

Singing *Girls and boys come out to play. The moon doth shine as bright as day.* Singing *Lavender blue, dilly-dilly! Lavender green. When I am King, dilly-dilly! You shall be Queen.* And Mommy's favorite which she sang at the piano, but also when I was in bed and slipping into sleep *Hush-a-bye baby in the tree-top! When the wind blows, the cradle will rock. When the bough breaks, the cradle will fall. Down will come baby, cradle and all!* But Mommy laughed, and showed how she would catch me in her arms if I fell.

But later. When I was bigger. When the voices came into the room. And Mommy said *There's nothing. Stop!* And Mommy pressed her hands against my ears, and against her own ears. And next morning if I said the voices had come into the room, Mommy would scold me; or would stand up suddenly, and walk away. And one of my brothers would take care of me.

For Mommy ceased to love me when I was no longer a baby. Too big to be carried in her arms like a doll, and too big to fit on her lap at the piano. I think that was when. Calling out *Mommy!* in the night. And Mommy didn't want to hear. And I learned finally to hide such cries in the pillow. But the pillowcase became stained which Mommy didn't like and which disgusted Mommy, like other stains I could not help. And I would crawl away to hide. And when they called me, I would not answer. The voices were whispers sometimes, I pressed my ear against the wall to hear, or against the windowpane, or the floorboards. Royall tried to hear, but could not. Royall said there was nothing, not to be afraid. That time I went where Mommy said not to go, into the cellar, in the dark, and fell from the steep wooden steps and cut my lip and crawled away to hide from the voices mixed with the wind and the freight cars and it was Zarjo who found me; except Zarjo didn't know I did not want to be found, to Zarjo everything was a game. And so he poked me with his moist nose, he kissed and tickled me with his slippery tongue. Zarjo barked, which he rarely did inside the house and so they found me where I was huddled on the floor behind a stack of old rabbit cages. My brothers calling *Jully-ett!* And Mommy hurried downstairs shining the flashlight in my face, my eyes that were blind. Mommy screamed when she saw my bleeding mouth *Juliet, what have you done to yourself, oh you bad girl you've done it on purpose haven't you!* In her widened green eyes I saw that Mommy wanted to shake me, Mommy wanted to hurt me because I was not her baby daughter now, I had disappointed her not once but many times, and yet she was Ariah and not another woman in the neighborhood who would scream at her children, slap and spank them, she was Ariah Burnaby the piano teacher and she was not one to strike any child and so her hands seizing me were gentle, her voice was low and controlled telling me I must never disobey her again, I must never come down into this filthy place again, or Mommy would give me away.

It upset Mommy that I was laughing. Or made a sound like laughing. And I was dirty, and wet my panties. And there would be a scar like a starburst in my upper lip that would never go away, so people's eyes would always drift onto it and I would sense how they wanted to flick it off as you'd flick off a piece of dust, they would want to brush it off to make me a pretty girl and not a freaky girl with something pale and shiny on her upper lip. And later, when I was going to Baltic Elementary and Ronnie Herron pushed me on a swing too high, and wouldn't stop when I begged him, and I fell off, and the flying seat of the swing struck the left side of my forehead knocking me unconscious and cutting me so deeply I'd be covered in blood, taken to the emergency room of the Niagara Falls General Hospital by ambulance and the wound stitched up and ever afterward there would be a little sickle moon in my forehead that was pale too, and shiny. And Mommy came to be fearful of me believing me demented, a child who would hurt herself deliberately in order to hurt Mommy; a child who ran away to hide from her groveling in filth in the cellar Mommy could not bear, not the smell of, not the dirt floor that flooded when it rained and the ill-fitting stone walls oozing muck and the stacks of rusted, broken rabbit cages that smelled of rabbit droppings.

She isn't mine, sometimes I think she isn't mine Mommy would say and my brothers would tell her no that wasn't right, Juliet was their sister and Juliet belonged to Mommy just like they did.

Ariah too has long suffered from insomnia. And now in the rainy spring of 1978 as the anniversary of his death approaches, and the house is empty of her sons, now her insomnia rages like a malevolent fire. Not that she would ever acknowledge such a weakness, even to a doctor. All weakness fills Ariah with disgust, and her own with self-disgust. Her children, growing up in the house at 1703 Baltic, will recall hearing her stealthy footsteps on the stairs in the early morning, before dawn; hearing her in the kitchen setting a tea kettle on the gas stove. And in the chilly unlighted room at the rear of the house as she waits for the water to boil she sits at the spinet lightly touching the keys, depressing the keys as a devout Roman Catholic might it isn't just music that makes Ariah happy but the mere possibility, the promise, of music. *Music can be your salvation, Juliet. You will raise your-*

self from the worst in yourself. Have faith! But by nine in the evening Ariah is often so exhausted she falls alseep on the living room sofa, Zarjo drowsing across her knees, even as she listens to her much-anticipated broadcast of the New York Philharmonic on the radio. And her children exchange nervous glances wondering: Should we wake Mom, or let her sleep?—either way Mom will be annoyed with us, and embarrassed.

Did this house have a daddy I asked when I was old enough to know that houses like ours had daddys. And Mommy told me *No*. And I could see in Mommy's eyes that I shouldn't persist but I asked *Where did Daddy go?* and Mommy would press her forefinger against my lips and say *Shh!* And if I continued to persist Mommy would frown and say *Daddy left us before you were born, he's gone and he isn't coming back.*

And a cold heavy sickish feeling came into me like dirty water oozing through the cellar walls and I thought *Now you know. You asked, and now you know.*

3

Shame, shame. Your name!

Already in first grade the others seemed to know. (But what did they know?) Almost, you'd think they knew by instinct. Their eyes following Juliet in curiosity at first. Later, in suspicion. Later, in derision. And then Royall was in junior high, at another school, and Juliet was left behind. And alone. A strange dreamy stammering child with not one but two scars on her small pale face. Two scars! Her teachers considered her, not knowing what to make of her. *Burnaby? Is she related to—?* For she was one of those children who stammered in class, sometimes; at other times she spoke normally, and intelligently; at other times, unpredictably, she spoke in what seemed to them a sullen mumble. *A spiteful little girl. Not nice.* But when she sang, she never stammered. When she sang, her voice was remarkably clear, a lovely voice, though wavering, uncertain.

Burn-a-by. Burn-a-by. Hey!

On the playground, in the neighborhood, there was no protocol in considering "strange" children. There was no sympathy, mercy.

That one. Burn-a-by. Shame!

You spoke to her, she didn't hear. Stood close to her, she didn't see. Looked right through you, like she was listening to something far away. To get her attention you had to clap your hands in her face, pinch her, poke her, tug at her hair until she cried. *Burn-a-by. Your father drove his car into the river, your father was gonna go to jail. Burn-a-by, shame-shame!* Older brothers and sisters must have told them. Adults must have told these older brothers and sisters. (But what?)

So childhood was endured. She would think of those years in retrospect as if they'd been lived by someone else, a brave, stubborn little girl, unknown to her.

4

A shadow-child Ariah calls her. *Trailing a shadow-self.*

Speaking of her adolescent daughter critically yet with a look of perverse sympathy as if she understands such an affliction in a young female and can't entirely condemn it. Seated at the spinet playing one of her favored musical compositions, Debussy's mordant, mysterious *La Cathédrale engloutie*. Oh, the beauty of *La Cathédrale engloutie*! A breathless hushed beauty like that of The Falls in winter when the rushing water is muted and all is obscured in mist. Sonorous rising chords that seem to shimmer with life through Ariah's thin, skilled fingers. *Profondément calme.* Is it strange, Juliet will one day wonder, of a mother to call out to her daughter, fourteen at the time, who's just come home from school, "Juliet! Hear? This is your music. Your soul. You are the sunken cathedral, no one can reach you. This is the music you were born to sing." In a tone of stoic hurt suggesting *I've given up on you. Go away!*

Juliet slinks away, but only upstairs. She and Zarjo, huddling and murmuring together.

As Ariah continues to play Debussy, below.

(Why does Ariah say such wounding things to Juliet, whom in fact she loves? Does she, mother of an attractive adolescent daughter, imagine a secret, sexual life in the daughter; does she yearn for that secret, sexual life she long ago lost, ripped out of herself like an ungainly, unsightly weed? Is she frankly jealous of her daughter? Of that very voice, a rich warm alto, she has wanted so badly to "train"?)

Royall has seen. Juliet's *shadow-self*.

Most distinctive in slanted light. Close behind her, like a reflection of rippling water, an apparition that moves with the unconscious, slightly awkward grace of the girl herself.

Like a sleepwalker Juliet often seems, out-of-doors. Her heavy-lidded eyes, her wavy hair falling past her shoulders like an uncombed mane. This hair exudes an odor of something romantic and melancholy as wetted autumn leaves, or violets beaten and ravaged by rain; a fragrance that draws older boys and men to her. Royall has seen, and hasn't liked what he has seen: the stricken expressions on male faces in Juliet's presence, as if they are reminded of something crucial lost to them.

Royall, in late adolescence, now sexually active, and yet exasperated by his sister. Sometimes!

By chance Royall has seen Juliet on the street, occasionally with girls from school, but most often alone. Trailing home in that dreamy brooding way of hers. Seeing her, you'd wonder where Juliet's mind is; Royall guesses she's hearing music in her head, shaping notes in her throat. Yet: alone in Baltic Park, being covertly watched by men. Or, taking an inexplicable, perverse detour along Garrison Street (where the Mayweathers, Stonecrops, and Herrons live), or through a no-man's-land of tall grasses and briars adjacent to the Buffalo & Chautauqua yard. Another time following Juliet as she drifts along a brackish, evil-smelling ditch beside the chain-link railroad fence, a solitary, alluring figure, no more conscious of herself than a cat is conscious of itself, yet stepping with deliberation, fastidiously, pausing to examine—what? (Blue chicory flowers? Something impossibly alive, skittering on the surface of the brackish water? Or is it Juliet's own reflection she stares at, without recognition?) Royall would swear he can see the *shadow-Juliet* floating just behind his sister.

Royall isn't imagining this. It's as Ariah has said: there's something sunken, secret about Juliet. Something feral and untrustworthy. Royall feels a stab of embarrassment, seeing his sister at such an intimate moment. Yet he can't leave her, he's her brother and he loves her; he understands how vulnerable she is, in this rough neighborhood, unprotected except for him.

The fatherless Burnaby children.

Shame, shame. We know your name!

(Strange: no one has ever dared tease or taunt Royall Burnaby about his name. Yet he knows that Chandler was once harassed, and that Juliet is now, sometimes.)

(Royall is offended thinking about this. *His* name?)

He follows Juliet at a short distance, marveling that she hasn't glanced around, noticed him. Anyone could approach her: any predator! She crosses a field, crosses railroad tracks and slides down a graveled embankment and comes out at Forty-eighth Street which is partly a residential neighborhood of shabby brick and brownstone rowhouses like theirs, and partly a commercial neighborhood of small stores, taverns, a gas station. He sees, or believes he sees, the *shadow-Juliet* hovering beside her. And he sees guys watching her. Guys his age, and men. Some of these men are old enough to be their father. If not older. Bastards! Juliet walking without haste, listening to music inside her head, dreamy, distracted. Her lips are moist and slightly parted and there's the small scar on her upper lip and another, only just visible, at her left temple. Her breasts are clearly defined by the purple cotton sweater she's wearing, which is too tight for her, like her black flannel skirt, a year or more outgrown. Royall is offended: doesn't their mother notice how Juliet looks, leaving the house? Is he the only one who *sees*?

Juliet is passing the gas station where guys in their early twenties are hanging out, guys Royall knows, Juliet is unaware of them staring openly at her, nudging and grinning at one another. *Jully-ett. Burn-a-by. Oh baby!* Royall can't bear this any longer, he catches up with his sister, jarring her shoulder with his own. "Oh, Royall! Where'd you come from?" Juliet smiles, mildly startled, as a cat might blink when touched by a familiar hand, in an unfamiliar place.

Royall smells that Juliet-fragrance, wetted leaves, or bruised flowers. This, too, is maddening! Probably Juliet hasn't washed her heavy, windblown hair in a few days, or bathed. A flame passes over Royall's brain, of protest, outrage. He can't bear to see his sexually alluring younger sister so unconscious of herself, on Forty-eighth Street. Doesn't she know what guys are like? Doesn't she have a clue what sex *is*?

"Juliet. Where the hell are you going?"

"I'm going home."

"The long way around?"

Juliet smiles uncertainly. "Is it?"

Royall tries to keep his tone light, he loves his kid sister and maybe he's exaggerating, a little, the danger she's in, he doesn't want to offend or alarm her, but saying, "Hey, I'm serious: you need to wake up, see how guys are watching you. Don't you know where you are?" And Juliet says, hurt, "Royall, don't scold. I know where I am: Forty-eighth Street. Where are *you*?"

One of the guys watching Juliet Burnaby is the shaved-headed boy. Tramping through the undergrowth in the no-man's-land beside the railroad yard, following Juliet at a distance, discreetly, so that not even her jealous sharp-eyed brother Royall has seen him.

5

Shame, shame!

In the late winter of 1977 when the thaw began. When the monkey-voices began their jabbering and jeering. When Juliet wasn't happy with her classes, and with a song by Robert Schumann she was trying to learn ("An den Sonnenschein") and so abruptly she walked out of school, without an excuse cutting two afternoon classes and girls' chorus which was the most important single thing in her life (of which she dared speak) and she hitched a ride to the river (was hitch-hiking dangerous for a lone girl of fifteen in the waning years of the druggy 1970's in Niagara Falls, New York, climbing into a car with a stranger behind the wheel giving you a sidelong smile like a cat contemplating cream?) and hiked along the steep embankment above the river breathless in the wind, behind the guard railing (approximately eighteen inches high) that must have been replaced (where, exactly?) when Dirk Burnaby's car swerved out of control in a heavy rainstorm fifteen years ago and smashed through the railing to career into the river.

"I'm here. This is it."

Never had she come to this place before. A forbidden place. Her heart beat violently, in exaltation. Ariah hovered near, furious with her.

"If I love you, must I hate him? I won't."

There, it was said.

On the highway connecting Niagara Falls with Buffalo, by way of l'Isle Grand, traffic passed in a steady stream. It was mid-afternoon, and no rain. Vehicles in the outside right lane passed close beside the rushing Niagara River, separated by a gravel shoulder, the guard railing, and a few yards of steeply banked soil.

Juliet didn't know where her father's car had skidded and left the highway. It must have been somewhere along here. The guard railing appeared weathered and rusted uniformly, as if no section were newer than the rest. Of course the accident had happened long ago.

The car had plunged into the river just below the Deadline, where the river accelerated its speed, rushing by in a churning white-water rapids. And now with the spring thaw, the river was high. Juliet found herself staring at it, mesmerized. You could think that at any moment out of sheer exuberance or malevolence, the river might overflow the bank and flood the highway.

You could almost believe as the Indians once believed, that the Niagara River was a living thing, a spirit. There was a god of the river, and a god of The Falls. There were gods everywhere, invisible. Chandler said that the old gods were human appetites and passions and that these were never vanquished, only re-named. Yet the river required no name. "Naming" was silly, ridiculous. Useless. The river might come alive and all that you would know was that its nature was nothing human, and that no human being could survive for more than a few minutes, or seconds, in it.

A terrible death, in such a place. And alone.

Juliet felt weak suddenly. Her strength of defiance, arrogance, walking out of Niagara Falls High and hitching a ride and not giving a damn who saw her, faded. She understood the horror, for the first time. *It did happen. Here. A man died. My father.*

What a relief to think these words! Even the pain of the words, that left her faint, confused, was a relief.

For the next several minutes Juliet lost track of her surroundings, and of time. Slipping into one of her trance-like states, that often accompanied her music. When she sang, when she breathed, in a specific way. Dreamy though open-eyed. Unconsciously she moved from side to side, keeping a deliberate beat. *If I love my mother, I can love my father, too. And he needs me.*

The sound of the rushing water entered her trance. Juliet perceived a subtle, secret rhythm in this sound. Consolation, solace. *Juliet! Burn-a-by! Come to your father in the river.* She had never heard this voice so distinctly. In a tone so urgent yet matter-of-fact. The sun shifted in the sky. It had become a wan sullen sun, withdrawing. On the highway, truckers slowed to get a closer look at the solitary girl with the windblown hair standing so still at the edge of the river; but the girl was oblivious of them. Attentive, fiercely concentrating on something she heard, the girl was oblivious of her surroundings.

A male voice sounded harshly—"Miss? What are you doing there?"

A police cruiser marked Niagara Falls Police Department braked to an abrupt stop on the highway shoulder and one of the officers called to Juliet who seemed not to hear. For there was the wind, the incessant wind, and Juliet's hair whipping in the wind. "Miss? Stay where you are."

A male voice, loud. A voice accustomed to giving orders and to being obeyed without question.

If Juliet had begun to hear, she gave no indication at first. A sullen teenaged girl. Stubbornly not-hearing a cop yelling at her from a few yards away, and not turning to him; though seeing now the moving uniformed figure in the corner of her eye. He was approaching his quarry cautiously, as he'd been trained. He didn't want to frighten her and cause her to throw herself into the river.

"Miss? I'm talking to you. Look here."

The spell was broken. Already the voices had faded, withdrawn. Juliet turned, and climbed the embankment as if finally she'd heard the harsh authoritative voice. But her eyes were heavy-lidded, downcast. She refused to look up. Her mouth worked, silently. The police officer stood squarely in front of her, bulky in his steel-gray uniform. She saw with disdain his booted feet. She saw his polished belt, his holster. The pistol in the holster. She saw his ridiculous badge, conspicuously shiny as a sheriff's badge in a Hollywood movie. But she would not acknowledge his face, his eyes upon her. Not yet.

He was asking her sternly: why wasn't she in school? what was she doing in this dangerous place? didn't she see the warning signs? what was her name?

Juliet stood silent, staring at the ground. She was trapped, she couldn't escape. You can't run from a cop. He'd take her into custody, the power of the State was his.

Juliet swiped at her eyes, in a childlike gesture. In this instant she became a child, her mouth tremulous. She murmured she'd just come to the river to be alone—"To think about some things."

"Miss, didn't you see the signs out here? 'Warning: No Pedestrians.' 'Dangerous Area.' You don't want to get too close to this river, miss. You should know better."

Juliet nodded, trying not to cry. Oh, she would not cry! And how badly she wanted not to tell these hostile strangers her name.

In the back of the cruiser, separated from the police officers by a crude wire mesh, she wanted to ask *Am I under arrest?* But the mood was somber, a joke would be misunderstood.

And the police were being unexpectedly kind to Juliet. Once she'd obeyed, given in to their authority. The one who'd accosted her on the embankment was telling her now that he had a daughter her age, at St. Mary's; the driver, a younger man, observed her in the rearview mirror, and told her it wasn't "one hundred percent safe" for a girl like her, her age, and pretty, and alone, to be wandering in such places even in the daytime. "You understand what I'm saying, miss?"

How like Royall he sounded! Juliet murmured, "Yes, sir."

They drove her home to Baltic Street. She'd had to tell them her address, and her name. She'd seen a flicker of recognition in their faces when she told them *Burnaby*.

6

SUDDENLY IN THE HUMID, gnat-infested summer of 1977 there came into their lives Joseph Pankowski of whom Ariah would speak, with fond derision, as the "shoe-repair man"—"the Jew who likes music." Sometimes, "the Polish Jew, with the Irish setter."

It was difficult to discern how Ariah felt about Mr. Pankowski. She forbade Juliet to "breathe a word" of him to Chandler and Royall. Chandler would brood, and make too much of a casual, inconsequential friendship between two "left-behinds"; Royall would tease. And, Ariah warned, she was in no mood to be *teased*.

Juliet, who was more comfortable with adults than with people her own age, had never met anyone like Joseph Pankowski. He fascinated her as a being from another planet would fascinate. You would wish to tell such a being nothing of yourself, for your "self" could be of little significance; all that mattered was him, mysterious and elusive; yet you dared not be rude, and ask questions. And there was the man's wounded, stitched-together face, that drew the startled eyes of strangers, and made children stare.

And the tattoo on his left wrist. Of that, Juliet would never ask.

Yet Joseph Pankowski was not reticent. He talked freely, happily, of certain subjects. He was nervous, ardent, stammering in his enthusiasms. He had a weakness for Hollywood movies of the 1930's and 1940's, which he watched on late-night TV. He counted himself a baseball "fan." He was vehement in his belief that Eisenhower would prove to be the "last, great" president of the United States. (Years after the senator's death, he spoke bitterly of Joseph McCarthy as the "ugly face of the American Gestapo.") In his heavily accented English he embarrassed Juliet by telling her that her singing, especially of German lieder, gave him much joy. That Ariah's "brave" piano playing gave him much joy. That meeting them had "given hope" to his life.

Mr. Pankowski had been a widower for several years. He lived alone above his shoe-repair shop on South Quay. (A "mixed" neighborhood east of downtown.) His children, two sons, were grown and long gone from upstate New York. And no grandchildren, though both were married. "These young people whine, 'Why should we bring children into such an evil world?' As if they were us, and had lived their parents' lives in Europe. They break our hearts." Ariah, uneasy at such personal revelations, said, "Isn't that the role of children, to break their parents' hearts?"

But Mr. Pankowski wished to speak seriously. That was the man's failing, in Ariah's eyes: he could not, or would not, make jokes where jokes badly needed to be made.

In Prospect Park where they went for open-air summer concerts, Ariah walked swiftly ahead, impatient to find three seats. Juliet lingered with Mr. Pankowski who walked stiff-legged, rubbing pensively at the nape of his neck. He said, " 'Evil,' 'good'—what is this vocabulary? God allows evil for the simple reason that God makes no distinction between evil and good. As God makes no distinction between predator and prey. I did not lose my first, young family to evil but to human actions, and—only think!—a marvel of its kind, unspeakable!—the actions of lice, devouring them alive in the death camp. And so you must grant to God what is God and not try to think of what you have lost, for that way is madness."

Juliet would pretend she had not heard some of this.

No, she had not heard. The man's speech was unreliable, especially when he spoke passionately.

Not that evening in Prospect Park but another evening, when Ariah was out of earshot, Juliet asked boldly to see the tattoo on Mr.

Pankowski's wrist that looked like nothing more than dark ink beginning to fade. Yet it would never fade for it was stitched into the man's very skin.

B6115

Wanting to ask *Why live, then? It's God that is mad.*

7

YET, IN SECRET, Juliet wishes to believe. Desperately, Juliet wishes to believe.

A vision! Such visions came, sometimes, to Christians who were special, "devout."

Ariah had taken Juliet to a dozen churches in Niagara Falls by the time Juliet was twelve, and in each of these churches Juliet had watched the others, the "worshippers," through her linked-together fingers brought up to partly hide her face, thinking *Are they serious? Is this real? Why can't I feel what they are feeling?* Especially, Juliet was baffled by worshippers sobbing with evident joy, tears streaming down their contorted faces. And Ariah tried to believe, too. Often Ariah volunteered her services as an organist or a choir director. But within a few months, or weeks, Ariah would grow bored, restless. *Such silly people. I can't respect them.*

Growing up in Niagara Falls, Juliet has been aware for years of the local legend of Our Lady of The Falls. The story of the little Irish dairy maid and the Virgin Mary who appeared to the dairy maid in the mists of the Horseshoe Falls. In ninth grade, she made a (secret) pilgrimage to the shrine three miles north of the city, on foot; she has brooded over the dairy maid's fate, which was to have been taken in by well-to-do Catholics who took care of her during her pregnancy and adopted her baby when it was born, and found employment for her in a family-owned canning factory. With a part of her mind Juliet is skeptical yet with another part of her mind she identifies with the fifteen-year-old scorned by everyone, even relatives; the girl who'd been drawn to the river hoping to cleanse the world of herself but who was granted, instead, a miraculous vision.

Ariah has said there is no God, and numerous are His prophets.

Juliet is too much Ariah's daughter to believe in Roman Catholic superstitions and yet: in her loneliness she has fantasized that a vision might come to her if she were utterly sincere about wanting, needing, intending to die.

I would not need to be saved if the vision came to me. The vision would be enough.

She has wondered if, at the instant of his death, as his car skidded into the guard railing, smashed through and plunged into the river, her father, Dirk Burnaby, had experienced a vision.

And what that vision might be.

She has wondered *Is Death itself a vision?*

Luckily, Ariah never learned that Juliet had made a pilgrimage to the Shrine of Our Lady of The Falls. Or Chandler, or Royall who would have teased her.

The shrine was a stunning disappointment. Naively Juliet had expected something very different, more inward, spiritual. But Our Lady of The Falls swarmed with tourists. There were chartered buses, enormous parking lots, the "Pilgrim Center Restaurant" and souvenir shop; curiosity-seekers toting cameras, ailing individuals of various ages and degrees of disability in wheelchairs being pushed gamely up ramps, and the faithful on their knees reciting the rosary with bowed heads, conspicuously meek and adoring of the colossal Virgin Mary, thirty feet high, looming above them from the basilica dome. The statue was solid white marble, visible for miles, grotesque as a mannequin amid the hilly countryside; promotional material for the shrine boasted it weighed more than twenty tons. Juliet stared at the Virgin's vapid female face with its blind eyes and smile bland as that of a woman in a TV commercial. "You! You are not the one."

What a betrayal of the dairy maid's vision of 1891! Juliet was angry on behalf of the girl, a girl so like herself, yearning and helpless.

The Irish girl had had her vision and it had been stolen from her, debased even as it was magnified, just as the girl had had her baby and the baby was taken from her.

Nothing to forgive. Love, and you do God's will.

On this mist-shrouded June morning as she makes her way barefoot as a penitent to the river Juliet is thinking not of the shrine, not of the tourists and the ugly looming statue but of the dairy maid, her lost sister; and of the vision that is promised. *Come! Come to your father in The Falls.*

8

"WHO IS—?"

Ariah wakes with a start, thinking there's someone in the room with her. Or in her bed.

Among the twisted sheets. (Which husband? Which year is this?)

Her ridiculous heart is thudding. Like most chronic insomniacs Ariah often lies awake for hours, wretched interminable hours, then falls into a stuporous sleep for an hour or two only to wake exhausted, with a thudding heart and a parched mouth as if she's been dragged by nightmare-horses across an acrid, stony plain.

This day in June. These days. Infamy. Oh, if she could sleep her stuporous sleep for a solid month!

A freight train has wakened her, damned *Baltimore & Ohio* boxcars rattling through her skull. And something scratching at her bedroom door, with shy persistence. Zarjo?

Ariah would snap, "Bad dog!" Except she knows that this intelligent, sensitive animal who has lived with her for sixteen years, trained by Ariah herself, would not dare wake her for a trifle.

What time is it? Just past 6 A.M. An overcast morning. A few birds call tentatively to one another in the jungly back yard. For a dazed sullen moment Ariah can't recall if this is supposed to be a season of warm weather, or cold; if both her sons have left her, or only just Chandler.

No. Royall has left, too.

But there's Juliet: her daughter.

And there's Zarjo, her best friend, sensing she's awake, scratching more emphatically at the door, and beginning to whimper.

9

Between us there's a secret.

For years he has been watching her. Not continuously, not every day. But often. Juliet has never consciously looked for him, sensing that she should not, she must not. Ariah has warned her not to "make eye contact" with strangers or any others "who might do a young girl harm." And so Juliet has shyly looked away, Juliet has purposefully turned away, learning to be unknowing, unconscious. More and more she lives inside music. In her head music plays continuously, coming from a mysterious source as light comes from a mysterious source called "sun"—"the sun."

Yet, he's there. The shaved-headed boy. Waiting.

Juliet first became aware of him, the something strange, something special about him, when she was in fifth or sixth grade. The slow realization, gradual as the change of season, that she sees him just a little too often, at approximately the same distance, observing her in silence: on Baltic Street, on Forty-eighth, on Ferry. On Garrison (where he lives in a barn-sized clapboard house at the intersection of Veterans' Road). Sometimes she sees him when she's waiting at the bus stop, to go downtown. And outside the public library downtown. Perhaps she sees him most frequently when she's trailing dreamily through Baltic Park, coming home from school.

Rarely, in fact never, has Juliet noticed the shaved-headed boy watching her when she's with other people. Only when she's alone.

A big boy, impassive, ugly. Unsmiling. She glances up to see, at a distance of thirty or more feet, something fixed and fanatic in his eyes.

Between us there's a secret.

One day you will know.

Why hasn't Juliet told anyone, not Ariah, not Chandler, not her brother Royall, about the shaved-headed boy? She might have told a teacher at school. She might have told a classmate, a girlfriend.

Why, Juliet doesn't want to think.

From childhood she seems to have known that to speak of the shaved-headed boy to another person would be futile.

He has never approached her. He has never spoken her name in derision, like other boys. He has never harassed her, threatened her.

One day you'll know.

This past year, Juliet has seen the boy, now grown into a hulking young man, at her choral concerts at the high school and elsewhere. She has even (this is more alarming, of course) seen him at rehearsals in the high school auditorium. Stonecrop always sits by himself in the last row, in the shadows. He's big, but can pass still for a high school student. Juliet wants to think that he doesn't hate her, doesn't want to harass her or ridicule her. Where other boys murmur *Jully-ett! Burn-a-by!* making lewd sucking noises with their mouths, the shaved-headed boy is silent. Waiting.

This, too, is a secret: how, several years ago when Juliet was twelve, in seventh grade, Stonecrop intervened when a gang of older boys were tormenting Juliet on her way home from school.

These were ninth graders with surnames like Mayweather, Herron, D'Amato, Sheehan. They teased and harassed other girls, not exclusively Juliet, but Juliet had become their favorite target. *Why do they hate me, is it my face? My name?* The boys were noisy and gregarious and resented it that Juliet Burnaby seemed indifferent to them. Her dreamy distracted manner provoked them. Her way of staring at the ground, or into the distance. (Hearing music in her head?) The scars on her mouth and forehead seemed to intrigue them. They were boys with their own scars. They brushed near her, jostled her. Like dogs crowding her. *Jully-ett. Hey: who bit your face?* Not knowing if she was a disfigured girl, a freak, or if she was attractive, sexy. They dared one another to kiss her. *Scar-face! Burn-a-by!* If no adults were around their play became rougher. Their faces became flushed, their eyes shone with a greedy hunger. That afternoon Juliet had not been able to elude them and they'd forced her into an alley just off Baltic Street, hardly two blocks from her home. The Mayweather boy tugged at Juliet's hair, the Herron boy tugged at the collar of her new sweater. If she'd been hearing music in her head, imagining her own voice lifted in song, it was a crude awakening now, these grinning boys surrounding her. Why couldn't she scream, why did her throat shut up in panic? She was desperate to escape but could only push and shove and weakly slap at their busy hands. When she tried to run they blocked her, encircling. Loudly laughing and jeering, egging one another on. *Jully-ett! Jully-ett! Burn-a-by! Who bit your face?* Juliet's sweater was ripped, her school books knocked to the ground and kicked about. The attack by these boys was more protracted than it had ever been before, Juliet was beginning to panic. She knew what boys can do to girls: if the girls are alone, and helpless. She had no clear knowledge yet she knew.

Yet she was trying not to cry. Never give your enemies the satisfaction, Ariah warned. Never show them tears.

"Hey. Little shits!"

There came into the alley, on the run, fists swinging, Bud Stonecrop the cop's son, bearing down on the boys like a pit bull. He moved swiftly and without warning. He seized Clyde Mayweather's head in one big hand, as you'd grab a basketball, and slammed it against Ron Herron's head. He struck the D'Amato kid with his fist, breaking and bloodying his nose. He kneed the Sheehan kid in his puny groin, followed this with a kick to his belly. The boys stumbled back, astonished by the attack, and by the ferocity of the attack. Those who could run, ran scattered and bawling. Stonecrop outweighed the biggest of the ninth grade boys by more than thirty pounds. He stood panting and wordless above Juliet who crouched, still shielding her head against her assailants. Her sweater, a pink embroidered cardigan she'd bought with baby-sitting earnings, was torn at the neck, and buttons were gone. Stonecrop mumbled what sounded like, "Shit-faced fuckers. Should of killed 'em." He stooped to retrieve one of Juliet's buttons on the ground. And another. These were pink mother-of-pearl buttons, tiny in the palm of Stonecrop's massive hand. Seeing that Juliet was trying awkwardly to hold her ripped sweater together, Stonecrop swiftly removed his T-shirt, and handed it to her grunting what sounded like, "Here."

Juliet took the shirt from the shaved-headed boy and numbly pulled it over her head. A gray cotton T-shirt, not clean, damp beneath the arms, voluminous on Juliet as a tent. The right sleeve hung over her shoulder at half-mast. Embarrassed, Juliet murmured, "Thanks." The shaved-headed boy was a little older than Royall, no more than eighteen, but with the thick muscled torso of an adult man. Juliet had a fleeting impression (she was looking away, not at him) that he was covered in a bear-like pelt. His shirt, on her, smelled of briny sweat and fried onions. Juliet would wear it home and enter the house at 1703 Baltic undetected by her usually vigilant mother (Ariah was at the rear, with a piano student) and later that evening she would launder it tenderly by hand and hang it to dry in her room and next day return it in a plain paper bag addressed BUD STONE-CROP and placed on the front porch railing of the ramshackle house at 522 Garrison Street.

There would be no further close contact between the shaved-headed boy and Juliet Burnaby, no words exchanged, for more than four years.

10

STONECROP! In the Baltic Street neighborhood of Niagara Falls, New York in the late 1960's he'd begun to acquire a reputation while still in junior high. He was *Stonecrop the cop's son.* Sometimes, to those who knew his family, and his father the NFPD sergeant, he was *Bud, Jr.*

But you never called Stonecrop by that name. You never called Stonecrop by any name. You avoided Stonecrop, even looking at him. You didn't want Stonecrop to look at you, to register you in what would appear to be his dim-flickering yet vigilant consciousness, as you would not want a predator of any species, a shark for instance, to register your existence. In childhood, that early instinct to survive by becoming invisible.

By the age of twelve Stonecrop had grown to a height of nearly six feet and a weight of one hundred eighty pounds and he would continue growing through adolescence. Even among the big-boned Stonecrops he was distinctive. He had the build of an upright, engorged blood sausage about to burst its casing, and his face was of that hue, hot and hard. His natural smile was a grimace. His head suggested the density and durability of a concrete block. His hair, stone-colored, was brutally shaved at the back and sides of his head (by a barber who happened to be an uncle) and was short-cut at the crown, harshly stubbled as a winter cornfield. His eyes were small, steely and alert and antic as pinballs. His discolored teeth were spade-shaped and his nose had been flattened at birth, and could not be broken or made to bleed by any blow. It was said of Stonecrop that already in elementary school he'd begun to sprout ominously thick, wiry hairs on his stocky body. His cock grew weekly. In the boys' locker room it was observed to be always semi-erect; the other boys soon learned to avoid looking at him with the instinctive terror of an individual armed with a three-inch penknife confronted by an adversary with a machete. Yet, in the presence of girls, Stonecrop was withdrawn, aloof or indifferent. Girls said of him he made them *shiver*.

Stonecrop was the youngest son of NFPD sergeant Bud Stonecrop, a locally known, controversial police officer who'd retired young. The Stonecrops were a large Niagara Falls clan, married into the Mayweathers and the O'Ryans, but alliances between families, especially boy cousins, were inconstant. The Stonecrops of Garrison Street were not invariably on good terms with the Stonecrops of Fifty-third Street or their Mayweather neighbors. Bud, Jr. was a reliable friend only when he wished to be; but he could always be counted upon to be a reliable, treacherous enemy. While in school he ran with a select gang of boys of his approximate size, background, and temperament, but more often Stonecrop was alone, a brooding boy. He cut classes frequently but never received any grade lower than C—. No teacher would have wished to flunk him, and "teach" him another year. Yet he was often earnest, even somber in his classrooms. He scowled at textbooks as if they were printed in a foreign language in which he could pick out familiar words now and then. He quit school abruptly after his sixteenth birthday, in his junior year, but before quitting he'd insisted upon being allowed to take a much-derided girl's course known as "home economics"; in this course, to the surprise and delight of his girl classmates and their teacher, Stonecrop excelled as a cook.

A cook! But no one laughed.

It was said that Stonecrop's windpipe had been injured in a street fight and that was why he spoke in mumbles and grunts; in fact, Stonecrop had a deep, hoarse voice but a tendency to stammer, out of shyness. It was Bud, Sr., his father, who'd been severely injured in the throat, as well as elsewhere on his body: the sergeant had been ambushed in Mario's parking lot, beaten nearly to death with tire irons by assailants described as "coke-crazed Negroes" with a vendetta against him. (This was the official police report. At the first precinct, where he'd been assigned for most of his career, and among Stonecrop's relatives, other facts were known about the beating and his subsequent physical and mental condition.) He'd been retired from the NFPD with honors and a full disability pension at the age of forty-two.

It was expected that Bud, Jr. would go into police work, like his father. There were police officers, parole officers, prison guards among the relatives. But from the age of eleven Stonecrop had been drawn to his uncle Duke's Bar & Grill on Fourth Street; after quitting school he began working there full-time. Duke's Bar & Grill was near the first precinct and the City-County Building and had long been a popular hangout for NFPD officers and staff and for burnt-out veterans from the district attorney's office. Always there was a shifting contingent of women at Duke's, many of them lonely divorcées. Already by early evening the atmosphere in both the bar and the adjoining restaurant was boisterous, smoky and convivial. Jukeboxes in both favored elemental rock music of the 1950's and country-and-western, turned up high. The TV above the bar was always on, broadcasting sports events, though no one could hear it. In the kitchen of the restaurant, Stonecrop and co-workers listened to deafening 1970's rock music on a portable radio. The older kitchen workers appeared to be fond of Stonecrop, the owner's nephew; he was willing to do what they called shitwork, scraping plates, hauling out garbage, scouring away grease and washing dishes. To reward him, the cook sometimes let him prepare meals, under his supervision.

Of course no one in the Stonecrop family approved of Bud, Jr. as a kitchen worker. Was this a joke? A kid that size, and not dumb? (Anyway, not so dumb. He was at least as bright as his old man who'd graduated from Police Academy and made quite a lucrative career as a cop "with connections.") There was continual pressure on Stonecrop to get a "real" job, a "serious" job, a job "fitting for a man." Through relatives he began working with Parks & Recreation but nearly amputated his right foot working with a chainsaw. For a hellish winter season he was a rescue worker for Niagara County, going out with snow removal trucks on ten-hour emergency missions. One of his better-paying jobs was at a local quarry but he'd hated such zombie work and wound up drinking with older guys though he was under age at the time, returning home drunk, or not returning home. By the age of seventeen Stonecrop had grown to six feet two, two hundred twenty pounds, and so there was talk among the relatives of training him as a boxer. Stonecrop's semi-invalided father Bud, Sr. began to fantasize Bud, Jr. as the next heavyweight champion of the world, returning the crown to the Caucasian race where it belonged. (There had been no American white champion since Rocky Marciano who'd retired undefeated in 1956.) But Stonecrop was a reluctant boxer. He was a street fighter by instinct, with a tendency to throw powerful round-house rights from the shoulder, and so he had no patience, let alone skill, for more devious strategies of jabbing, slipping punches, moving adroitly on his feet. Stonecrop could intimidate an opponent with his size only if his opponent was not his size, or larger. At the gym on Front Street, training half-heartedly for his first Golden Gloves tournament (which would be held in Buffalo), Stonecrop became sulky, sullen. His small antic eyes became bloodshot, his lips swollen and cracked. He had difficulty breathing through his nose, which was all cartilage, now flatter than ever; after a few rounds, he panted like an ox. His eighty-year-old trainer admonished him as you'd admonish a young ox: "Boxing isn't about getting hit, kid. It's about hitting the other guy. See?" Stonecrop lacked the language to protest. Flat-footed and mute he stood in the ring allowing blows to rain upon his unprotected head, face, torso. His big white body, covered in the damp pelt, exuded an air of stoic, wounded dignity, brooding upon its curious fate. *I don't want to hit some guy. I want to feed him.*

In his first Golden Gloves bout, at the Buffalo Armory, Stonecrop went down in fifty seconds of the first round, felled by a sixteen-year-old black heavyweight, and was counted out by the appalled referee.

In this way, Stonecrop was allowed to quit the gym forever and to return to Duke's Bar & Grill, working longer hours. (Still, his uncle paid him hardly more than the minimal wage.) Stonecrop's father, sinking by degrees into more serious illness, often semi-paralyzed, would not forgive him, and never asked after Stonecrop's work at the restaurant. When the cook quit, Stonecrop stepped in. He learned to execute orders swiftly and with increasing confidence. Though within a few months he became restless with the grill menu, preparing fatty hamburgers and cheeseburgers, pork sausage, fried eggs, bacon, buns, and toast, frying everything in shimmering grease. As a boy of ten he'd begun preparing meals at home in the absence of his mother and he had his own ideas about food, in defiance of his Uncle Duke. Lost in scowling concentration in grease-splattered apron and cook's hat, slope-shouldered, head bowed over the chopping block, Stonecrop ventured to insert chopped Bermuda onions, green peppers and chili peppers into ground beef; he experimented with novel ways of preparing even Canadian bacon, Birds Eye frozen fish, chicken wings and chicken-in-the-basket, french fries. Stonecrop annoyed his uncle by using new types of pickles, potato chips, cole slaw. He developed his own spicy version of Campbell's tomato soup, a staple of the restaurant's menu, laced with spices and chunks of fresh tomato. He developed his own Italian dishes, primarily spaghetti and meatballs. His corned-beef hash and special chili began to find customers. In time, Stonecrop would develop an interest in "greens" other than iceberg lettuce, and in fresh vegetables instead of canned or frozen. Perversely, he came to prefer chunk cheddar cheese to sliced process American cheese for burgers, which narrowed Duke's margin of profit. He had his own ideas about rib steaks, "chicken-fried" steaks,

London broil and pork chops. Pork and beans, breaded halibut and cod cakes, even mashed potatoes. When customers began to remark upon, or to complain of, the new, exotic taste of Stonecrop's burgers, his Uncle Duke lit into him in fury. "You little cocksucker, what's this? What kind of shit is this?" The older man, shorter than Stonecrop by inches and slighter by perhaps thirty pounds, stabbed open a hamburger to reveal incriminating chips of onion, pepper, chili pepper in the meat. He took a bite, chewed suspiciously and took another bite, shook ketchup onto what remained of the meat and tasted it again. He conceded, "Well. It ain't bad. It's different, a little like dago food. But this goes on the menu as a special—Bud's Burger. And next time you experiment in my kitchen, kid, tell me beforehand, or I'll break your ass." Red-faced, sullen, Stonecrop wiped his sweaty face on his apron and mouthed *Screw you*, so that the kitchen laughed loudly.

As the months passed, Stonecrop began to acquire customers who liked his food. The burnt-out ADAs and the lonely divorcées were among the first.

As Budd, Sr.'s health deteriorated, Bud, Jr. spent more time away from the house on Garrison. When he wasn't working at the restaurant he cruised the city, along the river and into Buffalo and back in a meandering loop. He had a second-hand Thunderbird he'd bought with the intention of repairing but neglected instead. Sometimes he prowled the neighborhood on foot. He asked no girls out, had no apparent interest in girls. (That anyone knew of. It was speculated that Stonecrop might have had a secret life.) A hulky boy with a scowling, flattened, blemished face, dishwater eyes and that brutal shaved head, Stonecrop exerted a perverse attraction upon certain of the female customers at Duke's, some of whom were observed waiting (in the bar) for the kitchen to close at 11 P.M., to take Stonecrop home with them. Though the shaved-headed boy's mother had been missing for more than a decade, yet Stonecrop was frequently spoken of, by such women, as a "motherless boy"—"that poor, motherless Stonecrop boy."

Stonecrop's father was an invalid at home, tended primarily by an older, unmarried sister. When he'd been in better condition, Bud, Sr. had made everyone in the family sign a document promising never to check him into a nursing home. Among the Stonecrops, as among most families in the Baltic Street neighborhood, such a desperate measure was rarely taken. *Better to die at home, with your own kind.*

Better for whom, wasn't asked. There were some things you just didn't do, out of duty and guilt.

It was observed that Stonecrop had become increasingly tense and short-tempered over his father's decline. He'd fought with Bud, Sr. for years but maybe he loved the old man after all? Stonecrop was a mysterious boy, evolving into a more mysterious young man. By this time he'd dropped his old friends. Sometimes he took a weekend off from the restaurant and disappeared. At Duke's, as his cooking came to be more appreciated, and new customers joined the old regulars, Stonecrop had a way of storming out of the kitchen if his feelings were hurt by his uncle. Duke fired him, and rehired him; and fired him again. But there were local restaurants keen to hire him, at good wages, so Duke hurriedly rehired him, grudgingly raising his salary. Stonecrop's sense of family obligation must have been such, he kept returning to Duke's Bar & Grill, like a kicked large-breed dog warily returning to his seemingly repentant master. "The little bastard has a mind of his own," Duke said, with grudging approval. "But the premises are mine." The Stonecrop men were not given to tactful speech, especially in their business dealings. When Duke called his hulking nephew "asshole"—"little shit"—"piss-pot"—"cocksucker"—Stonecrop reacted with indifference, knowing these to be backhanded forms of endearment; but when his uncle called him "stupid"—"retard"—"deaf-mute" in front of witnesses, Stonecrop reacted with violence. He might rip off his apron, throw it down and stalk out of the restaurant. He might smash plates, overturn platters of hot steaming food, or plates piled with garbage. Once, Stonecrop was observed seizing a heavy, hot iron skillet off a stove and advancing upon the older man with the apparent intention of killing him. The shaved-headed boy had had to be forcibly restrained by several NFPD officers who happened to be eating in the restaurant. "If we hadn't stopped him, the crazy kid would've broke Duke's skull." This episode quickly became part of the Stonecrop family legend, recounted frequently, with mirth.

One evening, Royall Burnaby and his sister, Juliet, were having dinner at Duke's, seated in a booth against the outer wall, and there hovered Stonecrop in the kitchen doorway, brooding and impassive. This was an evening in November 1977, several weeks after Royall had moved away from home; Juliet had come to visit him in his apartment on Fourth Street. Brother and sister were talking quietly together. "Mom misses you," Juliet said. "She keeps sighing as if her heart is broken." Royall shrugged. With a knife and a fork he was idly beating out a rock rhythm on the Formica tabletop, accompanying Bill Haley's classic "Shake, Rattle, and Roll" on the jukebox. Since moving out of the house on Baltic Street, Royall seemed older; even to himself he seemed more self-sufficient, and more secretive. He wasn't nearly so lonely as he'd thought he might be. "I guess I miss you, too," Juliet said, ducking her head as if embarrassed.

The record ended abruptly, leaving Royall exposed. Awkwardly he said, "It doesn't mean anybody loves anybody less, not living with them. It just means . . ." Royall's voice trailed off, uncertain.

Royall had ordered a large bowl of chili, into which he'd crumbled a handful of oyster crackers, and Juliette had ordered a Spanish omelette. Both Royall's bowl and Juliet's plate had been heated. On Juliet's plate, in addition to the omelette, was a garnish of baby carrots and parsley, and thin sliced cantaloupe arranged like petals. The omelette was so exotically spiced and so packed with stir-fried tomatoes, onions, chopped green and red peppers, Juliet was having difficulty finishing it. What an enormous meal! It was like opening a familiar drawer, and something magical balloons out, you can't quite recognize. And the cook had sent out a hefty basket of baking powder biscuits, hot from the oven. The waitress said, "He says it's for you, it's extra. No charge." Royall regarded Juliet's plate doubtfully. In an undertone he said, "That looks sort of runny. Is it any good?" Juliet said, "I think an omelette is supposed to be soft inside. Folded over, and soft inside." Ariah, a hasty cook, had always prepared omelettes for the family by simply scrambling eggs and dumping them into a frying pan and letting the mass puff and whiten and congeal to something resembling a pancake; often, Ariah's omelettes tasted of scorch. Royall had grown up with simple, crude tastes; he trusted only eggs that were toughly textured, even rubbery. Juliet said, "This is the most delicious omelette I've ever had. Want some?"

"Thanks, no! I'll take your word for it."

They saw that Stonecrop, the shaved-headed cook who was only a year or two older than Royall, had emerged from the kitchen to the rear and was behind the counter now, preparing to clean the grill. He'd been watching Royall and Juliet covertly but now he appeared to take no notice of them. Royall called over, meaning to be polite, "Hey, Bud. This is terrific. Both our dinners. *You* made this?" Royall meant well, but Stonecrop's warm, flushed face darkened with blood as if he'd been insulted. He returned to the kitchen abruptly, the door swinging shut in his wake. Royall stared after him, struck by Stonecrop's steely, anguished stare in the instant before he'd turned away. Juliet was folding her paper napkin, in silence. She'd eaten about two-thirds of the omelette and most of a biscuit and all of the lovingly arranged garnish.

Royall muttered, "Shit. I guess I said the wrong thing."

Driving Juliet home to Baltic Street, Royall said, "That guy, Bud Stonecrop. He looks at me funny sometimes. What about you, Juliet?" Juliet murmured she wasn't sure. "Like there's something between us," Royall said. "But—what?" Royall was uneasy thinking that the shaved-headed Stonecrop, of whom it was rumored he was built like a horse, had a thing for Royall's eighty-nine-pound sister, at this time fifteen years old.

11

Shame, shame's the name. You know your name.
    Come to your father in The Falls.

It's the anniversary of his death. The voices are clearer now. Less confused, and less reproachful. As if what Juliet will do, she has already accomplished. Like the fifteen-year-old Irish girl. Penitent, breathless, numbed bare feet in the wet grass.

Juliet! Burn-a-by! Come come to us.

Now at the railing above The Falls. Her hands gripping the wet railing. Her face wet with blown mist. Thrashing white-water rapids like the muscles of a great beast rippling beneath its skin. How many times Juliet has seen the Niagara River at close range and yet it's different at this twilit time before morning, the eastern sky banked with cloud like dirty concrete yet laced with a faint golden-bronze light, it's different, or Juliet is different, light-headed yet somber, yet smiling. Regretting only that she didn't leave a note for her family, and now it's too late.

No turning back from The Falls.

Burn-a-by! Burn-a-by! Come.

The voices are more sympathetic, at close range. Juliet isn't so frightened now. She isn't unhappy. It isn't unhappiness nor even sorrow or grief that has drawn her here. It's knowing that this is right, this is the right place, and this is the right time. The voices in The Falls are not threats, and not admonitions. She hears them now as music. Like *My country 'tis-of-thee* she'd sung with other children at Baltic Street Elementary and the music teacher had singled her out for praise though Juliet had not known what *'tis-of-thee* meant. Like *Silent night holy night round yon virgin mother-and-child* which was the most beautiful of the Christmas carols she'd sung but she had no idea what *round you virgin* meant, nor even, somehow, for she'd heard it as a single phrase, *mother-and-child*, and there were *heavenly hosts* and *hallelujah* utterly mysterious to her, codified, like the vast world itself, in adult speech. Have faith, trust in that vast world to give comfort to you and to protect you, Juliet had tried, she'd tried to have faith, but she had failed. But now she would redeem herself, as others had redeemed themselves, in The Falls.

It isn't yet 6:30 A.M. Except for the overcast sky, it would be dawn. The embankment along the river, facing Goat Island, which will be crowded with tourists in a few hours, is deserted now. A heavy yellowish fog has been slowly lifting but billowing clouds are being blown westward from The Falls and as Juliet stares there's a sudden schism in the cloud-impacted eastern sky and a glow as of phosphorescence in the river and in her mesmerized light-headed state Juliet wishes to believe that this is a sign; this is the vision meant for her alone, as the Irish dairy maid had a vision meant for her alone, long ago; a lightning-stroke of sunlight, and rising from the Gorge a giant, shapeless figure, nearly opaque columns of mist teasingly forming, dissolving, and reforming continuously out of the great Gorge. Amid the deafening roar of The Falls the near-inaudible but unmistakable murmur *Juliet! Juliet! Come come to me it's time.*

Juliet smiles. It's time!

Blindly, she's been edging along the railing, gripping it tight in both hands. By instinct, like a trapped creature seeking the most pragmatic way out. As if there might be a little gate as in a fairy tale, she might open, and step through. But the railing is waist-high and there is no little gate and so she will have to hoist herself over it and her young, ardent muscles tense to execute this feat as she has held her body in thrilled readiness drawing breath to sing and she has sung her heart out and been redeemed in singing, all shame obliterated, even her curse of a name forgotten. It's time!

And then, someone swiftly approaches her. So swiftly, Juliet hasn't seen him until now. He speaks words she can't decipher. He's gripping her hand, prying her fingers loose from the railing. It must be—Royall? Her brother taking hold of her so familiarly, as if he had the right? Juliet struggles frantic as a trapped cat, it isn't Royall but the massive shaved-headed Stonecrop, twice her size and looming over her, grunting what sounds like, "No! C'mon." Within seconds he has pulled Juliet away from the railing. Back from the embankment, and onto the grass. Stonecrop is so strong, and so unhesitating in his strength, it's as if Juliet has been lifted by an elemental force, wind or an earthquake, her individual will blotted out, of no more consequence than a struck sparrow. Juliet protests, "Leave me alone! You're not my brother." She's furious, this young man has no right to interfere, no right even to touch her. He's panting through his mouth like a winded animal. Hasn't shaved in some time, the lower part of his face glints a smudged, steely blue. His expression is embarrassed, dismayed, stoic and determined. He isn't going to release her though she's struggling against him, slaps and kicks at him, tries to claw his knuckles. "Let me go! Leave me alone! You have no right! I hate you!"

But it's too early. Prospect Park is deserted. No one sees, and no one will prevent Stonecrop from lifting Juliet as one might lift a small, resisting child, walking with her kicking and trying to elbow him, his massive arms closed about her, awkwardly yet unhesitatingly Stone-crop walks Juliet across an edge of parkland, to his parked Thunder-bird and safety.

12

"MOM? Where's Zarjo?"

"In the back yard."

"No. He isn't there."

"Of course he's there, honey. Don't be silly."

"Mom, he isn't! He's gone."

That terrible time. Those days of misery, anguish. Never will the Burnabys forget. Calling, crying *Zarjo! Zarjo!* imagining that at any moment the dog would reappear panting and repentant and anxious to be hugged. In the neighborhood, in the park and the railroad yard and along the smelly drainage ditch, along streets and sidewalks and alleys desperately peering into neighbors' yards, daring to ring door-bells, stopping strangers on the sidewalk, asking, pleading *Have you seen our missing dog, his name is Zarjo, he's a mixed cocker spaniel and beagle, a small dog, four years old, a friendly dog but shy with strangers, no he doesn't bite, he barks sometimes if he's nervous, he slipped his leash and ran away and we think he must be lost* showing snapshots of Zarjo, to us he seemed such a beautiful dog and yet to strangers only just a small buff-colored dog of no distinction, immediately forgettable *His name is Zarjo, we love him, we want him back, if you see him here's our telephone num-ber*. Our throats hoarse, and eyes reddened from crying.

Even Ariah cried, in terror of losing Zarjo. On this raw, awful oc-casion, it seemed that Ariah was allowing tears.

Ariah, panicked and pale with emotion! Grief, shock, a wild look in Mom's face, and her dull-red hair unplaited, messy. On the tele-phone, her voice rising, pleading. We had never seen our mother in such a state and we were frightened of her and our fear of her and for her was mixed with our fear that Zarjo was gone, we would never see Zarjo again. We had not known how we loved the feisty little dog and now our love for him hurt like acid clawing at our flesh.

Ariah's piano students rang the front doorbell and one of us went to answer, explaining our mom isn't feeling well, she's got a bad headache and is lying down, she says to practice the same as last week and she'll see you next week, she says she's sorry.

This terrible time. At first Zarjo was missing for just part of a day and then Zarjo was missing for an entire day and then for a day and a night (except none of us could sleep, we kept vigil for Zarjo on the front porch believing he might wander home in the night ravenously hungry) and at last Zarjo was missing for forty-eight hours and our tears were depleted, or nearly. We roamed ever farther from home, in concentric circles fanning out beyond Veterans' Road, beyond the high school, the hospital, crossing Sixtieth Street and into a zone of fierce citrus-flamey smells that stung our eyes more cruelly than salt tears had done. *Zarjo! Zarjo! Where are you, what has happened to you, please come home.*

None of us thinking whose puppy Zarjo had been. Who had brought Zarjo into our lives. None of us uttering such a fact aloud.

We were shameless ringing doorbells. Showing the wrinkled snapshots again. Interrupting women vacuuming their houses, nursing babies, watching TV. Strangers' dogs trotted eagerly to us, sniffed our extended hands. *Zarjo! Take us to find Zarjo.*

Of the children, Juliet cried the most. Helpless, hopeless, her little-girl heart broken.

"Honey, don't cry. It doesn't help a thing. It just tears at us all. If crying helped, we'd have Zarjo back by now."

There was Ariah bravely trying to maintain some semblance of calm. Ariah, the mother. The responsible head of this unmoored abandoned near-destitute family living in a crumbling rowhouse on Baltic Street. Oh, Ariah wanted to be strong, stoic, a model for her children in this time of anxiety.

One of us found her lying half-dressed on her bed. Thin white arms shielding her face. Saying in a slow halting voice she didn't know what was wrong with her, she was so tired, could barely lift her head. *If Zarjo doesn't come back I don't want to live.*

Later, Ariah would deny having said such a thing.

Later, Ariah would deny the hysteria of these hours.

Her children were discovering the remarkable friendliness of certain of their neighbors. In fact, most of their neighbors. And strangers, too.

Come in, sit down, you're not interrupting us at all, we know what it's like, losing a pet you love. This is the dog? Sweet little thing. Zar-jo? That's an unusual name, a foreign name? We haven't seen him I guess but we'll keep an eye open, I'll put your telephone number right here, sure I can't get you anything? No?

An older woman on Ferry Street took us into her grassy back yard where among tangled briars and wild-growing sweetpeas there was a cemetery for her lost babies. Bobo, Speckles, Snowball, Laddie. Each had a grave marker made of birch wood and their names had been burnt into the wood with her son's wood-burning equipment. When Laddie died, a beautiful long-haired tortoise-shell who'd lived to be seventeen and had shrunk to half his size, she'd decided she could not bear to have another pet, it hurts too much when they leave us. *But this is my quiet place. Here, we're all at peace.*

We ran home. Zarjo was still missing.

Ariah was still lying on her bed. Her eyes were open, vacant.

Chandler was beginning to be frightened. It would be Chandler who'd have to call the emergency number. *H-Hello? My m-mother isn't well I guess. My m-mother needs help I guess?*

Juliet snuggled beside Ariah who was breathing hoarsely, mouth agape. Juliet, four years old, was yet a baby eager to press against Mommy, arranging Mommy's floppy arm over her. Shutting her eyes and sucking her thumb pretending she and Mommy were napping together the way they used to nap together a long time ago.

And there was Royall, why did Royall run downstairs and slam a door, shutting the smallest finger of his left hand in the door so that he cried with pain, whimpered and moaned with pain, why did Royall feel he was to blame that Zarjo was gone, had Royall tied him carelessly to the clothesline in the back yard? Had Ariah cried at Royall

It's your fault, you were the last to see him, I'll never forgive you, I will send you away and never see you again.

Next morning, Zarjo returned.

Gone for nearly three days, but we'd never know where. We were weak with happiness! Hearing Zarjo bark in nervous excitement, a harsh staccato bark new to him, and when one of us stroked his ears he turned and snapped as Zarjo had never done before so almost you could think *This isn't Zarjo, it's a strange dog*. Yet a moment later Zarjo was himself again, whimpering with love and licking our hands and faces desperately. We took turns lifting the squirming dog and kissing his warm pug nose and even Ariah who'd been dazed and slow-moving revived and tried to open a can of dog food but her hands trembled so badly, Chandler had to take over. And fresh water for Zarjo's red plastic water dish. The dog's fur was snarled and muddy and his eager thrashing tail was stiff with burdocks and a wicked smell of tarry sewage lifted from him as if he'd been rolling in filth, Ariah insisted that we wash him, immediately we must wash him to get the stink of death from him, and so we did, in a laundry tub carried up from the cellar and into the kitchen, and while shampooing Zarjo's fur we discovered that the pads of his paws, though tough as cartilage, appeared to be burnt, as if he'd had been prowling in chemical waste, Zarjo whimpered and shrank from our touch initially so we were fearful he might bite us but after a while he grew calmer, his paws soaking in the warm soapy water, we rinsed him, gently we lifted him from the tub dripping onto outspread sheets of newspaper on the floor, we squatted beside him wrapping him in a big beach towel and in gratitude Zarjo licked our hands again, especially he licked Ariah's hands, and within seconds he sank into a merciful sleep, a harsh labored sleep, a sleep of exhaustion; collapsing onto his side, with his wet, slick fur he appeared a skeletal creature, shivering and whimpering in his sleep, deeply unconscious as if comatose.

In this way, Zarjo was returned to us. Ariah would claim never to have been seriously worried. She laughed at us, chided us. "You babies! I told you, that damned dog would come back. He wandered off, and he wandered back. And if he hadn't, it would be no great loss. He's just a mongrel. He won't live forever. Caring for a pet is like pouring money down a rat hole, you'd better wise up, life breaks your hearts, next time it will be the real thing, he'll be hit by a car or poison himself or drown in a bog and I don't want you ridiculous children bawling and sniveling and hanging on to your mother, I won't hear of it, *I'm giving you warning*."

13

THIS MISMATCHED COUPLE!

Abruptly in the summer of 1978 they began to be sighted together: the six-foot-two hulking shaved-headed Bud Stonecrop, high school drop-out and cook at Duke's Bar & Grill, and sixteen-year-old Juliet Burnaby, the daughter of the late Dirk Burnaby. The broodingly silent young man and the dreamy high school girl with the beautiful alto voice. They were observed driving together in Stonecrop's battered black Thunderbird, and they were observed walking together (not holding hands, and not much talking) on the windy bluff overlooking the Niagara River, and on the sandy beach at Olcott, thirty miles away on Lake Ontario. They were seen at odd hours at the movies, often mid-afternoons. They were seen at local malls, improbably shopping together. (New clothes for Stonecrop? Suddenly he began to wear sports shirts instead of exclusively T-shirts. In the pitiless heat of summer he consented to wear khaki shorts and sandals instead of his usual long pants and ankle-high sneakers.)

More than one woman neighbor of Ariah Burnaby dared to knock at her door to inform her that her daughter was seeing "that Stonecrop boy, from that Stonecrop family on Garrison." White-lipped Ariah listened politely to these informants and murmured, "Thank you!" without inviting them inside.

(Did Ariah speak with Juliet? She did not, dared not. The news of her daughter seeing a boy, any boy, let alone a dangerously hulking Stonecrop boy, filled her with terror, but she was shrewd enough to recall the mutinous emotions of her own adolescence; she knew how a well-intentioned parent could inadvertently stoke such emotions to a frenzy by saying the wrong thing at the wrong time. And there was the likelihood, as Ariah consoled herself *Whatever it is between them won't last long. It never does.*)

Melinda Aitkins, a nurse at Grace Memorial Hospital, with whom Chandler was now reconciled, and deeply in love, hesitantly reported to him that she'd seen a girl who very much resembled his sister Juliet in the company of "a brute-looking guy twice her size." She'd seen this mismatched couple at the Niagara Mall gazing into a pet shop window at a litter of gamboling kittens, not speaking but just standing there, not quite side by side, but together. Quickly Chandler said that the girl couldn't have been his sister, Juliet was too immature and too shy around boys to date.

Royall's friends began to report back to him having seen the mismatched couple, which aroused Royall's alarm and disapproval. Stonecrop! The son of the NFPD officer who'd been retired from the force under the kind of vague sullied cloud that had accompanied Dirk Burnaby to his death, and beyond. When Royall asked Juliet about Bud Stonecrop she blushed guiltily, and looked away, and said in a small, stubborn voice, "Bud is my friend." Royall was livid. " 'Bud' you call him? 'Bud'? 'Bud is your friend'? Since when? For Christ's sake, Juliet, Bud Stonecrop is—" Royall searched for the precisely defining word but failed to find it, as if Stonecrop stood before him jutting-jawed and glaring. "—a Stonecrop. You know that family."

Juliet said, still not meeting Royall's eye, "Bud's family isn't my friend. Just Bud."

Just Bud. Even in his state of aroused dread, Royall detected a tone of tenderness here.

Juliet said, "Bud isn't what people think. He's shy. He's quiet. He's happiest cooking for people intelligent enough to appreciate it. And he respects me, and our family. Not like other people who scorn us."

"Our family? What the hell does Stonecrop know about our family?"

"Ask him."

This was a remarkable answer, from Juliet. Royall sensed his sister's alliance with the other, with Stonecrop. Hotly he said, "He's too old for you. You're too young for him. He sleeps with women older than he is, he picks up in his uncle's bar." Royall's breath was coming fast, he felt a choking sensation in his chest. None of Ariah's children was comfortable speaking of sex with one another, though they were living in the most giddily sexually liberated decade in American history; or so it was believed. A fierce blush came into Juliet's face. She said, stammering, "Bud doesn't ask anything of me—he isn't like other guys—he isn't, probably, like *you*."

Royall said, hurt, "What's that mean?"

Sleep with a girl, give her a ring, break the engagement and break her heart.

"We're talking about you, Juliet. Not me. Come on!"

"You want to know about Bud, well—you can't know Bud. He isn't what he looks like. And if he doesn't want you to know him, you can't."

"Bullshit."

But Royall wasn't so sure. It alarmed him, how unsure he was. And how emotional: like Ariah, years ago, flaring up into a mysterious "fugue" state and lashing out at her children.

Juliet said, in her still, stubborn voice, "Bud is like someone I've known all my life. Someone I can trust. He's—my only friend."

Now Royall was hurt, and baffled. Protesting, "Bud is not your only friend! I'm your friend, Juliet, and I'm your *brother*."

14

Between us there's a secret.

We have something in common, you and me. That will never change.

Stonecrop never spoke so directly. Yet Juliet understood.

The shaved-headed young man communicated as much in phrases of silence as of speech. In mumbled asides, grimaces, shrugs, grunts. He sighed, he scratched his stubbled head. He was forever tugging at the ragged collar of a T-shirt, as if his baggy clothes were too tight. His smiles were cast sidelong, with the air of one uncertain that a smile from him was welcome. There was eloquence in Stonecrop if you knew how to read him. There was subtlety in his soul however clumsy; tongue-tied, and menacing he appeared to others.

Allowing Juliet to know on that first morning they were together, when he'd carried her bodily away from The Falls and into his Thunderbird speeding north and out of the city *We have something in common you and me. We always have. We always will. That will never change.*

By midsummer Stonecrop began bringing Juliet home with him to the sprawling gray clapboard house on Garrison Street. In a neighborhood of faded brick-and-stucco rowhouses, the Stonecrop house stood out like a beached ocean vessel. The broad front yard was mostly grassless, and littered. Stonecrop had tried to keep it clean—cleared—but had soon given up, as he'd given up on the weedy, overgrown back yard. The front porch was cluttered with furniture and other objects cast off from the interior of the house, also with children's bicycles, scooters, sleds. Several of the front windows were cracked and conspicuously mended with tape. The roof had the perpetually damp, rotted look of a roof that leaks in the mildest of rains; so close to The Falls, the mildest of rains might be torrential. Juliet had often wondered, passing this house: who lives inside? She'd seemed to know beforehand that this was a family very different from the family living in the squeezed-together rowhouse around the corner at 1703 Baltic.

Stonecrop's mother, whom he called, in his embarrassed mumbly way his mom, had "gone away somewhere, south"—"maybe Florida"—a long time ago. When Juliet exclaimed he must miss her, Stonecrop shrugged and edged away.

Well: it was a thoughtless remark, probably. And stupid.

Later, not minutes or hours but days later, Stonecrop took up the subject of his mom, as if he'd been brooding all this time, and carrying on a conversation with Juliet in his head, saying, with a fierce swipe of his nose, "—it's better than her dead. Going away. Like she did. Before—" Stonecrop searched for the remainder of this phrase, but came up with nothing. Juliet wondered if he'd meant to say *Before something happened to her*.

The big gray clapboard house was the property of Stonecrop's father who was spoken of, on the premises, as The Sergeant. Only his older sister and his mother called him Bud, Sr.; Stonecrop referred to his father as "Dad" or "my old man"—"the old man." Stonecrop never spoke of his father without grimacing, scowling, twitching or grinning. He tugged at the soiled collar of his T-shirt, he picked at the scabs and burns on his battered cook's hands. It was impossible for Juliet to gauge whether Stonecrop loved his father, or felt very sorry for him. Whether he was upset by his father's condition, or furious. Stonecrop often seemed ashamed, and angry; maybe he was angry because he was ashamed, or ashamed because he was angry. She wondered uneasily when she would meet The Sergeant. But she knew better than to ask.

A shifting population of Stonecrops lived in the big clapboard house, including a half-dozen lively children who were presumably Stonecrop's young nieces and nephews. There were surly, unshaven young men Stonecrop's age who appeared downstairs, yawning and scratching their underarms, drinking from bottles of beer, then disappeared, shuffling away upstairs. Stonecrop made no effort to introduce Juliet to this shifting population and she soon learned to smile brightly and say, with a high school cheerleader's sincere-seeming enthusiasm, "Oh, hi. I'm Juliet. Bud's friend." The first time Stonecrop brought Juliet home, he introduced her to his aunt Ava, his father's oldest sister who was a registered nurse and took care of The Sergeant; the second time he brought her home, he introduced her to his grandmother, his father's eighty-year-old mother; at last, after much hesitation, and a good deal of sighing, scowling, and nose-swiping, on Juliet's third visit he took her to meet his dad. By this time Juliet had become mildly anxious.

It was a warm July afternoon, shading into evening. Juliet wore white shorts, a soft pink floral shirt, her long untidy hair fastened into a tidy ponytail. She hoped her facial scars weren't glistening as they sometimes did in humid weather.

The Sergeant was in the weedy back yard, dozing in the waning sun beside a portable plastic radio blaring primitive pop music. On the grass beside his canvas lawn chair was a pile of comic books, Captain Marvel and Spider-man on top. And scattered glossy pages of automobile and boat advertisements. Juliet's sensitive nostrils pinched at the smell—bacon, cigarette smoke, stale tired flesh, dried urine.

Oh, she was trying not to be distracted by the loud, brainless music. (It wasn't even rock. It was some confectionary teenage pop of the 1970's, jingly repetitive tunes and rhythms stolen from the Beatles.) The Sergeant half-lay in a soiled canvas lawn chair, his hairless head drooping. He was a shocking sight, like a bloated baby. His face was flaccid and oily, his scalp looked as if it had been singed and smoked, his eyes were dull, vacant. There were curious scabs, gnarls and knots in the veins of his bare legs and forearms. His arms and legs were spindly but his torso bulged as if he'd swallowed something large and indigestible. He wore filthy shorts and a dingy undershirt and lay without moving, only just breathing harshly, until Stonecrop approached him. When Stonecrop's massive shadow fell over The Sergeant, the older man stirred uneasily, squinted up at him. His eyes that had seemed vacant showed now a quick glisten of fear.

Stonecrop mumbled a greeting. "Dad. Hey. You O.K. out here?"

The Sergeant blinked at him, and smiled hesitantly. His lips drew back from big, stained teeth damp with saliva. Stonecrop repeated his question several times, louder, leaning over his father, before the older man seemed to hear.

"Hey Dad? You been sleeping, I guess."

Juliet saw a slow dull flush rise in Stonecrop's bulldog neck, of the kind she saw sometimes at the restaurant, when Stonecrop's irascible uncle bullied him. Her heart went out to her friend, he was trying so hard. Always, it seemed, Stonecrop was trying hard.

Saying now, stooped to his father's red-veined ear, "Hey, see? Got a visitor, Dad." Stonecrop cleared his throat loudly.

Like a singer dreading her performance before a difficult audience, in terror of failing and yet determined not to fail, Juliet came forward smiling foolishly and licking her lips that felt dry and cracked. She had no idea why Stonecrop had brought her here, but here she was. She would try not to let her friend down. Raising her voice to be heard over the din of the radio she said, "H-Hello, Mr. Stonecrop. I'm—Juliet."

What a hopeful, pretentious name! The hope and the pretension had been Ariah's.

(Yet: hadn't Juliet committed suicide, a reckless young teenager?)

The Sergeant now took notice of Juliet, the diminutive pony-tailed girl he might have supposed was a child inhabitant, a relative of some kind, of his ramshackle house. He blinked, scowled, stared at her uncomprehending as if she'd spoken foreign words. Juliet wondered what the poor man could possibly see, seeing her materialized beside him: his eyes looked so ruined, his vision must be askew. And he'd been wakened rudely from a comfortable doze, his thoughts scattered like scraps of paper blown by the wind. Juliet almost could see Stonecrop's father frantically chasing these scraps, trying to fit them back together into some kind of coherence.

And there was the distracting pop music on the radio. Melodies simple and repetitive as nursery tunes given a synthetic erotic beat and bizarrely amplified. Stonecrop said, disgusted, "That shitty stuff, Dad likes. It's music he can hear, I guess."

Since The Sergeant continued to stare at her in silence, Juliet had no choice but to smile again, a little harder, in that bright American-girl way that hurt her face, and extend her hand tentatively. "Mr. Stonecrop? S-Sergeant? I'm h-happy to meet you."

The Sergeant made no response. Juliet glanced sidelong at Stonecrop in dismay.

Stonecrop grunted, and turned down the radio. He fumbled with the knob, and turned the radio off. The Sergeant reacted like a hurt, insulted child, by lashing at Stonecrop with his feeble fist, which Stonecrop ignored, with such cool aplomb that, a moment afterward, Juliet, a witness to this exchange, might doubt that it had ever happened. Stonecrop cleared his throat again and loomed tall over his father and said stubbornly, "This is Juliet, Dad. My friend Jully-ett."

The Sergeant looked suspicious, and then intrigued. His damp lips moved as if he were shaping a mysterious sound. *Jully-ett?*

Stonecrop was unrelenting. You could see him shouldering a boulder twice his size, pushing it up a hill. Up, and up, panting and wheezing and unrelenting. "My friend Juliet. Lives on Baltic."

" 'Jully-ett'?" The older man spoke doubtfully, in a voice like dried rushes being shaken. Juliet recalled that, in the tales told of Sergeant Bud Stonecrop, he'd been beaten with tire irons, his windpipe crushed. " 'Bal-tic'?"

Stonecrop said patiently, "That's where she lives, Dad. You know where Baltic is." Though it wasn't at all clear that The Sergeant did know. "Her name is Jully-ett Burn-a-by, Dad."

Another awkward pause. The Sergeant now seemed to be focusing his eyes on Juliet, with an effort that appeared to be muscular.

Stonecrop repeated "Jully-ett Burn-a-by" in an aggressive sing-song that grated at Juliet's nerves like the strings of a piano crudely plucked. He then added, to her alarm, "Dirk Burnaby's daughter. Dad."

Now suddenly The Sergeant was alert, vigilant. Like a blind man roused from sleep. He gaped and blinked at his son's friend as if he wanted badly to speak, but could not; something was wet and snarled in his throat. In a voice unusually firm and clear, Stonecrop repeated "Dirk Burnaby"—"Dirk Burn-a-by's daughter"—while Juliet stood blushing and mystified.

It wasn't like Stonecrop to put Juliet into uncomfortable situations. There was something here she didn't understand, and didn't like.

"Maybe we should leave, Bud? Your father is—isn't—in a mood for—"

But The Sergeant was making an effort now to respond to Juliet, blinking at her with watery, ravaged eyes. He lifted a shaky hand that Juliet forced herself to touch, with a little suppressed shudder, and he drew his lips back again into a smile. With great effort he managed to say, enunciating each syllable like a man picking up grains of sand with a tweezers: " 'Burn-a-by.' "

Juliet asked with childlike candor, "Did you—know my father? I guess—lots of people did?"

But The Sergeant fell back into the lawn chair exhausted. He was wheezing as if he'd been running uphill, and a faint froth showed on his lips. His hairless baby-head lolled on his bony shoulders. Stonecrop turned to yell over his shoulder a single word, or name, which Juliet couldn't decipher, but concluded afterward must have been "Ava" or the run-on "AuntAva" because his middle-aged aunt appeared, smoking a cigarette, and suggested that the young couple leave now. The Sergeant had had enough of the back yard for the day.

He'd have to be helped inside. It was time for his supper. And, obviously, he had to be "changed."

As Stonecrop led Juliet away, around the house to his car in the driveway, Juliet asked, " 'Changed'? What's that mean?"

Stonecrop mumbled, "Diaper."

This first visit with The Sergeant, which Juliet would have estimated had lasted at least an hour, had in fact lasted less than ten minutes. *She* was exhausted!

They drove away. Juliet saw that her friend was deeply agitated. Rivulets of sweat ran down his big blunt face and a smell as of something rank and wetted exuded from him. He seemed hardly aware of her. He drove the Thunderbird fast, braking at intersections so that the car cringed and rocked. Tactfully Juliet dabbed at her own damp face before passing tissues to Stonecrop who took them from her, wordless.

After a while Juliet said, for there seemed no way not to say such a thing, "Your poor father, Bud! I had no idea he was—well, so sick."

Stonecrop, driving, made no reply.

"But he isn't old, is he? I mean—" In her distress and confusion Juliet almost said *Like your grandmother*. It was a bizarre fact: those two Stonecrops, The Sergeant and his eighty-year-old mother, might have been the identical age.

15

THE VOICES! The voices in The Falls were mostly gone now. Remote as faded radio stations. You realize one day you haven't been hearing these radio stations for a while, you cease to search for them on the dial.

16

YOU DON'T NEED TO, if you don't want to.

Yes but Juliet wanted to. If it meant so much to him.

Casting his hopeful sidelong look at her. His forehead creased in worry, and in yearning. So that Juliet could not bring herself to protest *Why are you doing this, what is the point?*

She halfway thought he wanted her to meet his only parent, as a way of knowing him. And so perhaps she must introduce him to Ariah, in turn.

Juliet smiled to think of such a meeting. She shuddered!

In all, Stonecrop would take Juliet to the ramshackle clapboard house on Garrison Street to visit with The Sergeant just three times that summer. And at last Juliet would know why he'd brought her. And she would never see The Sergeant again.

The second time, ten days after the first visit, The Sergeant was in the back yard as before, lying motionless on the lawn chair with a wetted cloth on his head, listening to the radio. Again it was turned up high. But to a different station, at least. Not teenaged pop but country-and-western. As the young couple approached, The Sergeant took no notice of them. His eyes were shut and he was smiling and humming with the radio music in a high quavering voice. Stonecrop re-introduced Juliet to his father who gave no sign of remembering who she was and this time he told his father that Juliet was a singer, and she was as good as anyone on the radio, and somehow it happened that Juliet sang for The Sergeant. It must have been Stonecrop's suggestion. Always she would recall the invalid's mouth gaping in childlike wonder and his rheumy, staring eyes fixed avidly upon her as she stood before him clasping her hands like a choir girl, singing a song she'd first sung for school assembly in fifth grade.

According to Stonecrop, this was his dad's favorite song:

> "My country 'tis of thee
> Sweet land of liberty!
> Of thee I sing."

What came next? What were the words? Juliet was unnerved by the old man's painfully intense stare and by Stonecrop's look of adoration. Juliet never dared confront, let alone acknowledge. She wasn't certain of the words but like any professional musician she glided past the fault-line of error so smoothly, with such assurance, you wouldn't have detected error, or even uncertainty.

> *"Land of the pilgrims' pride!*
> *Land where our fathers died!*
> *From every mountain-side*
> *Let freedom ring."*

Later that evening Juliet brought up the subject of Stonecrop's father, for it seemed unnatural not to speak of him. She asked Stonecrop what was wrong with his father exactly, had it been the beating, so severe that his brain was injured; but Stonecrop wasn't yet in a mood to speak of his father. Shifting his shoulders in such misery, snuffling and swiping at his nose, so that Juliet quickly backed away from the subject. But a few days later, Stonecrop told her in his dour sidelong way, " 'Dementia.' My dad. It's called."

" 'Dementia'? Oh." Juliet had heard of this medical condition. But she knew virtually nothing about it. Was it senility, or something worse? She shuddered to think of it: *dementia*. The term must spring from the same root as *demon*.

Juliet's heart went out to Stonecrop. Gently she touched his brawny forearm. But she said nothing, for there seemed to her nothing to say that was adequate to these painful circumstances.

Juliet's third visit to Stonecrop's home, the final visit, took place the following week, on a Sunday. This time it was raining and The Sergeant was indoors, where his smells were more concentrated, and his ravaged yet bulky body seemed to take up more space. He seemed to have been napping with his eyes open on a shabby plaid sofa whose seat cushions were covered prudently in oilcloth; his flaccid, boiled-looking face had been freshly washed by Stonecrop's aunt Ava, and his jaws shaved, to a degree. A small black-and-white TV, tuned to a baseball game, blared in a corner of the room and when Stonecrop entered he went without a word to switch it off. Roused from his nap, The Sergeant made no protest. He seemed hardly surprised that his son was in the room, with a pony-tailed girl in a yellow print dress he stared at, trying to remember. Stonecrop winced and grunted, "Hey Dad. How ya doin'." When The Sergeant grunted a vague reply, still staring at Juliet, Stonecrop said, "Remember Juliet, my friend?" Juliet smiled but said nothing. Stonecrop, uncharacteristically verbal, repeated to his father that Juliet was a singer, she had as good a voice as anyone on the radio or TV, she lived just around the corner on Baltic, her name was *Jully-ett Burn-a-by*. Stonecrop paused, breathing through his mouth. The Sergeant continued to stare at Juliet as if he'd never seen anything like her, working his mouth as if he were chewing, chewing, chewing something tough and cartilaginous he couldn't swallow.

Her face warming, Juliet murmured hello and tried to smile as if this were an ordinary visit to an ordinary invalid. A sick man who was convalescing, and would become well again. She was determined to endure the visit for Stonecrop's sake, it seemed to mean so much to him. She guessed that he must love his father very much; she was reminded of her own father, whom she hadn't known but of whom she thought almost constantly. *He could be alive now. After that accident. He could be alive like this, a living death.*

The thought made her light-headed, the heat and airlessness and stench of this place made her feel faint.

Stonecrop had brought cold drinks for the occasion. A can of cherry soda for Juliet and beers for him and his father. But Stonecrop's father could no longer drink from a bottle and even drinking from a cup was a challenge, so Stonecrop ended up having to lift the cup to his father's mouth, and to wipe his jaws when beer spilled over. Juliet hated the chemical taste of the cherry drink. The sensation of faintness grew stronger. Oh, she hoped Bud wouldn't ask her to sing!

" 'Burn-a-by.' " The Sergeant spoke in wonder, and in dread. Something flared up in his bloodshot eyes. He slapped the cup out of his son's hand, and began screaming at Juliet, quaking and quavering on the sofa like a giant infant in a tantrum. His mottled skin flushed red, his teeth flashed like a pike's. Juliet leapt back instinctively out of the range of The Sergeant's flailing hands. Never had she seen such raw terror, such loathing in another's face.

Stonecrop reacted unhesitatingly: with the flat of his hand he shoved his father down, knocking him against the back rest of the sofa as he might have swatted a fly. He muttered what sounded like, "Old fuck." Within seconds he and Juliet were outside, headed for Stonecrop's car.

Out of Niagara Falls they drove, north past Lewiston, past Fort Niagara, to Four Mile Creek. On the bluff above Lake Ontario they walked.

". . . it's from syphilis. What's wrong with him. 'Dementia.' People think it was the beating he took, which wasn't by any Negroes but by fellow cops turning on him, but it was this other, the last stage of syphilis when you haven't had the shots for it, your brain rots away, see? He can't remember new things. He won't remember what happened today. You won't see him again but if you did, he wouldn't remember any of it. Older memories, maybe. For a while. But the new things, it's like a clock hand moving but there's no hours on the clock, just the hand moving, see?—and nothing adding up.

"The doctor says he just forgot how to go to the bathroom. He forgot. It will get to be, in a while, he'll forget how to eat. Some food in his mouth, on his tongue, he won't know what it is, they spit it out. The doctor says not to be surprised.

"Fuck him, it's O.K. with me. See, he wasn't ever a nice guy. He wasn't a decent man. That was his actual soul you saw, I wanted you to see. I wanted you to know him. There's a reason, you need to know. He used to beat us kids. It wasn't that rare in the family, or in our neighborhood, probably you know this, but he was purely a bastard. He beat my mom. She used to be pretty, he broke her face with my brother's baseball bat. Another time he would've strangled her but we stopped him. Being a cop, he got away with it. And a lot more.

"He got promoted in the NFPD because he was smart, he knew to look the other way. Lots of the top-rank cops that was true of. It's supposed to be a cleaner department now. But the same bastard is still police chief. He's on the mob payroll, the Pallidino family in Buffalo. This is no secret. Everybody knows this.

"Him and his buddies, they'd pistol-whip Negroes for just the hell of it. A fourteen-year-old kid almost died. They said it was a gang thing. Might've been a riot, this was around the time Martin Luther King was shot, but it blew over here. The kid's family disappeared from here. They knew, you don't fuck with the cops. Dad used to brag about this. It was what you did, if you were a cop.

"He beat me till I got too big. I don't tell people, I'm almost blind in my left eye from him slugging me. 'Detached retina.' I'm O.K. now, I don't hardly notice it. I'm grateful not to be blind, see? If I was blind I couldn't be a cook. I'm always cutting myself anyway. Burning myself. What the fuck, it's O.K.

"Once, he shot a dog in the neighborhood that was barking too much. It was his story, the dog attacked him. So he had to shoot it. This was around the time he killed your father.

"Him and this other guy, driving a truck. My dad was driving a police cruiser. They ran him off the highway into the river. That's how your father died, in the river. I guess you know that. Somebody wanted your father dead, see? My dad was contacted and took the job.

"People say 'Stonecrops.' I know that look in their faces. Well, they're not wrong. And they don't know the half of it.

"I always knew it. I mean, I knew something. Living in the same house with him, you picked it up. I'd hear him on the phone. He was never worried he'd be caught. Who'd catch him? Where was the evidence? He did other jobs like that, probably. Then he started getting weird. More weird than the department could handle. Nobody knew it was the syphilis. He'd never go to a doctor, he was scared shitless of doctors, hospitals. He still is. Practically we have to tie him down, taking him to the doctor.

"He got weird, and pissed people off in the department. So they beat him. Should've killed him but they didn't. It was written up in the paper when my old man retired from the force. The mayor, the police chief, all these guys praising him. What a laugh! You have to laugh. I'm going to kill him for you, Juliet.

"See, I been thinking about it for a long time. My aunt Ava and me, we've discussed it. I mean, sort of. Him dying 'by accident.' Or his heart stopping, in his sleep. Nobody would give a fuck. A few times I've almost strangled him, he starts screaming and breaking things like he did today. But I wouldn't, my hands would leave marks. I'd use a pillow. He isn't strong, I'm a lot stronger. A few minutes pressing a pillow over his face, he'd be dead. And nobody would know.

"How I knew about your dad for sure, he told me. My aunt Ava came to see me, she says the old man is bawling, saying he did something bad. I asked him what it was and he's shaking his head like he can't remember. So I asked him about your dad, and he caved in and told me yes that was him. He's bawling, he's kind of crazy. My aunt says maybe we should call a priest, he could confess to the priest, but I said fuck that, no way a fucking priest is coming into our house. So she agreed. So he just told me. 'This thing I did.'

"The other guy, driving a truck, he's dead. I couldn't make much sense of what my dad said. Maybe he killed the other guy, to shut him up. Or maybe somebody else ordered the hit. The other guy is nobody whose name I know. I only know my dad. I want to kill him for you."

Stonecrop ceased speaking. The lake was cobalt-blue below them, white-capped waves washed against the pebbly beach. Juliet had been listening to her friend in astonishment. Never had she heard Stonecrop speak more than a few muttered words, now he'd spilled his guts to her. He was earnest, and anxious. Juliet understood that he was making a gift of his father's life to her, or wished to make such a gift. It would be the most extraordinary gift offered to her, in her life. She understood that Bud Stonecrop loved her, and this was a declaration of love. Not just that he was in love with her, as anyone might fall in love with her, but he loved her, too. As a brother might love her, out of long knowing, intimacy. As if they'd grown up in the same house. In the same family.

Juliet said, "Bud, no."

"No? You sure?"

Juliet took Stonecrop's hands in hers. They were twice the size of hers, big-knuckled hands, with discolored nails, marred with fresh scabs, older scratches, burns from years of kitchen work. She smiled, she'd never seen such beautiful hands.

"I'm sure."

Epilogue

In Memoriam:

Dirk Burnaby

21 September 1978

1

I can't be part of it. Don't make me."

It isn't like Ariah to beg. Her son Chandler stares at her in disbelief. Later, he'll feel guilt. (How natural guilt seems, to a devoted elder son of Ariah Burnaby.) When first he tells her about the memorial ceremony being planned to honor Dirk Burnaby. For, as Chandler reasons, someone has to tell her: and soon.

Poor Ariah. Staring at Chandler as if he has uttered incomprehensible yet terrifying words. Deathly white in the face, groping for a chair. Her eyes wild, glassy-green, unfocused.

"I can't, Chandler. I can't be part of it."

And, later: "If any of you love me. Don't make me!"

In the intervening weeks, as September approaches, and plans for the memorial for Dirk Burnaby are becoming more ambitious, and are written of in the *Niagara Gazette*, Ariah will not speak of it. She shrinks from speaking of the future, of the imminent autumn, at all.

Does the telephone ring more frequently at 1703 Baltic? Ariah refuses to answer it. Only her piano students engage her deepest, most intense and abiding interest. And her piano: at which she sits for long hours playing those pieces, some of them mournful, some of them vigorous and passionate, her fingers have long ago memorized.

You are gone. You abandoned me. I am not your wife. I am not your widow. No one can make me. Never!

2

ALWAYS, Royall will remember: how on the balmy afternoon of September 21, when he pulls his car up to the crumbling curb at 1703 Baltic, there is Ariah waiting with Juliet on the front porch. Like the high school kid he believes, he knows, he has outgrown, Royall exclaims aloud, "Holy shit."

Later, he'll ask Juliet why she hadn't warned him. Given him a call. And Juliet will say, But I didn't know, really. Until the very last minute I didn't know myself that Mom would come. I did not.

Ariah Burnaby wearing not stylish black, nor even somber dark blue or gray, but a white cotton shirtwaist of a kind fashionable in the 1950's, with embroidered pink rosebuds scattered in the fabric and a pink silk ribbon-belt and a wide-brimmed straw hat, lacy white gloves, white patent leather pumps. Though by the calendar the season is officially autumn, the weather in Niagara Falls today is warm, sunny, summery, and so Ariah's eccentric costume is not inappropriate. (Has the dress been purchased at the Second Time 'Round, or discovered at the rear of Ariah's crammed closet?) And Ariah has made up her wanly freckled middle-aged girl's face to look almost robust, and glamorous; and Ariah has had her shamefully straggly faded-red hair professionally cut into a glossy bob, to astonish her children.

Too surprised to be tactful, or mindful that neighbors might overhear, Royall calls out, "Mom? You're coming with us?"

In the car, seated beside him, Ariah says dryly, with dignity, "Of course I'm coming with you. How eccentric would it appear, if I did not?"

3

SHE'S FIFTY-SEVEN YEARS OLD. She lost him so long ago. Fifty-seven! And he died, vanished, in his forty-sixth year. For a woman who accepts it that, yes she is damned, if not doomed, Ariah has lived a stubbornly self-reliant life bringing up three children in the very city of her outrage, sorrow, and shame; and never, so far as she has wished anyone to know, wanting to look back.

Saying to Chandler, "I told Joseph. You know: Pankowski, with the dog. He's a widower twice over, fine for him. But I am not a widow. I refuse the status. I think that self-defined 'widows' should commit suttee on their husband's funeral pyres, and give the rest of us a break." An intake of breath, a wicked smile. "Oh, the look on his face!"

(Chandler wonders: What is the relationship between Ariah and Joseph Pankowski? He has asked Juliet, who must know, but Juliet insists she does not. She doubts that Ariah knows, either.)

Chandler worried that his mother would blame him for the memorial ceremony, since he's acquainted with the organizer; not just the fact of the memorial, but its highly public, publicized nature. Yet, unexpectedly, Ariah has said nothing about blaming him, has not accused him of betraying her trust. Responding so weakly to the news, Ariah surprised us all. At first we were relieved, and then concerned.

"This isn't normal for Mom."

"This isn't natural for Mom."

"Well. Maybe it means—"

Maybe what? We had no idea.

We had no idea.

Even Chandler, who'd believed he'd been kept informed of the progress of the Love Canal Homeowners Association lawsuit.

Reading, in July 1978, the astonishing front-page interview in the *Buffalo Evening News* with Neil Lattimore, the aggressive young lawyer who'd recently made national headlines when a Niagara

County jury found for his clients in the re-instated Love Canal lawsuit; and seeing, on the front page, beside Lattimore's photograph, a photograph dated 1960 of Dirk Burnaby.

"Daddy."

The word escaped Chandler, involuntarily. His eyes stung with tears.

It was repeatedly said that the Love Canal lawsuit had been "reinstated" but in fact the 1978 case, though built upon Dirk Burnaby's 1962 case, was far more complicated. Many more plaintiffs were represented in the Love Canal Homeowners Association than had been represented in the original Colvin Heights Homeowners' Association, and they were far better organized, with stronger political ties to the local Democratic party and access to the media. More industry defendants had been named including now Parish Plastics, long a major Niagara Falls polluter, and there were many more lawyers and assistants on each side. The $200 million award, the verdict after a fourteen-week, highly publicized jury trial, was a sum that would have astonished Dirk Burnaby.

Yet there was Burnaby's photo on the front page. Through tear-dimmed eyes Chandler stared.

The photo showed a youthful, bluntly good-looking man of forty-three with a large, broad face, an assured smile, and kindly, slightly shadowed eyes. You could see that he was a man accustomed to being treated with a certain degree of respect; you could guess that he thought well of himself, as others thought well of him. Yet he was dressed casually, in a white shirt with sleeves rolled to his elbows. He was tieless, and his hair appeared to be windblown. Strange it seemed to Chandler that this man was reputed to have been a famously belligerent litigator; that this man had had enemies who'd wished him dead. Neil Lattimore spoke extravagantly of him as "heroic"—"tragically ahead of his time"—a "crusading idealist"—a lawyer of such intellectual and moral caliber, he'd been "persecuted, pilloried, and driven to his death" by an unholy alliance of chemical manufacturing money, political and judicial corruption, and the "ecological blindness" of an earlier decade.

Anxiously Chandler skimmed the remainder of the interview. But there were no more references to Dirk Burnaby. He was weak with re-lief, that Lattimore had chosen to say nothing about Dirk Burnaby being blind himself to the "moral rot" of his class, and to his "falling apart" during the trial. Lattimore had said nothing about the possi-bility, unless it was the probability, of Dirk Burnaby having been murdered.

4

Royall. You didn't, did you.

Didn't what?

I realize, of course you didn't. Couldn't.

Couldn't what, Chandler?

I'm not asking you. This isn't a question. I have no right to ask such a ques-tion. And no reason.

Are you asking a question?

No. I'm not.

But if you were, what's the question?

This enigmatic exchange, Chandler has never had with Royall. He will not have with Royall. Having read in the papers the shocking news of the midsummer disappearance of Chief Justice Stroughton Howell. Formerly a Niagara Falls resident, more recently a resident of the Albany area, Howell was reported by his wife to have "van-ished"—"in thin air"—somewhere between the private parking garage reserved for chief justices at the state capitol complex and his home in Averill Park; his car was found abandoned, keys in the igni-tion, on a service road near the New York State Thruway. As of September 21, Judge Howell has been missing for seven weeks.

This Chandler knows without having to ask Royall: Royall no longer works for Empire Collection Agency. He has become a full-time liberal arts student at Niagara University and his part-time employment has been on campus, as an assistant in the geology de-partment. During the past summer Royall worked, not as a Devil's Hole pilot, but for the university; his plan is to major in geology. He no longer carries a gun. He no longer has any need to carry a gun. Since that evening in his apartment on Fourth Street, when the brothers spoke together so frankly, Royall has never alluded to any gun, and Chandler has never asked him about any gun. Chandler almost might think *Was there a gun? Was it real?* He'd been drinking that night, and his memory was muddled.

5

AS STONECROP HAS SAID *They don't live forever.*

By which Stonecrop has meant to be optimistic: The Sergeant, that sick old bastard, won't live forever. But Juliet interprets the remark as a warning to her, that Ariah won't live forever either. She must try to love Ariah while Ariah is still living.

"Oh, Mom. You look beautiful."

Ariah makes no reply. Doesn't seem to have heard. Since her brave remark, settling into the passenger's seat beside Royall, Ariah has been subdued on the drive downtown to Prospect Point. Juliet, in the rear of the bumpy car, observes the back of her mother's head uneasily. She feels both exasperation and tenderness for Ariah. Since the beginning of the fall term at Niagara Falls High School, and since she has begun voice lessons at the Buffalo Academy of Music, Juliet has felt both detached from her mother, and more affectionate toward her; less intimidated by her, and more forgiving. *I am not you. Never will I be you again.*

"Must be my Burnaby face. No I.D. required."

Royall has only to utter the name—"Burnaby"—at the parking lot entrance, to be waved inside and directed to a section reserved for special guests.

Crossing into Prospect Park to the Victorian gazebo where the memorial is to be held, Royall and Juliet realize for the first time how stiffly anxious Ariah is. A gathering crowd of mostly strangers, folding chairs arranged in a semi-circle in the grass. And the grass is freshly mown, as for a special occasion. Ariah clutches at both her children, suddenly pleading. "There won't be photographers, will there? Please, I can't endure that again."

Royall consoles her: Chandler has promised, no pictures. He'd extracted a promise from the organizers, no pictures without Ariah's permission.

Though Royall wonders: how can anyone make such a promise? How reasonable is it for the family of Dirk Burnaby to expect privacy, at a public event? And this can't fail to be a controversial event, for local feelings run high, on both sides, regarding Love Canal, and environmental lawsuits and legislation generally. The new mayor of Niagara Falls (who'd won the election on a reform ticket, beating out veteran Republican and Democrat candidates) is scheduled to speak at the memorial, as well as members of the County Task Force on Urban Renewal, the chair of the New York State Board of Health, an officer of the Love Canal Homeowners' Association. Lawyer friends of Dirk Burnaby will speak, one of them a fellow World War II veteran. Dirk Burnaby's eighty-nine-year-old Jesuit Latin teacher from Mount St. Joseph's Academy for Boys will reminisce fondly of Dirk as a schoolboy known as the "Peacemaker." Clyde Colborne, Dirk's old friend, now a highly successful local entrepreneur and civic booster, will reminisce, and make the announcement that he is establishing a professorship in Dirk Burnaby's name at Niagara University, in the new field of ecological studies. The organizers failed to locate Nina Olshaker, but one or two others from the original Love Canal lawsuit will speak. Neil Lattimore, the fiery radical, will be presiding. There is even the possibility, excitedly noted by local media, that the consumer-rights crusader Ralph Nader will appear, if his schedule permits, to speak of Dirk Burnaby's "legacy."

Nader! Who never knew Dirk Burnaby. Royall's heart sinks. He resents it, this will be more a political rally than a memorial for his father.

Still, it means a validation of his father and that is what matters: isn't it?

Royall says, "Mom, pull down your hat brim. That's why you're wearing that silly hat, isn't it?"

Juliet protests, "Mom's hat is not silly! It's stylish, and beautiful. Like something in a Renoir painting."

" 'Renoir painting'! That's classy. Are we all in this painting, or just Mom's hat?"

Ariah laughs, wanly. Being teased by Royall usually revives her spirits, but not, somehow, this afternoon.

Dirk Burnaby's widow and three children had been invited to speak at his memorial, of course. Ariah had declined immediately but each of the children tried to imagine what they might say, or do; Juliet had even fantasized singing. (But what would Juliet sing? Bach, Schubert, Schumann? Or something more American, and contemporary? She had no idea what sort of music her father liked: did that matter? And how appropriate would such a gesture be? And who would be Juliet's accompanist, out-of-doors? The audience would feel that they had to applaud such a sentimental effort, but was applause, at a memorial service, appropriate?) In the end, they'd politely declined.

"There!" Ariah speaks grimly, pointing. "The vultures, waiting."

A few photographers in the area of the gazebo, no more than five or six. And two local TV camera crews. Juliet thinks they hardly look like vultures, only just like everyone else.

6

CHANDLER DRIVES ALONE to Prospect Park to join his family. He isn't to blame for the memorial but he does feel responsible.

Those hurt, stricken looks Ariah has been casting him, for weeks. *Can't be part of this. Don't make me. If you love me.*

The pain had gone so deep in her. Chandler sees that now. Being in love with Melinda, loving Danya as if she were his own child, Chandler has begun to understand something of his mother's grief sixteen years before. She has never hated Dirk Burnaby, only the loss of him.

Can't speak of such loss, can't acknowledge it, you are paralyzed, yet you must live.

Reserved parking! Chandler smiles at being so singled out as a

Burnaby, the first and no doubt last time. He has let Melinda out of the car, she'll be sitting with friends in the audience. He, a Burnaby, is a VIP for the occasion. He parks amid other VIPs and takes up the necktie he'd brought to wear: a gift from Melinda. It's silvery-blue with a pattern of subtle geometrical shapes, a classy Italian silk tie he'd been so pleased to receive he'd nearly wept.

"How did you know, darling: trilobites?"

" 'Trilo-'—what?"

"My favorite species of fossil. These shapes here." Chandler laughed at Melinda's expression as she caught on, he was being funny. "Darling, I'm just saying I love the tie. Thank you."

Hurriedly he puts on the necktie, over a freshly laundered pale blue shirt. It is a beautiful tie, and he loves it. Seeing with surprise his furrowed forehead in the rearview mirror. His fish-scale eyes behind smudged glasses. Yet Melinda loves him: has forgiven him.

Maybe, love is always forgiveness, to a degree.

Melinda had time to think him over, the puzzle of him. His Burnaby soul. And possibly his postcards persuaded her. She'd laughed at the crudely drawn cartoon of the nurse extracting blood from a prostrate male's arm. *Have mercy!*

Chandler has vowed, he'll change. He intends to marry Melinda within the year and adopt Danya and he intends to resign his position as a junior high teacher and go to law school and he's feeling, yes he will do these things, and his life will change, he will become the son Dirk Burnaby deserves. Today, following the memorial, when he's alone with his family he will tell them.

Crossing into the park, beginning to hear music, Chandler feels both dread and exhilaration. He would never have predicted that such a day might come: never, as a boy, shrinking in resentment at the careless ways in which the name Burnaby was uttered. Well, there would be no *Shame shame Burnaby's the name* any longer.

Yes, this is good. Ariah will be upset, but the memorial is a good thing, and important. The vindication of Dirk Burnaby in his home-town. At last.

Bastards. Murderers. Cheating him even of dignity.

He does wonder, about Stroughton Howell. The esteemed state judge. But he seems to know, he will never know.

That music! At the memorial site, a brass quintet playing something solemnly brisk by Purcell. The site is a familiar Prospect Park structure, used for open-air summer concerts and other public events. Chandler is relieved, the music sounds good. Stately, yet not pompous. Beauty tinged with melancholy. Chandler has always liked the Victorian gazebo, with its steep gabled roof and ornate fretwork, painted several shades of lavender and purple like something in a child's storybook. Many years ago Dirk Burnaby brought his young family here, to a summer concert. They'd sat in the grass, on a blanket, Ariah was the only one bitten by mosquitoes . . . hadn't that been their family, the Burnabys?

Another time, further back in time, so far back that Chandler could hardly recall it, like looking through the wrong end of a telescope, Mommy had sent Chandler out to push Royall in his stroller. This was in Prospect Park, too. Nearer The Falls. Chandler recalls the cold spit-like spray, little Royall's infant docility. And Mommy who was so beautiful with her red hair glinting in the sun, stretched out on a park bench lazy and luxuriant as a big sleeping cat. *Do as Mommy says! Go away.*

Chandler stops dead in his tracks. Trying to think. What?

Seeing American flags, of some shiny synthetic fabric, jutting from the gazebo's eight-cornered roof and fluttering in the breeze. His heart sinks, just a little. The patriotic atmosphere in this place, outdoors in Prospect Park. Fourth of July fireworks at the Gorge.

"Chandler? Hey."

It's Royall. Grabbing at Chandler's arm, smiling.

In Royall's blunt handsome face a look of apprehension. Beyond the smile, and the crinky good-heartedness of Royall's smile. As if the brothers are greeting each other on an ice floe in some bizarrely public place. Not daring to glance down, to see if the ice has begun to crack.

"Guess who's here."

Chandler's mind is blank. He can't even recall the name of the high-profile consumer-rights activist whose presence at the memorial has been vaguely promised.

Then Chandler sees: Ariah.

He's so surprised to see their mother here, he can't think what to say. Stammering, "Mom! You look—" (But how does Ariah look, in fact? Feverish, distracted. Crimson lipstick outlining her usually pale, small mouth. And a new hairstyle. And what is this fussy, so feminine dress she's wearing, a bridesmaid's costume?) Chandler hugs his mother, wincing as the sharp brim of her hat strikes him above the eye, and feeling her stiffen just perceptibly in his embrace. (Yes, Mom blames him. He knows.) Urgently he says, "Mom, it's going to be all right. We'll take care of you."

Ariah pushes at Chandler as if, even in her benumbed state, she must chide. "And who's going to take care of you, smartie?"

And there's Juliet: beautiful Juliet.

Chandler is relieved to see his young sister so attractive. The shy, shrinking girl who'd tumbled facedown the cellar stairs into a rusty rabbit cage and cut her mouth and bled and bled and hardly cried. The shy, shrinking girl with the scarred face at whom neighborhood children stared. Juliet is sixteen, taller than Chandler has ever seen her, in stylish high-heeled shoes. Her usually windblown hair has been fastened with clips and she too wears lipstick, which suits her. Her dreamy-lidded eyes fasten upon his in a look of appeal. But she seems poised, not ill-at-ease. Her dress is sheath-like, made of some iridescent green fabric so dark as to appear nearly black; chic and sexy, in contrast to Ariah's floral-print shirtwaist. Around Juliet's neck glitter mysterious smoked-glass beads which Chandler has never seen before but seems to know are a gift from a male friend. (Chandler has never met Stonecrop face to face. But he knows who Stonecrop is. In fact, Chandler believes he just saw Stonecrop here at the park, the shaved-headed young man scowling and pacing at the edge of the crowd, too restless to sit down. From Royall, Chandler has heard that Stonecrop quit his uncle's restaurant for the last time and is cooking now at Mario's.)

Chandler squeezes Juliet's hand to reassure her. That this isn't a terrible mistake. The Burnabys of Baltic Street blundering out into a public place, naked and exposed.

Juliet smiles slyly at Chandler, biting her lower lip. "Too late now."

"Too late—?"

"To have not come here."

The program is scheduled to begin at 4 P.M. It's nearly that now, still people are arriving; mostly strangers, with here and there a familiar, startling face. In case of rain the event is to be held in a nearby hall but the sky is reasonably clear, only to the north above Lake Ontario are there banks of dark cloud. Chandler realizes he's been digging his fingernails into his palms, with worry that no one will turn out for Dirk Burnaby's memorial but there appears to be, thank God, a decent audience. His scientist's rapid brain counting sixteen rows of folding chairs, twenty-five chairs in each row, four hundred in all.

Four hundred! Chandler feels a fresh stab of panic, so many seats will never be filled.

Neil Lattimore, high-energy, thrumming with adrenaline, the quintessential lawyer-activist, comes to shake Chandler's hand, nearly breaking his fingers, wanting to be introduced to the Burnabys. But Ariah is frowning and distracted, listening with cranky attentiveness to the brass quintet: is it Ives they're playing now? Copland? A slow march that sounds a little too American-optimistic for Ariah's refined taste. Programs are being passed out: DIRK BURNABY 1917–1962. Young volunteers for an organization called the Niagara Frontier Coalition are soliciting signatures on a petition. Glaring-yellow buttons urging VOTE YES AMENDMENT "CLEAR WATER" are suddenly conspicuous in the audience. Lattimore has a request to make, murmured into Chandler's ear, all right, Chandler hasn't much choice but to ask Ariah to consent to be photographed, it's unavoidable, might as well respond graciously. To Chandler's surprise, Ariah agrees. But she will not speak with the half-dozen reporters who are hovering nearby, and she will not pose alone. "Royall! Juliet! Chand*ler*! Come here." This is one of the few privileges of motherhood, that you can summon your brood in a public place like a hen summoning her chicks, and they have to obey.

Beside the flower-garlanded gazebo Ariah stands between her tall handsome sons, her slender arms linked through theirs; Juliet, the youngest in the family, stands partly in front of Royall, the tallest. Flashbulbs, TV cameras. The Burnabys of Baltic Street, impossibly exposed. Ariah will avoid searching out these images in the media with one exception: it's impossible to avoid the flattering front-page picture in the next day's *Gazette* where she and her children will appear with solemnly smiling faces above the caption—

Family of Dirk Burnaby attends Prospect Park memorial.

This simple declarative statement will be read and reread by each of the Burnabys as if it were poetry of surpassing beauty, containing a hidden meaning.

7

Champagne has a strange effect upon me.
   How so?
   A wicked effect.
The consequence is, Ariah is seated with three children, apparently hers, in the first row, center of the audience at the memorial for Dirk Burnaby 1917–1962. Should she smile? Laugh aloud? A screaming laugh, or a laughing scream? Or should she sit quietly, with her unwieldy straw hat now removed, between Chandler and Juliet, clutching their hands in hers?

The quintet is concluding its last piece. The slow march has turned, in its final movement, into something brisk and distinctly American, as Ariah foresaw.

The microphone is being adjusted. It's 4:12 P.M. Miles away at the lake there's a drum-roll of thunder. Unless it's a freight train closer to home. The Burnaby children recall their father's legendary sense of

humor, possibly this sound is distant laughter? You do have to laugh.
Vindication, validation, redemption, and so forth. Sixteen years too
late.

Chandler hears Juliet whispering to Ariah, "Mom, it's going to be
all right. We'll take care of you." Chandler waits for Ariah's cutting
retort, and is hurt when none comes. *Always, she has loved them both, bet-*
ter than me.

Before he sits beside Juliet, Royall turns to scan the crowd for her:
the woman in black. The woman he met, made love to, in the cemetery on Portage Road. Since that morning Royall has not seen her
though he has seen women who resemble her, teasingly and fleetingly.
He almost could believe the meeting, the intense lovemaking, had
been a dream. A dream of that cemetery, and that time. Yet so real,
he's sexually aroused, stirred to the point of pain recalling it. In public places like this he habitually looks for her though guessing, nearly
a year after their meeting, that he won't ever find her. He sits now
with his long legs outstretched, jamming his fists into his trouser
pockets. His heart beats hard and sullen, but why? He knows that
this is a happy occasion. His pale blue eyes, skeptical, yet yearning to
believe, glance upward. Those strangers on the gazebo platform, who
are to speak this afternoon of Dirk Burnaby's "legacy." He should be
grateful for them, he knows. There's Lattimore (whose crushing
handshake Royall made certain he countered with a more crushing
grip of his own), and there's the "reform" mayor of Niagara Falls, adjusting the microphone, inquiring is it on? Yes, yes! The damned
thing is on.

Flags fluttering in gusts of wet air. Smelling of the Gorge.

Earth, water, rock. A mysterious *livingness* to these, that seem to
superficial eyes inanimate. One morning Royall woke to the excited
realization that he would study these phenomena; that he preferred
them to the world of mankind. Law, politics. Men in their futile striv-
ing to conquer men. How strange for Royall Burnaby of all people,
who is, but mostly is not, his father's son.

And for a brief hallucinatory time was not Royall either, but Roy.
Roy, working for Empire Collection Agency. He'd had a permit to
carry a gun but he had not ever fired that gun—had he? And now the

gun has been returned safely to his employer and Roy has ceased to exist.

Royall remembers, with a faint smile. Sure he's a university student now, much better off. He has a future, not just a past. He isn't a desperate young man. But sometimes at moments like this, quiet, meditative, a little restless, he misses the weight of that revolver in his hand. And he misses Roy.

It's a fact: elsewhere in Niagara Falls the air of September 21, 1978 is muggy, hardly breathable; of the texture of rotted fabric filtered through a corrosive mustardy sun. But here in Prospect Park, close by the Niagara Gorge, the air is fresh as if charged with electricity. You want to live: you want to live forever. The brass players, withdrawing from view, shaking spittle out of their gleaming instruments, are emissaries of wonder. On the gazebo platform, as the first stranger speaks, a vase filled with ice water glows with refracted light. Airborne particles of moisture, blown from The Falls, quiver with light. From time to time during the ninety-minute memorial for Dirk Burnaby 1917–1962 as the sun disappears and reappears between strips of tattered clouds, rainbows become visible above the Gorge. So faint, so frail, hardly more than optical illusions they seem. Look a second time, they're gone.

P.S.

Ideas,
interviews
& features …

Joyce Carol Oates:
A Profile

By Eithne Farry

ON THE WALL above Joyce Carol Oates's desk is a 1957 quote from the film director Alfred Hitchcock. It says: 'It's only a movie, let's not go too deeply into these things.' These simple words of advice were given to Kim Novak when she was feeling agitated and despondent on the set of *Vertigo*. 'I thought it was good advice,' says Joyce Carol Oates. 'Writers can get too intense and too emotionally involved with their work. Sometimes I tend to get a little anxious and nervous about my writing, and I can make myself unhappy, so I look up at that quote and think, it's only a book, don't worry, it's not your life.'

But writing is an intrinsic part of Joyce Carol Oates's life, the biographical details overshadowed by her literary output. To date, Oates has thirty-nine novels, nineteen collections of short stories, and numerous plays and nonfiction works (including monographs on boxing and the artist George Bellows) to her name – as well as those of her pseudonyms Rosamond Smith and Lauren Kelly. By the time this interview appears that number, in all likelihood, will have increased. 'I like writing, and I'm always working on something; if it's not a novel, then it'll be a short story, or an essay, or a book review.'

From an early age Oates was fascinated by words; she began writing when she was very young. 'Even before I could write I was emulating adult handwriting. So I began writing, in a sense, before I was able to write.'

Her first stories were about cats and horses. 'I love animals. I'm very close to animals.' Born on Bloomsday – 16 June 1938 – she grew up on a small farm in Lockport, New York, and studied at the same one-room school her mother attended. Her grandparents had a hard life: Joyce's father and his mother moved frequently 'from one low-priced rental to another'; Joyce's mother was handed over to the care of an aunt when her father died suddenly and left the family impoverished. 'Is die too circumspect a term?' asks Joyce. 'In fact, my maternal grandfather was killed in a tavern brawl.'

Oates is the eldest of three and her childhood territory was mapped out in books. She was a voracious reader; by the time she was in her teens she was devouring Henry David Thoreau, Ernest Hemingway, Emily Brontë and William Faulkner – and she can track the influence of these major writers in her own work. She explains: 'I think we are most influenced when we are adolescents. Whoever you read when you're fifteen, sixteen, seventeen, eighteen are probably the strongest influences of your whole life.' She adds, 'I think it's true for all artists: as an adolescent you don't have much background, you don't know much. I can imagine a young artist who's, say, thirteen years old and seeing Cézanne for the first time being very, very overwhelmed. But it's not going to have the same impact when you're forty.' ▶

ELEVEN FAVOURITE BOOKS

The Collected Poems of Emily Dickinson

Ulysses, James Joyce

Moby Dick, Herman Melville

Walden, Henry David Thoreau

Madame Bovary, Gustave Flaubert

The Sound and the Fury, William Faulkner

The Odyssey, Homer (translated by Robert Fagles)

The Turn of the Screw, Henry James

Collected Stories of Franz Kafka

King Lear, William Shakespeare

Collected Stories of D. H. Lawrence

Joyce Carol Oates: A Profile *(continued)*

◄ Oates majored in English at Syracuse University (to which she won a scholarship) and won the *Mademoiselle* 'college short story' competition when she was just nineteen (Sylvia Plath received this coveted award several years previously). She gained her master's degree from the University of Wisconsin in just a year, and had already embarked on her prolific writing career at this point, at times publishing two or three books in the space of twelve months. In 1962 she and her husband Raymond Smith moved to Detroit and stayed there until 1968, witnessing at first hand the civil unrest that overtook many American cities. She was 'shaken' by the experience, and 'brooded upon it'. She is now a professor at Princeton, but the violence and unease of the Detroit years still make their unnerving way into her fiction some thirty-six years later.

The sheer amount of Oates's output can be bewildering. Her biographer Greg Johnson recalls his first visit to the Oates archive at Syracuse University, when he was beginning research for *The Invisible Woman*, his book on Oates. 'My overwhelming impression was of the sheer amount of labour represented by these manuscripts ... the novel manuscripts in particular were astonishing in their complexity.' Oates explains, 'I like writing. I'm not a person who thinks in terms of her career. I think in terms of the work I'm doing.' She adds, 'I don't think I'm incredibly disciplined. I write in the mornings, I sometimes write through the afternoon, even the evening, but not every day. It's not a schedule that's rigid.'

> ❝I think we are most influenced when we are adolescents. Whoever you read when you're fifteen, sixteen, seventeen, eighteen are probably the strongest influences of your whole life. ❞

Her earlier fiction was written in 'one headlong plunge', a rush of words across the page. Then she would 'systematically rewrite the entire manuscript, first word to last … and this was the triumph of art … control imposed upon passion'. Oates still writes every manuscript in longhand first, and then continues her work on a typewriter, editing each book as many as five times before she is happy. 'I don't have a computer. And I won't let things go until I'm happy.' She doesn't have hobbies, but likes to run, hike, and cycle in the summer, before heading back to the study to get back to her writing. 'I'm just trying to do the best work I can. Most writers are trying to do the best they can. You hope someone responds to the work, but then you move on to a new project.' It's a pragmatic attitude to a prolific career. 'People can get depressed and suicidal and upset with their work, but I look at that Hitchcock quote on my wall and remind myself it's only a book. It's a good cautionary tale.' ∎

> ‘I'm just trying to do the best work I can. Most writers are trying to do the best they can. You hope someone responds to the work, but then you move on to a new project. ’

Life at a Glance

© Marion Ettlinger

BORN

16 June 1938, Lockport, New York

EDUCATED

BA from Syracuse University; MA from the University of Wisconsin

CAREER

Lecturer at the University of Detroit, 1962–8; Lecturer at the University of Windsor, 1968–78; Distinguished Professor of Humanities at Princeton University, 1978 to the present day.

SELECTED BACKLIST

Most recent novels
The Tattooed Girl (2003)
I'll Take You There (2002)
Middle Age: A Romance (2001)
Blonde (2000)
Broke Heart Blues (1999)
My Heart Laid Bare (1998)
Man Crazy (1997)
We Were the Mulvaneys (1996)
Zombie (1995)
What I Lived For (1994)
Foxfire: Confessions of a Girl Gang (1993)
Black Water (1992)
Because It is Bitter, and Because It is My Heart (1990)

Most recent short story collections
I Am No One You Know (2004)
Faithless: Tales of Transgression (2001)
The Collector of Hearts: New Tales of the

Grotesque (1998)
Will You Always Love Me? (1996)
Haunted: Tales of the Grotesque (1994)
Where Are You Going, Where Have You Been?:
Selected Early Stories (1993)

Novellas
Rape: A Love Story (2004)
Beasts (2002)
First Love: A Gothic Tale (1996)
The Rise of Life on Earth (1991)
I Lock My Door Upon Myself (1980)
The Triumph of the Spider Monkey (1976)

'Rosamond Smith' novels
The Barrens (2001)
Starr Bright Will Be With You Soon (1999)
Double Delight (1997)
You Can't Catch Me (1995)
Snake Eyes (1992)
Nemesis (1990)
Soul/Mate (1989)
Lives of the Twins (1987)

'A Very American Novel'

Joyce Carol Oates Talks About
The Falls

Q: Niagara Falls truly comes alive in the story; you describe its power and beauty in exquisite detail and during different seasons. How did your connection with Niagara Falls contribute to writing the book?

A: I grew up in the countryside not far from Niagara Falls and we often visited there. Even in western New York State, a region that is haunting to me, Niagara Falls was always special.

Q: For those who have never been to Niagara Falls, would you recommend it? What would you say to encourage people to visit?

A: The Falls at Niagara is an extraordinary experience. It's at once a visual spectacle and sociological phenomenon, one of those natural wonders that seems to grip us on a primitive, visceral level as well as aesthetic. What we experience is beauty tinged with mystic terror.

Q: The reader knows things about Gilbert that Ariah does not, including a first-hand account of what drove him to commit suicide. How does having this information enhance the reading of the story?

A: Many suicides, especially in the past, have surely been as a consequence of sexual anxiety. The reader understands Gilbert's 'secret' to a degree Gilbert doesn't understand himself, while Ariah can only feel guilt, shame, and humiliation as the bride of a suicide.

Q: The Love Canal lawsuit was an actual legal case and plays a pivotal role in the storyline of *The Falls*. How much do the facts and circumstances of the real-life case mirror what takes place in the book?
A: Except for Dirk Burnaby's personal intervention, and changed names, much of the Love Canal material is historical. Obviously, I have had to select details in order to enhance them. Virtually all of this section is wholly realistic.

Q: The epitaph to the book is an excerpt from *A Brief History of Niagara Falls* (1969) and includes this passage: 'By 1900 Niagara Falls had come to be known, to the dismay of local citizens and promoters of the prosperous tourist trade, as "Suicide's Paradise". Why do you suppose suicide is synonymous with the Falls? Did you uncover any statistics on the suicide rate at the Falls?
A: There are a number of very beautiful scenic sites, most famously the Golden Gate Bridge, Japan's Fuji, and a cliff in, I think, Cornwall, as well as Niagara Falls, that have drawn potential suicides. Only in recent decades have statistics on such suicides been kept. ▶

‶Niagara Falls is at once a visual spectacle and sociological phenomenon, one of those natural wonders that seems to grip us on a primitive, visceral level as well as aesthetic. ›

'A Very American Novel' *(continued)*

◄ **Q: Where did you derive the inspiration for *The Falls*? Did the story flow from the plot, the setting, or a particular character?**
A: I always begin my novels with precisely identified characters in environments that have, in a sense, given birth to them. From characters, as from individuals in life, inevitable stories flow that constitute the formal 'plot' of the novel.

Q: Ariah is a character likely to incur both empathy and exasperation. Do you think readers will identify with her?
A: I identified with Ariah in many ways, imagining what it would have been like to be married in the early 1950s, to a 'nice' man who is, unknowingly, homosexual. ('Gay' did not exist.) Ariah's intense happiness in her second marriage, initially at least, I very much understood. She is a favourite of mine, eccentric and headstrong, self-hurting and yet truly loving of her children (if smothering).

Q: Families have their own unique characteristics, like the Burnabys in this story, but are there certain universal truths that apply to every family?
A: Where there is intense love, whether erotic or parental, it is likely to become possessive and stifling, provoking rebellion. Upsets may occur, even painful misunderstandings and separations, yet the essential love remains, and might again flourish, more temperately.

Q: What message do you hope readers will get from *The Falls*?

❝ I always begin my novels with precisely identified characters in environments that have, in a sense, given birth to them. ❞

A: I don't write to convey 'messages' since I am not a propagandist. Obviously *The Falls* is a very American novel of the second half of the twentieth century with which I hope readers might identify in the crises of family life threatened by 'outside' forces.

Q: What books would you recommend for people who would like to learn more about the history of Niagara Falls?

A: There are many books about the Falls. My favourites were a combination of history and photographs. The saga of Love Canal, that environmental disaster area and class-action litigation, has also been written about copiously, but for a personal, memoirist account I would recommend Lois Marie Gibbs's *Love Canal: My Story* (1982) and *Love Canal: The Story Continues . . .* (1998). ∎

❛*The Falls* is a very American novel of the second half of the twentieth century with which I hope readers might identify in the crises of family life threatened by "outside" forces. ❜

Have You Read?
Other titles by Joyce Carol Oates

I'll Take You There
Anellia is a student at Syracuse University, and away from home for the first time in her life. Headstrong, vibrant, and occasionally obsessive, she embraces new experiences with a headlong enthusiasm for life and love. In her quest to belong, Anellia discovers the risks and rewards of confronting the world so passionately.

'Seethes with Oates's trademark intellect and psychological insight' **Elle**

....

Middle Age: A Romance
When Adam Berendt collapses suddenly, his death sends shock waves throughout his hometown, the affluent hamlet of Salt-on-Hudson. Its inhabitants are beautiful, rich, and middle-aged, and, following the demise of Berendt, suddenly forced to confront their own mortality and morality in this richly comic study of middle-class mores.

'A stylish and wise chronicle of transformation and regeneration' Jonathan Bates, *Books of the Year*, **Sunday Telegraph**

....

Faithless: Tales of Transgression
In this collection of twenty-one stories, Joyce Carol Oates explores the darkest territory of the human psyche – these stories are shot through with sexual and emotional violence. The characters consider suicide, plot murders, are both the victims and

perpetrators of sexual assault and stalking. *Faithless* is a startling look into the grim heart of contemporary America.

'Again and again [Oates] finds new language to describe the immensity of desire . . . She twists back against our assumption, seeking always the grisly pop of revelation'
The New York Review of Books

Blonde

Blonde is the deeply moving exploration of the inner life of the woman who became Marilyn Monroe, and a portrait of an American culture hypnotized by its own myths. Poetically sensual and compulsively readable, it traces the destruction of a cultural icon, but never loses sight of the real woman behind the invention.

'*Blonde* is an epic achievement, a masterpiece, a piece of art so shatteringly well-conceived and lavishly wrought that at times it does not seem like a mere book'
Julie Myerson, **Independent on Sunday**

We Were the Mulvaneys (1996)

Selected by the Oprah Winfrey Book Club
In her twenty-sixth novel Joyce Carol Oates has written a rich, complex saga about a seemingly ideal family that is almost destroyed by the date-rape of sixteen-year-old Marianne Mulvaney. This shattering event touches off a heart-breaking journey into twenty-five years filled with shameful ▶

❛Again and again [Oates] finds new language to describe the immensity of desire.❜

Have You Read? *(continued)*

◄ secrets and despair, but ends with an unforeseen miracle which emotionally reunites the troubled family. Making *We Were the Mulvaneys* her first Oprah's Book Club™ selection of 2001, Oprah Winfrey said, 'I read this book over a year ago, but this family still haunts me.'

'It is a book that will break your heart, heal it, then break it again every time you think about it' **Los Angeles Times** ■

Find Out More

www.joycecaroloatesbooks.com
visit HarperCollins's official Joyce Carol
Oates website, with book information,
reading guides, and all Oates-related news

http://www.usfca.edu/
fac-staff/southerr/jco.html
for a wealth of information on Oates's
oeuvre, log on to the Celestial Timepiece
website – intended as a resource for 'fans
and students and scholars of Joyce Carol
Oates's work', this site has news, photos,
and biographical detail, as well as a comprehensive overview of Oates's work to date

http://www.city.niagarafalls.on.ca
http://www.infoniagara.com
http://www.tourismniagara.com
http://www.niagara-usa.com
for anyone wishing to visit Niagara Falls
themselves, these websites give you all the
information needed to plan a trip, whether
to the American or Canadian side

http://ublib.buffalo.edu/libraries/projects/
lovecanal/
for a comprehensive library of documents
and writings related to the Love Canal trial.
From newspaper clippings to a clear
chronology, everything anybody could want
to know about the facts of this case can be
found here

http://www.brainyquote.com/quotes/
authors/j/joyce_carol_oates.html
for some of Oates's most famous and stirring
lines collected together in one place ▶

Find Out More *(continued)*

http://www.ontarioreviewpress.com
for information about the literary journal
that Oates and her husband, Raymond
Smith, founded in 1974, and that is still one
of the best around ∎